LEAH NASH MYSTERIES

BOOKS 1-2

SUSAN HUNTER

Severn River
PUBLISHING

ALSO BY SUSAN HUNTER

Leah Nash Mysteries

Dangerous Habits

Dangerous Mistakes

Dangerous Places

Dangerous Secrets

Dangerous Flaws

Dangerous Ground

Never miss a new release! Sign up to receive exclusive updates from author Susan Hunter.

SusanHunterAuthor.com/Newsletter

As a thank you for signing up, you'll receive a free copy of *Dangerous Dreams: A Leah Nash Novella*.

DANGEROUS HABITS

LEAH NASH MYSTERIES BOOK 1

For Irene, who always believed.
For Gary, who always loves.

1

I've seen a lot of really ugly things happen in my 10 years as a reporter. Good people suffer, bad people thrive, and it all seems pretty random to me. A friend of mine keeps telling me I have it wrong. Life is a tapestry woven with the threads of all that is good and bad in each of us. But in this world, we're limited to viewing it from the underside, full of knots and tangles and hanging threads that seem to have no connection or purpose. It's only after we reach the next world that we can see how everything fits together in an amazing, beautiful picture.

Maybe. But what I know for sure is that when I started to pull on one of those tangled threads last spring, a lot of lives unraveled, and I almost lost my own. It was pretty hard to see a Grand Design in that unholy mess.

My name is Leah Nash. I'm a good reporter and an even better smartass who, as it turns out, isn't all that smart. That's why, instead of driving around sunny Miami chasing leads, I was slip-sliding down a riverbank in Himmel, Wisconsin, on a particularly nasty early April day last year. My assignment—and I had no choice but to accept it—find some wild art to fill a gaping hole in the front page layout of the *Himmel Times Weekly*.

Wind and sleet riled the normally placid Himmel River into foaming whitecaps. Miles upstream the force of the current had uprooted a dead oak and carried it on a collision course with the dam supplying hydroelectric power to the town of Himmel. Now, city crews in two boats were trying to harpoon the tree with hooks and ropes before it wreaked havoc at the dam. I was hoping to get some action shots before deadline.

When I reached the bottom of the steep incline, I saw that a massive winch had been set up to haul the tree in. As I shifted my camera bag from my shoulder, a fresh gust of wind sent an icy trickle of water down my neck.

"I'm gonna kill Miguel." Miguel Santos is the other staff writer at the *Times* and a much better photographer than me. It was his turn to follow up on the scanner chatter that had alerted us to the renegade tree photo op, but he'd begged off with a dead car battery. So, I was the one shivering and reaching for the telephoto lens.

"Whatsa matter, Leah, Ricky Martin afraid the rain will mess up his coiffure?" Darmody asked, pronouncing it cough-your and then guffawing.

"Quiet, would you, Darmody?" I said, though I was more distracted than annoyed. The boats were already halfway to the tree by the time I got the lenses switched. Dale Darmody, the Himmel Police Department's oldest, but not smartest, cop was still droning on.

"That tree must be 80 feet long. And lookee all that stuff hangin' from the branches. Musta picked up a load of crap goin' downriver." His chapped red nose wiggled as he talked. Little tufts of gray hair sprang from it and from his ears. His watery blue eyes blinked in the wind.

"Darmody! Make yourself useful and help Bailey with the winch." The order came from Darmody's boss, David Cooper, now striding toward us.

"Right, LT," said Darmody, scurrying off.

"Hey, Coop. What good's a promotion to lieutenant if it doesn't keep you warm and dry behind a desk? What are you doing here?"

"Crowd control," he said, clapping his hands together to warm them and glancing up at the high bank above us.

"Right." The nasty weather meant only a fraction of the usual gawkers were on hand, and all were neatly contained behind yellow police tape. But the faithful few who kept watch were about to be rewarded.

A sudden shout from the water signaled the tree had been hooked, and we both turned our attention to the river. As the winch roared to life, I focused the camera and started shooting pictures but soon realized I needed a better angle. I glanced around for a higher vantage point then spotted a half-dead birch jutting from the bank a few yards downstream. I sprinted behind the winch and shinnied up to a Y-juncture in the tree. It wasn't a very sturdy perch, but I only needed it for a minute.

I looked through the lens and zoomed in. As I did, the winch groaned against the weight of the tree and gave a banshee wail. The men in the boats pushed hard at the trunk with long poles topped by metal hooks. The tree began bobbing up and down and rolling side to side, slowly at first, then picking up speed. The pressure from the poles, the pull of the winch, the force of the current, and its own growing momentum caused the tree to rock faster and faster. It began to buck, one side dipping low in the water as the other raised higher with each rolling motion.

"Look out! Look out! She's going over!"

Poles dropped and motors roared as the boats pulled away from the wake of the giant tree. With a lurch, the part of the oak that had been underwater shot upward. Branches that had been submerged lifted toward the sky. Hanging from one of them was what looked like a flapping sail. But as the tree bounced up and down more slowly, the horrifying truth became clear.

"Somebody's caught; someone's on that tree!" came a shout from the onlookers.

Tangled in the web of branches was a body bobbing up and down in awful rhythm as the winch groaned slowly on and the oak neared the shore. The crews moved back in quickly to steady the tree and free the body. By the time they pulled it into one of the boats, someone had already radioed for EMTs. The other crew and the guys on the bank continued to maneuver the tree to shore, but our eyes were on the boat speeding in with the unknown victim.

I scrambled down from the birch and waited in silence with everyone else as two men carried the body to a grassy spot a few feet from where we stood and laid it gently on the ground.

Rivulets of dirty river water ran down a narrow face above a once white collar now muddy and askew. Wide open eyes didn't blink as sleet fell on their sightless stare. The veil that had once covered curly black hair was gone, and the gray color of the long robe had gone black with water and river grime. For a minute, no one said anything. Then an anonymous voice broke the silence.

"Holy shit! It's a goddamn nun."

Two EMTs came up behind me with a stretcher. "Ma'am, you'll have to get out of the way." Nodding, I took a step backward. Stumbled. A hand under my elbow kept me from falling.

"Leah? You OK?"

I grabbed the arm and looked up. "Coop. I know her. She—" I stopped and looked again at the battered body, the blank eyes and slack mouth, and remembered the last time I saw her. I looked away.

"Leah?" Coop repeated. "Who is she?"

"Sister Mattea Riordan. She's a nun at DeMoss Academy. How could this happen? She was fine the last time I saw her." An irrational wave of anger rose in me. What? Like the mere fact of seeing her alive a week or so ago made it impossible she was dead now? I gave my head an impatient shake, sending droplets of water flying off my hair and into Coop's face.

"Sorry. I'm all right. Really. I need to grab the rescue guys before they get away." I looked at my watch. "What will you have for me before deadline?"

He shook his head. "Nothing official before you go to press, I'm sure. Probably not even confirmation that she's dead."

I gave him an incredulous look.

"I know, I know." He held up his hands to ward off my scorn. "But a body pulled from cold water isn't dead until a doctor says she's warm and dead. Then we have to contact her order, her next of kin; there'll be an autopsy, and, well, you know the drill."

"Coop, are you serious? A dead nun floats into town on a tree and the *Times* has nothing but 'no comment' from the police?"

"Yeah. I'm serious. Nothing official. I mean it. And don't try any 'highly placed sources in the police department' bull either. The last time I gave you a heads up, the chief nearly took my head off. I got nothing for you, Leah."

"I already know who she is. Remember? I just told you."

"True, but you're not going to print the name of an accident victim before the family gets notification, are you?"

I pounced. "So, you're saying this is an accident?"

"Am I talking to Leah Nash or Lois Lane?"

"I just want to know what you think. Not officially, just as a regular person. You are still a regular person sometimes aren't you Lieutenant Cooper?"

He took off his HPD ball cap and ran his hand through short dark hair, a sure sign that he was irritated. I was a little irritated myself. After two months back in town, I still had a hard time accepting the ways of the local police department. Everything was on a need-to-know basis, and the chief's point of view was that the paper never needed to know anything. I could rarely even get anything attributable to an anonymous source, because the department was so small it was easy for the chief to pinpoint a leak.

"Off the record, right now I can't see anything but accident, but that's not official. We still have to investigate. Look, when I have some answers I'll make sure you have them too. Is that good enough?"

"I guess it'll have to be."

2

I got what I could at the scene, then headed back to the office. The unexpected death of someone I knew and liked had left me unsettled. It wasn't that Sister Mattea's absence would leave a hole in my life. We barely knew each other. But her death did feel like a tear in the fabric of the universe that I vaguely believe holds us all together.

Funny, smart, not much older than me, she was someone I'd planned to get to know when I had time. But we don't hold time in our grasp. Time holds us and often as not lets go when we least expect it.

The rain beat steadily as it had for days. My normal route back to the paper was blocked by flooded intersections, forcing me to go the long way round. The resulting drive was a small-scale sociological survey of Himmel that added to my depression. On Worthington Boulevard, upscale homes rested safe and secure behind high hedges and wrought iron fencing, seemingly unaffected by the weather or the changed fortunes of my hometown.

Further on the southeast, things were definitely different in the once well-manicured subdivisions, where middle class managers, young professionals, and factory workers with plenty of overtime bought their homes. Now, many of the houses were fronted by frayed, raggedy lawns with weather-beaten For Sale signs swinging in the wind. Driveways were empty and curtains were closed.

A few blocks later I turned onto a street in Himmel's poorest neighborhood. There, slapped together rentals still bowed under the burden of sagging roofs. Ancient asphalt siding still curled and peeled on the houses. Scrappy lawns were still littered with broken bicycles and rusty lawn tools. The major difference from years past was the number of vehicles crowded into the rutted gravel driveways and parked on front yards, a sign of extended families huddling together, one paycheck away from financial disaster.

A turn north through town took me past empty storefronts that once housed the hardware store, the shoe store, Straube's Men's Wear. They were all going businesses when I was a kid, but our small town was living on borrowed time even then. A couple of big box stores moved in with lots of choice and low, low prices. We didn't realize what the bargains would actually cost. Specialty stores began closing their doors, unable to compete with one-stop shopping.

By the time the first of Himmel's several manufacturing plants closed, the town was already in trouble. Jobs left, then families left, then one morning we woke up and Himmel was a struggling community of 15,000, not a bustling town of 20,000. The citizens who remained were frustrated and not quite sure who to blame.

"Much like me," I said out loud, as I pulled into the newspaper parking lot and turned off my car. But that wasn't really true. I knew exactly why my fortunes had changed. The fault, dear Brutus, lies not in my stars but in myself, that I am a stubborn smartass. But I had neither the time nor the inclination for self-reflection just then. I had photos and final edits to do if we were going to make our Thursday night deadline. I grabbed my stuff and slipped through the side door of the building.

Max Schrieber, owner and publisher of the *Times Weekly* was nowhere to be found, and Miguel was still among the missing. I filed cutlines for the photos, wrote up a brief on the officially unidentified female found in the river, and went out to the front desk to check for messages. We have a lot of walk-in traffic at the *Times* as well as a fair number of callers who would rather leave word with a live person at the reception desk than record a voice mail. Though that can only be because they don't know Courtnee Fensterman, our receptionist.

Courtnee's slightly buggy blue eyes peered out from under a feathering of light blonde bangs as she gave me a wad of pink message slips from the spike on the corner of her desk. Then she patted my hand.

"Wow, Leah. That is so weird. It's like you're one of those middles. You know, getting messages from dead people."

"What are you talking about, Courtnee?"

"The Sister. The dead Sister. Sister Mattea, the one in the river."

"How—" I cut myself off. There was no point asking how she found out about the death, let alone how she knew the identity of the body. The *Himmel Times* can't compete with the Himmel grapevine.

"My cousin Mikey was at the hospital with my Aunt Frances, she had another spell. He saw them bring Sister Mattea in, and he told my mom, and she called me. But anyway, like I said, Leah, you're like a middle or something. Kind of."

"You mean a medium?" I asked, mystified but game.

"I'm pretty sure it's called a middle, Leah," she said kindly. "I mean, because they're in the middle of like two worlds, right? The living and the dead."

"OK, I'm a middle. But what are you talking about? Messages from the dead?"

"Well, the Sister. She's dead. And she gave you a message. Only wait, maybe that's not right. She wasn't dead when she was here, so that probably doesn't count. Right?"

"Sister Mattea? When was she here? What kind of message? Where is it?"

A blank stare from Courtnee told me my rapid-fire questions had caused a temporary interruption in brain service.

"Well..." her light blonde eyebrows pulled together in a frown of concentration, and she bit her lower lip. Taking a deep breath, I tamped down my impatience and altered my approach. I became the Courtnee Whisperer.

"Courtnee, Sister Mattea stopped by and left a message for me, right?" I said in a low, measured tone. I all but started stroking her withers.

She visibly relaxed and nodded.

"Well, she had this book she wanted to give you. But then you weren't here so she was going to leave it. She asked me for a Post-it, so she could write you a note. Then she asked me to give it to you. But then I thought, no, I'll put it in a manila envelope so the book and the note will stay together."

She paused for a lump of sugar.

"That was a great idea, Courtnee. Now, can you think where you put the envelope?"

"I put it on your desk, silly. What else would I do with it?"

What indeed. "Actually, no, Courtnee, you didn't. I didn't have an envelope left on my desk any day this week. Do you think maybe the phone rang before you could take it to my desk, and maybe you set it down somewhere and forgot about it?"

She turned slowly around her cubicle and patted papers on her desk like a horse pawing the ground. After shifting a few issues of the *Himmel Times*, lifting a couple of flyers and picking up a stray box from Amazon.com, she gave a small whinny of happiness. Then she faced me, holding a large manila envelope in her hand.

"Here you go!"

My name was neatly written across the front in Courtnee's carefully rounded handwriting. I grabbed the envelope wordlessly and headed back to my desk.

"You're welcome!" she said in a reproachful tone as I closed the door behind me.

The newsroom was still empty. I sat down and tore open the sealed flap, reached in and pulled out the contents, a paperback edition of *Echo Park* by Michael Connelly, with a sticky note attached to the cover.

Leah—sorry I missed you. I need to talk with you about something as soon as possible. It's quite important, and I'd rather do it in person. Please give me a call to let me know when we can meet—M

P.S. Here's the book I told you about.

I went back to the front desk.

"Courtnee, what day did Sister Mattea stop by?" She looked up from opening her box of Milk Duds and took a couple before answering.

"This week or last week?" she asked, her voice a little muffled by the need to talk around the sticky caramel.

"She was here last week?"

"Mmmph," she said nodding, then swallowing her candy.

"She was looking at the bound volumes, and I made some copies for her."

"What was she looking for?"

She shrugged. "I don't know. Some old stories about the school the Sisters run for criminal kids, you know, Dumbass Academy?"

"It's DeMoss Academy," I said coldly. "She didn't say anything about me or wanting to see me?"

"It's not all about you, Leah, you know," she said. "We had a really good talk about my cousin Andrew. He just got busted for weed, and now my Uncle Don thinks he's a drug addict. Sister Mattea was really nice. She said Uncle Don might be over-reacting, but at least he cares. Most of the kids at Dum—DeMoss Academy, their parents are just a waste of space, my dad says." Clearly Courtnee had forgotten that my sister Lacey had spent time at DeMoss, but there was no point in pointing that out.

"She said not everybody is cut out to be a mom or dad. And then I told her about Max. How he's a great dad to Alex, even though he's like so old. And crabby. It's kinda cute, him and Ellie. But it's probably good she already had her own baby when they got married, because I mean like, could Max even, well, you know, have sex? I mean you'd always be thinking is he having a heart attack? What if he, like, dies right on top of me! Then I thought, whoops, maybe I shouldn't be talking about that to a nun—"

"You think, Courtnee?" I shuddered at the thought of Sister Mattea subjected to Courtnee's oversharing about Max's love life. Though it was a nice story. Max and his first wife Joyce never had children, and he was so lonely after she died. Then he met Ellie on a trip to Ohio. It was a love-at-first-sight romance. At age 50, he became a newlywed with a toddler and a whole new, happier life. A lot of people had a lot to say about the 20-year age difference, but it didn't seem to matter to them.

"I don't really need a line by line of your chat, Courtnee, just the essentials. So, Sister Mattea left, and she didn't say anything about wanting to see me. Then she came back on Monday, and she wanted to see me, but I wasn't here, so she left the book and the note for me. Is that right?"

"Well, I have to think, Leah. I don't keep everything, like, right at the top of my head." She tilted said head to the right and squeezed her big blue eyes to narrow slits.

"Courtnee?"

She batted her hand at me, lest I further disturb her concentration, then began speaking, her eyes half-closed like a psychic in a trance.

"It wasn't Monday, because the day she came in we were real busy. Mrs. Barry was yelling at me because I mixed up the numbers on her classified and everybody that called got a phone sex message. It wasn't my fault. My mom says I have undiagnosed dyslexia and—"

"Right, Courtnee. This was what, Tuesday?"

"I'm trying to tell you." Her eyes flew open in exasperation. "I was telling Sister Mattea you weren't here, and she asked could she leave you this book and a note and blah, blah, blah. Then Mrs. Barry busted in and started yelling. I handed Sister Mattea a Post-it, and out of the corner of my eye I saw Max coming in, and I didn't want Mrs. Barry telling him all about my mistake. So, I sorta pushed Sister Mattea off on him, and Brad came in to fill the Coke machine.

"Then the phone rang, and I accidentally knocked my water over onto my keyboard, and Brad jumps over the counter—he's really sweet—and he helps me." She paused for me to celebrate Brad's heroic action, but the look on my face got her back on track.

"Well, then Mrs. Barry starts again, so I gave her a refund and a free ad for next week to get her to leave. Then both lines start ringing, and, like I've told Max before, I can't do everything. And I look over to see if he'll help, but he's walking out the door again without even helping me, and Sister Mattea hands me the book, and she leaves, and then after she's gone, I notice—"

"Courtnee! What. Day. Was. It. That's all I want to know."

"Well. Pardon me for trying to give some context." She pouted for a few seconds as I stared at her and briefly wondered where she'd picked up that phrase. Then she continued in an injured tone, as though waiting for me to beg forgiveness. That would not be happening.

"I told you. It was Tuesday. Brad always fills the Coke machine on Tuesdays. Why does it matter when she came in anyway?"

"Because, Courtnee, she asked me to call her, and two days went by and I didn't. And now she's dead, and I never will."

"Well, it doesn't matter then, right? Like you said, she's dead."

"Find your silence, Courtnee. Please."

I stepped back into the newsroom, closed the door, and sighed. Courtnee had a point. Sister Mattea was dead and whatever was on her mind didn't matter anymore. Still, her note bothered me. Why did she want me to call?

I'd met her briefly when I first got back to town. Then I ran into her again at the bookstore a few weeks ago. She was buying a Michael Connelly paperback, and I kidded her that Connelly didn't seem like typical nun fare. She laughed and said she loved the way he wrote about LA. Then she offered to lend me one of her favorites. But time went by, and I assumed she'd forgotten, like people do.

I picked up *Echo Park* and started leafing through it. Something fluttered from between the pages to the floor. I grabbed it, unfolded it, smoothed it straight. It was a two-sided copy of a page from the *Himmel Times*. A photo in the lower left caught my eye—Max, Ellie and Alex grinning above a cutline naming them St. Stephen's Family of the Year.

Above that was a story about water line replacement on Main Street, a grip and grin check-passing photo of some Rotary Club donation, an ad for Bendel's Ford. Typical page two copy. I flipped it over and read the front page headline. The air rushed out of my lungs as though I'd been punched in the gut.

Missing Teen's Death Ruled Accident
By Mike Sutfin, Times Staff Writer

Himmel, WI – The death of Himmel teenager Lacey Nash has been ruled accidental, according to Grantland County District Attorney Cliff Timmins, speaking at a press conference on Wednesday. Nash, 17, disappeared last November from DeMoss Academy, a residential facility for troubled youth run by the Daughters of St. Catherine of Alexandria. Her body was discovered two weeks ago in a ravine on the 300-acre estate owned by the nuns.

"The autopsy indicated cause of death was a head injury sustained in a fall. The sheriff's department has re-interviewed witnesses, and its findings, coupled with the autopsy results, have led us to conclude the death was accidental," said Timmins in a prepared statement. There will be no inquest.

Nash had been a resident of DeMoss Academy for approximately 6 months at the time of her disappearance. She was reported missing the morning of November second by a representative of the school. At the time authorities believed that Nash, a student with a history as a runaway, had left on her own. An undisclosed sum of money was also reported missing at the time.

Timmins declined further comment, but turned the press conference over to Sheriff Lester Dillingham.

"Now, I want to make this clear. In no way did we not do a professional, thorough investigation of Lacey Nash's disappearance. At the time, we had every reason to believe she had run off like she did other times," Dillingham said. However, a witness, who had previously not made a full statement, came forward after the body was discovered.

The witness, whom Dillingham refused to identify citing her status as a minor, told investigators that she and Nash had both attended a party at the abandoned Lancaster farm adjacent to the nuns' property. The site is popular with underage drinkers, Dillingham said.

"We can't be everywhere. We patrol that area as much as we can, but kids do gather there to drink; it's a fact. Our witness said Lacey became highly intoxicated and belligerent and said that she was leaving that night and never coming back."

Nash left the party, and the witness assumed that she had made good on her threats. She didn't come forward at the time out of fear that she would get herself in trouble, and she believed that Nash had run away, Dillingham said.

"It's a sad story, but you get a kid with some booze and drugs inside her —it'd be easy to get disoriented in those woods at night. Then she trips, falls down the gully, hits her head on a rock, and that's all she wrote."

The sheriff confirmed that an empty liquor bottle was found near the body. An unlabeled bottle containing several hydrocodone tablets, better known by the trademarked name Vicodin, was found in Nash's purse. However, the autopsy report does not indicate Nash was intoxicated.

"Well, I don't want to be crude, but a body exposed to the elements for better than six months, you've got your accelerated decomposition to deal with. And out in the woods, you've got your animal factor. Let's just say there wasn't much left for testing and leave it there."

Sister Julianna Bennett, director of DeMoss Academy, issued a formal statement. "We are saddened at the loss of Lacey, and our hearts go out to her family. She remains in our thoughts and in our prayers." Representatives of the order refused any further comment.

The funeral for Lacey Nash will be held May 5 at St. Stephen's. (See Nash obituary, p. 10)

After I finished, I took a deep breath that ended on a ragged note. Why did Sister Mattea have this clip about my sister Lacey tucked in the book she gave me? Was that what she wanted to talk to me about in person? Did she want to tell me something about her, or how she died?

When Lacey disappeared, she and I were barely speaking. But it wasn't always that way. Lacey wasn't even a year old when Annie, our middle sister, died. I was 10. Not long after that, Dad left. He just couldn't deal with the sadness, Mom said. But my mother pulled it together, and we survived. Her parenting style was closer to Roseanne Connor with an English degree than to Carol Brady, but it worked for us.

Lacey used to dissolve in giggles that gave her the hiccups, when Mom would belt out "I Am Woman" and point to us to come in on the chorus. Mom said we were the three Nash women, and we could take on the world. Only it turned out after Lacey turned 14, we couldn't.

I had just taken a job at the *Green Bay Press-Gazette*, after spending the first year out of college working at the *Himmel Times*. It was only a few hours away, but a small daily that's short on staff doesn't leave a new reporter much free time. Lacey and I emailed and talked a lot on the phone, but she was as busy with school and her activities as I was with mine. The next year when I took a position at the *Grand Rapids Press,* a mid-size daily in Michigan, Lacey and I had an even harder time connecting.

By then I was caught up in my first serious relationship. So caught up that it took a while before I realized, that when I did call, Lacey didn't always call me back. When I asked her about it, she brushed me off. But then things got worse. Lacey started lying about where she'd been, staying out past her curfew, skipping school, hanging out with kids she never used to like.

It was as though someone had taken our Lacey and dropped a demon child in her place. Her behavior escalated for almost three years—drinking, smoking weed, doing other drugs. She stole, she ran away, she blew off the counseling sessions Mom set up for her. And lying. She was always, always lying.

When I questioned her, she was evasive. When I talked to her, she was sullen. When I yelled at her, she was defiant. Nothing I did could reach her. She caused Mom a hundred sleepless nights and me a hundred furious days. It just kept getting worse. I dreaded answering the phone or opening my email, because there was always some fresh crisis that I couldn't seem to fix. When she was 17, she stole my credit card, took my mother's car, and headed for parts unknown with her boyfriend. That was it. I was done. I had to be. Trying to save her was killing me.

She was headed for juvenile detention, but my mother's parish priest, Father Lindstrom, intervened. He got her into DeMoss Academy, a residential school for hard case kids run by an order of nuns outside of Himmel. I didn't care where she went as long as it was out of the house.

No more screaming fights, no more nights driving around looking for her, no more missing cash, no more futile attempts to comfort Mom, no more feeling like I couldn't breathe. I hated my sister and what she had done to our lives. Or, maybe more truthfully, I hated that she made me realize we're never safe. Nothing lasts. No matter what dues you think you've paid, they're never enough to keep the next bad thing from happening.

I drove, and Mom sat tight-lipped but dry-eyed all the way to DeMoss. Lacey lounged in the back with her ear buds in, listening to her music and staring straight ahead. I wasn't mad, I wasn't sad, I wasn't anything. I just didn't care anymore. All I wanted was to get it done.

There was only one minute when I felt anything at all. After we finished the intake and met the staff, Lacey was her usual self: defiant, angry, sullen. She endured Mom's goodbye hug and ignored my "See you."

I watched her go down the hall with her counselor. She looked so small. She held her body stiff with her shoulders squared and her chin high. She walked the same way the first day of kindergarten, trying not to show how scared she was. Just before they reached the end of the corridor, she half-turned and our eyes met. The lost look I saw there hit me so hard it took my breath away.

Later, after her body was found, I saw her in my dreams for months— the way she used to be. Running toward me with soft black hair flying, dark blue eyes shining, laughing, holding out a flower or a pretty stone or a butterfly she caught.

But as she got closer, the flower turned into a phone and she was crying into it, "Lee-Lee, Lee-Lee." I reached down to pick her up, but she slipped right through my arms. And she kept running. And crying and crying and crying. I would wake up in a cold sweat and know that I was only fooling myself. I never stopped caring about Lacey. In my unguarded dreams, it all came flooding back—the guilt, the anguish, the sorrow, the love.

That's why I had to know what Sister Mattea was trying to tell me with that newspaper clip.

3

"Refill?"

"Definitely." I was sitting in McClain's Bar & Grill waiting for Max and Miguel to join me for our usual Thursday night post-deadline drink. I'd already downed one Jameson.

"Better bring me a hamburger with that, too, please, Sherry."

"Are you waiting for Coop?" the waitress asked, casually tucking a strand of curly brown hair behind her ear.

"No, but Miguel and Max are supposed to be here shortly. Will they do?" Though I knew they wouldn't. Sherry made it pretty obvious that she had a thing for Coop. We had gone to high school together. She was a cheerleader and I wasn't. She still had rosy cheeks and round brown eyes, and she looked good in the bar's requisite clingy t-shirt and tight black pants—despite two kids and a divorce. I became conscious of my baggy sweater and jeans and my hair jammed up under a red Badgers baseball cap.

"Do you mind if I ask you something?" she said, then asked without waiting for my assent. "Why are you in town, really? I know you're filling in for Callie Preston while she's on maternity leave, and I know your mom's here and all, but you've been back for what, a year? You always said you were getting the hell out of Himmel and never looking back. I heard you were some big shot reporter at a paper in Florida. But here you are, Leah. Back. How come?"

Ouch. That was surprisingly malicious. And bonus points for the repeated use of "back" to emphasize the direction my life had taken. There was more going on than I had credited behind those big brown eyes. I looked at Sherry with new respect. Dislike, but respect.

"Two months, Sherry, not a year. I've been filling in for two, and I promised Max I'd stick it out for six." Then I decided to yank her chain a little. "And, besides, it's been great seeing Coop again. No matter how long it's been, we always just pick up right where we left off," I said, with what I hoped was the right touch of innuendo. I wasn't sure though. I don't do subtle very well.

The truth was that Coop and I had a low-maintenance relationship that suited me perfectly—long periods of limited contact, but no recriminations, no apologies, just slipping back into an easy friendship based on shared history but no romance. OK, there was a beer-fueled hook-up once during college that neither of us ever talked about again, but that hardly constituted a romance.

"Now, if I could have that refill and my burger?" Her color rose, but she just grabbed the empty glass and walked away.

—————

My triumph in the mean girls skirmish didn't count for much though, because Sherry was dead-on about my career. *A problem ignored is a problem solved*, is engraved on the Nash family crest, but this one stubbornly refused to go away. Over a year ago I'd had a blowup with my editor. My threat to quit was unexpectedly accepted, and suddenly I had no job.

I searched for months, but with papers folding and cutting back and an extremely negative reference from my last employer, I had no luck. My patchwork of freelance and stringer work wasn't enough to pay the rent, and I was up against the wall when Max Schreiber, the man who got me started in journalism, called. I suspect my mother put him on to me, but he never said. He just asked if I was available to do him a favor and fill in for his senior reporter while she was out on maternity leave. So, there I was, back in Himmel at the job I'd left for bigger and better things 10 years earlier.

I didn't plan to stay, but I was pinning my hopes on a long shot. During my long exile from regular employment, I'd outlined a nonfiction crime story about a murder I'd covered several years earlier. I'd finally found an agent willing to take me on when Max called. So far, he hadn't had any luck placing my book, but hope springs eternal. Especially when it's all you have to hold on to.

All I ever really wanted to do from the time I was 13 was to be a reporter on a big daily newspaper. I made it, too, until my temper finally got me into real trouble. If I couldn't find a way to write about something more than county fair board meetings and school talent shows, I—well—I didn't know what I was going to do.

"*Chica*! Hellooo, are you in there? Why isn't your phone on? Did you lose it again? Is your battery dead?" A graceful hand waving in front of me broke my reverie. I looked up into the face of the *Himmel Times* junior staff writer, Miguel Santos. Six feet tall, shiny black hair, dark brown eyes, long thick eyelashes, a wide full mouth, and skin the color of a chai latte. Miguel is also witty and charming and almost ten years younger than me. And gay. There is that, too.

"Sorry. I forgot to charge it last night and—"

"Yes, yes, I know your sad story. You need to go retro and get a beeper for back up," he said, pulling out a chair and neatly folding his lean body into it. He was wearing a bright yellow cotton sweater under a brown leather jacket and looked like my favorite candy—chocolate with a lemon cream center. I must be getting hungry.

"Coop called right after you left. They released the identification of the nun and confirmation of death. I just had time to squeeze it in your story before Max said we had to go to press."

"Nothing else? Like how she got in the river?"

He shook his head. "The autopsy is tomorrow. Coop said no official word yet. Good thing you were on the scene, or we wouldn't have anything.

Oh, and the pictures—*muy bien, chica.* Almost as good as mine," he said, and winked. That's how good looking he is—he can carry off a wink.

Sherry returned with my Jameson and burger.

"A Kir Peche for me, *mi bonita,*" Miguel said.

She rolled her eyes. McClain's is a dark paneled lair of scarred wooden tables, duct-taped vinyl booths, and the after smell of a million cigarettes. It runs more to Leinenkugel and JD than to Miguel's exotic cocktail orders, which are a source of wonder and amusement to the staff.

"You know this is just a working class bar. If you want fancy drinks, they have them over at the Holiday Inn."

"Ah, but they don't have you, my Sherry," he said, taking her hand in both of his and flashing a smile with his perfect teeth. She pulled away, laughing, and went to confound the bartender with Miguel's cocktail order. He turned back to me.

"*Chica,* when you gonna let me take you to see my *Tía* Lydia at her salon? Those lips, those eyes, that hair!" He reached over and tugged off my ball cap, causing my reddish brown hair, badly in need of a trim, to fall in a shaggy curtain round my face and shoulders.

"A little liner, some mascara. What Aunt Lydia could do. It's a shame. No, it's a crime. I know you got it goin' on, but not everybody has my eye. No wonder you're sleeping alone."

"Shut up," I said, laughing and yanking my cap out of his hand. I grabbed a handful of hair and shoved it back under my Badgers hat. "And who says I'm sleeping alone?"

"Your *mamá.*"

That was probably true.

"My mother talks too much."

"She cares about you, *chica,* that's all. You have the beautiful hazel eyes, the million dollar smile. But you don't do anything with them. You got no game, Leah."

"OK, OK. Enough." He was hitting a little too close to the bone to be comfortable.

"So, where were you all day today? I'm not sure I believe that 'my car was in the shop' story. Very convenient when the wind chill was about 90 below out on the river today. And Max was missing in action too. He—"

"Bad mouthing the boss again, kid?" A chair scraped noisily across the floor and groaned as the owner, editor, and publisher of the *Himmel Times* dropped heavily onto it. Max flagged Sherry down and ordered his favorite, a Manhattan made with cherry juice, before I answered.

"I was just saying it seemed more like the Nash News today than the *Himmel Times*. Miguel took up residence at Parkhurst's garage most of the afternoon, and I had to cover the Milk Producers Association meeting for you this noon. That was a lot of fun, I can tell you. Hey, what happened to your pants? And your shoes?" I asked, noticing the streaks of mud on his khakis, the dried dirt on his loafers. "You look like you've been playing in mud puddles."

"Yeah?" He pushed his glasses up on his forehead, then rubbed his temples for a minute. Max has an unruly mop of grayish brown hair and brown eyes that droop at the corners. He looks a little like a weary Basset Hound wearing a short-sleeved white dress shirt and an ugly paisley tie. But when he smiles, he has a certain charm. Though he hadn't been very charming of late. The last week or so he groused at everything.

"I never even made it to the office this morning. Got a flat on the way in, and then I fell on my can in the mud trying to get the lug nuts off. Finally got the spare on, went back home to change, and the basement was flooded. Ellie was at some committee meeting, so I was on the phone trying to get a plumber for an hour. I hadda wait around for him to show, and wait while he routed out the line. What a mess.

"It was past two by the time I got out of there. I almost missed my interview with the president at the technical college, and I forgot to change my clothes. Don't give me any more grief. I had enough today." As he waved his arm for emphasis, I caught a gust of a powerful but pleasant, almost grassy scent.

"Well, at least you smell outdoor fresh. I like your cologne."

"From Alex," he said momentarily distracted. "He made it himself from some recipe he found online. Gave it to me and Ellie for our anniversary. Said it's "gender neutral." What kind of 10-year-old says things like that?" He shook his head, but the pride in his voice was unmistakable. "I know you can smell it a mile away, but I'm glad today, because whatever I fell in changing my tire, the smell was like—"

"OK, OK. You win. You had a worse day than everyone."

"Except for that dead nun in the river," Sherry injected as she set the drinks down, then moved on to the next table.

That shut us up for a minute. Max took a gulp of his Manhattan, Miguel sipped his cocktail, and I took another bite of my burger. Then I said, "You know, something odd happened with Sister Mattea."

"What do you mean odd?"

"She left me a message, but I didn't get it 'til after she died. Thanks to ditzy Courtnee." I told them the story and added, "I'm pretty sure she wanted to tell me something about Lacey. Maybe she found something of Lacey's, or maybe there was something new about how she died."

"You already know how she died, Leah. What could Sister Mattea have to add five years later?"

"I don't know, and now I can't ask her. But, come on, she left me a book and inside the book was a photocopy of the front page of the *Times*. The lead story, the only story that has any connection to both me and Sister Mattea, is a report on Lacey's autopsy. The one where Timmins says her death was accidental."

"You don't think it was, *chica*?" Miguel asked, intrigued.

"Well, I have to ask."

"No, Leah. You don't. How's Carol gonna feel if you go digging all that up again?"

"Mom will be fine. She'll want to know if there's anything new."

"There isn't anything new. You may not like it, but you know it."

"Max, Courtnee said you talked to Sister Mattea on Tuesday. Did she say anything, give any hint at all why she wanted to see me?"

"Just small talk. How busy we were, what a nice day it was, were we gonna cover the fundraiser for DeMoss. That's all." He paused a minute and tried to reason with me again. "That was a rough time for you and Carol those last years with Lacey. She was a mixed-up kid. She made a lotta bad choices, and she paid the price. You all did. But you can't go back. Let it go."

"Sister Mattea had a message for me. I just need to find out what it was." I could feel my chin setting and hear my voice getting louder.

"Leah's right, Max, what does it hurt to ask?" Miguel said.

Max ignored him.

"How? How you gonna find out, Leah? What are you gonna find out the police didn't already? Where you gonna even start?"

"I'll start at the nuns' place. That's where Lacey was when she died. What are you so crabby about? I'm not asking you to do anything. I just thought I might get a little support from my friends."

"Christ almighty, what makes you so stubborn? If I don't support you, I don't know who does. What are you trying to prove, Leah, and to who? It's not your fault that Lacey's dead. Let it go."

I slumped back in my chair, stung. Miguel looked nervously back and forth between us.

"So, I was telling Leah—the pictures on the river today, *fantásticos*. One of them, there's a break in the clouds. A little light comes through—everything glows: the water, the river, the tree, the yellow slickers on the police. Like a Thomas Kinkade picture. Only beautiful."

"Hey, I like Thomas Kinkade." Sherry arrived at that moment. "*I* think his pictures are beautiful."

Miguel gave her a pitying look and shrugged his shoulders.

"My mother gave me one of his paintings for my birthday. He's very famous. They're collector's items." She gave a little flounce and walked away without checking on refills.

I finished off my Jameson, put some money on the table for drinks and dinner. "I gotta go. G'night."

Max nodded but didn't say anything. He was pissed. That's OK. So was I.

"Hey, *chica*. Great pictures. See you tomorrow."

"Leah? Is that you?" a sleepy voice called from the far end of the house as the latch on the front door clicked. I had closed it as carefully as I could, but my mother can hear a snowflake fall at 50 yards.

"Yes, Mom," I said, watching her walk down the hallway toward me, tying the belt on her blue chenille robe. Her black hair is shot through with silver, and she wears it short and spiky. Her eyes, slightly out-of-focus without her contacts, are the same midnight-blue color as Lacey's. In fact, in that light she looked so like my sister that I started talking to rush past the sudden lurch in the pit of my stomach.

"Sorry. I tried not to wake you. Max and Miguel and I had a few at McClain's."

"Don't call me to bust you out of a drunk driving charge."

"Mom, a couple of drinks after work, that's all. Plus, I ate dinner too. I'm good. Besides," I said to divert attention, "we had a pretty big, pretty sad story today."

"You mean the nun who was found dead this afternoon in the river?"

Why did we even bother to publish a paper?

"Who told you? Never mind. Doesn't matter. Yeah. It's Sister Mattea Riordan." I hesitated, thinking about Max's warning, but plunged ahead. "A weird thing. She left a note for me at the paper a couple of days ago. But I didn't get it until today."

"Was she a friend? What was the note?"

"I've run into her a few times since I've been back, but no. We weren't really friends, more like friendly. But she went out of her way to see me, and her note asked me to call. Said she had something she wanted to talk to me about in person. And that's not all." I explained about finding the old *Times* story on Lacey in the book Sister Mattea left, and waited for my mother to tell me to leave it alone.

She had padded into the kitchen and was turning the burner on under the tea kettle, setting out cups and reaching for chamomile tea. Then she stopped, took the Jameson out of the cupboard and poured me some over ice. Then one for herself. We both pulled up stools and sat down at the bar separating the kitchen from the living room. Finally, she said, "What are you going to do?"

"Max thinks I should let it go. He thought you'd be upset if I started asking questions."

She waved off Max's concern with a lift of her hand. "Of course it upsets me, but that doesn't mean we should just ignore it. It sounds like Sister

Mattea wanted to tell you something about Lacey. Why else would she give you the clip and ask to talk to you in person?"

My mother is awesome. "Exactly. I was thinking about starting with the Catherines. Do you think Sister Julianna is still in charge at DeMoss?"

"I know she is. The bishop said Mass at St. Stephen's last Sunday and she was there. We took up a special collection for DeMoss. Leah, what do you think it is? Maybe Lacey told her something, gave her a message for us?" She shook her head. "No, that can't be it, Sister Mattea would have told us right away. Maybe she found something of Lacey's and wanted to give it back, or—"

"That's just it. It could be anything. Or nothing. Maybe she just wanted to say that Lacey didn't really hate me after all."

"Leah! Don't say that. Your sister didn't hate you."

"Really? She gave a pretty good imitation of it."

We were both quiet for a minute, each following our own train of thought.

"You know it wasn't your fault. None of it. I was the adult in charge. I was her mother and a piss poor one as it turned out."

"I'm gonna have to cut you off. Quit crying in your whiskey. And quit fishing for compliments. You were a great mom. You still are." I couldn't imagine trying to raise a smart-aleck, stubborn kid like me, or the pain of watching Lacey turn from sweet kid into monster child, but my mom just kept on doing what she did —loving us and believing in us and always, always being there for us.

"All right, Leah. All right. I'm going to bed." She drank the last of her Jameson. "You should think about it too."

"I will." It's not true that you can't go home again. You can as long as you're willing to regress from 32 to 13.

But I didn't go to bed. I took my drink and moved to the rocking chair in the living room. I found what Miguel calls my "sad bastard" playlist, because it's composed mostly of singer-songwriters in a melancholy mood. I turned the volume down low.

I went over to the mantel and took down a framed photo of me and Lacey going down a giant waterslide in the Wisconsin Dells when she was about seven. Her face was a mix of terror and delight. I closed my eyes, and

I could feel her sturdy little body leaning back against me as we barreled down the slide laughing and shouting.

I carried the picture over to the corner chair with me and held it in my lap, slowly rocking, listening to Big Star and Bon Iver and Lucinda Williams until I finally fell asleep.

4

"So, she just fell into the river? That's the conclusion of Himmel PD's crack investigation team?"

"You're in a pleasant mood," Coop said. We were sitting in his office at the Himmel Police Department on the Saturday after Sister Mattea died.

"Sorry. I haven't been sleeping very well. So, what's the story?"

"She drowned, according to the autopsy. There was water in her lungs. Body had bruises and contusions—she must have bounced off the rocks and bushes sticking out of the bluff, and then hit the water. Even if she was a strong swimmer, her habit would have pulled her down and the current is powerful right now."

"But how did she even wind up in the river in the first place?"

"Sister Julianna said Sister Mattea always took an early morning walk on the trail that runs along the river from the edge of their grounds toward the county park. Every day, same time, no matter what the weather she never missed. A couple of people saw her set out from the convent that morning, same as always."

"We checked the trail after the body was recovered. It was a mess. Any tracks that might have been there were washed away. That whole area should've been cordoned off all week. The ground is unstable."

"So, what do you think happened?"

"I think she stopped at the Point, went to the edge to take a look at the river rushing by there. She watched for a minute, then turned, pushed off, and a chunk of ground broke loose under her foot. She tried to catch her balance, got hold of a branch. It bent, held for a minute, but then she went over the edge. She kicked out with her feet, tried to get a toehold, but the limb broke. There were gouges in the dirt just below the overhang."

An image flashed into my mind of Sister Mattea, panicked, clutching onto a flimsy limb, feet flailing as she tried to get a foothold. Then the sharp crack of the branch and the tumble down the steep side. I shuddered and pushed it away.

"How long was she in the water?"

"She left for her walk around 6:45, probably got to the Point by 7 at the latest. Given the current and the way the river flows, that fits with her getting down to the dam in six hours or so."

I needed caffeine. The bookshelf behind me held a selection of mugs and the coffee-maker. As I poured a cup and dug around for a spoon to stir in some sugar, I glanced at the titles on the shelf above. Lots of cop manuals and procedurals, a thick notebook marked City Ordinances and assorted books on managing and supervising. Slightly unexpected, but not out of character, were a couple of mysteries by James Lee Burke. What threw me off was a small paperback called *Buddha's Little Instruction Book* and a hardback copy of *The Collected Poems of Robert Frost*. I caught Coop's eye, then gestured toward the books.

"David Cooper, man of mystery. What's up with these?"

He shrugged. "I have eclectic tastes."

I had been kidding with the 'man of mystery' line, but it was true in a way. We moved in and out of each other's lives easily, using the foundation of our 20-year friendship, but we weren't kids anymore. We each had things that we hadn't shared.

I sat back down and took a sip of thick and bitter coffee, and wished I'd added another pound of sugar to my cup. "What about Sister Mattea's family? Have you talked to them?"

"Parents are both dead. She had a brother in California. I talked to him yesterday. He's making arrangements with the Catherines. The body was released to the nuns this morning."

I forgot myself and took another sip of coffee, then used the subsequent coughing fit to decide whether to mention the newspaper clipping and the note from Sister Mattea. Coop beat me to it.

"So, aren't you going to tell me about your message from beyond the grave?"

"Sounds like you already heard about it."

"Yeah, I ran into Miguel yesterday morning."

"So, I suppose now you're going to tell me it's stupid, let it alone, it doesn't matter now, blah, blah, blah."

"Nope," he said, shaking his head and reaching into his desk drawer. He pulled out a manila file folder and tossed it across to me.

"What's this?"

"A copy of the files on Lacey's case from the sheriff's department. I went over and got them after I talked to Miguel. I knew you'd want to see them."

I stared at him. "So, you don't think I'm crazy? You do think Sister Mattea was going to tell me something about Lacey?"

"Well, those are two different questions. Sure, I think you're crazy." He raised an eyebrow and gave me a half-smile. "But, yeah, maybe Sister Mattea wanted to tell you something. I'd want to know if I were you."

"Did you look at the file?"

"I haven't had time. I tried to talk to Charlie Ross, the investigator on Lacey's case, but he wasn't around when I picked this up."

"Doesn't matter. I remember him. He makes Darmody look like Sherlock Holmes. Coop, does it seem weird to you that Lacey died in a fall and then five years later Sister Mattea dies in a fall, and they're both accidents, and they both happened at or near the Catherines' place when no one else was around?"

He was quiet for a minute considering his response.

"No, Leah, it doesn't. It's like asking if I think the drunk driving accident on High Street five years ago is linked to the fatality last year when the traffic light malfunctioned. Two totally different things."

I started to answer, but he wasn't finished.

"I'm just gonna say this straight. Your sister had a history of drug and alcohol abuse. She was found with hydrocodone in her purse and an empty bottle of booze near her body. She was on the road to that accident a long time before it happened, and she was driving herself. Sister Mattea was different."

"Oh, because Lacey was a drug addict slut, and Sister Mattea was a saint?" I snapped out the words without thinking. Where does that atavistic urge to defend the family honor come from? I knew Coop was right, but it was like I can say whatever I want about my sister, but don't you try it mister—even if it's true.

He started over in the calm voice I hate, especially when I need calming.

"Leah, what I'm saying is that the circumstances surrounding Sister Mattea's death—the weather, the soft ground, the high wind—those circumstances came together in a way that made for a freak accident. Take any one of them away and it might not have happened. But Lacey's case is different."

He could see the anger rising in me. "Get as mad at me as you need to, I can take it. But like I said, Lacey's case is different. Her high risk behavior—drugs, bad decisions, worse friends, finally, that party in the woods—take any one of those factors away and she's still on a collision course with an unhappy ending. I think Sister Mattea's death was just plain bad luck. Lacey's death was predictable for the last three years of her life. I'm sorry. I don't think they're the same at all."

"Well, if Lacey was just a waste and her death was her own fault, why did you bother to get me the files?" I knew I was being unreasonable, directing at Coop the anger I felt at myself for not taking care of Lacey, but I couldn't seem to stop.

"Quit putting words in my mouth. I never said and I never will say Lacey was a waste. Like I told you, I got the files because I knew you'd want to see them, and because maybe Sister Mattea did want to tell you something that might help you and your mom feel a little more at peace with things. Maybe if you look at the records now that time's gone by, something will strike you that helps you figure out what that might have been. I didn't get them for you because I think there's some *DaVinci Code* plot linking the two deaths." I should have laughed off his slight sarcasm, but I didn't.

"You're such a patronizing jerk sometimes I—"

My cell rang. I stopped, looked at the caller ID. Miguel.

"I should take this."

"Sure, feel free to stop ragging on me anytime."

"Miguel? What's up?"

"Leah—Alex is hurt. He's in the hospital. Max is freaking out."

"What? What happened? When?"

"He fell out of a tree, and he's in the ER. That's all I know."

"OK, OK. Are you at the hospital?"

"Yes, I drove Max over. We were at the paper when Ellie called. I don't know what's going on." The usual teasing note in his voice was gone, and he sounded sober and scared.

"OK. It's all right. I'm on my way."

I turned to Coop. "Alex is in the hospital. I'm going over there."

Alex cracked me up. He was only 10, but he'd already announced he was going to be a forensic architect. Seriously, how many 10-year-olds even know what an architect is, let alone one who specializes in determining how and why buildings fail? Last time I talked to him, he showed me the plans he and his best friend, Lincoln Methner, had drawn up for their tree house—excuse me, tree condo. Max built the platform for them, but the boys had big expansion plans. Their version looked more appealing than my last apartment.

I pulled into the parking lot, ran to the ER and headed for the desk, but Miguel intercepted me.

"How's Alex? What's going on?"

"I guess he tied a rope to a branch so he could swing down from his tree house like Spiderman. The rope broke and he fell. Then his friend ran in and told Ellie Alex wasn't breathing. She called 911, then Max. He was so freaked out, I drove him here. It feels like they've been in there a long time."

At that moment, the doors from the ER swung out, and Max's wife Ellie came through. She had the bright blue eyes, long curly red hair, and impossibly perfect body of an animated Disney heroine. Normally, I kind of hate her. To my surprise, as soon as she spotted us, she ran straight toward me and flung herself into my arms, tears streaming down her face. People don't usually turn to me for comforting hugs, but I tried to step up. I noticed in a distracted way that she exuded the same grassy fragrance Max had. Alex's signature scent.

"It's OK. He's going to be fine," I murmured, though what did I know?

She hiccupped as her sobs subsided and then pulled back from me. Miguel, who had been hovering anxiously on the sidelines, brought her a wad of tissues big enough to sop up the Mississippi.

"I know, I know. Alex is fine. That is, he'll be fine. It's just. Oh—" Her eyes welled up again, and she blew her nose.

"That's good, that's good," Miguel said, gently leading her over to the couch and adroitly sitting them both down. I pulled up a chair across from them.

"What did the doctor say?"

She took a deep breath, held it in for a minute and got her thoughts together.

"He has a concussion, but the doctor thinks he'll be fine. He had the wind knocked out of him, and he was a little woozy, and that scared him—and me. But he's alert, and his memory seems fine. I'm sorry to be such a hysteric. I was just so scared when Lincoln came running in and said Alex couldn't breathe. Then, I saw him lying on the ground, gasping for air, and I thought, 'Oh, God, what if he broke his back or—"

"*Pobrecita*, poor baby," Miguel said, patting her hand.

"But the doctor said he's going to be OK?"

"Yes. They're keeping him overnight just for observation. We were lucky. So, so lucky. If anything happened to Alex, I just couldn't go on. I just couldn't," she repeated. From the look on her face, I believed it.

She made a shaky attempt at a smile. "You'd never know I was a nurse in a past life, would you? The way I fell apart."

"Cut yourself some slack, Ellie, it's your kid. You're allowed to fall apart a little. Hey, you got him here, he's fine, and it's all good. Can we stop in and say hi, just for a minute?"

"Let me go and see if he's settled in."

In a few minutes, we were hovering in the doorway of Alex's hospital room. I peeked inside. He was sitting up in bed, a small bandage on his forehead, talking excitedly. His brown eyes grew large as he used his hands to make a point. A piece of dark brown hair fell forward, and he pushed it out of the way.

On either side of him, Max and Ellie stood gazing at their only son with such intense, naked love that I had to look away. But then Alex spotted us and shouted hello.

"I didn't really fall, Leah," he asserted.

"Oh? You gave a pretty good imitation of it, I hear."

"Well, yes, I fell, but the rope broke, so it really doesn't count. I mean, it's not because I didn't do the jump right. How could I know the rope was going to break?"

"How about you were told not to put one up at all?" Ellie made an attempt at sternness, though the fact that she was gently pushing his hair back from his forehead took a lot of the oomph out of it.

"I know. I'm sorry, Mom. We just thought—I just thought—it would be so cool, and Dad told me how when he was my age he used to swing out over the Himmel River and drop in and so I—"

"Hey, I can get in enough trouble with your mother without you helping me," Max said. "You're supposed to be smarter than me." He gave Alex a fierce look that didn't faze the kid a bit.

"Leah, I got an MRI and a CT scan. I have a first degree concussion. That's the minor kind. Good thing I had my lucky dog tags, right?"

"Lucky tags?" Miguel asked.

"Yeah, didn't you ever see them, Miguel?" He reached over and pulled a set of silver tags on a chain from his bedside table and motioned Miguel to come closer.

"Cool, huh? They were my dad's. I mean my first dad. Ian. He died before I was born."

Ian McCallister
    493 Waterford Way
    Los Angeles, CA

Blood Type O negative
Religion Presbyterian

"See, my dad was O negative. I'm B positive. The nurse told me I should always 'be positive.' Get it? B positive and 'be positive.' That's a pun."

For a second I flashed back to Lacey. She loved puns, too, when she was a kid, and as she got older she loved wordplay and puzzles of all kinds. She was so smart. And so lost. I gave myself an internal shake and turned my attention back to Alex.

"Mom gave me these tags to wear so I'd know my birth dad was always looking out for me."

I glanced at Max to see if he was bothered by Alex's obvious attachment to the tags, but he just rubbed his son's head and said, "Buddy, I'm glad Ian was watching out for you, but those things aren't magic you know. You have to make smart choices. And swinging out of a tree isn't a smart choice."

"I know, Dad. But still, they *are* my talisman. That means lucky charm," he added, lest Miguel and I not understand.

"You're lucky, that's for sure. I hear you have to stay tonight though, yes?" Miguel asked.

"Yeah. The nurse said they have to observe me tonight, so I have to stay. Mom thinks she has to stay, too, but she doesn't. I can be here by myself," he said, enough anxiety creeping into his voice to make it clear he hoped she would insist.

"Of course, you could stay yourself, no doubt about it," Ellie said. "But let me put my nurse's training to use a little. I could use some practice just to keep my hand in. You can be my guinea pig."

"Did you know a long time ago, like the 1700s, scientists used to almost always use guinea pigs for experiments, instead of rats or mice like they do now? That's why people started saying 'guinea pig' when they were going to try out something new. And, besides, it sounds better than saying, 'You can be my rat,' " Alex informed us.

"Little man, nothing wrong with your brain. How you come up with that stuff?" Miguel asked, giving Alex a light tap on the shoulder.

"It's a gift."

"And, on that note, I think we'll take off." I moved closer to Max and gave him a sideways shoulder squeeze—neither of us would have been comfortable with a full-on hug, but I wanted him to know that any tension between us was over—at least as far as I was concerned.

"Don't worry about anything at the paper. Miguel and I can handle it. And Courtnee, of course we have Courtnee to count on, too."

Max smiled. "Hey, before you go, why don't you take Ellie down to the cafeteria for some dinner? I'll keep Alex company, and then we can get things squared away for the night."

"Max, I don't need—" Ellie started to protest.

"Yeah, you do. Besides, me and Alex are gonna catch the last inning of the Brewers game."

"OK." She threw up her hands in surrender.

Miguel had excused himself because he had a date, so it was just me and Ellie at the small round table. She picked at a chef salad, and I dug into a surprisingly good cheeseburger.

"Ellie, are you all right? Seriously?"

"Yes, I'm fine, Leah. I know Alex will be OK. It's actually Max I'm concerned about."

"You mean because he's so worried about Alex?"

"No, not that. Has he talked to you at all about the paper? Never mind, you don't need to answer. I'm sure he hasn't. He's barely talked to me."

"You mean the finances? He hasn't said anything, no, but I can see ad revenues keep falling. When I left the paper, we had three sections of the *Times* every week. Since I've been back, we're lucky to have enough advertising to support two. And Max hasn't been himself lately. He's been pretty cranky."

"I know. He's even been a little short with me, which isn't like him at all. It would hurt him so much to lose that paper, the paper his grandfather started."

Her words gave me a sick feeling. "I knew it wasn't good, but I didn't realize things had gone that far."

"He has a meeting with Miller Caldwell next week, trying to get some kind of business loan from the bank. But he's worried about it. Max thinks Miller isn't going to be supportive, and there's another board member who thinks it's a bad investment."

"Who's that?"

"His name is Reid Palmer. He's a retired lawyer or investor, something like that."

"What's he got against the paper?"

"I don't know. Max said he met Miller for lunch last week, and they ran into Reid, so he joined them. Max was sort of testing the waters about the loan, but Reid wasn't very encouraging. Talked about online newspapers and how every change brings some casualties. Max didn't think it went very well."

"Max is a really smart guy, and he's got a lot of friends in this town. This Reid Palmer guy won't be the deciding factor."

"He could be. He has a lot of influence, not just with Miller but with other people on the bank board. And he's a big contributor to Miller's campaign for the senate." She hesitated, as if deciding whether to say something, then went ahead. "Max told me you're planning to dig around at DeMoss Academy, question the nuns and things. Reid Palmer is on the board there, too."

"And so?"

She sighed in exasperation. "So, think about it from Max's point of view. We don't need the paper stirring things up, maybe upsetting the nuns—the board, Reid Palmer."

"I don't want to stir things up, Ellie," I said, a little puzzled at the direction our friendly conversation had taken.

"But you *will* stir things up if you go out to DeMoss, asking the Catherines questions about your sister, implying they didn't take proper care of her, and they were keeping something from you. That's not going to go over very well. What if they complain? What if Reid Palmer gets upset and pressures the bank not to loan Max the money? Have you thought about that?"

"No. Why would I? Why would he get mad at Max or the paper?"

"Oh, don't act so naïve. You don't think the Catholic Church might be just a little sensitive these days to a reporter nosing around?"

"I'm not going as a reporter. I'm going there as Lacey's sister. I won't pretend I'm representing the paper. I'll make it clear the only thing I'm representing is my family. I can't see why you and Max are so worked up about it. I think you're a little over the top on this one."

"My family is the most important thing in the world to me. I would do anything to keep Max from being hurt. And it will kill Max if he has to close that paper. So, I really don't care if you think I'm 'over the top.' If Max thinks it's a bad idea, I think you should respect that. Surely you owe him that much."

"I understand."

"Then you'll drop this?"

"I'm sorry. I wouldn't hurt Max for the world, but my family is just as important to me as yours is to you. And I need to find out what Sister Mattea wanted to tell me."

The look on her face made it pretty clear it was just as well I hadn't brought any of my Leah Nash Fan Club membership forms with me.

5

My mother took off early Sunday morning to go antiquing with Paul Karr, so I was alone with the file that Coop had given me. Paul had been our family dentist forever. Then, after he and his wife Marilyn divorced a few years ago, he and my mother started seeing each other. He's a nice guy; they seem to enjoy each other's company, and that's as far as I want to go in thinking about my mother's romantic life.

With the house to myself, I sat at the bar and spread out the material. I looked over the crime scene photos, then put them in a pile turned upside down. They weren't something I wanted to keep seeing. I settled in to go over the written summaries, most of which had enough misplaced modifiers and missing punctuation to make reading very slow going. Like most cops I've encountered, the sheriff's department personnel were men of action, not words.

There were references to Lacey's drug and alcohol use, her history of running away, the long string of minor and major infractions that ultimately led up to her placement at DeMoss. Charlie Ross, the lead investigator, had interviewed the school staff, my mother, me, Lacey's old boyfriend, her roommate; but it was as clear now as it was to me then, that he was convinced Lacey had simply run away. And, I had to admit, I thought the same thing at the time.

As I read the reports filed after her body was found six months later, I grudgingly gave Ross a little credit. He had stepped up his game a bit. He re-interviewed witnesses and expanded the file to include a lot of the people who had been at the annual fund raiser held at the school that night. I knew many of the names: Miller Caldwell, his wife Georgia, Paul Karr and his then-wife Marilyn, Father Lindstrom, the priest at St. Stephen's, Ellie's bogeyman Reid Palmer, plus dozens of others, including most of the staff and many of the nuns.

And, of course, he had talked to the woman who found the body, Vesta Brenneman. Vesta is a local eccentric who lives in a tumbledown shack at the edge of town and spends most of her time pedaling around the county on an ancient Schwinn bicycle. Her little dog Barnacle sits in the bent metal basket attached to its handlebars. She found Lacey's body on one of her rambles in early spring. A groundskeeper heard her screaming in the woods.

When he got there, she was at the bottom of the ravine, her dog going nuts, and Lacey's body just feet away. But Vesta couldn't tell them much, just kept repeating Bible quotes. The investigators at the scene surmised that Barnacle had gotten loose, and she'd gone after him, finding Lacey's body in the process.

The follow-up reports were peppered with references to Lacey's drug use, her past misdeeds, even the general character of the kids at DeMoss Academy. The contents of her purse were listed: the unmarked bottle of pills that turned out to be hydrocodone, a cell phone with no contacts or texts or anything useful on it, her wallet with only her ID and a few bucks, her MP3 player, a little sketchpad with some random drawings. Lacey liked to sketch and was almost as good at drawing as she was at singing.

Then I found what I was looking for. The revised statement from the last-minute mystery witness, Lacey's roommate Delite Wilson. She reversed her earlier insistence that she had not seen Lacey that night and knew nothing about her disappearance. The second time around, she admitted that she and Lacey had snuck out to a party at the old Lancaster farm next to the Catherines' property.

She said that Lacey was really upset and kept repeating she was going to get away from DumbAss Academy as soon as she could. At the party she got pretty wasted, pretty fast. When she wanted to leave, Delite wasn't ready to go. Lacey got mad and took off on her own back toward the school.

"That's the last I seen her. I figured she just did what she kept saying she was gonna do—took off. I couldn't afford any more trouble. This is my last stop before juvie. But now I know she's dead, well, like I had to come forward. Her family should know what happened. For closure, like."

Delite named a college student who was working off community service hours tutoring at DeMoss as the source of her invitation to the party. When questioned, he denied inviting her, then confessed that he didn't remember for sure; he'd told a lot of people about the party. He didn't remember seeing Lacey there, but the party was pretty big and he didn't know a lot of the kids who turned up. He offered up a few names, but police drew a blank there, too.

Most said they didn't know Lacey; they didn't recognize her picture either. A couple said maybe they talked to a girl who looked like her, but they couldn't be certain. Not surprising. You put a bunch of drunk teenagers together and you're not going to get much in the way of recall, especially six months later. Ross's conclusion was that Lacey went to the party with Delite, got drunk, tried to walk home, slipped, fell, and died of head wounds and exposure.

But there was something in the file that didn't quite fit. I skimmed the medical examiner's report. Then I re-read the crime scene description, and then riffled back through the original report on Lacey's disappearance. I stopped mid-paper shuffle as the doorbell chimed "I Will Survive."

"*Tu mamá* is so cool." Miguel stepped inside, but not before hitting the buzzer once more to fill the front hall with the '70s anthem. Some days it was Gloria Gaynor, some days it was Motown or Carole King. After my mother installed a digital doorbell that used tunes from her MP3 player, there'd been no stopping her. Mom has always marched to a different drummer.

"At least she's not here to bust out her disco moves."

"C'mon. You know you love it. Hey, what are you doing, *chica*? I thought we were going to see *Mama Mia* at Himmel Tech. Abba? It doesn't get better. What is all this stuff?" He pulled up a stool and picked up one of the crime scene photos, then quickly put it back.

"It's the police report on Lacey. Coop got it from the sheriff's department for me. I'm just trying to see if there's anything...I don't know...odd I guess."

"Is there anything about your nun in there, Sister Mattea?"

"Not really."

"So, maybe Max is right. There's nothing to investigate?"

"Probably. Except there is one thing that's bothering me a little. It's not what's there, it's what isn't there. The night Lacey disappeared, so did $1,500 from the administrative offices at DeMoss Academy—money from a raffle that should have been deposited but got left in an unlocked drawer instead. Everyone assumed Lacey stole the money to fund her runaway adventure."

"So?"

"So, if Lacey took the money, where did it go? There's no mention of it in the crime scene report, nothing about it in any of the follow up interviews after her body was found."

"Maybe whoever found her body took the money."

I shook my head. "Vesta found her. I'm not sure she even knows what money is. Besides, Lacey's purse was under her body. There's no way Vesta would have poked around to find it."

"Maybe the deputy took it. Or maybe some *pendejo* found your sister and took the money and never reported the body?"

"That's pretty cold."

"It's a cold world, *chica*. That's why I got my friends to keep me warm."

"There's another possibility. Maybe Lacey didn't take the money. Maybe that's what Sister Mattea wanted to tell me. That there was one crappy thing my sister didn't do. Like steal from nuns. One thing that wasn't her fault, that she shouldn't be blamed for."

He nodded. "You could be right, *chica*. The money was gone, Lacey was gone, but there were a bunch of other mixed-up kids living there. Maybe one of them took the money, and when Lacey disappeared, they let her take the blame."

"I think it's worth checking out. It might be that whoever took it saw the light or found the Lord and confessed to Sister Mattea. Maybe they told her something else, something good about Lacey. And too bad if Max and Ellie think I'm obsessed for asking."

"Hey, I'm with you, *chica*. Lacey, she's your sister. She matters."

On Monday, I talked to Sister Julianna to get some information for a fuller story on Sister Mattea's death, but I didn't mention anything about the note she'd left. I felt virtuous. Separation of the job and the personal—isn't that what I told Ellie? Who said I wasn't professional? And sensitive? Then we got so busy that I didn't have time until the paper came out on Friday to follow up on my personal quest. Publication day always gives you a little breathing space at a weekly. No matter what happens, you still have six more days to get things together for the next edition. That afternoon I headed to the Catherines' place about 10 miles from town.

The Daughters of St. Catherine of Alexandria order is actually head-quartered in upstate New York where it runs a small Catholic college. A branch of the group wound up in Himmel in the late 1920s, after a bene-factor gave the order 300 acres and a spare mansion. Her instructions were to set up a school for the faith formation of young women. The Catherines chose not to dwell on the source of the donor's wealth, which was mostly amassed through illegal whisky runs from Canada during Prohibition.

The colonizing group that went west to Wisconsin did a pretty good business with a boarding school serving the daughters of the rich and Catholic for a number of years. But after Vatican II, the Catholic Church's major rebooting of 2,000 years of tradition, their fortunes declined. Most religious orders lost numbers, and recruits were hard to come by. Boarding schools for young ladies also began to fall out of fashion, and the one-two punch forced the closure of the school.

The order replaced its long habits with more modern garb and sent its nuns to work in social agencies, schools and hospitals in the area, but membership continued to decline. After flailing about trying to find their niche in the world, the Catherines decided to return to a more traditional approach. The order abandoned pantsuits and social justice for traditional habits and semi-cloistered living. That move proved very appealing to some. Finances improved, the college in Brampton, New York, achieved greater stability, and the number of new entrants to the order itself began to rise.

Fortunes changed so dramatically that the Wisconsin site was not only maintained, but the school was reopened with a new mission thanks to an infusion of money from the alumna for whom the institution was named. DeMoss Academy was established as a residential facility for troubled youth of both sexes and various income levels. Over the years it gained a reputation for achieving results with some hardcore kids. Just not Lacey.

The school grounds were beginning to show signs of spring as I turned through the entrance gates and onto the winding drive leading to the main part of the campus. Trees and bushes were sprouting buds and yellow daffodils poked up in flowerbeds. The paved road led me by the original mansion, which served as the convent, and past the main classroom facility for the 200 or so students in residence. Then a jog to the left took me past a chapel, a couple of dorms, and a counseling center, according to the signs. It looked like a prosperous New England prep school. Or, at least what I thought one looked like based on repeated viewings of *Dead Poets Society.*

The main artery, St. Catherine's Way, ended at the central administration building, which housed the director and various staff. I walked through the door of the one-story T-shaped building and flashed a confident smile at the elderly nun sitting behind an enormous wooden desk in the center of the reception area.

6

"I don't have an appointment, but I wondered if Sister Julianna might be able to spare just a few minutes for me? It really won't take long, Sister Margaret," I said, glancing quickly at the nameplate in the corner of her desk.

"She's in a meeting right now, but if you can wait a few minutes, she might be able to see you. She does have a little free time. That doesn't happen very often. Are you a family member of one of our students?"

"Not a current student. My sister was Lacey Nash. I'm Leah Nash."

"Oh, Lacey. Oh, yes." Was that good or bad? Given Lacey's track record, odds were on the "not good" side. I offered a neutral response.

"You remember her?"

"Of course. She was a lovely child and such a beautiful voice. She could sing like an angel. Are you a singer too, Miss Nash?" She settled back a little in her chair and perched her hands lightly on the desk, tilting her head slightly, her dark eyes as bright and blinking behind wire-rimmed glasses as a robin's.

"Call me Leah, please. No, I'm afraid Lacey got all the musical talent in our family."

"What was it you wanted to see Sister Julianna about, dear?"

"It sounds a little weird, I know, after all this time, but I'd like to talk to her about Lacey."

"Not weird at all. When someone so young dies, it's very hard to let go. Death is something we're built to resist, even though it opens the door to all that we've been living for. I'm sure you know we just lost one of our own far too young. Sister Mattea," she said, her eyes dimming a little with tears.

"I'm so sorry for your loss. I knew Sister Mattea a little. I've been wondering if she knew Lacey—though she never mentioned it to me."

"Oh, I doubt she did, dear. Sister Mattea was working on her MBA when your sister arrived. She wasn't working with our students at all."

"I didn't know she had a business degree."

"Whip smart she was. I was so happy when she was named Sister Julianna's assistant director. Sister Julianna works far too hard, does everything here, academics, student discipline, finances. Sister Mattea was so enthusiastic, so eager to lift some of that burden. She did so much in the two short months before she died. She would have been Sister Julianna's successor someday, no doubt about it."

"I didn't realize she had such an important job at DeMoss."

"Oh, yes. And so many plans she had. Right away she got working on a surprise for Sister Julianna. She got her brother to donate some big wheelie dealie software to revolutionize—that's what she said, 'revolutionize'—our accounting system. To hear her tell it, the new program would do reports, fraud audits, inventory control, time sheets, payroll, and then shine your shoes for Sunday Mass. She was so excited to do that for Sister Julianna. She was such a dear girl, a wonderful person. And a real firecracker, too."

She laughed and repeated, "Oh, a real firecracker. It seems so unfair. Ours is not to question God's ways, but I confess I have raised an objection over this one." She was quiet for a minute and so was I. Then I brought the conversation back to Lacey.

"Sister, I feel the same way about Lacey. She was so young. It seems unfair that she didn't really get a chance to turn her life around. I'm just trying to understand. What do you remember about the day she disappeared?"

"I recall that Friday very well. Very well. It was the same day Mary disappeared."

"Another student took off when Lacey did?" I asked in surprise.

Inexplicably, Sister Margaret chuckled. "No, no. I meant Mary, the Virgin Mary. The statue I kept on my desk."

"I'm not sure I – ?"

"I'm being a little silly, I know. But I loved that statue. It belonged to my dear father. Large and clumsily made, but in its own way, rather beautiful. For all it was a bit battered with the years. Had a long white scratch at the base. I was going to have it fixed, then I thought no, it's just like Papa. Because aging gave him character and it gave my Mary statue character, too.

"Anyway, she was there when I left for the day, I'm sure, because it was a very difficult day and I gave her a little pat on the hand like I did some-times, just for a bit of comfort when things had been especially trying. The next afternoon when I came in, I noticed right away she was gone."

I wanted to get her off the Virgin Mary track and back to Lacey, but then I thought maybe the best way to get her to tell me what I wanted was to listen to what she wanted to talk about first. So I nodded.

"There was a lot of hubbub that day. Sister Julianna thought one of the cleaning staff or a visitor must have broken it and thrown it away. But I don't see how it could have broken, really. It was heavy enough to stop a door. It was marble, you see. I had one of the younger nuns look through the trash bins, but it wasn't there. No, I suspect one of the students took it for a prank, and with all the commotion, forgot about it. Strange that young people feel things so deeply, but they're so often careless about the feelings of others, isn't it?"

I nodded again, then made an effort to get the conversation back where I wanted it to go. "So, you were saying things were very intense the day Lacey disappeared?"

"Oh yes, that was a wild and wooly day. We had intake for three new students and one of them was very unhappy to be here, and there was a little ruckus. Actually, he turned out to be one of our best students. He just graduated last year and—"

"And so there were lots of things going on. Did you see Lacey that day?"

"Yes, I did. She came in to see Sister Julianna, and she sat right over there waiting. She had her little sketchpad with her. I remember that because she drew a little picture of me and gave it to me. Not the most flattering I must say, but the young are fearless truth-tellers, aren't they?" She gave a rueful grin, and I had to smile back even though I was anxious for her to get on with the story.

"Anyway, it was such a busy day Sister was running behind. We had the annual fundraiser that night and that is always a command performance. All hands on deck. Everyone was running around like crazy getting ready, and all staff had to be there. And then as I said, there was all the ruckus with the student and such a to-do, and Sister Julianna needed copies made for the Board packets. And I can tell you that old copier was just one step above a mimeograph machine. And she was getting quite impatient and—"

I felt a flutter of sympathy for Sister Julianna.

"Yes, well, it sounds like a lot of commotion that day. But you said Lacey was here. Do you know why?"

Sister Margaret seemed a little flustered as she tried to bring herself back from the meandering story I'd interrupted.

"Ah, well, I think Sister Julianna wanted Lacey to sing at St. Catherine of Alexandria's feast day. Our order is named after her, you know, and we always have a big celebration on her saint's day. But then what with all the commotion and things, Sister Julianna didn't get to see her at all. I think your sister was a little upset, and she slipped away. If I had known it was the last time I'd see her, well I—" she paused as though trying to think of exactly what she would have done.

"Well, I don't know, but you like to think you could have done something, said something that would have made a difference, don't you? I tell you, I usually count every day a blessing—at my age you have to. But that day—well, that was one of the worst days I've had since I started working here as receptionist and that's been almost 15 years."

The door to the director's office opened then with a sharp click. A slender middle-aged man with close-cropped dark hair emerged and walked toward the desk. He wore an expensive looking gray suit, a shirt so white it seemed to glow, and a navy tie patterned with tiny gold *fleur-de-lis*.

"Sister Margaret," he said, with a nod and a quizzical look at me. He smelled of some expensive and very subtle men's cologne that made me want to lean in for another whiff.

"Mr. Palmer!" she said with obvious pleasure. "I didn't know that was you with Sister Julianna. How are you today?"

"Well, Sister Margaret. Extremely well." His voice was tinged with a slight Southern drawl. He wasn't much taller than me, and as he turned my way I saw that his eyes were an unusual silvery blue. The contrast with his dark brows and dark lashes was disconcerting. "And you are?"

"Oh, my manners. Mr. Palmer, this is Leah Nash. Leah, this is our Board Chairman, Mr. Reid Palmer. Leah is the sister of one of our former students, Lacey Nash. She was also a friend of Sister Mattea's."

"Ah. Pleasure, Miss Nash," he said, taking my hand in a light but firm grasp, then quickly letting go.

"Leah is here to get some closure. You remember the story of poor Lacey, I'm sure. Sister Mattea's death brought back the memories for Leah," Sister Margaret happily volunteered for me before I could speak.

"Yes, well—" I said, trying to stem the information flow, but Palmer jumped in himself.

"Closure. Ah. A worthy goal, but one that I have found most difficult to achieve. I wish you success in your quest, Miss Nash." His speech was oddly formal, but appealing. I quashed the sentiment as I remembered that this was the man who stood between Max and his dreams. But he did smell really, really good.

"Thank you." We looked at each in silence and then he said—perhaps to stave off another tidal wave of chatter from Sister Margaret— "I must be going. Wonderful to see you, Sister Margaret. Delighted to meet you, Miss Nash." With a nod of his head, he was gone.

"Such a kind man. He's a very good friend to DeMoss Academy. Very good. Of course, his grandmother gave the money that reopened the school. I don't know what Sister Julianna would do without his advice. Well, I do know. We were that close to closing the one time, just before he came on the Board." She held up thumb and forefinger with an infinitesimal gap to demonstrate just how near to the financial edge the school had been.

"Really? I thought your order had loads of money."

"Not us. That's the motherhouse in Brampton," she said with an unexpected note of tartness in her voice. "We're responsible for our own funding to keep the school open. It was touch and go there for a while. Then Mr. Palmer stepped in and set things right. And they've been right ever since."

Riding to the rescue didn't sound much like the action of a rampant capitalist ready to grind Max's business under his heel. "Mr. Palmer is a pretty good guy then?"

"The best. As I say, everything has been right as rain since Mr. Palmer took over on the Board. Now, that's not a criticism of Sister Julianna, she just has so much on her plate. She travels so much you know, always presenting papers and making speeches all over the country at conferences and such. She's very high up in her profession. Just last month she—"

"I'm sorry, Sister Margaret, but do you think Sister Julianna might have time to see me now?" I interrupted as gently as I could, afraid that I'd miss the narrow window of opportunity to talk to the director.

"Oh, yes, of course. Let me just pop in and ask her." She sprang lightly from her chair and hopped with quick little steps to the office, tapped on the door and went in. Within seconds she came out smiling.

"Go right in. Sister can give you a few minutes."

7

I had met Sister Julianna at Lacey's funeral, and saw her again briefly when I attended the rosary for Sister Mattea. She was about my height, 5' 7" or so, and her perfect posture made her seem even taller. Her jaw was square, her nose short and straight. Her eyes, the color of cognac, were warm as she smiled and stood up to greet me. But when the smile left, the warmth was replaced by something in her gaze that made it clear she'd have no problem keeping a school of tough kids in line.

She took my hand in both of hers and gave it a light squeeze with long cool fingers before releasing it and gesturing toward a chair opposite her desk.

"Please, sit down. I want to thank you again for the lovely obituary you wrote for Sister Mattea."

"You're welcome. Thank you for seeing me without an appointment."

"What can I do for you, Leah?"

"This might sound odd," I began, feeling less certain of my mission under her intent gaze. "But I've been thinking a lot about my sister lately, and it's because of Sister Mattea. I have to ask, was there a connection between them?"

She looked surprised. "Not that I know of. I'm not even sure they knew each other. Sister Mattea was finishing her studies, traveling back and forth to school. She wasn't assigned to any direct student contact at the time Lacey was here. Why?"

"She left a message for me before she died. I think she was trying to tell me something about Lacey's death."

"A message? What kind of message?"

I explained about the note and the clipping in the book. She listened attentively, then drew a breath and sighed.

"Leah, I'm so sorry that Sister Mattea's death has stirred up painful memories for you, but whatever she may have wanted to ask or tell you, I'm sure it wasn't about your sister. How could it be?"

"I know it seems unlikely. But there is the thing with the money."

"Money?"

"The $1,500. You told the investigator, Detective Ross, that the day Lacey disappeared, $1,500 went missing from the school. But if Lacey took the money, where was it when her body was found? Couldn't Sister Mattea have found out something about that—that Lacey didn't take it, maybe she was just a scapegoat for one of the other kids? Or, maybe there was something else that she had learned, maybe she found something of Lacey's, or one of the other students confided something to her—"

She raised a hand. "Leah, I'm afraid there isn't any mystery, but I'm not sure it will help to tell you what I know."

"But it will, Sister. I really need to hear it."

"All right, Leah, if that's what you want." She sounded reluctant but resigned.

"Early the morning of the day Lacey disappeared, Father Hegl reported to me that he had found her lurking around the dispensary. It looked to him like she was trying to get into the locked prescription drug cabinet. She denied it. She told him she was just looking for the nurse, but he felt she wasn't telling the truth. I called her into the office immediately."

She stopped for a minute as though gathering her thoughts, then looked directly at me again.

"I was very stressed that day. It was the annual fund raiser as well as the Board meeting. There was a great deal to be done. I've gone over the events in my mind several times. I do believe I handled it as well as possible given everything that was going on."

"What? What did you do?"

"I was very direct. I told Lacey about Father's suspicions and that she would be required to undergo regular drug screening and increased counseling sessions. She became very angry and stormed out of the office. On a normal day, I would have gone after her immediately, but there were so many issues that morning."

"Wait. So, you did actually see her, speak to her?"

"Yes, of course."

"But Sister Margaret said Lacey was waiting for you and that she left without seeing you. She said you wanted to talk to Lacey about singing for St. Catherine's feast day."

She hesitated as though searching for the right words. "Sister Margaret is very important to us here, but as she's gotten older, she's become less— discreet. I may have implied to her that the meeting was about Lacey singing for us. Your sister did have a remarkable voice. But that wasn't the topic we discussed. Sister's recall isn't always reliable, and in the five years since Lacey's disappearance, she's obviously confused her memories. It was a very chaotic day."

"I see. So, you told Lacey you were on to her, and she got belligerent and left."

"Yes. I think it's only logical to believe that Lacey took the money. It was in an unlocked cupboard behind Sister Margaret's desk. Another example, I'm afraid, of Sister's memory problems. It should have been deposited in the bank, not left to tempt the students.

"As for why it wasn't found with her body—she was at a drinking party and in a highly intoxicated state. She could have given the money to someone or bragged about having it and someone at the party took it from her. Does it matter now? Frankly, the money was the least of our concerns, and I would think of yours as well."

"I'm not 'concerned' about the money. I just think it's odd that Lacey would have lost $1,500 without leaving the grounds."

"Perhaps she connected with her supplier."

"You say that like you know she had one."

"We know that there were no drugs missing from the clinic, yet there was hydrocodone found in her purse. And we don't know how long she'd been pursuing her prescription drug habit."

"If that's true, she must have been getting them from someone here."

"Our staff are screened and the students are monitored. But we can't prevent every breach. We're not a maximum-security prison, Leah. You'll see no armed guards or barbed wire fences here."

"You didn't answer my question. Do you know who her supplier was?"

She leaned forward and brought her fingertips together, pressing them against her mouth and the tip of her nose, her elbows resting on her desk. She looked at me as though weighing carefully what she was going to say.

"After Lacey's body was discovered, our head maintenance man, Leon Greer, came to me and admitted that he had hired a temporary grounds employee without vetting him to help with fall clean up."

"And?"

"He was fired a few days after Lacey left when Leon found him smoking marijuana on the grounds. Sometime later he heard that the man had been arrested on a drug charge. When Lacey's death became known, and the paper reported her drug use, Mr. Greer became concerned that this Cole person may have been her supplier."

"Cole? Not Cole Granger? Lacey's boyfriend?"

"Yes. I believe that was his name."

"He's the one who got her using in the first place. What were you thinking?"

"I didn't even know he had worked here until Leon informed me. And I certainly didn't know anything about his history with drugs."

"Did you tell the police?"

"Of course I did. I called Detective Ross. He investigated and later assured me that Mr. Granger had denied being her supplier, and that his time the night Lacey disappeared was accounted for."

"Sister Julianna, Charlie Ross couldn't investigate his way out of a roundabout."

"Leah," she said in a patient voice, "You're playing a guessing game in which there are no answers. I've worked with troubled children and their families for many years, and I've seen this sort of thing before. The desperate need to find a reason, the refusal to accept that not everyone can be saved. I understand why you came but believe me when I tell you that refusing to face facts won't change them."

"Why didn't you call at the time and tell my mother and me that Lacey was suspected of trying to steal drugs? That seems like a pretty big thing to ignore."

"I didn't ignore it, Leah. I would have informed your mother, of course, but Lacey disappeared the day Father Hegl came to me. I would never have called without gathering the facts. Then, when she ran away, or we thought she had, there seemed no point in further upsetting you or your mother. Without drug testing, I had no proof. It was a suspicion, but there were no drugs missing. In hindsight, I can see that may have been an ill-advised kindness."

"Sometimes kindness is just a cover for what's convenient. Maybe it wouldn't be so good for word to get out that prescription drugs were getting passed around, and donated money was getting stolen by kids that are supposedly rehabilitated." OK, so that wasn't exactly fair, but her refusal to even consider that Lacey wasn't the culprit was making me mad.

She stood up then, saying, "I really am sorry for your pain, Leah, and I understand it. We've just lost a sister, too. But I can't agree with your theory that Lacey was wrongly accused. I don't see what more I can say. I'll continue to keep you and your mother in my prayers." She walked over and opened the door. Clearly, this interview was over.

I stood up. "Sister, Cole Granger is a known drug dealer. If Lacey was back on drugs, he was the logical supplier. And if you're wrong and Lacey wasn't using again and didn't take the money, I'd really like to know that. I'd think you would, too. Thanks for your time." With that, I walked through the door, nodded to Sister Margaret, and left the building.

I yanked open my car door and dropped down onto the seat. I hate being condescended to and, in my book, Sister Julianna was the patron saint of patronization. I pulled out my cell and punched Coop's speed dial number.

"Is Cole Granger still in town?"

"Yeah. He got a job at Jorgenson's Tire. Been there awhile, ever since he got out of jail. Why?"

"I'll tell you later. Gotta go. Thanks."

All right, that would be my next stop. Right after I had a chat with Father Hegl. I rolled down the window and asked a passing staff member where I could find him. Per instructions I took the first turn to the left, and a short way down the graveled side road, I spotted a small bungalow. As I pulled in the driveway, a man in sweatshirt and jeans rounded the corner of the house carrying a rake.

"Father Hegl?" I asked, leaning out the car window.

"That's right," he said, walking toward me and smiling. "How can I help you?"

"I wonder if I could talk to you for a few minutes," I said, getting out. "I'm Leah Nash. Lacey Nash was my sister."

He looked puzzled and something else—uncomfortable, maybe?

"Really, it won't take long."

He hesitated still.

"Please? It's important to me."

"All right. Come on in." He leaned his rake against the side of the house, and led me through the front door and into a large living room. The first thing I noticed—it would be hard not to—was a floor-to-ceiling shelf on the west wall, filled not with books but with the largest collection of kitschy religious statues I'd ever seen.

"Wow."

"A little overwhelming, isn't it?" He flashed a disarming grin. "It started as a joke gift from my sister when I entered the seminary. She gave me that little dashboard Jesus up there in the corner. Then, over the years, people kept adding to it. Now, it's a kind of competition among friends and family to see who can gift me the most garish saint."

There must have been dozens of plaster, plastic, wooden, marble, painted, carved, cast statues. Most that I could see were hideous.

"Who's winning? The contest, I mean. There's some seriously wrong stuff up there."

"It's ongoing. And I guess it could be worse. She could have started me a Beanie Baby collection."

I liked the way the corners of his mouth turned up when he smiled and his blue-green eyes crinkled at the corners. He had light brown hair that fell casually onto his forehead and gave him that boyish appearance a lot of women like. He looked a few years older than me, maybe late 30s. He pointed me toward a worn leather chair, sat down himself in its counterpart, and waited for me to begin.

"Father, I was speaking to Sister Julianna, about my sister Lacey's death—"

"Sister Julianna sent you here?"

"Not directly." I explained to him about my failure to connect with Sister Mattea before she died, and the cryptic message I was trying to decipher, and my puzzlement over the missing $1,500. I may have implied that Sister Julianna was as intrigued by the mystery as I was.

"Sister Julianna seems convinced that Lacey was using drugs again, based in part on your story about finding Lacey trying to break into the dispensary drug cabinet."

"It's not a story, Leah. It's what I saw. And I was very sorry to see it. Your sister had a lot of promise. A beautiful voice, one of the best I've ever coached. I tried to get her to join our choir. We perform nationally, you know. But I'm afraid she wasn't ready to give up the things that brought her here."

I started to follow-up with a question about Cole, but his cell phone began to ring.

Digging it out of his pocket, he glanced at the number and said, "Sorry, I need to take this," and stepped into an adjoining room.

I seized the opportunity to snap a picture of the wall of saints and texted it to Miguel. He would love it. Then I glanced around the room while I waited and noticed another unusual decorating touch—for a priest anyway. A lighted display case on the wall behind his desk contained a selection of handguns. I walked over to peer in closer, then jumped when I heard a voice in my ear.

"Are you a collector?"

Startled, I took a step back to reclaim some of my personal space. "No. I'm kind of surprised you are. Handguns and priests don't go together very well, do they?"

He smiled. "I agree. The collection was my dad's. He was a handgun enthusiast. I'm not, but we spent some quality time together at the shooting range, and he left the collection to me when he died a few years ago."

"Isn't that a little dangerous to have around with all these troubled kids?"

He shrugged. "Students aren't allowed in staff housing. I doubt if anyone even knows the collection is here. Besides, it's locked—and wired with an alarm. If anyone tried to break in, security would know right away. Now, where were we?" He moved back to his chair and indicated I should resume my seat as well.

"I wanted to ask you about Cole Granger. Did you ever see Lacey with him?"

"Cole Granger?"

"The temporary groundskeeper, the one who got fired for smoking weed on the job?"

"That's right. I forgot about him. As a matter of fact, I did see him once with your sister."

"When was this?"

"A few days before she disappeared."

"Did you report it?"

"No. Why would I?"

"Because he's a known drug dealer. Because he was Lacey's ex-boyfriend. Because maybe, if she was using, he was supplying her."

"I'm sorry, but I didn't know any of that. So no, it didn't occur to me to link Lacey's drug use with Cole Granger."

"Suspected."

"What? Oh, all right. Her suspected drug use."

"What were they doing—Lacey and Cole?"

"Just standing on the sidewalk talking."

"You didn't hear what they were saying, can't remember how they looked? Was Lacey agitated, or was Cole threatening in any way?"

"Leah, I'm sorry. I don't think so, but I don't really remember much about it. It was just a few seconds and I went on. I only remember it because Cole left a rake laying across the walk, and I tripped and almost broke my neck."

"All right," I said, down but not defeated. "What about Sister Mattea, can you tell me anything about her? Can you think of anything, anything at all that she might have wanted to tell me about Lacey or the way she died?"

He shifted in his seat a little, clasping his hands together and leaning slightly forward.

"Leah, I'm very sorry that your sister is dead. But Lacey died because she wasn't able to overcome her demons. We offered her help, just as you and your mother must have offered help before she wound up here. But no one, not you, not me, not Sister Julianna, or any of the staff here can force someone to be saved if they don't want to be. Do you really think Sister Mattea had some knowledge that would magically make you and your mother feel better? You can't rewrite history." His words were a little harsh though his voice was not.

"You don't get it. I'm not trying to rewrite her history. I'm trying to understand it. I think Sister Mattea had a piece of that, and I'm going to keep asking questions until I get the answers I need. The fact that nobody else gets that doesn't change my mind at all."

"Obsession isn't healthy, Leah."

"I'm not obsessed."

"Five years after your sister's death and you're still looking for answers? Be careful."

What was he getting at? Be careful of obsessing? I didn't need his advice.

"Meaning?"

"Meaning your sister's life is over. Yours isn't. God always answers our prayers, but sometimes the answer is no."

"What's that, the Catholic version of a fortune cookie?"

To my surprise he smiled and shook his head, raising his hands in a gesture of surrender. And there was that crinkle around his eyes again. This time I didn't find it so appealing. Why was everyone talking to me like quick-fix therapists from some reality TV show?

8

The faded black and white sign for Jorgenson's rested on top of a pea-green cinderblock building that wasn't flaking so much as molting. A rusty purple Camaro, with "Bad to the Bone" stenciled on the side over a skull and cross-bones, was the only car in the lot. I parked and went inside, but there was no one behind the scratched and dented Formica counter.

An out-of-date State Bank of Himmel calendar on the wall announced that it was December 2009. I opened the door on the left and was immediately hit with mixed smells of rubber, oil, and gasoline. Rows of tires lined one wall. The concrete floor was sticky with accumulated layers of grease and dirt. On the far side of the garage, a pair of legs on a rolling cart protruded from beneath a green van.

"Hello? Have you got a minute?" I called.

There was no answer, but after a few seconds the cart came rolling out from under the van. A man in greasy jeans and dirty t-shirt stood and swaggered toward me.

"You need your tires rotated, sweetheart? You oughta make an appointment, but I might be able to fit you in." He gave me a look that I guessed was supposed to be sexy. It wasn't.

"Forget about it. It's me. Leah. Lacey's sister?"

We hadn't exactly been friends, so I wasn't surprised that he didn't recognize me. But I wouldn't forget him. Thin, petulant mouth, yellow-flecked green eyes, slicked-back mud-colored hair, thick-chested, muscular body. A dragon tattoo started under his sleeve and ran all the way down his hairy forearm.

He did a double-take, and his demeanor went from flirtatious to surly.

"Huh. Whadya want?"

"I want to know if you were supplying Lacey with drugs after she went to DeMoss Academy."

"What're you talkin' about?"

"Let's cut the crap, Cole. I know you worked there. I know you saw Lacey there. I know you got fired for smoking weed on the job. And I know you spent time in jail on drug charges. What I want to know is, did you sell to Lacey while she was at DeMoss?"

"I ain't got time for this."

"I'm aware that you and my sister were in a relationship."

"In a relationship?" He snorted. "Me and your sister wasn't in a relationship. We was hook-up buddies more like." He watched to see my reaction. What had Lacey ever, ever seen in this guy?

"I know you and Lacey had sex; you're not shocking me. I'm pretty sure that's all you had. But she spent a lot of time with you before she went to DeMoss, and I know you saw her there. It's a simple question. Did you sell her drugs?"

"No. And I never hooked up with your sister at her junior jail. And I ain't no drug lord either. Would I be workin' here, if I was? Or at that lousy job they fired me from at the nuns?"

"You might. Nice potential customer base there. And if you weren't selling how'd you wind up in jail?"

"Somebody had it in for me, that's all."

"Right." I tried changing tactics. "Look, Cole, I'm trying to find out what happened the day Lacey died. I'm not here to bust your balls, or get you in trouble. I just want to find out the whole truth about my sister." I explained briefly about Sister Mattea's message.

"Mattea. She the one used to walk out to the Point every day?"

I nodded.

"She was all right. Least she'd say hello like you was a human being." He seemed to be softening a little.

"Cole, you told the police you didn't see Lacey the day she disappeared. I think maybe you did."

"Yeah? Why's that?"

"If she was running away, she'd need someone to help her at least get into town so she could catch a bus, or to the highway so she could hitch a ride. Who could she call, but you? And you were talking to her just a few days before she left. Did she ask you to help her?"

He looked at me, seemed to be weighing something in his mind, then shrugged.

"All right. Yeah. I seen her. But I ain't tellin' the cops that because I don't know nothin' about what happened to your sister. She told me she was bustin' out of there. Said could I give her and a friend a ride, and we could have a little party before she left town. Lacey always was a party girl. So, I said yeah."

My heart started racing but I tried to look calm. I didn't want to spook him. "So, what happened?"

"I meet her like we planned at that big rock, Simon's Rock they call it, off the Baylor Road entrance around 10:30. I ask her where's her friend, and then this snot-nosed little kid, he comes creepin' out from behind the rock. I didn't want no part of some whiny brat. I said no way. She tried to sweet talk me. When that didn't work, she pitched a fit. I grabs her arm, just to calm her down like, but then she hauls off and kicks me in the nuts. Then she and the kid took off. Your sister was batshit crazy."

"What kid? What was Lacey doing with a kid? Who was it?"

"How should I know? I didn't want to get mixed up in anything then, and I sure as hell don't want to now."

"Did she go to a party that night with her roommate?"

"Like I said, I don't know what happened to your sister. Alls I know is I had nothin' to do with it. She took off, and I went over to my girlfriend Amber's. I told the police that's where I was, and she did, too. Except for the part about seein' Lacey."

"Nothing to do with it? Don't you realize that if you had given Lacey a ride like she asked, she might still be alive? Or, if you at least had told the police—they could've found that kid. Maybe he had something important to tell them.

"My mother and I put up flyers at bus stops, and haunted teen runaway centers and jumped every time the phone rang for six months, trying to get word on what happened to Lacey. Until we got the call that my little sister was dead! If you had helped her, maybe she wouldn't be!" My voice was loud and ragged, and my nails bit into the palms of my hands.

He stepped in so close I took an involuntary step back. His face was contorted with anger and he spat out the words. "You always did think you're better'n me and your shit don't stink. Well it does lady, and there's a pile of it in the middle of your nicey nice little family."

"What do you mean?"

"I mean Lacey's problem wasn't drugs. And it wasn't me. It was whoever made her his little baby doll. You had to know. You just didn't want that kind of mess in the middle of your perfect little life."

What was he talking about? That I wasn't there for Lacey? I already knew that. I didn't need this jerk to tell me. "What are you saying?"

"I'm saying somebody raped your little sister and kept on doin' it, and you didn't do nothin' about it."

"You're lying." My brain refused to process what he was saying, but my stomach had dropped like I'd stepped off a cliff.

"You ask yourself, why would that nice little girl from nice little family USA start hangin' out with the likes of me and my friends? Why'd she start smokin' weed and poppin' pills? Why did little princess turn into such a mad little bitch. Somebody turned her into one. I ain't lyin.'"

"Stop it. You are. You're lying. Lacey would've told me something like that. She would've told me. It's not true."

"Would she now? Seems like she didn't though. Maybe you was too busy with your big, important career. Cause you're so important ain't you, Leah? And you're so much smarter'n the rest of us, ain't you?"

"You're lying," I repeated in a flat voice. I pressed my lips and swallowed hard against a wave of nausea. Could it be true? Had Lacey been sexually abused? Was that why she was so angry, so self-destructive? But why wouldn't she tell me? It didn't make sense. But why would Cole even say it? Why would he lie?

I realized that he was still talking. This time, though, there was a smirk on his face and pseudo sympathy in his voice.

"It sure would be upsettin' to me. Thinkin' I let my little sissy down like you did. The guilt must be killin' you. I'd help if I could, but I can't tell you much except it happened. See, Lacey talked a lot. She was one of those drunks that just can't shut up. But me, I'm not what you'd call a real good listener. But I bet your Sister Mattea was. Maybe that's the big secret she wanted to tell you."

"Shut up. Shut the hell up." My head had begun to pound and a warm flush spread through my body. I needed to go.

He leaned in close again, and I felt his hot, fetid breath on my face. He grabbed my wrist and in a rasping whisper said, "Alls I know is, if it was me, I wouldn't be wasting time botherin' a poor, workin' man like myself. I'd be askin' to find out who messed with my little sis. Cause maybe that's the one who really knows what happened the day she died. And don't be tryin' to drag me into it. I said all I'm gonna say, and I ain't sayin' nothin' to the police."

He flung my wrist down so forcefully it cracked. Then he said in a normal voice, as though we'd been doing normal business, "Tell your boss we been holdin' his spare here for two months. He needs to pick it up. He gets a flat, he'll be shit outa luck. Besides, we ain't a storage locker."

9

I must have stopped at traffic lights, and yielded for pedestrians, and driven the speed limit, and parked my car, and passed for a normal person on the drive from Jorgenson's to McClain's, because I didn't get pulled over, but I had no awareness of the trip.

Coop was waiting when I got there. I guess I looked as bad as I felt, because within seconds of spotting me walk through the door, he led me to a booth, ordered me a drink, and sat down across from me. "What's wrong?" His eyebrows were drawn together in a concerned frown.

"I'm all right. Stop looking at me like you expect me to keel over."

"Take a drink," he said as the waiter put down a Jameson on the rocks. "Then tell me what's going on. Something is up." His dark gray eyes searched my face.

"I think Lacey was sexually abused when she was 14."

There. Saying it out loud should make it go away, right? I mean, it was crazy. If I said the words, I'd hear how ridiculous they were. But they weren't.

"All right. OK, take it easy. Why would you think that?" His voice was carefully neutral, but he couldn't conceal the shock in his expression.

I told him what Cole had said. He rubbed the side of his jaw with his thumb and waited for me to go on.

"I know Cole lies as easy as breathing, but think about it, Coop. Why this lie, why this time? What's the purpose? It's not getting him out of anything, in fact, it's getting him in deeper. He could've just kept denying that he saw Lacey at all. What he said, I just have a gut feeling it's true."

I waved away Sherry who had come to take our order, apparently having ousted the waiter when she realized Coop was sitting there. But Coop overruled me and asked for two burger baskets and water for both of us. Sherry tried a little flirting, but got nowhere. For once I didn't have the stomach for even a small victory smirk.

"What do you think?"

"I think you're putting a lot on the word of a punk."

"But it's not just him," I said, eager to make my point. "It's not just what he said. Look at the rest of it, Coop. I did a story on sexual abuse of adolescents a couple years ago. The sexual acting out, the drug use, the withdrawal from family, those are all symptoms. Lacey was a textbook case.

"She didn't morph into a demon child. Somebody made her that way. I just don't understand why she never told us, or at least me." Except, maybe I did. I had been really wrapped up in my own life then. Involved in my first serious relationship, anxious to prove myself at work, to get ahead. I didn't have as much time for my family as I should have. Maybe I didn't want to hear anything that would disrupt my happy new world.

"Slow down, Leah. For the moment let's say you're right. There are lots of reasons for a teenage girl not to talk about sexual abuse. Shame, guilt, fear. Her abuser can convince her it's her fault. Tell her that no one will believe her, maybe even threaten her or her family."

"I should have seen. I should have known. She should've been able to trust me."

"It's not a matter of trust. Are you listening to me? Kids that age, they've got so much going on, they don't think straight. She may have been trying to protect you. Or your mom."

"I should have figured it out."

"Leah, c'mon. You don't even know that it happened." He was right, I didn't *know*, but somehow it felt true.

"I know it might not make sense to you, but I have a feeling—all right, maybe it's more like a fear—I don't think Cole is lying."

He tried another tack. "OK, even if it did happen. You can't do anything about it. Lacey is gone and without her, how could you prove anything? Timmins isn't about to prosecute on behalf of a dead sexual abuse victim."

"No. But he'd have to if she were a murder victim." Where did that come from? I didn't even know I was thinking it until I said it, but Coop's immediate negative response didn't dissuade me.

"Whoa. Whoa, whoa, whoa. How did we get from suspected sexual abuse to murder?"

"Did you read the investigation report?" I reached across the table and grabbed his arm, trying to shake him into the growing sense of certainty I felt.

"I looked at it. It wasn't as thorough as it should have been—"

"Not as thorough? You must've just skimmed through it if you didn't see the gigantic holes. Look, Lacey disappears on the night of the big DeMoss fundraiser. Half the town was out there, coming and going all night. No nuns, no staff, no students, no visitors, nobody noticed Lacey where she shouldn't be? OK, give that it was a big night. Maybe most people wouldn't realize anything was wrong even if they saw her.

"But Ross does a half-assed investigation and doesn't even ask the right questions, because he's sure slutty little Lacey Nash just took off on her own. And pretty much everybody, including me, thinks he's probably right. Then, when her body is found, oh-oh that doesn't look so good. How to explain it? Oh, well, suddenly her roommate decides to come clean and confesses that Lacey went to a party with her and got wasted. Then, Ross and the medical examiner and Timmins all agree, she fell down the ravine in a drunken stupor and died of head injuries and exposure. Everything all tied up nice and neat.

"Until Cole finally tells me the truth. She met up with him that night. She wasn't going to any party. She was taking off, but for where? And she had a kid with her. What happened to him? Why didn't he come forward? And where's the money? She stole $1,500. She didn't leave the grounds, but it's gone? And her phone. What about her phone?"

"What about her phone?"

"It didn't register until now. She wasn't even supposed to have a phone. Students aren't allowed."

"She wouldn't be the first kid to get hold of a contraband pay-as-you-go phone."

"Sure, I know. But why wasn't there anything on it? The police file said there were no emails, no texts. No record of calls. Really? No emails? No texts? What teenage girl isn't texting? Where was her music, her pictures, or at least a few contacts?" I felt like I was channeling Sherlock Holmes, because I hadn't even thought of those anomalies until that very minute.

"If Lacey had a phone, why would she bother with Cole to get her out of there? Why wouldn't she call your mom and ask for help?"

"Because she'd be afraid Mom wouldn't believe her. That she'd call the school and they'd stop her. Maybe it had something to do with the kid she had with her. I don't know. But I know she did make a call. And it should have shown up on her phone. She called me. Only I didn't pick up. I didn't recognize the number. She left a voicemail." I let the words hang there, stark and ugly. I'd never said them out loud. To anyone.

Coop waited, not saying anything.

"I was covering a big accident, lots of casualties and chaos. We worked all evening and into the night. I just flopped into bed when we finished, didn't check my voicemail until the next morning. The connection was bad and kept breaking up. Lacey was talking so low, and she didn't make any sense. It was kind of a drunk whisper. I thought—" I stopped for a minute, took a big drink of Jameson. Coop still didn't say anything.

I finished in a rush.

"I thought she drunk dialed me. She just said Lee-Lee and then something like 'It's legal.' It didn't make any sense. I just felt so mad at her, Coop. I thought she had thrown out her last chance at DeMoss—that she was right back at it. And I couldn't jump back in with her. I deleted the message and didn't even try to call her back.

"When Mom told me she was missing, and it looked like she'd run away, I didn't say anything about the call. I didn't want Mom to think I could've stopped her, and I didn't bother to answer my phone. It didn't seem to matter. It was just like all the other times, and she'd surface after a few days or weeks."

Only, of course, it wasn't. I knew I should have picked up or at least called her back. That's why when her body was found, I felt so guilty, I was physically ill. Maybe, if I'd called her back, I could've saved her.

"You should have told Ross."

"You think I don't know that? You—"

He went on as though I hadn't spoken.

"I think you've got way more guilt than facts lined up here, Leah. It's clouding your judgment. The things that don't add up? Yeah, they do. Lacey took $1,500 and somebody at the party took it from her when she was drunk. Or, I'll even give you that maybe she didn't take it at all. Some other kid did and got lucky when Lacey disappeared the same day and the blame fell on her.

"But the other stuff—this mystery kid and the sexual abuse—that's all from Cole, nobody else. And he's a con man who already told you he won't stand by his story. Lacey's rebellion, her drug use, her anger—well, sorry to tell you but that can be part of being a kid. And the phone call? You had reason to think she was drunk dialing—and Leah, do you get this? You still have reason to think that. Lacey backslid, got drunk, called you—same old, same old. That makes a lot more sense than this theory you're floating."

He paused for a moment to see if he was making an impact. My crossed arms and the set of my jaw told him he wasn't.

He leaned forward and put his head between his hands in frustration for a second. The jagged scar running the length of his left index finger made a pale zigzag against his skin. When he looked up, he spoke in a much less understanding tone.

"What are you doing here, Leah? You're going to make yourself and everyone else crazy going over and over this stuff. I get it. You feel like you weren't there for Lacey. But you were.

"You were there every day of that kid's life, and you and your mom gave everything you had to help her. But sometimes, some kids can't be helped. It's just the way it is. And making up some crazy idea about sexual abuse and cover ups and murder, for God's sake, that's not going to help anything. And no one is going to get behind you on this. Not the sheriff, not the D.A. —"

"Not even you? What about you, Coop? Will you get behind me?"

"Ahh, don't do that. Don't make this about our friendship. It's not personal. I'm trying to help you here," he said. The thing is, I knew that he was. But he was wrong.

"Oh. I get it. You think I'm a delusional idiot. But nothing personal."

"That's not what I meant, and it's not what I think."

"Let me ask you this. If your sister died, and you thought there was something suspicious about it, would you stop asking questions?"

"No, I wouldn't. But I wouldn't create suspicions either, just because I couldn't deal with my own guilt."

We stopped talking then. I picked at my burger and fries, and Coop demolished his. Finally, I dug in my wallet for my share of the bill, then put it on the table.

"See you."

He nodded, and I left.

Instead of heading home I found myself driving toward the south end of town. When I pulled into the parking lot of Riverview Park, it was almost dark, and the grounds were deserted.

The grass was shaggy and sparse, overcome by dandelions and brown patches and the shrinking Himmel municipal budget. I got out of my car and walked to a weathered wooden picnic table. The flaking brown paint bore scratched random messages: of devotion "AK loves JB," self-promotion "Kiley 2010," and judgment "John Z is an asshat."

I sat down and looked at the sun-faded plastic "safe" playground equipment that had replaced the multi-level jungle gyms and hand-over-hands of my youth. I got my first broken bone at the park trying to beat Coop's time on the hand-over-hands.

In the dimming light, I could see the railroad trestle crossing the river at the north end of the park's boundaries, and beyond that JT's Party Store, home of Sour Patch Kids, Charleston Chews, and Slush Puppies, as well as more adult treats. I stared into space thinking about Lacey and what I'd done wrong. How I could have tried harder, been more patient, listened better, just have been a better sister.

Why didn't Coop understand? I wanted him to back me on this, help me figure it out, find the truth. But maybe he was right. Maybe Cole was just jerking me around. Once a con man always a con man. But why would he do that? What was in it for him? No. He was telling the truth. I just knew it. But I'd feel more sure if Coop could see things the same way.

My thoughts went round in useless circles, until finally the repeated wailing of a train in the distance penetrated my consciousness and took my mind in another direction. To another spring evening when Coop and I were both 12 and he got that zigzag scar on his finger. We'd gone to the park after dinner and time got away from us. It was almost dark and we were supposed to be home before the street lights came on.

"C'mon, hurry up. I'm gonna get grounded if I'm late again," he said as I *stopped to tie my shoe. I was wearing a cool pair of Adidas that my mother had picked up for half-price. The only flaw was that they were almost a full size too big. I tried to remedy the situation by tying the laces extra tight and double-knotting them. They weren't coming off, that was for sure—though I was starting to lose circulation in my toes.*

"Chill. We can go the back way, across the trestle and save 10 minutes." The *trestle spanned a narrow spot on the Himmel River, just outside the park boundaries. It wasn't very high or very long—maybe 18 feet above the water and 60 yards or so across. It only took about 10 seconds to scamper across, and there was rarely any train traffic. Nonetheless, my mother had forbidden me to take the shortcut. Then again, she had forbidden me to miss curfew, too.*

"OK."

We took off at a run across the park. When we were almost at the trestle, we heard the long, plaintive wail of a train whistle.

"Crap, the train's coming. We're gonna have to go the regular way," Coop said, *turning to go back toward Main Street.*

"No!" I grabbed his arm and pulled him back. "We won't get home in time. That train's miles away, we can make it, c'mon."

"No, I'd rather get grounded than creamed by a train."

"I'm going this way. You do what you want. I'm not getting grounded!" I said, impulsively, daring him to be as brave as me. Or as stupid.

I ran onto the trestle. I could see the train way down the track ahead, but I wasn't worried about it. What bothered me more was the simple act of crossing the narrow bridge. I'd always been a little scared of it—there were no guard rails, just open air on either side, and when you looked down, you could see the river below through the spaces between the ties. Other times, I'd kept my eyes straight ahead, looking at Coop moving confidently in front of me and just imitated his stride. This time, I was on my own.

But buoyed by the notion that I was going to best Coop at something and beat him home, with my mother none the wiser, I felt agile as a mountain goat. I moved with quick hops over the wooden ties, skipping over scattered broken glass and sharp pieces of rusty metal.

The train wailed again much louder this time, but when I looked up it was still a non-threatening distance down the track, and I had almost reached the far side. I looked over my shoulder for a second to give a victory fist pump to Coop, still watching me from the spot where I had chosen the road less traveled. I flashed a triumphant grin.

But as I turned around again and took the last step, instead of landing lightly at the edge of the bridge, I sprawled forward, my arms flung out in front of me, my cheeks scraping the rough wood of the splintered railroad ties. I could feel the vibration of the train through the track and a corresponding shudder of fear ran through me. I scrambled up but only got as far as one knee.

My left foot was caught and refused to break free. My foot in its too-big shoe was firmly wedged between two railroad ties. I reached back and grabbed my ankle with both hands and gave a tremendous yank. My foot, and the shoe, stayed put. I dimly heard Coop yell, "Leah, Leah, the train!"

I looked up. The engine that had been so far from me was coming at warp speed. My fingers fumbled as I frantically tried to untie my knotted laces. Tears streamed down my face.

"Leah!" Coop was beside me. I felt the trestle shake as the train rumbled closer.

"Get out of here!" I shouted above the din of the train's whistle.

He shoved my hands out of the way and sawed at the laces of my shoe with a piece of rusty metal.

"Hurry, hurry, hurry, hurry!" I repeated in a frantic mantra, though he couldn't hear me. I put my hands to my ears to shut out the sound and squeezed my eyes tight against the terror, but my entire body was filled with the noise and throbbing of the oncoming engine. I couldn't tell where the pounding of my heart ended and the shaking of the trestle began.

"I'm sorry, Coop, I'm sorry, I'm sorry."

He kept sawing, then gave a fierce tug and the lace broke. My shoe loosened, and with a tremendous yank, I pulled my foot free. At the same moment, I felt a hard shove in my chest. Then I was floating in open space. A half-second later the hot breath of the diesel engine as it roared past hit me with the force of a blow, and I fell.

When I hit the water, it was with body jolting force. I plunged to the bottom of the muddy Himmel. I came up coughing, sputtering, and missing a shoe but otherwise fine. Wiping my eyes, I saw Coop clambering up the bank. I swam the few yards to join him. He was shivering and his finger was bleeding pretty badly.

"You all right?"

"You are such a dickhead," he said.

I had to agree.

What with the police coming, and half the gawkers in town converging on us, and stitches, and tetanus shots, and a chewing out from Officer Darmody, who was first on the scene, any hope of keeping our parents from finding out died.

Coop was grounded—though he was featured as a hero in the *Himmel Times*. I was under house arrest for a month with my Aunt Nancy keeping watch over me and Lacey, because as my mother said, "I can no longer trust your judgment, Leah Marie."

Coop had my back then, like he always did. And now, just because he didn't agree with me about Lacey's death, it didn't mean he wasn't on my side. Maybe it meant he was right. To be honest, this wouldn't be the first time I crossed the line from reasonable doubt to unstoppable obsession. I just can't give up when something doesn't make sense. That's what makes me a good reporter. It's also what lands me in trouble more than I like.

But this time I wasn't pursuing a story, trying to get an exclusive. This time it was about my little sister and what happened to her and why. The anger and resentment I'd felt toward her for so long was gone. Coop was wrong.

It wasn't guilt that was driving me, though I had that in spades. It was a burning need to resurrect Lacey the way she had been, and perhaps, underneath all the rage and rebellion, the way she'd remained. I wanted to see her again, I wanted my mother to see her again, the way she really was. And

I wanted whoever took that away from her, and took her away from us, to pay.

10

When I got home, my mother was loading the dishwasher.

"How was your run?" I asked. She tried to get in a couple of miles after work most days, and she was still wearing her running gear.

"I was on my way out the door, but I wound up not going. The blood drive called their list of O negative donors and asked us to come in because they didn't meet their quota or something. Ellie Schreiber was donating right next to me."

"Yeah?"

"She seemed really worried, Leah."

"About Alex?"

"No, no, he's fine. She's concerned about Max. She said he's worrying himself sick trying to keep the paper going."

"Yeah, I know. It's rough on him." I knew where this was heading and tried to distract her. "Too bad you had to miss your run. Your time has really improved. Of course, you'd probably pick up an extra 10 minutes if you dumped that lanyard you wear. It kind of makes you look like a preppie coach from 1980."

She lifted it off the little nail by the kitchen door and waved it in front of me, then pointed with her finger ticking off the items.

"I refuse to be shamed for being prepared. My front door key, my car key, my mini Swiss Army knife. I can get into my house, start my car, open a wine bottle, tighten a screw, defend myself or file my nails. Quit trying to distract me," she said, hanging it back up and walking over to lean on the bar where I had pulled up a stool.

"Ellie said Max got a call from Sister Julianna. She was concerned that the paper was questioning the school's role in Lacey's death."

"Yeah? Well, that's not what happened today. Ellie should mind her own business."

"I think she thinks it is her business. She's anxious. She's afraid you're making things harder for Max. She's worried about his health, too. Max is under a lot of stress. His father died of a heart attack at exactly his age. Did you know that?"

"Oh, come on. Ellie's trying to play the health card? And if she's really concerned, maybe she should make him cut down on his double burger baskets. Max will outlive all of us. And I'm just as concerned about Lacey as she is about Max. I found out some things today, and they're not very good." I struggled with how to tell her what I knew and what I suspected it meant. There wasn't any easy way to say it.

"What sort of things?"

I explained my questions about the missing money, and told her what Sister Julianna and Father Hegl had said about Cole and the drugs. I didn't say anything about the phone. I wasn't ready to face the look in her eyes if she knew I could've helped Lacey that night and hadn't.

"Leah, everything is so black and white with you, isn't it? First, Lacey is a monster child you can't wait to drop off at DeMoss. Now, she's an innocent scapegoat? You know how much I loved Lacey, but I've had to face the fact that it wasn't enough. Don't forget, there was hydrocodone in her purse. She was drunk the night she fell. I've known since her body was found that she must have been using again."

"I'm not saying she was innocent. I'm saying something happened to her, something really terrible, and we didn't see it. So, there was no way we could help her." I searched for a way to soften the blow, to keep her from feeling the sharp, searing guilt I'd felt when Cole told me. But there wasn't any way to make it less awful to hear than it was.

"What are you talking about?"

I dropped the bombshell and told her what Cole had said. She pulled out a stool and sank onto it.

"I don't believe it. I would have known. I couldn't not know something like that."

I put my hand on her arm. "I'm sorry, Mom."

She shook it off. Her expression had gone from stunned to angry. "It isn't true. It is not true."

"I think it is, Mom."

"No. Stop talking like that."

"I thought you wanted to know what really happened to Lacey."

"I know what happened to Lacey, and you do too. She wasn't sexually abused. She would have told me."

"Mom, you have to see it makes sense."

"No. It doesn't. This isn't some front page story you're trying to get. This is real. This is our family, and you are wrong. I won't listen, do you understand?" She stood up without another word and left the kitchen. In a second, I heard the door to her room close with a violent thud.

Well. That's what you call a first-rate day. A sleazeball drug dealer informs me my sister was sexually abused and hints she was maybe murdered, my best friend thinks I'm an obsessed conspiracy nut, and my mother is so angry, she can't stay in the same room with me.

The next morning, when I wandered into the kitchen, I found a note. "I bought you some Pop Tarts yesterday. Coffee is made. LOL." Which my mother persisted in thinking meant "lots of love" instead of "laugh out loud."

I tried to respond in kind. Food is the way we apologize, celebrate, comfort, and commiserate. Nothing says Nash family love like a heaping helping of something to eat. I took off early from work that day and hurried home to make the one thing I have in my cooking repertoire. Coincidentally, it happens to be my mother's favorite meal: Grandma Neeka's meatloaf and twice-baked potatoes. Her car pulled in the driveway just as I pulled the meatloaf out of the oven.

The kitchen was still pretty much a disaster. I'm not sure how it happens, but whenever I cook, things turn chaotic. Every cupboard door was open, there were pans on the stove, spills on the counter, measuring spoons and aluminum foil on the stove, and pans soaking in the sink. But I hoped the tantalizing scents of dinner would blind her to the post-Katrina conditions in her kitchen.

"It smells great," she said, walking through the door. "What are you doing home already? And cooking?"

"I have a ton of comp time, and I was just hungry for some meat loaf." I moved around the kitchen shutting doors and sweeping errant utensils and cups into the sink.

"That's nice."

"How was work?"

"Busy. Karen's in the middle of a complicated probate case, and our secretary quit with no notice." My mother was a paralegal for a one-woman law practice, and her boss, Karen McDaid, was also her closest friend.

"Mom, about what I said last night—"

She interrupted me before I could finish. "No. Stop. I shouldn't have just walked out on you. We should have talked." She put her purse on the bar and cleared a space in the sink so she could wash her hands. Looking over her shoulder as she lathered up, she continued.

"Leah, I was in therapy for a year trying to figure out how I could make such a mess of two great kids. I finally got to a place where I could forgive myself for not being a perfect—or even a very good—mother. When you hit me with the idea that Lacey had been sexually abused, and I was too dense to see it, I—well, it took my breath away. I wasn't angry at you, not really, but it was just so hard to hear."

She wiped her hands and walked over to where I was standing. "I've been thinking all day, and I don't want to believe you're right. But I do want to know the truth. And there's a little part of me that says maybe, maybe. Lacey's behavior was so different, so self-destructive. There has to be a reason. Doesn't there?"

"I think so."

She helped me set the table and get the food on. When we were seated, she asked me, "What does Coop say about what you're thinking?"

"He thinks I'm crazy, like you do, and there's no point anyway, because Lacey is dead. And even if I found evidence, they wouldn't prosecute, and what can I expect to find after all these years, and don't be so stupid."

"Don't exaggerate. I didn't say you were crazy, and I'm sure Coop didn't either. Isn't he right, though? After all this time, what can you hope to find? And even if you do turn up something that supports Cole's story, they won't prosecute with Lacey gone."

"That's true." I paused a beat, then said, "Mom, there are so many off-kilter things about Lacey's death. It really bothers me. The missing money, her phone with no contacts or anything else on it, the convenient story her roommate suddenly came up with, everything Cole said. Sister Mattea's note with the newspaper clipping. Something is seriously not right with this whole thing."

"It seems like you're taking it for granted that what Cole said is true. Why do you believe him?"

"Because there's no advantage to him in making up that story. In fact, it puts him in line for more trouble if it's true. I know he's a liar. I just think this time he's telling the truth. I'm going to find out one way or another."

"How?"

"I'm going to start at the beginning. Eight years ago, when things started to go to hell. The summer she was 14."

"But who are you going to talk to? You can't think anyone we know, any of our friends could have molested Lacey."

"Most abusers are someone the victim knows, not some guy in a van with candy." I was already running and rejecting possibilities in my head, but the next words I spoke I hadn't intended to say out loud.

"What about Paul Karr?"

She looked stunned. I tried to backpedal. I didn't really think it was Paul —at least I had no reason to think he was more likely than any of the other men Lacey was around a lot.

"I'm not saying he did anything. I'm just thinking of adults she knew who had the opportunity."

"Not Paul."

I understood her reaction. I liked Paul too, though probably not nearly as much as she did.

"Nobody can be off-limits. Not even people we like a whole lot. The police didn't even try to find the pieces the first time around. I'm going to pick up every last one of them, and see what kind of picture I get." I leaned across the table and covered her hand with mine. I'd taken the conversation this far, I might as well go the whole way.

"Remember what Cole said? That whoever 'messed' with Lacey might be the one who really knows what happened the night she died? I don't think Lacey's death was an accident, Mom. You're right. The DA will never do anything about an eight-year-old sexual abuse case with a dead victim. But if I find enough evidence, he'll have to reopen it. This time as a murder investigation."

The word "murder" hung oddly in the air in our bright white and navy kitchen with the cheery yellow accents—as out of place as *The Scream* hanging on a wall of kindergarten drawings. But there it was.

Then the doorbell rang.

11
———

"It's Paul!"

We both jumped like guilty things surprised. Mom opened the front door just as Paul hit the buzzer again. He grabbed her hand and started an impromptu swing dance to the opening strains of *In the Mood*. I'm not much of a one for spontaneous dancing, and the sight of two late-middle-aged people engaging would be disconcerting under normal circumstances. In the current situation, it was all kinds of wrong. Paul caught my eye mid-twirl and his grin faded. He stopped, then looked at my mother and raised an eyebrow.

"Carol? What's going on?"

"Nothing," she said with an attempt at a smile that didn't get beyond a grim baring of her teeth. He looked back and forth between us, puzzled.

"What's going on?" he repeated.

"Come on in, Paul," I said.

He sat on the couch, then leaned forward with his long-fingered hands clasped in front of him. His sandy-colored eyebrows were drawn together in a frown that looked odd on his normally cheerful face.

"Carol?" he asked again.

"Paul, would you like a drink?"

"Do I need one?"

"I do," she said. I waited while she made two strong bourbons on the rocks and handed him one.

"Paul, you know that one of the nuns from DeMoss died last week."

"Sure, yes. Everyone knows. Someone's head should roll for not putting a barricade up at the Point. Never should have happened. Was she a friend of yours, Leah?"

"I knew her. The thing is, Paul, she left a message for me a few days before she died. A message about Lacey."

"Lacey?" His dark brown eyes registered curiosity but nothing more that I could see.

"Yes. I think she was trying to tell me that Lacey's death wasn't an accident." I explained about the clipping and some of the inconsistencies in the police report. "I've found out a few more things, too."

"I don't understand."

My mother, who had been tapping her foot up and down and fidgeting in her chair, could contain herself no longer. "Oh, for God's sake, Leah, just say it." Then she proceeded to say it for me. "Leah thinks Lacey was sexually abused, and that's why she started getting into so much trouble. And she thinks Lacey was killed by her abuser, because she was going to identify him."

If it weren't so serious, it would have been funny to watch the slow motion changes on his round open face as the words sunk in. His jaw dropped, and his eyebrows lifted on his high forehead. "You can't be serious! The police investigated—twice!"

"They did a bad job. I should have seen it at the time." I gave my increasingly familiar summary of what I believed had happened.

"If your friend the nun knew about this, why didn't she just tell you?"

"I don't know what she knew, Paul. Maybe she just had a suspicion, maybe she remembered something, maybe someone told her something. But she died before she could tell me."

"So now Leah is planning to investigate it herself," my mother said, in the same tone she might have used announcing that I was planning to become a pole dancer.

"How?"

"By talking to people. Somebody could be holding on to a piece of information they don't even know they have, or that they don't understand the significance of."

He shook his head, ran his hand through his curly hair and then turned to my mother.

"But if she were abused, wouldn't she have told you, Carol? Surely Lacey would have said something?"

"I don't know. Maybe not. Maybe she didn't feel like she could come to me. I don't know."

"That's ridiculous. Of course she'd come to you. You were her mother."

"Kids don't always find it easy to talk to their parents. Sometimes they confide in other adults they trust," I said. Now things were going to get really awkward. I mean, there's no easy way to question your mother's beau about your sister's sexual abuse. It wasn't that Paul topped my list of suspects by any means, but despite my mother's understandable distress, I had to start somewhere. I had to ask.

"Lacey didn't say anything to you, did she, Paul? She worked with you in your yard a lot that summer you put in your rose gardens. You spent a lot of time with her."

"Yes, but we didn't have that kind of relationship. She'd never confide something like that to me."

"She never said anything about a teacher at school, or a friend's father or anything that seemed maybe just a little odd, something out of the ordinary?"

"No, never."

"What about after she went to DeMoss? Did you ever see her? You used to volunteer with the mentor program there. Did you ever run into her? Did she seem any different?"

"No. I never saw her."

"That last night, the night of the fundraiser. You told the police you left early with Miller Caldwell, because he had a toothache. You went to your office. Did you go by the main drive? It would have been shorter to take Baylor Road."

"Miller drove. He took us down the main drive. It was a toothache, not life and death. We didn't need to save three minutes going the back way. Why?" His voice sounded puzzled.

"You didn't see anything, any parked cars where they shouldn't be, any students walking toward the park trail?"

"No."

"What time did you leave?"

"I don't know, maybe 6:30, 6:45."

"So, did you go back when you were through with Miller?"

"I didn't. Miller did. His tooth was fine. Sometimes that happens, just a sudden jolt, but there's really nothing wrong. Those fancy dinners were Marilyn's thing, not mine. Once I escaped, I stayed at the office and did some work. Marilyn wasn't happy."

"How did you get home?"

"My car was at the office. But when I went to leave, it wouldn't start. I wound up walking five miles home. She was just pulling in when I got there, and she couldn't have been happier to see me coatless and freezing. I damn near caught pneumonia. Why does it matter?"

And here we go. Paul is not a stupid man, and he clearly got the implications of my questions. He was mad. I couldn't blame him. But, as is my gift and my curse, I pressed on.

"What time did you get home?"

"I don't know, somewhere around 11:30, I think." His voice had hardened. "What is this, Leah? Do you seriously think I sexually abused Lacey? That I would ever do anything to harm your sister? What's the matter with you?"

"I don't think anything, Paul, I'm just trying to gather as much information as I can. You're not the only person I'm going to talk to."

He had placed his drink on the table and was standing. I stood too.

"Strangely enough, it doesn't comfort me to know that I'm only one possibility on your list of suspects. I did not molest your sister. I did not kill her to protect my dirty little secret. For the record, I don't believe anyone did. I think you're chasing after a bad guy who doesn't exist. But you should be careful. Because if it turns out to be true and you ask the wrong person the right questions, you could find yourself in a very bad situation. Carol, I'll call you later."

Then he turned and walked out without another word.

I was afraid to look at my mother.

"Could that have gone any worse? You really hurt Paul. Do you intend to interrogate every adult male who knew Lacey that summer? Miller Caldwell? Father Hegl? Max? Dr. Steffenhagen? Don't let the fact he's been in a wheelchair for 15 years stop you."

"I won't."

"You can't randomly accuse people we know, people who have been our friends for years, people who would never—"

"I didn't accuse Paul. Why don't you ask yourself why he was so uptight?"

"Why wouldn't he be? He comes to what he thinks is a friend's house and instead he walks into the lion's den. He is not going to forget this. Neither is anyone else you talk to. This is going to hurt people, change lives. Our lives, if you go ahead."

"Mom, our lives are already changed. They've been different for the last five years. The only way I know how to go ahead is to go forward with this. I have to know."

We both sat quiet for a minute, then I said, "What did you mean just then when you asked was I going to talk to Father Hegl? Why him? "

"Because he was Lacey's director on *The Wizard of Oz*, that summer she turned 14."

"He never said that he knew Lacey before she went to DeMoss."

"Well, he did. The first year he was here they asked him to step in when the regular director got sick. It was just after he arrived at DeMoss. He probably forgot."

"Hmm." I was following another train of thought. "Remember how Lacey was babysitting for the Caldwells all the time that summer? She was either at rehearsal or at their house. Saving money for her Spanish Club trip to Spain. And then, boom, she stopped. No reason, just didn't want to anymore."

She sighed and stood up, taking her glass to the kitchen and putting it in the sink before she said, "Could you please stop, just for tonight? You do realize that you waltzed in here this evening and told me that my youngest daughter wasn't only sexually abused, she was possibly murdered. And, oh yes, maybe by a man I really like. Someone who's been a friend for 30 years.

Or by one of our other friends. Once you get an idea nothing else matters. You're ready to mow down everyone with a machete to prove you're right."

"Mom, I—"

"I really can't talk about this anymore tonight. I'm going to bed."

"I'm sorry. Really. I just don't know how else to do this."

She nodded, then turned and walked down the hall. It wasn't until after I heard her turn off her light that I remembered something she'd said earlier. "I was in therapy for a year trying to figure out how I could make such a mess of two great kids."

Make a mess of two great kids—what did she mean by that? I wasn't a mess. Was I?

12

The interview with Paul had turned really ugly, really fast. And my mother and I were at odds again. Was I obsessing instead of investigating? I wandered around picking up the glasses, loading the dishwasher, and wondering if I'd have any friends—or a mother—left by the time I was done. I looked at the clock. 11:15.

On impulse, I grabbed my wallet and keys and headed out the door. In a few minutes, I was pulling up in front of a small brown brick bungalow. Through the curtains I could see the gleam of lamplight in the living room. I knocked on the arched wooden front door. I heard footsteps coming and the door swung in, revealing a short little man with fluffy white hair and a surprised but welcoming expression on his face.

"Leah! How nice. Come in, come in."

"Hi, Father Lindstrom. I'm sorry it's kind of late, but I know you're a night owl."

"Yes, yes I still am. In fact, I'm just having a cup of tea," he said. "Can I interest you in one?"

"Sure, that would be great."

Father Gregory Lindstrom was the parish priest during most of Lacey's troubled years. He's been a good friend to our family. I really like him, even though I haven't been a practicing Catholic since I was 12.

He led me into the kitchen, and as he fussed around putting the kettle on to boil I asked, "How's retirement? Everything you hoped for?"

He half turned as he set the gas flame to the right height and gave me a rueful smile.

"I'm afraid I've found that my expectations and the reality are quite different. When I was serving as a parish priest, I was anxious for the time when I could spend my days fly fishing, researching, reading and thanking God for the privilege. But after a few months, I found myself praying to Him for some real work to do.

"It seems I value leisure only when it's measured out in small doses. So, when the bishop called and asked me to return to St. Stephen's while Father Sanderson is undergoing cancer treatments, I was only too happy."

The kettle whistled, and he prepared the tea, handing mine to me in a cup bearing the image of Mr. Spock. As he sat down at the table with his own mug, I saw it bore the phrase *The Truth Is Out There.* He noticed my glance. "Father Sanderson is a diehard *Star Trek* fan. I've always been an *X-Files* man myself."

We sipped for a few minutes in companionable silence, and then Father Lindstrom spoke. "Leah, I'm delighted to see you, of course. But a visit at this hour is unusual. Is there something on your mind?"

I was finding it unexpectedly hard to get started. I began by dancing around the topic.

"Did you know Sister Mattea Riordan, the nun who died recently?"

"I had spoken to her once or twice but, no, I can't say that I knew her. Was she a friend of yours?"

"More of an acquaintance. It's quite an operation they have out there. The Catherines. DeMoss, I mean. Why do they wear those old-fashioned habits, do you think? Most of the nuns I know—well, actually I only know two other nuns—but both of them dress pretty regular, you know, pants and blouses and things."

He gave me a look that said he knew the clothing preferences of religious orders had nothing to do with what was on my mind, but he gave my inane question the same thoughtful attention he gave to every conversation.

"There are quite a few orders that either never gave up or have returned to traditional habits. It's a form of identification as a community, and it signifies a new way of life, like taking a new name when you take your vows, as I believe the Catherines do. A habit is a sign of commitment and perhaps a sort of protection."

"Protection? From what?"

"We all wear habits, Leah, physical or emotional, as a way to protect our secret selves. I have a habit of dispassionate observation to preserve the illusion that my soul is untouched by the messier pangs of human emotion." He paused and took a sip of his tea.

"You have a habit of cynical wit to mask the pain of a loss-filled life. The physical habits the Catherines wear may be important to them as a way to help protect their integrity as a community of faith. But they are far less interesting and certainly far less dangerous than the emotional habits we all use to cover ourselves. Don't you agree?"

And, we're done. A look-see at my psyche was definitely not where I wanted to go then. Or ever. But Father Lindstrom's incisive observation did have the benefit of plunging me right into the subject I'd come to discuss.

I set down my cup and opened the floodgates, telling him everything that had happened since Sister Mattea's body was found. He didn't say anything, just let me unload my suspicions, my guilt and my theories.

"So, everyone thinks I'm overreacting. Mom is really mad, because I questioned Paul Karr tonight, and Ellie thinks I'm going to give Max a heart attack, or make him lose the paper, or both, and Coop just thinks I'm on the wrong track and too stubborn to admit it. And what if I am? What if all of them are right, and I'm all wrong?" I wound down. I half-expected him to tell me something about letting go and forgiving myself and letting God take care of things and blah, blah, blah. But I should have known better.

"What about you, Leah? What does your experience, your instinct, your heart tell you?" He had taken off his black plastic rimmed glasses and was carefully polishing the lenses.

"That Lacey's death wasn't an accident. That she was crying for help for years but I didn't hear her. That now I do, I can't ignore it. I have to find the truth. I have to know the answers."

"Well, then. Does it really matter what others are telling you? Keep your heart with all vigilance, for from it flows the springs of life."

"You know I'm not much into the Bible stuff. That is the Bible, right?"

"Yes. Proverbs 4:23. Follow your heart, Leah, but be careful. It can lead you toward the darkness as well as toward the light." His eyes behind his thick lenses were steady and serious.

A little shiver ran through me and a sudden suspicion arose. "You know something, don't you, Father?"

He shook his head. "About Lacey's death? No."

"What then?"

He took a last sip from his mug of tea. "Finding the truth isn't always the same as finding the answers, Leah. It requires great discernment to know which is most important."

"I don't understand."

"When you need to understand, you will." He stifled a small yawn, and though I was far from satisfied with his answer, I felt guilty when I looked at my watch and saw it was nearly 12:30.

"I'm sorry for keeping you up, Father. I'd better get going. Thanks for, well, thanks for being here."

"My door is always open, Leah."

Finding the truth about Lacey was always on my mind, but work that week didn't give me much chance to do anything about it. In addition to the regular paper, we were putting out a special section: *Summer Fun in Grantland County,* allegedly a celebration of the wonders of Wisconsin—our piece of it, anyway. In reality, it was an attempt to generate additional ad revenue. Max and the sales guys had been beating the bushes for business from the local pontoon factory, the festival and fair committees, restaurants, canoe rentals, and any other business remotely linked to summer activities.

That meant writing a ton of puff pieces designed to please the advertisers who purchased space in the section. It went against every journalistic bone in my body—and it used to Max's, too. It was a sign of how desperate he was for revenue. Other times I might have mouthed off, but things were not that great between us at the moment, so I shut up, hunkered down, and cranked out the copy.

On Saturday morning, I was at the office writing a piece describing the joys of kayaking down the Himmel River, with quotes from expert kayaker Punk Onstott. Punk, not coincidentally, was the owner of Onstott Hardware & Sporting Goods selling a full range of quality kayaks and accessories. I paused for a minute and leaned back in my chair for a good stretch, then jumped when I saw a figure looming in the doorway. "You scared me! What are you doing here, Miguel?"

He looked perfect, even on a weekend morning, wearing dark wash skinny jeans, a navy striped shirt, a close-fitting gray vest and a pair of Converse sneakers. He sat down on the corner of my desk.

"I could ask you the same, *chica*. If I knew you were here, I would've brought you a chai latte. Of course, if you showed up to meet me and Coop at the Elite, like you were supposed to, you could've got your own."

"Oh, I'm sorry, I forgot! I just—"

"Hey, I'm cool. Coop's the one who was not so happy. What's with you two?"

"He thinks I should leave Lacey's death alone. That I'm not being objective, I have too much guilt to see things clearly."

"Well, do you?"

I shook my head. "Of course, I feel guilty. I am guilty. I did about a thousand and one things wrong, and if I hadn't maybe Lacey would be alive. But that doesn't mean that everything I've found out doesn't count."

"*Dígame*. And don't leave anything out."

I'd done my best to avoid Miguel since my meeting with Cole. I didn't want Max getting mad at him for getting caught up in my Lacey drama. I should have known that wouldn't work for long. I told him my current working theory. Miguel was a much more receptive audience than anyone else had been to date.

"So, if I accept that Cole is telling the truth, which at the moment I do, then I have to find out who abused Lacey, because there's a damn good chance that he had something to do with her death. So far I've talked to Paul Karr—"

"Your *mamá's* boyfriend?" His eyes widened.

"He's not her boyfriend."

"No?"

"Well, she's a little old for a 'boyfriend,' don't you think?"

He laughed. "*Chica*, just because you got no social, don't try to step all over your *mamá's*. She's a pretty lady. She should have some fun. So should you, but you, you are so *obstinada*! But I'm not giving up."

"Yeah, well, whatever. I want her to have fun. And I know that Paul's always seemed like a good guy, but..."

"So why did you accuse *mamá's* boyfriend?"

"You sound like my mother," I snapped. "I didn't accuse him. I just asked some questions; that's what reporters do. Don't you want to be one of those when you grow up?"

He looked surprised. And hurt.

"I'm sorry. That was nasty. I should be snapping at myself. I'm so frustrated. I feel like I'm going nowhere. Maybe I'm too close to this. Maybe I shouldn't do it."

"*Chica*! Don't talk crazy. You have to try. You always have to try for your family."

I knew he understood in a way that Coop couldn't. When he was 16, Miguel's older cousin was collateral damage in a robbery gone wrong in Milwaukee. Miguel was a witness, and got a beatdown to keep him from testifying, but he did it anyway. Afterward, his mother sent him to Himmel to live with his Aunt Lydia and Uncle Craig.

"You can do it. I can help you. I'm a professional reporter, *mi querida*. It says so right here on my notebook." He held up the narrow flip-top pad most journalists use to take notes. The brand we used at the *Times* had the words *Professional Reporter's Notebook* on the front cover. I laughed.

"You're right, Jimmy Olsen, it does."

"So, who do you think besides Paul Karr?"

"Miller Caldwell."

"The bank guy? The one who's running for senator? You think he abused Lacey?"

"He could have. He had plenty of opportunity. Lacey took care of the Caldwell kids all the time. She even went on trips with them once in a while."

He still looked skeptical.

"But Miller Caldwell—he gives big money, I'm talking serious *dinero*, to that foundation for abused kids."

"I know. He's also on the board at DeMoss Academy. But think about it. Maybe he protests too much. Maybe he does so much good to make up for doing so much bad."

"I don't know, *chica*, I think—"

"Look, I'm not saying he's the one. But you asked. Then there's Father Hegl."

"The priest at DeMoss? Why?"

"He knew Lacey before she went there, and he never said a word to me. He had plenty of opportunities to be alone with her when he was directing *The Wizard of Oz*. And he's a charmer if you like the type. He'd be able to manipulate a teenage girl, and smart enough to figure out what would keep her quiet after."

"OK, well, let me help. I'll take the *padre*, see what I can find out about his back story."

"No, seriously, I can't let you do that. I'm likely to make a lot people mad, including Max, and I don't want you tangled up in that."

"Too late, *chica*. I already wrote it down in my notebook. Now, it's official. I gotta follow the lead."

I hadn't talked to Marilyn Karr since Lacey's funeral, and then it had been a stilted thank-you-for-coming conversation. She had looked very *Vogue* in a black dress, her carefully highlighted auburn hair pulled back in a French twist, her expert make-up unmarred by tears of sympathy. She didn't reach out to hug me the way most people did, just held out her hand for me to take, then withdrew it and gave me a slight nod.

I had never gotten over the habit of calling her Mrs. Karr, and around her I always felt as though I should be apologizing in advance for social errors she could see in my future.

But for this conversation we needed to be on equal footing. I wanted to check Paul's story. If his car really wasn't working, and Marilyn really did get home around 11:30 just as he was getting there too, that would mean he hadn't been back at the Catherines' running into Lacey after Cole dumped her. I practiced calling her Marilyn in my head until the name came easily before I punched in her number.

"Marilyn? Hi. It's Leah, Leah Nash."

"Leah?" she sounded surprised as well she might. The last time I had called her was never.

"Yes. Hey, I'm sorry to bother you on a Saturday afternoon, but do you have just a minute to talk?"

"I am rather busy—"

"This will just take a minute."

"Well," she hesitated, but curiosity got the better of her. "Yes, I suppose so, Leah."

"Great." A brief but awkward silence fell as I tried to summon up the appropriate tone for the questions I was going to ask.

"Great," I repeated.

"Yes," she said with some impatience. "I really would appreciate it if you got to the point?"

"Right. Sorry. Marilyn, do you remember the night of the DeMoss fundraising dinner, the night my sister Lacey disappeared?"

"Your sister? Leah, I don't understand—"

"You do remember that she disappeared the night of the dinner, right?"

"Yes, yes, I suppose so. It's been so long—"

"You were at the dinner with Paul, and he left early with Miller Caldwell."

"Yes," she said, obviously puzzled. "What has that got to do with anything?"

"Was Paul just getting home when you got back from the dinner around 11:30? Was he walking because he had car trouble?"

She didn't answer immediately, and in the pause that followed I heard what sounded like wine glugging into a glass and then a long swallow. Possibly Marilyn enjoyed a late afternoon cocktail hour. "Why don't you ask your mother about Paul's whereabouts that night?"

"My mother?"

Another swallowing sound. "I know Carol Nash is seeing Paul. Probably was seeing him for years before our divorce."

"That's not true. My mother wouldn't do that."

"Oh really? Well, all I know is Paul left me at the dinner with some ridiculous excuse about taking care of Miller's tooth. And he never came back. It was humiliating. I'd like to forget everything about that night. I wasn't even seated at the bishop's table. Sister Julianna was. And Reid Palmer was. But not me. No, not the person who served as fundraising chair for three years. No. I was seated next to Sister Margaret and one of the DeMoss scholarship winners. It was unbelievable!"

She said it as though she'd been relegated to sit in the fireplace ashes next to Cinderella. I tried to get her back on track with Paul's movements that night, but she was determined to air her grievances.

"You must have been glad when the night ended. When you got home—"

"It was an interminable evening. Sister Margaret could not stop bleating about her mundane duties, and that scholarship child talked of nothing but her pathetic 'future.' And then Reid deliberately undermined me.

"He said he 'forgot' the large-scale drawing of the new rec center I wanted to use in my after-dinner speech. He said he'd go to the administration building to get it right away, but he didn't come back until my speech was over. In fact it was after eleven and the dinner was over before he showed back up. Everyone was leaving.

"Oh, he was *so* apologetic, said he had trouble locating it. He poured on that phony Southern charm. But I wasn't fooled. I was a threat to his dictatorship on the board, so he ruined the recognition I should have gotten that night.

"I resigned the next morning. And I take great pleasure in knowing they still haven't raised the funds to complete that center."

"I'm glad you found the silver lining. I'm sorry the evening was so disappointing."

"I never think about it. I've moved on." Another long swallow.

"I don't want to keep you, Marilyn, but I did just want to clarify that after the dinner, Paul arrived home about the same time you did, around 11:30."

"He wasn't home when I got there. I have no idea when he got in, but his car was in the driveway when I got up the next morning. I don't have any more time for this now. Or ever. If I were you, I'd ask your mother where she was that night. Goodbye, Leah."

And we're done. Or at least Marilyn was.

Paul's tone was frosty when I called to check Marilyn's version of the story.

"I'm sorry to bother you, Paul. I just had a conversation with your wife —your ex-wife—that has me confused."

"I think you're confused about a lot of things, Leah."

"Marilyn said you weren't there when she got home, and she didn't see you again until the morning. And your car was in the driveway when she got up."

"Of course it was. I called the garage, and they jumped it and drove it back for me."

"You didn't say that before."

"You seem to be under the impression that I owe you some kind of minute-by-minute accounting of my life. I don't. Marilyn is either misremembering—an unfortunate side effect of her drinking—or she's lying."

"Why would she do that?"

"She enjoys wreaking havoc. Maybe she has that in common with you."

"Paul, I know this is awk—"

"It's more than awkward Leah, it's insulting. Don't call again."

13

When I got home, I didn't bother to tell my mother what I'd been up to, and she didn't ask. We had been tiptoeing around each other for days, neither wanting to get into it again. So, she pretended that I had heeded her advice and dropped things, and I pretended that she had decided to let me do what I had to do. We Nashes are skilled in the art of denial.

However, as soon as I walked in, she pounced on me with a box of groceries and some old clothes and said, "Good! You're home. Could you deliver these to Vesta Brenneman? I have to go back to the office. Karen's out of town and needs some information from the files ASAP."

"What is it?"

"Just some summer clothes from St. Vinnie's and a few groceries and treats."

"You know Vesta hates it when people go to her house. The last time I delivered something, she threw crabapples at me. She's crazy."

"What are you, 12? She's not crazy. And you're not kind. She's old and she's eccentric. It's not a crime."

"Eccentric? Mom, she stares right through you when you talk to her, or she starts shouting Bible verses. She rides around on her bicycle all day, scares little kids—and some big ones, too. She looks—and smells like—she hasn't taken a bath in months. Is it really 'kind' to let her fend for herself? Maybe she needs social services help, not random charity."

"She's living as she wants to. What's wrong with that? And if we can help her do it with just a little effort, shame on us if we don't. If you go now, she won't be home. She'll still be out riding. You can leave the things by her door."

"OK, OK. I'll fill in for you, Mother Teresa, but remember, I'm just the understudy. Don't plan on me taking over your starring role. Give me the stupid box."

She grinned because she got her way. She usually does. "Kid, you're walking out there an understudy, but you're coming back a saint!"

I laughed because I have the same stupid sense of humor she does, and because it felt nice not to be quietly tense with each other as we had been for the past week or so.

She handed me the box, gave me a shove, and sent me out the door.

Vesta lives in the only house on the last block of Birch Street before the metropolis of Himmel gives way to country roads. It's not much of a street, cracked asphalt instead of concrete, and there isn't a birch tree in sight, just a few scraggly box elders. My heart sank as I turned in her driveway and saw her faded red Schwinn leaning next to the front door. She was out on the front step before I got the box off the back seat, her little mixed-breed terrier tagging at her heels.

She wore a shabby gray cardigan over a flowered print house dress of the kind someone's grandma might wear on *The Waltons*. Underneath was a pair of tan men's work pants rolled up to her ankles, and on her feet were black high top tennis shoes with no laces. Her stringy gray hair was pulled back in a long ponytail, but wisps trailed across cheeks that were as brown and wrinkled as old ginger root. She stared at me, arms folded across her bony chest.

"Hey, Vesta. Remember me? I'm Leah Nash. Carol's daughter. Just dropping off a few things Mom was hoping you could take off her hands."

"You got any tin foil?"

"Why, yes, yes I do. As luck would have it, here's a nice roll of it."

Her eyes lit up the way mine would if you offered me a box of chocolates. She came down off the step and rooted around in the box. I struggled to balance it on my knee to give her easier access as she dug through the contents. Apparently satisfied, she said, "In there," pointing to the front door, then motioned for me to follow her. I'd never been invited in before.

It was dark and crowded inside, but relatively neat. A metal bed with springs was set in the corner, covered by a pink chenille bedspread. A wooden rocking chair was next to it and beside that was a basket full-to-overflowing with balls of aluminum foil of various sizes. A table made out of an old door and two saw horses were in the middle of the room, bowed under the weight of glass jars filled with rocks and gravel. Beside them was a large family-style Bible. Plastic bags filled with feathers lined the window ledge above her kitchen sink. She had a mini fridge and an ancient apartment-sized electric stove in the corner.

I let out a gasp when I turned to the left and saw a chest of drawers piled high with dozens of babies, then quickly recognized them as naked plastic dolls.

"My collections. You got collections?"

"No, not really."

She nodded as though it were to be expected.

"Well, can I set this here?" I nodded toward the table and she nodded back. "There, that's that then."

"*Charity never faileth: but whether there be prophecies, they shall fail; whether there be tongues, they shall cease; whether there be knowledge, it shall vanish away.*"

"Absolutely. Well, I'd better get going. See you, Vesta."

"My Dorrie is dead."

I wasn't sure if Dorrie was a daughter or a sister or a friend—or a figment of Vesta's imagination.

"Dorrie?"

"My Dorrie," she said a trifle impatiently, as though she'd explained all this to me before. "My sister. Your sister is dead."

"Yes." I wanted to get out of that hot, musty room, away from the uncomfortable presence of this suddenly intense, more than slightly crazy lady, but my mother's words, "if we can help her with just a little effort, shame on us if we don't," inconveniently came to mind.

"I'm sorry about your sister. When did she die?"

"You were there. In the twilight, in the evening, at the time of night and darkness."

"No, Vesta, I wasn't there. Do you mean you were with your sister when she died?"

"Her feet go down to death; her steps lead straight to the grave."

Oh boy. Had I just encouraged her into a full-blown psychotic break?

"Vesta, are you all right? What's wrong?"

"And I looked, and behold a pale horse: and his name that sat on him was Death, and Hell followed with him."

Her eyes were unfocused, and she started making little humming noises.

"Vesta!" I said as sharply as I could. She looked at me in surprise.

"Don't take my collections."

She pushed at me with unexpected strength.

"It's OK. I'm leaving. Just dropped the box off from Carol Nash," I repeated trying to reorient her in reality. "But I'm going now."

I backed out lest she bash me in the back of the head with a jar of rocks and then beat me to death with a dead doll baby. I got in my car and shoved it into reverse, while she stood on her front step and watched me. An involuntary shudder ran down my spine as I sped down the street. That was spooky.

And that was the last time I was running this particular errand for my mother. I took the corner onto River Street just a hair too fast, and the squeal of my tires reminded me I needed to get air in them. There was a gas station just a few blocks away, but within several yards of my *Fast & Furious* turn, I saw a blue light flashing in my rearview mirror.

Great. I pulled over and watched as the cop got out and came toward me. Darmody. Even greater.

I rolled down the window, and he leaned in. "Where's the fire?"

"Nowhere. My tires are just a little low, so they squealed when I rounded the corner."

"Uh-huh. I clocked you at 45 in a 25."

"Come on, Darmody. I was just doing a good deed. Took some food and stuff to Vesta."

"You want to watch it out there. She's kinda unpredictable. Where you been lately?"

"Oh, pretty busy at the paper." I tried to be pleasant in the hopes he wouldn't write me up, but I wasn't anxious to pass the time of day with Darmody.

"Yeah? I heard you and the lieutenant got into it at McClain's the other night. Sherry said that—"

"Yeah? Well Sherry doesn't know what she's talking about."

"I get it. You got a little cat fight going there, Leah?"

"Darmody, I think you need a refresher course from HR on sexual harassment. Are you going to give me a ticket or what?"

"Nah. I'll let you off with a warning. Don't use a hair dryer in the bathtub." He then laughed so hard he started snorting and had to wipe the tears from his eyes. I shook my head.

"Thanks."

Seeing Darmody reminded me how much I missed Coop. But I wasn't ready to talk to him about Lacey again. Not until I had enough to tell him so that he couldn't blow me off.

To my surprise, I'd had no trouble booking an appointment with Sister Julianna when I called, though Sister Margaret warned me the director was on a tight schedule. I'd have to be there before eight o'clock, so she could make her flight to a conference. Early mornings are no problem for me, but when I arrived at 7:30 Sister Margaret wasn't at her desk, and the door to Sister Julianna's office was closed. I walked to the reception desk and called, "Hello? Sister Margaret?"

There was a thudding sound from the direction of the small room that housed the copy machine behind the reception desk. A second later a little nun came scurrying out, a guilty look on her face.

"You caught me! I was just closing the window in the copy room before Sister Julianna gets in."

"You're not allowed to open the windows? Sister Julianna runs a tight ship."

"It's not a problem during the day, of course, but when the security system is on at night, we shouldn't," she said, in a voice that sounded like a small child repeating a parent's reprimand.

Then she grinned. "But it's just a small window, and I open it just a smidge. It makes such a nice little bit of fresh air here in my corner in the morning. I just turn that zone off on the alarm system and no one is the wiser."

"Your secret is safe with me."

She sat down and wiggled around on her chair for a minute like a bird getting comfortable in its nest, then looked at me with her bright eyes. "So nice to see you again. Sister should be here in just a few minutes. Did you get a chance to talk to Father Hegl about Lacey?"

"I did, thanks. And I've talked to a few other people as well. It sounds odd, I know, but I really don't think I knew my little sister as well as I thought I did."

"Well, we all have our secret selves."

I wondered what dark depths might be hidden beneath Sister Margaret's cheery persona. "Sister, do you remember Lacey's roommate?"

"Oh, yes. Delite Wilson. She was a tough cookie, that one."

"Did she finish out at DeMoss?"

"Yes, but it was touch and go, I don't mind telling you. Sister Julianna didn't want to give up on her though, especially after she came forward and told the truth about going drinking with Lacey that night. Sister thought it showed some evidence of conscience. I wasn't convinced."

"Why was that?"

"Well, it sounds unkind to say, but I'm afraid Delite didn't have much spiritual integrity."

"You mean like faith?"

"No, not exactly. I've seen many children come and go, and the ones who make it have what I think of as spiritual integrity. You know, a core of basic decency. I pride myself on being able to spot it. Sister Julianna may be the expert, but I know what I know."

"What happened to Delite?"

"If I remember correctly, she moved to Appleton to live with a sister after she graduated. I hope I was wrong about her, but I'm usually not," she said, with more regret than complacency in her voice.

"I'd really like to talk to her. Do you think you could get me her sister's name and address?"

"Well...," She hesitated.

"Please? It's just that she was the last one to see Lacey."

"We're not supposed to give out student information, but I suppose in this case...well, it's not really student information, is it? It's just her *sister's* address." She struggled with her conscience for a second, then said, "All right dear, I'll see what I can find."

"And, I wonder, could you give me Father Hegl's phone number? He was really helpful, and I'd like to talk to him again."

"Oh, I know that one by heart. 292-5731."

The light on her phone blinked, and she picked it up. "Yes, Sister. She's here. I'll send her right in."

She saw my puzzled expression. We'd both been standing in the middle of the room, and Sister Julianna had definitely not passed us on her way to her office.

"Sister has a door with direct access to the outside in her office. There's a nice little courtyard there just off the side drive."

Sister Julianna smiled as I walked in and moved around the corner of her desk, her hand extended. I shook it and said, "Thanks for seeing me, Sister, I understand you have travel plans this morning."

"That's quite all right. I know you weren't very happy with our last conversation, Leah. I'm hoping to hear that you've found some peace of mind." She surprised me by sitting down in one of the chairs in front of her desk and motioning me to the other, instead of moving back to her power seat.

"Really? I thought that you called my boss to complain that I was harassing you."

"I did call," she said, showing no sign of embarrassment. "But not because I felt we were being harassed. I was worried about your state of mind. And I suppose when you tried to link Lacey's disappearance with Sister Mattea's death, I was a little concerned that you were trying to sensationalize things for the paper."

"Sister, if I wasn't clear before, let me be now. I'm not representing the *Times* in any capacity here. I'm asking questions as Lacey's sister, not as a reporter."

"That's what your editor said. I'm sorry if I caused you any problems there. It's just an upsetting time for everyone. Are you feeling more at ease now that you've had time to reflect on things?"

"Actually, I've got more questions now than I did before."

"Oh?"

I plunged right in.

"I think that Lacey was sexually abused before she came to DeMoss. I want to know if there's anything in her records or counseling files that would confirm that."

She flinched, but she answered calmly. "That's very serious. If we had had any knowledge of sexual abuse, it would have been reported to the police. It's both a legal and moral obligation. Are you sure about this?"

"Pretty sure. Lacey showed all the typical signs of sexual abuse in adolescence—the behavior changes, the anger, the sexual acting out, drug use. It all fits."

She relaxed a little and put her hand on my arm. "Leah, you must know those behaviors are common in troubled adolescents. Sexual abuse is far from the only cause."

"I understand that. But Lacey confided in someone at the time. Just not in me. I blame myself for that."

"And you blame DeMoss as well?"

"No. But I'm hoping DeMoss can help. Are there any case notes or a counseling file I could look at? Maybe I'd see something there that wasn't apparent to the counselor at the time, or maybe—"

She was shaking her head before I even finished. "Our counselors are professionals, trained to help children in crisis. It's highly unlikely that you'd find anything in a file that they had overlooked. In any case, we purge the records of minors five years after treatment ends. There are no counseling files to look at."

"What about talking to her counselor?"

"Our professional staff comes and goes—it's not a very well-paid job, I'm afraid. They usually leave for more lucrative practices once they get some experience. I don't believe we have anyone here now who was on staff then. And I really can't recall who Lacey's counselor was. We have over 200 students and that was almost six years ago."

"So, you're saying there's no one in the whole school who can tell me anything about what Lacey might have been thinking while she was here?"

"I'm sorry. I really am."

"I'm going to find out who sexually abused her."

"To what end, Leah? And how can you even hope to know for sure that she was abused after all these years and without her corroboration?"

"Sister, do you know who the young boy Lacey was seen with that last night might have been?" If she was startled by my abrupt shift she didn't show it.

"This is the first I've heard of a young boy. You think another student was with Lacey? I doubt that. I would have known about it at the time."

"But you didn't know about Lacey. I think there were a lot of things that none of us knew. Someone got away with sexually abusing her. I'm beginning to think they may have gotten away with killing her as well. And I have to wonder if that isn't what Sister Mattea wanted to tell me."

"You can't be serious." Her mouth had dropped slightly open in astonishment.

"Oh, but I am."

There was a light tap on the door, and Sister Margaret stepped in. "I'm so sorry to disturb you, but Sister Esther is waiting in the side drive. You'll miss your plane to the conference if you don't leave right now. Here are the reports you wanted to take. Your luggage is in the car." She thrust a brown leather briefcase into Sister Julianna's hand and gestured toward the door that led to the side drive. Uncharacteristically, Sister Julianna dithered. "Ah, Leah, just—Sister Margaret—please—"

I took the opportunity to slip through the main door. "No problem, Sister Julianna. I think we covered everything. Don't miss your flight on my account."

In a few seconds, Sister Margaret came hop-stepping into the reception area where I waited by her desk. "I'm sorry I had to interrupt. But Sister Julianna has no sense of time. As it is she's cutting it fine to make her plane. I don't envy her. I couldn't stand all that flying around the country giving speeches. But, like she says, the board does like the recognition it brings DeMoss. Oh, I did get the name and address of Delite's sister for you." She tore a sheet from a pink notepad and handed it to me.

"That's great, thank you. Just one more thing, Sister Margaret. Do you remember if Lacey was friendly with a blonde kid, a boy somewhere around 9 or 10?"

"Oh yes. That would be Danny Howard. Beautiful child, small for his age though. He was actually 12, I think. She stepped in when one of the bigger boys was bullying him one day. He was devoted to her. Just devastated when she disappeared. He became very withdrawn and uncooperative. In fact, he was outplaced not long afterwards."

"Outplaced?"

"Yes, sometimes the children who aren't doing well in the group environment here are sent for one-to-one intensive family care. Some of the students do better in that setting."

"And Danny, did he do well?"

Her chipper expression faded.

"No. I'm afraid he didn't. Eventually, he ran away. He was never found."

I thanked her and turned to leave, clutching Delite's phone number in my hand. I had almost reached the door when she called me back.

"Leah, wait! I'd forget my head if it weren't screwed on." She waggled back and forth in a gesture of self-exasperation that sent her veil fluttering.

"What is it, Sister Margaret?"

"You should talk to Mr. Palmer. He had Lacey in his office the day she disappeared. Maybe she said something to him that would help you."

"Isn't disciplining students a little below the Board Chairman's pay grade?"

"Oh, he wasn't disciplining her. He was rescuing her. Remember, I told you one of our new intakes kicked up quite a ruckus that day? Sometimes that happens and with this boy there was a lot of shouting and some language, I can tell you. The things I've heard would make my father blush, and he had quite a salty tongue.

"I had to call security. Lacey was sitting in that corner chair over there waiting to see Sister Julianna, and Mr. Palmer had come out to see what the commotion was. He spotted Lacey and right away he went over and took her to his office to get her out of the fray. It was a good 20 minutes or more before things calmed down. So, when I remembered, I thought maybe you'd like to speak with him."

14

As I walked to my car, a gust of wind caught hold of Delite's address while I was trying to tuck it in my purse. After a few undignified stoop-and-runs across the concrete, I nabbed it with my foot and bent down to pick it up. When I stood and turned around, Reid Palmer was directly behind me.

"Wow. *The Secret* really does work," I said.

"I'm sorry?"

"I was just wishing I could talk to you, and here you are."

"I saw you on your paper chase and came to offer my assistance. It's an unexpected pleasure to see you again so soon. Not thinking of joining the order, are you?" It was a lame joke and the delivery suffered from his oddly formal diction, but still, he was trying to be pleasant.

I smiled. "No, I'm pretty sure I'm not Catherines material, Mr. Palmer. I just had an appointment with Sister Julianna." I dropped the note in my purse.

"About your sister again?"

I nodded.

"Was she able to help you?"

"Not really. But I wonder if you might be able to. Sister Margaret just told me that you spent a little time with Lacey the day she disappeared."

He frowned in thought for a second, then his brow cleared.

"Yes, of course. That was the day one of our new students precipitated an incident in the reception area. I do remember now. I brought your sister into my office until things calmed down." His slight drawl was very comforting to listen to. He smiled.

"Would you like to come to my office for a cup of coffee, Leah? If I may call you Leah? And you must call me Reid. I have a special French roast I think you'd like."

"Sure, that would be nice." As we walked I asked him, "Why do you have an office in the administration center? I thought you were a lawyer or investor or something like that."

He smiled. "Something like that is quite right. I am a lawyer, but it's been years since I practiced. I have been fortunate in my life to have the means to indulge myself by doing things I enjoy. One of those things is helping DeMoss and the students here."

Sister Margaret looked up as we walked back in, but she was on the phone and just nodded.

His office was large and well proportioned. It included built-in book-shelves holding equal parts books and things that looked a little too classy to be called knickknacks. I sat down at a small round table while he went to a credenza behind his glass-topped desk. He poured water from a carafe into a high-tech coffee maker. While he searched out his French roast, I got up to look closer at a pencil sketch matted in gray and resting on a minia-ture silver easel on his bookshelf.

The drawing featured a kneeling boy offering water to an eagle. The artist had used hatching, shading and shadows to give depth and life to the sketch. The child's body looked smooth and supple, and the eagle feathers were so detailed the bird looked three-dimensional.

"Do you like it?"

"Yes. Who's the artist?"

"Thank you." It took me a second to get the implication. "You?"

He nodded. "I do a little sketching. Purely for stress relief."

"It's amazing. It looks...Greek?"

"Very good. It's actually a drawing of a sculpture in the Thorvaldsen Museum in Copenhagen. It depicts a scene from Greek mythology. The boy Ganymede offering water to Zeus, who has appeared to him in the form of an eagle. I made the sketch some time ago on a trip to Denmark. I have a copy of the sculpture in the gardens at my summer home."

"Did you make that too?"

"No," he said as he handed me coffee in a gold-rimmed china cup with saucer. "I'm afraid my artistic talents end with a little pencil scratching on paper. I commissioned a sculptor to make the piece for my garden. You can see it if you look closely in that picture," he said, pointing to a large photograph on the wall opposite his desk. "That's Highview. My summer home. I host an outing there every year for DeMoss students and staff. Perhaps you'd like to come this year."

A beautiful garden ablaze with summer blooms was in the foreground of the photo, and to the left, part of the sculpture was visible. In the background, a white two-story Greek revival mansion sat atop a hill. It looked like something out of *Gone With the Wind*.

"That's your *summer* home?"

He smiled.

"It is. A trifle ostentatious, I know, but my great-grandfather was a Southerner to his core. He grew up in Florida, but his wife, my great-grandmother DeMoss, was from Wisconsin. He fell in love with the north woods and built Highview for her as a summer place to showcase his Southern heritage. My grandfather was born there in 1910."

"So, it passes from one generation to the next?"

"It has, but unfortunately I'm the last of the direct line. My wife died several years ago. We never had children. Perhaps that's why I put so much energy into the school here."

"Didn't your grandmother start DeMoss?"

"Helped to fund it is more accurate. Yes, she spent summers in Wisconsin and went to boarding school here when the Catherines ran an academy for young ladies. She was very fond of the order. When they decided to reopen the school with its current emphasis on helping troubled children, she set up a trust to support it."

"Very generous."

"Giving back is a tradition in our family. What about you Leah, and your family? You wanted to ask me something about your sister?" He sat down and began drinking his coffee as I put my cup down.

"What did you and Lacey talk about after you brought her to your office that day? Was she upset? Did she tell you anything?"

"She didn't. I tried to engage her a little. I like to talk to the students and find out something about them when I have the opportunity, but your sister was... uncommunicative. She answered all my questions with yes and no and didn't volunteer anything. I could see she didn't want to talk to me. So, I just brought her a Coke and left her here while I tried to help settle things out front."

"Did she seem upset? Anxious? Afraid?"

"Upset? Yes, I'd say so, but that was understandable. The scene out front was unsettling. But afraid? No. I wouldn't have left her if I'd thought that. Why would she be?"

I debated how much I wanted to say. But no doubt Sister Julianna would tell him everything I'd told her anyway, so I might as well. "It's not very pretty. I'm afraid that my sister Lacey was sexually abused, and her death was a direct result of that."

"You think someone at DeMoss molested your sister?" He looked shocked, and I almost felt bad for upsetting his Southern gentility with my bluntness.

"I didn't say at DeMoss. Actually, I think it was before that."

"But even if that were true, how would that have led to her death?" He paused then answered his own question. "You mean because she responded to the abuse with her drinking and reckless behavior?"

There it was again. The underlying implication that Lacey had only herself to blame for a tragic but predictable end.

"No. I mean because someone killed her. Probably the person who abused her."

"Ah. To keep her from revealing the secret?" Well, bonus round to Reid Palmer the first person whose immediate reaction wasn't, "You're crazy, Leah."

"Exactly."

"Interesting theory, but what evidence do you have that your sister was abused?"

I told him what I'd told Sister Julianna, but I couldn't guess what he was thinking. His colorless eyes made him hard to read. For some reason, it felt really important that I convince him I was on the right track.

I found myself going into detail about Sister Mattea's note and outlining for him the inconsistencies in the police report: the fact that Lacey had confided in someone else about the abuse, and finally, that she had been seen with a young boy, a student at the school, the night she disappeared.

"I agree with the original police assessment—she was running away. But everyone was wrong about why. She wasn't just trying to get away from DeMoss rules and restrictions, she was trying to save herself. I think she was afraid she was in danger. And I think Sister Mattea learned something about that—I don't know how. She died before she could tell me."

He had sat perfectly still while I spoke, his eyes fixed on my face and an unreadable expression on his own. When I finished, he took a sip of coffee, placed the cup down to his left, then leaned back in his chair, his arms casually crossed. I waited.

"You're certain the source who told you about Lacey and about the child is reliable? More reliable than the young woman who was her roommate and related the story of their illicit drinking party?"

"Reasonably sure. My source isn't exactly above reproach, but has no reason to lie, and telling me was unplanned, I think."

"But what reason would your sister's roommate have to lie?"

"Maybe she was smart enough to know that Sister Julianna was a sucker for a sinner who'd seen the light. It could be that she saw an opportunity when Lacey's body was discovered. There wasn't anyone to dispute her story. And it worked. She wasn't transferred."

"Possible, I suppose."

Encouraged, I pressed. "The little boy is the kicker. I mean, why would Lacey have a little kid with her if she was going out to get wasted? She wouldn't."

"That's a valid question. Do you know who the child was?"

"Yes. Danny Howard. Trouble is, I understand he was shipped out for bad behavior not long after Lacey left, and he ran away from there. Sister Margaret said the school wasn't able to find him, and no one knows where he is now."

"Yes. Quite possibly he's living on the streets. It happens more often than people realize. That's why DeMoss is so vital. Unfortunately, we can't save everyone. This Danny must have been a particularly hard case." His pale eyes seemed to darken a little—with sadness? "What about your sister's abuser? Do you have any idea who that might be?"

"A few." He waited, but I'd done enough sharing.

"Well. I'm sure anything DeMoss could do to help, we'd be happy to."

"You might want to check with Sister Julianna on that. I don't think she's so keen on it."

"I'm sure she's just concerned that the reputation of the school not be compromised. That doesn't mean she wouldn't want to know the truth as you find it."

"Maybe." It was hard to keep the doubt out of my voice. "Reid, are you certain that Lacey spoke with Sister Julianna that day?"

"When things calmed down, I took her from my office to Sister Julianna's myself, so I'm fairly certain."

"It's just that Sister Margaret thought that Lacey left without speaking to her."

"As I said, there was a great deal of commotion that afternoon. I suspect she's just misremembering. Is it important?"

"No, no. I'm sure you're right."

I felt a twinge of disloyalty toward the little nun who had been so helpful. I stood to go, and he rose as well. Then he said something that made me take a step back.

"Leah, if you think your sister was killed, and you believe Sister Mattea had some knowledge of that, do you also think Sister Mattea was killed?"

"It crossed my mind. But so far, I'm the only one who even thinks Lacey's death is suspicious. Everyone would think I'd really lost it, if I started questioning Sister Mattea's death, too," I said, thinking of Coop's deflating skepticism when I tentatively brought it up with him.

"You don't strike me as someone who seeks approval before taking action, Leah."

"Are you saying you think I should be linking the two deaths?"

"No. Definitely not. I was just wondering if that's where your thoughts were heading. On the one hand, the story you present is quite fantastical."

He smiled, perhaps to take the sting out of his words.

"On the other, the inconsistencies you point out are puzzling. I've always been fond of puzzles."

"Be straight with me, Reid. You think I'm on to something. You think Lacey's death is suspicious, don't you? And you agree Sister Mattea knew something about it?"

"I don't know if you are 'on to something,' or not, Leah. I do believe you have a curious mind, in the best sense of the word. But as my grandmother was fond of saying, 'Curiosity killed the cat.' Not very original. Still, there's a good deal of wisdom in the old sayings. Do consider that, if you're right about your sister, pursuing this could put you in danger as well."

He stepped aside so I could leave, saying in clear dismissal, "Please keep me informed of your progress. Perhaps I can help at some point."

15

When I walked in the front door of the *Times,* Courtnee was redoing her makeup. I don't mean opening her compact and dabbing some powder on her nose. I mean sitting in front of the makeup mirror she keeps in her bottom drawer, reapplying shadow, eyeliner, and mascara. From the look of the supplies in front of her, that was only the beginning.

As soon as she saw me, she jumped up. Not because she felt guilty about turning her cubicle into a Mary Kay consulting room, but because she had something to impart. I could tell by the light in her baby blue eyes.

"Max wants to see you as soon as you get in. I think he's mad," she said in a conspiratorial whisper, leaning over the counter as I checked the spike for messages.

Gossip is the real coin of the realm in Courtnee's world, and she clearly felt like she was about to make a killing on the market.

"What's he mad about?"

"He got a phone call from someone, and after while came out looking for you, and then he said to tell him as soon as you got back."

"Who called?"

"I was on another line, wasn't I? I think he said Rick Panther or something like that, but I had to get back to my mom, so I didn't really listen that well. Aren't you going to go and see Max?"

"Yes, don't worry about it." I grabbed the box of baklava—Max's favorite —that I'd picked up on impulse on my way back from the Catherines and headed down the hall.

Max's office looks like Miss Havisham's house without the decaying wedding cake. Open bags of snacks on the desk, stacks of newspapers on the floor, M&Ms (plain, not peanut) in every available container, manila file folders piled high at crazy angles, bowling trophies on dusty bookshelves, Kiwanis Club plaques on the wall, and a clock that shows the time in six different time zones. All incorrect.

"What's up?" I asked, moving a pile of papers off the chair in front of his desk.

He had been tilted back in his seat, his favorite death-defying balancing act. Now he leaned forward, bringing the front casters down with a thud.

"What the hell are you doing?"

"Bringing you baklava?" I smiled and held out the box, but without much hope that it would placate him. It didn't. He set it down on top of a pile of old newspapers.

"Leah, it's not funny. I asked you. No, I told you. Stay away from the Catherines. Leave your crazy theory about Sister Mattea and Lacey alone. There's no story there. Why can't you just once do what I tell you? I'm not gonna let you cost me this paper." A little vein on the side of his forehead had popped out and throbbed for emphasis.

"But, Max—"

He continued as though I hadn't interrupted. "I talked to Reid Palmer a little while ago."

Of course. Rick Panther. "Oh?"

"You know anything about that?"

"No. Well, that is, I saw him this morning, and we had coffee, but I don't know why he'd call."

"Because you're poking around bugging the Catherines, and that's bugging him!"

"Is that what he said?"

"He *said* that he wanted to talk with me about my refinancing plan. He *said* that there are a lot of things to consider. And then he said he saw you this morning at the Catherines.'"

"Max, what's wrong with that?"

"Read between the lines, Leah. Guys like Palmer don't come out and say things. They hint, they imply, and you better understand, because they're not spelling it out for you. He's telling me I might have a chance to get the money, but there are 'a lot of things to consider.' Like whether we do a story that makes it look like DeMoss was responsible for Lacey's death."

"Max, you're losing it. I talked to him, and I talked to Sister Julianna this morning, and they both know that this has nothing to do with the paper, that I'm pursuing my own theory. And besides he was sympathetic to me, he didn't seem threatened. I told him I didn't blame DeMoss. I—"

He ignored me, and his face got redder as his voice got louder. "I'm warning you, Leah, and I am serious as a heart attack, you'd better damn well stay away from the Catherines, stay away from DeMoss Academy, and stay away from Reid Palmer. Otherwise, you're gonna have plenty of time to work on that true crime book of yours."

I sat back in my chair and stared at him without speaking. I'd seen him angry before, plenty of times, and more than a few of those times it was at me. But never like this. In the face of my silence, he calmed down a little.

"I'm sorry. I know you think I'm going off the deep end. But I can't let anything get between me and the loan I need. Not even you. If I do, the paper is going to close. For the first time in more than 75 years, there won't be a *Himmel Times*. This has to be it. Period. End of discussion."

Courtnee was lurking in the hallway, and I nearly knocked her over as I beat a hasty retreat.

"Wow. Max really got after you for bothering the nuns, didn't he? I thought he was gonna fire you!"

"Max isn't going to fire me," I said, with more confidence then I felt, because there was no way I was going to stop trying to find the truth about Lacey, and no way that truth didn't somehow involve the Catherines. I dropped the camera bag and my purse on my desk and realized that Courtnee had followed me into the newsroom.

"Don't you need to be out front?"

"I'm on break. What are you wearing to Miguel's *Cinco de Mayo* party on Saturday?"

"I don't know."

"You know how I have this little dress with red and white stripes and blue stars that, like, I wear for the 4th of July? I thought I'd do, like, that. Only for Mexico, with this really cute red skirt and a yellow top. Like, my outfit will be the same color as their flag for their Independence Day."

"Mexico's flag is green, white, and red, Courtnee. Spain's flag is red and yellow."

She stared at me for a minute. "But my outfit is red and yellow. Are you sure?"

"Yep. And Cinco de Mayo isn't Independence Day for Mexico—that's September 16. The 5th of May is the date the Mexican Army won the Battle of Puebla."

"You always know everything, don't you? Well, I think it's stupid that they have a different day for the 4th of July than we do. I mean all Independence Days should be the same no matter what country you're in. Like, how can they just pick any day they want? It doesn't make sense. I mean, Independence Day is Independence Day, like Christmas is Christmas, right? It'd be like we go, Christmas is December 25th, but Mexico goes, our Christmas is the 3rd of March."

Now it was my turn to stare.

At that moment Miguel came through the door wearing a stack of sombreros on his head and carrying two large bags from Pat's Party Palace. He put the bags on the table and the sombreros on his desk. Then he grabbed one of the hats, put it on Courtnee, and danced her across the newsroom, singing a salsa version of "Careless Whispers," finishing with a swooping dip that sent her into a fit of giggles.

"Miguel, Leah told me my yellow and red outfit is the wrong colors for Mexico."

"Courtnee, you will be *muy bonita* no matter what you wear."

She gave me an I-told-you-so look, as though I had banned her ensemble and Miguel had issued a pardon. "Courtnee, I don't care what you wear. I don't even care what *I* wear."

"Well," she sniffed, looking over my khakis, white t-shirt and black blazer. "That's pretty obvious."

Which was a pretty good comeback for Courtnee. Miguel is on Team Courtnee when it comes to my clothes.

"She's a little bit right, *chica*. Look at you today. You look like an Amish lawyer." He shook his head in mock despair. I started to protest, but before I could, he went on. "Never mind. Both of you, wear whatever you like. You will be beautiful. Is your boyfriend, Trent, coming, Courtnee?"

"Trent? I thought his name was Brad."

"I broke up with Brad. We looked too much alike."

"What?"

"My grandma said couples who look too much alike never last. Like Brad Pitt and Jennifer Aniston. Or Ellie and her first husband."

"Ellie's first husband died, Courtnee."

"Well, but they're not together, are they? And she told me once people used to tease them about looking like twins. And Brad and I both have blonde hair and blue eyes and we're both hot, so I'm just sayin.' "

"You're just 'sayin' nothing that makes any kind of sense and—"

I was interrupted by an uncertain-sounding voice calling from the reception area. "Hey? Is anyone there? I'd like to place a classified ad? Hello?"

The phones had been ringing nonstop while Courtnee took her break and dispensed culture lessons with fashion accents. But now the in-person request rescued her from my coming rant, so she happily returned to her rightful place at the front desk.

When she was gone, Miguel said, "You know, *chica*, Courtnee is right. It wouldn't hurt to add a little color, maybe a nice green to bring out your eyes? I promise you, it's gonna be so worth it. Lots of hot guys coming to my party. Coop is gonna be there," he said, hopping up and coming to rest on the corner of his desk.

"And so? Right now, we're barely speaking to each other."

He lifted his shoulders in a shrug.

"OK. But if you don't want him...I wonder if he's heteroflexible?"

I couldn't help it. I tried not to let it, but a laugh snorted out.

"Knock it off," I said. "I've got serious stuff going on here. Max just about fired me 10 minutes ago."

I gave him a brief recounting of my Catherines adventures, and he agreed that Max was overreacting. Then I told him about my conversation with Marilyn Karr.

"Do you think she's telling the truth?"

"I don't know. Paul says she just wants to stir things up."

"Well, I got something else for you to think about."

He pulled a notebook out of the inside pocket of his denim jacket and flipped it open.

"Father Hegl used to be the priest at San Carlos parish in Florida. Then one day—poof he's gone. Didn't say *adios* to anyone and didn't stay in touch."

"Caught with an altar boy?"

He shook his head. "I don't think so. The church secretary, she was very helpful."

"Of course she was." I have yet to meet the woman Miguel couldn't charm.

"She said that Father Hegl was very close to the Perez family. *Especialmente* to their beautiful teenage daughter Olivia. He was her voice coach. She died in a car accident just before the *padre* left."

"When was that, Miguel?"

"May 2004. I checked. That's when Father Hegl showed up in Himmel."

"Yeah. That's the summer Lacey was 14. Were Hegl and this Olivia having an affair?"

"Rosa, the church secretary, didn't want to say, but yes, I think so. Olivia was just 18, but already she was married. Sad, so young. Her family didn't like the husband, Vince Morgan. He was wild, and he was white. Not good. And worse, he was not Catholic. But the *chicas* sometimes they like the bad boys, yes?"

"Or the bad priests? Hegl, another beautiful young girl and another death. What about the accident, was Olivia alone?"

"The police report says yes. She was over the limit and drove off the shoulder. The car rolled. She got thrown out. Massive head injuries. Died in the ambulance on the way to the hospital. She had a younger sister, Carla.

I'll call her. Sometimes the sisters, they know things the *mamá* and *papá* don't, right?"

"You did great, Miguel, thanks. But let me call Carla. I might be able to make a connection because of Lacey."

He looked disappointed. No one likes a lead taken away.

"No worries." He smiled, but I knew I'd hurt his feelings.

Sometimes I can't believe what a jerk I can be. Most of the time I can though. Miguel busted his butt to get background on Hegl, and then I snatched his lead right out from under him. Max threw me a job lifeline, and I tied it to a personal investigation that could sink him. Coop disagreed with me, and I cut him off at the knees. I hit my mother with the news that Lacey was abused and possibly murdered, and I suggest that Paul might be involved. Then I wonder why she's not on the same page with me.

It's true. I can be bossy, overbearing, arrogant, know-it-all, stubborn, single-minded (I really should write that down for my online dating profile). But it's not because I don't think other people are competent or smart. I do. I really do. It's just that no matter how hard I try, I can't believe that anyone else is really going to care as much as I do, or get it done the exact way I think it should be done. So, I have to rely on myself.

The catch is, despite my confident exterior, I don't really believe that I'm going to do it right either. And if you make the mistake of thinking I can do it, then how dumb are you? Which just proves I can't trust your judgment, and I better do everything myself. I shook off my circular self-reflection and pulled out the number Sister Margaret had given me and tried Father Hegl's cell phone.

"Yes?"

"Father Hegl? This is Leah Nash."

Silence, then a business-like but not unfriendly greeting. "Yes. Hello. How can I help you?"

"I just had a quick question for you, Father. I wonder if you remember seeing anything unusual the night of the fundraiser. That was the night

Lacey disappeared. I've been reading the police report, but I can't seem to find an interview with you."

"That's because I wasn't interviewed. I wasn't there the night of the fundraiser."

"But I thought everyone at the school, all the staff, had to go. A command performance, I think Sister Margaret called it."

"Yes. Normally, that's the case, but I had an unexpected call from an old friend who needed my help on an urgent personal matter. Sister Julianna gave me permission to miss the dinner."

"Oh, I see. So, you weren't there at all?"

"I got back quite late, long after everyone had left. So, I couldn't have seen anything that would help you, Leah. I'm sorry. Are you having any luck elsewhere?"

"Father, why didn't you tell me you knew Lacey before she came to DeMoss?"

"Didn't I? I'm sure I mentioned it."

"No. You didn't."

"It must have just slipped my mind. Well, if there's nothing else—"

"Just one more thing. Your friend, was it someone you knew in Florida?"

Silence. Then "I, uh, I really can't say. As I said, it was personal. And confidential. I have to go now, Leah. Goodbye."

Well, something was making Father Hegl nervous. Was it getting caught lying about knowing Lacey? Was it the Florida reference? Or was it to do with his mystery friend? Or were they somehow all connected?

16

Early the next morning I stood shivering in the early morning cool on the doorstep of Miller and Georgia Caldwell's tasteful brick colonial. Dressed in jeans, a UW T-shirt and my favorite Keens, I hoped my downscale ensemble would emphasize that I was not working; I was not representing the *Himmel Times*; and nothing I did or said could be held against me in a court of Max. I wasn't even the one who set up this little *tête-à-tête* with Miller. He had called me the night before.

I know Miller in the way I know most high-profile people in Himmel, because of my job. We don't exactly travel in the same social circles, although he and his wife both go to St. Stephen's like my mother. When he called and asked me to come by, he said it wasn't for a story, but he'd rather talk to me in person. Since I had some non-story chatting I wanted to do with him, too, I accepted.

I rang the bell and waited for a maid or housekeeper to answer, but it was Miller who stood there when the door swung open. At well over six feet tall, his muscular frame filled the doorway. His carefully cut brown hair was touched with gray; his eyes were a shade of blue so bright, they might have owed their hue to colored contacts. The smile he gave me was the broad grin required of every candidate. I was surprised when he shook my hand to find that his was calloused, more like a farmer's than a politician's.

"Thank you for coming, Leah."

"Sure, no problem." He led me through the large entrance hall to his study. Rows of books in ceiling-high glass-fronted cabinets lined one wall. An ornate mahogany desk dominated the far end of the room and, in the other end, two wing-back chairs upholstered in a rich looking burgundy fabric flanked a sofa with striped silk cushions. An Oriental rug of intricate pattern covered the oak floor. The room looked like a photo spread for *We're Old Money* magazine.

Miller sat down on the edge of the sofa. I took the chair nearest him. I accepted a cup of coffee and waited as he poured one of his own. He added sugar. Stirred it. Offered me biscotti, and when I refused, put the platter back down without taking one himself. I maintained a politely curious expression as I waited for him to speak.

He finally did.

"I understand you've talked several times with Sister Julianna and Reid Palmer about your sister's accident."

I didn't respond. It's a technique Max taught me a long time ago. If you just let the silence hang there, most people can't stand it. They have to fill the gap.

"I was very fond of Lacey. We all were."

Again, I didn't say anything, but this time I nodded.

"We were so upset when she," he hesitated, picked up his coffee and put it back down without taking a drink. "When she lost her way."

"That's a pretty delicate way to put it."

"May I ask why you're going back over things, so long after Lacey's death?" His fingers played with the gold band of the wristwatch on his left wrist.

"I've learned something that casts a different light on Lacey's death— and on the last few years of her life. I'm just following up on it."

"You mean the note from Sister Mattea?"

"You're well-informed. Yes. That and some other information. I'm pretty certain now that Lacey was sexually abused. I'm going to find out who did it."

"Leah, that's appalling." His face registered concern.

"You don't seem that surprised. I suppose Sister Julianna or Reid Palmer already told you. Isn't that what lawyers do, ask questions you already know the answers to? Did they also tell you I believe it happened the summer before she went into ninth grade? Lacey spent a lot of time with your family back then. Did she ever talk about anyone, a teacher, a coach, anyone who had a lot of contact with her?"

"Surely you or your mother were in a better position than me to notice anything like that."

"Yeah, that's true. But for a while there it seemed like she was here more than she was at home. That's what Mom said anyway. One time, didn't she even spend the night with you?"

"I'm not sure I understand."

"I'm just trying to think if I'm remembering that right. You and Lacey got stranded on your way to your cottage up north when the car broke down. You had to stay overnight, just the two of you at a motel, right?"

"Are you insinuating—"

"Miller, why did you ask me here? Why do you care if I'm talking to people about my sister?"

"Lacey was like a daughter to me, an older sister to Charlotte and Sebastian. When I talked to Sister Julianna, she said you seemed over-wrought. She was concerned about you, and that you might inadvertently cause some damage to the school. That's why she turned to me, because I'm on the board."

"That's funny, because when I spoke to Reid Palmer, who is also on the board, he didn't seem worried about my questions."

"Reid is inclined to take a detached view of things. I'm not sure he real-izes how much doubts and rumors could affect the reputation of DeMoss, or of the Catherines for that matter."

"And so you offered to step in and what? Soothe the troubled waters, shut down the inconvenient questions?"

"Leah, please. I was just trying to ease Sister Julianna's mind, just trying to do a kindness. Nothing more. What are we here for if not to make life less difficult for each other?"

"Very inspiring. But you shouldn't worry. I don't think Lacey's sexual abuse will reflect on DeMoss. She wasn't there when it happened. Though that's not to say her abuser didn't track her down there. In fact, I think he must have. Because I think that's why she died. Did you ever run into Lacey there?"

"No. I didn't see her again after she stopped caring for the children. I heard about her ... troubles ... of course, in a small town like this, you do. But I never spoke to her again."

"I see. So, the night she disappeared, the night of the big fundraiser for DeMoss, did you go back after you left with Paul Karr?"

"Back? Yes, I think so. I can't be sure. That was five years and at least 50 charity fundraisers ago."

"Did you see anything when you were driving back in, or even later when you left for the night?"

"What sort of thing?"

"Maybe a little boy wandering the grounds? A car leaving from the side entrance? A girl, maybe Lacey, standing near the Baylor Road entrance?"

"Leah, what's the point of this? I was interviewed by the Sheriff's Department at the time, and whatever I said then was fresher than what I could hope to remember now. Do you really think anyone will be able to tell you anything useful at this late date? Is it worth reminding people all over again about Lacey's problems, worrying good people who are trying to help other children like Lacey, risking the school's reputation and its funding for an unprovable theory? Do you think your sister would want that?"

"My sister would want justice. I don't believe she got it. Why are you so interested in stopping me?"

"I'm not trying to stop you, Leah. I'm just trying to get you to think through what is really in the best interest of you, of Lacey's memory, and I admit, of DeMoss Academy."

"And you, Miller? What's in your best interest?"

"Dad? Dad! Telephone. It's grandma." A girl's voice sounded from somewhere upstairs.

"I have to take this call, my father's not been well. I think we're finished here. Can you see yourself out?"

"Yeah, sure. Thanks, Miller."

He nodded and walked out of the room and down the hall. As I left, a pretty girl in running gear came clattering down the stairs.

"Oh! Hi," she said. "I didn't know Dad was with anyone."

"That's OK, we were finished. Could you possibly be Charlotte?" I asked, as I noted her big brown eyes and remembered the solemn little girl Lacey used to bring to the house sometimes.

"That's me," she said, sweeping silky blonde hair into a ponytail and securing it. "Who are you?"

"Leah Nash. Lacey's sister."

"Oh sure, I remember you now."

"It's been awhile. The last time I saw you, I think Lacey brought you over to see her cat Zoey. You couldn't have been more than—"

"Ten. I was 10. That was just before Lacey stopped coming. Sebastian and I felt really bad. We loved her."

We had walked through the door and were standing on the flagstone path leading to the drive where my car was parked.

"Did she ever tell you why she stopped babysitting?"

She shook her head. "No. We used to see her at least twice a week— Mom and Dad are pretty social. I thought she liked us. Then one day Dad said Lacey told him she wouldn't be coming anymore. She was too busy. I called her and asked if she could visit us some time, but she just said no, she didn't think so.

"I was really bummed. And Sebastian cried that he wanted his 'Wacey' every time a new sitter came. He was only five. For a long time, we thought we did something wrong and she didn't like us anymore. But when I got older, I figured it out."

"What did you figure out, Charlotte?"

"Mom fired her because we all liked her so much—me, Sebastian, even Dad. Mom doesn't like it when she's not the center of the universe."

"But Lacey wasn't fired, she quit. That's what she told us—my mother and me."

She shrugged.

"Well, then she quit because Mom was such a bitch to her. Mom told us Lacey wasn't our friend, she was only nice because she was paid to be, and we should get over it. I'm sorry about what happened to Lacey, Leah. She was always great to us, and that's how I remember her, no matter what people said."

A car pulled into the drive just then and a very beautiful woman, the image of Charlotte in 20 years, got out. Georgia looked surprised—and not in a good way.

"Leah, what are you doing here? Charlotte, I really need you to go back inside and change into something more suitable."

Her daughter's tight-fitting tank top and shorts were more revealing than I'd choose, but with her lithe body and long legs, Charlotte looked good, and she was dressed pretty much like other girls her age.

She had begun inserting her earbuds as Georgia approached, and now said, "Sorry, Mother, can't hear you. I've got to run. Literally." She gave me a small wave and took off with a steady stride, her ponytail bouncing behind her.

Georgia trained her icy gaze back on me and repeated her question. "What are you doing here?" She pressed her carefully outlined lips into a thin pink line as she waited for my answer.

"Miller asked me to stop by. He wanted to talk about Lacey."

"I don't believe it."

"Why would I lie?"

"Why do reporters do anything? To dig up dirt. To make trouble. To ride on the coattails of people who are better and smarter than they are. But I'm sure my husband did not initiate a conversation about your delinquent, dead sister."

"Why did you dislike her so much?"

"Dislike a predatory, oversexed teenager who couldn't leave my husband alone? What's not to like?"

"That's not true, Georgia. Lacey was a kid. She was 14 years old when she babysat for you."

"Lolita was 12, right?"

"You really are a horrible person, aren't you?"

"You don't know the half of it. And trust me, you don't want to know."

The carefully cultivated mask of wealth and privilege fell away for a minute. Underneath I could see the viciously ambitious girl from the poor side of Himmel. Not Georgia then. No, she was plain old Crystal Bailey before she clawed her way up the social ladder and snagged the son of the wealthiest family in Himmel along the way.

"Your sister was a little bitch who tried to worm her way into my family and turn my own children and my husband against me. I knew her game. I'm telling you, you'd better not make any trouble for us. I didn't get here by playing nice. Miller is going to win his state senate race and that's only the beginning. I won't allow you to tie him to that little slut and her drunken death."

"Do you even know how pathetic you sound? Lacey was in ninth grade! She was into Justin Timberlake, not some guy old enough to be her father, like Miller. You know what, Georgia? If I were you I wouldn't invest too much in my campaign wardrobe. Because it could be that when I get the answers I'm looking for, Miller might be fighting for his life, not for a state senate seat. You may find that your future is not very bright at all."

I had nothing to base it on. I was just trying to give back a little of the trash talk she had thrown at me.

I was too slow on the uptake to see it coming. She stepped back to give herself room then shoved so hard she knocked me on my butt. As I sat staring up at her in surprise, she turned and marched to her front door, high heels clicking on the pavement.

17

I'd been calling and leaving messages at the number Sister Margaret gave me for Delite Wilson's sister, Brandee Holloway, for a few days, but she wasn't picking up, and she wasn't answering my voicemail. When I got home from the Caldwells to change for work, I gave it another try. After three rings, someone answered, but it sounded more like an adolescent boy than an adult woman.

"Yeah?"

"Hello. May I please speak to Brandee Holloway?"

He didn't answer, but there was a slight clunk as the phone was tossed down, and I could hear him yell.

"Ma! Phone!"

"Who is it?"

"I dunno. Sounds kinda like the counselor from my school."

"Whadya been doin'? I told you I ain't got time to go runnin' to your damn school every day. And I told you, don't answer my phone!" There was the sound of a *whap!* And a sharp cry of "Oww!"

Then, "Who is this?"

I talked fast, trying to get my question in before she hung up on me.

"Hi, Brandee, this is Leah Nash. I left a couple of messages. I'm trying to reach your sister Delite. Does she still live with you?"

"No. Whadya want her for?"

"She was my sister Lacey's roommate at DeMoss Academy. I don't know if you know this, but Lacey died in an accident there, and I'm trying to talk to some of the people who knew her then."

"What for?"

"Lacey and I weren't close when she went to DeMoss, but I miss her a lot. I just feel if I could talk to people who knew her then, I might feel closer to her, might understand her better. You know how it is with sisters." I'd decided to play the we're-all-sisters card, but now that didn't seem like such a great idea.

"I know how it is with my husband-stealing, lazy, lying half-sister, if that's what you mean. I threw Delite out two months after she got here from Loserville. Right after I caught her screwin' my old man. Him, he's a piece of shit. But my own flesh and blood? I tossed her little bitch ass right out, and I ain't talked to her since."

"Uh, I'm sorry to hear that. Do you know where she went?"

"Last I heard she was workin' at a casino in Michigan up to Mixley. I gotta go. I don't know nothin' about Delite. Don't call me anymore."

Before she clicked off, I could hear her yelling at her kid again. "Don't you goddamn pick up my phone you little fucktard! I don't have time for your—" and she was gone.

My mother walked into the kitchen dressed for work as I hung up.

"Leah? What are you doing home? I thought I heard you leave over an hour ago," she said, tilting her head as she fastened a silver hoop earring.

"You look good, Mom." She did, dressed in a bright green blazer and knee-length skirt—she still has great legs. I thought of Brandee and her harangue at her unknown son, and I walked over and gave her a hug.

"What's that for?"

"Because you've never called me a little fucktard."

"At least not when you could hear me."

"Funny."

"But what are you doing back home at 8:30? I did hear you leave once already, didn't I?"

"Yeah, I had an early coffee date."

"Hmm. Dressed like that I guess it's safe to assume it wasn't with one of the royal family."

"Actually, it was. Himmel's, anyway. Miller Caldwell asked me for a coffee at his house this morning."

"Miller called you?" The look of astonishment on her face changed to suspicion. "Why? Leah, you didn't accuse him of hurting Lacey, did you?"

"I asked him a few questions. Look, Mom, like I said, he's the one who called me. He heard I was asking about Lacey and wondered why. Sister Julianna put him up to it."

"Leah, you haven't said anything about that for the past few days. I was hoping you'd dropped it."

"I haven't said anything, because I don't want to fight with you. I know you're angry, and I'm sorry if I messed things up for you with Paul I—"

"Leah, it's not just that—have you thought at all about what Paul said? This could be a lose-lose situation. If you're wrong, you can hurt a lot of innocent people. Like Paul. If you're right, ask the wrong person, and it could be dangerous. I'm worried about you."

"Well, maybe if someone tried to kill me, I'd finally convince you and Coop and Max that I'm on to something."

"That's a terrible thing to say, Leah."

She was right, but I never stand stronger than when I'm wrong.

"Look, let's not talk about it anymore, OK? We're not going to agree, and neither of us is going to change her mind. Besides, you'll be late for work."

"We're not through with this conversation, Leah. You don't need to be sarcastic with me and treat me like I'm some kind of overprotective nitwit. Karen is worried too. And she mentioned something I hadn't even thought of—possible libel or slander suits. You think you've got career and money problems now—you ain't seen nothin' yet if Georgia Caldwell decides to take a swing at you."

Now didn't seem the time to confess that indeed Georgia already had.

"Mom. I don't think you're a nitwit, and Karen isn't either."

Karen had been like a second, less-guilt-wielding mother to us growing up. She tried to help Lacey almost as much as Mom and I did, but Lacey cut her off just like she did us. I knew it hurt her, but she never said a bad word about my sister. She stayed a good friend to us when some others didn't.

"But just think about this, Mom. You're afraid I'm not being objective, that I'm seeing connections that aren't there, because I feel guilty. Isn't it possible that you're refusing to see things that *are* there for the same reason? I'll be late tonight. There's something I have to do after work."

————————

Instead of heading to McClain's for our usual post-production drink and dinner, I jumped in my car after we put the paper to bed, ready to head out for a four-hour drive to Shining Waters Resort Casino in Mixley, Michigan. According to the staff person I spoke to, Delite Wilson was working a 9 p.m. to 3 a.m. shift. That was my best chance of catching up with her. A rap on my window made me look up from buckling my seatbelt.

"*Chica,* where are you going?" Miguel's expression was similar to that of a golden retriever hoping for a trip to the park.

"To the casino in Mixley. I've got a line on Delite."

"That's at least an eight-hour round trip. You won't get back here until morning!"

"That's OK. I don't have any assignments until afternoon. If I get too tired driving back, I'll just pull into a rest area and catch a nap."

He ran quickly around the car and jumped in the passenger seat before I could say anything. "I'm coming with you. We can split the driving."

I turned to face him and started to protest but he waved me off. "No. You need me. You don't see Frodo without Sam, Buffy without Willow, Abercrombie without Fitch."

"No. Seriously. Thanks, but no. You've already done enough." He continued as though I hadn't said anything.

"Lilo without Stitch, Holmes without Watson, Jerry without George—"

"OK, OK, OK. Enough. Buckle up and let's go."

I reached over to plug in my iPhone for some music, but Miguel grabbed it away. "No-no. I am so not listening to Adele for four hours. I'm in charge of the tunes for this road trip. Hey, don't you believe in security, *chica*? Your phone should be password protected."

"I know. But it's too much trouble. I don't like to keep putting the pass code in every time it's idle for a few minutes."

"Oh, *dios mío*. It's worse than I thought. *Journey*? Seriously?" he said as he scrolled through my song list.

"You know my secret, now I have to kill you. Besides, you're the one with Susan Boyle on his playlist."

"I'm not ashamed. The voice of an angel. Ohh, OK, here we go, let's go retro."

Soon the Bee Gees started pouring out of the speakers, and by the time we pulled out of town, we were both singing and car dancing to *Stayin' Alive*. Almost four hours later when the lights of the casino lit up the night sky, we weren't quite as lively. It was about 11 when we pulled into the parking lot.

If you've never been to a casino in rural Michigan, let me hasten to assure you it is not Monte Carlo. Or Las Vegas. Or even Atlantic City. There is no glamour and precious little excitement, unless it excites you to watch people who look like they haven't a dime to spare, wheezing their way around game tables and slot machines on electric carts. There's an air of noisy desperation about the whole scene that I find extremely depressing. Miguel, I discovered, did not share my feelings. Bouncing out of the car, he almost danced his way through the big double doors and immediately pulled me over to the dice table.

"C'mon, *chica*, let's roll the dice. I feel lucky tonight."

"Roll away, buddy. I've got work to do. Life's a big enough gamble for me, thanks. Besides, I haven't the faintest idea how to play craps. It looks way too math-y to me."

"No, no, *chica*. It's so easy. You've never played?" His eyes lit up. "Then you'll be super lucky. Here, just roll the dice, please?"

"No. Seriously. You go ahead and make new friends. I'm going to look around for Delite."

The room was dark and the air redolent with smoke despite the air purifying system. I wasn't sure I'd recognize her. I'd only seen her once before, when DeMoss brought a contingent of kids to Lacey's funeral. I remembered her as a pale ash blonde with flat blue eyes and a discontented mouth. I scanned the gaming tables. Outside of the dice table only three were open; a raucous three-card poker game staffed by a skinny young guy with glasses, a let-it-ride game with a balding dealer and two hard-bitten women playing, and an empty blackjack table with a female dealer. Something about her cocky stance made me think I'd found her. As I got closer, I could see that her nametag read Delite. Jackpot.

Her hair wasn't ash blonde anymore, instead it was a streaky yellow-orange color not found in nature. Her eyes were the same though, hard and dull.

"Delite. Hi. I'm Leah Nash. Lacey's sister."

"Yeah, so? You wanna play or what?"

"Yeah, sure." I placed a bet and then said, "Actually I wanted to talk to you. To ask you about Lacey. Lacey Nash," I added, as she showed no sign of recognizing the name.

"What about her?" She shuffled the deck and dealt me a car and turned over her own.

"You and Lacey were roommates. You must have talked a lot. Did she ever tell you that she was worried, or afraid?"

"No," she said, giving me another card.

"Did she seem unhappy?"

"Everybody was unhappy. We was at Dumbass Academy, wasn't we?" She looked at her second card. Ace. I busted.

"She never said anything to you about before she came to DeMoss? About what happened to her when she was younger? Did she ever say anything about being sexually abused?" Her face kept the same disinterested stare.

She shrugged. "She mighta said somethin' about some big shot makin' her screw or something. Too bad, so sad, we all got somethin'."

"Lacey said she was abused? Think, did she say who?"

"I don't know. It's not like I really cared, I got my own problems. You gonna play another hand or not?"

"Yeah, yeah, sure," I said, putting another $5 on the table. "Did she say why she didn't tell the police?"

She dealt me a card and turned her own over.

"Delite?"

"Look, I don't know why she didn't tell. I don't know if she was gonna. I don't know anything. Except your sister stole my phone. And that was f'n' hard to get, too. Had to have it sneaked in, cost me a lot in trade. And I had some pretty special pictures on there, if you know what I mean." I signaled for another card.

"Are you saying it was your phone the police found with her body?"

She shrugged and laid down cards for both of us.

"I'm sayin' I had a phone and then I didn't. I'm sayin' I shared a room with your sister. I'm sayin' if she had one on her, and mine was missin,' which it was, she took it."

"Do you know if Lacey was using drugs again?" I signaled and she dealt me another card before answering. I busted again.

"I got hold of some Vicodin one time, offered to sell her some, but she didn't want any."

"They found drugs in her purse when they found her body."

"Don't know anything about that."

"Did you ever see Lacey and Father Hegl?"

She shook her head. "She couldn't stand him. He was always buggin' her to be in his stupid choir. Your sister could sing," she added with a grudging note of admiration.

"Why did you lie and say you didn't see Lacey the night she disappeared, then come forward after her body was found and claim she was at a party with you?"

"Like I told the cops, I didn't want to get in more trouble. One more screw-up and I was going to juvie."

"Weren't you afraid of that when you finally did confess?"

Her face had a sly expression, and she answered as if tutored by Dr. Phil. "I wanted to give your family, like, closure, right? I couldn't cover for her anymore. It was dysfunctional. For me. Mentally, like. I didn't want to be doing codependent behavior anymore."

"But Lacey wasn't with you, was she? You made that up."

Her eyes hardened as she said, "Look, I'm workin' here. If you're not gonna play, you better move on."

Two men, one wearing a Brewer's T-shirt that rode up on his belly and left a hairy gap above the top of his droopy jeans, and the other sporting a Green Bay Packers sweatshirt, lumbered up to the table and put down a stack of chips.

"No. I'm done, thanks. But if you do think of anything," I reached in my purse and found a business card. "That's my cell phone, you can reach me anytime."

"Hey, honey, you got one of those for me?" said hairy belly.

"No."

Delite hesitated for a second, then scooped the card off the table and put it in her pocket.

"See you."

She didn't answer.

18

I was ready to go, but I saw that Miguel was the center of a group of players urging him on at the craps table. He'd come all the way up there with me. I couldn't make him walk out on his run. Instead, I wandered over to a video poker machine near the cashier's window. I put $5 in a nickel machine and settled down to play some draw poker, but all I did was stare at the screen thinking about what Delite had said.

I still didn't believe her story, but I no longer thought she had offered a fake confession to demonstrate she was a reformed sinner who should be allowed to stay. No. That sly look on her face, those psychobabble words she used, "closure" "codependent"—someone was feeding the rationale to her.

But who and why? She said Lacey was abused by a "big shot." What would a big shot be to Delite? A doctor? A lawyer? A dentist? Miller Caldwell was a lawyer. Did he connect with Delite, get her to lie when Lacey's body was found to wrap things up quickly, keep the police from doing an actual investigation, instead of the pro forma walk-through Ross had led? Or, there was Hegl. Would a priest be a big shot to Delite?

Miguel walked up just then with a big grin, waving three $100 bills.

On the ride home I told him about Delite and speculated a little more about Miller Caldwell, but I was hit by a sudden wave of sleepiness and begged off further chatting. Miguel drove all the way back. I was a little coma-sleep groggy when I woke up as we pulled into the parking lot at the *Times*. But by the time I pulled in my driveway, I had started to perk up a bit. I opened the front door quietly, but knew that my mother and I would have to do our usual call and response.

"Leah?"

"Yes, Mom."

"You're awfully late."

"Sorry, I know. I'm fine. Go back to sleep."

"Goodnight, sweetheart."

"G'night."

It was 4 a.m. but no way could I go back to sleep. Instead I got my phone and switched over from Miguel's playlist to stream a mix of old-school folk/rock—Joni Mitchell, Joan Baez, The Band—singers my mother had conditioned me to like growing up. I turned it down low, so I wouldn't wake her. I made some tea and sat down in the rocker to think. After a few minutes, I got up and set my laptop on the kitchen table, and typed in www.delaneysmemorialgarden.com.

When the site came up, I clicked on *For Always*. From the list there I chose "Lacey Nash," and then there she was in a smiling school picture, wearing the silver locket I gave her for her 13th birthday. Delaney's Funeral Home, for a fee, provides permanent memorial web pages with photos, condolences, memories, and comments for its "clients." Mom and I never talked about setting one up for Lacey, but she must have wanted something she could go back to. I'd only visited it once.

I reread the obituary that Max had written for her.

I had tried to write it myself, but the anger and sorrow got so tangled up in me that I couldn't make it work. I wanted people to remember the good about her, but it felt like a lie to ignore all the terrible things she'd done. I couldn't strike the balance between tribute and truth. Max did a beautiful job.

Lacey Nash, 17, daughter of Carol (Collins) Nash and the late Thomas Nash, died November 2, 2007. Cremation has taken place and the funeral Mass for Lacey is scheduled for 11 a.m. Tuesday at St. Stephen's Church with the Reverend Gregory Lindstrom officiating.

Lacey was born in Himmel, Wisconsin, where she spent her entire life. She loved singing. She was also a talented artist, often sketching pictures of her family, friends, and pets.

As a member of the Himmel Community Players, Lacey found an outlet for her vocal talent. She was chosen for a role in the Sound of Music at age 10. She performed with the local theater group for several years and was always a crowd pleaser. Her last appearance was as Dorothy in The Wizard of Oz.

Lacey was also active in swimming and church choir, and she enjoyed helping others. At age 12 she organized a carnival for Muscular Dystrophy in her back-yard that raised more than $1,000. After a heavy snow, she often rounded up neighborhood kids to help her shovel the driveways of elderly neighbors.

As a youngster, Lacey's favorite author was Dr. Seuss, and her favorite book was Horton Hears a Who. As a middle schooler, she loved Madeleine L'Engle and she read A Wrinkle in Time multiple times. She also loved the movie The Parent Trap and is believed to hold the world's record for number of viewings.

But this bright, talented, kindhearted girl entered a very difficult period as a teenager. She spent her last years troubled and isolated, and that was a great sorrow to the people who loved her.

May she be remembered for the happy and loving spirit inside her and granted compassion for the tragic ending of her too-brief life.

Lacey is survived by her mother Carol Nash of Himmel, her sister Leah Nash of Grand Rapids, Michigan, her aunt Nancy Taylor of Wadley, Michigan and several cousins. She was preceded in death by her sister Annie and her father Thomas.

I scrolled down through the comments. Lots from old classmates, stuff about school and favorite class trips, and I'll-never-forget-the-time stories. They were fun to read, because they reminded me of a time when Lacey was like any other kid.

There were some nice tributes from teachers and old neighbors, and as I moved on through I noticed over the years people periodically posted things, though far less often, of course, than when the page first went up. Most were signed by name but a few weren't.

And then as I read through them, I realized there was one that had recurred each year since Lacey died. The same quote, no signature.

"Thank you for making life less difficult." Earlier I would have skimmed right over it. But this time the phrase set off an echo in my mind, and I heard Miller Caldwell say as we sat sipping coffee in his sumptuous home, "What are we here for if not to make life less difficult for each other?"

First thing in the morning, I stopped by Delaney Funeral Home and talked to Mary Beth. She co-owns the business with her husband Roger.

"Mary Beth, is there any way to tell who posts anonymous comments on a memorial website?"

She looked startled, though with her carefully drawn in and unnaturally high arched eyebrows, Mary Beth always appeared somewhat surprised.

"I don't know, Leah. I suppose maybe. I wouldn't have the faintest idea how to do it. And don't even think about Roger. He still doesn't really get what the online site is. Our oldest boy talked him into it. Why?"

"There's a comment on Lacey's site that I'd like to track down. Thank the person, you know. They've posted it every year, so I know Lacey must have been special to them. Could I talk to whoever set up the page for you? There's probably something that could be done through the host site to track messages."

"Well, I don't know. Really, the page kind of belongs to the person who paid for it, and I wouldn't feel right without talking to him." She started twirling a strand of copper colored hair that had escaped from the old-fashioned bun on the back of her head. Her eyes blinked rapidly.

"Him? Don't you mean her, don't you mean my mother?"

Mary Beth's discomfort increased. "I promised it would be anonymous. I thought it was such a nice gesture. A lot of our families would like to do it but, well, it's no secret funerals are expensive, and so many people just don't have the extra money. Not that we're overcharging, mind you.

"There's a lot involved with keeping the online memorial garden up. I just thought it was such a nice thing, to set up the perpetual site for a family in need. Not that your family is in need, I didn't mean, that is—" If she could have blinked me away, it was obvious she would have.

"Ahh, of course. I should have realized right away. How nice of Miller," I said, taking a guess that I knew Mary Beth would confirm.

She looked relieved. "Exactly. That's what I thought, and to pay in advance. We charge the yearly fee you know, and really $200 is a good rate, I think, but he asked how much it would cost to keep it up indefinitely. We do offer the perpetual package for $5,000. He wrote me a check for the full amount right on the spot. Such a good man."

I nodded. "Did he say why he did it, Mary Beth? Just a random act of kindness or what?"

Now that her secret was in the open through almost no fault of her own, she could indulge her natural inclination to chat.

"That's what I wondered when he came in. 'Miller,' I said, 'that's really nice of you, but can I ask why?' And he said that he and his family were so fond of Lacey and wanted to be sure her memory stayed alive. But he didn't want you and your mother to feel uncomfortable or obligated or anything. That's why he swore me to secrecy. You just don't see that kind of thing often enough, do you? I mean, just doing good for the sake of doing good. You're not upset are you, Leah? You wouldn't even know about it, if you hadn't come in here and tricked me. Now, don't tell him I told you."

"Sorry, Mary Beth, I can't promise that."

I went into the office for meetings with two school board candidates and got their views on test scores, and school improvement, and the importance of an upcoming referendum vote. And when they left, I wrote up the story, but my mind wasn't on any of it. By then it was nearly noon, and I decided to take a run over to the cop shop. The bare bones activity log is online, but I wanted an excuse to run into Coop, and see if we could end the weirdness that had sprung up between us.

I pushed through the double doors and into the scruffy reception area. The Himmel Police Department is on the first floor of the city hall and looks like it hasn't been redecorated since 1975. The avocado green and beige tile floor is cracked and chipped. On one side of a scarred, wooden counter is a row of orange plastic chairs bolted together, apparently to

prevent someone from absconding with valuable late-20th-century arti-
facts. On the other side is a large metal desk where Melanie sits. Coop's
office is down the hall.

"Hey, Melanie. How's it going?"

She looked up from her computer screen and didn't answer. Instead,
she frowned at me and shoved reading glasses onto the top of her curly,
gray hair, then laboriously lifted her heavy body off her chair. She walked
slowly over to the counter with a side-to-side gait. Reaching underneath it,
she pulled out the logbook and shoved it toward me, then went back to her
desk. Still without speaking. Sometimes she was friendly, other times not.
This was apparently a "not" day.

"Hey, I see Harold Dane had his house TP'd again. Wouldn't it be easier
for him just to quit yelling at kids to get off his lawn?"

She looked up, but just shrugged.

"I'm thinking about doing a story on vandalism, maybe how neighborhoods can get together to help prevent it, that kind of thing." It sounded
lame, and Melanie didn't bother to respond.

"So, is Coop around? I thought I might get some ideas from him."

She picked up her phone and punched in his extension. "Leah's here."

I prepared to stumble through my story all over again. But when Coop
came through the door, he smiled and said, "Hey. Hi. C'mon back." He
lifted up the pass-through in the counter so I could follow him. Relief
rushed through me as I realized how easy it was going to be to get back to
our old familiar footing.

I dropped down in the chair opposite his desk and shook my head
when he offered me coffee. He sat in his chair and leaned back a little.

"Haven't seen much of you lately. Nice special section you guys did on
the summer recreation stuff."

"Thanks. *Grantland's Summer Wonderland* isn't exactly the high-water
mark for Himmel journalism, but it generated some ad revenue for Max."

He nodded. I nodded. This was the most stilted conversation I'd ever
had with Coop. We waggled our heads at each other like bobbleheads for
another few seconds, and then I took the plunge.

"Look, I haven't called you back because I didn't want to hear you tell me how ridiculous I am, and how I'm wasting my time, and how my ideas are stupid, and I should just let things go."

"I don't recall saying you're ridiculous. Or stupid."

"You might not have said it in so many words, but admit it, you think tracking down the truth about Lacey is a waste of time."

"Leah, c'mon. I don't want to fight with you again. But I'm not going to lie to you either. So yeah, I still have serious reservations about what you're doing. I'm hearing things, and it worries me."

"What things?"

"Like you're stirring things up, harassing people even. I saw Mary Beth at the Elite today and she was all shook up because you pressured her into giving out confidential information. Max is scared to death you're pissing the bank board off, and Georgia Caldwell is telling people you're trying to sabotage Miller's campaign. You're setting yourself—or the paper—up for serious trouble. Maybe a libel suit."

This wasn't going the way I planned at all. "Slander. It's only libel if it's printed."

"This isn't funny, Leah."

"Coop, listen, just for a minute. I know when I talked to you before I wasn't connecting the dots. I didn't even know where the dots were. But I do now, I've found out a lot more."

I told him about Hegl hiding the fact that he knew Lacey before she went to DeMoss, about his abrupt departure from Florida after another young girl died; about Miller paying for Lacey's perpetual memorial and posting to it every year; how I was sure Delite had lied about going to the party with Lacey, how she confirmed—sort of—that Lacey was sexually abused; and that I knew the name of the kid who'd been with Lacey. I finished in a rush, as though by spilling it out fast I could speed by his skepticism and bring him over to my side again. Where he had always been before.

Only it wasn't working.

"Leah, I wish you could see yourself, hear yourself. You look like you haven't slept in days. You drove eight hours round trip to the UP for a 10-minute conversation with Lacey's old roommate? You just said yourself she wasn't changing her story about the night Lacey died. She didn't admit to lying; you're basing that on the look in her eye?" His tone was mocking.

"And she didn't give you a name for this alleged sexual abuser, did she? As far as the young kid with Lacey, you still have no proof that Cole even saw her, let alone that she had a kid with her. All you know is the name of a boy who was a friend of hers. And what were you doing dragging Miguel along with you? If you don't care about your job, you should at least give a thought to his."

I recoiled as though he'd hit me. He'd been leaning forward with his hands resting on the desk. Now he lifted them up in obvious frustration.

"Leah, you're so fixated on—I don't know, making up for not saving Lacey?—that you can't think logically. You're tearing through this town hurting people, whether you mean to or not. It's reckless, and it's cruel. Look what you're doing to Max, to Paul Karr, to Miller and his family. You and your mom are at odds too. If I thought you were right, I'd be behind you a hundred percent. But I think you're wrong, and somebody's going to get hurt. I don't want it to be you."

I felt tears stinging my eyes and blinked hard to keep them from falling. I was so angry my voice shook.

"Just stop it. I came here to try and make things right between us. But you won't even listen. I don't know if somebody got to you or what—obviously, you've been talking about me to half the town. I may not have it all right, but I know in my gut I'm damn close. Don't worry. This is the last time I'll bother you with my obsession." I stood up and headed for the door.

"Leah! Stop. I'm just trying to help you see—"

"Don't bother. I can see just fine."

Darmody was in the front talking to Melanie.

"Hey, Leah, where's the fire? Should I call 911?" His laugh filled my ears as I pushed through the double doors and ran to my car. I pulled the door open and tumbled into the front seat. For a full minute, I pounded my fist on the dashboard, waiting for the sick feeling in my stomach to subside. Finally, it did.

19

All right, fine. I couldn't count on Coop, but he was right. I shouldn't be dragging Miguel into this. I had an idea of what I wanted to look into next, but first I had to do some "day job" work.

I stopped by the fire hall to take a picture of the chief with the department's new truck, then went to the County Extension office to talk to the agricultural agent, Jerry Grosskopf, about the potato-crop outlook. It was good. Unless the weather didn't hold. Then it was bad. I could feel another cutting edge story in the works. It was 4 p.m. when I finished and called in to tell Courtnee I wouldn't be back.

"Must be nice to be a reporter. You can, like, just come in when you want and you don't even have to stay until 5."

"That's right, Courtnee, reporters have it easy. I mean after all, it's so much fun to go to a county commissioner meeting that doesn't end until 10 p.m., then come back to the office, write up the story, and then get called out to a fire that lasts until 4 a.m. Then go home to sleep for two hours so you can be on time at the Rotary Pancake breakfast. All said, it's really a cushy job."

"Whatever. I just know I have to be here, like, from 8 a.m. until 5 p.m. It would be nice if I had some flexibility."

"I'll see you tomorrow."

Despite Courtnee's efforts, I didn't feel guilty at all. It was a rare week at the *Times* when we didn't put in 50-60 hours, and weekends didn't really exist. Neither did evenings off, if it was your turn to take home the scanner and monitor police and fire calls.

When I got home my mother was still at work. She didn't have a "cushy" job like me either. I sat down at the kitchen table and scrolled through my phone for the number of Sister Mattea's brother. I had met Scott when I stopped by the rosary for Sister Mattea, and I got his business card. I always save contact information, because as a reporter, you just never know. Scott worked in San Francisco, so it would be around 2 p.m. there. I tapped in his number, and on the second ring, a woman answered.

"Riordan Software Development, Miss Adams speaking. How may I direct your call?"

"Hi, Miss Adams, this is Leah Nash. May I speak to Scott Riordan please?"

"I'm sorry, Miss Nash, Mr. Riordan is away from the office. Can someone else help you?"

"Not really. Actually, this is a personal call. I need to speak to Scott."

"I see," she said, in a voice that conveyed she did not approve of this personal intrusion during business hours. "I'm afraid that's not possible. As I said, Mr. Riordan is away. Perhaps you'd like to try his cell phone?"

"That would be great. Can you give me his cell phone number?"

"Oh no, I couldn't do that. We're not allowed to give out personal cell phone numbers. When you said personal business, I naturally assumed you were a personal acquaintance and would have Mr. Riordan's non-work number."

"Right." Self-important flunky, I thought but realized it was a good time to use my filter. "Well, can you tell me if he'll be in later?"

"Oh, I hardly think so. Mr. Riordan is in China on a business trip. He has an open-ended return date."

"Could you give him a message?"

"That's my job," she said noncommittally.

I spelled my name, gave my number, and asked that Scott call me on a matter related to his sister. I'd been hoping to get some insights into Sister

Mattea—anything that would help me find the elusive link between her and Lacey. That plan would have to wait.

I had better luck following up with Miguel's information on Father Hegl. If I hadn't been a reporter, I definitely would have been a librarian. I love the research. I love trying first one tactic then another, searching out unexpected connections, going at the problem from all angles. Once I'm on the Internet trail, I can't let go.

I opened my computer and typed "Sean Hegl" into Google. Multiple pages popped up, but the first listing that caught my eye was the obituary for Noreen Holcomb Ramsey of Naples, Florida, whose survivors included a son, the Most Rev. Joseph Ramsey of Braxton, Florida, a daughter, Rita Ramsey Hegl of Jacksonville, Florida, a granddaughter, Claudia Hegl Patterson, and a grandson, the Rev. Sean Hegl. Neither grandchild's address was given. But Hegl's uncle was a "most reverend," which translated to bishop in Catholic speak.

Next, I bounced around between several aggregating sites that compile public information and can provide you with a person's age, address, phone number, relatives, and sometimes even roommate names.

Hegl didn't have a Facebook page that I could find, which was too bad because you can find a lot of stuff there. It's amazing how many people don't restrict access to their photos or their list of friends. Between the two of those and professional sites like LinkedIn, you can collect a lot of intel.

But I did pretty well even without Facebook. I found Sean Hegl, age 38, with possible relations Rita Hegl and Noreen Patterson, and several addresses in Florida, though nothing in Wisconsin. The first address was the same as that listed for Rita Ramsey Hegl, so that was probably the family home. The second one I checked turned out to be a Catholic seminary in Boca Raton. The third was what I was looking for—when I typed the address into Google, I got a nice little map with an arrow pointing to San Carlos Catholic Church.

I went to the church website which listed all of the pastors and the years they served under the "Our History" tab. The welcome page identified San Carlos as part of the Leesville Diocese and its bishop was the Most Reverend Joseph Ramsey. Well, well, well, Father Hegl had worked for his uncle.

I could call the diocesan office, but my gut told me it wasn't a good idea for Uncle Bishop to know someone was tracking his nephew.

I switched gears for the moment and looked for a number for Carla Pérez, the sister of Hegl's teenage "protégé" Olivia Pérez Morgan. No luck. I found some info on Carla—the school she graduated from, a couple of jobs she'd had, but no phone number. That's one of the current obstacles to tracking people online—the lack of a decent cell phone directory to take the place of the old-fashioned phone book.

But, fortunately, the elder Pérezes, Carlos and Laura, had not cut the cord, and they still had a landline. I called their number as I mentally readied my story. The phone was answered by a woman with a soft, pleasant voice.

"Mrs. Pérez?"

"Yes?" she said, in the tone of someone ready to give a thanks but no thanks as soon as I identified myself as a telemarketer. I started talking fast, a slight uptick in the end of each sentence.

"My name is Andrea Lawson, I'm on the All Class Reunion Committee at St. Francis High School? We're trying to get a database of everyone's email and phone numbers? It's driving me a little crazy?"

Pause for a slightly airheady giggle.

"Could I get Carla's cell phone number from you?" I put all I had into sounding like a cheerful, school spirit-filled alumna.

"Oh, that sounds like a good way for all of you to keep in touch. I'm sure Carla will want to be included. What was your name again?"

"Andrea Lawson?"

"Were you a friend of Carla's in school?"

"More of an acquaintance? How's she doing?"

"Very well. She's in the RN program at the community college, and she'll graduate next year. What about you Andrea, what are you doing?"

"I just got a new job in Orlando? I start next week at Sea World as a dolphin trainer?" When I'm making up a back story I won't need again, I like to fill in with jobs I think would be really cool, and for which I am not remotely qualified or suited.

"Oh, that sounds so interesting. Well, I'm sure Carla will be glad to hear from you. Hold on just a second. I have to scroll through the menu here. I have her on speed dial, so I can never remember her number."

She was quiet for a second and there were several beeps, and then she came back on the line with Carla's cell phone number.

"Thanks so much for your help, Mrs. Pérez? You have a great evening now?"

"You're welcome, Andrea, you too."

For my conversation with Carla, I opted for the truth, partly because I couldn't use the same lie, but mostly because it would be easier and cleaner.

"Hello?"

"Carla? Hi. My name is Leah Nash, I'm from Himmel, Wisconsin, and if you have just a few minutes, I'd like to ask you some questions about Father Sean Hegl."

The line went so quiet, I checked to see if we were still connected.

"Hello? Hello? Are you there, Carla?"

"Yeah. Yeah, I'm still here."

"Carla, this might sound weird, but please hear me out. My younger sister Lacey died five years ago. She was 17. I know your sister Olivia died when she was very young as well. And I know that she was connected to Father Hegl. I'd like to hear anything you can tell me about Father Hegl and your sister."

I heard a sharp intake of breath, then, "Why?"

"Because I think there's more to the story of how my sister died. I'm trying to find out if Father Hegl had any link to it. And I'm wondering if you think he had any connection to Olivia's death. She died in a car accident, right?"

"Yeah. They said she was drinking and driving too fast. She hit the shoulder and rolled her car. She got thrown out, hit her head. She wasn't wearing a seat belt."

She paused, and I waited, trying not to signal how badly I wanted the information I knew she was about to give.

"She was meeting him that night. Father Hegl. She took her car, because he didn't want to take the chance that someone would recognize his where it shouldn't be. But he always drove. He liked to be in charge, Livy said. She thought it was romantic."

"Always? She was in a relationship with Hegl?"

"Yes, for months. I knew it; her husband Vince suspected there was someone, but my parents were clueless. They always were with Olivia. She was my father's little princess."

"Was the affair serious?"

"Olivia thought it was, but she thought Lifetime movies were real. I mean, even a 15-year-old like me could tell he wasn't that into her. She was always talking about how they were going to get married and move to New York. You know, daydream stuff."

"What happened the night your sister died?"

"Olivia said she was going to tell Hegl she wanted to go public—you know, tell her husband Vince and Hegl tell his bishop, and then they'd be together forever. She never thought things through."

"So, that night..."

"Olivia did her hair, make-up, put on this sexy new dress, gave me a cover story to give to Vince in case he called to check on her."

"But the police report said she was alone in the car."

"Maybe. Maybe Hegl just let her drive off drunk after he dumped her, but I don't think so. I think he was right behind the wheel driving drunk himself. Tell me this—what was she doing on that dark country road in the middle of nowhere in the middle of the night? Alone?"

"Who found her?"

"An anonymous 911 call reported the accident. She might not have been found for days otherwise. It was way out in the country."

"The 911 call was anonymous? How do you know?"

"A deputy told my parents the call came from a pay phone at a gas station on the main road a mile away. He said one of the local weed growers probably spotted the car but didn't want to risk getting busted.

"What I want to know is, why did Hegl leave town right after the accident? He didn't even go to her funeral. And why did Olivia's husband Vince all-of-the-sudden have enough money to buy a boat and move to the Keys?

That *perezoso* deadbeat couldn't get enough money together to buy a fishing pole, let alone a fishing boat."

"Carla, did you tell anyone you suspected Hegl might have been involved?"

"I was 15 years old, nobody cared what I said. I told the cop who came to the house to tell us Olivia was dead, but he didn't listen. My mother was hysterical, and my father slapped me when I said Olivia was going to meet Father Hegl that night. They're old-fashioned, and they couldn't think a priest or their little princess would do anything like that. My parents were grieving, but they were embarrassed, too, ashamed about Livy drinking. They thought it was their fault. They told me to pray and quit talking about it."

"But, Carla, the crime scene reconstruction that must have been done, it would have shown if anyone else was in the car."

"Would it?" she asked in a tone that told me, if I were there, I'd see a sardonic sneer on her face. "Could they really tell? The sheriff's department isn't exactly *CSI Miami*. And they started out thinking they knew what happened. Drunk girl, drunk accident, dead drunk girl. End of story."

"So, you think someone helped Hegl cover-up the fact that he was involved with Olivia, and maybe even that he was driving the car that night?"

"That's right. And somebody must have been a little worried about my 'hysteria,' because Father Herrera, my mother's cousin, who works in the diocese office, came to visit. When my mother left to make coffee, he talked to me. Told me that it was a sin to spread rumors. Said that I would only hurt my sister's memory and my parents. Said making up stories wasn't the way to get attention.

"He told me Father Hegl couldn't have been with her, because he was at dinner with the bishop and a very important donor the night Olivia died. The bishop told Father Herrera so himself. After that, I knew it wasn't any use, so I did shut up. It made my parents happy, and it made my life easier."

"But you've never been convinced."

"No. My sister was a naïve kid with too many *telenovela* plots running in her head. She always fell for the good-looking guy—whether he was riding a motorcycle like Vince, or wearing a priest collar like Hegl. She could spin a fairy tale for any situation. With her as the heroine. Only this time, she was the victim. What I can't forget is that she was still alive when the EMTs got there. It was just too late. She didn't have to die."

"But you don't have any proof?"

"If I did, maybe the cops would've done something. But maybe not even then. This is like little Vatican here. The priests are like saints to people like my mom and dad. It was just easier for everyone if drunk Olivia had a terrible accident and crazy Carla—who doesn't even go to Mass!—just lied for attention."

"Did your priest happen to mention the name of the bishop's friend, the donor he and Hegl supposedly had dinner with that night?"

"I don't remember, I'm sorry."

"That's OK."

"It's been so long. Why are you calling now?"

"Because of my sister. Her story is a lot like Olivia's. It's possible Hegl was involved, but no one wants to hear it."

"So, what are you going to do?"

"I'm not sure."

So now, although Miller was still the odds on favorite, Hegl had just moved up a length.

20

On Saturday, the last thing I wanted to do was go to the *Cinco de Mayo* party, where, according to Coop, half the guests thought I was unbalanced, and the other half thought I was a malicious character assassin. But I had promised Miguel I'd be there, so I had to show up at least for a little while.

The May night was unseasonably warm. Cars lined both sides of the street, and I could hear laughter and music when I parked and turned off my engine a few houses away. The party had spilled into the backyard where the fence was strung with white lights and a large *piñata* hung from the branch of an oak tree. I rang the front bell. The door was opened by a guy around my age that I hadn't seen before.

"Hi, come on in. I'm Ben Kalek. You're Leah, right?" he said in the kind of husky voice I find quite appealing. He smiled and revealed well aligned and very white teeth. His blonde hair was short and a little messy, and his eyes reminded me of the periwinkle blue in a box of crayons. Miguel's latest conquest?

"How did you know?"

"Miguel's talked about you. You look just the way he described you."

"So you were expecting an Amish lawyer?"

"I'm sorry, I didn't catch that?" he said, tilting his head down toward me.

"Nothing. Never mind. So, how do you know Miguel?" I asked as we stood in the front hall.

"We met at the gym a while ago."

"Ah," I nodded. "So, you haven't been together long?" I fished, wondering why Miguel hadn't told me about his crush. He usually can't contain himself when he meets someone new, which is about every other week.

"What?" Ben said, looking confused. "No, no I'm not gay—"

"Not that there's anything wrong with that," we both said at the same time and laughed.

"No, we just hang out sometimes. A bunch of us play pick-up basketball on the weekends."

Hmm. I didn't get why he was playing host/doorman for Miguel. But he was very pleasant to look at. Nice enough that I wished I'd worn something besides jeans and a white oxford shirt with rolled up sleeves. But I had gotten a haircut that day, so there was that.

"How about a drink? Miguel mixed up a big batch of margaritas, and they're pretty good."

"Sure, thanks."

"Be right back."

I wandered into the living room and sat down on a folding chair near the fireplace. As I did, Miguel spotted me and came dancing over. He leaned in and gave me a big hug.

"*Chica*! I saw you talking to Ben. Nice, yes?" he nodded his head up and down.

"Yeah, he seems pretty nice."

"Pretty nice? I special-ordered him for you."

"What?"

"You need a little spice in your life. Ben, he's perfect for a little spring fling." He grinned broadly and lifted his eyebrows up and down in mock lechery.

"You didn't! Miguel, I hate set-ups and I don't have time for one now. I can't—"

Instead of listening, he reached over and undid a button on my shirt, shaking his head. "This a party, *chica*, not a deposition. You gotta work it a little. C'mon. I can't do everything. Ben's hot and hetero. Get in the game."

Before I could answer, someone yelled to him from across the room that the *empanadas* were running out. He patted me on the shoulder and said, "I'll be back. Now get out there and make the magic happen."

I was mortified. Who knew what he had told Ben—take pity on my desperate, lonely friend? I headed through the patio doors and out to the backyard in hopes of avoiding him. I made a beeline for a punchbowl set up on the picnic table, filled a plastic cup to the rim, and took a big gulp. Whoa! That was one strong margarita. I found an empty chair in a corner of the yard and sat down to nurse my drink and watch the revelers.

Several couples were salsa dancing with varying levels of skill, and I recognized Courtnee's flag of Spain colors swirling around. She and her boyfriend Trent were actually pretty good dancers. The stars were out, the music was lively, and the embarrassment over Miguel's matchmaking began to fade as I downed my margarita. I started to feel a pleasant glow that ended abruptly as my benevolent gaze picked up Ellie steaming across the yard toward me.

"Leah, is it true you confronted Miller Caldwell at his home and accused him of being involved in Lacey's death?" she demanded without preamble. A fresh grassy smell wafted off her.

"Miller asked me to stop by for coffee. He invited me. I didn't call him. We talked about Lacey. I didn't accuse him of anything. I just asked a few questions."

She shook her head, making flame-colored hair swirl around her shoulders and land in charming chaos above her close fitting purple tank top. I had the urge to tell her she looked like the Little Mermaid and smelled like a field of clover, but fortunately my prefrontal cortex hadn't yet surrendered to the tequila.

"I've asked you, begged you, and Max has ordered you to stop this stupid attempt to rewrite your family history. It's bad enough to fool yourself, but your selfishness is hurting my family. I won't have it." She was actually shaking her finger at me.

"You know, I'm getting a little tired of you telling me how to live my life.

How is me finding out how my sister died hurting your family, Ellie? I mean, seriously. I make sure everyone I talk to knows this is my deal, not Max's."

"I wouldn't care what you're doing, Leah, if it didn't affect Max. I don't know why he's so fond of you, because you sure don't seem very fond of him. All you care about is what you want to do, what you think is important, and to hell with everyone else. But I care that my husband is juggling creditors, and cutting his pay in half, and dodging old friends, because he owes them money. I care that he has to take Ambien every night to get to sleep. I care that you're a major part of the stress he's feeling.

"And no matter what you tell the nuns, or Miller, or anyone else connected with DeMoss, nobody likes feeling they're under investigation. Least of all the Catholic Church. And that kind of people take care of their friends, and they don't leave fingerprints. They won't have to refuse Max's loan to punish him. If they delay acting on it long enough, Max will go under. And I hope you can live with that, knowing it's partly your fault, after all he's done for you."

I didn't know that about Max. I didn't realize he'd cut his own salary.

"Look, Ellie, I'm sorry. I really am. But Max's problems with the paper started long before I got back. You know that. I'm finally getting somewhere with this, and I can't stop now. Things are starting to make sense. I'm even beginning to see how Sister Mattea fits into the picture." OK, so I was exaggerating, but in the face of Ellie's anger I guess I was trying to justify myself.

She looked at me nonplussed.

"You are unbelievable! Now we'll have every Catholic in town cancelling his subscription to the paper because you're trying to dig up dirt on a nun!" Then she turned on her heel and strode away. Ellie's rant shook me up. It made me sick to think of Max's situation. Maybe there was a little truth in Ellie's fears. If someone like Reid Palmer or Miller Caldwell thought I was going to hurt something they cared about—in Palmer's case the DeMoss family legacy, in Miller's his political future—they might put pressure wherever they thought it would help. No matter what I said about Max not being part of it.

I became aware that someone was watching me.

"I've been looking for you. You're not trying to avoid me, are you?" Ben asked, but in the teasing tone of someone who knew he never had to worry about being ditched. He held a plastic cup toward me. I accepted and took a big gulp. One and a half margaritas in, I was a little less uptight about Miguel's matchmaking efforts.

"Hey. Thanks. I just saw someone I know, and we got talking."

"Ah." He nodded as he pulled up a lawn chair and sat down beside me. "It's a beautiful night, isn't it?"

"Yeah, it sure is." We were both silent for a minute, then both started talking at once.

"So Miguel says—"

"So where are you—"

"No, you go," I said.

"All right. Miguel said you're a big-time journalist. What are you doing back in Himmel?"

"He's exaggerating, as usual. I'm back to take care of some family stuff. You know," I said evasively and took another sip. His hand accidentally brushed against my arm as he leaned over to reach for the chips sitting on the table next to us. He really was good looking. Or did I just think so because I was in the middle of a long dry spell, tempered now by a wet margarita haze?

"Yeah, I hear you. So, you're from here then?"

"Born and raised. How about you?"

"I live in Chicago, but I used to spend summers here with my grandmother. She died a couple of months ago. I'm staying at her house, trying to fix it up to sell."

"I'm sorry."

"Yeah. Well, she had Alzheimer's. It was pretty hard to have her go like that. She was a special person."

"I'm sorry," I said again. I changed the subject.

"So what do you do, Ben? When you're not fixing up houses?"

"I'm an IT security consultant."

"No way."

"Way. Why not?"

OK, I wasn't so far gone that I was going to tell him he looked too hot to be a computer geek. But I was close. "You just seem too, too, uh—social. You seem too social."

"C'mon. You don't seriously think all IT people are awkward social misfits?"

"Um, kind of."

"You're a very biased person, Leah. I'm surprised. I thought journalists were supposed to be all about getting the facts, no judgments, just the facts."

"I think you're thinking of Joe Friday."

He looked blank.

" 'Dragnet.' 'Just the facts, ma'am.' 1987 Tom Hanks/Dan Aykroyd movie? Old-timey TV show? Really bad remake with Ed O'Neill 2003?" Oh boy. He looked dreamy, but he was dropping in my esteem. I put a lot of store by old movie and TV references.

"Sorry."

"I forgive you." He really was very pretty. "So how long will you be here?"

"Couple more months, I think. Until the house is in shape to put on the market. Right now the interior needs a lot of work."

"I hope you're handy."

"I've been told I am," he said with a grin. I was glad it was dark as I realized I'd walked right into that double entendre and felt a flush rise on my cheeks. And remembered Miguel's comment about picking Ben out special for me. I was going to make an excuse to circulate, but he said, "Would you like another drink?"

Suddenly, that seemed like a really good idea. Why couldn't I just once, just let things happen? I wasn't judgmental. I wasn't obsessed. I knew how to have a good time. I could get in the game.

"All right. Sure."

As he left, I heard a burst of laughter from across the yard. Coop was walking toward my little corner of the party with Sherry holding so tight to his arm she looked like a third appendage. He caught my eye, then we both looked away. Sherry must have seen the glance, because she gave his arm a proprietary squeeze, then leaned her head on it for just a second. As they turned and changed direction toward the house, she cast a triumphant smile at me.

Dumbass. Coop could date all the bimbos he wanted. I wasn't interested in him as a boyfriend, but I sure did miss him as a friend. I stood up to stretch my legs and someone tapped my shoulder from behind.

"Karen! I haven't seen you in forever."

"I know. But I hear all about you from Carol," she said, leaning down from her 6-foot height to give me a hug.

"I bet. You look great. Your hair is super cute." I was used to seeing her silver-blonde hair in a no-nonsense short cut, but she'd grown it out to a layered bob that suited her narrow face.

She waved away my compliment, then hit me with what was on her mind.

"Leah, what's goin' on with you? Your mother is really worried. She told me," and here she leaned in a little and dropped her voice almost to a whisper, "she said you're convinced that Lacey was sexually abused, and you're risking your job and Max's business to prove you're right."

"Karen, don't you start on me. Despite what everyone seems to think, I didn't just dream this up." I gave her the shortest version I could of what I'd discovered, and to my surprise, instead of telling me I was crazy and irresponsible, she nodded her head.

"I see. That's not exactly how your mom explained it."

"No doubt. Look, I get she's concerned, but I've been doing investigative reporting for 10 years. I know when something is off. Yeah, yeah, so I'm emotionally involved in this. That doesn't mean I'm not on to something, does it?" I tried to keep my desire for her validation out of my voice.

"Kiddo, if you say there's something wrong with Lacey's death, then I have to take you seriously. But at this point, it looks to me like you know too much for your peace of mind, and not enough for a court of law. And Carol's right you're treading on dangerous ground.

"Miller is very powerful, and Georgia is very protective. She's not going to let a threat to his election go. And DeMoss Academy has influential friends. This priest you're after, the Catholic Church is going to protect him, too. You're out on your own on this one. Max has taken a clear step back. You could be sued for slander. And that could be a very expensive, career-destroying court case. Your professional and personal life, everything will be up for grabs."

"It doesn't matter. If it's true, it isn't slander. I just have to prove what I'm saying is true. And, Karen, I don't know all the answers, but I'm getting closer."

"Leah, are you getting enough sleep? You look so tired. You know, you're all your mother's got. You need to take care of yourself. She loves you like crazy. And so do I," she said, reaching out and putting a hand on my shoulder.

A warm glow infused me, and I thought, take that Coop, everybody else loves me. I had moved into a very mellow place in Margaritaville, and all things seemed possible. I reached up and pulled her down in a hug. "Karen, it's OK. I'm OK. And you're OK. And everything is A-OK. Don't worry."

"How much have you had to drink, Leah?"

"Oh, a couple. Small ones. I'm good," I assured her. I really was. I've heard that drinking brings out the side of your personality that you keep under wraps—that's why some people who are jovial, funny types turn into mean drunks. In my case, drinking turns me from a cynical smartass to an affectionate extrovert. With each sip, I become more enchanted with everyone.

At this point I found it hard to keep from giving Karen a pinch on the cheeks, because she looked so darn sweet with her face all scrunched up with worry lines, looking at me with big sad eyes.

"Look, give me a call tomorrow. I want to walk through this with you when you're fully functional. You need to understand what could happen if you're wrong. And maybe even more important, what could happen if you're right. Now, you settle down and eat something. I'll talk to you later."

As she started to move away, Ben came up with our drinks.

"Wait, Karen, this is my new friend Ben. He loves his grandma. Ben, this is Karen. She's really nice. Do you like her hair?"

They exchanged glances. "Nice to meet you, Ben. Take good care of your new friend."

"Don't worry. I've got it covered."

"Who was that?"

"My mom's boss. Karen. She's a good lawyer."

He nodded. "I'll keep that in mind if I need one."

He sat down next to me, and I drank freely from my replenished margarita while he started on a long story, which I vaguely remember had to do with a road trip with a friend in a 1982 Plymouth Reliant. I absolutely remember I found it hilarious. Toward the end I noticed I was getting cold. And I was hungry.

I stood up a little woozily and reached down to pull Ben up beside me.

"Whoa, steady there. You all right?"

"Yeah, yeah. Just hungry. Let's go in and get something to eat."

Inside I excused myself and headed for the bathroom. "Be right back." Of course, there was a line up. When I finally got through and headed for the kitchen, I saw Karen and Ben in conversation. Walking up to them, I said, "Hey, you guys. I really like you. Did you know that?"

Miguel came up just then, and I threw an arm up and pulled his head down and gave him a big kiss on the top of his head. "Miguel! Ben and Karen this is my Miguel." Which struck me suddenly as very funny, especially when I began to sing the Beatles "My Michelle," replacing it, of course, with "My Miguel."

In the middle of the chorus, I saw Coop in the doorway. I broke off mid-song. "Coop!" I shouted, so happy to see him. Then I remembered. "You're an asshat. This is my new friend, Ben. And this is my true friend, Miguel. And, Karen." I fixed him with a withering stare. Or at least what in my mind was a withering stare.

"Leah, don't you think it might be time to go home and get some rest?"

"Quit telling me what I think. I think you should just go call your best friend Miller Caldwell. I think you don't know who I think you aren't. Are. Thought you were. Think you know!" I finished incoherently, but with an unwarranted sense of triumph, as though I had scored a major verbal putdown. "I am going. I am going with my new true friend Ben."

From somewhere in the dark recesses of a childhood spent listening to my mother's *Best of the '70s* albums, I dredged up the Michael Jackson song "Ben." None of the words came to mind, but that was OK. I settled for humming and ad-libbing something along the lines of "*Ben, my new best friend. And I will not pretend. That you are not my friend. And I will never bend...*" And then, mercifully my lyric machine ran dry, and I sat down abruptly in the nearest chair. From there memory dims.

21

I woke up to the nauseating smell of bacon frying. I was in a bed I didn't recognize in a room I'd never seen before. Not a good feeling. I remembered the party. I remembered Ben and drinking margaritas and laughing and maybe singing and maybe, sort of, coming back here with Ben. But nothing was very clear.

I threw back the cover, saw that I was still wearing my jeans and oxford shirt. That seemed like a positive sign. I sat up. Then promptly lay back down and closed my eyes. My head was pounding. Was this Ben's house? I tried again to get myself upright, this time more slowly. I opened my eyes carefully and looked around.

The room was small and held only the bed I was in, a battered nightstand, and a threadbare rug. The wallpaper was a faded dark green festooned with big pink cabbage roses. The bed itself was the kind you see in old Westerns, a metal frame and springs topped by a blue ticking mattress. Well. No one could say I wasn't a cheap date.

OK, OK, pull yourself together. I swung my feet onto the floor and felt around for my shoes, which I located tucked under the bed. As I leaned over to put them on, a wave of nausea hit me, and I stopped mid-reach and took a deep breath. By employing this torturous start-stop-start method, I was able to get my shoes tied. I rose from the bed and grabbed my purse, which was sitting on the night table, and slowly made my way to the door.

The bacon smell now mingled with the scent of strong coffee. I made a stop in the bathroom across the hall, where I repeatedly splashed cold water on my face. I squeezed toothpaste on my finger and ran it across my teeth and tongue a few times. I studied myself in the mirror. There were huge bags under my eyes, and my hair was sticking out as though I was a cartoon character with a finger stuck in an electric socket. I dug around in my purse for a hairclip, yanked my hair back and clipped it up, searched within my soul for the few shreds of dignity I could muster, and followed the breakfast smells down the stairs.

I walked through a formal dining room and into a kitchen that looked like it came straight from the set of a 1950s sitcom. A big roundish refrigerator was set against one wall, next to a white stove with a solid door and chrome knobs. A dinette set with yellow Formica top and yellow-padded chrome chairs held center stage in the room. That's where Ben sat drinking a cup of coffee, as I trudged shamefacedly in.

"Hey, good morning, how're you feeling?" he asked in the hearty voice of someone who had not consumed way too many margaritas the night before. His eyes were clear, his smile bright. He was disgusting.

"OK," I whispered. "But could we talk in our indoor voices for a while?"

He grinned. "Here, a glass of water and a cup of coffee. That'll start you on the road to recovery. I've got some over-easy eggs, bacon—"

I shook my head rapidly, then dropped into the nearest chair to ride out a sudden wave of dizziness. "No, no thanks. Dry toast if you have it. That would be great."

I took a huge drink of water and ate a couple of bites of dry wheat toast before I said, "Look, about last night. I, uh. That is, I don't want you to think...uh, I don't usually...I didn't sleep with you last night, did I?"

"You don't remember?" he asked, a hurt look on his face.

Oh no. Oh hell. I took a deep breath, "Ben, I—"

Then I realized he was shaking with laughter. "I'm sorry. I couldn't resist. The expression on your face—" He lost control and started laughing again.

"You know, you're kind of an ass."

"Hey, now. Last night you told me I was your best friend. You even sang me a song about it."

I lowered my head into my hands and muttered, "Stop. Please. Just stop."

"C'mon Leah. Don't be embarrassed. No. We didn't sleep together. You were in no condition to drive. When we got in my car you couldn't give me your address. Said you didn't want your mom to see you. So, I brought you here, took your shoes off, tucked you into bed, and now here you are safe and sound."

"Thanks," I said. Then, anxious to change the subject, "So, this is your grandmother's house? It's pretty, uh, vintage."

"I know. Every time I come into the kitchen, I expect to see Lucy and Ethel having coffee. It's gonna take a while to update it."

"Well, it made a nice B&B for me. Thanks. But I should get going. Could you give me a ride to my car, and then I'll just head on home?"

"Nothing more to eat?"

"No, I'm good, thanks."

***

I've done the walk of shame a few times in my life, but this was the first time strolling into my mother's kitchen was part of it. As I pulled into the driveway, I noticed Miguel's bright red Toyota parked across the street. Yay.

I squared my shoulders and did my best to appear nonchalant and clear-eyed.

"Hey! Morning, Mom. Hi, Miguel. What are you doing here?"

"Miguel just brought me some *tamales* left over from the party last night. I could put a couple in the microwave for you," she said with an evil glint in her eye.

"No, no, that's OK," I said, as my stomach did a quick lurch.

"So, Miguel was telling me you had quite a good time last night, Leah. You don't look like you're having so much fun now." Her voice was filled with faux concern.

"Whatever, Mom. Let's just move on, OK? Got any coffee? I saw Karen last night."

"Oh?"

"Mom, if you're so worried about me asking questions, maybe you shouldn't be telling everyone what I'm doing."

"Karen isn't 'everyone,' and, besides, I already told you I talked to her. Don't get surly with me because you're hung over."

I held up my hand. "Sorry. Can we take it down a notch? My head is killing me."

"Serves you right," she said, but handed me a glass of water and some aspirin at the same time. "You're old enough to know better. Did Lacey's roommate reach you last night?

"Delite? She called here?"

"She said she lost your card, and she wanted to talk to you. I gave her your cell number. I thought about not doing it, but I knew that would only postpone the inevitable."

I unzipped my purse and started pulling things out and setting them on the table as I rooted around. Camera batteries, my wallet, a battered compact, a bottle of water, geez, my purse was way too big. "Damn!"

"You lost your cell again? Your *mamá* needs to make you one of those strings little kids use for mittens, only you can hook it to your phone," Miguel said.

"You know what's not funny? You. Help me think. I must have taken it out at your house?"

"Sorry, *chica*, I cleaned up everything this morning. If it was there, I would've found it. Maybe it's in your car?"

I dashed out and started ransacking my Focus. Not on the seats, not under the backseats, not in the door pocket, not in the glove compartment, not on the floor, not in the center console storage box.

"It's not there. Why am I so careless?"

My mother didn't say anything, but it was killing her.

"Maybe it's at Ben's. Do you have his number, Miguel?" He nodded and punched it in, then handed me his phone.

"Ben, Leah Nash. Hey, could you do me a favor and take a look around and see if I left my cell phone at your house, or maybe in your car?"

"Sure, I'll call you back in five."

As I waited anxiously, I grilled my mother.

"What exactly did Delite say?"

"I told you. She lost your card, and she wanted to get in touch with you."

"But did she say what about? Why?"

"She didn't say, and I didn't ask. You're going to do what you want to do, I know. But I don't have to be part of it."

"Don't you get it, Mom? Delite knows something, I'm sure of it. She as good as admitted that she lied about going with Lacey to a party that night. Maybe she's ready to tell me why."

"Now, Leah," she said in the tone she's used to correct me since I was two years old. "You need to settle down. You need to get some sleep. You need to take a step back. Honey, I'm worried about you."

"Don't be, Mom. I'm fine. I—"

Miguel's phone rang, and when he looked at the caller ID, he handed it over to me.

"Ben? Did you find it?"

"Sorry, Leah, no luck. I checked all the rooms you were in—bedroom, bathroom, kitchen. It's just not there."

"Well, thanks for looking. Talk to you later." I handed the phone back to Miguel.

"Hell to the max. It's got to be somewhere. I can't go without a cell phone. If I don't find it today, I'll have to get a new one tomorrow." Another roadblock loomed. "I don't have Delite's number!"

"Yes, you do, just look at the recent call list on Carol's phone," Miguel said.

My mother and I exchanged looks—hers slightly defiant, mine definitely I-told-you-so. "That would work, if Mom's phone was made in the 21st century. She's still got a 1994 Trimline phone—that one on the wall over by the bar. No tracking phone calls there, right, Mom?"

"It's a perfectly good phone. It does what I want it to do, and I don't leave it lying around all over town. I have an answering machine, isn't that enough? Don't get snarky."

At that moment, the phone in question rang. My mother answered it. "What? Yes. Of course. Yes, Max. She's on her way, I think. No, she's just running late. She lost her phone. All right. Tell Ellie good luck."

She hung up and glared at me.

"What?"

"Max is at the Fun Run at the county park with Ellie and Alex and half the town. He wants to know where you are. Leah Marie Nash, I lied for you, and I don't like it. I told him you were on your way. It's bad enough you get drunk and go home with a stranger last night, but I don't want Max to think you're so hell—"

I shot a glance at Miguel who was suddenly studying with rapt attention a recipe for curried chicken stuck to the refrigerator with a magnet.

"Sorry, Mom, sorry, sorry. I just forgot about it," I said, throwing things into my purse.

"It seems to me you 'just forgot' about everything except your current obsession. No one said you shouldn't be trying to find the truth about Lacey—"

"Oh, no. We're not going there are we? 'No one?' How about Max, Coop, you, Paul, everyone in this town except Miguel," I hissed back.

"Just a minute, missy—"

"Missy? Really, Mom? You haven't hauled that one out since I was 10 years old."

"Well, you're acting like a 10-year-old! A belligerent, willful—"

"OK, great as it's been talking to you, I've got to go. As you know, I'm late." As I banged the door shut, I heard her say, "Wait, Leah, please. I'm worried about you, I—"

But I didn't wait, I kept going.

22

The 5K Fun Run—which name seemed to me an oxymoron, fun and run being diametrically opposed activities as far as I was concerned—was an annual event to raise money for DeMoss Academy. The course skirted the county park, looped around a section of the Catherines' property, then came back by the river bluff where just weeks ago Sister Mattea had plunged to her death. Judging by the chattering crowd waiting for the race to start, and the runners joking and doing warm-ups, no one seemed to mind—or remember.

A bank of clouds advancing from the west suggested a storm in the offing, but if so, it was still miles away. Meanwhile, a few hundred yards from the finish line, volunteers fired up charcoal grills, set up serving tables with paper plates and plastic cups, and unloaded tubs of baked beans and coleslaw, mountains of hotdogs, buns and condiments. Farther over in the park, kids were playing on swing sets and slides. It was the first major event of the almost-summer, and the turnout was great.

As I got out of the car, Helen Sebanski, publicity chair for the event, spotted me and came bustling over with her characteristic half-walk, half-trot, a gait that left her perpetually breathless. She was resplendent in a purple track suit over a T-shirt imprinted with the MGM Grand logo. Her soft white hair was held back by a glittery gold headband.

"Leah, I'm so glad you're here. I was beginning to worry. I should have known we can always count on the *Times*," she said, panting discreetly and smiling as she took my hand in both of hers. I felt a stab of guilt that I tried to assuage with a hearty, "I'm happy to be here, Helen. Looks like a great event. Did you have fun on your senior excursion to Las Vegas?"

"Oh yes. I won $500 on the slot machines. It was just marvelous," she said, as she took my arm and fox-trotted me over to Sister Julianna and Reid Palmer.

"Sister Julianna, Mr. Palmer, this is Leah Nash with the *Himmel Times*."

"We're already acquainted, Helen," Reid said, smiling at her.

"Well, that's a small town for you, isn't it? But then it's a small world, too, I always say." She turned to me. "You won't believe this, but I ran into Sister Julianna when I was in Las Vegas. You brought me luck, Sister. I won $500 after I saw you."

"That's wonderful, Helen. Can I count on you to tithe 10 percent of that for the DeMoss development fund?" She winked to show she was kidding. Then she must have noticed the puzzled expression on my face. Las Vegas and Sister Julianna went together in my mind like the pope and McClain's Bar & Grill.

"I was attending a conference on adolescent dysfunctional behavior at the Bellagio," she said to me.

"Sister Julianna is being modest. She was the keynote speaker. She's a nationally recognized expert on adolescent behavior," Reid said.

"Well, we're just so proud of all the wonderful work you do," Helen said. "I—"

"Helen! We can't find the starting pistol!" someone shouted from the starting line.

"Oh dear, I have to go. But thank you both so much for all you do for the children. And, Leah, I'll look forward to seeing the write-up in the paper," she spoke from over her shoulder as she trotted off with a little wave.

"So, maybe I could do a feature about you and your work on the national level," I said to Sister Julianna. That might be an avenue for access to the Catherines that wouldn't upset Max.

She shook her head. "Reid is exaggerating. I just like to stay current and make a contribution. Actually, Leah, we were talking about you when you walked up with Helen."

"Oh?"

"I think you've mistaken my feelings about your inquiries. I understand that you need—we all need—to know the truth."

That was a 180. Had Reid engineered her change of heart? Mine not to reason why, mine but to step up and take advantage of it.

"I wonder then if you know why Delite lied to you about Lacey going to a party with her the night she disappeared?"

"You talked with Delite? She said she had lied?"

"Yes and no. Yes, I talked to her, but, no, she didn't admit she lied. She was clearly hiding something, though. Her story just doesn't fit when you factor in Danny Howard. When I pressed her on it, she got pretty belligerent. She also said Lacey couldn't stand Father Hegl. Do you know anything about that?"

"I don't think she can be right about that. They were both so interested in music and both such beautiful singers. And Father Hegl loves teaching, especially talented performers like Lacey. In fact, he's teaching a music class Wednesday nights at the technical college this semester, in addition to everything he does at DeMoss."

"Father Hegl is, as am I, a believer in the transformative power of music," Reid added.

It seemed to me that this sidebar on Hegl's devotion to music was a diversionary tactic to get away from the topic of Delite and her lie. "Why do you think Delite would have made up a story about going to a party with Lacey? Do you think it's possible she was trying to make you believe she was trying to be a better person by accepting responsibility for her behavior? So she wouldn't get shipped off to juvenile detention? Or, is it possible someone put her up to lying? Because—" My query was cut short.

"I'm sorry but I believe Helen is trying to get our attention, Reid. It looks like the race is about to start. Leah, you'll excuse us?" She started moving away before she even finished her sentence.

As Reid turned to go he said, "Please call me, Leah. I'm curious to hear more about your investigations." As they left, I saw Max striding toward me.

"Hey, Max. I saw Alex and Ellie headed to the starting line a few minutes ago. You're not running this year?" The last time Max ran anywhere was in 1989, when I accidentally hit a softball through his picture window. He ignored my attempt to keep things light.

"I hope you were talking to Reid Palmer and Sister Julianna about the race and nothing else."

"Don't worry, I've got it covered. It's all good." A lie by omission is still a lie, I know. It just doesn't feel quite as bad.

He fixed me with his fierce eyebrow stare. I stared right back, and then he surprised me. He put a hand on my shoulder.

"Leah, please don't make me do something I don't want to do."

Before I could ask him what he meant, the loudspeaker crackled and runners were ordered to the starting line. He dropped his hand. "I gotta go. I want Ellie to hear me cheering."

As the runners took to the course, I talked to committee members, got a tally on sponsorships and tickets sold, and how many runners had entered —the usual drill for an event like that. As I worked the crowd, I saw Miguel wandering around shooting photos. He must have taken pity on my unprepared state this morning, even though it wasn't his weekend to work. That was a good thing, because even with the foolproof idiot camera in my bag, I wasn't confident I could hold it steady enough to take any decent shots.

The first runners started coming in about 20 minutes after the race began. The last ones trailed in about half an hour after that. Ellie took first place in her group. Paul Karr finished 5th for the over-60s, and Miller's daughter Charlotte got a first. Helen Sebanski was in her glory on the dais, putting medals around the winners' necks, and Reid made a nice speech about the work DeMoss Academy did, and how grateful everyone on the board was for the community support.

People were still eating and talking as the sky got darker and darker. The more experienced committee members, used to the vicissitudes of Wisconsin weather, had begun packing up supplies when the wind started to pick up. By the time the first drops of rain fell, the tables were cleared and the vans loaded. After a few more tentative drops, the pace picked up and people scrambled to their cars.

Thunder rumbled to the west and I dove into my Focus just as a flash of lighting forked across the sky. I was blocked from leaving by an SUV filled with squabbling children and irritated parents who apparently elected to punish them—and me—by sitting in place until the kids stopped crying. By the time they left, the rain was pelting my little compact with such force that the windshield wipers couldn't keep up even on high speed.

I decided to stay where I was until the storm passed. A few other cars had the same idea, but I moved away from them toward the center of the lot to be out of range of any falling trees. Then I turned off the motor and tilted my seat back. The rain hit the roof and slapped at the windows with a hypnotic rhythm. I reached into the backseat, pulled out the raggedy blanket I keep there, and snuggled under it. I closed my eyes, safe from the storm in the warm cocoon of my car.

With no sound but the rain and my own breathing, my body relaxed and my mind quieted. I fell into a kind of trance. The tangled knot of regret, anger, and guilt that had been tightening around my heart since Sister Mattea's death, seemed to loosen. My failure to save Lacey, Max's problems, Coop's defection, Miller's involvement, Delite's stonewalling, Hegl's role, the mystery of what Sister Mattea knew—everything fell away, and I was just breathing in the semi-darkness of the storm.

At some point, I must have drifted off into sleep, because when I opened my eyes, the rain had stopped. I sat up with a start and looked around. It was still light but the shadows were long. I looked at my watch—eight o'clock. I'd slept for hours.

Stiff and groggy, I got out of the car to stretch and pull on my oversized hoodie. The area was deserted. A scattering of puddles in the parking lot and a few clouds overhead were the only evidence of the storm. I stood there in a post-sleep stupor, yawning, and staring blankly out across the river.

Gradually, a movement near the edge of the bluff caught my eye. Squinting in the dim light, I saw something that made my mouth go dry and my heart contract with quick thumping beats. At the spot where Sister Mattea had fallen something—or someone—was rising up over the ground.

I ran toward the edge of the cliff, my feet pounding the trail. I blinked my eyes to make the shape take form in the gloom as it moved slowly side-to-side. When I came within yards of the edge, I saw it clearly.

My heart slowed down considerably as I realized that the "ghost" of Sister Mattea was actually a Mylar balloon, one of those that had been on sale at the Fun Run. Some kid had probably let it go, but instead of soaring off into the stratosphere, its long string got tangled on one of the bushes that jutted out beneath the overhang of the bluff. It had just enough play to let the balloon rise up and float in the air, embodying in my fevered imagination the spirit of Sister Mattea.

I shook my head at my idiocy and then walked over to the edge myself. I looked down at the river running fast and deep more than 70 feet below and said a silent prayer for her. A light breeze tickled the back of my neck and carried the scent of spring with it, grassy and fresh. I inhaled deeply and closed my eyes. They flew open as a strong thump in the middle of my back threw me off balance and sent me hurtling over the edge.

23

I plummeted in a terrifying tumble down the sandstone bluff, flailing out to latch onto a jutting rock, a tree, a bush, anything to stop my relentless downward plunge. It happened in seconds that seemed to last hours. I was going to die just like Sister Mattea, and I didn't know why. Halfway down I felt a sharp yank on my neck and shoulders. My body swung out away from the bluff, then slammed back into the welcoming arms of a scraggly tree.

My baggy hoodie had snagged on a branch. That beautiful scratchy outgrowth was just tenacious enough to hold on and pull me into its rough embrace. I burrowed into the small tree, heedless of the nips and scratches inflicted by its bristly limbs. I stayed there motionless until my heart slowed, my ragged breathing returned to normal, and I could think clearly enough to assess my situation.

"Well, this is another fine mess you've gotten us into," I said out loud. I looked up and could see I had fallen maybe 30 or 40 feet. I didn't let myself look down. My only option was to try to climb back up, using whatever hand and footholds I could find.

It took everything I had to force myself to let go of the scrappy little limb I clung to. I put a tentative hand up, stretching my arm as far as it would extend. My fingers found a medium-sized handhold large enough for me to grab. I swung my body to the right to adjust my center of gravity, then pushed up and away from the security of my rescue tree. Thank you, ex-boyfriend Josh, for making me go to the climbing wall at the gym with you every Saturday for three months.

I found a toehold with my left foot and pulled up, then reached out again, fingers twitching and fumbling as they found a hold that let me insert them an inch or so. I moved methodically, feeling for the next outcropping or tiny crevice that would give me enough of a hold to move upward. It was a lot easier doing it on the climbing wall. With a safety harness. But I was making slow progress. I was almost up to another tree. I felt a surge of confidence.

I reached out and pushed off, but one leg slipped out from under me and scraped against something sharp. I scrambled to get my balance, throwing my body forward into the face of the bluff. All my weight rested on my right leg as my left foot kicked up and down, searching for something to land on. By the barest of inches, I found a tiny ledge under my foot and got my toes on it. I was splayed out on the side of the bluff, both arms outstretched, afraid to breathe let alone move. Involuntary tears sprang to my eyes, and I felt panic rising.

How could I possibly do this? A self-pitying sniffle snuck up on me. I snuffled it back and heard my mom saying, "Leah, you might not win by trying, but you'll always lose by giving up." Easy for her to say, she wasn't clinging like a bug 50 feet above rocks and a rushing river.

I leaned out more carefully this time, moving my leg, poking gently for another toehold, searching for any way to get purchase. Finally, when I extended my leg to the farthest reaches of my tendons, I found it. A shallow crevice I could wedge my foot against to give me leverage. I looked up, and in the faint light of the rising moon, I could see what I had to do. I shoved off with my leg and prayed for a sprinkling of fairy dust to fly me up to the swaying branch of a small tree. I stretched up, swung my body over and clung as the limb bent and creaked, but held. I twisted and wriggled and shinnied myself far enough up to reach the sturdier central trunk.

Once again, I found myself in a one-sided relationship with a tree. I gave a half-sob of relief and let out the breath I'd been unconsciously holding. I wrapped both arms around the tree and pressed my back into the crevice from which it sprung. My feet rested on a small outcropping. Then I felt something warm running down my leg. I looked and saw that my jeans had ripped and an ugly gash on my thigh was bleeding profusely. Now that the adrenalin jolt had departed, it hurt. The sweat I'd worked up was evaporating, leaving me chilled and shivering.

"Damn, damn, damn!" I yelled, just to hear a human voice. It rang out into the night, but what did it matter? There was no one to listen. I yelled it again even louder.

Then a voice called my name through the darkness.

"Leah? Leah? Leeeeaaaaahhhhh!!!"

Was it God? If so, He had a distinctive Latin lilt to his voice.

"Leah, *chica,* where are you?"

"Here, down here, Miguel, down here. Miguel! Miguel! Miguel!" I screamed as loud as I could, and the voice came closer.

"Leah!"

"Down here! Down the bluff!" The beam of a flashlight shone over my head, then on my face.

"Are you all right?"

The look on Miguel's face didn't make me feel any better than the involuntary "*ay, mierda*" he uttered when he took in my predicament.

"Yeah, sure, I'm fine. Well, no, actually. I can't get up any farther. And my leg hurts kind of bad."

"Hold on, *chica.* Hold on. I'm calling 911. Hold on, hold on." He swung the flashlight away, and I was surprised by how much I didn't want to be alone in the dark as I heard him give directions and urge the operator to hurry.

He hung up and focused the beam of light on me again. "What happened?"

"Somebody pushed me."

"What? Who? Why?"

"I don't know, I—Miguel—" An unwelcomed thought popped into my head. "Be careful up there. Whoever pushed me could still be around."

I was starting to feel a little woozy. The breeze that had been playing around the rocks was on its way to becoming a full-fledged wind. It was getting harder to maintain my balance with my bad leg, and I tried to press myself further back into the rock.

"Leah, hang on. I can hear the siren. Just a minute, *chica*. Just hang on. You can do it. Look at me, *chica*, just look up here. We can do this. You can do this."

I looked up again, and I could see Miguel had laid down on his belly so he could lean over the bluff. His face was directly above mine as he shone the flashlight for me. "You're like Cat Woman. Like Wonder Woman. Just another minute. You OK? You're OK."

"Great, I'm great," I croaked in a voice that sounded nothing like my own. The branch I was leaning on so heavily swayed. My bad leg slipped. My arms wrenched as my body dropped. I was treading air. Above me, Miguel shouted.

"*Chica*, listen, you just gotta swing to the left. Come on now. Just swing in, get back on the ledge. You can do it, I know you can."

"I—I'm so tired." My arms were burning, and I was hanging just like I did the instant before I fell from the hand-over-hands and broke my wrist —but that drop was only a few feet, not 50.

"You are not letting go, you are not letting go. You hold on. *Escuchame.* You hold on!" Miguel shouted. "*Mirame*! Look at me! I can hear the sirens. The rescue team, it's here. It's here. You will not let go," he said.

I looked up at him, and from that distance our eyes locked. And I held on. And I tried once more to swing to the left, and this time my toes landed, and I threw my weight forward and wriggled back into the tree and willed myself to stay there.

And then I heard a truck come roaring up, and the blackness lit up with headlights and floodlights, and someone barked orders and then hours later, or so it seemed, when I just couldn't hold on one minute longer, I felt arms wrap around me and a voice said, "There you go, sweetheart. Let go. It's all right. I've got you. You can let go now."

Only I couldn't. The fireman who had rappelled down in his harness had to pry my hands loose from the branch. When he did, I started to shake convulsively.

"Too much caffeine," I said weakly. He wasn't listening. He concentrated on getting us to the top. As soon as we were on firm ground, he got me on a gurney and under a warm blanket. An EMT did some preliminary poking and prodding, and then Miguel was beside me, his eyes suspiciously bright.

"Oh, *chica*, you scared me so bad."

"And you saved me so good," I said, reaching up weakly and ruffling his hair, perfect even in life and death circumstances.

"All right, sir, you have to step back," said the EMT, but then a familiar voice reached me.

"What the hell, Leah?" Coop came striding toward me, a mix of concern and exasperation on his face. Miguel stepped forward and started talking

"She was here alone up on the bluff and some—"

I interrupted before he could finish, giving him a look that I hoped said, *We speak not of this.*

"Coop! I'm OK, just had a little fall. Miguel found me and called 911. It's fine."

"What were you doing out here in the dark? Alone?"

"It's no big deal," I croaked, trying to sit up. It's hard to make your case lying down.

"What happened? Did you trip? Is the ground soft there? Damn it, there should be a guardrail." I tried to answer, but instead sank back down on the gurney.

"I was waiting for her at the paper so we could put together a story for the web edition on the Fun Run. When she didn't come, I thought maybe she had car trouble. I knew she didn't have her phone. I came looking for her. When I got here, I saw the car but no Leah. I started walking around, and then I heard someone shouting and swearing and I found her."

"Leah, you know how lucky you are, right? This is where Sister Mattea fell. You realize that?" The EMT who had stepped aside in deference to Coop asserted himself at that moment.

"Sorry, Lieutenant. We need to get her to the hospital."

"Wait a minute. I don't need to lie down. I don't need a stretcher. I don't want to go to the hospital. I just need to go home." I felt like I was talking really loud, but no one seemed to hear me. And it suddenly seemed like a really good idea to just be quiet. Before I knew it, we were on our way and the EMT—Phil, I read on his name tag—was expertly hooking me up to an IV.

"Phil, why?"

"Don't talk, Leah. You'll be fine. We just want to get some fluids in you, keep you warm, get that heart rate stabilized at a nice steady pace. It's a cold night for climbing, and you've got a nasty cut on your leg. Just lie quiet."

And I did. Just to be polite.

At the hospital, there were x-rays and blood work and stitches and a tetanus shot, which actually hurt more than anything else they did, before I was released to go home. In the waiting area, my mother gasped as they wheeled me in. I was surprised to see Miguel and Coop still there, and Karen had shown up as well.

"Mom! It's OK. Just protocol. See, I'm standing. I can take it from here. Thanks," I said to the aide who had pushed me out in a wheelchair. "Hospital rules are—" She saw the expression on my face, shrugged, and left me with my posse.

"You guys shouldn't have waited. Except for you, Mom. I think that falls under other duties as assigned in the mother job description. It's after midnight, Karen, geez, Mom shouldn't have called."

"She didn't. I was on my way home from dinner in Omico, and I saw the ambulance pulling away from the county park. Then I saw Coop's car. And then Miguel's. I stopped one of the deputies, and he told me what happened. Don't be so full of yourself. I'm here to take care of your mother, not you," she said, but with a smile.

"*Chica*, of course we stayed. We had to make sure you were OK. *Especialmente* with—"

He caught himself and stopped, but Coop had heard it.

"Especially with what?"

"Nothing, especially with a cut so deep, you know."

Coop looked about to pursue it, but Karen said, "All right, enough talking. Time to catch up tomorrow. Right now, I'm driving Carol and Leah home."

At home my mother fussed around making me tea and cinnamon toast, while Karen hovered over me as I changed from the scrubs the hospital had given me in place of my torn and bloody clothes. I pulled a long-sleeved T-shirt and a pair of sweats out of the closet and was surprised at how good their worn and soft fabric felt against my bruised body. I winced as I wiggled the top over my head and didn't object when Karen helped me with it as though I were a toddler.

Then she settled me on the couch with an afghan tucked round me and my comfort food and drink next to me on the end table. She and my mother both brought their cups of tea into the living room and watched as I devoured the toast, and then sipped slowly on my tea, letting the heat from the mug send a pleasant warmth through my hands.

My mother sat in the rocker across from me, and Karen occupied the wingback chair next to her. She drew her long legs up under her chin, wrapped her arms around them, and looked at me intently.

"All right. Now tell me. What happened tonight?"

"Like I said before, I was just out for a walk and—"

"OK, I'm cutting you some slack because you almost killed yourself tonight, but do not treat us like we're doddering idiots. Why were you teetering on the edge of a precipice alone in the dark?"

"It's not a precipice. It's just an overlook," I said crossly.

"Leah, stop it. Karen is right. There's something you're not telling."

I heaved a sigh. Then, my guard down from post-shock, the warmth of home, and a really effective painkiller that was kicking in, I went for broke.

"I fell asleep in the car during the storm. When I woke up, I thought I saw Sister Mattea. I ran over toward the bluff, and it turned out to be a stupid balloon. I was just standing there when someone pushed me off that bluff. I think it may have been Miller Caldwell."

"Leah! That's it. It's either the drugs talking, or you are certifiable."

Karen put a hand on my mother's arm to stem the flood. "Carol, let's let her talk."

I went through the evidence step by step—at least it seemed like I did. The pleasant haze I felt may have made me less cogent than I wanted to be, but my mom and Karen seemed to get the drift. I pointed out how much time Lacey spent with the Caldwells, then her abrupt cut-off of contact, Georgia's hostility and her insinuation that Lacey had seduced Miller.

I highlighted Delite's vague recollection that Lacey said "some big shot" had abused her, Miller's out-of-the-blue meeting with me, and his fishing expedition to discover what I knew. Then I told them about Mary Beth

Delaney's admission that Miller had funded Lacey's memorial site, and about the quotation that appeared every year on the site, the one that mirrored what Miller had said to me when we spoke. Finally, I pointed out Miller's lack of an alibi the night Lacey disappeared.

"It all adds up. He saw me at the park today. Maybe it was just chance that he came back and found me, or maybe he was waiting somewhere and watching. Either way, when I walked out by the bluff, it was the perfect opportunity. And I think he did the same thing to Sister Mattea." They were both quiet, but then it was Karen who spoke.

"Leah, I know how hard you've been working to find out what really happened to Lacey. And I have to give you credit. You've turned up a lot of things the sheriff's department overlooked or ignored."

I was liking how this was going. Karen was the first person other than Miguel to concede that I was on to something.

"But think for a minute. None of it is really evidence. It's circumstantial, it's speculation and, kiddo, it's not actionable. Leah, hon, you've got no proof that Lacey was abused, let alone that she was killed. No evidence that Sister Mattea knew anything about it, and no hard data that supports your theory that Miller was her abuser and possibly even her murderer."

"But what about her behavior changes? What about the money Lacey supposedly stole? What about the missing data on the phone? And Sister Julianna is hiding something. I could tell when I talked to her today. Maybe she's protecting Miller Caldwell. He's on the board, and he's got a lot of power. Maybe she even knows what really happened to Lacey." I heard a pleading note creep into my voice and willed it away.

Then my mother spoke.

"Leah, you've run yourself ragged since Sister Mattea died. You're not eating, you're not sleeping, you've put so much pressure on yourself. You carry the weight of the world on your shoulders—you always have. Look what happened today—you fell asleep for four hours in your car. That's how exhausted you are. No one can blame you if your judgment is skewed, but you can't, you just can't, accuse Miller of trying to kill you."

"Why would he risk killing you when he's not in any real danger? You don't have any evidence that he did anything to Lacey, and you haven't found any connection between Lacey and Sister Mattea. I'm sorry, hon, but there are alternate explanations for everything you've found," Karen said.

"But it wouldn't *be* risky for Miller. All he had to do was run up behind me, and give a quick push, and run away. And it worked, right? Because no one saw him and you don't believe me."

I didn't like the way my mother was looking at me, and the gentle way Karen said, "You need to take a step back. Think a minute, Leah. If a source came to you with this, there's no way you'd run with that story. You'd demand the facts, and the facts just aren't there."

"I didn't imagine that someone pushed me off that bluff. And I'm not imagining that Miller abused and then killed Lacey. I'm getting closer to proving it every day. You want facts? Wait and see. I'm going to make sure everyone knows what he did and that he pays for it. And then you can thank me for finding the truth. I'm going to bed."

My angry exit was marred somewhat by the fact that it hurt like mad to stand, and I wound up doing more of an old lady shuffle than a righteous reporter strut down the hall to my room. Out of the corner of my eye, I saw Karen put a hand on my mother's arm as she started to get up and come after me.

24

I came awake gradually the next day, until I tried to execute a slow stretch that quickly ended in a yelp of pain. Every part of my body ached and the cut on my leg both throbbed and itched. I realized that the sun was streaming through my windows. The windows on the west side of my bedroom. What time was it?

I sat up cautiously, but it didn't seem to have any impact on the pain level. About a 7 on a 10-point scale. I leaned slightly to reach my watch on the nightstand and was rewarded with a protest twinge from my rib area. I looked at the time. Squinted. Looked again. It was 2 p.m. I'd slept for 12 hours straight.

Inch by inch I managed to get up, maneuvered into a clean T-shirt and jeans, but didn't even try to bend over and put on a pair of shoes. Instead I slid my feet into some flip-flops and clopped my way to the bathroom. I brushed my teeth and then looked closely in the mirror.

My face was a mass of scrapes and beginning scabs. I had a dime-sized purple bruise on my right cheek. My hands were in worse shape—nails broken, fingertips cracked and split, knuckles abraded and my arms, though relatively unscathed, felt like someone was pulling them out of their sockets every time I forgot and extended them too far.

My thigh was covered with a bandage above my knee where the stitches were and judging by the generally oozy looking state of it, a dressing change was in my future. I just didn't have the stomach for it. On the counter was the Vicodin the doctor had prescribed, but I decided to tough it out. Instead, I grabbed a couple of ibuprofen and washed them down with a glass of water. Then I began the thousand-mile journey down the hall with a single step of my lime green flip flops.

I found my mother drinking a cup of tea at the bar.

"What are you doing here? Why aren't you at work?"

"Like I'm going to work without being able to check if you're still breathing. You get at least 24 hours special treatment. What can I fix you?"

"Mom, you don't—"

"I know I don't have to. How about eggs? Toast? A grilled cheese sandwich and tomato soup?"

"Grilled cheese and soup would be great. I can't believe I slept so long. Why didn't you wake me up?"

"Obviously, you needed it. You should still be in bed. Your poor face. You look like Rocky. The first movie. How does your leg feel?"

"It's OK. I'm all right. I look worse than I feel. The story of my life." I lied, because she looked so worried. "Oh boy, I better call Max."

"I already talked to him. In fact, you had a steady stream of visitors this morning. Max stopped by; Miguel came to see you; Karen ran in on her way to work; Coop called and said he'd be by later, oh, and he had one of his officers bring your car back. Even Ellie stopped after she took Alex to school to see how you were doing."

"Ellie came by? Wow, I must have been closer to dying than I thought if she came to check on me. She was pretty mad last time I talked to her. Of course, maybe she was hoping for bad news."

"That's not funny," she said, looking over her shoulder as she buttered two slices of bread. She placed one into a hot iron skillet, topped it with sliced cheddar and then the other piece of bread. The sizzle made me realize how hungry I was. She reached in the cupboard for a can of tomato soup before saying, "About last night. I need you to understand. It's not that I don't believe you—"

"It's just that you don't believe me," I said. "No, it's OK, Mom. I get it. You think I'm overwrought, and I've gone off the deep end about Miller.

Fine. I don't want to fight about it. I'll just prove to you how wrong you are."

She didn't answer, and it took me a minute to realize that she was crying.

My mother almost never cries. Carol Nash will yell, nag, rant, croon, cajole, but not cry. Not unless her heart is breaking.

I stared in horror, finally getting it. What I was putting her through, why she kept negating my findings, trying to get me to stop. She was really, seriously scared. I heaved myself up, wincing as my muscles cramped in protest, and lumbered over to her.

"Mom, it's all right. I'm all right. Nothing happened. Nothing is going to happen. I'll be careful."

"It already did happen, Leah. Something did happen. Someone pushed you off that bluff, and if it weren't for the fact that you're so damn stubborn, you'd be at the bottom of the river."

"You believe me?"

"Of course I do. Do you think I'm an idiot?" She snuffled and reached for a Kleenex.

Just then we both smelled something burning. "Damn!" She picked the pan handle up without a potholder and dropped it with a clatter. I grabbed a dish towel and lifted it from the burner, then turned off the stove.

"What are you going to do?"

Before I could answer, the front doorbell rang. The opening bars of "I Shot the Sheriff" were playing as I looked through the glass panel.

I opened the door and said, "Hello, Detective Ross."

He flashed his badge. "I got a few questions for you, Leah. Can I come in?"

"Actually, how about we sit on the porch?" I was mindful of my mother with her tear-stained face and burned grilled cheese.

He cocked his head, making little fat rolls ooze over the tight collar of his shirt. "You sure about that? You might feel more comfortable if we talk inside, private like."

"No, that's all right. It's a nice day, and I could use the fresh air." I pointed him to one of the chairs on the wide wooden porch. I leaned against the railing facing him. It seemed easier than the struggle to sit down and get back up again. I didn't want Ross to watch me wince. He didn't say anything about my bruises.

"All right then, let's get right to it. Leah, we got a complaint about you today from Mrs. Miller Caldwell."

"What, she didn't like a headline in last week's edition? She couldn't just write a letter to the editor?"

"It's a little more serious than that. Mrs. Caldwell says you been stalking her."

"What?"

"Two or more unsolicited contacts is stalking in Wisconsin. Mrs. Caldwell says you showed up at her house uninvited on Thursday. Says you accosted her daughter there, too. And she says you texted her 15 times on Sunday with threatening messages."

"That's ridiculous."

"You weren't at the Caldwell's on Thursday?"

"I was, but—"

"Did you accost Mrs. Caldwell in the driveway?"

"No! I—"

"You didn't tell her that she didn't have a very bright future?"

"I may have said something like that, but I—"

"You didn't send her threatening texts on Sunday?"

"Of course I didn't. What did they say?"

"Well, now, why don't you tell me?"

"How would I know? I didn't send them. I didn't even have my phone on Sunday. I lost it Saturday night. I still don't have it. Check with my mother, check with Miguel Santos."

"Lost your phone. Huh." He stared at me for a minute, his dull mustard-brown eyes narrowed. He wasn't wearing a hat, and there was a faint sheen of oily perspiration on his mostly bald head.

"Mrs. Caldwell says you were in her driveway where you proceeded to harass and threaten her on Thursday morning. She says you accused her husband of criminal sexual conduct. What do you say to that, Leah?"

"I say she's lying, or you are."

His fat cheeks burned bright with two red spots, but he didn't react otherwise.

"Are you denying you went to the Caldwell's on Thursday?"

"No, I'm denying I was uninvited. Miller Caldwell asked me to stop by and talk to him. So, I did."

"Let me get this straight now. It's your story that you weren't waiting for Mrs. Caldwell, and didn't approach her and threaten her?"

"How many times do I have to tell you? No!"

"Did you post a comment on the Miller Caldwell for Senator website suggestin' that he had sex with a minor?"

"No."

"Leah," he said, standing up as though finally realizing he'd lost his power position while he sat and I towered above him, "you know, and I know, your sister was a druggie who died because she was drunk and high. You can't change that by telling people all over town that I screwed up the investigation."

"Is that what this is really about, Detective Ross? Did I hurt your feelings? Are you trying to arrest me for slander? Because last time I looked, that's a civil offense not a criminal one, and you should know—it's not slander if it's true. And I'm doing nothing but telling the truth when I say you screwed up the investigation. Or, to give you credit, maybe you were persuaded to give it less than your best by Miller or his wife?"

His right fist clenched, and I watched him willing himself not to grab me and shake me—or smack me. I knew the feeling. He waited a minute, and as his hand relaxed he said, "Nash, we can clear this up quick and easy, or we can do it slow and painful. Are you willing to give me a look at your phone?"

I knew I'd gotten under his skin when he switched from calling me Leah to calling me Nash.

"I told you, I lost it. When did you say Georgia got those threatening texts?"

"Between 5 p.m. and 11 p.m. yesterday."

"Interesting. During a big chunk of that time I was hanging from a branch 50 feet over the Himmel River. Then I spent a couple of hours semiconscious in the hospital, surrounded by medical personnel, then I was back home with my mother and a friend. You should do your homework, Detective Ross."

"I'm a good investigator, and I always do my homework, Nash. See, I know that you can get an app that sends out texts for you at a preset time."

"You can?" I asked, temporarily diverted.

"Yeah. So, you set up your little alibi, and then while your phone is 'missing,' it sends out the texts."

"You think I threw myself over a cliff, and almost died, to set up my alibi?"

"You're a smartass. That don't mean you're smart. What's your cell number, Nash?"

"I'm sure you know."

"As a matter of fact, I do," he said, pulling his own phone out of his pocket and punching in numbers.

In a second, the sound of "Rumor Has It" came tinnily from the direction of my car, parked next to us in the driveway.

"Aren't you going to answer that?"

A triumphant smile sat on his piggy little mouth.

Heaving myself off the railing and down the three steps to the sidewalk, I Frankenstein-walked over to my car and opened the door. There was nothing in the front seat, but the phone kept ringing. Louder now. With an effort, I opened the back door and at first glance didn't see it. Following the sound, I shifted the blanket I'd tossed in the back. There on the floor behind the passenger seat was my phone. Ross was looming behind me.

"It wasn't here. I looked all through my car. Ask my mother, ask Miguel."

"So how come it's there now?"

"Anyone could have put it back here. My car was in the parking lot at the county park all night. It's been in the driveway unlocked since this morning. Anyone could have had access to it."

"So, your story is someone stole your phone, sent threatening texts and emails to Georgia Caldwell, and then they just put it back in your car, all nice and neat. Why would anyone do that?"

"I don't know. To cause me problems, to distract me from finding out what happened to my sister."

"We know what happened to your sister. She got drunk, fell down and died. End of story. But now we got a new story. This ain't exactly your first rodeo is it, Nash?"

"What are you talking about?"

"It says here," he said, ostentatiously pulling a small notebook out of his jacket pocket, "it says right here that you don't play nice with others, Nash. A couple of your old bosses said you were," and here he paused to read from his notes "not a team player, impulsive, stubborn, unpredictable."

He shook his head in a parody of sad disapproval.

"The picture I got is that you're too bullheaded and full of yourself to hold a job for very long. Yeah, a few said you were good, but it seems like you're one of those types that are more trouble than they're worth. Pain-in-the-ass types. High maintenance. And, oh, let's see here." He made a minor production of flipping through the pages of his notepad. "It says you got fired from your last job for harassment." He gave me a little smirk.

"See, I told you I was good at homework. Seems your boss, Ms. Hilary McKay—your ex-boss that is—got some scary texts from you, after she started dating your ex-boyfriend. Some sick, angry stuff, Nash. You ever been in anger management?"

"Oh, come on, that's ridiculous. It was just a joke. It's not even what happened."

"No? Ms. McKay says it is. She says you were unstable, and she had to fire you, and she feared for her safety."

"Oh, really? Then how come she didn't press charges?"

"She felt sorry for you."

"That's not true. She didn't press charges, because the texts were sent anonymously and she couldn't prove they were from me. Which they weren't. She jumped to the conclusion it was me, and never really let go, not even when the guys that actually did it FOR A JOKE came forward when she came unhinged.

"I didn't know anything about it until she came unglued and freaked out at me in the office. I didn't do it. Maybe you should have had your mother check that homework you did. Didn't you learn anything after you botched Lacey's investigation?"

The angry red spots had spread so that his entire face was suffused with a dark maroon color. I started to walk back to the porch, but his bulk blocked my way. He was close enough for me to see a few drops of spit spray from his mouth when he said, "Button your lip, you wiseass."

The front door opened, and my mother stepped out onto the porch. "Everything all right out here?"

Ross turned and nodded to my mother, "Everything's just fine, Mrs. Nash. Just getting some information from your daughter."

"I wonder if you wouldn't want to come up here on the porch to wait, Detective."

"Wait ma'am?"

"Yes. I've called our lawyer. She should be here any minute."

As if on cue, Karen's SUV pulled into the driveway, and she was up and out beside us almost before the engine turned off.

"Detective. What are you doing here?"

"I'm investigating a complaint."

"Leah, you don't need to say anything."

"Detective Ross, are you arresting my client?"

"Not at the moment."

"Then I suggest you leave. She has nothing more to say to you."

"Wait a minute. Arrest me? You've got to be kidding."

"Leah, be quiet."

I shut up more out of surprise than compliance. Karen had never spoken that sharply to me before. I guessed that was the difference between friend Karen and attorney Karen.

"Don't think you can erase anything off your cell phone. We can get the records, you know. And, trust me, I'm gonna do a very thorough job investigating. Just like I did on your sister." Then he turned and left.

"Leah, inside."

Once we got into the living room, Karen said, "What did you tell him?"

"Nothing. He said Georgia Caldwell had accused me of stalking her, that I'd shown up at her house and threatened her, and that I sent her a bunch of threatening texts."

"Did you?"

"No! I wouldn't do something that stupid. Besides, my phone's been missing for two days. I just found it in the backseat of my car."

"But didn't you look there before?"

"You don't seriously think I did this?"

"You were very upset about Miller. This might have seemed like a good way to get under his skin."

"Oh, I'm so stupidly upset that I'd set myself up for a slam dunk conviction by using my own phone to stalk his wife? Come on, Karen."

"Take it easy, Leah. I had to ask. But if you didn't do it, who did?"

"Somebody had to have taken my phone. Probably Saturday night at Miguel's, and then put it in my car either last night at the park or today."

"Who would do that? Why?"

"To set me up, to damage my credibility, to get Max to turn against me, to prove I'm a mad, crazy troublemaker. In other words, Miller or Georgia would be perfect candidates."

"Who might know that you suspect Miller of being involved with Lacey?"

"Max, Ellie, Mom, you, Miguel, Miller, Georgia, Coop, Marilyn Karr, maybe Mary Beth Delaney, anyone she told in her family, anyone that overheard me talking to you at Miguel's—"

"Why didn't you just take out an ad that said, 'Miller Caldwell Killed My Sister'?" my mother asked.

"I thought about it."

"Who had the opportunity to take your phone—and get it back to you?" Karen asked.

"Dozens of people wandered in and out of Miguel's on Saturday, you know that. A lot of them were at the Fun Run the next day. Plus, I'm not one hundred percent that I lost it at the party, it just seems most likely. The last time I remember using it was mid-afternoon. I got a text from Miguel to make sure I was coming. Then I ran some errands, got my hair cut. I could've dropped it somewhere maybe, but that party seems like a place where I might have set it down."

She waved her hand impatiently. "How many people knew about your problem last year with your ex-boss?"

"I didn't think anyone but Mom knew, and I asked her not to say anything. I see she shared with you."

I raised an eyebrow at my mother. She had the grace to look abashed.

"Since she already told you about it, I hope she also said it wasn't a problem, Karen. Not like Ross made it sound. It was just a dumbass joke that got out of hand. My boss Hilary was a real piece of work. She didn't know a good lead from a lift quote. She had this bad-tempered, mouth-breathing little dog that she dressed up in a Dolphins cap and carried around the office in a baby harness for God's sake.

"Once she found out I used to date her fiancé, she wouldn't get off my case. She was almost as bad with the rest of the reporters. Nobody liked her, and a couple of them actually hated her. They got pretty wasted one night and decided it would be hilarious to make a fake ransom flyer for her dog Shadow—only she spelled it C-H-A-D-E-A-U-X—you can see what a pretentious idiot she was.

"They texted her a bunch of dumb things like 'I'll get you and your little dog, too.' One said, 'Who knows what evil lurks in the hearts of men? Your Chadeaux does.' With a picture of the hat her little dog used to wear."

I couldn't stop a little grin at the memory.

"Leah, are you laughing about this? Because it's potentially very serious."

"No, no, I know. I'm sorry. She thought the stuff came from me, and she freaked and she called me in and started screaming. That's when the guys who did it confessed, but Hilary didn't believe them. Thought they were covering for me. The police didn't pursue the complaint. They could see it was ridiculous. But she wouldn't let it go.

"We got into it. I was fed up. I threatened to quit. She said fine. So, I thought, all right then. I let her have it—verbally only. But it got pretty heated. After I left, she spun it like she had to fire me, because I was emotionally unstable. And I guess the scene I had with her in the office—but it was justified, I swear—I can see how some people might have thought she was right. And when your ex-boss tells every reference check that she fired you because you're crazy, well it's kind of hard to shake."

"Did you ask Ross how he found out?"

"He said he was a good investigator who does his homework. Ha."

"Would your ex-editor have talked to him?"

"Oh, yeah. But how would he know to check with her? You really think Ross has that much initiative?"

"Don't underestimate him, Leah. Or the initiative a push from the Caldwell family can give."

"Well, what do I do now?"

"Nothing. Don't speak to him again without me. I'll talk to a friend of mine in the DA's office, see how serious this is. I'll be in touch when I know something."

"Thanks, Karen."

"No problem."

As my mother walked out to the car with her, I hobbled over to the couch, thought better of the challenges of getting back up from its cushiony depths, and opted for the rocking chair. I opened my phone and looked for the text from Delite that should have come in on Saturday. Nothing. In fact, all my texts were gone—those I sent and those I received. I thought a minute, then decided to call the casino and see if I could get her supervisor to give me her home number.

25

"She doesn't work here."

"What? I just saw her there a few days ago."

"Well, she isn't here now."

"Did she quit?"

"I'm not allowed to say."

"You mean she got fired."

"I didn't say that."

"I'm an old friend. I've really got to get in touch with her. Could you please give me her number?"

"We don't give out personal information about employees. Or ex-employees."

"Please, it's about her sister. She's in a bad way, and I know Delite would want to know. It could be her last chance to talk to her. Ever."

"Her sister doesn't have her number?" she asked, suspicion replacing truculence.

"They had a falling out. It's been years since they've talked. If I don't reach Delite, she'll never have the chance."

"I don't know. I don't want to get in trouble—"

I heard the hesitancy and pushed. "Seriously, that's all I want to do. Just let her know about her sister. Brandee is hanging on by a thread. No one needs to know how I got the number. Please."

Sigh. "All right. It's 293-555-0124."

"Thank you, thank you. It will mean so much to Brandee."

I called the number immediately.

"This is Delite. You know what to do."

"Delite, this is Leah Nash. My mother said you tried to reach me Saturday. I lost my phone, so if you called or texted, I didn't get it. But it's back now, so please call me when you get this."

My leg was throbbing again. The effort not to let Ross see me sweat had taken a lot out of me. I caved then, and let my mother give me a Vicodin along with my grilled cheese and tomato soup. Soon I nodded in the chair, alternately dozing and floating in a Vicodin fog.

When I re-entered consciousness, I heard my mother talking to someone in the kitchen. I stretched without thinking, shooting a sharp pain through my shoulders and sending my phone clattering from my lap to the floor. I reached for it, but a large hand with a zigzag scar on the index finger beat me to it.

I looked up and smiled at Coop.

"Hey, you." He gave me the phone, then offered the plastic cup with straw he held in his other hand.

"Diet Coke, extra ice?"

"Absolutely. How you doin'?"

"Not so bad. A little stiff. And I'm gonna have a mark on my leg that'll put your wimpy old finger scar to shame. Otherwise, OK."

"So, how's your friend Ben? You want to sing me a verse or two?"

"Shut up. I don't know. He's OK, I guess. How's Sherry?"

"Fine."

"When did you guys become a thing?"

"We're not a thing. We just ran into each other at Miguel's."

"Huh. Looked more like she was welded to your arm."

"You know Sherry. She's affectionate," he said, giving me a half-smile. "Where did you and Ben meet? You two seemed to be getting on pretty well."

"You don't know the half of it," my mother said as she came into the room and rolled her eyes at Coop.

"Oh?"

I gave her a look that could freeze an open flame, and she shrugged.

"Nothing. Mom's being what she thinks is funny."

"What's his last name? He looked kinda familiar," Coop said.

"Kalek. He's not from Himmel. He's just here to fix up his grandmother's house for selling. She died a few months ago."

"Ah. How does Miguel know him?"

"How does Miguel know anybody? He met him at the gym and decided to take him home as a pet, I guess."

He laughed, and my mother excused herself and went down the hall to the laundry room.

"Are you going back to work tomorrow?"

"Yeah. Unless of course, Ross comes back and arrests me."

"What?"

I explained what had happened.

"Can't you just stay away from the Caldwells?"

"What? You think I'm some psycho stalker?"

"No, but I know how far you'll go to prove you're right."

"What's that supposed to mean?"

"You've been pretty pissed off, and I don't think your judgment is the best right now. I'm just thinking if you were a little out of it—like you were Saturday night—well, if you did anything stupid, maybe I can help get it straightened out."

"I didn't send those texts. Maybe Georgia sent them herself. Or maybe Miller did."

"Why would either of them do something like that?"

"To land me in a mess. Worst case scenario, I could wind up with a Class I felony, a fine, and maybe even jail time. Nothing like a stint in prison to enhance your resume. Best case scenario, charges are dismissed, but I'm remembered as the obsessed reporter who crossed the line and can't be trusted. It casts doubt on everything I do, and especially on anything I turn up related to Miller and Lacey."

"But wouldn't pressing charges just put attention on what you think they're trying to hide?"

"If Miller can make everyone think I'm a nut job, he won't have to worry about that. Nothing I find out will be taken seriously."

He tried a different approach.

"How would Miller or Georgia get your phone?"

"Maybe I dropped it somewhere?"

"Oh, and they were just trailing along after you, waiting for that lucky break?"

"At the party, then."

"They weren't at the party."

"Someone who was there gave it to them."

"Really?"

"They have money, they have influence. They could have someone working for them to get me."

"Leah, I'm gonna give you the benefit of the doubt and say it's the pain-killers talking. You sound like you should be in a steel bunker with a sliding panel, waiting for me to whisper the password to you."

"I am not paranoid."

"All right."

"Somebody pushed me. That's real."

"What are you talking about?"

My mother came in just then. "Oh, she finally told you."

"Not exactly, Carol. Why didn't you say anything before?"

"Who'd believe me? You don't."

"You could've at least told me."

"Why? So, you could dismiss it like you have everything I've told you for the past month?"

"Tell me now."

When I finished, he said, "You were lucky this time. If Miguel hadn't come—"

"I know. Like I know it was Miller who pushed me. Or maybe his crazy wife."

"Coop, talk to her. Tell her she needs to stop."

"She won't listen, Carol. She never has."

"Hello? She's right here. Listening."

"Good. Then you'll hear me when I tell you the push in the park isn't what you think. If you don't back away from Miller and Georgia, things could get ugly."

"What does that mean?"

"It means back off. It means trust that someone besides you knows how to do their job."

I stared at him, then all the tumblers clicked into place. "You've got something on Miller. All this time you've been jerking me around, telling me I'm way off base, practically telling me I'm mentally unstable and you were sitting on information."

He shook his head in frustration. "I'm not gonna get into this with you. Look, I'm asking you. Please leave it alone. You'll understand. I'll call you."

As he turned to leave, my mother grabbed his arm.

"Coop, just tell me. Is Leah safe? What if the person who pushed her last night decides to try again?"

"It's all right, Carol. I've got it covered."

"Mom, just let the great big man protect us. We women folk don't need to know about anything scary."

"Leah Marie, that's enough. Coop has had your back more times than I can count. Probably more times than I want to know."

I was still mad, but her words hit home.

"All right. Yeah. Fine." That's me, grace under fire.

"I'll see you later," he said, leaving by the kitchen door.

I was getting tired of apologizing every time I turned around. Of course, I guess if I didn't talk without thinking so often, I wouldn't be in that position. Still, Coop was holding out on me and I couldn't help feeling betrayed.

"Is your leg hurting you?"

"It's OK, not bad."

"Then there's no excuse for you to behave like such a little brat."

"OK, I'm sorry. I said I was sorry."

"Oh, really? That was your version of sorry, 'all right, fine, yeah'?" She shook her head in disgust.

"Okaayyy. I'll talk to him tomorrow. But you can see, can't you, that he's on Miller's tail? That he knows about him? He didn't have any right to keep that from me."

"In case you haven't noticed, you're not a member of the Himmel Police Department. You're really not even a member of the press on this. And the way you've steamrolled ahead, I can see why he didn't say anything."

"But—"

"No. We're not going to argue about this. You need to relax, eat a good dinner, and get a good night's sleep."

I sank back onto the chair without another word. I was ticked, but too tired to argue.

"Stay where you are, I'll bring you a tray."

"Mom, I'm not an invalid. I'm going to work tomorrow. I think I can walk two feet to the kitchen."

"Just stay there. Tomorrow is tomorrow; tonight, I'm taking care of you."

26

We ate off tray tables in the living room, neither one of us saying it, but both thinking how we used to do that every Friday night when Lacey was little. I guess current parenting theories say you should sit down around the dinner table to a nice meal, but we had some of our most fun times eating crock pot dinners on the couch and watching old movies on Friday nights. My mother loved classic films, so we learned to, too. My favorite was *Notorious* with Cary Grant and Ingrid Bergman. I loved how tough but vulnerable she was. And the closing scene, best ever.

Lacey and my mother liked the MGM musicals. The three of us would sometimes sing songs from the movies around the house—I know, corny, right? Can I help it if I got the music in me? Unfortunately, I don't have the voice in me, too. Lacey got her voice from Mom. I got mine from our father.

Sometimes when I joined them in a spontaneous song or bellowed out a solo in a particularly heartfelt off-key rendition, they would look at each other and Lacey would start to giggle, and eventually she'd laugh so hard she got the hiccups. I'd pretend to be insulted, and then she would feel bad.

Once in a fit of compassion, she said, "That's OK, Lee-Lee, you don't have to sing. Your talking voice is nice. Like caramel corn. Sweet and crackly. And everybody likes caramel corn." We laughed so hard.

And that night with Mom was fun, too, in a weird out-of-time-and-space kind of way. We watched *Notorious*. And repeated in unison the closing lines, "Alex, will you come in, please? I wish to talk to you," as a very wicked, but very scared, Claude Raines made the lonely walk to his doom.

———

Getting up the next morning was tough, but I'd set the alarm to give me enough time to stand in the hot shower for a while, and by the time I got out, I was feeling fairly loose. I lifted my arms to pull on my T-shirt without wincing and changed the bandage on my leg without grossing myself out. It had stopped seeping and actually didn't look too nasty, though it still gave me the willies.

When I got to the office, everyone was out except Courtnee.

"Wow. You look terrible, Leah. If you want, I could try to cover up those scrapes and maybe that bruise on your chin," she said, pulling out her drawer and grabbing a bag presumably filled with make-up cures. "I don't really have anything for that puffy spot over your eye though."

"No, that's OK, Courtnee, I'll just stay *au naturel* today. Where is everybody?"

"I don't know. Nobody ever tells me where they're going."

Max was old school, and even though everyone had cell phones and was accessible day and night, he still insisted we use the sign-in sheet at the front desk so Courtnee could keep track of us. As if that were going to happen.

I swung the clipboard over and scanned it. Max was at a Chamber meeting, Miguel was at the Middle School Awards Assembly, Duff, an advertising sales rep, was at a Rotary breakfast.

"Courtnee, it says right here where everyone is."

She rolled her eyes. "If you already know, Leah, why did you ask? I'm too busy to play your games," she said, turning back to the Facebook page that was up on her computer.

"You're right. Sorry."

Back in the newsroom, I lowered myself gingerly onto my chair and went through my messages, then pulled up the copy for the week's paper and started editing. I dimly heard Max come in, but he didn't stop by the newsroom. It was close to noon when I heard the excited voices of Miguel and Courtnee in the front.

Then Max yelled for me from the back. He didn't sound happy. Apparently, I wasn't going to get even a one-day get-out-of-trouble-free card, despite my battered body. His door was open, and I gave a slight knock. He turned from his computer screen. His face was as red and angry as I'd ever seen it.

"What the hell is wrong with you?"

"I—"

He turned up the volume on his computer and moved so I could see a blonde anchor staring into the camera and speaking with local news gravitas. An unflattering photograph of me loomed in the background over her left shoulder.

This just in. Local reporter Leah Nash of the *Himmel Times Weekly* is the subject of a Himmel County Sheriff's Department investigation. Ms. Nash, 32, has been accused of stalking by Georgia Caldwell, wife of prominent businessman and state senate candidate Miller Caldwell. Nash allegedly sent multiple texts and email of a threatening nature to Mrs. Caldwell and showed up uninvited at the couple's residence. No arrest has been made. Police are refusing comment on what they say is an ongoing investigation.

However, KNET News has learned that Nash left a position at the *Miami Star-Register*, a Florida daily newspaper, following similar accusations. Nash did not respond to attempts to contact her. We'll keep you posted on this developing story.

"How did they get that story?"

"How did they get it? How could you do it? Christ, Leah, this is your idea of taking it down a notch? You just tanked your career. I hope you haven't taken the *Times* down with you."

"But, Max, I didn't do it. Somebody set me up."

The little vein above his right eye was pulsing again. His hands pressed down so hard, he had to be leaving indentations on the top of his wooden desk.

"Enough. I've had enough. Clean out your desk. You're done."

"What? But, Max, please, listen, I—"

"No! No more talk, no more chances. I don't want your excuses. I don't want your side of things. I don't want anything from you. You've got the writing chops and the smarts, but it's a waste, because you've got no judgment and no self-control. And no loyalty either."

"Max, I'm sorry. You have to believe me. I didn't do this. But listen, Miller is the person who abused Lacey. I think he's the one who pushed me off the bluff. Probably Sister Mattea, too, I just don't have—"

"You don't have anything, Leah. Most of all, you don't have a job here. You're done." He turned his chair around to face his computer as though I'd already left, his solid back a bulwark against any attempt to explain.

I turned and went to my desk. Courtnee and Miguel were there, their eyes wide with sympathy and shock. I didn't say a word, just walked to the copy machine, dumped a ream of paper out of the box sitting next to it, and carried the empty container to my desk.

"*Chica*, what happened? What was Max talking about?"

I shook my head. I didn't trust my voice not to shake as well, so I said nothing as I pulled open drawers and threw their contents into the box.

"When my boyfriend Jace broke up with me, I sent his new skank girlfriend some texts like that. Didn't you know you can buy a phone at Target for, like, really cheap for stuff like that?" Courtnee gave me what I guessed was her version of comfort and solidarity.

"I know you didn't do that. You wouldn't do anything so crazy?"

The slight uptick on the end of his declaration made me feel as bad as anything Max had said. He wasn't sure I hadn't.

"No. I didn't do it. Someone set me up."

"Ohhh." Courtnee nodded with sudden comprehension. "I've seen that on *Pretty Little Liars*. You know, where somebody wants like Hannah or Aria or somebody to get blamed, so they make it look like she did something only she didn't. Only sometimes she did, so it's not really fake, but—"

"Who would do that?"

"You know who. The same person who pushed me off the bluff."

Courtnee's eyes got even bigger. "Somebody pushed you? Who?"

I didn't answer, just swiped my arm across the top of my desk and swept everything into the box. Then I slung my purse over my shoulder, picked up my belongings, and awkwardly tottered out. Before I got down the hall, the box was lifted from my hands, and Miguel was beside me.

"I know you didn't send those texts. I know you didn't stalk the Caldwells. But *chica*, I don't think Miller abused Lacey."

"*Et tu*, Miguel?"

I took the box from him and tossed it in the backseat. I got in the car and drove away.

27

My cell phone rang. I let it go to voicemail. Then it rang again, and again, and again all the way home. I ignored them all. I pulled into the driveway, then trudged in the house with my box of stuff and set it down on the counter. Thank God, my mother was out of town, delivering some legal papers in Appleton. She wouldn't be back until late, and I wouldn't have to go over this with her—as long as she didn't catch the news or hear it on her car radio.

I pulled out my phone and saw the missed calls were from Miguel, from Coop, from Courtnee, one from Rich Givens, a KNET reporter, even one from Ben. Great. He probably wanted to tell me what a nice photo that was of me on the noon news.

Nothing from Karen. That was weird. She should've called by now to tell me what was going on with Georgia's complaint. I punched in her number, but it went straight to voicemail. I tried the office line, then realized it was lunch time and they were closed.

How had KNET gotten the story? It had to be Ross. That jerk. He had to know it wasn't true by now. He also knew that once it was out there, no matter what retractions and corrections were made, all people would remember was that Leah Nash was some kind of stalker, wasn't she?

I sat down on the rocker and closed my eyes. I woke when my phone rang an hour later. Before I could say hello, the caller started talking.

"Leah, I promised Ben I wouldn't forget to tell you, but then I did, but it's not really my fault, because it was kind of crazy with you getting fired and all. And I called before, but you didn't answer."

"Who is this?" I shook my head to clear the grogginess, then immediately regretted it.

"It's me. Courtnee. Are you having a concussion? I'm talking about Ben. Ben Kalek. You know, Miller Caldwell's nephew. He came to see you, but it was kinda awkward, 'cause we could hear Max yelling at you. I mean, everyone in the building could hear Max yelling, right? So, he said he'd come back later, but I said you might not be here later, right? And—"

"Wait. Ben Kalek is Miller Caldwell's nephew?"

"Well, duh, yeah—"

"How do you know that?"

"Well, his grandma lives next door to my grandma, doesn't she? Of course, his grandma is dead, so she doesn't live there anymore. I mean, he's not blood nephew, just marriage nephew. His mom is Georgia Caldwell's sister. His grandma is their mom. Or she used to be—"

Courtnee droned on, while I tried to grab just one of the dozen thoughts flashing through my befuddled brain. Ben was Georgia Caldwell's nephew. Ben had easy access to my phone. Ben just happened to meet me at Miguel's. It made sense that Miller or Georgia would use him.

Ben was an IT guy. Who knew what kind of damage he could do? Even if the stalking set-up fizzled out once Karen dealt with the DA, the Caldwells could keep making major trouble for me. With access to my phone, Ben could screw up my whole life—identity theft, ruined credit scores, bad recommendations, huge debt. The worst-case scenarios of the wired world danced through my head as Courtnee yammered on.

"So, like, I promised Ben I'd tell you he stopped and wants you to call him. He's a hottie, Leah, and you should know you don't get that many chances at your age—"

"What's his number, Courtnee?"

"987-555-0136."

I hung up without saying goodbye.

I just sat there for a minute, thinking about what to do. I should call Karen, but she'd just try to talk me out of what I wanted to do. Which was confront Ben. Though I could see where that might not be a good idea just yet. Maybe I should call Karen and tell her that I wanted her to come with me to talk to Ben. She could be a witness and—my internal debate was cut short by the ringing of my cell phone.

It probably isn't the smartest thing I've ever done. I'm sorry to say it's not the dumbest either. But once my caller asked for a meeting, I had no choice.

The EAT diner is one of the worst restaurants in Himmel, but one of the best places for a quiet meeting, because it's almost always empty. As I pushed open the door, I spotted my quarry and headed to the last booth on the left. There was no one else in the diner.

"Leah, thanks for coming. I got you a coffee," he said, pushing it toward my side of the table before blurting out, "My God, what happened to your face?"

I lowered myself into place, ignoring the screams of all my major muscle groups as I tried to make it look natural and easy. No way did I want him to know how bad I was hurting from the other night.

"I'm sorry, that was rude."

"Not as rude as shoving someone over the river bluff though, is it? Why did you call me, Miller? Should I be expecting Ross and his minions to jump out from the kitchen and arrest me for stalking you?"

"Leah, that's what I want to talk to you about. Or part of it—"

"Really. Actually, there's one or two things I want to talk to you about. But you go first." Under the table I hit record on my phone.

"I don't know quite how to start."

"How about with what you did to my sister?"

"Leah, I know what you think, but you have to believe me, I never touched Lacey, never thought of her that way, I never would. I couldn't."

"Oh, really? Then why did you pay for her online memorial? Why did you post on it anonymously every year since her death, thanking her for making your life less difficult? Did you meet her that night, Miller? Was it planned, or did you just run into her on your way back to the dinner?

"Did she tell you that she was going to expose you? Is that why you killed her? Or was it not you at all, Miller? Was it Georgia? Did she find out about you, and decide to take care of the Lacey problem, so nothing would ever come out that would affect your political career or her social position?"

"No, Leah, no. Just hear me out, then I'll answer anything you ask."

He started speaking in a low monotone, looking down as his hands turned his coffee cup in half circles to the left, then to the right.

"It was the last weekend in June. Lacey was supposed to take Charlotte and Sebastian to a movie, and they were very excited. At the last minute Georgia decided to take the children with her to her mother's for a few days. I didn't know she'd forgotten to call Lacey and cancel. I thought I was alone for the weekend."

He paused, looked at me, cleared his throat then looked back down and continued.

"A friend stopped to see me. We were together, and I didn't hear Lacey when she knocked on the front door. She came in. She saw us in the study. We were in a ... compromising position. For a minute, our eyes met. Then she turned and ran out. I went after her, but she'd ridden her bicycle over, and she was already too far down the path for me to catch her.

"I panicked. I could see my whole life crumbling, everything I worked for, everything I loved. All in the power of a 14-year-old girl. I didn't know what to do, what to say, how to fix it. Every time the phone rang, I expected it to be Georgia saying Lacey had called her. By evening I was a wreck.

"Finally, I called Lacey. As soon as she came on the line, I said, 'I want you to know. Whatever you saw this afternoon, it isn't what you think. It was just a mistake. I don't want you to—' I don't even know what excuse I was going to make, but she cut me off. I'll never forget what she said.

" 'Mr. Caldwell, I'm sorry. I was going to call you to apologize. I forgot all about babysitting this afternoon. My mom says I have too many things on my plate. I guess she's right. I don't think I'll have time to babysit for you anymore.'

"I knew she was there. I saw her. Yet it sounded like she wasn't going to say anything about it. I had to be sure. 'Lacey, I just want to say that sometimes things are very different from the way they look. And if anyone were to misinterpret things, well, they might not mean to but they could hurt innocent people. And I'm trying to say—'

"She wouldn't let me finish. She just said that her mother said she needed to set priorities, and she was really sorry she forgot to come over. That was it. And there I was, my entire future resting in the hands of an adolescent. But she never said a word to me about it again, or, I presume, to anyone else.

"I heard about her problems later, of course, but then when she died so shockingly, I was stunned. I wanted to do something to mark the passing of your truly remarkable sister, so I funded the online remembrance. I asked Mary Beth to have your mother think it was just part of the services she'd paid for.

"When I talked with you last week, and it became clear you suspected me and that you weren't going to stop asking questions, I spoke to Georgia. I told her you were investigating and that you had mistaken ideas, but that there was something I did need to tell her. She wouldn't let me. She got hysterical and I—I backed away. Then she got the texts from you and she went to the police.

"I'm sorry. I understand how angry you are. I know you were just trying to force the issue, but you don't need to do that anymore. I've decided to come out with the truth. And I'll see the investigation into your texts is dropped."

"Uh-huh. I suppose this girlfriend can give you an alibi for the night Lacey was killed? She'll say you were meeting her, not Lacey, the night you walked out on the fundraiser?"

"Leah, you don't understand."

"Sure I do. You may get burned a little for having an affair, but you confess, say a few *mea culpas* with Georgia by your side, and you're good to go. It works for politicians all the time, doesn't it? And look what a great guy you are, taking pity on crazy stalker Leah Nash and forgiving her for sending those nasty texts to your wife."

"You're not listening. I wasn't having an affair with a woman. I was with a man. My lover is a man. I'm gay."

I was shocked into silence.

"I'm gay. And I'm coming out. I'm ending my marriage, hurting and possibly alienating my children, ruining my political career, and breaking my father's heart. But I've spent every day of my life since I was 13 years old fearing exposure, humiliation, and exile from my family and my faith because of who I am. I can't do it anymore."

I was having trouble reconciling what I thought I knew with what he was telling me.

"But Miller, all these years—you supported the anti-gay marriage amendment. Georgia chairs the Mothers Against Same Sex Marriage coalition. How—"

"How could I be such a fraud? Please, Leah, you have no trouble accusing me of heinous sexual crimes, and even murder, but you can't bring yourself to think I'm a hypocrite?"

"You're saying that you wouldn't have abused Lacey, because you're sexually attracted to men."

"No, I'm saying I'm not sexually attracted to children. That I have been unfaithful emotionally and physically to my wife many times, but always with adult men. I'm saying that the night I left Paul Karr's office, I was going to meet my lover. If necessary, he has agreed to make a statement, but I hope I don't need to invade his privacy as mine is stripped bare."

He spoke with such weary resignation that it was hard to hold onto my conviction that he was guilty. I wondered how his children would cope with the news, and I even felt a twinge of sympathy for Georgia.

"All right, say it's true. You didn't have anything to do with Lacey's abuse or her death. But, Miller, I didn't send those texts to Georgia. In fact, up until a minute ago, I was convinced that you or Georgia got your nephew Ben to steal my phone and set me up."

"Ben? I don't understand. What does he have to do with anything?"

"I'm not sure now, but I met him at a party Saturday night. The next day my phone was missing. I searched everywhere, and Ben had plenty of opportunity to take it."

"But, why would he? And why would he send messages to Georgia, suggesting that if I didn't get out of the race, I'd be sorry, that she was married to a fraud, that both of us were going to be sorry?"

"I thought you two had asked him to do it, so you could get me off your back. I'd get arrested, or at the very least, fired and have my credibility destroyed. Good plan, by the way. Whoever designed it. Max canned me today, and I made the noon news as crazy stalker."

"I'm sorry, Leah."

"Yeah, well, just don't take it out on Max. I know he's got a loan application at the bank, and he's been taking heat for me."

"Leah, you said earlier that someone pushed you off the river bluff? Is that true?"

"Yeah. Sunday night."

"Who? Was it to do with Lacey's death?"

"Well, I don't think it was someone unhappy with my coverage of the Elks Pancake Breakfast. I thought it was you. Or Georgia. If it wasn't, I don't know who. Or why. Just for the record, where were you Sunday night?"

"I was at St. Stephen's rectory, talking with Father Lindstrom, from around 8:30 to midnight."

"Pretty good alibi. How about Georgia?"

"You can't seriously think—" but looking at my face, it was clear I did seriously think. So he added, "She was with my campaign manager, going over a speech she gave yesterday at the Omico Women's Club."

"That can be verified?"

He nodded.

"Miller, I'm sorry that my investigation into Lacey's death has pushed you to the brink like this. I only want to find the truth."

"And that will set us free, Leah? I'm not so sure."

28

I felt sick. Confused. And mad as hell. Coop must have warned me off Miller because he knew who really molested Lacey. He knew, and he didn't tell me. Did that mean he knew who killed Lacey? Did he even believe Lacey was murdered? Or that I was pushed? Or that Sister Mattea was?

How could he stand by and let me waste so much time on the wrong man? I reached for my phone to call him, then put it back down. To hell with him. If he didn't trust me enough to tell me what was going on with my own sister's case, I wasn't going to beg him for information. If he figured it out, I could too.

Who else had means, motive, and opportunity? There was still Paul Karr, but really? I had nothing but Marilyn's assertion that he wasn't home when he said he was. And she was a bitter, vindictive woman who hated my mother. It was Marilyn's word against Paul's, and I just didn't think it was Paul.

But Hegl now, that was entirely different. He lied about knowing Lacey before she went to DeMoss. He had plenty of opportunity there to try and start up with her again, or to try to ensure she kept their secret, or both. If Lacey said no, if she threatened to tell, or even if her daily presence was just too threatening to him, he could have decided he had to get rid of her. And there was his history with Olivia Pérez Morgan. But if he was involved, did Sister Julianna and Reid Palmer fit in the picture, too?

It was so frustrating. What did Coop know that he wasn't telling me? I tried to think of inadvertent hints he might have dropped. What about Cole Granger? Coop had warned me the first time I talked to him about Lacey's abuse that Cole was a con man.

What if Cole had told me just enough of the truth to sound plausible, but he was actually covering up his own involvement? What if he met Lacey, like he admitted, and they got into a fight, like he said. But there wasn't any kid with her. And she didn't kick him in the balls, he knocked her in the head, hard enough to kill her. Then he panicked and took her body into the woods and dumped her. He could've told me about the sexual abuse both to distract my attention from him and to point me in the direction of the abuser as the killer.

I had driven all the way back home, and still I didn't know which way to go now that Miller was out of the picture. I sat in the driveway staring blankly. It took a minute to realize my phone was vibrating. I looked at the caller ID. Delite Wilson.

"Hello."

"I seen you on the news. Looks like you're screwed."

"Yeah. Delite what did you call me for on Saturday?"

"I had some bad luck. Your fault."

"My fault?"

"Yeah. My boss saw me talkin' to you that night. She fired me."

"She fired you for talking to me?" I asked, not hiding my skepticism.

"Maybe not exactly that. I missed my shift a coupla times, and she was pretty mad about that. Anyway, she fired me and I'm sorta short of funds."

"What's that got to do with me?"

"Well, I was thinkin' you're lookin' for information and I figure maybe it's worth somethin' to you."

"You picked the wrong door, Delite. I don't have any money."

She snorted. "I thought you wanted to know the real story about the night your sister disappeared. Isn't that worth somethin'? Like maybe $5,000?"

"$5,000? I don't have that kind of money. But if you know something about Lacey's death—"

"I'm not sayin' anything unless I see the money. I'm not tellin' for free. I'm tired of everyone takin' advantage of me."

"Who's taking advantage of you?"

"Never mind. Just bring me the money."

"I can't get that much. It's not possible. I might be able to scrounge up $1,000?"

"$1,000? For what I got to tell you? No way."

"Look, maybe I can get $1,500 bucks together, and that's it, take it or leave it."

She went quiet, but I thought I heard another voice in the background.

"Hello? Delite? Are you there?"

"Yeah. Meet me at 6 tonight at 229 Elm."

"You're here, in town?"

"I'm stayin' with a friend. I gotta go. Bring the money if you want the information."

I drove straight to an ATM. I pulled out everything I had and still I was $600 short. I didn't want to ask my mother—she'd only try to stop me, or call in Karen or Coop, and if Delite really had information, the fewer that knew about it, the better. Miguel.

"*Chica*, I've been so worried. You didn't call me back."

"I'm fine. I'm OK. Can I borrow $600?"

"To take out a hit on Detective Ross? I don't know if I'm down with that."

"I'm not kidding, and I hate to ask, but I really need it."

"Sure, of course. But only if you tell me what's going on."

"I don't want you involved."

"Then I guess you don't want my money."

I hesitated, and he stepped into the pause.

"I'm going to the ATM, I'll be right over. And then you're gonna tell me everything."

Which is why, two hours later, there were two of us in the car as I pulled into the drive of 229 Elm Street, a rundown house with a cobbled together appearance. A sagging screened-in front porch, a patchy lawn strewn with bits of broken things—a cracked clay pot, a bicycle wheel, a rake with most of its tines missing. A drooping maple, more dead than alive, bent toward the gravel driveway where a rusty purple Camaro was parked.

"I'm going in with you."

"No. You're not. I don't want to spook her. I shouldn't have let you come."

"You had to. I'm a shareholder."

"Whatever. I'll be fine. Just wait here for me."

I reached for the doorbell until I noticed it was only loosely connected to the doorframe by a frayed wire and opted instead to rap loudly on the peeling front door. It opened, and a figure stepped out from the shadows.

"Well, well, well. If it ain't big sis."

"Cole. Is Delite here?"

———————

"Welcome to my humble home," he said, ushering me in with a mock bow and a wave of his arm.

Inside was even more depressing than outside. A stained and scarred wooden floor, bare light bulbs in the ceiling, a sagging, threadbare blue couch patterned with big pink and white flowers sitting in the middle of the room. The air smelled faintly of burning weed though none was in evidence. Delite looked at me and sat up from her semi-reclining position.

"Delite, look who come to visit. Sit down now, won't you, Leah?" he said, pointing to a metal folding chair and pulling up another for himself.

"I didn't come to talk to you."

"But I'm what you might call Delite's personal representative. Like her lawyer, kind of, just to make sure her interests are safe."

I turned away from him and looked at Delite. "OK, so what's the information?"

"Now hold on there. Let's just see some evidence of your part of the deal," Cole said.

I reached in my purse and pulled an envelope out, opening it slightly so he could see the bills within. He nodded.

"All right then. Delite, you go ahead now, darlin.'"

"I wasn't with Lacey that night. We didn't go to a party. I never saw her after lunch."

"Where were you that night?"

"With Hegl. He got a car from the carpool and sneaked me out under a blanket. We went and saw *Knocked Up* and got a pizza, like a date. Then we hadda go back to DumbAss Academy. I did his bj in the car. If we'da got caught, they woulda bounced him, and Queenie prob'ly woulda killed him herself. Me, well straight to juvie for sure. But he liked to do stuff like that. He wanted to do it twice. The second time in Queenie's office."

"You had sex with Father Hegl in Sister Julianna's office?"

"Not sex," she said in an annoyed voice. "Just a bj." She shrugged. "I got pizza, didn't I? And I liked that movie. He sat in Queenie's chair. He wanted me to crawl under the desk. So, I did. He finished, then we heard like a door openin.' I ran out Queenie's side door while he was zippin' his pants. I don't know what happened after that."

Lacey. Lacey had gone to the administration building to get a car after Cole refused to take her with him.

"What time was this?"

"We got there a little after 10:30. I could see Queenie's clock from under the desk. I hadda get down there, he hadda get in the chair; I was there maybe 10 minutes or so. Hegl wasn't exactly pre-jack but he never lasted very long. Queenie's clock chimed when I was leavin' just like Cinderella leavin' the ball." She gave a scornful laugh.

I turned to Cole. "What time did you leave Lacey?"

"Hold on a minute. My information ain't part of this deal. If I'm gonna give you anything, I got to get somethin', too, don't I?"

"Tell me, or I'll call your parole officer and we'll see how a drug test comes out. I'm pretty sure smoking weed will get you kicked right back to jail."

"Don't be such a high and mighty bitch."

"Just tell me."

"I got a speedin' ticket, right? When I was on Dunphy Road. That was 10:50 p.m. according to Officer Asshole who wrote the ticket. So, I musta left there about five minutes before that."

"The files say you told Ross you were with your girlfriend Amber all night. They don't say anything about you getting a ticket that night just a few miles away from DeMoss."

"I guess he didn't check with the state po-lice, did he? Cause that's who give me the ticket. And that ain't my problem. I told you I didn't need to get mixed up in any of that shit."

I turned back to Delite. "You're sure you didn't see who came into the reception area? You didn't hear anyone speak?"

"Nope."

"Why did you come forward with that story about Lacey and you being at a party?"

"After they found her body, Hegl said with all the pokin' around they were doin', they could find out he took a car and took me out that night. Maybe even that we hooked up in Queenie's office. He said I should say Lacey went to a party with me and got wasted. That'd quiet things down, and he promised to make sure I got to stay outa juvie."

"Didn't you realize that by lying you altered the whole course of the investigation? If you hadn't made up that story, then they might have actually tried to find out what happened, and Lacey's murderer wouldn't be walking around."

"She's dead either way, right?"

"Delite here was just protectin' her own interests. Now, as I see it, you got what you wanted, and if you hand over what we want, this deal is concluded."

"No. Not yet."

"You're not tryin' to back out on us, are you? 'Cause I gotta tell you, I don't see that you have a real strong negotiatin' position here." He moved in closer, his body odor strong enough to make my nostrils flare, and his fists clenched with latent menace.

I ignored him. "Delite, what do you know about Danny Howard?"

"Ralphie. That's what your sister called him. 'Cause he looked like that loser kid in the Christmas movie. Used to follow her around. Little wussy kid."

"Do you know what happened to him? Do you know where he is now?"

"I seen him once."

"Where? When did you see him?"

"Me and Cole seen him at a truck stop at the Dells a coupla months ago."

"Did you get his number?"

"Yeah. We're gonna get together next week and plan the DumbAss Academy reunion. No, I didn't get his number. I said I seen him. I didn't talk to him. He was kinda busy."

"Do you know how to reach him?"

"Look, he was workin,' and it's not like we was big buddies. That was him and your sister."

"He was working at the truck stop? Is he a bus boy? A server?"

"I s'pose you could call it that," she said with a smirk. At my confused expression she said, "He was hustlin', OK?"

"You mean he's a male prostitute?"

She made a sound between a laugh and a snort.

"Yeah, he's a 'male prostitute'," she said, mocking me with a simpering, prissy tone.

"Do you know how I can reach him?"

"What do I look like? 411? I told ya, we didn't trade phone numbers."

"I think that about wraps up our business, Leah. Me and Delite got plans. Now, if you'll just hand over the cash."

"Delite, what did you mean when you said you were tired of 'all of them' taking advantage of you. Who is all of them?"

"After you came sniffin' around, I figured there might be somethin' in it for me. I reached out to Hegl for a loan, like. He treated me like dirt. Told me if I tried to spread lies about him, I'd regret it. Said he could make more trouble for me than I ever could for him. Nobody would believe a liar like me. Asshole. I don't have to take that anymore. Then Cole said maybe I should call you. Now, I'm thinkin' maybe I even got a bonus for you," she gave me a sly grin.

Cole cut her off.

"Shut it, Delite. Nothin' is free. Now, if Leah comes up with a little more cash—" I had no scruples about paying for information, obviously, but I was tapped out.

"I haven't got anything more. This is it. But—"

"Then our business is done here." He reached out and snatched the envelope from my hand. "And don't think any of this is on the record, cause it ain't. And we definitely ain't standin' behind it. You're on your own."

29

I had refused to talk on the ride back home, waiting until we were seated at the breakfast bar, each with a bottle of Supper Club lager in front of us. I had barely ended with Delite's hint that there could be "bonus" information if I came up with the cash, when Miguel started peppering me with questions.

"Hegl is the *pendejo* who molested Lacey? But how could she go to DeMoss and see him and know what he did? Wouldn't that be *muy* hard for her?"

"Yeah, I'm sure it was really hard for her. But Lacey was a strong kid. Stronger than we knew. By the time she got to DeMoss, seeing Hegl every day maybe made her more angry than afraid. So angry, she decided she had to come out with the truth no matter how he threatened her."

"So, what do you think happened the night Lacey disappeared?"

"I think she wanted to get away before she outed him, and she thought Cole could take her into town, to our house. Then when Cole wouldn't go along with it because of Danny, she had to come up with a new plan."

"But what could she do?"

"Steal a car. That was her fallback position. She took Mom's car a few times, and her last hurrah before she got sent to DeMoss was trying to get to Chicago with it. I'm guessing that after Cole let her down, she figured her last option was to get the car keys from the administration building and take one of the pool cars. The keys are just hanging there on a board behind the reception desk. She left Danny to wait for her while she got the car."

"Only Hegl was there with Delite."

"Exactly. Maybe Hegl left the front door unlocked, on purpose, to heighten the 'danger,' or maybe Lacey just busted in. Either way, she got in, made a beeline for the keys, and Hegl heard her and came out to reception. He confronted her, asked her what she was doing there.

"She snapped. Told him she was going to go forward, tell everyone the truth, and she didn't care whether anyone believed her or not. Maybe he stepped in too close, maybe he taunted her—maybe she slapped him. He was backed into a corner and he was furious."

I could see the scene in my mind's eye. Lacey, small, defiant, lashing out verbally and physically. Hegl, enraged and motivated by self-preservation, hitting right back.

"Oh, wait a minute—"

I jumped up, and ran down the hall to my room, searching through my desk for the case folder, then flipped quickly through the papers. There it was, the medical examiner's signature: Donald Straube, M.D.

I went back to the kitchen and grabbed my phone to look up Dr. Straube's number. "What? What is it, *chica*?"

I waved my hand to shush Miguel as the call rang through.

"May I speak to Dr. Donald Straube?"

"Speaking. Who is this?"

"Leah Nash, Dr. Straube. You were the medical examiner on the case for my sister, Lacey Nash, five years ago. I just want to ask you a couple of questions. It won't take a minute."

"Young lady, I'm retired. Have been for four years. I can't remember details at this date. You should be able to get a copy of the autopsy from the sheriff's department."

"No, no, that's OK. I have a copy. I just wanted to ask you, in your report you say the cause of death was head trauma from a blunt object, probably from her head hitting a rock or a tree stump when she fell down the ravine."

"Yes, yes. I do remember now that you specify. Sad case, very young girl."

"Dr. Straube, is it possible that my sister didn't die from the fall? Could she have been struck in the head, and her body transported to the location where it was found?"

He got a little ouchy then. "Miss Nash, I am a qualified medical doctor who met every standard of the state of Wisconsin for medical examiner. A licensed pathologist conducted the autopsy. Are you suggesting our findings were not correct?"

"No, please, not at all. I'm just wondering if there was specific evidence that proved she died at the site where the body was found."

"The site was trampled by the unfortunate woman who found the body, as well as by some of the more inexperienced members of the sheriff's department. Furthermore, your sister's body was badly decomposed."

"I understand. I'm not criticizing your findings. I just want to know if it's possible that she could have received a blow to the head, and afterward her body was dumped at the location where it was discovered. Is there anything in the findings that would say that wasn't possible?"

He sighed. "No, nothing I recall from the autopsy or the crime scene investigation that would preclude that. But given the findings of the investigators and the location, the most likely cause of the head injury seemed to be her head striking a rock or tree stump as she fell. Perhaps you should be talking to the detective in charge of the case. He would have managed the crime scene and would be able to help you better than I."

"No, you've helped me a lot. Thank you, doctor. I'm sorry for disturbing you."

I hung up and turned to Miguel, who was bursting with the effort of not talking.

"I know. I know how Hegl did it." I looked back down at my phone and clicked on photos. Nothing. "No!" I had forgotten that everything on my phone had been deleted.

"What? What? *Dígame.*"

"Miguel, do you still have that text with the picture I sent you? The one I took at Father Hegl's?"

"I don't know."

"Look, look, look!"

"OK, OK, chill." He pulled out his phone and started scrolling back through texts, and then handed it to me. The wall of religious statues at Hegl's popped up crisp and clear. On the second shelf from the bottom, in the corner, there it was. I zoomed in on the photo, then showed it to Miguel.

"The murder weapon. Taken from Sister Margaret's desk the night Lacey was killed. The Virgin Mary, with a long white scratch on the base."

"*Ay, Dios mío!* Are you sure? But why would he keep the murder weapon?"

"Haven't you ever heard of hiding in plain sight? Think about it. He kills Lacey and then he's in a panic. He's got to get rid of a body, a phone—he doesn't know what she might have on it—and a murder weapon. He can reset the phone to factory settings, no problem. He can take one of the 4-wheelers and dump her body in an out-of-the-way place on the property and plant some pills and bottles with her.

"If he's lucky, the weather and animals will take care of things. If he's not lucky, and she's found right away, well, there are the pills, the empty bottle. And running away fits her pattern. She's just another kid who couldn't turn her life around.

"But what can he do about this big, old statue? He can't throw it with the body. That would raise way too many questions if it was found. He can't throw it in the trash; he knows Sister Margaret will be having a fit when it's missing, and someone is sure to look there. He makes a bold move. He puts it right on the shelf with a hundred other statues."

"That takes *cojones, chica.* What if Sister Margaret or one of the other nuns saw it?"

"Unlikely. The nuns don't drop in on Hegl. And even if they did, he could say that one of the students must have put it there as a joke, and he has so many statues he didn't notice. Anyone else who might visit—they wouldn't see it among all the other statues. I didn't. And even if they picked it out, it wouldn't mean anything to them."

"What are you going to do now? Call Coop?"

"No. I botched things with Miller. I don't think Coop has much faith in my crime theories just now, and I think he's working on one of his own. Maybe it involves Hegl, maybe not. He's not telling me anything. Once I get the statue, though, he'll have to believe me. Then he can work it with Ross. I sure as hell am not going to that nimrod."

"How you going to get the statue? 'Please, Father Hegl, give me the statue you used to kill my sister?' " His teasing grin turned to dismay when he saw the look in my eyes. "No, no, no. Don't even think about it."

"I'm not thinking it. I'm doing it. I'm going out to Hegl's, and I'm coming back with that statue."

"No," he repeated.

"Yes. He teaches a music class at the community college tonight. He shouldn't get back home until 10:30 at the earliest. It's only 7:30 now. Plenty of time for me to get in and get out. I know right where the statue is," I said, walking over to the kitchen drawer to pull out a flashlight. It was still daylight, but it would be dark before I was done.

Miguel followed me out to the garage, still protesting while I rummaged through a disorganized workbench before finding the canvas Piggly Wiggly bag and plastic gloves I was looking for. He continued arguing as I headed toward my car, but as I reached to open the door, he grabbed my arm. "No, let's take my car. I'm behind you."

30

We drove into the county park and left the car at the far end of the lot, then took the path that wound along the edge of the Catherines' property. About a quarter of a mile in, we cut across a field that rose gently to a modest hill. When I got to the top, Miguel was trailing behind, stopping to wipe something off his very expensive shoes.

"If you're coming, come on!"

"You know how to show a boy a good time. If I knew we were going mud bogging on foot, I wouldn't have worn my new boots," he grumbled.

"You don't have to be here, you know, but if you are here, I need you to not be whining." It was a little sharp, but I was more nervous than I was letting Miguel know.

"I'm in, I'm in," he said, giving up on his shoes with a shrug and a half-grin.

Spread below us, the campus of DeMoss Academy looked idyllic.

"There's Father Hegl's, that cottage to the right, see it?"

"Yes. But how we gonna get there without anyone seeing us?"

"Geez, Miguel. I didn't know you were such an old lady. Just follow me. It's half-dark now. Do you see anyone out there? All the little children are tucked in their dorms. The cottage is dark; Father Hegl won't be home until 10:30. It's 8:30 now, so it's all good."

We were quiet then as we hurried down the hill and cut across the bumpy, muddy ground. It wasn't until we reached the back door of Hegl's small house that either of us spoke.

"Oh-oh." In my haste to get there, get in and get out, I forgot about the possibility that Hegl's door might be locked. The knob turned, but when I pushed, it didn't open.

"OK, then I guess we better *vámanos*. Try again another day." He turned and was already moving across the backyard.

"Wait a second, wait." I turned and pushed, putting some force into it. "Sometimes these old locks don't really click into place and with a good— oof!—shove. There we go! See, the door is open. I'll just give a shout."

"Father Hegl? Anybody home? Your door was open." When there was no answer, I motioned for Miguel to follow me in. I turned on the flashlight and led the way down the short hall to Hegl's small living room. There, tucked away in a corner near the bottom of his shelf, was the statue of Mary. I pulled on the gloves I'd taken from home and reached out to pick it up, but Miguel said, "Wait, *chica*, wait."

He turned on a lamp, looked around, and grabbed a copy of *USA Today* lying on the coffee table in front of the sofa, and handed it to me. "Go there by the statue. No, don't pick it up, just kneel down off to the side. Hold the paper so I can see the date. *Bueno*, now point to the statue."

He snapped two pictures, then switched to video. "Stay there a sec. I want to get the room in the video, so you can see it's really the padre's house." He panned around the room and for good measure zoomed in on the newspaper again with me holding it, and then the statue, which I had picked up to show that it did indeed have a long scratch down the side, as Sister Margaret had described it.

"OK, I think we've got enough." I had turned to put the statue into my canvas bag when we heard it. The sound of tires on gravel. A millisecond later headlights flashed on the wall. We both froze. Then the slamming of a car door threw us into frenzied action. I snapped off the lamp, handed the bag to Miguel, and shoved him toward the kitchen, whispering, "Go, you've got to go."

"Aren't you coming?"

"You're way faster than me, and we've got to get the statue out of here. I can handle Hegl. I'll catch up." The front door opened, and there was movement in the living room. I gave him a push out the door, and he took off. I stepped out right behind him, pulled the back door shut and immediately began knocking loudly—or maybe that was my heart pounding. Either way, it brought a surprised Hegl to the door.

I had positioned myself to block his view of Miguel's retreating figure in the gathering dusk.

"What are you doing here?"

"I need to talk to you."

"Not a good idea." He started to pull the door shut.

"No, wait, please. Just for a minute, that's all." I wanted to turn and see how far Miguel had gotten, but I didn't dare. If I could just keep Hegl talking for another minute or two, I could be sure Miguel had gotten away.

"Where's your car? How did you get here?"

"I came in the back across the fields. Please, it's been a really bad day. I'm just asking for a minute to talk to you."

Bizarrely, he smirked.

"Yeah. Saw you on the news." I noticed then his words were slightly slurred. As he turned his head, I got a whiff of JD. I realized then that he was drunk, but one of those drunks practiced in the art of appearing sober.

"Do you have just a minute? I wanted to ask you about Olivia Morgan."

That got his attention.

He opened the door wider and grabbed my arm. "You better come in."

I tried to pull back, but his grip was firm and his lean frame was deceptive. He was very strong. Up close his eyes were red-veined and bleary. I opted for feigned nonchalance. "All right, thanks."

In a painful imitation of gentlemanly behavior, he force-walked me toward the living room with a vise-like grip on my elbow, then deposited me roughly in a chair. He bumped the edge of his desk as he tried to navigate around it on his way to the sideboard holding several bottles of whiskey. He poured himself a generous shot, then tipped the bottle toward me.

I shook my head. But I was happy to see he was still thirsty. The more he drank, the better chance I had around his befuddled wits and out the door. He pulled up a chair and took a long gulp. He was facing me, directly across from his wall of statues. If I didn't keep him distracted, he'd see the gaping hole where I removed Sister Margaret's Virgin Mary from his collection. I needed him to focus on me, fast.

"Carla Pérez says you were having an affair with her sister Olivia. She thinks you were with Olivia the night she died."

"She's lying." He stared into his glass.

"Why would she lie?"

"To make trouble."

"Like her sister Olivia? Did Olivia try to make trouble for you?"

He had dropped his head down and was silent so long I thought he might have fallen asleep. When he raised his glass to take another swallow, a little bit of the dark amber liquid spilled on his shirt. "Wasn't my fault. An accident." He had a defiant look on his face.

"What happened the night Olivia died?"

"It wasn't my fault," he repeated. "She shouldn't. She should. She." He stopped to gather his fuzzy thoughts.

"What happened?" I prodded.

"She, she—" He paused again and took another drink. "She grabbed the wheel. Not me. It wasn't me. She did it. It was raining so hard. She."

His voice had dropped to a whisper, so I had to lean in to hear. Staring into his glass, he said, "I tried to stop. We rolled. We rolled and I —I—I—"

I couldn't see the expression on his face.

"What about Olivia? What happened to Olivia?"

His head jerked up, and his voice was anguished now. "There was blood. So much blood. I couldn't. I couldn't." He started to cry, reaching out his hand and grabbing my wrist. Tears were running down his face.

"I couldn't help her."

I wasn't moved. "So, you left her, lying on the road. Olivia was still alive when the ambulance got there. You left her to die alone."

"No, no, no. I had to go. I had to go. My rib. I broke my rib," he said pitifully, as though by his injury he could absolve himself of his culpability. "I called the ambulance. I called."

"You called? But you didn't use your cell phone, did you? You waited until you got to a pay phone. A mile away. You waited, what? A half an hour? All the while Olivia's life was bleeding out because you didn't want to get caught."

His mouth quivered, and he wiped the thin line of mucous running from his nose to his upper lip with the back of his hand. "I couldn't help it."

"You keep telling yourself that, Hegl. It's a first-degree felony in Florida to leave the scene of an accident when someone dies. And you were driving. You could go to prison for 30 years."

The tears stopped. He stared at me sullenly. When he spoke, his voice was harsh.

"Prove it. Nobody can prove it."

"Yeah? Then why have you been hiding out here for years? Something's got you scared."

He was suddenly cautious, a sly expression on his face. "God. God protects drunks. Drunks and fools, don't you know that?" He started to laugh then went into a coughing jag. When he finished, I tried again.

"Why did you come to DeMoss?"

" 'Can't afford a scandal, Sean.' " He had lowered his voice and was attempting to look out from under his eyebrows in what I assumed was an imitation of someone. His uncle?

"Who knows about the accident? Your uncle the bishop? Who else?"

He didn't answer. Instead, he stood abruptly and staggered toward the hall. For half a second I considered waiting on the chance I could talk to him about Lacey, get more out of him, but my reptile brain was saying "Run! Run! Run!" It won. As soon as I heard the bathroom door close, I ran.

Miguel was waiting at the top of the hill.

"*Chica*, what took you so long?"

I huffed for a few minutes, then panted out an answer. "Hegl was drunk. And talkative. He admitted he was driving the night Olivia died. He was drunk, and he left her there. He left the scene of the accident. His uncle got him out of it."

"But why would his uncle send him here?"

"I don't know. Maybe Uncle Bishop didn't want to deal with **Drunken Priest Kills Lover in Car Crash** headlines. If his uncle wanted him stashed away in a backwater, he couldn't find a much better place. And Hegl would have a good reason to settle down and play nice up here. Maybe his uncle has something else on him, something even worse, who knows? But if the bishop's buddy ever rescinds his alibi, Hegl's in big trouble."

"I get that. But why here? What's the connection?"

"I don't know. Sister Julianna? Reid Palmer?" I bent over and tried to catch my breath.

"You didn't ask him about Lacey?"

"No, I just tried to keep him distracted, so he wouldn't notice the statue was gone."

"Look—your *amigo* is looking for you." He pointed in the direction of the cottage. From our vantage point we could see Hegl, silhouetted in the light flooding out his open back door.

"*Ádale!* Let's go. Maybe he noticed his statue is missing." We took off.

31

My mother was sitting up at the bar drinking a cup of tea when I tried to sneak in the house without waking her. I hadn't returned her calls after my surprise appearance on the noon news, just texted to say I was all right, it was a mistake, and I'd talk to her.

"How was your day?"

"I would guess a lot better than yours. At least I didn't lose my job."

"Who told you?"

"Courtnee. When I called the paper."

"I'm sorry, Mom. I just needed a while before I could talk about it, can you understand that?"

"Frankly, Leah, there's very little I understand about you these days." She sighed, then said, "All right, yes, I guess. But I want to hear about it now."

I stood uncertainly for a minute. She hadn't asked about the canvas bag I was carrying, so I pulled out the stool next to her and casually set it down, pushing it off to the side. I gave her a scaled down version of the day's events leading up to my trip to Father Hegl's.

"I had to get proof, Mom."

"Proof of what?"

"Proof that Father Hegl is the one who abused Lacey—and the one who killed her."

She just sat there.

"Did you hear me, Mom? I said Father Hegl—"

"Yes. I heard you. I heard you when you said it about Paul. And about Miller Caldwell. Leah! You've been thrown off a cliff, investigated by the police, nearly arrested, publicly humiliated, fired from your job, and now you seem determined to get yourself killed. I am so angry at you right now, I can barely speak."

"Why are you so mad?"

"You broke into Father Hegl's house! What if you're right, what if he did kill Lacey? Why wouldn't he kill you too? Do you realize the chance you took? Don't you care about anything but what you want to do?"

"Mom! Of course I do. Miguel was with me. Weren't you listening? I didn't break in; the door was open ... pretty much. We had to get the statue out. And we did." I lifted the bag and opened it slightly.

"First thing tomorrow I'm taking it down to the police station. I'm giving it to Coop, along with proof that it came from Hegl's, and then he can get it to Ross and the DA—I don't think I'd get far with either of them until this Caldwell thing is straightened out."

"So, you're saying that once you give the statue to Coop, you're done? No more questions, no more investigating?"

"Well, no, not exactly. I still need to—"

She shook her head, and put up a hand for me to stop talking. "You do what you want, Leah. You always do."

Then it was my turn to get angry. "Oh yeah, that's me, Leah livin' large, back in my old bedroom, roomies with my mother, working at the crappy weekly where I started. Or I was 'til I got fired. That's me, doing what I want. You think I want to go over and over this in my head every night? You think I want to face the fact that I let Lacey down, that I was too busy to take her call, and maybe if I had, she'd still be alive?"

"Lacey called you?"

"Yes, Mom, she did. And I didn't pick up, and by the time I listened to her message, she was already gone. I didn't tell you because I didn't want you to know what I'd done—or hadn't done. I didn't want you looking at me the way you are right now."

"What did she say? What was the message?"

"She kept breaking up, there was lots of static. I thought she said something about legal—like maybe she was in trouble again. That's why I thought she was drinking and had run away again."

I paused to take a breath. My mother continued to stare at me.

"I can't bring her back. But I can make sure the person who did it pays. And I'm sorry if that upsets you, or worries you, or pisses you off. I'm not feelin' so happy myself right now." And I grabbed the statue and went to my room, slamming the door behind me. There had been more door slamming in that house in the last month than in all of my teen years and Lacey's combined.

Once in my room, I checked my Facebook account. It was blowing up with people asking me about the stalking charges. I was hearing from classmates I hadn't talked to in years. As I scrolled through the commiserations and questions, I suddenly realized that this might be a way to reach Danny Howard. I tried a search and didn't find him under his own name, but I didn't really expect to. I hit it though, when I typed in a search for RalphieP. The kid from *A Christmas Story*.

He didn't have any identifying information I could look at beyond the fact he was from Wisconsin. But I felt pretty confident. I made a friend request, and I hoped the name Leah Nash would pique his interest. And then I had to wait.

The next morning Melanie was at the front desk when I walked into the police station. She gave me an odd look. Maybe it was the Blessed Virgin poking her head out of the Piggly Wiggly bag under my arm that caught her eye. I shifted it discreetly toward my back and said, "Is Coop in? I need to talk to him."

"He's in, but he's busy right now."

"How long will he be?"

"Not sure."

"Well, I guess I'm gonna wait."

"Suit yourself."

She turned back to her computer screen, and I settled in on one of the hard plastic chairs.

But I noticed that instead of returning to her own dimension, where only she and her computer screen existed, Melanie kept sneaking glances at me. What was up with that?

I sat for a while, replaying the scene with my mother, and wishing I'd just kept my mouth shut. Thinking about what I could have said, and should have said, and what actually came out of my mouth. Why did I tell her about Lacey's phone call? She was never going to forget—or forgive me. How could she? I couldn't forgive myself.

Finally, I got up and paced the small waiting area, then walked up and leaned on the counter to talk to Melanie.

"Hey, Melanie, what's taking Coop so long?"

She shrugged. "He's interviewing a suspect."

"What's going on?"

"I couldn't say. But what's goin' on with you, Leah? You're gettin' pretty famous. I saw you on the news yesterday."

"Yeah. That. Well, it wasn't true, I didn't send those texts and stuff to Georgia Caldwell."

"I figured. So, now you're writing the news and in the news this week, eh?"

"No. I won't be writing the news this week. I don't work at the *Times* anymore."

Before she could ask the question so clearly on her face, her phone rang.

"Right. OK. Oh, Leah's here to see you. Yeah. Sure." She hung up and came over to lift the counter for me to walk through. "Coop's in his office. He wants to talk to you."

"Not as bad as I want to talk to him."

"Don't be so sure of that."

I hustled down the corridor, mentally counseling myself to stay calm, to lay out the facts clearly, not to lose my cool if Coop didn't get on the same page with me right away. I could convince him, I knew I could, if I didn't push too hard.

"Leah, I was just goin' over to the paper to see you."

"Don't bother. You won't be able to catch me there. I got fired yesterday."

"What?"

"Yeah. When KNET got hold of the story that the sheriff's department was questioning me about stalking Georgia Caldwell, Max lost it. He fired me on the spot."

"Ah, geez." He ran his hand through his hair. "I'm sorry. C'mon in."

I pulled up the chair across from his desk and set my evidence bag on the floor.

"Coop—"

"Leah—"

We both spoke at the same time, then both gave the polite, slightly nervous laugh of strangers caught in an awkward two-step while trying to pass each other on a sidewalk.

"Let me go first, please. I know I was wrong about Miller. I've been wrong about a lot of things, but this time I have it right. If you'll just listen, you'll see."

"All right." He sat back and waited, but the look he gave me was so sad, it threw me off stride.

"OK. OK then." I was surprised that my hands were sweating. I wiped them nervously on my jeans. "Do you have some water?"

"Sure." He reached around to the small refrigerator behind his desk, pulled out a bottle, opened it and handed it across to me.

I took a big swig and then started in. I laid out everything I knew about Hegl, including ground we'd covered before to try to make him see the big picture—starting with his involvement with Olivia Morgan, the fatal car crash, his sudden departure from the parish, his bishop uncle, and the role he played in getting him out of a felony charge.

I reminded him about Hegl's opportunity to connect with Lacey during the production of *The Wizard of Oz*, Lacey's subsequent downward spiral, her animosity toward Hegl at DeMoss, his involvement with Delite, his lie about where he was that night. I told him Delite's story about someone interrupting them in the administration building the night Lacey disappeared. Her admission that she'd lied about the party.

"And finally this, Coop." I reached into my Piggly Wiggly bag and pulled out the statue.

"What is it?"

"It's what he killed Lacey with. Sister Margaret's marble statue—the one that went missing the night Lacey disappeared. The one I found on a bookshelf in his cottage." I set it on his desk.

"You found—Leah, tell me you didn't break into Hegl's house."

"I didn't break in, not technically. We knocked, the door was open. Stuck maybe, but definitely open."

"I assume 'we' means you and Miguel. Was Hegl there?"

"Not at first. He came home before we expected him though."

The look on his face told me I'd better talk faster if I didn't want to get another—probably deserved—lecture on using commonsense, and not jumping in feet first without thinking.

"I got Miguel out with the statue before Hegl showed up. And I didn't accuse him of anything, if that's what you're worried about. But, Coop, he has the motive. And look! This is the murder weapon. I'm sure of it. I thought if you could get it tested, there might still be some DNA on it. It's been cleaned, no doubt, but see this crack here? If blood got in there—"

He had stopped listening to me. He pushed the heels of his hands into his eyes and rubbed for a minute, his long fingers resting on his scalp. Then he brought them down, took a deep breath and heaved it out so forcefully, the papers on his desk fluttered.

"Leah, we've arrested the person who sexually abused Lacey—and at least two other girls."

"What? When did you make the arrest?" How could he have let me go on and on when he already had Hegl in custody?

"Early this morning." He stopped, came around his desk and sat on the edge so that he could reach out and touch my shoulder. His voice was gentle as he spoke, but the sound echoed in my head as though he'd shouted through a megaphone.

"Leah, it's not Hegl. It's Karen. Karen McDaid was Lacey's abuser."

32

"What?" I heard what he said, I just couldn't process it.

"I'm sorry, Leah. A senior at the high school came forward a few weeks ago and told us Karen had a sexual relationship with her for over a year when she was a freshman. We've turned up two more since then."

A wave of nausea so powerful surged through me so fast I couldn't do anything but grab the waste basket and heave. Tears came to my eyes as I gagged and coughed, and I felt the pressure of Coop's warm hand on my back.

"Sorry," I choked out, my head still half in his wastebasket.

"Take a breath and hold it a second. That's right, hold it, now let it out slow and easy. That's right. That's good." I focused on the sound of Coop's voice, and my breathing came under control. I sat up and took a small sip of water.

"Are you sure? Are you sure someone's not setting her up? I mean, who's saying this? Who's corroborating it?"

"It's a solid case—we've been building it for weeks. Leah, there are pictures on her computer. They—well, it's very clear the girls are telling the truth."

"Pictures? Is—are there pictures of Lacey?"

He nodded.

"Did Karen—did she kill Lacey?"

He shook his head. "She couldn't have. Karen was in Arizona for the whole month of November that year. That's when her mother died."

I remembered then. Karen had called every day to ask if there was word on Lacey. She was so kind, so helpful, such a rock for my mother.

There was a knock on the door, and one of the detectives I knew slightly stepped in without waiting for an answer. He looked at me, then quickly looked away.

"Not now, Randy," Coop growled.

"Sorry, Lieutenant, but it's Ms. McDaid. Darmody told her Leah was here when he brought her coffee. She says she'll sign whatever we want, if we let her talk to Leah. She says she doesn't want a lawyer, she just wants to talk to Leah."

"This isn't a hostage negotiation, she's not getting anything—"

I knew he wasn't just taking a stand on proper police procedure with a suspect; he was trying to protect me, too. I appreciated it, but I actually needed just the opposite. I had to see Karen.

"Coop, wait. I want to. Let me talk to her."

"That's not a good idea."

"Please."

Something in my eyes must have told him that I had to do this. That I wouldn't be able to eat, or sleep, or breathe until I could confront Karen and stop this rising tide of fury that was building up inside me.

"I've got to talk to the DA first. Wait here, Leah." Then he leaned down and pulled the liner from his trash, knotted it and handed it to Randy, whose face had shown a growing awareness that something unpleasant had happened here. He took it and left the room behind Coop, holding it at arm's length.

When I walked through the door, Karen was sitting on one side of a metal table, an empty chair across from her. Devoid of make-up, her skin was ashen and seemed to have collapsed in on itself. There were hollows and wrinkles on her cheeks, little lines around her mouth and chin. Her eyes, those slightly uptilted blue topaz eyes that had always sparkled with intelligence and humor, were dull and sunken. Her shiny silver-blonde hair was flat and lifeless. Her hands holding a coffee cup looked corded and old.

Her eyes met mine as I sat down.

"Leah, you came. I was afraid you wouldn't."

"I had to, Karen. I had to look at the person who destroyed my sister."

Her head recoiled. "Leah, don't say that. I loved Lacey."

"You loved her?" Under the table my hands clenched into fists and I held them on my knees by force of will. "You ruined her life!"

"No, no, no." She started shaking, and tears ran down her cheeks. "Don't say that. Just listen, please, please, please just listen a minute."

I pressed my lips together to keep more invective from spilling out, and then I nodded.

"Lacey was such a beautiful child, so bright. She reminded me of a little butterfly. She used to make me laugh, and I loved to hear her sing. I always enjoyed it so much when she stopped to see your mother after school." Karen's eyes had a faraway look.

"Of course, I always loved you, too, Leah," she added, as though I might be jealous that I hadn't made the Pedophiles Pick of the Week list.

"But Lacey was special. I remember that day we became more than friends. Your mother had a weekend retreat, and you were away with that boyfriend nobody liked. What was his name? Zach? Carol asked if Lacey could stay with me for the weekend. We had such a wonderful time. She was so sweet, so unsure, so...." Again, she seemed awash in memories that I didn't want her reliving.

"She was 14 years old, Karen, and she trusted you. She looked up to you. She was 14. Don't try to make this some special, loving thing. You molested her, and you kept on doing it, and you are a sick, hypocritical monster!"

"But I told you, I loved her. I would never harm Lacey. We both wanted it. I didn't force her. I never forced her. But later, she got very upset. Said she was going to tell people. I begged her not to, I knew no one else would understand. So, I had to help her see what could happen to her, to me, to your family if she did."

"What did you do, Karen? Did you threaten her? Did you tell her it was her fault? Did you say no one would believe her? Did you kill her to keep her quiet?"

"No, no!" she said sharply, a horrified expression on her face. "I would never harm Lacey. But I had to convince her to keep quiet."

"How did you do that?"

"I told her we didn't need to hurt each other. Someday, she'd realize how special our relationship was, but some people wouldn't. You and your mother for instance. That you would be disappointed in her, angry. Like you are right now. And I could lose my law practice. Then your mother wouldn't have a job.

"And then I told her I would publish the photos I'd taken of her online, if she wasn't sensible. But she was." Her voice was barely a whisper now, and I had to bend forward because her head was hanging down, and she was staring at her hands folded in front of her on top of the table.

"You put all that on a 14-year-old kid? How could you do that? And how could you work with my mother every day? How could you pretend to be her friend, her best friend?"

"But I am her best friend. I knew Carol wouldn't understand. I didn't want to hurt her. I didn't want to hurt you. What Lacey and I had was beautiful, but it was just for us. What harm did it do?"

"What harm? Are you really that insane?" An idea came to me. "You sent those texts to Georgia Caldwell, didn't you? And you gave Ross an anonymous tip about me getting fired in Florida. It was you, trying to frame me."

"You wouldn't leave it alone. You kept asking and asking about Lacey, and I knew when you realized it wasn't Miller, you'd keep asking. I had to do something to make you stop. I took your phone when you set it down at the party that night. Then I put it back in your car on Monday morning, when I stopped by your house."

"You pushed me off the bluff that night. You almost killed me!"

She shook her head, "Leah, no! I wouldn't do that to you. I couldn't. I love you."

"Yeah? Like you loved Lacey, like you love my mother? You make me sick. And whatever feeling is festering in that garbage dump you call a heart, it sure as hell isn't love."

"No! No! I love you, Leah. And I love Carol. You have to believe me."

I stared at her, trying to reconcile the self-deluding, twisted predator that sat before me with the kind, generous woman I had loved and respected. What was it that Father Lindstrom had said? Something about all of us wearing habits to hide our secret selves. Karen's habit of warmth and humor had been the perfect disguise to hide the twisted ugliness within.

"Actually, no. I don't. And I don't have to listen to another self-justifying word you say. Goodbye, Karen."

I could still hear her calling my name as I slammed the door and walked down the corridor.

I went back to Coop's office, collapsed in a chair and put my head in my hands. Karen with Lacey. Karen taking advantage of Lacey's trust, her enormous respect and love for Karen. Then the confusion and the shame she felt. Trying to break free, longing to turn to Mom, or to me, but thinking she couldn't because of Karen's threats. She must have felt so helpless. So hopeless. And me too busy and too blind to see. No wonder Lacey lashed out against the people who should have protected her. Me and my mother.

"How could I not have seen that?" I must have spoken out loud, because walking into the room just then, Coop answered.

"Stop, Leah. Lacey didn't want you to see it, she worked damn hard to protect you and your mother. When you did suspect, you acted on it right away. You wouldn't let go."

"But I had it all wrong. Even when it was staring me in the face. Delite told me it was 'a big shot,' and I knew it had to be someone who spent a lot of time with Lacey. No other adult was with her more than Karen. But I never even considered her. This is going to kill my mother."

"Don't underestimate Carol. You two are a lot alike."

"How long did you know? And why didn't you say anything? Why did you let me think you thought I was crazy?"

"You thought that up all on your own. I admit I did try to steer you away from the investigation. And I felt bad, real bad, when you thought I didn't have your back. But it wasn't true. Not for a second."

"Then why didn't you tell me?" The shock was wearing off, and I was starting to feel both stupid and ill-used. "Didn't you trust me?"

"Leah, come on. It was an open investigation, and you were very personally involved. You couldn't be objective. I barely could. We had to be very careful. You were so determined to get justice for Lacey. Karen was a close friend of yours. I couldn't take the risk."

I leaned forward and opened my mouth to yell at him, tell him he had no right to keep that from me, tell him that he should have trusted me, should have known I wouldn't do anything to jeopardize his investigation. And then I slumped back in my chair and didn't say anything, because I knew he was right. I'd been crazed since I suspected Lacey was abused, and I doubted I would have been able to stay away from Karen, or keep from telling my mother. He was right. It hurt to admit it.

"Who else knew about it?"

"Just me, my team and the DA."

"Not Ross?"

"Not at first, not until we realized there was more than the original victim involved and we started putting it all together. Lacey was his case, the county's case. We had to put him in the picture."

"How many girls did she hurt?"

"Don't know yet. She's writing a statement now. So far, we have the three, counting Lacey."

"What do you think will happen?"

"You know her better than I do. Do you think she'll recant her confession and contest the charges?"

"I thought I knew her. Clearly, I didn't. I have no idea what she'll do." I stood up to get a cup of coffee. My foot bumped against my forgotten bag. In the immediate aftermath of the Karen revelation, I'd forgotten all about my original mission.

"Coop—what about Hegl? You're going to check out this statue, aren't you? Get it tested? I understand Lacey wasn't killed because she was abused. But she was killed. I know it. And that statue is going to help prove it."

"I can't, Leah."

"Hegl lied about knowing Lacey; he lied about where he was the night she died; he got Delite to lie; he warned her against talking to me; he admitted he was driving the night Olivia Morgan died—and even if I don't have proof, it has to be investigated. And what was this statue—Sister Margaret's missing statue, the statue that disappeared the same night Lacey died—doing in his house? He's in it up to his neck."

"I'm not arguing with you. I'm saying this is Ross's case. He's gotta take the lead. I already called him. He should be here any minute."

"I'm not talking to that asshat."

"You're going to have to. I'm not playing your middleman here. You're a big girl, and you can handle it. Just know that Ross is already royally pissed off at you. He's going to give you a hard time about illegal search and seizure. Hold firm. The door was open; you went in to ask Father Hegl about the statue. He wasn't there; you saw it and seized it as possible evidence of a crime. You're a civilian, you don't have to follow the same rules we do."

He gave me a warning look.

"If there's anything there, the DA will be able to get it into evidence. For God's sake, Leah, don't snatch defeat from the jaws of victory. Just stay away from Hegl and the rest of them, and let Ross do his job."

33

An hour and too much caffeine later, I sat in the conference room, the Virgin Mary on the chair by my side, both of us waiting for Coop to bring Ross back.

He came truculently into the room, running his finger around his too tight collar in a vain effort to give his neck roll some breathing space.

"Nash, why is it every time something smells bad, there you are in the middle of the stink? All of a sudden, Mrs. Caldwell drops her stalking complaint—even though we could nail you on that. Now, Coop tells me you got some kinda statue supposedly used to kill your sister. I ain't buyin' it."

"I'm not selling, Ross. If you'd done your job, you wouldn't have wasted time on that stupid stalking complaint at all. And if you had half the brains of an amoeba, you wouldn't have done such a half-assed job investigating my sister's death when it happened. Maybe the smell is the crap I have to shovel to clean up after you."

"That's it, that does it."

"Both of you, knock it off. Charlie, Leah's got some information for you. Leah, just give him a statement without editorializing." Coop turned on the tape recorder.

I gave Ross the story.

"Miguel can corroborate. And he has the photos that prove the statue was at Hegl's the first time I visited back in May, and still there where we found it last night. I wore gloves when I picked it up, and it hasn't left this bag except to show it to Coop."

"Let me get this straight. You broke into the priest's house—"

"I didn't break in. The back door was open. I thought he'd be there. I wanted to talk to him." I lied without guilt or hesitation.

"And you just walked in and stole property from his shelf," he continued as though I hadn't said anything.

"We went in, and when I saw the statue, I seized it as evidence of a crime. I didn't steal it. I knew it had been taken from Sister Margaret, and I had reason to think it had been used to kill my sister. I'm just a private citizen. I don't need to have a warrant. Look it up. Now are you going to take the statue and have it tested, or do I have to do everything on this case myself?"

"I don't need to tell you what I'm going to do. I was solving crimes when you were still watching *Scooby Doo*. I'm warning you, Nash, stay out of this case and away from Father Hegl, or you'll regret it. You got lucky on the criminal sexual conduct thing, but that's a long way from a murder investigation.

"You still haven't convinced me there's anything but an accident involved in your sister's death. It's the DA's call if we go to the expense of testing this statue, and right now, Nash, your track record ain't so good."

"Only an insensitive jerk like you could call it 'lucky' that I was right about my sister's sexual abuse. Just do your damn job this time, Ross, and don't worry about what I'm doing."

"Which should be sendin' out your resume from what I hear, Nash."

I left without saying anything else. But I wanted to.

***

My mother's car was in the driveway when I got home. She jumped me as soon as I walked in the door.

"Something strange is going on. When I got to work this morning, Karen wasn't there. I tried to reach her, but she isn't answering her cell. I drove by her house and her car is there, but she isn't. The house was locked. I knocked, but no one answered. She had two client meetings this morning, and she didn't show up. She never misses a meeting! I cancelled the rest of her appointments, but I'm getting really worried about her. I think we should go back over and try to get in through a window. Maybe she—"

"Mom, Karen's been arrested." She kept on talking as though she hadn't heard me.

"She could have fallen in the shower or—wait, what did you say? Arrested? Is that supposed to be funny? I'm seriously concerned, Leah." I grabbed her by her shoulders and looked straight into her eyes.

"Karen was arrested this morning on criminal sexual conduct charges involving two high school students. She's confessed. And she—she," I struggled to get it out. "She told me she had a sexual relationship with Lacey, too. Karen is the one, Mom, the one who abused Lacey."

At first, she didn't react, just tilted her head and drew her eyebrows together in a frown, as though I'd said something she didn't quite catch. Then she grabbed my arm and pulled me over to the couch and sat us both down. "I don't understand. It just doesn't make any sense."

"The police found pictures on her computer—some of them were Lacey. I was at the police station this morning, and when Karen heard I was there, she wanted to talk to me. She said if she could talk to me, she'd sign a statement."

Again, there was that look of confusion, as though I were speaking in a language she was familiar with, but not quite fluent in. "But that can't be right. Karen loved Lacey. Loves you. Remember how strong she was for us when Lacey died?" She paused, and I could almost read her thoughts from the growing horror on her face.

"She didn't kill Lacey, Mom. At least not directly. She was away the whole month of November that year, with her mother in Arizona."

I told her what Karen had said, her self-serving explanation, her feeble attempt to justify what she'd done, and how she'd kept Lacey quiet with guilt and threats. The longer I talked, the tighter my mother gripped her hands together, until her knuckles were white with effort.

"Oh, God," she moaned when I finished. "How could I have been so stupid? I thought it was wonderful that Karen took so much time with

Lacey. I thought it was so good for Lacey to have a strong, professional woman as a role model. Why did she do this? How could she do this?

"How could she look me in the face every day? How could she pretend to care when Lacey started getting into trouble, or when she ran away, or when she went to DeMoss? She always acted so concerned, so kind, so...." Her voice trailed off as she tried to make sense of the betrayal.

"She's sick, I guess, and she couldn't stop herself—or wouldn't stop herself. I don't understand how she could compartmentalize her life that way, but that's what she did. She believes she loves you and me and Lacey too, but it's a crazy kind of love. She couldn't admit, especially to herself, that what she rationalized as beautiful was toxic. But another part of her knew—that's why she begged and finally threatened Lacey to keep it quiet."

"It makes me sick, physically ill. And it makes me want to kill her." She jumped up and went to the cupboard, pulled down the Jameson and poured it in a glass and drank it straight down in one gulp. Then she got some ice and poured another.

The phone rang. I answered and handed it to her.

"Mom, it's Paul."

I got up, went into the kitchen and banged around in the freezer for a while getting ice out. Then I got a glass and some Jameson. By the time I went back to the living room, she was off the phone.

"Paul's coming over to get me. He said you should come, too. He wants to fix us dinner."

"That's nice of him, but no, I don't think so."

Things were still pretty awkward between me and Paul, and the thought of going over and over things with my mother and him was more than I could bear. I knew that for Mom, talking was the only way to vanquish the falling-to-the-bottom-of-a-mine-shaft feeling. But I wasn't ready to hear all the guilt and recriminations and what ifs and whys—I had my own battle. Paul was much better equipped to be her listener, and they didn't need me there.

As we finished our drinks, his car pulled in. My mom ran out to the driveway with me trailing behind. He opened his arms wide, and she collapsed against his chest and started to cry. I realized then how much he cared about her, and how hard my suspicions had been on both of them. He stroked her hair and looked at me over the top of her head.

"Leah, I'm so sorry."

"No, I'm sorry, Paul. I—"

"No. You were right. I didn't believe you when you started out, and then when you came after me—or it felt like you came after me—well, I lashed out. I understand you had to ask, Leah. I still wish you hadn't, but—well—I get it, and I'm not mad anymore."

I gave my best attempt at a smile.

"Thanks, I appreciate it. And I'm glad Mom will be with you tonight."

"Are you sure you don't want to go with us, Leah?" Her voice was thick with tears yet to come.

"I'm sure, I'm fine. Yeah. I'll be all right."

"Try to eat, don't just drink Jameson all night."

"I'll make a sandwich or something. Don't worry."

After several more attempts to get me to join them, they got into Paul's car and drove off. I went back inside to think about the question my mother hadn't asked, but which had been on my mind since I left the PD. If Hegl wasn't Lacey's abuser, what was his motive for killing her? And if he didn't do it, what was he doing with the statue?

34

I sat down in the rocking chair and moved slowly back and forth, talking out loud to myself.

"OK, Hegl is a ladies' man who likes them young—Delite was 17, Olivia was 19, who knows how many others? He's having fun with Olivia, but he wants out when she wants to get serious. When the car crash happens, he cuts and runs and that makes things get a whole lot more serious. He could go to jail on this one. With his position of supposed moral authority and his chickenhearted behavior, chances are good he will. So, he runs to Uncle Bishop, who provides an alibi and a witness to corroborate it."

I got my laptop out and googled the Most Reverend Joseph Ramsey.

Twenty minutes later, I had it. A website set up for the St. Lucian School alumni. Lots of old photos and reminiscing, and in the middle of all that upper-class male bonhomie there they were, their arms jauntily slung over each other's shoulders. The pride of the Class of 1978, the most Reverend Joseph Ramsey and Reid Palmer, then known as Joe and Reeder.

The class update noted that Joe was now the Most Reverend, and Reeder was now Reid Palmer, attorney-at-law, retired hedge fund manager and benefactor of too many charities to mention. It also contained a quote from the Bishop: "The older I get, the more I value the days I spent at St. Lucian's. *Fratres in vitam.* Brothers for life."

And so, when his nephew got into some bad trouble with a girl, a drunk girl, who wound up dead, Joe turned to his old friend Reeder.

What if Reid Palmer supplied an alibi and a refuge for Hegl, and maybe even some money to persuade Vince Morgan that a slow boat to Key West was the best way to get over his dead wife? Carla could be right about everyone ignoring things. With a little nudge from the bishop, the sheriff could have fast-walked his investigation right into an accidental death finding, no one involved but the drunk girl herself.

Much the conclusion that Ross reached just as speedily up here. But even though Hegl walked away from a felony, he was now and forever under the thumb of his alibi provider, Reid Palmer. If he ever recanted, Hegl was in a world of hurt.

But what was in it for Reid Palmer, beyond the joy of doing a helpful turn for an old friend? And how did Sister Julianna fit in? Did she? If Palmer suddenly thrust a choir director priest on her, wouldn't he have had to offer some explanation? And what had Delite been about to tell me when Cole cut her off?

I got up and did some nervous eating—a peanut butter and honey sandwich, a chocolate cupcake with about an inch of frosting. Then I stretched out on the couch as my sugar buzz bottomed out. My eyelids started to droop, and I was sound asleep for the next hour. When I woke up it was 8:30, but my mind was clear and I knew my next step. I pulled up the recent call list on my phone and selected Delite's number.

"Yeah?"

"Delite, this is Leah Nash."

"I know who it is."

"Is Cole with you?" I was going to try to persuade her to give me the "bonus" information she had hinted at before. It would be easier if Cole wasn't around.

"No. He ain't. That asshole took my money and took off. Left me with nothin'. Not even enough for bus fare. My brother in Minneapolis said I could crash with him, but I don't even have enough for a ticket."

"I might be able to help with that," I said cautiously, trying not to sound too eager. She needed cash pretty bad and didn't have much of a negotiating position. "If you tell me what you meant by 'bonus' information that night I met with you and Cole."

"That'll be 500 bucks."

"Come on, Delite, get real." As we were talking, I pulled up bus fare from Himmel to Minneapolis. $52. "I can give you $75. That's it." Which it was. I had an emergency $50 tucked in my wallet. My other source of bribery funds would have to be the $25 or so my mother kept in a miscellaneous cash cookie jar.

She sighed, but she must have been really desperate, because she didn't try to bargain.

"Meet me at the bus stop. I can catch the 10:30 if you move your ass."

When I pulled up, she was leaning against the brick wall of the all-night diner that served as Himmel's bus stop. She looked small and tired as she smoked a cigarette with quick, impatient puffs.

She saw me and straightened, throwing aside her cigarette and assuming her usual aggressive stance.

"What happened?"

"I told you. Cole took the money and cleared out. Left me with nothin'. I'm goin' to my brother's. He said he can get me a job at the factory where he works. You got the money?"

I reached in my purse, and she put out her hand. "No. Wait a minute. First I want to hear the information."

"Fine. I seen Queenie up at the casino. More than once."

"What was she doing there?"

"Do I gotta draw you a picture? She was at the casino. Playin' the slots."

"Sister Julianna was gambling?" I was dumbfounded. "Are you sure it was her? Did you talk to her?"

"Yeah, I'm sure. I spent enough time in her office starin' at her while I was gettin' yelled at, didn't I? She didn't see me, and I didn't talk to her. She never had anything to say I wanted to hear."

"Why would she drive all the way to Mixley to gamble? There are closer places."

"Duh! So nobody would see her, whadya think?"

"That doesn't make sense. A nun in a habit playing the slot machines would attract a lot of attention no matter where she was."

"Are you retarded or what? She wasn't wearin' her nun clothes. Now, are you gonna give me the money or what?"

I thrust it into her outstretched hand.

"It still goes, ya know. This ain't on the record. I'm not gettin' mixed up with any of that crowd again."

"I'd stay away from Cole Granger, too."

"Don't worry. I can take care of myself." Then she turned and walked into the restaurant/bus stop to buy her ticket. She didn't say goodbye, and she didn't look back.

At home, I typed Sister Julianna Bennett into Google. She popped up in conjunction with multiple professional associations and conferences. I pulled up the program for her recent Las Vegas conference, the one where she had run into Helen Sebanski at the slot machines. There was her bio with highlights from her vita. As Sister Margaret had said, Sister Julianna did a lot of professional traveling.

Funny thing, almost all the papers she presented and the keynote speaking listed took place in cities that also boasted casinos with conference facilities. Well-known gambling meccas like Las Vegas, Detroit, Reno, Albuquerque, as well as a number of smaller towns like Mt. Pleasant, Michigan, and Black Hawk, Colorado featured heavily in Sister Julianna's professional life.

I thought for a minute, then typed in gambling nuns. Soon I'd read several stories about Catholic nuns and priests who had embezzled money —big money, like millions of dollars in some cases—from their order, their parish, their school. They used it to buy vacations, purchase condos, give lavish gifts to friends and family, and to cover gambling sprees. The fraud went on for years, in many cases, before it was discovered.

Clickety-click went my little brain as I recalled Sister Margaret telling me how precarious the school's finances used to be. Clickety-clack it picked up speed, thinking of her recounting the arrival of Reid Palmer and the subsequent stabilizing of funds. And then clickety-clackety-click-clack-click, we rolled into the station. I heard Sister Margaret saying that Sister Julianna did everything herself. That Sister Mattea's surprise revamping of the accounting system would take such a burden off her.

Sister Mattea's brother. I had to get ahold of him.

Scott Riordan hadn't called me back, but maybe his snotty receptionist hadn't given him the message. I looked at my watch. 10:00 p.m. It would be 7:00 p.m. in California. Miss Moneypenny would be gone for the day, and maybe I'd be able to leave a message directly on Scott's voicemail. I crossed my fingers and called.

After three rings, I was readying a coherent message to leave when an actual male person answered. "Riordan Software."

"Oh! hello. My name is Leah Nash. May I speak to Scott Riordan please? It's very important."

"Hello, Leah. This is Scott. What can I do for you?"

"Scott—I didn't expect to connect directly to the boss. Last time I called, I couldn't make it past your receptionist."

"Miss Adams takes her job seriously. I've been out of the country actually, just stopped in on my way home from the airport to see what my desk looked like. You're lucky. I can't stand to let a phone go unanswered. What is it you need?"

"It's sort of complicated, so I'm going to skip a lot that I can fill in later. I know you were donating a new online accounting system to DeMoss Academy."

"Yes. I still plan to. What about it?" His tone of voice had gone from friendly to curious.

"And Sister Mattea, your sister, that is, did she provide you with financial records to be entered into the new system, so you could get it operational and ready to go when she presented the system as a surprise to Sister Julianna?"

"Yes."

"Did you find anything unexpected?"

"Leah, I can't really talk about this to you. The financial data is confidential."

"I understand. I'm not asking for particulars. I just wondered if there was anything that concerned you at all. Please. It's important."

"I guess I can say that there is some information I plan to bring to the board's attention."

"Don't! Not yet, please!" I blurted out.

"Excuse me?"

"Your sister trusted me. I need you to trust me too."

"What do you mean?"

I told him about Sister Mattea's note, and that I'd been working for weeks to figure out why she reached out to me and what she wanted to say. "I think part of what she wanted me to know was personal to me. But part of it might have had to do with financial problems at DeMoss. Have you found anything that indicates there could be fraud or embezzlement going on at the school?"

"You're putting me in a tough position."

I held my breath. Finally, he spoke again.

"The proprietary software my company developed is very sophisticated. I asked my sister to give me records going five years back in order to demonstrate all the program could do for the school."

"The software detects fraud?"

"Yes, but it's not that simple. It uses data mining and algorithms to classify and segment information, find associations and determine patterns and deviations in behavior. When a dissimilar behavior is identified in a pattern of transactions that should be similar, for example, it can signal a problem."

"Like fraud or embezzlement, right?"

"I want to be clear here. These pattern anomalies are not proof of fraud, Leah. They are indicators. Further analysis and additional information is always required."

"Has your software ever identified real-life fraud, for other companies, I mean?"

"Oh yes. Absolutely. We had a situation last year where a vice president for finance at a nonprofit had embezzled more than $3 million dollars over a 10-year period. He wrote checks to himself, forged signatures, destroyed cancelled checks the bank provided. He covered losses by inflating the number of unfulfilled pledges, and he was able to get away with it because there were no checks and balances.

"He reconciled the books and handled everything. Then, while he was seriously ill for an extended period, the organization brought in an acting manager who was familiar with our software and convinced the board to purchase it. The system revealed the indicators of fraud and within months the man was caught."

"So, you think that could be happening at DeMoss?"

"I didn't say that."

"OK, but it could be right?"

"I'm comfortable saying that nonprofits and religious organizations have among the highest rates of fraud. They rely on trust rather than verification, and they invest too much authority in one person."

"But Sister Mattea never said anything to you about it? You didn't talk to her?"

"No. I didn't pinpoint any problems until after she died. And truly, I'm not comfortable talking to you about it, Leah. As I said, I intend to talk to Reid Palmer and suggest some areas for additional data gathering and alert him to potential problems."

"Scott, please don't, not yet. Just give me a few days before you do."

"I really don't understand."

"And I can't explain. Yet. But if you give me just a week or so, I will."

"I don't know...."

"No one but Sister Margaret knows you're working on this, right? It's not like anyone's waiting to hear from you. I promise you what I'm doing is exactly what your sister would have wanted me to do. I know it is. Just give me a week. Whatever is or isn't wrong with the DeMoss accounts—a few days isn't going to make any difference, right?"

"I suppose not, but I—"

"Thanks, Scott. I'll be in touch as soon as I can. I promise."

Sister Julianna was stealing money. Had Reid Palmer found out? Was he covering for her like he was for Hegl? But why would he do that? And what did any of that have to do with Hegl, Lacey, and the statue?

"Damn." The more I found out, the less I knew.

Discouraged, I slumped back in my seat.

There was a light tap on the kitchen door, and when I looked up I saw Miguel peering through the window. I waved him in.

"*Chica, que va?* What did Coop say about the statue? And what about Hegl? And Karen! Did she—Lacey, was she the one who—"

"Coop turned the statue over to Ross, who gave me grief about breaking into Hegl's, which remember we absolutely did not do. And he'll give me nothing about the investigation. If he even does one. Karen swore she didn't kill Lacey—and she was out of town, so that's probably true. But she did admit she was the one who sent the texts to Georgia."

I got up and went to the refrigerator and got us each a beer. We both sat down at the bar, drank, and didn't say anything for a few minutes.

"You knew it wasn't Miller all this time, didn't you?"

"I didn't know it was Karen. I never thought—"

"No, but you *knew* it wasn't him. Not just you didn't think, you actually knew."

He shifted on the stool and looked down, staring at his Supper Club.

"It's all right. I know he's gay. He told me. And he told me he's coming out. But why didn't you tell me? You let me go after him, and all the time you knew he was gay?"

"I tried to push you in a different direction. It's hard to turn your boat around, *chica*. But I couldn't tell you about Miller. *Lo siento*. I'm sorry. It wasn't my secret."

I waved away his apology. "I probably wouldn't have listened to you anyway. I've pretty much had my head up my ass for the last month or so, I think we can all agree."

"So, what's next?"

I was a little hurt that he didn't fight me on the head up my ass thing.

"Well, I've just spent the last hour backing myself into a corner of this godforsaken maze, and I can't seem to think my way out of it."

"*Dígame.*"

I explained my attempts to link Hegl, Palmer, Sister Julianna, and Sister Mattea together. I told him about my phone conversation with Scott, and my belief that Sister Julianna was an embezzler with a gambling problem. Miguel was as excited as I was at first, and then his face fell. Just like mine.

"So—what does Lacey have to do with all that? And the statue? You still think Lacey was killed, right? That it wasn't an accident?"

"Yes. But I don't know why."

"Maybe she found out about the embezzling?"

I shook my head. "I don't see how she'd even stumble across something like that. And if by some wild chance she did, I doubt she'd get the significance. She was just a kid."

"What are you gonna do?"

"I don't know. Think some more, I guess. It's not like I have a job taking up all my time anymore."

"That could be good." The encouraging note he tried to inject in his voice was sweet, but kind of comical at the same time.

"Hey, it's gettin' late. You don't need to babysit me, I'm OK. In fact, I think I'm going to put all this stuff away for now and listen to some music and try to get some sleep. Maybe something will come to me in my dreams."

"OK, *chica*, if you're sure."

"I am."

35

After Miguel left, I fussed around in the kitchen for a while, putting stuff away, doing the dishes, wiping down the counter. I'd told him I wanted to get some sleep, but I was too restless. On the other hand, my brain felt too fried to figure out anything coherent. I walked down to the hall closet and reached way back on the top shelf and pulled out a sturdy banker's box marked *Lacey*.

I carried it into my bedroom, set it on the bed, and sat down next to it. Sometimes, Mom would get the box down and look at the things inside, but I rarely did. It was just too hard. But that night I wanted to remember.

I took the top off and started sifting through the contents. Cards she'd gotten from me and Mom, a wall poster of *Wicked*. A small notebook filled with quick drawings of things that caught her fancy. I flipped through a few pages—a tree with bare branches, her cat Zoey, Mom sleeping on the couch, a bird, the swing on our front porch.

I put it aside to look at later, with the half-formed idea of pulling out some of the pictures to mat and frame for my mother's birthday, then resumed my digging. A book of word puzzles. She loved crosswords, word search, anagrams, all that stuff. Some old report cards. The next thing I pulled out was a half-bald, one-eyed, matted, stuffed dog she called Fluffy

Pete that I gave her when she was three. For years, she wouldn't go to sleep without it.

That's when I started to cry. Once I began, I couldn't stop. It went from tears running down my face to shoulder-shaking sobs. I cried for Lacey and the life that was stolen from her, for my mother and the pain she had endured, and for myself and my inability to save her. I cried until my nose was stuffy, and my eyes were swollen, and my throat hurt. And then I cried some more.

When I finally stopped, I reached in the box for one more thing. Lacey's MP3 player. If I could listen to what she loved, maybe I'd feel connected to her again. Maybe somewhere, somehow, she'd know how sorry I was. I fumbled to turn it on, but, of course, it wasn't charged after all this time. I plugged it in the charger, and put the rest of the stuff away except for the sketch pad and Fluffy Pete. Then I layed down on my bed with the tattered stuffed animal beside me and fell asleep.

The next thing I knew my iPhone pinged. I leaned over and looked at the time: 7 a.m. When I saw that RalphieP had accepted my friend request, I shook off my sleepiness. He was still online. I started typing.

Danny—I'm Lacey's sister.

I know who you are.

Can we meet or can I get your number and call you?

Not a good idea.

Why were you with Lacey the night she disappeared?

I hated DeMoss. She said I could go with her.

Why didn't you?

You tell me.

What do you mean?

She left me. Went to get a car. Never came back.

She didn't leave you. Lacey was killed that night.

He didn't respond for so long I wondered if he left his computer. Then the cursor started moving.

I got outplaced. Off the grid. No TV, no Internet. Home schooled. No one told me.

How long were you there?

Two years. Ran away.

What happened after Lacey's friend Cole took off?

Lacey went to get the car. She didn't come back.

What did Lacey know that would make someone want to kill her?

I don't know. I have to go.

And that was that. He went offline. But I learned three things from our chat: he was scared, he knew something, and I was right, Lacey *was* in the administration building the same night Hegl and Delite were there. But why would Hegl have had to kill her? All he'd need to do was call security and report her. If he wasn't her abuser, what was the motive?

But what if it wasn't Lacey coming in at 10:45? Maybe Hegl and Delite heard someone else enter the building, not Lacey. Not yet. If Sister Julianna or Reid Palmer—or both—were on the scene, Lacey could have walked right into the middle of something when she got there. And never walked back out.

I got out a pencil and paper and made a timeline. Delite and Hegl get to Sister Julianna's office just after 10:30. They have round two of their romantic tryst, and as they finish up, they hear a noise in the outer office. Delite runs out the back door at 10:45, leaving Hegl with his pants down. Literally.

According to Cole, he got his ticket on Dunphy Road, a five-minute drive from Simon's Rock, at 10:50. If that was true, then he must have left Lacey at 10:45. It would take her at least 10 minutes to get to the administration building from the Baylor Road entrance, especially in the dark. And Delite was very sure it was 10:45 when they heard the noise. If it wasn't Lacey coming in, who was it?

Everyone else was at the dinner, which didn't end until after 11. Including Sister Julianna and Reid Palmer, except maybe not. I recalled the bitter words of Marilyn Karr. How he had sabotaged her. How he had offered to retrieve the drawing he'd forgotten in his office. How he didn't get back until it was too late for her. Had his unexpected arrival at the administration building ensured that it was too late for Lacey, too? But why?

"Damn it!" I shouted out loud, then immediately shut up so I didn't wake my mother. I sighed and pulled Lacey's MP-3 player out of the charger, inserted my ear buds and hit play. I picked up the notepad of drawings I'd set aside the night before, intending to leaf through it while I ate my breakfast. My mother's door was still closed as I passed down the hall. I set the sketchpad on the bar and went into the kitchen.

The songs on Lacey's player moved from Avril Lavigne to Justin Timberlake and on to the Black Eyed Peas. I had to smile when Simon and Garfunkel showed up. We are our mother's daughters, I thought, as I put bread in the toaster, poured a glass of orange juice, cracked an egg into the frying pan. Then a song came on that made me stop in my tracks.

Except it wasn't a song at all. It was two people talking. And what they said turned my stomach.

Danny, what are you doing in here all by yourself? The unmistakable soft Southern drawl of Reid Palmer.

Listening to my player. A young boy, nervous and high-pitched.

Well that's fine, Danny. I know that's a favorite pastime of boys your age. But wouldn't a nice soak in the hot tub after all our exercise today feel good?

That's OK. I want to stay here.

Danny, what's wrong? Didn't you have fun today? Didn't you like the horses? Didn't we have a grand time?

I guess.

Danny. Let's go now. Everyone is waiting.

Silence. Then Danny's voice came in a rapid-fire burst.

I don't want to. Just take me home. I just want to go home, Mr. Reid.

Home, Danny? You mean back to DeMoss? Well, of course, you can go, anytime you want. But I would have to tell Sister Julianna that I think you are having some adjustment problems. And that could mean you need to be outplaced. Then you wouldn't be able to stay in touch with your little brother. What is his name now? Justin?

You can't do that!

Of course I can. Not that I want to. I hope you'll realize that my friends are your friends, too. They all like you very much. Is it the camera, Danny? Does that worry you? Don't even think about it. We all like to remember special times, don't we, Danny?

I just don't want to do it. Please, Mr. Reid.

It's up to you, of course. I can take you back to DeMoss. And you can abandon Justin. Like your mother abandoned you.

The small voice of a frightened and defeated 12-year-old whispered, *Fine. I'll stay.*

That's wonderful. Why don't you put away your music now?

That's why Danny wanted to run away. That's what Lacey knew. And that's why she died, to stop Danny from suffering the same way she had.

I went to my laptop and Facebooked Danny with my phone number and a message: I know what Palmer did to you. I have the recording. Call me.

Then I waited. Within 10 minutes my phone rang.

"It's Danny."

"I know about Reid Palmer. Why didn't you tell me?"

"My little brother is only 10. He thinks I'm in technical college. He can't know about what happened. What I did. What I am."

"Danny, I need your help. We can stop this. Stop Palmer."

"No. You can't. Lacey thought she could, and she's dead."

"Is it just Palmer, Danny? Do Sister Julianna and Father Hegl know what he did to you? Are there others?"

"They know. Sister Julianna picks out the kids. The ones like me, with nobody who gives a crap about them. If you go along, you get special privileges. If you don't, you get outplaced. And if you tell, nobody believes you. And they have pictures, video, stuff that shows what you—that you—everybody can see what you did. Anyway, you're just a lying screw up. That's why you're at DeMoss, right? After Lacey left—died—Hegl said, if I kept my mouth shut, they'd take me off the website. And they'd let me stay in touch with Justin."

"What website?"

"Where they post the videos. For the SLB."

"The SLB?"

"His club. His friends. The St. Lucian Boys—that's what they call themselves. The ones he brought us for."

I almost dropped the phone. "These friends, Danny, they were people Palmer went to school with?"

"I guess."

"How many are there? Did you know any of their names? Was there a Joseph?"

"There were different ones. Mr. Joe. He was the worst."

"If I showed you a picture, would you recognize him?"

"Yeah."

"Just a sec." I pulled the diocesan website up on my phone, did a screen capture and texted it to him. "Have you got it?"

"That's him. Mr. Joe." Danny had just identified the Most Reverend Joseph Ramsey.

"Did you tell Lacey about the website?"

"She said if we could find it, prove there was a website, we could go to the cops. They'd have to believe us. They'd shut the SLB down. I'd be safe. But we didn't know how to get to it. So, she gave me her MP3 player to record Palmer. I was supposed to get him to say something about the website, but I was too scared, I couldn't."

"You were really brave just to record him, Danny."

"I wasn't brave like Lacey. The night we tried to run, I started to cry when her friend left us. She put her arm around me and she gave me this big smile. She said, 'Don't worry, Ralphie. The eagle has landed. I've got what we need.' Then she went to get a car, but she never came back. It started to snow. I waited two hours, and she never came."

"I don't understand. Did she mean she found the website?"

"I don't know. Look, all I have left is my little brother. And the only way I can keep him is to lie to him. I can't help you. Please, leave me alone."

"But, Danny—"

It was too late. He was gone.

I called him back but he didn't pick up. I texted. "Danny. Please. I need you."

I got one back almost immediately. "This ain't Danny."

I called again, and a woman answered.

"I'm trying to reach Danny Howard?"

"Well, I'm not him. Quit callin' my phone and textin' me, will ya? I let him borrow it for 10 minutes. I wasn't plannin' on startin' a dating service." The call ended.

I tried Facebook, but he was gone. Not just not online, gone. He'd unfriended me or deactivated his account. Either way, he wasn't interested in talking to me again.

36

So that was it. Reid Palmer had some kind of freaky pornography site that he shared for fun—and maybe profit—with his friends from prep school. Their housemother was Sister Julianna, strewing throwaway kids in the path of the St. Lucian's Boys in exchange for Palmer helping cover up her own crimes. And Lacey had died because she found out and tried to rescue Danny.

Palmer probably uncovered the embezzling when he joined the DeMoss Academy Board, and "set things right," as Sister Margaret had said. But he set them right in exchange for Sister Julianna's help in securing suitable boys for himself and his SLB friends. Palmer and Sister Julianna knew about Hegl's felony. Sister Julianna and Hegl knew about Palmer's sexual crimes. The three of them were an unholy trinity of mutually assured destruction.

It was 8 a.m. Mom was still sleeping. I couldn't stand to sit at the kitchen table a minute longer, my mind running in circles. I cleared away my dishes, went to my room and threw on jeans, a T-shirt, and pulled my hair into a ponytail. Then I put on a Badgers cap, wrote her a note, and let myself quietly out the kitchen door.

The streets were full of traffic. People who hadn't lost their jobs all had somewhere to go. I wondered if Miller Caldwell would be making his big announcement today. Odds were he'd be losing his job then, too, and probably a whole lot more. I tried to stop thinking and focus on just moving ahead, one step at a time. I walked through familiar neighborhoods, past my old elementary school, the park, JT's Party Store.

I walked until the sidewalk narrowed and the concrete squares were heaved up at crazy angles by erupting tree roots. In some places, there was more dirt than cement showing, and, finally, at the edge of town, the sidewalk stopped altogether. The street petered out, ending with a broken-down wooden barricade topped by a Dead End sign.

I sat on a downed tree that lay half across the road, facing the fields beyond the barricade. As soon as I paused my forward motion, the peaceful non-thinkingness I'd cultivated on my walk disappeared. I had to find that website. And, somehow, I had to get Hegl to tell me what really happened the night Lacey died. I considered my options.

I could talk to Coop and tell him what Danny had said and what I'd figured out. But could I trust him not to go to Ross? Probably not. It was Ross's case, Ross's jurisdiction, and Coop would have no choice. And Ross would just screw things up.

I could boldly go out to the Catherines' and run a bluff on Hegl. Tell him I knew everything. Tell him Delite was coming forward, and Danny was going to testify. Tell him he couldn't trust Palmer, that he'd already tried to throw him under the bus. Tell him he needed to get ahead of the curve, or he'd be saddled with Lacey's death. But he was up to his neck in everything, and I couldn't be sure he wouldn't turn on me like a cornered rat.

Then there was the X factor. Was Sister Mattea's death an accident? Or, was she killed not because she knew about Lacey's sexual abuse, but because she had figured out something about the financial fraud even before her brother had used his super-duper software?

And there was also me. Who pushed me off that river bluff? It had to be Hegl, Palmer, or Sister Julianna, and I sure wasn't going to let any of them get away with it.

And what did Lacey mean *the eagle has landed?* What kind of word game was that? Why couldn't she just say, "It's all good, Danny. I have the address, and here it is."

I was so intent on trying to untangle the threads and formulate a plan that I didn't hear the approaching sound of bike tires behind me. But the little hairs on the back of my neck began to prickle and I whipped my head around. There was Vesta straddling her bike, flowered grandma dress riding high on nonexistent hips, decorum preserved by the pair of rolled up men's khakis she wore underneath it. Her little dog was asleep in the basket attached to her handlebars, snoring gently.

"Vesta! Hi. I didn't hear you," I said, in the overly loud and cheery voice I sometimes use with very small children and the elderly. "How are you?"

"*Lord, dost thou not care that my sister hath left me to serve alone? Bid her therefore that she help me.*"

I blinked. That was a little too apropos to be entirely comfortable. She got off her bike and put down the kickstand. I stood up from my tree seat as she walked the few steps toward me. She kept coming until she was well within my personal space comfort zone. Her hair was damp with sweat, and she had a pungent, garlicky smell. I took a half-step backward, but the branch at my back didn't give me much room.

"Your sister is gone."

"I know, Vesta. I know you found her. That was a long time ago."

"*For nothing is hidden except to be made manifest; nor is anything secret except to come to light.*" She was getting that agitated look again, the way she had when I dropped the box off at her house. I took care to speak in a low, almost crooning voice.

"OK. Right, that's true, I know. You're right about that. It's good to see you, but I'll let you get back to your riding. I've got to get home myself. If I could just scoot around you here?"

I tried to move past her, but as I did she clutched my arm. Her dog woke with a start and emitted a sharp little bark. I tried to ease out of her grasp, but she was stronger than she looked.

"*For the prophet and the priest are defiled: and in my house I have found their wickedness, saith the Lord.*"

Her faded blue eyes were big and almost beseeching. Vesta spent long hours—both day and night—rambling the county roads. Fences and property lines meant nothing to her. She was such a common sight, and had been for so long, that people didn't even see her anymore. But that didn't mean Vesta didn't see them.

"Vesta, did you see something the night Lacey died?" I asked with an urgency that seemed to scare her.

She released my arm and started to shake her head and back away. Her little dog Barnacle began softly growling.

"Vesta! Vesta! Is it Father Hegl? Are you talking about Father Hegl? What did you see?" This time it was my turn to grab her. I held her twitching fingers in my hand. I shook her, and she jumped and pulled away. She looked at me, eyes wide with fear.

"I'm sorry! I'm so sorry!" I said.

She began to scuttle backward as I repeated, "I'm sorry, please. I didn't mean to frighten you." Tears were streaming down her face, and I felt horrible. "I'm so sorry, don't cry, please." I took a step toward her and she moved with surprising agility and speed. She jumped on her bike and turned it so rapidly Barnacle, who had begun barking frantically, almost fell out. She pedaled down the road, leaving me calling after her.

When I got home, a note on the table said my mother had gone into work to try and organize things, and let clients know that the office would be closing. It hadn't occurred to me until that moment that my mother, like me, was now out of a job. I sighed as I put the kettle on for tea.

What had Vesta tried to tell me? Had she been there that night? Had she seen Lacey being carried through the dark woods, to be dumped like an old mattress or a sack of trash at the bottom of the ravine? Did her tangled thoughts and her fear prevent her from describing it? But she hadn't abandoned Lacey. She'd gone back until Lacey was found.

I heard my mother's car pull in the driveway. When she came in, I said, "You better sit down, Mom. I know why Lacey was killed, and I know what's going on at DeMoss Academy, and it's really, really bad."

37

I told her everything—Sister Julianna's embezzlement, Hegl's complicity, Palmer's perversion, Danny's recording, the website, my encounter with Vesta. She listened without saying a word. Then she went to the cupboard, got out the Jameson and two glasses, and poured it for us straight over ice. By the time I finished this investigation, we'd both be candidates for detox.

"Mom. It's only one o'clock." But I took a sip anyway.

We carried our glasses into the living room. She took the couch, and I took the rocker. In the back of both our minds was the image of Karen sitting on the now empty wingback chair. Neither of us wanted to go there.

"What are you going to do?"

"I don't know what to do. I've got the recording, but I'm not sure we'd be able to prove it's Palmer. And without Danny's cooperation, I won't even be able to prove he's the boy talking. If I could get to that website, I'd have something solid. Without something tangible like that, Ross is not going to listen or do anything. He hates me, and I hate that everything I have is circumstantial, and I'm going to be up against a nun, a priest, and a rich guy. And I'm already not the most credible source in the world, thanks to Karen's texting on my behalf."

I stood up and started pacing around the room. When I got by the bar, I stopped and pounded the top three times shouting, "Damn it, damn it, damn it!" As I did, the force of my blows sent Lacey's sketch book flying off the bar, and it fell to the floor with pages fluttering.

"Well. That was productive," my mother said, getting out of her chair and stooping to pick it up.

"Sorry. It's one of Lacey's old sketchbooks. I found it in the box of her things."

She started leafing through it and smiling. I stood looking over her shoulder as she paused to study a page. It was the drawing of a bird, only now that I was paying closer attention, I saw it wasn't a random bird. It was an eagle. I stared at it. Hard. *The eagle has landed.*

"Mom, what's the legend about Zeus and Ganymede?"

"The god Zeus fell in love with a mortal boy, Ganymede, and took him to live with him in Mt. Olympus. Zeus is sometimes shown as an eagle or a swan." She waited for me to explain my out of left field query.

"So, basically Zeus was a pedophile and Ganymede was his boy toy?"

"That's one way of putting it. But the ancient Greeks thought that a relationship between an older man and an adolescent boy was a good thing. Leah, what—"

"I'm sure that's what Palmer and his St. Lucian Boys tell themselves. They're not sick predators. No, they're wise mentors to young boys, like the ancient Greeks. This eagle Lacey drew. It's rougher, not as detailed, but still it looks a lot like the one in a pencil sketch of Zeus and Ganymede that Palmer has in his office. He has the same statue at his summer home."

"But why did Lacey sketch the eagle? And how would she know Palmer had the drawing in his office?"

"She was in there for almost half an hour when Palmer "rescued" her from the scene with the kid who flipped out the morning she was waiting to see Sister Julianna. Palmer's sketch is very good. It would have caught her eye. It did mine."

I paused lost in thought. Lacey loved the hand-drawn Christmas cards my mom's friend Adrienne sent every year. Adrienne always cleverly concealed her name somewhere in the picture—in the mane of a horse, the bark of a tree, the curl of a wisp of smoke—the feathers of a bird.

"Remember how Lacey loved to find the hidden letters in Adrienne's cards? You and I missed them half the time, but Lacey could always see them."

"Yes, but—"

I took the sketch pad from her hand and stared at it, willing my eyes to see what had to be there. After a few seconds letters and numbers began to disentangle themselves from the shadows and hatch marks that made up the eagle's feathers. I grabbed a pen and frantically wrote them down.

"Leah, what are you doing? What do you see?"

I shook my head, intent on my task, searching carefully to make sure I had found them all. Then I looked at what I had written and groaned in frustration.

"What's the matter?"

I shoved the paper over to my mother. She read it out loud.

"4PzsLBe?.onion. What is this, Leah?"

"I thought it was going to be the URL for Palmer's pornography site, but it doesn't make any sense. The domain should be ".com," or ".net," or ".org," or something like that. I've never heard of ".onion" as a domain. This can't be right. We're back to nowhere." I slumped down on the bar stool.

"Just try it, see what happens," my mother said.

"It's not going to work, Mom. There's no kind of address like this, or else it's some kind of code. And Lacey was the word game code breaker, not me." I sat mired in frustration and self-pity for a minute before my mother spoke. When she did, it shook me up.

"Leah, think about Lacey sitting there alone in Palmer's office. Wondering if Sister Julianna was on to her plan to get Danny out, probably scared out of her mind. She notices Palmer's sketch. Goes over to look at it to distract herself. Then she sees it, the numbers, recognizes it's a web address. She starts a quick sketch, not knowing when he'll be coming back, roughing out the bird, inserting the letters and numbers, maybe finishing it just before she hears him coming down the hall.

"It's the key to everything, Leah, it has to be. It's what she was saying when she called you that night. Not 'legal,' she was saying 'eagle.' She trusted you, and I trust you, Leah. You can figure this out. You've come all this way on your own, but Lacey's with you now, you know that, don't you?" She had gripped my arm and was holding so tightly it hurt.

I don't share my mother's faith in the belief that our dead continue as benevolent presences in our lives, watching or encouraging us from afar— or at least I didn't used to—but I knew she was at least partly right. Lacey had trusted me. And the answer was here somewhere for me to find.

I got my laptop, and I typed the URL in my browser. Nothing. "Cannot find." I tried a browser with a different search engine. This one brought up a list of sites for *The Onion* a satirical newspaper, and recipes for onion rings, and nothing remotely related to perverted sex sites. I tried inserting http// in front of the string of letters. Still nothing.

"Nothing. I am so sick of this!"

My cell phone rang. My mother picked it up and glanced at the caller ID.

"It's your friend Ben."

Ben. I'd forgotten all about him. He called when? Was it really only two days ago?

"Hi, Ben."

"Leah. I've been trying to get hold of you." His voice was tight and clipped.

"I meant to call, but a lot's been happening. Look, I have to call you back I—"

"I wasn't sure you got my message. But after talking to Miller this morning, I'm pretty sure you did. Leah, you seriously thought I stole your phone and tried to set you up? What the hell?"

I didn't have time for this.

"Listen, Ben, I'm trying to find out who killed my sister. Someone pushed me off a cliff the other day, I got fired from my job, and the one thing I was counting on to give me the answers turned out to be a bust. I can't deal with your hurt feelings right now. I'm sorry I suspected you. Truly. I was misinformed. Now, I've got to—"

"Wait, wait, hold on! Don't hang up. Is that for real? Someone tried to kill you?"

"It's not the next freaking installment of *Scandal*. Yes, it's real."

"What were you counting on to give you answers?"

"A URL. Really, Ben, I have to go."

"Wait, maybe I can help."

"How?"

"What do you mean the URL doesn't work?"

"I typed it in, and it goes nowhere. I've never seen one like it before. It ends in .onion. I think it might be some kind of code."

"Did you try the dark web?"

"Dark web? That sounds like something Harry Potter would get caught in."

"No, I'm serious. If your URL ends in .onion, Google won't get you there. You need to download the Tor browser."

"I don't have any idea what you're talking about, but I need your help. Now."

To his credit, he didn't ask for any more explanation than that.

"What's your address?"

I gave it to him, hung up, and turned to my mother.

"Ben said the URL is part of some, I don't know, underground web or something that you can't get to just Googling. He's going to come over and show me what to do."

When his car pulled in the drive, I was waiting with my laptop open on the bar. If he was startled to hear "Puttin' On the Ritz" as he rang the door-bell, he didn't show it.

"Ben. Hi, c'mon in."

I took him into the kitchen.

"Mom, this is Ben. Ben, this my mother, Carol Nash. Here's the address."

"Good to meet you, Ben. You can see we're a little anxious to get started."

"No problem. I'm glad to help if I can."

"What about the URL?"

He glanced quickly at the paper I'd thrust under his nose. "All right, yeah, that's part of the Tor network, I'm sure. The first thing to do is down-load the Tor browser on your laptop."

"What does that even mean?"

"Like I started to tell you on the phone, the web most people use every day only accounts for a small percentage of what's out there on the Inter-net. The dark web or deep web—some people call it the invisible web—is a huge storehouse of information that's not accessible to regular search engines."

"Why not?"

He had pulled up a stool next to me and was already tapping on the keyboard, checking security configurations and my computer's RAM and storage capacity while he talked. My mother hovered on the other side of the bar.

"Search engines send out spiders—essentially roving algorithms—that constantly scan the web, indexing pages. When you type in a query, the engine matches your query with its indexed pages on the topic and gives you a list of sites to choose from. But any password-protected sites, or private networks, or paywalled content, or pages without hyperlinks—anything like that won't show up when you do a search, because the spiders can't index them.

"That's where the dark web content lives. Most of it's benign and boring. Academic databases, scholarly research, directories, raw data, stuff like that. But some of it isn't. There's criminal activity going on there too—like selling drugs and guns and pornography, and it can all be done anonymously using the Tor network."

"How?"

"When you use the Tor browser, basically, you're assigned a false identity. Your search is routed through dozens of computers in sites all over the world. Your real identity is buried under so many layers, it becomes impossible to find you. That's where the .onion domain came from—Tor hides you behind layers, like the layers of an onion."

He had continued typing and now he turned the computer to face me and said, "There. I downloaded Tor, that should let you find this address. Go ahead."

I looked at the paper, typed it in and waited expectantly.

"Damn it!"

"What's the matter?"

I turned the laptop around so my mother could see the screen. A little box blinked politely, asking me to please enter the password.

I flipped it over to Ben.

"You don't have any idea what the password could be?" he said.

"None. I don't suppose you're a code breaker as well as an IT consultant, are you?"

"Sorry."

"Me, too."

Ben's face was crestfallen, and I realized I hadn't been as gracious as I could have been, given that he'd dropped everything and come over to help, no questions asked.

"It's OK, Ben, I'll just have to come at it from another direction. But thanks for your help. And for the dark web lesson."

"I could stick around, see if we could play with it a bit. Maybe we'd come up with that new direction for you."

"No, thanks anyway. I need some time to think this out."

"But you haven't told me what's really going on."

"I can't." I stood up. "Thanks again, Ben."

"Well, OK," he said, standing finally and moving toward the door as I all but pushed him there. He seemed surprised, but then a guy who looked like him probably didn't get shoved aside very often.

"Ben, thanks so much for your help," my mother said, adding her own polite verbal nudge.

"Yeah. Sure. Call me if I can do anything."

38

"OK, OK, Mom," I said when he left. "Help me think. What do people use for passwords? Birthdays, anniversaries, their mother's maiden name ... none of which we know for Palmer."

"What about a pet?"

"As far as I know he doesn't have one."

I sat staring morosely at the blank screen on my computer. And then I turned to her.

"Mom, maybe it has something to do with the eagle. That's why Lacey didn't just write the URL down, she replicated the eagle sketch because both things were part of it—the URL was hidden, and the eagle is the password!"

I opened the Tor browser and typed in the dark web URL again. When I reached the password box I typed Eagle. Nothing. OK, just a setback. I started on a round of variations. EagleGanymede, EagleZeus, ZeusEagle, GanymedeEagle. Nothing. ZeusGanymede. GanymedeZeus. All caps. All lower case. Alternating upper and lower case. Nothing. Nothing. Nothing. It had to work. But it didn't. My brilliant idea was a bust.

I started to exit the site in defeat. Then, though I never told my mother this, I heard a password in my head as clearly as if Lacey were whispering it in my ear. I typed SLBeagleganymede1978.

Bingo. I was in. And immediately wished I was out. The screen was filled with thumbnail images of boys and men in various states of arousal, engaged in a variety of sexual positions. A click on any one led to video footage. Most of the boys looked to be between 10 and 14. Their faces were clearly visible. However, the men, who seemed to be mostly middle-aged, judging by the flabby muscles and sagging posteriors, had their backs to the camera, or their faces blocked, or were so far out of the center of the frame that it was impossible to identify them.

My mother came up behind me, and I heard her gasp. I kept checking video, hoping for something that would connect with Palmer. I half-heard her cell phone ring, and after a few minutes she came back over and touched my shoulder.

"That was Paul. I forgot he offered to help me pack up more of the files. I just want to get done and out of that office. We were going to grab a late pizza when we finished. I told him to skip it tonight."

"What? No, Mom, seriously. The sooner you're done with everything to do with Karen, the better. Go ahead. I'm fine, there's nothing for you to do here, really. Call Paul back. Have him come and get you. There's no reason both of us have to make ourselves sick looking at this garbage."

"You'll be all right? You'll call Detective Ross, and tell him what you found? Or at least Coop?"

"Yes, absolutely. As soon as I really have a handle on this."

"I'll call Paul." I didn't hear any of her conversation, but a few minutes later she tapped me on the shoulder again.

"Paul's coming by to pick me up. Will you meet us later? Say around 10 at McClain's?"

"Mmmm, maybe. Depends on how long this takes me. Maybe I can grab something with Coop, when I fill him in. Who knows, I might still be going over files when you get back."

"Leah, you are going to turn this information over? You're not going to pursue this yourself?"

"Of course. I just—"

"I know. You just can't let go."

"It's not that, really."

"Yes. It is. Really. I've half a mind to call Coop myself."

"No! Mom, I'll call him. I will, all right? When I'm ready."

A horn tapped lightly in the driveway. She sighed. "I have to go. But if you don't call him, I will. This is too big and too dangerous for you to be playing around with on your own."

I nodded, but didn't look up as the door closed behind her. I turned back to the videos. After a few more minutes of viewing the sad, sick variations on a theme, I admitted the truth. Palmer was way too smart. I was not going to find anything on that site that would remotely link to him. I shut it down.

I had gone as far as I could. I had to turn over everything, I knew. I felt a pang about Danny—once Ross got onto him, there was scant hope he'd be able to hide his current life from his brother. But he was key to bringing down Palmer and the rest, maybe some of the St. Lucian's Boys as well.

I picked up my phone and hit Coop's speed dial number, but I got his voice mail. I didn't leave a message, instead I called Melanie to see where he was.

"He's over to a meeting with the prosecutor, then he's got a Law Enforcement banquet in Omico. He's not coming back in the office this afternoon. Did you try his cell?"

"Yeah, it went to voicemail. I'll just text him later."

"Hey, after Miller's press conference this morning, it looks like you're not the big story anymore. Think you'll get your job back?"

"I don't know, Melanie. I really don't know." In truth, I hadn't thought about it at all. The stalking fiasco was the last straw for Max, but he'd been building up a steady list of my offenses for a while. Maybe the fact that I wasn't guilty wouldn't matter that much to him. "Well, I gotta go. I'll catch you later."

I tried to imagine what Coop would say when I told him about the site. I tried to address all of Ross's potential objections. The voices on the MP3 player could be anybody. My star witness was, by my own admission, a teenage hustler.

The dark website was real. They might even be able to identify DeMoss boys on it, but there was no other connection to Palmer or Sister Julianna.

If I was right, and Lacey picked the address out of the sketch in Palmer's office, that would be a direct connection, provided I could get the original.

And really, why couldn't I?

39

OK, I probably shouldn't steal the sketch. Palmer would notice that immediately. But I could get a good photo of it, sitting on the shelf in his office.
Good enough so a person could pick out the numbers and letters. If they
were there. They had to be there. An idea took shape. I made a quick phone
call and got the information I needed. Then I paced back and forth down
the hall between the kitchen and my room, waiting for darkness to fall.

Finally, a little after 9, I left a note for my mother telling her that after
viewing all that filth, I needed to get out in the open air. I was going for a
drive to think and clear my head. And not to worry. I might stop by Coop's
before I came home. That way, by the time she started to worry, I'd be back.
I had to take her car, though, because she'd blocked me in.

I grabbed the lanyard with her car key from the hook by the door and
put it around my neck, then hopped in her Prius and took off. My plan was
simple, and if I was lucky, easy. I would enter the Catherines' property at
the Baylor Road entrance and park at the Rock, the same spot where Lacey
had met Cole. Then I'd walk down the road, which was little more than a
track, to the administration building. As long as Sister Margaret hadn't
been busted yet for leaving her window open "for a bit of fresh air," I
should be able to slide into the building that way.

I cut the lights as I left the main road. I pulled in next to Simon's Rock and turned off the car. The night was cloudy and cool and it was lightly sprinkling. I looked at my watch as I started out. I thought about Danny, shivering there as the night turned cold, and the snow fell along with his hopes, as he slowly came to believe that Lacey had abandoned him. I pictured Lacey hurrying along the trail, black hair flying behind her, determined to get Danny out, not realizing she was running toward the last few minutes of her life.

I felt a fresh surge of anger. Anger that my smart, brave sister and a scared little boy were crushed by that triad of ruthless hypocrites. The fury powered me forward so that I practically flew down the unfamiliar terrain. The bony fingers of slender branches caught in my hair and snapped on my cheeks. I flung them away impatiently. Something small and furry darted in front of me and I jerked, my heart thumping. I flashed my light, and it scurried into the bushes.

When I reached the building, I checked my watch again. Twelve minutes—and I was really hustling. It would have taken Lacey at least that long. I surveyed the scene. Security lights in the drive lit the front of the building, and in the rear more illuminated a small parking lot for staff. Darmody's brother, Delbert, a security guard at DeMoss, had happily divulged his entire nightly routine when I called him earlier.

Guards walked the perimeter of the campus, checked doors of the main buildings—academic, counseling center, library—every two hours, starting at 9. By 9:30, they were back in the maintenance building watching video feed from the newly installed security cameras and eating junk from the vending machine. He didn't question why I was asking. He even volunteered the location of the security cameras.

It was just ten o'clock, so I had over an hour before a guard was due. And I knew just where to go. The security camera in the back of the building was mounted on a light pole and aimed at the back entrance. I wasn't planning on using the back door, and as long as I didn't cross in front of it on my way to Sister Margaret's secret window, I should be golden.

I slipped around the back, staying close to the wall. Sister Margaret's window, cracked just a few inches, was well away from the security cameras. Keeping my body pressed along the side of the building, wary of motion sensor lights Delbert may have neglected to mention, I crept to the opening. The sash lifted easily and silently, no doubt from regular illicit use by Sister Margaret.

I tossed my flashlight through but getting in myself took a little more effort. Even opened as far as it would go, the window was small and required some origami-like body folding and flattening. For a few minutes, it looked like I might be found lodged half-in and half-out during the next security guard rounds. I gave a final desperate push with the leg I'd managed to get onto the floor, and that popped me through like a cork shooting out of a bottle. I landed in a heap and added yoga classes to my mental list of future fitness activities.

I picked up my flashlight and paused in the doorway. My breathing and the thumping of my heart were the only sounds. I moved forward out of the small copy room and patted Sister Margaret's chair for luck as I passed it on my way to Palmer's office.

I'd come prepared to jimmy his office lock with a credit card trick that a source once taught me. No need. Not only was Palmer's door not locked, it wasn't even shut. Arrogant bastard. As though no one would dare violate his sacred space. No ambient light from the parking lot or plugged in electronics relieved the cave-like blackness of his office.

I took a couple of steps inside and shined the beam of my flashlight on the far end of the room. There it was. The eagle sketch sitting on its easel. I hurried over, grabbed it and focused the flashlight on it. I stared at it with single-minded concentration, until gradually the distractions of the dozens of fine lines, cross-hatching and shadows fell away, and the numbers and letters of the deep website came into clear view.

I dug my phone out of my pocket. Took a second to double check that the ringer was off. Then I set my flashlight on the shelf and angled it toward the picture. I zoomed in and took a shot. Not great, but I could make out the letters. I zoomed out and took another shot that showed the sketch sitting on the shelf with the rest of Palmer's tchotchkes to put it firmly in context. For good measure, I emailed the pictures to myself and copied in Miguel.

I turned to leave the office. My eyes were hit with a blinding flash as the overhead light flicked on. I was still blinking and squinting when Sister Julianna said, "Hello, Leah. I'm surprised to see you. Especially since Reid is in no condition to visit."

She nodded her head to the left, and I turned in the direction of what had been the darkest corner of the office when I entered. Sitting at his desk was Reid Palmer. And he was very, very dead.

I couldn't take my eyes away from the gaping hole in his head, out of which oozed blood and brain matter, or from the spattered wall behind him. I swallowed back a sudden urge to throw up.

"Leah, do you feel faint? Help her, Sean." I turned and saw that Hegl was standing in the doorway as well.

I waved him away, and shook my head. "I'm all right. What happened?"

"Isn't it obvious? Reid has committed suicide. After leaving a note confessing to heinous crimes. Including killing your sister and engaging in pedophilia with some of our most troubled students. It's truly shocking."

I wasn't firing on all cylinders. "Palmer confessed? How? Why?"

"Well, I think you have to take some of the credit, Leah. Your relentless pursuit of your sister's death really put a great deal of pressure on him. He was extremely depressed and despondent and apparently—at least according to his note—he had a great deal to answer for."

"Wait a minute, wait a minute. You're saying that Palmer was responsible for everything?"

"Who else?" It was then I saw the glint of mockery in her eyes and realized just how much trouble I was in. Did she know I'd pieced together everything—including her embezzlement?

"I know I shouldn't be here—"

"No, but you seem to make a habit of being places where you shouldn't be. I wonder, what were you looking for in Reid's office?"

When there's no other option, the truth will sometimes work. "I was trying to find something incriminating on Palmer."

"And did you?"

"No."

"I see."

"Aren't you going to call the police?"

"Yes, certainly. Just not this very moment." She inclined her head slightly, as though making up her mind about something, then said, "Sean, let's take Leah to the reception area. We all need to get away from this office."

I had no choice but to move down the hall with them. When we got to reception, Sister Julianna stopped and turned to face both of us. "Leah, where is your car?"

"I parked by Simon's Rock and walked from there."

"I see. Sean, walk Leah back to her car, would you? Then I think you should drive her home. She's had a very upsetting evening. I'll follow and bring you back."

I didn't care for the look that passed between them at all. Sister Julianna seemed perfectly normal, clear-eyed and calm. Hegl was another matter. He'd had at least a fortifying shot of whiskey not too long ago, judging from his breath. The sour odor that wafted from him spoke of recent heavy drinking, as his red-rimmed eyes did of sleepless nights. He was wearing jeans and a Henley t-shirt that looked and smelled as though it had been pulled from the bottom of a laundry basket.

"That's OK, I'm fine. I don't need a ride."

"Nonsense. It's very late, and you've had a shock. I insist."

"No. Really. I don't." I made a fast break for the front door. I thought if I could reach it, I might be able to set off the alarm. But hung over or not, Hegl was fast on his feet. He grabbed me roughly by the arm and yanked me back.

"Leah, don't make it so hard for us to help you."

"Sister, I'm not the only one who knows what's been going on here. I've talked to other people."

"I'm well aware, Leah. I told you Reid was driven to his death by your hounding. Not that he didn't have a great deal to answer for. The confessions in his suicide note are horrifying."

I tried to keep her talking, playing for time until I could think of some way out of this.

"Sister Margaret was right. You really did set up the appointment to ask Lacey to sing, but she got spooked after being in Palmer's office and took off. Later, after Palmer killed her, you made up the story about her using drugs again, and the missing money, to make it seem more plausible that she ran away."

"Really, Leah. You should try your hand at fiction. Mysteries or suspense thrillers perhaps. But I'm intrigued. Do go on."

"At first I thought that Sister Mattea was killed because she knew who killed Lacey. But that wasn't it at all. She was killed because she found out about your embezzling. Palmer knew too, didn't he? And about your gambling. And you knew about his young boys. He covered for you, and you found boys for him, isn't that right?"

"Absolutely not."

"You killed Sister Mattea. You pushed her off the bluff."

"I didn't kill Sister Mattea. You should harness that imagination of yours. It's going to get you into trouble someday. We need to go, Sean."

She reached behind Sister Margaret's desk and hit a few buttons on a keypad, presumably disarming the front door. Hegl had my arm pinned up against my side, and he marched me roughly out the door.

"Sean, I'll wait for you at the Baylor Road entrance. We'll be taking River Road."

"That's not the way to town," I said, though I already knew they had no intention of taking me home. "The police are reinvestigating. They've got the statue. You won't get away with this."

She looked at me then and smiled. "It's a long shot, I agree, Leah. But as the saying goes, you'll always miss 100% of the shots you don't take. Goodbye." She stepped up into her black SUV and was off on the road leading out of the campus.

40

A car accident on River Road may not have been the original plan for getting me out of the way, but it wasn't bad improvising. The lanes are narrow, the curves are poorly marked, and the puny wooden guard rails wouldn't stop a bicycle, let alone a car. Accidents happen fairly often. And everyone knew how stressed I was, how tired, how bad my judgment had been. And I had so thoughtfully laid the groundwork by lying to my mother about going for a long drive to clear my head. Another tragic accident in the making.

Hegl yanked me along the trail, and I struggled to keep up with his long strides. Why had Sister Julianna allied with him? He seemed more logical as the fall guy than Palmer. Maybe she was tired of Palmer running the show. Maybe she wanted someone she'd have under her thumb. So, she persuaded Hegl to turn on Palmer. His death and the fake suicide note would save them.

But maybe not. Because in choosing Hegl, Sister Julianna disregarded one of the hard truths of life: you can't manage stupid. And Hegl's inability to control his appetites rendered him stupid.

The rain was coming down steadily as Hegl and I reached Simon's Rock. He pushed me up to the car, staying close behind me, then released my arm so I could open the door.

I brought both elbows down hard and back and jabbed him in the stomach. He wasn't prepared, and it knocked the wind out of him. I turned and ran toward the woods, thinking I had a better chance there than on the main road, where by now Sister Julianna would be waiting.

I only got 20 yards or so before my legs were jerked out from under me. I landed on the muddy ground face first and felt the pressure of something hard and cold in my back. I lifted my head and turned my neck. Hegl was leaning over me, pushing something into the small of my back. He had a gun.

"Get up!"

I moved slowly onto my hands and knees, then lifted my hand to rub my throbbing jaw. "Get up!" he yelled a second time.

"Get the damn gun out of my back so I can stand up."

He took a step back, but the gun was still pointed at me as I struggled to my feet. He waved me toward the car.

I used to wonder why victims ever obeyed their killer's orders to get in the car, or walk to the edge of the cliff, or kneel and raise their hands, when clearly, they were going to be murdered no matter what they did. Why make it easier?

But walking at gunpoint to the driver's side of my car, I finally got it. Because every fraction of time I bought with my compliance was a minute, or a second, or a millisecond when I wasn't dead. And if I wasn't dead, I still had a chance to figure out how to stay alive.

So, I did as Hegl said, and I got behind the wheel.

"Start the car."

I pushed on the starter button, and then turned on the lights and wipers. The rain was coming down so hard it looked like someone was throwing buckets of water at the windshield. His cell phone rang, and he dug it out with difficulty while keeping the gun trained on me. Sister Julianna gave him specifics on our ride in the country.

"Where are we going?" I asked.

"Drive out to Baylor. Keep going until you get to River Road."

I backed up, did a three-point turn, and drove the short distance to the Baylor Road entrance. Sister Julianna's black SUV was waiting on the shoulder. I braked and hesitated, then felt the nudge of the gun in my ribs.

"Go on. And don't try anything."

"I wasn't. I just didn't know if she wanted me to go first or follow her," I said in a small voice to convey that I'd given up, and I was putty in his shaky hands. We pulled out, and Sister Julianna followed. Baylor Road was fairly straight, but once we turned onto River, things were going to get interesting.

The question was, where did they plan to do it? My guess was the overlook. It would be easy enough to have me park the car with the engine running. A knock on the back of the head to put me out, a good push and it would be too bad, so sad, Leah must have driven off the road and drowned.

I stole a glance at Hegl. He was on the ragged edge. The gun was in his lap, his trembling hand still clutching it.

"How far are we going?"

"Until I tell you to stop."

"All right, I was just wondering." I was silent for a few seconds, then I gambled on the one thing I was sure of. Hegl was the weak link. This was my only chance to break it.

"You know, Father Hegl, I realize now, everything that's happened, none of it was your fault." It almost gagged me to give him the honorific 'Father,' but I wanted to convey a respect and sympathy I didn't feel and remind him just a little of what he was *supposed* to be. He didn't say anything, so I continued.

"I know you didn't want Olivia to die. And I know you didn't mean to hurt Lacey either. I understand that now." I waited.

"I didn't want anyone to get hurt. I didn't."

"But you haven't done anything, not really. Palmer made you hurt Lacey. He found you there, didn't he, the night you were with Delite? Then Lacey came in and she...." I trailed off, hoping he'd fill in the blank space. He did, talking fast as though the words had been damned up inside for a long time.

"She was stealing the car keys. Reid said he'd call the police. She said she knew about Danny, and she had proof. Then she kicked him hard, trying to get away. He went crazy. It wasn't me. He went crazy." He was still pointing the gun, but his hand was shaking so much I was afraid it might go off by accident.

"What happened then? What did Palmer do?"

"He took the statue, and he smashed her. He hit her so hard, she fell and she didn't get up."

My eyes filled with tears, but I had to keep going. I had to try and turn him. "Father Hegl, who took Lacey to the woods? Was it you?"

"Reid erased her phone. Sister Julianna brought the Vicodin to put in her purse and the empty liquor bottle, so it would look like she was drunk and fell. She said we should say money was missing, so the police would think Lacey stole it to run away. They made me take the four-wheeler to dump her body. It wasn't me. I didn't want to do it. But Reid said he'd recant his story about me having dinner with him and my uncle the night Olivia died. It wasn't my fault. None of this is my fault."

"What about the statue?"

"Reid told me to hide it in my collection for a while, then later get rid of it."

"Why didn't you?"

"I forgot about it."

I almost lost it then. That narcissist could sit in his living room across from the piece of marble that had crushed my sister's skull, and not have one moment's discomfort because he "forgot about it."

"Why did you have Delite lie for you?"

"To give us more protection when they found the body. I thought if she came forward the police wouldn't look any farther. And they didn't. Reid and Sister Julianna weren't happy. They didn't trust her. But it was fine until you started poking around."

His hand steadied a little. So did his voice. This wasn't going like I hoped. He wasn't swinging to my side. He was focusing his anger on me.

"Did Sister Julianna make you kill Palmer?"

"Quit asking questions."

"She did, didn't she? She told you he could be the fall guy. But don't you get it, Father? You're going to be the fall guy."

His brain, dulled by anxiety, alcohol and fear, was slow to process what I was saying. I glanced in the rearview mirror. Sister Julianna was a good fifty yards behind us. We had reached River Road. I had no choice. I turned.

"We'll be at the overlook soon. That's where she told you to do it, isn't it?

What's the plan? Have me park the car? Hit me in the head like Palmer did Lacey? You going to shove my car over and watch me drown?"

He shook his head slowly and raised one hand, swatting at the air as though trying to still the buzz of my angry questions like a bear trying to rid himself of angry bees. I pressed on, but changed my tone.

"Father, don't let yourself get dragged any further into this mess. You can still get out of this. It's all on Palmer and Sister Julianna. And now she's going to put it on you. Don't you see? She's not going to let you go. She can't afford to."

The rain had lessened to a light patter, but I could see thin wisps of fog starting to curl around the edges of bushes and trees.

He tightened his grip on the gun, and I knew I had lost him. He was too cowed by her, too befuddled by fear and guilt. He couldn't do anything but what she planned for him. My hands were sweating on the wheel. I was running out of time. We were nearly at the overlook.

"Slow down. Pull over here."

As I started to brake, I looked in the mirror again. Coming very fast toward us was Sister Julianna's SUV. She was rolling the dice again, betting on taking us both out at once. She wasn't going to give Hegl time to make trouble. She was sending him over the edge with me. The big heavy vehicle banged into the back of my mother's car and sent us hurtling through the guard rail and out into space like Thelma and Louise.

For an instant, we were suspended in midair. Then we dropped, hitting the water with a huge splash. The airbag deployed and I took a solid punch in the face. It deflated immediately. We were still floating when I hit the button to lower the window. The car started filling with water. I lifted the latch on my belt, but instead of retracting, the thick nylon restraint refused to budge. I tugged, and as I struggled, Hegl slipped out the window and into the river.

The water was up to my waist, but instead of seeing my life pass before me, I saw my mother standing in the kitchen, extolling the virtues of her lanyard. I grabbed at my neck for the mini Swiss Army knife. I tugged so hard it came right off the cord.

My fingers fumbled as I tried to pull out the blade. My breath came in short gasps. Cold water rose to my armpits, and the car rocked in the current. With a last urgent tug, I got the blade free, but the knife flew out of my hand.

Frantic, I flailed with my arms underwater, on the seat, between my legs; it wasn't there. The hood of the car began to tilt forward. *Where the hell was that knife?* I took a last gulp of air before the water rushed past my head, and the car began to nosedive. I felt something bump against my hand. The downward motion had dislodged the knife from whatever cranny it had settled in. My fingers reflexively curled around it, and I grabbed it blade first into my palm. I turned it over. With two desperate strokes, I cut the strap and pulled it free.

I thrust my arm out to the side. My hand felt the window frame. With fear-fueled strength, I pushed myself through and started furiously kicking my legs and clawing through the water. My lungs were screaming to exhale. I broke the surface wild for oxygen. I blew out the pent-up air in my lungs and took a big breath.

Treading water, I fought the current as I tried to orient myself and regulate my breath. Hegl was nowhere in sight. I was alone, and not getting any warmer or stronger in the fifty-degree water.

Then I saw a flash of lights, white at first, then red and blue. It had to be cars on the River Road. Police too. Someone had called in the "accident."

I struck out for shore with a shaky crawl. The Himmel River is deep, but not very wide at that point. I kept repeating my survival mantra—it's less then 100 yards, it's less than 70 yards, it's less than 50…

With each stroke, my arms got weaker. My legs were barely kicking, and the urge to keep going was fading. I felt so weak. And so cold. If I could just rest. From a distance, I heard voices.

Was that in my head, or was it real? It was just too hard to lift my face out of the water. I took in a gulp of river instead of air.

I started to choke. I wanted to shout for help, but my throat was seizing up. I couldn't breathe.

My body bobbed straight up and down for a second. I began to sink as a bright white light washed over me.

41

When I came to, puking and coughing, I was on the shore, sharp rocks cutting into my back. My eyes flew open as someone rolled me on my side. My head was lifted. Fingers rammed into my mouth and did a sweep. That started a gag reflex, a fresh round of coughing, a little more puking. Either the white light I'd seen had been an emergency police floodlight, or heaven was not living up to its advance PR. I tried to talk, started choking again, and sank back down and out.

When I woke, I was in a dimly lit hospital room hooked up to a monitor and an IV. The equipment emitted soft, periodic beeps, and the blood pressure cuff on my arm inflated and deflated at regular intervals. For some reason, my hand was wrapped in a big white bandage. I thought I saw my mother, but I wasn't sure, and I was floating too high to ask. My eyelids fluttered back down.

The next time I opened them, sun was streaming through the window. My mother was seated beside the bed, her head down, her hand touching mine.

"Hey, what does a girl have to do to get some breakfast around here?" I croaked.

She squeezed my hand, and her eyes were bright with tears. "How about a late lunch instead? It's two o'clock."

"A drink of water would be great." She held a Styrofoam cup with a straw up to my lips. The cool water washing over my parched throat felt so good, I began gulping on the straw, until my mother moved it away. "Easy there, the nurse said a few sips when you woke up. You'll make yourself sick if you drink too fast."

"Mom," I began, "I'm sorry. I didn't—"

The door opened wide, and Miguel came bursting in, followed by Coop at a more measured pace.

"*Chica*! What am I gonna do with you! What were you thinking? Why did you go out there alone? What happened? You know Palmer is dead, right? You feel better now, yes?" He was fairly oscillating with pent-up anxiety as he stood next to my mother.

"How did anyone know where I was?"

Coop, who had come to stand by the other side of my bed, nodded in Miguel's direction. "You can thank your partner in crime."

I looked back at Miguel, who was smiling broadly. "I told you—there's no Frodo without Sam, no Lilo without Stitch –"

"OK, OK. Seriously. How did you know I was out there?"

"Your email. The eagle sketch. I called to ask *que démonios*! You know, what the heck is this? But you didn't answer. I knew you were awake, because you just emailed me. I called your *mamá's* landline and no one answered. So, I tracked your iPhone."

"You have a tracker on my phone?"

"No! Well, yes, a little. I activated the Find My iPhone app for you. After you got yours back."

"You can follow me with that? What are you, the NSA?"

He was unrepentant. "Are you going somewhere you shouldn't be, *chica*?"

"I think we know the answer to that is a big fat yes," my mother said.

"All right. We're losin' the thread here," Coop said. "The point is, Miguel got worried when he saw your phone was at the Catherines' at 10:30, then on River Road. He called me, and I called central dispatch and asked them to send a car over to that end of the county.

"A deputy got there just in time for Sister Julianna to pass him like a bat outa hell. He radioed in and kept going in the direction she'd just come from to see what was chasing her. He found the busted guardrail, and then saw your mom's car in the river, sinking fast."

"Yeah, about that, Mom – "

She shook her head. "We'll talk about that later. What I want to know is what were you thinking? Why did you go out there? How did you wind up in the river?"

I explained that I wanted to get the sketch as a tangible piece of evidence that linked Reid Palmer to the dark website, and how I stumbled onto Palmer's staged suicide.

"Hegl was supposed to drive me to the overlook—he thought he was going to push me over, but Sister Julianna double-crossed him and tried to take us both out. Did you get them both, Hegl and Julianna?"

"The deputy caught up with Sister Julianna as she was pulling into the Catherines' property. She's a cool one. She asked him to come with her, said she was worried about Reid Palmer. She was afraid that he might be planning to harm himself. She led him to Palmer's office. He was dead, complete with a suicide note admitting that he'd killed Lacey, was abusing boys from DeMoss, even that he'd been embezzling money."

"Go big or go home, I guess. She let it all ride on Palmer's number."

"She might have gotten away with it. If Hegl had died like he was supposed to, she could have made a case for him being in with Palmer and said that he'd abducted you at gunpoint. But her luck ran out. Hegl has the survival instincts of a ship rat. And you—" He stopped and shook his head.

"You know what they say. Weebles wobble but they don't fall down. How did you get Hegl?"

"He was stumbling around about a mile from where your car went in. Tried to get a ride from a car full of teenage girls. They called 911. When the deputies picked him up, he was pretty talkative."

"Did he confess? Did he tell you what they did to Lacey? Did he admit to killing Palmer? Who pushed me and Sister Mattea, him or Sister Julianna?"

"Hegl waived his right to an attorney. He admitted what happened the night Lacey died, but he wouldn't cop to pushing you or Sister Mattea off the bluff. Sister Julianna lawyered up right away, and so far, she's not talking. But I think her luck has pretty much run out. A player from one of the big casinos in Vegas saw her on the news. He had some interesting things to say about her gambling losses."

"I think *she's* the one that pushed me off the cliff. Then she tried it again at the overlook with her SUV. You know, if at first you don't succeed, try, try again. She probably pushed Sister Mattea, too. That asshat Hegl left me to drown. I couldn't get tht stupid seatbelt off. I hate to admit it Mom, but your lanyard saved my life. And the Grantland County EMTs."

"It wasn't an EMT who pulled you out of the water, Leah, it was Coop."

I didn't know what to say. To any of them.

"You know. I just. All of you. Well, thanks." I stumbled over the words. Why was it so easy for me to be a smartass and so hard to be real?

"Forget it," Coop said.

"No, *chica*, I want you to remember it. And don't go running off without me next time."

There was a light tap on the door. Ellie, Max, and Alex walked in.

"Hey you guys!" I felt a bubble of happiness rise at the sight of them. Max looked embarrassed, and Ellie was uncomfortable as she thrust a bouquet of flowers at me, but Alex ran right up and put a small packet on the bed.

"Leah! You're on TV! I saw you on Channel 9! Oh, wow!" He paused and examined me closely. "You look like a cage fighter. You got a black eye! And what happened to your hand?"

I looked down in surprise. I'd forgotten about the bandage, and with the pain killers I was on and the high of not being dead, my hand really didn't hurt. But I flashed on the water over my head, the frantic search for the knife. I shivered, but before I could answer, Ellie stepped up.

"Leah, I'm glad you're all right. And I'm sorry about Lacey, and that I was so hard on you. I know you were just doing what you had to for your family."

I felt awkward and ill at ease. Apologies usually affect me that way. "Never mind, Ellie. It's OK. It wasn't anything."

"Yeah, it was," Max interrupted, his voice gruff. "I'm sorry, too, Leah. I was just so uptight about the business and the bank. I didn't act much like a newsman. Or a friend."

This was getting excruciating. "No, it's OK. Forget it. We're good." I had to make it stop. "So, Alex, what's this you brought me?"

"It's a book I made. I thought you'd like to read it. It has stories about my family. Ancestors and stuff in it. We did them for school. The cover's awesome, isn't it?"

The hand-drawn cover featured a red-haired man with a superhero physique brandishing a sword, inscribed with the name McAllister, over his head. Next to him was an equally buff warrior woman wearing a crown emblazoned with the name Cameron.

"See, they're Scottish because my mom and my birth dad's families come from Scotland. That's their names. But look on the back." He flipped it over, and there was a picture of a sturdy looking man in short sleeves sitting at a computer.

"And that's my dad Max. He's a writer and that's what Schreiber means in German. Awesome, huh? So, there's some German stuff in there, too. It's pretty great."

"Alex! Don't brag."

"But, Mom, it is pretty great."

"That's right, *hombrecito*. Own your excellence!" said Miguel.

Alex started giggling and chanting, "Own your excellence." As Ellie tried to settle him down, I remembered something.

"Coop have you talked to Scott Riordan yet? He's been doing some accounting voodoo on the DeMoss books, and I think he's got proof that money was being embezzled. I asked him not to tip off Reid Palmer. He's not going to believe it when I call and tell him why."

"It's not my case, Leah. All that stuff is going to Ross. For the moment, anyway."

I latched on to the bone of hope he threw me.

"For the moment?"

"A joint investigation is in the works. And the Internet Crimes Against Children task force is in the picture now. The higher-ups have been fielding calls from the bishop—the local, not your guy in Florida. The media are going crazy. No way the sheriff's department is going to ride herd on this one. So be nice. Let Ross get his statement. He won't be the only one you'll be talking to, I'm sure. I'm kinda surprised he hasn't been here already."

And as if on cue the door opened, and we all looked up expectantly. But it wasn't Ross who walked into the room. Instead a slight young woman wearing blue hospital scrubs hesitated in the doorway, holding a tray which immediately held my attention.

"I'm sorry to interrupt. I'm just delivering some lunch?"

"I'm starving! Come in, please."

"We should get out of here and let you eat," Ellie said.

"Yeah, we should go, let you get some rest. I'll call you later, kid," Max said, patting me on the leg.

"Don't forget to read my book. You'll love it!" said Alex.

Coop and Miguel pulled up stakes as well, and I sent my mother down to the cafeteria. As the aide set up my tray, she introduced herself as Angela and got me fresh water.

"Your nurse will be in soon to change your dressing and check your vitals. Do you need anything else? Are you in pain?"

"Nope, I'm good, thanks, just hungry." I found it a little awkward to eat with my left hand, particularly since my meal consisted mainly of spoon-reliant foods—tomato soup and jello. She hung around waiting to make sure I could manage. Then, as she was leaving, Ross walked in.

"Nash."

"Ross."

"Hey, Angela!" I called to her retreating back. "Tell the nurse I need some pain medication, please."

42

They released me from the hospital the next morning with strong admonitions to stay home and take it easy for a few days. I wasn't inclined to argue. I was physically and mentally beat, my hand ached, and I was sporting some pretty spectacular bruising, not just the shiner that impressed Alex.

I tried to reach Scott Riordan the first day I was home, but he was out of town, and I had no more luck with Miss Adams than I had the first time I called. I kicked myself for not getting his cell phone number the last time we talked. But not too hard, in light of all my bruising.

What hurt worse than my injuries was having to sit back and see the story I'd uncovered reported on by other journalists. It irritated me that the 24/7 cable "news" channels spent more time on speculation and hype than on the facts. Though maybe I didn't have much room to complain. Reporters had called begging for interviews, but I didn't answer, and I didn't call them back, even though I itched to set the record straight. I knew it wasn't wise to start feeding the sharks.

On Friday, I assured my mother I would be fine, and after much protesting, she agreed to go with Paul to a Brewers game in Milwaukee. As they pulled out of the driveway, I got a call from Clinton Barnes.

Clinton was the one agent out of about a million I'd sent my book proposal to who had agreed to represent me. I hadn't heard anything from him for a while. But his last email had made me think he was just about to cut me loose, after a very tepid response from publishers to my proposal. But the DeMoss story reawakened his interest.

"You have the inside track, Leah—the journalist out to avenge her sister's death. You've got some really great stuff to work with—depraved millionaire, gambling nun, homicidal priest! Great stuff. And that dark web thing is a really on-fleek angle. It puts a new spin on the whole Catholic altar boy thing, which is getting a little tired, right? Anyway, I know I could sell your story. Do you think you could work up an outline, maybe a few chapters? There could be some serious money involved."

"What about my book on the Mandy Cleveland murder?"

"Oh, well, that's still out there, sweetheart. But this is the one that could really be epic. It's your story, your sister. You should be the one to tell it. What do you say?"

"I don't know, Clinton. I'll think about it."

"Don't wait too long. Somebody is going to write this book. It should be you!"

"I'll get back to you."

When I started out, I had no intention of writing a story, getting a scoop. I just wanted to find out what happened to Lacey. If I turned around and did it now, was I as much of an exploitative jerk as the hungry reporters that were driving me crazy? Or was I even worse, because she was my sister?

On the other hand, if I wrote the book, I could tell Lacey's real story. How smart she was, how brave. How because of her no more kids from DeMoss would be exploited by Palmer and his friends. Besides, if I didn't try to write it, what was my alternative? Callie Preston, the reporter I was filling in for, would be back from maternity leave in another few weeks, and then where would I be? It wasn't like I'd been fielding job offers.

I went to the kitchen and made a sandwich. On my way back to the living room, my eye fell on Alex's history of his family sitting on an end table. I knew I'd better read it while I was thinking about it, because there was no way he wasn't going to ask me for a reaction the next time I saw him.

It was typical Alex—research and writing skill beyond his years coupled with young-kid imagination and enthusiasm. His stories wove his ancestors into historical events in Scotland. Mixed in among actual family photos were Photoshopped pictures of Alex next to a fierce spear-wielding Scotsman in a kilt, and swimming with the Loch Ness monster.

A standard family tree showed no aunts, uncles or cousins. I hadn't realized both his parents were only children. I paused at a photo of his "real" dad, Ian McAllister. He had fiery red hair and bright blue eyes the same as Ellie had. His cocky grin reminded me of Alex.

My eyes began to droop. My need for sleep seemed to go up in inverse proportion to the amount of work I did. But what else did I have to do? I lay down on the couch and surrendered. I woke up when my phone rang. Finally, a return call from Scott Riordan.

"I just got back from Singapore. I've been reading some of the stories online. Is it true?"

"Most of it. Pedophilia, pornography, priests, gambling nuns—it's the stuff cable news dreams are made of."

"No wonder you didn't want me to contact Reid Palmer about the accounts."

"Scott, I asked before, but now that everything's come out, can you think of anything Sister Mattea—that is, your sister Teresa—said that might have been a hint about embezzling at DeMoss?"

"I've gone over it and over it since we talked, but honestly, Leah, I can't think of anything. All Teresa said was she wanted to bring the order into the 21st century. If she suspected anything, she didn't tell me. But then maybe she wouldn't have."

"Why's that?"

"Her membership in the Catherines was the one big thing in life we didn't agree on. If she was worried something wasn't on the up and up, maybe she thought I'd give her an I-told-you-so."

"You don't like the Catherines?"

"It's not the order in particular. I just don't have much use for organized religion in general. An order of nuns dressed up like something out of the Middle Ages it just seems, well, ridiculous to me."

"Obviously, your sister didn't feel that way."

"She used to. Neither of us grew up religious, but then 10 years or so ago she changed."

"Why was that?"

"I always thought it had something to do with a friend of hers. Elise."

"She was a nun?"

"No, no. It was, well, I guess it doesn't matter if I tell you the story now."

I waited for him to go on.

"Teresa had an abortion when she was 18. Our mother insisted. It was tough on her, but I thought she was OK with it. She never talked about it until years later when this nurse at the hospital where she worked had a baby that died.

"Then it was all Teresa could talk about—how unfair it was. How Elise had lost her husband in Iraq, and then her baby died, too. I mean, I was sympathetic. It was a sad story. But Teresa went off the deep end. All this guilt I didn't even know she had, shame, regret about her abortion—she just couldn't shake it. Even when Elise moved to Ohio, Teresa couldn't let it go."

"So, what happened?"

"She hooked up with the Catherines somehow, I don't remember exactly. Went to a retreat, and the next thing I knew she was signing up. She gave up her whole life—a great job at Regent Hospital in LA, friends, a nice guy she was dating. She just threw it all away to join some outdated cult."

"That's a little harsh."

"I know. You're right. She needed answers I didn't have. I guess she found them at the Catherines. As time went by, we sort of agreed to disagree. We just didn't talk about it when she came out to visit. Numbers make sense to me. Religion doesn't. But I had to accept that was her choice. That's why I agreed to donate the software, really. I wanted to show her that I respected her right to decide, even if I didn't agree."

"If it's any consolation, she seemed happy to me."

"Yeah, I think she was. And that's good." He was quiet for a second, then said, "There were just the two of us you know. Now there's just me. You'll let me know if you find out anything else?"

"Yes, sure, of course I will, but I'm pretty much out of it now. There's a big deal task force investigating everything to do with the Catherines, DeMoss, Reid Palmer. I'm sure someone will be talking to you soon."

Then he asked me the question I didn't have an answer for.

"Leah, if Teresa did know about the fraud and she mentioned it to someone there, is it possible that her death wasn't an accident?"

"I don't know, Scott. Any more than I know why she left me a note and an old newspaper clipping about my sister's death. And maybe we have to accept we'll never know."

I didn't feel near as Zen about things as I'd pretended to Scott. In truth, I couldn't stop thinking about the why. Everything else had fallen into place except that. Why, why, why had Sister Mattea left that note and that clipping for me? I hadn't turned up anything that linked her to Lacey or even to Palmer or Hegl.

I got up and vacuumed. I dusted. I loaded the dishwasher, and still I couldn't sit still. Something was nagging at me like an itch you can't reach, or a TV actor you can't place, or the words of a song you can't quite remember. I just couldn't settle down.

I went to my room and started cleaning up my files. My desk was a mess. I tend to favor a horizontal filing system—everything I'm working on spread across the top of my desk in little piles. But after a while, when the piles start to slide and the whole thing is in danger of landing on the floor, I have to do some re-ordering.

I picked up a fat folder, but it slipped out of my hand, scattering its contents on the rug. The clip Sister Mattea had given me was on top. It had landed with the grinning picture of Alex, Max and Ellie face up. They all looked so happy. I gazed at it for a long time. Then I put it down and got out my laptop.

An hour later the itch had been scratched, the actor recalled, the song lyric identified, but I didn't feel any better. I felt much, much worse.

43

I was still struggling with what to do when the doorbell rang.

"Max! What are you doing here?"

"Hey, aren't you glad to see me, kid? I brought you something." He held up a bottle of Jameson and one of ginger ale.

"What's the occasion?"

"A celebration. Because you're coming back to the *Times* Monday morning, I hope."

"Let me get a couple of glasses."

"I'll do it. I know where they are. You go take a load off. You've still got a coupla days special treatment comin.' "

A minute later he came into the living room carrying two drinks and handed me one before sitting on the couch opposite me. I took a sip even though I prefer my Jameson straight. Between the fizziness of the ginger ale and the strength of the drink, I started to cough.

"This is pretty stiff. How much whiskey did you put in here?"

"Just enough. You can handle it. Besides, I know you're not driving. I saw Carol and Paul leaving town for the Brewers game in your car."

I took another sip. It went down smoother this time.

"It'll be good having you on the job again, Leah. I talked to Callie today, now she wants to stay off the job until September. So, if you're willing? And for the record, I want to say again that Ellie and I, we both feel bad we gave you such a hard time....”

I couldn't stand it. I couldn't sit there and pretend I didn't know what I knew. Not to Max, not to one of my oldest friends.

“Max, there's something I need to ask you. I talked to Scott Riordan tonight. Then I did some research online and made a few phone calls.”

The color drained from his ruddy cheeks. He leaned forward and rubbed the cold glass in his hand across his forehead for a second before he said anything.

“Ah Christ, Leah. You know, don't you?”

I nodded.

“I was worried the other day, when you said you were going to talk to Riordan again. I was afraid you might turn up something. How did you figure it out?”

“I've had most of the pieces all along, but I didn't realize it until tonight. How could you think no one would find out?”

“No one did. For almost 10 years.”

“But then Sister Mattea saw the picture of the three of you.”

He nodded. “She recognized Ellie. Only she knew her as Elise. She knew her baby had died. And she knew a baby Alex's age had been taken outside a neighborhood bar in LA the same time that Ellie left town.”

“Did you always know about Alex?”

His big, heavy featured face crumpled.

“No. Not 'til a couple months ago. I came home for lunch one day and caught Ellie packing. She broke down, told me everything. How her baby died after Ian was killed. How she went numb. For days, she couldn't eat. Couldn't sleep. Couldn't get rid of the baby's stuff. Couldn't do anything but drive and drive and drive all over Los Angeles. Didn't matter where, she just had to be drivin.'

“One afternoon she stops for gas in this little neighborhood. Sees a woman pull up and park across the street. Ellie goes into the convenience store to buy some water, and when she comes out she hears a baby crying. The sound is coming from the woman's car. Nobody else is on the street. She walks over to check.

“The rear window is open, but it's so hot that day the door almost burns her hand when she touches it. This little guy is wet and dirty and cryin.' his lungs out. She reaches in and picks him up, and he just grabs on her finger and looks right at her and stops crying. She can't let go. She takes him. Goes back to her apartment, packs everything up and leaves that night."

"But how did she explain having the baby when hers had died?"

"She didn't tell her aunt when her baby died. She couldn't bring herself to talk about it. Then when she gets Alex she calls and says she's on her way, that her baby had a few problems but he was ready to travel. She got to Ohio, and Alex was her baby. He still is. He's our son, our Alex. You get that, don't you, Leah? Nobody could love that boy like we do. That woman Ellie rescued him from, she didn't deserve to have a baby. You see, you understand, don't you?"

The anxious plea in his voice cut me to the heart.

"But, Max, Ellie stole another mother's baby."

"That woman left him in a hot car in the middle of the summer while she went into a bar. He could have died if Ellie hadn't saved him."

"What happened when Sister Mattea contacted Ellie?"

"She said she knew that she was really Elise, that Alex wasn't her son. Ellie panicked, but then she asked to meet with Sister Mattea to explain and talk things through. Sister Mattea agreed, but Ellie wasn't going to meet with her. She was just going to run.

"That's when I walked in on her packing to leave. I convinced her to stay. I told her that she and Alex were the world to me, and I'd walk away from everything else in a heartbeat, if we had to. But I thought I could explain things to Sister Mattea, so she'd understand. I convinced Ellie to wait. That day Sister Mattea came into the paper to see you, I set up a meeting with her early at the Point where no one would see us."

I knew what was coming next.

"When we met, I tried every way I could think of to get her to back off. I told her if there is a God, he gave Ellie and Alex to each other. They saved each other. I told her how happy he was, what a great job Ellie had done as his mother, how much better his life was. But she said it didn't matter. It wasn't right for Ellie to take Alex away from his real mother. And nothing good could come from it."

He stopped and took a drink from his glass, then looked at me steadily. "She was wrong, Leah. Everything good in my life came from that."

I thought about the other mother, the one who had come out to her car and found her baby gone. But I didn't say anything, just let Max keep talking.

"I told her it would kill Ellie to lose him. It would be even worse than when her baby died. She said she was sorry. That she'd help us in any way she could. Help? She was the one destroying our lives.

"We were out at the edge of the bluff. No one else was around. I put my hand on her arm just to make a point. She stumbled and lost her balance. It was muddy there, and she slid. She grabbed onto a bush at the edge. I reached for her, but she slipped again and I missed. She was hanging over the side, kicking with her legs. I stretched out to take her hand. But then I stopped. I didn't push her. But I watched her fall."

The words were devastating to hear. I imagined Sister Mattea, begging for help, struggling, terrified, then falling, falling, falling.

I said in a flat tone, "I thought it was Ellie. That night on the bluff, I smelled her cologne. Like grass and spring. But Alex made it for both of you. It was you, Max. You pushed me that night after the race, didn't you?"

"I asked you not to make me do something I didn't want to do. I warned you over and over, but you just kept pushing with Lacey and what did Sister Mattea want to tell you. I knew you wouldn't ever let go. You were getting too close. I couldn't let you find out."

"Does Ellie know what you did?"

He shook his head. "I told her that Sister Mattea agreed not to tell. That she must have fallen after I left. She doesn't know about your accident either. No one has to know, Leah. It's done."

I took a long drink. Maybe it was the Jameson, or maybe it was the surreal quality of the conversation, but my head was starting to feel fuzzy.

"I knew, but I didn't know, Max. There were all these shiny little pieces, like a kaleidoscope. You lied about your tire. You said you were late that morning Sister Mattea died because you were changing a flat. But you couldn't have changed it because you didn't have a spare. Cole told me it was at Jorgenson's for months."

I paused. I knew the words I wanted to say, but I was having trouble getting them out.

"Leah?" he prodded, his voice coming from a distance.

"Ian had O negative blood. Mom said she and Ellie were at the blood drive, because they were both O negative. Alex's blood is B positive. Two O negative parents can't have a B positive child. In Alex's book. The picture of Ian. He has red hair and blue eyes. Ellie has red hair and blue eyes. Alex has brown hair and brown eyes."

"But how did you connect that to Sister Mattea?"

"When I talked to Scott, he said a friend of his sister's had a baby that died. Her name was Elise. She was a nurse from LA. Ellie is a nurse from LA. Ellie's husband died in Iraq. Elise's husband was killed in Iraq. Ellie's son is 10 years old. Elise's baby died 10 years ago. Elise went to Ohio. You met Ellie in Ohio.

"Then I went online. Read the stories about a baby who disappeared from a parked car while his mother was inside at the bar. He was never found. I turned up an old online picture of Elise McAllister in a Regent Hospital newsletter. Different hair, younger, but it was Ellie."

"You've always been a damn good reporter. Too damn good," he sighed. "What are you going to do?"

"What am I going to do? Max! Ellie stole a baby. You let Sister Mattea die. You tried to kill me! What do you think I'm going to do?"

"Who else knows? Coop, Miguel?"

"Nobody. Max, how could you do that to me? I thought you cared about me?" My words were angry but I felt oddly as though I were floating above the scene.

His eyes were bleak. "I have to protect Ellie and Alex. I don't want to do this."

"Do what Max?" but I knew. Knew why I was feeling so detached and lethargic. Why Max had mixed Jameson with the sweet tasting ginger ale. To mask the Ambien or Vicodin or whatever he'd put in my drink to slow my reactions.

He wanted to find out if I was ready to let things rest, just assume Palmer, Hegl and Sister Julianna were behind Sister Mattea's death and the attempt on my life. If I was, I'd just have an extra-long sleep that night. If I wasn't, then—my mind couldn't hold onto the thought.

"Max, don't. Please. It won't work. Please." I tried to get up.

"I'm sorry, Leah. I'm sorry." Tears welled in his eyes as he leaned over me with a pillow.

I thrashed around as it pressed down on my face. I couldn't breathe. I twisted my head and tried to kick out my legs, but I was going down. No bright white light this time.

And then the pressure stopped and there was a thud. I pushed and the pillow lifted easily from my face. I struggled to a sitting position. Max was lying on the floor, gripping his left arm, his face twisted in a grimace of pain.

"Max? Max?" I forced myself to focus. I picked my phone up from the table and called 911.

"Heart attack. My friend is having a heart attack. 607 Fletcher Street." The operator was talking, but I dropped the phone. I knelt beside him. His breathing was shallow and tight.

"Leah."

I leaned in. I could barely hear him. I put my ear next to his lips.

"Don't tell. About Alex. Don't. Please."

When the EMTs arrived, I moved to the kitchen chair while they worked. Coop had heard the scanner call and got there as they were loading Max into the ambulance. He offered to take me to the hospital to wait for news, but I said no. I told him that Max and I had been drinking a Jameson, and I'd forgotten I'd taken a sleeping pill earlier. That I was having a hard time functioning. That I wouldn't be any good until it wore off. He stayed with me until my mother got home.

44

Max's funeral was three days later.

At the wake, I was sitting in a corner by myself when Courtnee came up to me. Her pretty face was streaked with tears.

"I'm gonna miss him, too, Leah. I can't believe he was, like, in the office Friday and now, I'll never see him again."

"Yeah, it's hard to take in."

"You know, Leah, I'm not saying this is for real. And I'm not blaming you or anything, but a lot of bad stuff sure happened after you didn't help Sister Mattea. Maybe it's not so good not to help a nun when she asks."

"What are you talking about?"

"You know, how she left that note asking you to help her write that history for the nuns, and you didn't do it. So, like, if someone, you know, *holy* wants your help, maybe you should just do it?"

"Courtnee, could you put the brakes on the stupid train just for today?" I snapped. "Sister Mattea didn't ask me to write a history of the nuns. That's not what her note was about."

"Well, she told *me* that she wanted you to help her write a history or something for the nuns' anniversary, and she left you a note. Don't you remember how you yelled at me because you lost the envelope?"

"She wanted to talk to me about my sister Lacey. That's why she put that page from the *Times* in the book she lent me."

"I know you're probably being so snotty because you're sad about Max, but you don't have to be such a biatch. Anyway, Sister Mattea didn't put that newspaper page in the book. I did."

"What?"

"After she left, I saw she dropped the copy of the *Times* page I made for her when she was in the week before. I put it in the book inside the envelope so you could give it to her."

"Why didn't you tell me that?"

"I tried, but you wouldn't let me finish. Remember? I told you I was trying to give you context, but you were so grouchy that day. Just like now."

I stared at her. Then I started to laugh.

"Leah, are you OK? Are you hysterical? Should I slap you?"

"I'm all right. It's just...I thought Sister Mattea was giving me a message about Lacey. It's why everything started. And now you're telling me it was all completely random."

"Oh. Sorry. I guess.

Ellie and Alex left town a week after the service. I saw her once before they went. She was angry. She said that I'd let Max down. That if I hadn't been drinking, I could have saved him. Maybe she was right.

I didn't tell her I knew about Alex. I didn't tell her what Max had done for her. I didn't tell anyone. I did find out that Alex's birth mother had died of a drug overdose eight years earlier. Sister Mattea was trying to reunite Alex with a ghost.

So, it was all good, right? Ellie had saved Alex from a sad and dangerous life. He had a mother who loved him and the memory of a great dad in Max. If I told the truth now, Ellie would go to prison and Alex would go into foster care.

Ellie's decision to take Alex had set off a series of events that resulted in the death of Sister Mattea, Max, and, indirectly, Palmer. Would my decision not to tell the truth set off another chain of unintended consequences?

I didn't know. But I couldn't do it. *Finding the truth isn't always the same as finding the answers.* I didn't understand what Father Lindstrom meant when he had said that to me weeks ago. But I was beginning to.

My mother thought I was mourning the loss of Max and should talk to a grief counselor. Coop thought I had PTSD and wanted me to see a doctor. Miguel thought I was depressed and should go for a makeover and a new wardrobe. They were all a little bit right. But I knew there was only one place I might find what I needed.

One night late I walked up the steps of a small brown house with an arched front door. The porch light was on as if I was expected. When I rang the bell, the door swung inward and a little man with fluffy white hair stood on the threshold. He was holding an *X Files* mug from which rose a wisp of steam.

"Come in, Leah. I've been waiting for you." Father Lindstrom smiled, and I stepped inside.

ACKNOWLEDGMENTS

It took a lot of family, friends and encouragement to launch the Leah Nash Mysteries series with this first book, *Dangerous Habits*. I owe thanks to all, but especially to my husband Gary, who patiently endured the many ups and downs of the writing and production process.

I also want to single out another person for special acknowledgement, my dear friend, Irene Pavlik. If not for her, Leah might have remained a ghost of an idea, flitting in and out of my imagination at irregular intervals, never to be given shape and structure. Irene died unexpectedly and tragically before this book was written. I'm sorry that she didn't live to see the fruits of her belief and encouragement.

DISCUSSION QUESTIONS

1. The setting of *Dangerous Habits* is a small town in Wisconsin. Is that important to the story? Why or why not?

2. The book is written in the first person, so the reader sees everything though Leah's eyes. Does Leah's view of other characters affect the way you feel about them?

3. Leah is "equal parts smart and smartass." How do these character traits motivate Leah through the story? Is she motivated by one more than the other?

4. What aspects of a mystery—setting, dialogue, characters, conflict, point of view, plot twists—are most important to you? Which aspects did you like most in *Dangerous Habits*?

5. Which plot twists were most unexpected? How did they change your suspicions of who was guilty?

6. Did you learn something from the book that you didn't know before? What?

7. Leah is quick to pass judgment, yet she seems to have no trouble forgiving Max, and keeping his secret. Why?

8. If it's true that we're known by the company we keep, what does Leah's choice of friends say about her? Who is she drawn to and why? What does this say about Leah's values?

DANGEROUS MISTAKES

LEAH NASH MYSTERIES BOOK 2

For Sara and Brenna

1

"ALL OF US ARE DYING."

"Well, yes, I guess I can't argue with that, Betty," I said to the slight, white-haired woman seated behind my desk in the newsroom. I had come barreling in to pick up a new notebook, late for my next assignment.

"Oops, sorry, if I could just get into that center desk drawer there." I gently rolled her away from the desk, edged my drawer out a couple of inches, and stuck my arm into the depths until I felt cardboard. I tweezered out the spiral-bound notebook between two fingers.

"All of us. Dying. It's not right."

I slipped the notebook into my purse and moved to scoot Betty back into position, mentally cursing our receptionist Courtnee for sending her back to the newsroom. Again. Betty Meier was a retired nurse in her 80s. Years ago, during my first stint at the *Himmel Times Weekly*, she often stopped by to drop off an ad for a garage sale, or a press release for the Sunshine Girls bazaar, or to put in a notice for one of the many other groups to which she belonged. But now she suffered from Alzheimer's, and when she came to the office, it was because she'd wandered away from home. This was the third time in the past two months that she'd ended up here. As I reached round her to slide the chair, she grabbed my arm, clamping on with almost desperate strength.

Startled, I looked down into her upturned face. The spark of life in her faded blue eyes caught me by surprise. I swallowed the placating answer I'd been about to give.

"No, Betty, it's not right. It doesn't matter how old we are. No one wants to go into that good night." I pulled up the visitor's chair and sat down so we were eye level.

"No, no, no! It's us. Everyone is dying. Where's Max? I want to talk to Max." The bright light had gone out as quickly as it had come, and her eyes took on a cloudy cast again. Her fingers released their grip, and her voice became querulous.

"Max isn't here anymore, Betty." Max Schreiber, the former owner of the *Himmel Times Weekly,* wasn't just gone, he was dead. How and why he died was something I didn't like to talk about, but never really stopped thinking about.

Just then a harried-looking woman in her early 40s burst through the door.

"Mom! I've been looking all over for you. Sweetheart, what are you doing here?" She knelt down and patted her mother's arm. In an aside, she said to me, "I'm sorry, Leah. The caregiver didn't show up. Mom's next door neighbor went over, but then her dog got hit by a car, and she had to leave. I rushed out of work. It was only 10 minutes, but when I got there Mom was gone."

"Don't worry about it, Deborah. It's OK."

"Sometimes she seems fine, you know? The other day, out of nowhere, she said, 'How was work, Debbie?' It almost broke my heart. She hadn't initiated a conversation in weeks, and then for a second, there she was. My mom. And just as quickly she was gone, and there was a confused old lady who didn't know who I was."

"I'm sorry," I said, awkwardly and inadequately. Two things I specialize in, awkward and inadequate. "She keeps saying all her friends are dying."

She nodded. "I took her to a funeral a month or so ago. I knew she'd want to be there, but I shouldn't have. She's been upset ever since." She turned to her mother again. "Mom, let's go home. Tandy's coming over tonight, and we'll have dinner and watch some family movies. That'll be nice, won't it?" She slid her arm under her mother's and helped her up. As they left, she turned to me. "Leah, again, I'm so sorry. I know we can't go on like this. It isn't safe for her."

"It's not easy," I said, though in truth, and thank God, I knew nothing about the pain of the parent–to-child reversal Deborah was experiencing. My mother–maddening, bossy, loving, funny woman that she is–still has full control of all her faculties, and would happily take charge of mine if I'd let her.

I followed Deborah out the door on a run, but I was already 15 minutes late for an interview with the incoming principal at Himmel High School.

"Really, Courtnee? Betty Meier sitting in the newsroom? At my desk? Why did you take her back there?"

It was nearly five when I got back to the office, and I was a little on the pissy side. Make that a lot. My interview with the principal didn't go well. He was unhappy because I was late and even madder when I left early. I had to, or I'd have missed shooting a ribbon-cutting ceremony at the new McDonald's franchise. That's the kind of cutting edge journalism we do here at the *Himmel Times*. On the way back to the office, the iced tea I'd bought at the drive-through tipped over, and half of it ran into my purse. In fairness, I couldn't blame Courtnee for that, but I think that fairness is far overrated.

Looking up from her Facebook account, Courtnee gave a shrug.

"I'm a receptionist, Leah. It's my job to receive. So, I received her into the newsroom. You were gone, and Miguel is out, and Rebecca wasn't here, and like always, I had to take care of things myself. She likes sitting at your desk."

Miguel Santos is the other full-time reporter, and Rebecca Hartfield is the publisher and micromanager at the *Times*.

"The next time she comes in, if there is a next time, 'receive' her in reception. Sit her down—out here—and call her daughter. OK?"

"Okaayy." She gave a flip of her silky blonde hair and turned to read the text that had just pinged on her phone. At the same time a loud static-filled squawk came from the scanner in the newsroom. I couldn't make out the words, but I didn't need to, because Rebecca was already out of her office to translate. She's a cool blonde—calm, measured, methodical. And, oddly, not that crazy about me.

"Good, you're still here. There's a working fire at 529 Halston. A residence. I need you to cover it."

"But I've got a Parks Committee meeting. Miguel is—"

"He's still in Milwaukee. You can do a phone follow-up on the meeting. Is there a problem?"

"No. Nothing," I muttered. I grabbed the camera and headed out.

My name is Leah Nash, and in the exciting, competitive, high-adrenalin carnival that is journalism, I operate the merry-go-round. I'm a reporter for a small-town weekly in Himmel, Wisconsin. It's where I started 11 years ago, and it's where I landed 18 months ago, after a series of bad career decisions. I had an exit strategy, but it hadn't come together quite yet.

The fire assignment was no big deal. Except it was. Though I wasn't about to confide my darkest fears to Rebecca, who, as far as I can tell, has the empathy and emotional range of a Popsicle. The truth is, I'm afraid of fires—to the point of hyperventilating and quaking in my shoes. Have been since I was 10 years old. I never willingly cover one. But sometimes I have no choice.

My hands were sweaty on the wheel, and I was repeating *"breathe in, breathe out"* in a frenzied mantra as I pulled up. Smoke billowed from the back of a small two-story house. Here and there yellow flames shot red-tipped tongues out the windows. Gray ash snowflakes floated through the air as firefighters wrangled hoses, flooding the fire into submission. Still, I sat in my car, unable to open the door and move closer to the burning house. Hard as I tried not to let it, my mind hurtled back to another fire, a long time ago. I squeezed my eyes tight to shut out the images. A second later they popped back open in surprise at the sharp rapping near my ears. I rolled down the window so that David Cooper could lean in.

"Hey, Coop."

"Hey. What are you doing here? Where's Miguel?"

"Rebecca sent him out of town. So, it's me." I struggled to put on an air of professionalism as I opened the door and hauled out my camera bag. Coop is my oldest friend and a lieutenant with the Himmel Police Department.

"So, what's the story? Anyone hurt? What are the damages? Do they know how it started?" I fired off questions, determined not to let him know how hard it was to force myself to walk closer toward the heat of the fire, to hear the snap and pop as it ate through dry wood, the crash as a section of roof gave way.

I didn't fool him. Coop doesn't say much. But he sees a lot. Which I find quite irritating when it's me he's looking at.

"Al Porter's over by the ladder truck. He thinks it's just about under control. I'll point him in your direction when he gets off the phone. No sense you going over there and getting in the way."

I try not to let my weaknesses show. If anyone sees what hurts or scares you, it makes you vulnerable. And, in my experience, that's not a good thing.

I shook my head. "I'm going over to talk to him."

He looked at me, but didn't say anything.

"Look, I'm fine."

"Yeah, I know."

"Don't patronize me. I hate it when you patronize me."

"I'm not. Just saying it's wet and slippery and crowded over there. Call Al over here, and you'd be out of the way. Suit yourself."

"I will."

"Oh, I know."

We could have gone on like 10-year-olds forever—at least I could have —but the fire chief walked up just then.

"Leah." He nodded and paused to wipe a rivulet of sweat running down the side of his face, smearing ash across his cheek. He had pulled off his yellow helmet, and I could see that his gray hair was wet and curling in wisps. Pushing 60, and about 30 pounds over fighting weight, Al isn't going to be September in anyone's *Fire Fighters Calendar*. But he knows how to run a crew, keep them safe, and put out the fire, and no one is in any hurry to tell him to hang up his turnout gear.

"You're a little late to the party. But Matt McGreevy got some good shots and video too."

I could've kissed Al and Matt both, but I played it casual. "Oh? Sure, that'd be great. Whose house is it?"

"Old gal by the name of Betty Meier."

Al picked up on the shock I felt right away.

"It's OK, Leah. You know her? She wasn't home. Nobody was. Well, except for one pretty mad cat, but we got her out all right. The old lady was at her daughter's, the neighbor said. I guess she's got some dementia issues. Might have left on the gas burner on the stove. But don't print that," he hastened to add. "We're gonna have the state fire marshal in."

A loud whoosh of water hit the house just then, spraying the charred remains. No flames were visible, but I knew that didn't mean the fire was out. Some of the crew would be on the scene for a couple of hours to make sure the blaze didn't start up again.

"She's wandered away a few times and come to the paper, asking for Max. I talked to her daughter today. I think she's probably going to move her to a nursing home." Poor Betty. Losing all her friends, her memories, and tonight it could have been her life. It's true. Old age isn't for sissies.

"Yeah. I'd say it's past time for that. Fire can move so damn fast. People don't realize how—" He stopped. Looked at me. Looked embarrassed. I helped him roll on past a subject I didn't want to delve into either.

"For sure. So, who called it in? What's the damage estimate?" I went through the standard reporter's litany of who, what, when, where, why questions, and when I had all the information Al could give me at the moment, I asked Matt to email me his photos and video.

Then I packed it in and went back to the office to post a few pictures and a news brief on the *Times* website. I stopped by the front desk and checked the spike on the corner of Courtnee's desk for messages. At 6:30 p.m. she was long gone.

I pulled off the notes for me and gave them a quick glance. Nothing looked urgent, so I stuffed them in my purse to read later. In the newsroom, I didn't bother to flip on the light, just turned on my desk lamp and used the blue glow of the computer screen. It was kind of nice there in the semi-dark. There was no jangle of Courtnee's unanswered phones in reception, no tap-tap-tap of other keyboards, no repeated clunking of cans of soda coming out of the Coke machine.

Before I started writing, I texted Coop and Miguel to see if they wanted to meet up for a beer and a burger at McClain's, then I filed a quick story. I uploaded two of the photos Matt had sent to my iPhone and a short video clip. When I finished, I leaned back for a long, satisfying yawn and stretch, my chair tilted and my arms reaching as far back as possible. I was right at that almost orgasmic point of satisfaction, when every muscle was extended and just on the edge of relaxing, when the light clicked on.

"Leah."

I all but tumbled out of my chair.

"Rebecca! Geez, how about some warning when you creep in on little cat feet?"

"Did you get the story?" Her eyes, the color of a blue-tinged icicle, blinked behind her black-framed glasses.

"Already written. Nobody hurt. Betty, the woman who owns the house, wasn't there. Property's totaled though."

"Photos?"

"Yep."

"All right, good. Pull the commission story from the front page and run with the fire above the fold—if the pictures are any good. Are they?"

"Matt McGreevy took them. They're great. It was really nice of him to share them, especially since you fired him last month."

"I did not fire him. Stringers aren't employees. They're independent contractors. Why didn't you take the photos?"

I flashed back to my near panic attack at the fire, my dithering around the edge trying to get my nerves under control. The shaming fear that had gripped me. "I got there too late. Matt rolled out with the fire department—he does their videography. And he's a good guy, so he shared them, even though you 'not' fired him."

"I don't cut costs for fun. It has to be done. That's my job." She spoke slowly, as though explaining something to a small child.

I gave in to the urge to get a rise out of her. "I thought you went to journalism school. Not bean counting academy."

"I was hired to get the *Times* in better financial shape, and that requires the counting of some beans. It might be easier if you didn't take every decision as a personal affront."

Something in her voice made me look up from putting away my stuff. She had taken off her glasses and was rubbing the bridge of her nose. Her shoulders had sagged a little, and for a minute I saw her as a woman with a tough job, who didn't have the luxury of casual banter with her staff or after-work drinks at McClain's. Her role was to be the bad guy, the naysayer, the buzz-killer. That had to be pretty lonely. She was only 36, just a few years older than me.

"Rebecca, would you like to—"

She cut me off before I could invite her to stop by McClain's with me. "Don't forget to turn your mileage in tomorrow. It's the cutoff, and you won't get paid this month if you don't get it in. I've already told Courtnee that."

As part of the general cutbacks and reassignments in Rebecca's lean and mean vision for the *Times,* Courtnee had been assigned the task of processing mileage and expense reports. It had proven to be one of the more effective cost-saving measures, because half the time Courtnee didn't finish the reports in time for us to get paid for the month, which she always insisted was our fault. The other half of the time, she screwed them up, and they didn't get processed correctly until the following month. I suspected there was some method to Rebecca's madness in giving the job to Courtnee, in that to some degree, expenses were always deferred.

"Right." I gathered my things and left before saying something I'd regret. Working at the *Times* wasn't exactly a step up the career ladder, but when Max was here it was fun. I missed the camaraderie, the kidding around, the messy, lively, frustrating, fulfilling business of putting out a paper. When Rebecca first started, I thought we might be friends. She's near my age, she's from Wisconsin like me, and she'd even worked at the *Grand Rapids Press* in Michigan, like I had, though at a different time. It just seemed like we'd have a lot in common. Instead, Rebecca sucked the happy right out of the air. If it weren't for Miguel, I might have done something stupid like I did at the *Miami Star Register.* Namely, leaving one job without having another waiting. I wanted to play it smart this time. But she was making it awfully hard.

2

I HADN'T HEARD from either Coop or Miguel by the time I got to the parking lot, and I didn't really feel like going to McClain's Bar anyway. So instead I drove my car to the north end of town and parked it in front of the wooden posts that form the boundaries of Riverview Park. The lights on their old-fashioned poles shone on the deserted park with its weather-beaten picnic tables and forlorn wooden benches. I turned off the engine and looked at the empty acreage, repopulating it with my memories.

As a little kid, I spent hours on the swings and the jungle gym with my sister, Annie. Later, in the middle school years, Coop and I would rendezvous here to ride our bikes at breakneck speed on the gravel path that circles the park. Sometimes we'd make forbidden treks across the railroad trestle spanning the Himmel River at the edge of the park. It was a shortcut to JT's Party Store, which held a child's mother lode of candy. Later on, when I was a teenager, I'd bring my youngest sister, Lacey, here too. We'd feed the ducks down by the river, and I'd spin her around on the merry-go-round until we both were dizzy with laughter.

As an adult, whenever I came back to town, I was drawn to this space. If the weather was fine, the park was filled with families. Parents pushing strollers, kids running and shouting, heady with the sheer joy of a bright, sunny afternoon. I liked to watch and listen to the happy hubbub all around me. Once upon a time, our family was like that. My mother, my father, Lacey, Annie, and me.

But then Annie died in a fire when she was eight and I was 10. Lacey was just a baby. My dad left shortly after that. Lacey died five years ago at 17. People know about her, because of the story I did last year. Most people forget about Annie. It was so long ago. When they do recall it, like the fire chief Al Porter had tonight, I change the subject. If pushed into a corner by someone more curious than kind, I usually offer an Oscar Wilde paraphrase. *To lose one sister may be regarded as a misfortune; to lose both looks like carelessness.* All but the most dense retreat then.

I'm pretty good at keeping others at bay, but I have a tougher time with my own thoughts. That's why I don't like to be near a fire. When I feel the heat, see the flames, hear the crash and crackle of burning wood, a pain I can't stop rises with choking force. It takes all I have just to breathe. When Annie died, it was the end of my family as I'd known it. Everything changed.

I stared blankly at the bleak early winter landscape in front of me, willing my mind to settle, to forget, to achieve the numbness that was gradually creeping into my toes and fingers as I sat in the unheated car. Finally, I turned on the engine and left the park to drive down Himmel's mean streets.

Leaves that only a few weeks ago danced gaily in the trees, sporting vivid orange, red, and gold colors, now lay scattered, curled and brown, on the pavement. They crunched under my wheels or skittered onto the windshield, borne up by gusts of wind in the cold November night. A shiver ran through me. We were going into another Wisconsin winter. My second one since moving back. I was determined to make it my last.

Himmel, like a lot of upper Midwestern towns, is a faint copy of its former self. The empty store fronts downtown and the shrinking memberships in churches and social clubs tell a story that long-time residents are tired of hearing. A changing economy brought about factory closings, small stores gave way to big box operations, and people who expected to live here forever had to move to find work. The population had dropped from the bustling 20,000 of my youth to its current 15,000. Even the Chamber of

Commerce has a tough time keeping a straight face when it promotes Himmel as a little piece of heaven on earth.

I wasn't one of the people who never wanted to leave. I couldn't wait to get away and get started on my "real" life when I graduated from college. I'd been gone for 10 years when my progress up the career ladder was halted by my own impulsive stubbornness. After clashing with an editor at my last job at a midsize daily, I made the grand gesture and quit. That didn't work out so well. In the struggling world of print media, there weren't a lot of newspaper openings. During a long, fruitless job hunt, I realized that smart and smartass aren't the same thing. I'd like to say I changed my ways, but I'm kind of a slow learner.

I finally had to take the lifeline tossed to me by Max Schrieber, my old boss at the *Himmel Times*. I had planned to be there for six months. Just enough time to get myself back on track. But I got caught up in an investigation with some serious personal stakes—the accidental death of my sister Lacey years earlier. By the time it was over, I had discovered that Lacey had been murdered.

The articles I wrote for the *Himmel Times* got a lot of play in the online media and on cable news. Pretty soon I had a publisher, a $10,000 advance, and a book in the works. It wasn't enough to quit my day job, but I was hoping the book would help me transition from reporting to writing true crime books. That way I'd have everything I loved about journalism—researching, investigating, finding leads, making sense of things, writing—and none of what I didn't—cranky editors, impossible deadlines, workplace politics, and compromises in quality caused by shrinking news budgets.

The manuscript was in page proof stage, the final step before printing. *True Crime: Unholy Alliances* was set for a February release. Who doesn't like a little murder for Valentine's Day?

In the meantime, I still had to eat and pay the bills, so I was still at the *Times*. It had changed a lot since the death of Max last year. His wife sold it to a hedge fund that specializes in sucking up the life force of small town papers until they're dried husks of their former selves, then selling them. Or shutting them down. So far, Rebecca had cut staff, cut overtime, micromanaged coverage, and increased our workload. I just wanted to hang on long enough to get my book off the ground.

As I pulled in the driveway of our house, a red Toyota pulled up behind me. Miguel.

"*Chica!* I've been following you since you turned the corner onto Main Street. Don't you ever look in your rearview mirror?"

"Hey, you. Come on in."

I hit the kitchen light as we came through the door, grabbed a couple of Supper Club beers and some sliced turkey and bread from the fridge, and put them on the kitchen table.

Miguel took off his brown leather jacket and laid it over the back of his chair. Under a dark green v-neck sweater he wore a shirt with tiny green checks and a skinny burgundy tie. Well polished brown shoes poked out from under his gray pants.

"You look cute." If he weren't 10 years younger than me—and gay—I'd seriously think about taking our friendship to the next level.

"*Gracias.* Just got back from Milwaukee. Good news! My uncle Craig, he made it. He's on the transplant list; we got the OK from the Kidney Transplant Team." His smile made me smile.

"That's great. Now what?"

"Now we wait. But at least we know if a kidney match comes up, he's in line."

Miguel had lived in Himmel since he was 16, when his mother sent him to stay with his aunt and uncle, to keep him safe from some nasty gang bangers who had it in for him in Milwaukee. He took to small town life and stayed on after college, when he got a job at the *Times*. I met him last year when I came back. If I had a younger brother and I got to choose, it would be him.

I reached over and rubbed the top of his head—I can never resist a chance to mess with his perfect hair. He laughed and pushed my hand away.

"Now, *dígame*, how did your day go?"

I told him about the fire—not the near panic attack part, just that I got there late, but we still had some good pictures thanks to Matt McGreevy. When I went to rummage in the fridge for mustard and mayo for our sandwiches, I knocked my purse off the bar. The entire contents spilled out, and as Miguel scrambled to help me pick it up, I grabbed the handful of pink message slips I'd meant to look at before leaving the office.

I stopped and read through them. A reminder call from my dentist's office, a request to speak at career day at Himmel High School—given the state of my own career, that would not be a very inspirational talk—and then something odd in Courtnee's well-rounded handwriting.

4:30. She called about murder. And, of course, because it was Courtnee, there was no phone number, or any clue who "she" was.

I tried to determine whether this was a request for me to kill someone, an inquiry about the murders I covered last year, or an invitation to a philosophical discussion on the taking of human life. I shared the message with Miguel.

"Murder? We can investigate again. Just like last year, *chica*." His dark brown eyes lit up.

I shook my head. "Think about it. Courtnee took the message from someone called 'she.' Who probably didn't say murder, more like burger, as in the burger eating contest on Saturday. Someone probably wanted us to take photos."

"Come on, *chica*—Courtnee's not that lame."

"Oh no? Last week she told me she bought an argyle for her mother's garden. She meant a garden gnome. She got the word gnome mixed up with gargoyle, and then somehow made it come out argyle."

He grinned. "You're like a Windtalker. You and your *amiga,* Courtnee, you speak a language only you understand."

"I'll try my translation skills out on her tomorrow. But don't start counting on a big story. Good thing, too. I'm barely keeping up with regular stuff, and I'm behind on my book. But after it's published, all the big stories in Himmel—the Farm Bureau meeting, the Highest Butterfat Content Milk Award, the sewer repair on Maple Street, even the burger eating contest—all those front-pagers will be yours, Jimmy Olsen." I smiled, but instead of smiling back, his face became serious.

"*Chica*, it won't be the same when you go. I'm so sad when I think about it."

"You should be thinking about moving on yourself. The writing's on the wall. That soulless hedge fund Rebecca works for is not going to leave anything standing. You've got a year or two at the most, I'd say."

"I can't do anything now. I can't leave my *Tía* Lydia now, with Uncle Craig so sick."

"Yeah, I know you can't. Well, I might be hanging on right along with you. Who knows what will happen with the book? Maybe I'll be at the *Times* until Rebecca kicks me to the curb. Which could be any time, actually. She hates me."

"No, she doesn't, *chica*. She just doesn't show her feelings. She's not so bad."

I stared at him in astonishment. "You're kidding, right?"

"She's not that bad. She's had a hard life. Her *mamá* committed suicide; she never knew her *papá*. Her adopted parents were *muy mal*. She was in foster care; she had no family!" As part of a large extended family with millions—or so it seemed—of cousins, aunts, and uncles, Miguel couldn't seem to wrap his head around Rebecca's aloneness.

"Hey, I'm sorry she had a Jane Eyre childhood, but that doesn't give her the right to make my life miserable now. She's impossible to work with, and the room temperature drops 10 degrees whenever she walks in."

"She'll warm up to you, if you let her."

I raised an eyebrow, but before I could comment, the doorbell rang and my mother and Paul Karr came in from the living room laughing and doing a disco move to *Stayin' Alive*. My mom installed a digital doorbell that plays tunes from her MP3 player, and she changes it up so often you never know if the *Barber of Seville* or the BeeGees will start up when you hit the buzzer.

"Miguel!" She grabbed his hand and executed a few quick dance steps with him, while Paul came over and gave me a side-shoulder hug. Then they both sat down and joined us.

"What have you two crazy kids been up to?" I asked.

"Carol and I went to dinner and a movie, and then we stopped by McClain's for a drink." Paul was talking to me, but his eyes kept straying to my mother, who was laughing at something Miguel had said to her. Paul has been our dentist forever and my mother's "special friend" for the past few years. He's definitely smitten—and why wouldn't he be? My mom is great-looking, small and trim, with spiky black and silver hair and the same dark blue eyes my sister Lacey had. She's smart too, but pretty bossy. Though Paul doesn't seem to mind.

"Guess who we saw at McClain's? Ben. With a date," my mother said.

"You and Ben broke up? Why didn't you tell me?" Miguel asked.

I shook my head. "We didn't 'break up.' We weren't ever a couple. We just went out for awhile, that's all."

"What am I gonna do with you? I find you a smart, good-looking boy and you throw him away. You know I can't go shopping for you every day, *chica*. I have to look out for myself, too."

"Don't worry about it. I'm fine, he's fine, we had fun and now we're done."

He and my mother exchanged resigned glances. They'd both had high hopes for Ben, an IT consultant I met last year through Miguel. But as time progressed, I discovered he never listened to cheesy pop songs, he didn't like old movies, and he had no idea who Jack McCoy was. It just wasn't meant to be.

"OK, OK, that's enough discussion about my love life."

"You mean lack of it, don't you?" my mother said.

Miguel came to my rescue and abruptly changed the subject. "Leah got a message about a murder today."

"What?"

"Miguel is exaggerating. Courtnee took the message, so it could be about anything." I shoved it over to my mother and Paul.

"She? Who's that? There's no phone number or anything."

"This is my life. I keep telling you. Courtnee was sent here to drive me mad."

"It doesn't seem like she could mean an actual murder, does it? I mean, aren't we past our quota for the decade in Himmel?" Paul asked, referring to the events of last year.

"I would think," my mother said over her shoulder. She was carrying out my original mission to make Miguel and me turkey sandwiches. As she set them down in front of us and pulled up a chair for herself she added, "Garrett Whiting's suicide last month was bad enough."

"Yes, that was terrible. Marilyn and I were friends with him and his wife Joan years ago," Paul said.

Marilyn was Paul's ex-wife. Anyone she befriended was suspect in my book.

"They had a couple of kids, too," my mother said. "The Whitings were clients when I first started working for Karen." My mother had been a paralegal at a law firm that closed last year. "The son's name was Jamie, really sweet little boy. And the daughter—now what was her name? She was gorgeous."

"Isabel," Miguel said around a mouthful of turkey sandwich.

"You know them?" I asked.

"*Un poquito*. We weren't really friends, but she was in my class. Jamie was a few years behind."

"Well, I'm sure she knew you. You can't walk into Aldi's grocery store without all the cashiers shouting hello."

"Hey, if you got it, *chica*, you can't help it." He grinned before taking an enormous final bite of his sandwich, then washing it down with a swig of Supper Club.

"Isabel must be what, 23, then? And Jamie can't even be 21 yet. It's so hard. Especially for the daughter," my mother said.

"Why do you say that?" asked Paul.

"She's the one who found the body," Miguel answered for her.

"That's really rough. I didn't know that," Paul said. "Joan and Garrett divorced years ago," he added. "Joan moved out west somewhere after the divorce. The kids were still pretty young. She died a few years ago, and from what I've heard, she never saw Jamie and Isabel again."

"Nice mother," I said.

My mother frowned. "Don't be so judgmental. Being a mother is tough, and Joan had other problems."

"Like what?"

"She had a prescription drug addiction. She went to rehab to kick it. Maybe she couldn't, so she didn't come back. Or maybe she did, but she felt too ashamed, or too guilty, or maybe her kids wouldn't have anything to do with her. Not everyone is as forgiving as you, Leah."

I made a face at her sarcasm. "My sympathy's with the kids, not the mother who ran out on them. Well, look, it's been a long day. You guys can rehash Himmel history some more if you want, but I'm going to bed."

"I gotta go too, *chica*," Miguel said, then bent to give my mother a quick kiss on the cheek and waved to Paul and me. "See you later."

I changed into a T-shirt and sweats, washed my face, then flopped down on the bed and fell into total coma sleep. It took me awhile before I realized that the annoying giant bumble bee buzzing my dream was actually my phone bouncing and vibrating on the night table next to my bed. I fumbled around for a second, then found it and answered without looking at the caller ID.

"Hello?" I said, following it with an involuntary and really loud yawn.

"I'm sorry, were you sleeping?" The voice was female, light and pleasant, but agitated.

"What time is it?"

"Um, it's, let me see. Oh no, it's 11:45. I'm sorry. I didn't realize it was so late. I shouldn't have called. Go back to sleep."

"Oh no. Hold on. You don't get to wake me up and then do a hang up. Who is this?"

"My name is Isabel Whiting. I left a message for you at the paper today, but you didn't call me back. And I—oh, this was a bad idea. I'm so sorry. I called Courtnee at home and got your cell phone."

I was fully alert now. "I got a note about your call from Courtnee, but the message was—" I hesitated. "A little ambiguous. And she didn't leave a phone number."

"I feel really bad calling you. It's just that I don't know what to do. And it's all I can think about. I thought maybe you. You know. Because of your sister. I'm sorry."

"OK, quit saying you're sorry for starters. I'm awake now, so talk to me."

"It's my father. Garrett Whiting. The police say he killed himself. But he didn't. I know he wouldn't do that."

In my experience, families of suicide victims often think that. They usually try to convince themselves that it was an accident. Sometimes the medical examiner helps them think that, usually when it's a solo hunting "accident." That wasn't the case with Garrett Whiting.

"Look, Isabel, this is a really bad time for you, I know. But I talked to the sheriff's department at the time it happened. There wasn't anything to suggest it wasn't suicide. It was pretty cut and dried, from their perspective."

"I know that, but he didn't kill himself. No one will listen to me. Somebody killed my father."

"OK, what makes you so sure?"

"Can't we just meet in person? I know you'll understand if I can just talk to you face-to-face. Please. If you don't, then there's no one. I've tried, but I don't know how to do this by myself."

It can be pretty lonely out there on a limb. I know, because I've been there myself more than a few times.

"OK, how about this? I could do coffee at the Elite tomorrow, around 10? We can talk and—"

"Oh, thank you, thank you so much. I'll be there. I'm sorry I woke you, but thank you."

"All right but—" Before I could finish my cautionary words against expecting too much, she had hung up.

I sat staring at the phone in my hand for a minute, wishing I hadn't given her false hope. I was just delaying the inevitable. More than likely, Isabel was going to have to accept that there were things about her father she hadn't known. There always are.

3

FIRST THING IN THE MORNING I went straight to an 8 a.m. Board of Supervisors meeting at the county courthouse, which is adjacent to the Grantland County Sheriff's Department. It was, as usual, way longer than necessary as they debated restrictions on a private airfield owned by Grady O'Donnell, a farmer who rented hangar space to a handful of private pilots in the area. It was nice extra income for Grady, but some neighbors were complaining about flight noise and lights at night. No decision was reached, also as usual, and I was not in the best mood when the aimless meeting meandered to a close.

Out in the hall, I ran into Charlie Ross, a detective with the sheriff's department. I mean "ran into" literally. He stopped short just ahead of me to adjust khaki pants that were losing the battle between his belly bulge and his belt. I was looking at my phone for messages, and I hit him from behind with a soft thunk. It barely shook his solid bulk.

When he turned and saw it was me, his pudgy red face got even redder.

"Nash. I already know you can't hear. Leastwise, I guess that's why you're always buttin' in when people tell you to stay out. Looks like you can't see either."

"Sorry, Ross, you're hard to miss, I agree."

"I hear the *Times* isn't doin' so hot. Tryin' to make the sheriff's department look like a bunch of screw-ups didn't work out so good for your paper, huh?"

"Not the sheriff's department. Just you, Ross. You're the one who screwed up the investigation of Lacey's death. But don't worry, you can read all about it, all over again, when my book comes out."

Now, why did I say that? Yes, Charlie Ross is an ass. Yes, his incompetence helped keep the truth about Lacey—and a lot of other really bad things—hidden for years. And yes, he'd come after me with both barrels blazing for something I didn't do. But in the end the facts came out, Lacey's killer was found, I was exonerated, and he was still stupid. Couldn't I ever resist antagonizing him? Apparently not.

His close-set mustard brown eyes narrowed. "Always got a smart answer, don't you, Nash?"

"That reminds me, I'm looking for some answers from you. I need a copy of the case file on the Garrett Whiting investigation."

"I already gave you the information last month. It was suicide. End of story."

We don't run suicide stories in the paper, unless the death occurs in a public place or the victim is a public figure. The obituary usually uses something vague like "passed away unexpectedly." And I'm OK with that. Some things should stay private. But Isabel had piqued my curiosity and a look at the file would be helpful.

"Whiting's daughter Isabel is pretty adamant that her father didn't kill himself."

"Yeah? Well, facts are facts. You find a guy sittin' in a chair, he's got a hole in his head, powder residue on his fingers, and a gun sittin' on the floor beside him. It doesn't take a genius to see he blew his own head off. Autopsy confirmed it."

"He didn't leave a note, right?"

"No. Lotta times they don't."

"Isabel seems to think—"

"Nobody wants to think their old man offed himself. She was a little hysterical when we got there. It happens. Family, they don't think so clear when somethin' like this happens. Maybe they don't want to. He's drinking his rum and Coke, mixin' it with some pills. He's got financial problems. His son's a druggie. Life don't look so good. So he takes the easy out and pulls the trigger. If it walks like a duck and quacks like a duck, it's a duck. And this duck is quackin' suicide. Plain and simple. Take my advice: You try to make somethin' outta nothin', all you're gonna do is look stupid. You don't want that, do ya? 'Specially with your big important book comin' out and all."

"It's an inactive investigation. I can get the file."

"Not from me, you can't."

"I'll go to the sheriff."

"Knock yourself out."

What I wanted to do was knock him out—or at least on his well-cushioned butt. What I said was, "OK then. I'll see you around."

"Not if I see you first."

As I walked through the front door of the *Times* Courtnee greeted me.

"So, did Isa-bitch get hold of you last night?"

"Who?"

"You know, Isa-bore Whiting? So last night she calls me up. Right in the middle of Sheer Delight Make-up Value Hour on the Buy network. Before I could get her off the phone, they ran out of the Pre-Prep Foundation Magic in Alabaster. I hope you're happy."

"Deliriously." Looking at her carefully filled-in eyebrows, heavily mascaraed lashes, and shiny pink lips, it was hard to imagine there was any make-up product not already in her arsenal.

"Why didn't you just put her name on the message you left me? Or her phone number? That would have been helpful. And why are you calling her such mean fourth-grade names?"

Her full lips started to protrude in a pout. If at 20 Courtnee represents the next generation of American workers, we are all in a lot of trouble. Self-confident without any basis, incompetent without any awareness, unencumbered by any sense of responsibility, she is perpetually aggrieved and slightly perplexed by job duties that pull her away from Tweeting, Tindering, and Snapchatting.

"You don't have to get all up in my grill. She's just like #I'm Awesome. She thinks she's like this, this Queen of Switzerland or something. I can't even."

Queen of Switzerland? Interesting, but I didn't have time to explore that peculiar turn of phrase.

"You know her father did die just a month ago."

"Oh. I know. Everybody does. She is such a drama queen."

"What have you got against her? She wasn't even in your class at school, was she?"

"No, but my brother Jared wanted to hang with her, and she totally burned him. Like she thinks she's so lit. She's not."

Ah. Never forgive, never forget. The Fensterman code.

"Well, it would have saved me a midnight call if you had just written down her name and number."

"It's not like I'm your, like, personal assistant, Leah. I do the best I can."

Sadly, I think that is true.

"And she was all like freaking and talking about how her dad didn't kill himself, and no one would listen to her, and could she talk to you and yada yada yada. So, I told her you'd call. Only you didn't." She glared at me, and suddenly her inept job performance had become my dereliction of duty.

"Courtnee, you—"

I was just about to launch when Rebecca came into the reception area. She fixed on me, and a frown crossed her face. Time for me to exit, stage left.

"What happened at the Board of Supervisors? Anything change with Grady O'Donnell's private airport? Did you lay out the editorial page yet? Make sure you put the letters below the fold."

I started edging toward the door. "No big action at the board. No ordinance on the books, neighbors are SOL on their noise complaints about the airport. Might be some interest in changing county regulations, if the neighbors get fired up, or they may just let it drop. That's all there was. As usual, the board didn't take any action. The pages are almost laid out. I'm just going to check out a lead. I'll be back before lunch."

"What lead?"

"She's going to talk to Isa-bi—Isabel Whiting. She thinks her dad was murdered."

Rebecca moves with surprising speed for a person with such a calm demeanor. She had one hand on the door and the other on my arm, so I had no choice but to turn around.

"This is the doctor who committed suicide last month?"

"That's what the sheriff's department and medical examiner said."

"Then what's this about?"

I really didn't want to get into it with Rebecca before I even knew what "it" was. I glared at Courtnee, but it bounced right off her guilt-proof armor.

"I got a call from the daughter. She's convinced her father wouldn't have killed himself, and the police are wrong. I'm meeting her for coffee at 10."

I was ready for her to tell me to forget it, that it wasn't an efficient use of my time or the paper's resources.

"I'm going to be out for the rest of the day. Make sure you're back by noon. And I want full disclosure after you meet the Whiting daughter."

"OK, sure." And I left remembering what Miguel had said about Rebecca's mother—that she had committed suicide. Maybe it made her feel sympathetic to Isabel. Wait a minute, Rebecca, sympathetic? No. Had to be some other reason.

4

THE BELL HANGING OVER THE DOOR jingled as I walked into the Elite Cafe. I scanned the room looking for Isabel, though I hadn't thought to get a description from Courtnee. Clara Schimelman, the owner, was bustling around the small wooden tables, a white tea towel tossed over her ample shoulder.

"Leah, you looking for your friend? She's over there." She pointed toward the corner to a table half-hidden by a large, somewhat shopworn artificial fern. "She won't take no rugelach. She only wants the black coffee. But you have chai and rugelach, or maybe raspberry linzer, is good today. Yes?"

The Elite Cafe and Bakery isn't very imposing to look at, but the menu of bakery treats and the deli case are to die for. Everyone comes to the Elite. It's like Rick's in Casablanca, without the gambling and the Nazis.

"Rugelach sounds like heaven." I moved toward the counter, but she waved me away with a flutter of her damp towel.

"No, you go sit with your friend. I bring to you."

The person who stood up to greet me was tall and slender with dark blonde hair cut in an elfin style. She looked at me out of thick-lashed brown eyes.

"Hi. I know you're Leah. I'm Isabel Whiting. Thank you so much for coming. You must have thought I was crazy last night." She was wearing a light pink sweater of some soft, fluffy yarn and a pair of faded jeans. A tiny gold bell on a delicate chain hung on her neck. She had a good handshake, firm and cool. She smiled and I smiled, and before it turned awkward, Mrs. Schimelman delivered my rugelach and chai latte and Isabel's coffee.

"You sure you don't want the rugelach?" She turned hopefully to Isabel.

"No, no thank you. I'm fine." She seemed anything but—uptight and nervous.

Mrs. Schimelman shook her head, sending a bobby pin flying and freeing several strands of gray hair. "You come back again, you try my poppy seed cake. Off the hook." Though she hasn't lost her German accent after more than 30 years, or learned the more subtle points of English grammar, Mrs. Schimelman delights in collecting and using bits of slang, usually several years out of date.

As she moved away, Isabel shifted her coffee from the right-hand side to the left.

"You're a lefty, huh? So's my Aunt Nancy." I was trying to ease into things, maybe take her tension down a notch. Nervous people are hard to interview.

"I'm the only one in my family, so I've had to adapt." She started sliding the little bell charm on her necklace up and down its chain.

Clearly, my effort to set her at ease was not working. Might as well jump in then. Maybe she'd relax as she told her story.

"So, Isabel, why don't you tell me why you think your dad didn't commit suicide."

She took a breath, let it out slowly, then leaned back in her chair and wrapped both hands around her coffee cup.

"OK. My dad died last month. I found him." She stopped.

"I heard that. I'm really sorry."

"I'm not asking for sympathy. I just want the truth."

"Isabel, according to the sheriff's department, the truth is pretty clear. Your father shot himself with a handgun." I tried not to sound too harsh.

"But it isn't clear at all. My father would never have killed himself. Never."

"People do some inexplicable things sometimes. We can't know what's going on inside someone else's head."

She gave me a frustrated look and then tried again, gripping her cup tightly in her hands.

"Look, I was adopted when I was only three. My parents had Jamie the same year. My mother left when I was seven. So, you see, I already lost a parent twice, my real mother and my adopted mother. There is no way that my dad would do that to me again on purpose."

She couldn't have hit the mark harder with me if she knew my whole history. My dad left when I was 11. I knew what it felt like to be abandoned by a parent. And I understood her need to believe that her father hadn't let her down, whatever his own situation. But maybe the kindest thing I could do was to try and lay it out for her and help her start to accept reality.

"I get why you feel like that. But I talked to Detective Ross. He said your dad had a lot on his mind—financial issues, your brother's drug problems. That night he was drinking, he mixed it with medication, and he decided he wanted out. Do you know what kind of money problems he was having?"

"He invested a lot of money in what turned out to be a pyramid scheme. Kind of like that man in New York. Bernie Madoff. Only not as big. My dad did lose a lot, but it's not like we were poverty-stricken. He knew he could recover. Money wasn't that important to him. He wouldn't kill himself over something like that."

"Isabel, one thing that's really hard to get around is the way he was found."

"I know. He was in his study, slumped in a chair. The gun dropped beside him on the floor. I can still see it when I close my eyes." She shuddered. "I understand how it seems. But there were other things. Things the police wouldn't pay any attention to."

"Like what?"

She let go of her cup and leaned forward.

"There was no suicide note. And he had appointments scheduled for the next day—a haircut, a massage."

"People don't always leave notes. And haircuts or massages, they could be standing appointments."

She plowed on, determined to make me see.

"There's more. He ordered a book online that night. It came three days later. I have the receipt. He printed it out and put it in his file. Who orders a book, files the receipt, then shoots himself? And that night he even took a pound of Hook's 15-year-old cheddar out of the refrigerator and set it on the counter. It was still on the cutting board when I went into the kitchen. If it was some kind of 'last meal,' like the sheriff's detective said, wouldn't he have eaten it?"

OK, she had me at cheese. In Wisconsin, we respect our cheese. To set out a hunk of Hook's cheddar and not even take a taste of it, that was sacrilege. Especially when it goes for $50 a pound.

"All right, maybe there are some inconsistencies. But remember, he had both Klonopin and alcohol in his system. He probably wasn't thinking all that clearly, and he may have been more worried than you knew."

"He wasn't drunk, if that's what you're saying. At least he wasn't when he called me. And he didn't use Klonopin."

"Wait a minute. Your father called you?" That was a detail Ross had declined to share.

She nodded.

"Where were you?"

"I was east of Cleveland, driving home from the Adirondacks. I'd been visiting my old roommate at Blue Mountain Lake, at her family's cabin. We were supposed to stay until Monday, but on Saturday night Lauren's grandmother had a stroke and she left right away. I took off Sunday morning. I got as far as somewhere outside of Cleveland when it started raining so hard I stopped for the night. Dad called me around quarter to 12. Well, 11, Wisconsin time."

"What did he say?"

"He was worried. About Jamie."

"Why?"

"Jamie had a problem with prescription drugs in high school, but he's been really good for a long time. My dad sent him to this therapeutic boarding school in Maine his senior year. You know, a school for kids with substance abuse issues. He did great there. Then he enrolled at Himmel Technical College after he graduated, to get his grades up. This fall he started at UW. He even decided to stay at home for the first semester, just to, you know, stay grounded. Everything was good. I thought."

"So what made your dad worried?"

"Jamie was starting to behave like he used to, sleeping a lot, taking off, acting kind of out of it. When Dad told me that, I asked him to look in my medicine cabinet. The Klonopin I had last year for anxiety was gone. I didn't use it, because I didn't like how it made me feel. I should've dumped it, but I forgot about it. I felt terrible, like I'd, I don't know, tempted Jamie. I told Dad I'd come straight home. He didn't want me driving that late at night that far, but I knew I wouldn't be able to sleep.

"I left right away, but I had to get gas and it was still raining pretty hard, so I didn't make as fast time as I wanted to. I got home around 8:30 in the morning. Jamie's car was in the driveway, and there was a light on in Dad's study. I went right in, and..." For the first time, she lost her composure. She gave a shudder and her voice trailed off. After a minute, she took a drink of her coffee and started again.

"Don't you see? My dad wouldn't call, ask me to come home, say we had to help Jamie, and then kill himself. He knew I was coming home and I'd be there by 8:30. He'd never, never make me be the one to find him. He wouldn't."

I felt sad and sorry and unsure I could offer her anything but the pity that she didn't want. She read my expression.

"It's no use, is it? You're not going to help me."

"I want to help you, Isabel. But I'm not sure helping you believe your father was murdered is the way to do it. You realize, the way he was killed, it would have to be someone he knew, someone he trusted. Someone who could get very close to him. It wouldn't be a random killing."

She looked surprised then, as though she'd been so determined to prove that her dad didn't shoot himself that she hadn't really considered who else might have. But she rallied.

"Well, sure, of course. I mean, you said it yourself. We can't know what goes on inside people's heads. Maybe it was a patient or a friend even, or maybe, I don't know, a neighbor?"

"All right, who then? Who might have had a reason to kill your father?

Did he have problems with a business deal, or a patient who died, or a relationship that ended badly? Someone who envied him, or resented him, or blamed him for something?"

She put both hands to her forehead and rubbed her temples, all the while saying, "I don't know. I just don't know."

"What about your brother Jamie? You said his car was there. Where was he?"

"He was passed out cold in his room. Didn't even know anything had happened, could barely remember getting home. Dad must already have been dead when he got there."

"He didn't see anything? Didn't he go by your father's study?"

"No. He always comes in through the kitchen and up the back stairs to his room on the third floor. Dad's study is at the front of the house, on the opposite end from Jamie's bedroom."

"What does Jamie think about things?"

"It's hard to tell what Jamie thinks. He doesn't want to talk. I think he feels guilty, because he and Dad weren't getting along, and he was in the house and didn't even know Dad was dead. I'm having a hard time communicating with him right now."

"And you've told all this to Detective Ross? You didn't hold anything back?"

"I told him. I told the sheriff. I even tried to get Mr. Timmins, the district attorney, to talk to me, but I never even got past one of his assistants. Everyone thinks I'm just a hysterical daughter who can't let go. You do, too, don't you?" Her voice held both frustration and accusation.

I didn't answer, thinking about Charlie Ross investigating Lacey's death, and how he had been content with surface appearances. And how he had resented me trying to dig deeper. And how people's patterns are hard to change. Maybe he had done the same with Garrett Whiting. I tried to talk myself out of what I already knew I was going to do, but I didn't succeed.

"OK. I'm not saying that you're right, or that I can do anything about it. But I will poke around a little. That's all I can promise."

She jumped out of her seat and came over to hug me, just as Mrs. Schimelman came by with coffees and an order of linzer for another table.

Long years of experience allowed her to swerve her large frame with a ballet dancer's grace. She set the pastry and drinks down without incident.

"I'm so sorry," Isabel said.

"It's OK. No worries. You need to chill. I bring you a rugelach. You say you don't want none, but you skin and bones." She shoved the pastry in Isabel's direction.

Isabel sank back into her chair, smiled the first really happy smile I'd seen from her, and took a bite of the crescent-shaped cookie filled with apricot jam. Satisfied, Mrs. Schimelman moved on.

"Do you want to come to the house? Do you want to meet my brother?"

"Well, to start, I'll need to talk to some of the people who knew your father pretty well. See what their take is on his mental state, anything he might have confided that could shed light on his death. Any ideas?"

"I suppose Dr. Bergman. He's my dad's associate in the surgical practice. I don't really know him, but he's worked pretty closely with my father for the past couple of years."

"OK. Who else?"

"Ummm, maybe Frankie Saxon? She's a counselor at Himmel High School. Maybe you know her?"

I shook my head. "Must have been after my time." Which now that I thought about it had been 15 years ago. How did I get so old so fast?

"She helped my dad a lot when Jamie got into trouble with drugs. She found the place for him to get straight. I don't know, but Dad might have called her about Jamie, too."

"Her name is Frankie?"

"Francesca, actually, but she goes by Frankie."

"Anyone else?"

She thought for a minute. "Not really. Dad didn't have a lot of friends. He was always so busy with his practice. Oh, probably Miss Quellman could help, too. She was my father's office manager forever. And then there's Miller Caldwell, the lawyer. The one who used to be president of the bank? He knew Dad for a long time."

I was familiar with Miller Caldwell. He'd been pivotal in my sister's case, and I was pretty sure he'd give me any help he could. "That sounds like a good start."

"Thank you, Leah, you have no idea what this means to me." She reached out and put her hand on my arm. I gave it a squeeze with my other hand. There was something about her that got to me, I had to admit.

"I'll be in touch."

5

"CHICA, I DON'T KNOW ABOUT THIS."

Miguel stretched his long legs out from under the scarred wooden table. It was Thursday night, and the paper was put to bed. We were having a post-production dinner and drinks at McClain's, an old-school bar I love. It's filled with duct-taped vinyl booths, rickety tables, and the faint acrid smell of cigarettes gone but not forgotten. The waitress doesn't kneel beside your table, introduce herself, and then interrupt you every 10 minutes to ask how everything is. At McClain's, they don't care how everything is. I respect that.

"What don't you know?"

"Dr. Whiting. The suicide. Isabel, sure, she doesn't want to think her *papá* killed himself. But..." his voice trailed off.

"But what would be his reason for committing suicide?" Nothing like an opposing viewpoint to throw me into devil's advocate mode. "Garrett Whiting was worried about his son. He wanted to help him. And he talked to Isabel that night and asked her to come home. He knew she was leaving right away. What kind of father would shoot himself in the head and leave his daughter to find him?"

"But how could someone else do it? And make it look like Dr. Whiting did it himself?"

I'd been thinking about that ever since I left Isabel.

"I have a theory," I began, but then I felt two large hands clamp down on either side of my neck and give a squeeze. My shoulders shot up and I gave an involuntary shiver.

"I'll bet you do."

I looked up at Coop looming over me.

"Quit it."

He let go and sat down in the chair next to me, shrugging out of his leather bomber jacket and pulling his HPD cap off his short black hair. Before he could say anything else a waitress materialized at his side.

Short and curvy with curly brown hair and round brown eyes, Sherry Young had a crush on Coop that had lasted through high school, marriage, two kids, and her divorce.

"Hi, Coop. Leinenkugel? You want a cheeseburger basket?"

"No, thanks. I'll just have a beer, Sherry. I've got somewhere to go."

"Oh, that's too bad. I get off in a little while. I thought maybe you'd like to play in the dart tournament with me," she said, giving him a big smile and touching him lightly on the arm. He ignored the amused looks Miguel and I exchanged, and as Sherry walked away he asked, "What's your theory about?"

"She thinks Dr. Whiting was murdered," Miguel said.

"How did you come up with that?"

"What if someone staged Whiting's murder to make it look like suicide?"

"That seems pretty unlikely. You've been watching *Law & Order* marathons again, haven't you?"

"No, listen. What if Whiting was kind of out of it? You know, he had his evening rum and Coke or whatever, and maybe he was anxious, upset about his son, so he took some Klonopin. Maybe more than he should have. That stuff can knock you out. I slept right through the dental surgery Paul did on me last month. And you know my primal dental fear. Sleeping in the dentist chair is not something I do."

"Yes, but you didn't shoot yourself in the head, did you?"

"The point is, I don't remember anything about it, from the time I sat down until they shook me on the shoulder and said it was over. And they had me turning my head and lifting my tongue and they were jabbing things into my mouth. They could have put a gun in my hand if they'd wanted to. Isn't it possible that if Whiting was under the influence of Klonopin plus alcohol, someone he knew and trusted could put the gun in his hand, move it up to his head and pull the trigger? And there's another thing, Isabel says her father didn't use Klonopin."

Then, before he could raise the objection, I did it myself. "I know, it wouldn't be hard for a doctor to get some if he wanted to. But it also wouldn't be hard for someone to give it to him, if *they* wanted to."

I could tell Coop was turning it over in his mind before he shook his head. Lots of times Coop and I don't agree, but I have to admit he usually gives my ideas a thorough think through before he shoots them down. "I haven't seen the report, but if you think Occam's Razor here—the simplest explanation is usually the right one—Charlie probably got it right."

"Occam's Razor is about probability, not fact. Shouldn't we make sure all the facts are present and correct before deciding on the probable explanation?"

"She's got a point, yes?" Miguel asked with a wink at me.

"Don't encourage her."

"Here you go." Sherry had arrived with his beer. She leaned in as close as she could without falling into his lap as she put the drink in front of him.

"Thanks." He moved almost imperceptibly to the left.

"Sherry, *mi bonita*, you are killin' it tonight. New highlights in your hair?"

"Thanks, Miguel, I'm glad somebody noticed. Can I get you a refill?"

"No, *gracias*, I'm good."

"Hey, what about me?"

"What about you?"

"A refill? Another Jameson, please."

"Drowning your sorrows, Leah?"

"What are you talking about?"

"Oh, I get it. Good for you. Who cares if your boyfriend was in here last night with a really hot redhead, and they were all over each other." She smiled sweetly.

"Yay for Ben. I'm glad he found somebody."

"If that's your story." She shrugged. "Another shot and you might even believe it."

I considered my range of rejoinders, but she left before I could get one out.

"I didn't know you and Ben broke up."

"We didn't. We weren't together. Not really. Not a big deal. Maybe I should have written it up for the paper." I returned to the main issue. "Whether it's probable or not, admit it's possible that someone staged Whiting's death to look like a suicide."

"Maybe. What about the victimology?"

"What?"

"Victimology, you know, looking at the victim's life, relationships, reputation, habits. Did he have future plans? Was he in financial trouble?"

"I don't know enough yet. I haven't seen the file, and when I ran into Ross he wasn't too keen on me getting my hands on it."

"I doubt that will stop you," he said. "When you do get a look, pay less attention to the weapon and the body—the sheriff's department and the M.E. will have that covered. You're not likely to see anything they didn't. But if Charlie made assumptions because it looked like suicide, he might not have asked all the questions he could have."

"Oh, I'm sure he made assumptions. Isabel said she tried to point a couple of things out to him, but you know what a dolt he is."

Coop shook his head.

"What?"

"It's not your job to ride to the rescue for this Isabel. And it's not going to make your life any easier if you get on the wrong side of the sheriff's department again. Do you really want to tangle with Ross?"

"I'm not rescuing her. I'm investigating her story. And the only reason I might 'tangle' with Ross is if he got it all wrong again. I'm just asking questions, that's all."

"Are you sure? Sounds like you already have your mind made up."

"Yes, I'm sure. I just don't think Isabel Whiting's concerns should be dismissed."

"Now you're mad."

"No." And I wasn't. Well, maybe a little.

As Sherry set my refill down, he asked, "What does Rebecca think about it?"

"I haven't told her yet. I have to figure out a way to swing her to my side first."

"Your boss? I'd be careful if I was you. You just might get yourself fired again," Sherry injected.

"And if I were you, I'd be talking to customers who cared. But, oh, you're not me. So, you'll probably just stand here annoying us."

"C'mon, Leah," Coop said, as Sherry sniffed and walked away. He finished his beer in one long swallow and set it on the table. "Well, I gotta go. Just think about it, will you? Make sure you're not just following up on this to piss Ross off."

"Why are you in such a hurry?"

"Maybe he has a mystery date," Miguel said.

"No mystery. Just places to go." He stood up and put his jacket on, then put some money on the table for his bill. "See you later."

"Right. See you."

Something was up with Coop, but I figured I'd find out sooner or later. After he left I finished my Jameson. "Time for me to go, too."

"*Chica*, hey, I'll give you a ride."

I started to protest, but two whiskeys in an hour and the level of tired I felt made me reconsider. I definitely didn't need a DUI.

"OK, thanks."

* * *

"Why are you always so hard on Sherry?" Miguel asked as we got into his car.

"I'm not."

"*Sí,* you are. Do you want Coop for yourself?"

I shook my head.

"Coop's my best friend. Since we were 12. That's how we like it, you know that."

"Then why do you always hate his girlfriends?"

"I don't," I said in surprise. "Why would you say that?"

"Sherry has a crush. So? Coop's a man steak, you know, lots of ladies want to eat him up."

"Well, I just think he could do better than Sherry, don't you?"

Miguel didn't answer.

"OK. OK. Maybe I do come on too strong with her. She just irritates me. I guess I could ease up. A little."

He smiled. "So, you don't want Ben, and you don't want Coop, who do you want?"

"I want a man I know I can't have." I raised an eyebrow in his direction to make my point.

"You have my heart, *chica*. It's just my body you can't get next to."

I laughed.

"As long as your heart's in my corner. You know I'm not just out to get Ross, don't you?"

"I know. What can I do?"

"You could tap into the gossip grapevine at your aunt's salon." Miguel's Aunt Lydia owns Making Waves, a trendy hair styling place with a wide-ranging clientele.

"Sure. I'm helping out there tomorrow while Aunt Lydia goes to Milwaukee with Uncle Craig."

"Another doctor's appointment?" Since his uncle's kidney issues had worsened, it seemed like all Miguel's aunt and uncle did was an endless round of doctor and dialysis appointments.

"No, not this time. He's feeling OK. They're going to visit friends. They have to take the good days when they come."

"I guess that's true. So, what are you going to do at the salon? Wax eyebrows, do some highlights, a few makeovers?"

"What? You think I can't handle it? Oh. I can. I'm the best shampoo boy north of Chicago. Believe it."

"I do, I do. Now listen good while you're massaging that conditioner through some Himmel matron's hair. See if you can find any Garrett Whiting gossip to give me."

"That's violating shampoo boy/client confidentiality. But for you, I'll do it."

"I appreciate it."

"Why don't you stop by?"

"Oh, no. Don't start," I said, as he reached over and lifted my baseball cap off my head, causing my hair to tumble down on my shoulders.

I leaned away and picked up a strand of my own hair. In an exaggerated version of Miguel's speech patterns, I crooned, "Oh, *chica*, some copper highlights. A little green eyeshadow, a wash of brown—your hazel eyes will spark."

"I don't sound like that."

"Yes. You do. I've only heard you say it to me about a hundred times. Why don't you love me the way I am?"

"You know I love you. But you could look so fierce. You just won't try. How can I get you with somebody if you won't even try? I'm not giving up."

"Oh, yeah, you are. Let it go. Hey," I said as we buckled in and he pulled on to the street, "how did you get Rebecca to let you off tomorrow?"

"I keep telling you. She's not so bad."

"Not how I see it, my friend. She just doesn't like me. How can that be? I think I'm very charming, don't you? Don't answer that."

As we rounded the corner, I saw a red SUV parked next to the curb in front of my house.

"Expecting company?"

I started to shake my head, but stopped when the door of the SUV opened. Illuminated by the cab light was a figure I knew very well. What I didn't know was what the hell he was doing here.

"I can stay, *chica*," Miguel said, seeing my shocked expression. I was already unbuckled and had my hand on the door handle.

"No, that's OK." I tried to slip away without further comment, but Miguel was not down with that.

"No. I'm not leaving you alone in the dark with a stranger," he said as he unbuckled his own seatbelt. Since I definitely didn't need a third party at this meeting, I came clean as I leaned my head back in.

"It's OK, Miguel. It's my husband. My ex-husband that is, Nick Gallagher."

Miguel's eyes widened and his mouth was working, but nothing came out. Before anything did, I said, "Thanks for the ride. I'll talk to you later. Bye."

6

I TURNED TO MEET Nick as he walked up.

"What are you doing here?"

"Nice to see you, too."

We had tripped the light sensor above the garage door, and as it came on I saw that years after the fact—the fact of our divorce—he looked just the same. A piece of fine, wheat-colored hair fell across his forehead in a way I'd once thought endearing. His sea-green eyes held a familiar glint of amusement, as though he were in on some joke the rest of us weren't. When he smiled, his eyes crinkled at the corners and he revealed a set of perfect teeth. He looked like a man confident and at ease with his place in the world. The only thing that betrayed a hint of discomfort was the way his hand slid the zipper on his open jacket up and down, making a faint sawing sound. Suitable background music to our conversation. He tried again.

"Leah, it's great to see you."

"Really? Why?" I opened my purse and started digging for my house key.

"Don't be like that. We're divorced. We don't have to be enemies." He reached out and touched my arm. I felt the involuntary little shock I used to get when he touched me unexpectedly.

"I'm not your enemy, Nick. But I don't want to be friends. So, thanks for stopping by and goodnight."

"Wait. Leah, come on. Can't I come in? Just for a minute. I've been waiting here for over an hour, and it's pretty cold. Just a cup of coffee, and I'm on my way. OK?"

Curiosity warred with my instinctive urge to say no. Curiosity won.

"All right." I pushed the door open, and over my shoulder added, "For a minute."

I turned on the light, dropped my purse on the table and hung my jacket on the hook near the kitchen door. As I put the coffee on, Nick took his coat off and draped it over the back of a chair, then went to the cupboard and took out two mugs and set them on the counter. Something about the easy way he moved around the kitchen annoyed me. Nick always made himself at home. No matter whose home it was.

He walked past the bar that separates the kitchen and living room, picked up a photo or two on the mantel and looked at them, then came back and sat down at the table.

"Looks like your mother has done some redecorating. The living room's a different color, isn't it?"

"She's had a hard time finding a job since Karen's law firm closed. She's been channeling her energy into fixing up the place. But you didn't come all the way from Michigan to have an HGTV moment with me. What do you want?"

I added creamer to his cup of coffee and set it down in front of him, then took the chair opposite, my arms folded across my chest.

"Oh-oh. I know that Leah look." He slipped into a Ricky Ricardo accent. "You've got some 'splainin' to do, Nicky."

I didn't crack a smile.

"You're not making this easy, you know."

"That's not my job description anymore. Making things easy for you."

"Are you really still so angry at me?"

To buy some time, I got up and poured myself a cup of coffee. When I sat back down, I spoke slowly, trying to figure out my truth as I talked.

"I'm not mad at you anymore, Nick. I'm surprised to see you, and a little curious. And a little annoyed, maybe, that you think you can just drop back into my life without notice. I guess I just don't care enough about you anymore to be angry with you."

"A little harsh. But honest as always, that's my Leah." His smile was so warm it reminded me of all the things I liked about him. Then he started talking again and reminded me of all the things I didn't.

"How did I let you get away?"

"You didn't let me get away. You cheated on me, and you lied to me, and then you blamed your affair with Seraphim or Cherubim or whatever her name was on me. I was too intimidating, I was too intense, I expected too much from you." I knew perfectly well what her name was. Seraphina. A tall, exotically beautiful graduate assistant in the psychology department where Nick had been a temporary faculty member. "You knocked me down. I got back up. But there's no need to cover old ground. Just tell me what you want."

"I want to say I'm sorry. I'm sorry I wasn't good enough for you. You were always so strong, so absolutely sure you knew the way things should be—the way I should be. You never needed my approval. But maybe I needed yours, and when I felt like I couldn't get it, I looked elsewhere. I'm sorry."

"A pro tip for you: When asking forgiveness, it's not a good move to tell your victim it was really all her fault."

"Victim? That's not something you ever were."

"Oh, yeah. I was."

I didn't elaborate. No way was I going to admit that I was a victim of my own insecurities. That when I met Nick, I wanted him to love me so much that I surrendered whole parts of myself. I pretended to be less smart, less vulnerable, less strong-willed, less driven. At the same time, I wanted him to see me as more than I was—more confident, more giving, more patient—more worth loving. Because I didn't believe then that anyone could really love me as I was.

I still have my doubts, but I'm a lot more attached to my sense of self now. My real self. That doesn't mean I don't realize there are things I need to change. Only now I try to change them for myself, not for anyone else.

"Wait. This isn't going the way I wanted it to. I'm not saying it right. Let me try again. You know, you really can be a little terrifying. I did some terrible things, Leah. Whatever the reasons, there are no excuses. I hope you can forgive me."

I had once longed to hear those words, to feel the satisfaction of Nick admitting he was a liar, a cheat, a hypocrite. Now though, when he uttered them, or came as close as he probably ever would, I didn't feel the thrill of victory I'd imagined. Instead, I felt the urge to back away from the moment, to retreat from the emotions threatening to burst to the surface. So I did.

"You drove seven hours to ask forgiveness for something that happened years ago?"

"I didn't come here from Michigan. I've been teaching a class on Thursday nights at Himmel Tech."

"You're living in Himmel?" I certainly don't know everybody in a town of 15,000, but it was hard to believe if Nick were here, somebody wouldn't have run into him and mentioned it to me.

"Not in Himmel. I have a tenure track position at Robley College in Clarkson. I'm covering a class at Himmel Tech for a friend of mine. He's out for the semester, and I can use the money."

"Tenure track? That's good, I'm glad for you."

During our brief marriage, Nick had been frustrated by his temporary faculty status at Grand Valley State University outside of Grand Rapids, Michigan, where I worked for the *Grand Rapids Press*. Tenure track positions aren't easy to come by, and he was always worried he'd be a temporary for life.

"You are? Really?"

"Yes, really. I know it's what you always wanted."

That smile again. "That's great to hear. But I need you to hear what I'm saying, however badly I've been saying it. I own what I did. I'm sorry I hurt you. I apologize."

"All right. All right. OK, I forgive you. I wasn't perfect either—though I never cheated on you." I couldn't resist adding that.

"I know. You wouldn't. If I had it to do over again, I wouldn't either, but, well, here we are."

"Yep. Here we are."

We were both quiet for a few seconds and drank our coffee as though that simple act took all of our attention. Then he spoke again.

"So, how are things going for you? I read about Lacey and everything last year, and I wanted to call, but I didn't have the courage. I didn't think you'd want to hear from me, and I didn't want to make things any worse for you. I didn't know what to say."

"That's OK. There really wasn't anything to say. I'm glad we know the truth, that's all."

Another strained silence ensued, during which we both focused on our coffee again, as though it were a magic elixir to promote small talk.

Finally, I said, "I got a book deal. I'm working on the final proofs now. Supposed to come out in February."

"A book? Really? That's great. So, you're not going to be staying in Himmel? I was surprised when I heard you were back here. You're too good to be stuck at a small-town paper."

"Yeah, well, thanks. I kind of blew things at my job in Miami and bounced back here to regroup. Hopefully the book thing takes off. We'll see."

"That's great," he repeated. "Really great."

"So, what about you? Do you like teaching at a small school?"

"Yeah, sure. Robley's a really good liberal arts college. We get a lot of top students. I've only been there a year, but I can see a future for me there."

"That's good. What about family? Are you married, kids?"

"No, not married. How about you?"

"No, nothing to report."

"Still love 'em and leave 'em, Leah?"

"Yeah, right."

"What about your friend Coop? Where's he these days?"

"He's back in Himmel, too. He's a lieutenant in the police department."

He nodded. "I'm not surprised. He seemed like a basic good guy."

"You say that like you think being honest, and reliable, and trustworthy is dull. Oh, that's right. You do."

"Hey, that wasn't a criticism. I mean, he seems like a capable, nice, guy. Seriously. So, how's life at the *Himmel Times*?"

"Oh, you know. A lot of meetings to cover, Cranberry Queen pageant, local elections, zoning board controversy, that kind of thing."

"Sounds pretty deadly."

"It's a living. Though I just started looking into something that could turn interesting."

"Really? What?" He lifted his eyebrows just a little and raised his cup to his lips.

And then, for reasons unclear to me—maybe I wanted to show off a little, impress him with my investigative know-how, make my life sound a little more exciting than it was—I started telling him about Isabel Whiting, and Garrett's death, and the odd things surrounding it.

"I might be a little dense, but how do you think someone could kill him with his own gun and not leave traces? Walk me through it." He leaned forward a little, as though nothing was more interesting to him than whatever I had to say. Nick could be a great listener when he wanted to be. And I find it hard to resist a receptive audience.

"It would have to be someone he knew, someone he trusted, OK? Maybe an old friend stops by to see him. Suggests they have a drink, maybe he offers to make it. Or," I said, warming to my subject, "maybe the friend brought a bottle laced with Klonopin with him. He makes a drink for Garrett, has something else himself. When Garrett gets woozy from the drug and alcohol mix, the friend slips on the gloves he has in his pocket, takes the gun out of the desk, puts it in Garrett's hand, holds it to his head and presses the trigger. Then he takes his bottle, washes out his own glass, puts it away, and goes. Doesn't matter if his fingerprints are in the room. He's someone Garrett knows, and it wouldn't be unusual to find his prints there."

"But how would he know Garrett had a gun in his desk? And that it was loaded?"

"He's a friend. Friends know things."

"What about motive?"

"That's what I have to figure out. You're a psychologist. Do you think a man like Garrett Whiting, who had a son who needed him, and a daughter who'd already been abandoned by her mother, do you think he would just suddenly kill himself and leave them totally alone?"

"Leah, I don't know anything about Garrett Whiting. It wouldn't be professional—or helpful—for me to guess at what motivated him. Not to get too technical on you, but people do crazy things."

True that. Before I could say anything, my mother came bursting through the door.

7

"I'M TELLING YOU, if Bernard Magnuson winds up dead, you can put me at the top of the suspect list." She had half-turned to slip off her coat and hang her keys on the hook by the door, and was so wound up she didn't notice Nick's presence.

"We had a knockdown drag out at parish council tonight. He's the most intolerant, self-righteous, hypocritical so-called 'Christian' I've ever seen. Everyone knows he can't keep it in his pants, but he thinks he can pass judgment on a woman who made a mistake, then worked her butt off to turn her life around. He doesn't think it's 'appropriate' for Kim Granville to serve on the school board. Because she has a son and she's never been married. He should be—" By this time she had turned back to face us.

"Nick! What are you doing here?"

"Still like mother, like daughter I see. Hi, Carol. I was just leaving. I stopped by to see Leah for a minute. I'm sure she'll tell you all about it." As he spoke, he'd risen, slipped on his jacket, and moved toward the door.

"Just think about what I said, Leah. I really mean it. Call me if you want to. Good to see you, Carol." And he was gone.

"Well, you are absolutely not calling him. Are you?"

"No, Mom. I'm not planning on it."

"What was he doing here? Why did you let him in?"

"Take it easy." I filled her in.

"I hope you're not going to fall for that man again. You had to move all the way to the ends of the earth to get over him."

"North Carolina is hardly the 'ends of the earth.' Don't worry, he wants me to forgive him, not get back together with him. I was pretty hostile when I first saw him—"

"Hold on to that feeling."

"No, I don't think I will. I'm glad he came by tonight, because while I wasn't looking, I guess I really did get over it. I'm not mad anymore, because I don't care anymore. And the time we were together taught me something important. That it's never worth giving up who I am."

She looked at me the way she used to when, caught with crumbs on my mouth, I had vigorously denied any knowledge of missing cookies. "I hope that's true. But, you know, if a nice, not-Nick man comes along, you could just disguise a few things, couldn't you? You know, like your smartass remarks, and your need to win every argument? I would like to have grand-children before I'm too old to play with them."

"Not listening. Let's move on." I had to give her something to get off Nick, so I filled her in on Isabel.

"You're all in already, aren't you? No matter what you're saying to me or telling yourself, you've made up your mind that Isabel needs you."

"Don't say it. Don't tell me Isabel isn't Lacey. I know that."

"That isn't what I was going to say."

"Oh really?"

"I was going to say that Isabel isn't you. You're drawn to her because she's on some hopeless quest and no one will believe or help her. Just like you were with Lacey."

"Yeah? And look what happened. Look what I found out."

She sighed. "You're responding to how bad she hurts. You know how that feels. I'm not saying don't help her. All I'm saying is know why you're doing it, and know when to stop."

"Don't worry, I've got this. I know what I'm doing and why. Like I know I'm going to bed now. I'm exhausted. See you in the morning."

Shortly after I got into bed, I heard my mother's door close, and about 10 minutes later the muffled sound of her regular deep breathing, just shy of a soft snore. I tried to sleep, but I couldn't. Too much going on in my head. Finally, I got up, threw on jeans and a sweatshirt, and headed over to the place I go when I need help thinking.

"How are things at work?"

It was 11:30 p.m. and I was sitting in the warm and cozy kitchen of the Reverend Gregory Lindstrom's brown brick bungalow. A little late for conventional visiting, but our friendship has never been conventional. He's a Roman Catholic priest; I'm a non-believer—or at least a skeptic. He's thoughtful, patient, and wise. I'm, well, not. But he listens, he doesn't judge, and he doesn't give advice unless I ask for it.

"Ugh. Same as they have been since Rebecca showed up. More work, less help. Rebecca's job is to cut costs, and boy has she ever. A friend of mine from J school works at a paper where they send all their copy to a 'pagination hub.' In Malaysia. They got rid of local copy editors and proofers and graphic designers and do all the editing and layout out for a bunch of papers from there. That's not us yet, but it could be, if Rebecca or her corporate overlords decide that's the next step."

"I suppose that's more efficient, to centralize things."

"Maybe, but copy editors in the hubs don't know the towns, the issues, the people being reported on. My friend said when his town's basketball team won the state championship, the hub copy editors misspelled the team name—twice. Local people don't like it. They want their local news, and they want it right. When they don't get it, they cancel. And when enough people cancel, the paper folds. That's what I see in Himmel's future. A town without a paper. And Rebecca couldn't care less."

"Aren't you being a little hard on her?" His pale eyes blinked behind his glasses.

I considered. "Possibly. I mean I get that it's her job to tighten things up.

But how can she like a job where her whole purpose is to prepare the paper for slaughter? The hedge fund that owns us and a lot of other papers—they just want to suck us dry, then sell or shut us down."

"Maybe she doesn't like it. Maybe she doesn't have another option. You know very little about her and the struggles she may have faced."

"I'll take favorite Gregory Lindstrom quotes for $250, Alex. 'Remember that everyone you meet is afraid of something, loves something, and has lost something.' Am I right?"

He nodded and took a sip of tea from his favorite *X-Files* mug. I felt a rush of affection for the compact little priest with his fluffy white hair and kind eyes. He always listened as though nothing I had to say, not any of my secret shames, or sorrows, or regrets, shocked him, or angered him, or moved him to anything but quiet compassion.

"OK. I don't know what she's going through, or has been through, or why she acts the way she does. I shouldn't personalize it." I waited. "Is that it? Is that what you're trying to get me to see?"

He smiled full-on then. He really has a lovely smile. It starts in the corners of his mouth and slides on up his chubby little cheeks until it rests right in the center of his light blue eyes.

"You'll see what you need to when the time is right, Leah. I have every confidence in you."

"I wish a few more people did."

He raised an eyebrow and gave me an inquiring look.

"I'm starting work on a story, and I'm the only one who thinks it could be a story. I got this call from Isabel Whiting, Garrett Whiting's daughter. You know, the doctor who died last month."

"And?"

I explained Isabel's conviction that her dad hadn't killed himself and her reasons.

"Garrett's behavior is a little odd, I agree. But I find people, especially troubled people, can do very inexplicable things."

"You say 'Garrett' like you know him. Were the Whitings part of St. Stephen's parish?"

"No. I knew Garrett years ago, when he was a young doctor in Milwaukee. I worked part-time as a chaplain at St. Cyprian's Hospital. But I haven't even had a conversation with him in many years."

"Was he the kind of person to get someone mad enough to kill him?"

"One could argue we're all that sort of person, depending on what someone else wants or needs from us, and what we're willing to give."

"Well, then do you think he was the kind of person who would kill himself?"

"That was a long time ago, and I certainly didn't know him well enough to judge. Suicide is a complicated affair."

"You sound like Nick." The words were out of my mouth before I could stop them. I hadn't come here to talk about Nick. Or had I?

"That's your former husband?"

"That's the one. He stopped by to have me grant him absolution."

"I see. And did you?"

"Yeah. Pretty much. I guess so."

Father Lindstrom is really good at the silence trick. You know, don't comment, just let the silence hang there. Most people can't stand it and will start babbling. Myself included.

"It's not like I think he's fundamentally changed. He'll always do what's best for Nick, but maybe it's best for me to let that anger go."

He nodded.

"I mean, how long can you stay mad at someone? We're not exactly BFFs now. He has his life, and I have mine. And now I feel like I can actually wish him well. That's all."

"That sounds like quite a lot."

I stood up and put my mug in the sink.

As he walked me to the front door, I said, "Who knows? Maybe I'm turning into a brand new me. All forgiveness, all the time."

He smiled, and just before he closed the door, he said, "I like the old you just fine, Leah."

I love that guy.

8

THE NEXT MORNING, I tapped lightly on Rebecca's office door with the hand that held a pastry bag containing two rugelachs from the Elite. In the other was a cardboard holder with a chai latte and an extra large, extra bold cup of coffee, black. Rebecca's favorite poison.

"Come in."

It still took me aback whenever I entered her lair. The office that my old boss, Max, had inhabited for almost 40 years was now unrecognizable. Gone were the teetering stacks of files, the dusty bowling trophies, the jar of M&Ms, the occasional petrified remnant of a bygone feast. Instead, there were freshly painted walls in a neutral beige with bright white moldings, wooden floors restored to their golden oak glory, and a sleek glass and metal desk. Even Max's favorite rocking/rolling cushioned office chair had been replaced by an ergonomically correct and aggressively modern version. The desktop was so clean, I hesitated to put my tributes on it.

I sat down without waiting to be asked.

"Hey. I got you a treat at the Elite. Coffee, just the way you like it. And rugelach fresh this morning."

"Thanks for the coffee. I don't snack. I have a high protein breakfast at home and nothing else until lunch."

I almost said, "Of course you do." But I held it in. *Keep your eyes on the prize, Leah.*

"Healthier, I'm sure."

"So, what do we have, Leah? A suspicious suicide or a delusional daughter?"

"I'm not sure yet." I gave her the rundown, and while I talked, she made notes on a yellow legal pad she'd pulled from a side drawer.

"Well, what do you think?" I sat on the edge of my chair, poised to launch a fusillade of reasons why it warranted further investigation.

She didn't answer right away. Instead, she steepled her fingers and looked at me, her eyes slightly narrowed. As I waited, I tried to figure out what was going on beneath the polished exterior. But I couldn't get past the surface: straight, white-blonde hair that swept the top of her shoulders, every strand falling into perfect alignment. A long, thin nose offset by a generous mouth. A faint v-shaped wrinkle between her eyebrows that deepened when she concentrated. I noticed it was just beginning to leave a permanent trace even when her forehead relaxed. But it was her eyes that demanded attention. A glacier blue rarely warmed by a smile. Her unwavering gaze warned a person not to trespass, not to get too close. What had happened to make her so wary? I wondered. Then, with a start, I realized she was talking to me.

"Sorry, what?"

"I said, all right. Go ahead. But keep it low key. You can do low key, can't you, Leah?"

"All right? You mean start interviews, get the file?" I had expected her to reject the idea, initially anyway, because it might upset people, hurt the bottom line, make waves, any of the things that a good, true story can do.

"That's what 'go ahead' means, isn't it?" She permitted herself a small smile, but it was gone in seconds, a flash of sunlight overwhelmed by a leaden sky.

"OK. Just so we're clear. You're saying I can ask for the case file, I can interview Ross or the sheriff. I can follow up on any leads I come up with. Is that right?"

"What's the matter, you can't take yes for an answer?"

"No. I mean yes. I just don't usually hear 'Go for it,' from you, that's all."

"Don't make me regret it. You did hear the 'low key' part, right?"

"Oh, yeah. Right. Absolutely." I stood up to go before she changed her mind.

As I reached the door, she said, "Leah."

I turned back to look at her. "Yeah?"

"Don't take any unnecessary pokes at Charlie Ross, all right?"

"Sure, OK. And, uh, thanks, Rebecca."

So that just happened. But why?

It had been easy to get an appointment to talk to Grantland County Sheriff Lester Dillingham. His secretary, Jennifer Pilarski, (née Naseman) is always in a sunny mood. She and I had been academically and alphabetically linked from kindergarten through high school. Almost everything about Jennifer is soft—her comfortable round body, her wavy, shoulder-length brown hair, her warm brown eyes, and her soothing voice. Everything except her laugh, a joyous, whooping, belly-shaking blast that causes an irresistible spasm of laughter in everyone around her. Everyone except teachers, principals, and other assorted authority figures. She thought I was hilarious, and I love a good audience. As a result, we spent a lot of quality time together in disciplinary settings, ranging from the kindergarten time-out corner to the high school assistant principal's office.

"Hey, Jen. How's Lester's quest for true love going?"

She giggled. "Not good. He keeps asking me to set him up with my mother."

"I've got one of those. Do you think 10 minutes of heaven with Carol Nash could get me access to the unredacted Garrett Whiting file?"

Jennifer knows my mother well. The thought of Carol and Lester together set her off, as I knew it would.

I couldn't help but respond in kind, and within seconds we were laughing so hard I could hardly stand up. Is there anything more fun than laughing 'til your cheeks hurt with someone you really like? We didn't hear the door to Lester's office open.

"What's the joke, girls?"

I attempted a quick recovery.

"Hey, Sh-Sheriff, noth—, no, nothing," I said in a half-gasp, half-giggle. "You know, just 'girl' stuff. I had the funniest thing happen when I was at the gynecologist—"

His face turned red with the kind of embarrassment some men still feel at the mention of women's sexuality in any context other than a dirty joke. I glanced at Jennifer, who was fighting to achieve sobriety, and I took pity on them both.

"Nevermind. On second thought, not that interesting. Or funny. Actually, if you have just a minute, I was hoping to talk to you about Garrett Whiting."

He ushered me into his office. His broad face, with its ex-hockey player's bent nose and thick gray mustache, was still slightly flushed from his near encounter with "female issues."

"I heard you might want to take a look at the Whiting file."

"You talked to Ross?"

"Yeah. He did mention it. You know, Leah, we got some things wrong on your sister's case, and I'm still real sorry about that. I told your mother and you both. But we're not a bunch of Barney Fifes over here. The Whiting case was suicide."

"I'm not saying it wasn't. I just want to see the file. What harm could that do?"

"No harm to us. None at all. Everything was by the book. But that's not exactly what Charlie said you were doing."

"Well, Detective Ross and I don't communicate all that well, I'm sorry to say."

"I've noticed. Now, how can I be sure you're not just going to try to find something in the file because you have it in for Charlie?"

The old boy tone that had crept in put my back up a little, and I responded in a way that Rebecca probably wouldn't like.

"Look, I can file an Open Records Act request and get it."

"Yeah, you could. And I could redact it so you wouldn't wind up with much of anything. But I'm not gonna do that."

"You're not?"

"Nope. Matter of fact, I already told Jennifer to get a copy made for you. Course the *Times* is gonna have to pay for it."

"Sure, of course," I said, but I was uneasy. I'm wired to expect things to go wrong. When they don't, it throws me off balance.

"Wait a minute. What's really going on here, Sheriff?"

He shook his head and chuckled. "You're sure not like your old dad. He was a real easygoing guy. Yeah, Tommy was always ready for a laugh. He was a heck of a guy. We played on the state championship football team back in 1973. Last time Himmel fielded a winning team."

If he was trying to throw me off my game, he did. I never talk about my father. To anyone. I didn't answer, and he returned to a favorite theme.

"Charlie Ross is a good investigator. He made some mistakes in the past. We all do. Even you. I'd hate to see you tryin' to make him look like an idiot again."

So many possible responses. All of them so unwise. I restrained myself.

"Thank you, Sheriff. I don't plan to." Whether that happened or not was in the lap of the gods. Sure to be dropped there by Charlie Ross and his own fumble fingers.

He picked up the phone and buzzed Jennifer, asking her to get the file for me. As I thanked him and left, he said, "You give my best to your mother now." Which made me wonder what else I might have gotten hold of, if I'd played the mother card.

9

FRIDAY IS ALWAYS A PRETTY SLOW DAY at the paper. The latest edition is out, and the next deadline isn't for another six days. I went back to the office feeling pretty good about having a nice chunk of time, and, with Miguel off, relative quiet in the newsroom to go over the Garrett Whiting file.

I looked at, but didn't linger over, the photos of the body. Dr. Whiting had been found sitting in an armchair, one of a set of two that flanked a small table holding a reading lamp. An empty glass with the remnants of a drink sat on its polished wood surface. The gun that shot him was on the floor, next to the chair. My untrained eyes saw nothing that the experts hadn't recorded.

I focused on the other photos of the room, hoping to get some sense of the person that he was, from the things he chose to have around him.

In front of an arched window on the north wall was a sparely elegant wood desk. A small extension on one side held a PC, its computer mouse neatly aligned on the left. A note in the file indicated that taped to the bottom of the keyboard was a list of passwords—Garrett's email account, Amazon account, pin numbers—the kind of stuff my mother keeps stashed near her computer in case of a "senior moment." Nothing exciting like the combination to a hidden safe or a Swiss bank account number.

In the center of the desktop was a leather portfolio and just above it a

Meisterstuck Mont Blanc pen in a silver and onyx holder. I recognized the high-end writing instrument only because I'd done a feature story once on a pen collector. Who knew you could drop $1,000 on a pen? A black phone sat within reach of anyone sitting in the well-padded black leather chair behind the desk. On the right-hand corner was a framed photograph. A close-up showed it to be a picture of Garrett Whiting, looking very JFK on a sailboat. There was nothing else—no photos of his kids, no desk art, no expensive paperweights.

The rest of the room was just as anonymous. The walls were painted a sage green; the floor was dark wood. A set of shelves, holding books that looked more of the scholarly than best-seller variety, was built into one wall. All that the furnishings and the room itself allowed me to deduce was that Garrett Whiting was a very tidy man who enjoyed a solitary drink in his study. Sadly, the crime scene evidence team had found no muddy footprints, no dropped cufflinks, no tell-tale bits of fiber to indicate the presence of anyone other than Garrett.

I put the photos aside and started scanning the reports. Isabel told police she'd found the body at 8:30 a.m. She'd called 911. She told Ross she had spoken to her father around 11 p.m. the night before. I flipped through the phone LUDs—the local usage details—for Garrett's landline. The details for Sunday showed the call Garrett had placed to Isabel. The one Ross didn't think to tell me about. There were no other calls from or to the Whiting house that night, and no calls at all on Sunday on Garrett's cell phone records.

Isabel's brother Jamie had told the detectives that he wasn't sure when he got home, but it was pretty late. He had spent the weekend at the family cabin near Eau Claire. He had planned to stay another night and go home Monday morning, but changed his mind when his cell phone died and he didn't have a charger with him. When he got back to Himmel around 11 p.m., he stopped to fill up his car and ran into a friend who invited him to a party. It turned out to be a "pharm party," where kids bring a variety of pills, throw them in a bowl and everyone at the party grabs a mystery drug. He wasn't sure what he'd taken, but with the weed he smoked, the pills, and the beer, he was in pretty bad shape.

He didn't notice anything when he got home, just went to his room and crashed. He didn't wake up until Isabel came in that morning. He said the friend who invited him was Keegan Monroe and he might remember more. When police contacted Keegan later that day, he verified inviting Jamie, and said they'd left the party around 4 a.m. He was certain, because he wasn't as 'f'd up' as Jamie, and he remembered a neighbor banging on the door, saying it was almost 4 a.m. and he was going to call the cops if they didn't shut up. The party broke up then, and Keegan walked home. Jamie drove off.

Ross had noted that Jamie's bleary eyes and the lingering odor of stale beer and marijuana seemed to support the story he and Keegan had told. The housekeeper, Evelyn Godfrey, said she came in at 9 a.m., Monday through Friday, and had the weekends off. The last time she saw Dr. Whiting was the Friday before he died. He seemed fine to her. He had stayed in his study all day working. She had fixed dinner and left the house as usual at 5 p.m. Jamie wasn't home. Dr. Whiting told her his son was away for the weekend.

The next thing I read was the autopsy. The medical examiner put time of death between 11 p.m. and 3 a.m., based on stomach content analysis, body temperature, and rigor mortis, and the fact that Isabel had spoken to her father shortly before 11 p.m. Then I found something I didn't expect. Something that cast a whole new light on things. I closed the file and made a couple of calls. An hour later I was on my way to the Whiting house just outside of town.

"Leah! Hi, come on in. What are you doing here?" Isabel's smile faltered when she saw my stormy expression. No one has ever accused me of having a poker face, and I wasn't taking any pains to hide my anger as she led me into the formal living room.

"What's wrong?"

I sat down on the edge of a cream-colored couch and waited until she had taken the chair opposite me.

"You lied to me."

The force of my words caused a physical reaction. She jerked back and her eyes widened. "I don't understand. I didn't lie to you. I wouldn't—"

I didn't let her finish. "Why didn't you tell me your father had Parkinson's disease?"

"I—"

"He had a reason to kill himself, Isabel. He was a surgeon. His career was over."

"He told me about the Parkinson's the night he called. But he wasn't suicidal. He was worried about Jamie. I thought if I told you about it, you'd dismiss me, too."

"Didn't you know I'd look at the case file, talk to the medical examiner, talk to the investigator?" Not that Ross had told me anything. Or the sheriff either. They were trying to teach me a lesson. That every case wasn't Lacey's, and I wasn't as smart as I thought I was.

Isabel had raised her hands to her mouth, her fingertips poking out from the overly long sleeves of the pale-yellow sweater she wore. "Please, don't be so angry, Leah. You're the only one who can help me."

"After I read the autopsy, I called Detective Ross. And then I ate a big, rancid helping of humble pie." It had been an excruciating call to make. He was gleeful, and I knew that he had set me up. Ross isn't as dumb as I thought. He figured out there's no better way to get me to move full speed ahead then to tell me not to do it.

So, I walked right into his funny little joke, and he couldn't stop laughing and insulting me. And I had to take it. In this case, he was right, and I was stupid. He was so happy, now that he had a story to spread to all his cronies. How that smart mouth reporter wasn't so smart. He even gave me a bonus to show how extra dumb I was.

"But wait. There's more. Detective Ross told me that your father had a life insurance policy. One that pays you and Jamie $1 million when he dies. Except, oops, it has a suicide clause. You don't get anything if he kills himself within two years of the policy taking force. No wonder you were so anxious to prove he didn't commit suicide. You missed cashing in by six months."

"No!" She had found her voice and she spoke so loudly it broke my rhythm. I shut up for a minute.

"No, you're wrong. I don't care about the insurance. I tried to get the sheriff's department to investigate before I even knew there was insurance or a suicide clause. It's not about the money! Please, you have to believe me. I know I should have told you everything. But I thought you'd start investigating, like you did for your sister. You'd find more about my father, and you'd know he didn't kill himself. And then it wouldn't matter. I could tell you then."

Tears had welled up and started running down her cheeks. She didn't even brush them away. I suppose I should have felt bad, maybe given her a little pat, or at least handed her a Kleenex. I didn't.

"Look, I can't help someone who can't be straight with me. I went out on a limb for you, and you sawed it off. That's it. We're done."

I stood and walked out, leaving Isabel quietly weeping on the chair. I yanked hard on the door and almost tumbled into the guy who was standing on the other side, arm up to open it from the outside.

I had the impression of someone young, late teens or early 20s, but he was wearing a red hoodie that concealed his hair and shadowed his face.

Jamie, I assumed. He stepped back as I lunged out.

"Excuse me." I brushed passed him. I heard the front door close as I reached my car. Snow, which had been falling sporadically as I arrived, had picked up speed and the driveway and my car were covered under a light layer. I backed out with the windshield wipers screeching across the screen and fishtailed a little as I pulled onto the blacktop.

It's not like a source had never lied to me before. They do it all the time to protect themselves, or to point you in the wrong direction, or because they don't want to get involved, or sometimes, the weirdos, just because they can. But I had invested something in Isabel. All right, maybe it was more accurate to say I had projected something onto her. I did see a little of myself in her. I knew how it felt to have everyone against you. And I had identified with her so strongly that I lost my objectivity. I hate it when my mother is right.

I was so focused on my thoughts that I didn't notice until the last minute that the big, white, grandma Buick coming toward me had crossed the center line. I swerved and she missed, but the sickening scrape and thump on my car door told me I'd just taken out someone's bright red mailbox. This was turning out to be a grade A day.

10

I PULLED MY CAR into the driveway that the mailbox belonged to and walked up to the door of a neat white farmhouse with a wraparound porch and green shutters. I rang the doorbell a couple of times before it was answered.

The woman who appeared wore a peach-colored T-shirt, knee-length black yoga pants, and a sweatband that could have been lifted from a 1980s Olivia Newton-John video.

"Hi. My name is Leah Nash. I'm sorry, but I just took out your mailbox."

She frowned, but not because of her mailbox.

"I'm sorry, dear, I'm a little hard of hearing. Come in, won't you?" She opened the door wider. A workout DVD was blasting in some corner of the house. It explained why she hadn't come running when I crashed into her mailbox.

"Just a minute, I'll turn that off. Go on into the kitchen." She pointed vaguely to her left, but I followed my nose, which told me that somewhere nearby were freshly-baked chocolate chip cookies. Music has nothing on cookies when it comes to soothing the savage breast. I resisted the urge to help myself.

"Now, what did you say your name was?" she asked as she came bustling back into the room.

"Leah Nash. I just ran into your mailbox." I upped my voice volume a touch to accommodate her hearing loss.

"Oh, dear. That's the second time in the last six weeks." A frown creased her forehead and she absentmindedly dislodged her headband as she moved her hand through springy silver curls.

"I'm really sorry. Of course, I'll pay for a new one and whatever it costs to get it put back in."

She handed me a plate with several cookies. "Milk?"

"Yes, please."

I couldn't wait and took a bite—just the right temperature, warm enough so the chips were gooey, cool enough so the cookie was crisping around the edges. She smiled at my evident enjoyment.

"Whenever I make a batch, I always do a workout to sort of even things out."

"These are great." I was feeling calmer by the minute.

"Thank you, dear. Now, about the mailbox—did you get the post too?"

"Yes, ma'am. Sorry."

"Well, that will set you back about $125 for both. Don't worry about the labor. My grandson Mickey will take care of it."

I got my checkbook out of my purse and realized I hadn't asked her name.

"It's Aurelia. Aurelia Wright."

I wrote out the check, pausing between lines for another bite. After I swallowed, I said, "If you give these to everyone who takes out your mailbox, no wonder it happens so often."

"Well, not everyone stops. Last time it was just the mailbox, not the post, but still he should have stopped. Really surprised me. Jamie is such a nice boy. Of course, when I found out it was the night his father killed himself, well, I just let it go. A mailbox didn't seem that important."

I nodded, still lost in the bliss of the cookie. Then I processed what she had said.

"Jamie Whiting drove by your house the night Garrett died?"

"Yes, it was late. Early morning, really. I was in bed but my dog Flash—" she pointed to a corner of the kitchen near the stove. I saw that what I'd taken for a rug was actually an extremely relaxed sandy-colored dog.

"He's a sweetheart. A cocker spaniel and poodle mix. No trouble at all, except that night he ate something that didn't agree with him. He woke me up to take him out at 3:15. I know because I looked at the clock and told him no more people food."

"Are you sure it was Jamie? It would have been too dark to see the driver, wouldn't it?"

She nodded. "Well, yes, but I know that Mini Cooper of his. My daughter has one. Ridiculous things with the kind of winters we have. Still, they are cute. I've seen Jamie drive up and down this road a thousand times. I know that car. I'm sure it was him."

"Was he driving away from the Whiting house, or toward it?"

"Oh, he was driving away from it. He had to be on the right side of the road in order to hit the mailbox. That's where it is."

"So at 3:15, he was driving from the Whiting's house toward town. And it was definitely the night Garrett Whiting died?"

"That's why I remember so well. Are you a friend of Jamie's?"

"No, I've never met him. I know his sister Isabel."

"I used to babysit for both the kids when they were younger. Jamie was such a sweetheart. I felt so bad when Isabel told me he was having a problem with drugs a few years ago. So sad."

My brain was racing.

"Were you surprised Dr. Whiting killed himself?"

"Well, I have to admit he didn't seem the type. He liked himself pretty well, that one." She gave little gasp and put her hand to her mouth. "Oh! I shouldn't have said that. He was always perfectly polite to me. Just sometimes was a little, snooty, maybe. Wasn't one to neighbor much."

"You said Jamie was a sweet kid. How about Isabel, what was she like?"

"She was a clever little girl. And very, very pretty. Always took special care of her little brother, too. Jamie could get into some mischief, but Isabel always tried to help him out of it. I used to love brushing that long blonde hair of hers."

My phone chimed, and I saw a text had come in from Coop. I clicked it off to read later.

I stood up and put my jacket back on and grabbed my purse. "Thank you so much for the cookies and milk. And I really am sorry about your mailbox."

"That's all right. Gives me a chance to change up the color. I've had red the last two times; maybe I'll try blue and see if I have better luck. Nice meeting you, dear."

After I got in my car and buckled up, I opened Coop's text.

Charlie Ross is messing with you. Talk to me about Whiting before you do anything.

Too bad I didn't get that about four hours earlier. It might have saved me from making a fool of myself for Ross. Though now, after talking to Aurelia, I was having the tiniest of second thoughts.

What had Jamie been doing driving toward town at 3:15 a.m., when according to him, he was still partying and didn't tumble into bed half-conscious until 4 a.m.? If he'd really been home much earlier than that, as Aurelia Wright insisted, then his alibi for his father's death wouldn't cut it. Garrett had died between 11 and 3, the medical examiner said. I drove slowly, as much because I wanted time to think as because of the snow-covered roads. When I pulled into the Himmel Police Department parking lot, darkness was already setting in.

I pushed through the double doors and into the scruffy waiting area, with its scuffed linoleum and orange plastic chairs. Melanie Olson, the HPD secretary, sat behind the pass through counter that separated the offices from the reception area. Her eyes were glued to the computer screen, and she didn't look up.

"Hey, Melanie, is Coop in?"

She didn't answer, instead clicked her fingers rapidly across her keyboard. When she finally acknowledged me with a barely perceptible raising of her eyes, I noticed that her wiry hair was swept into an improbable updo with a cascade of curls coming down on her forehead, something like a 1940s pin-up girl.

"Your hair looks amazing." Which was true, though not in the way I hoped she'd take it.

She raised her hand and cocked a thumb in the direction of Coop's office.

"I'll just run on back then."

She lowered her head back to her screen as I raised the pass through and went down the hall. Coop was on the phone, so I hovered in the doorway until he waved me in.

I flopped into the chair in front of his desk.

"How bad was it?"

"Bad."

"I figured. Darmody talked to Charlie Ross today, that's when I texted you, but too late, I guess."

Darmody is Dale Darmody, not the brightest guy in the Himmel Police Department, nor the most discreet. Which often works to my advantage. Not this time though.

"What did he tell you?"

"That Ross said it was about time you took a tumble off that high horse of yours and found out you weren't the genius you think you are. His words, not mine," he added at the look on my face.

"He's such an ass. I had to admit he was right, and he loved it."

"That was a pretty jerk move of his."

"I appreciate the solidarity. You tried to tell me not to play Rescue Ranger with Isabel. But I did, and I got burned." I told him about Garrett's Parkinson's and about the insurance.

"Parkinson's would be a good reason for a guy like Garrett Whiting to kill himself. Could be he wanted to be in control of how things would end for him. And a million dollars is a pretty good incentive for Isabel to want his death to be anything but suicide."

"I know. Except—"

"Except what? Whiting had a good motive to kill himself, and Isabel and her brother don't get any money if their father's death was suicide."

"Well, but look at it another way. The insurance policy is also a reason why Garrett Whiting wouldn't kill himself. He took out a policy to protect his children. He only had six months to go. Why wouldn't he tough it out to ensure financial security for his kids?

"And I didn't tell you this part. The Whiting's neighbor said she saw

Jamie driving away from the house toward Himmel around 3:15 that morning. But he told police he got home around 4 a.m., went straight upstairs to bed, and more or less passed out until Isabel woke him in the morning to say their father was dead. He's got a buddy who corroborated his story, but he wouldn't be the first person to get a friend to lie for him."

"How reliable is the neighbor?"

"I don't know, she seemed pretty certain. She said he hit her mailbox with his Mini Cooper. She saw him because she was letting her dog out, and she had just looked at her clock."

"He can't be the only person with a Mini Cooper."

"That's true, but she saw it coming from the direction of the Whiting's house."

"Would it do me any good to point out that you just got burned by Isabel? And that you just got punked by Charlie Ross?"

"I know, I know. You're right. But it's just kind of bugging me."

"Is it bugging you because you don't want to admit your instincts were wrong, or because there's actually something there?"

"I think there's actually something there. Even if Ross did do his job. For once. Trouble is, the guy doesn't have any imagination."

"Some might say you have too much."

"Oh, some might, might they? C'mon, Coop. Besides a Mini Cooper driving away from the direction of the Whiting house when Jamie was allegedly passed out—which by the way Ross did *not* investigate very well —there's the fact that Garrett asked Isabel to come home, because he was worried about Jamie. Why would he decide a few minutes later, screw Jamie and too bad if Isabel finds me dead in my chair? And forget about providing for them. I can't wait even six months to take myself out. I'll just shoot myself now. And the cheese. Don't forget he left a pound of Hook's on the counter."

He smiled a little, as I had intended him to do. Then he got serious again.

"Those are odd things. But do they add up to murder? Maybe that call to his daughter was as close as he could come to saying goodbye—asking her to take care of her brother. Maybe Isabel heard things the way she wanted, or needed to hear them." He paused to see if his words had any impact. "Are you even listening to me?"

"I hear you, but I'm not listening."

"You're impossible, you know that?"

"Thank you."

"All right. I give up. Moving on. Anything else you want to tell me?"

I was genuinely mystified. "No, nothing else going at the moment. Unless you want to talk about the startling developments in the case of Melanie's new hair."

"Oh. I thought you might want to mention that your ex is in town."

"How did—OK, Miguel, right?"

"He's an excitable boy. I saw him downtown this afternoon. He was pretty shook up that a piece of your past stopped by to say hello last night. What's goin' on?"

"Nothing, seriously. Nick was there when Miguel dropped me off and I didn't have time to explain things to him. Actually, I didn't know what was going on. But, you know Nick."

"Not really. I only met him a few times. You didn't exactly have a long marriage."

"Thanks for pointing that out. He's in Wisconsin, teaching at Robley. He's been coming down to teach a night class at Himmel Tech, but he said he had to work up the courage to talk to me. Now why would that be? Nice, approachable, open-hearted me?"

"So, what did he want?"

"Forgiveness."

"Huh. Did you give it to him?"

"Yeah, I guess. Hey, you want to come for dinner? Mom's cooking. Mac and cheese, then we're gonna watch an old movie. Cowboy flick. *The Big Country*. Fun times."

"I'd like to, but I've got plans."

"You had plans the other night, too."

"What? A man's not allowed to have plans?"

"Sure. You're just being kind of mysterious about yours lately."

"Not really."

"Yes, you are, but whatever. I better get going. I'll talk to you later."

I waved to Melanie as I left, but she didn't notice. On the way home, I tried to think what might be making Coop so reluctant to divulge his "plans." And what could be a bigger attraction than my mother's cooking? The only thing I could come up with was that he was doing some kind of police operation he didn't want me to know about. He wasn't very trusting when it came to my ability to keep the lid on a story.

And with good reason. I couldn't guarantee anything. The worst thing a reporter can do is get too cozy with the cops. When you start identifying with sources, you can't do your job. We'd had a couple of tussles stemming from that before—him doing his job, me doing mine. It didn't always mesh. He might be thinking it was easier just to avoid me, unless and until he could tell me what was going on. But it was my job not to be spoon-fed information by the police, not even when they were my very good friends. I'd have to do some digging soon.

11

TRUE TO HER PROMISE, my mother had my favorite meal, four-cheese macaroni and cheese, waiting on the table when I got home, along with a big
salad and apple crisp for dessert. Over dinner I told her about Isabel's
grievous omissions.

"So, you're dropping this?"

"That was my plan."

"But I can see why Isabel left those key points out. She was afraid you'd
react like you did."

"Wait a minute. Weren't you the one who told me be careful, don't get
caught up in this, consider my motivations, remember it's Isabel's fight, not
mine?"

"Hmm. I do give good advice, don't I? But I'm just saying, I can understand why she wasn't completely upfront with you."

"I don't remember you having this relaxed approach to the truth when I
was younger. And I'm mad as hell that Isabel wasn't straight with me."

"But?"

"But nothing. That's all."

She waited.

"OK. I've got a gut feeling that something isn't right. And maybe it
wouldn't hurt to take another run at this." I looked at her out of the corner

of my eye to see how she was taking it. She started to speak, then cut herself off.

I stood up and started loading the dishwasher. She gathered up our leftovers and packaged them for the refrigerator. As she reached around me to grab a plastic container from the cupboard, she stopped and instead put a hand on my arm and turned me around to face her.

"I don't want to tell you what to do."

"That would be a first."

She made a face, then got serious. "It's kind of hard to know the right thing to do, isn't it? You feel sympathy for Isabel. I do too. Then again, you don't need to get tangled up in something right now. You've got the page proofs for your book sitting on the coffee table. Aren't they supposed to be going back? I thought I heard you tell your agent two days ago that you were all over it."

"I am. I'm just about done," I said, with the same amount of righteous indignation I used to use when she accused me of not doing my math homework. And the same amount of truth. I'd actually have to pull an all-nighter soon to get the page proofs back to the publisher by the promised date.

She looked at me skeptically but didn't say anything.

"I just can't let it go, Mom. Not yet. Something's off; I just don't know what."

—————————————

A half hour later we were both in our pajamas, sock-clad feet propped up on the coffee table, afghans in place and a bowl of popcorn in each of our laps. We were ready to watch *The Big Country* for the hundredth time. Nobody rocks a Friday night like the Nashes.

Truthfully, I enjoy the occasional early night at home, and there is worse company than my mother and Gregory Peck. The opening credits were running when Miguel knocked on the door. I paused the DVD player and called to him.

"Come on in, it's open."

"*Chica*, nice jammies. Where are your fuzzy slippers?"

I had my usual winter sleep uniform on: a tan oversized long-sleeved T, slightly ragged on the sleeves, and a pair of blue flannel pajama bottoms with sheep on them.

"Shut up." I threw a piece of popcorn at him. "What's your look called?"

He wore a plaid flannel shirt unbuttoned over an olive-green T-shirt, dark wash jeans, and hiking boots. Quite a change-up from his typical style.

"Lumbersexual," he said with a grin.

"What is that?" my mother asked.

I answered for him. "It's for hot hipsters who want to walk on the rough side and dress like a lumberjack. I see you had to draw the line at a beard."

"I think you look very nice, Miguel," my mother said.

"And you look *muy linda*, Carol, as always."

"You are such a suck-up," I said.

"*Gracias*, Miguel. For that you can grab yourself a bowl and have some popcorn. Do you want to watch a movie with us?"

"No, thanks. I'm meeting my *amigos*. We're going to the *Caliente* Club in Milwaukee tonight. I just stopped to tell Leah what I found out today."

"Anything good?"

"No-no-no. You get nothing. *Nada*. Not 'til you tell me about your *husband*!" He'd contained himself remarkably well up to that point, but now he squeezed onto the couch beside me and took both my hands in his.

"I never even knew you were *married*! How could you keep that from me? What is he doing here? When did you get married? Married, *chica*. I can't believe it. He's very hot. *Dígame*. Tell me everything."

"Nothing to tell. We were married for half a minute when I lived in Grand Rapids. It didn't work out. We got divorced and I haven't seen him for years."

"You never even mention him to me? Carol, you tell me. What's the real story?" he asked, dropping my hands and leaning around to get a good line of sight with my mother.

I answered before my mother could. Lord knew what she'd say.

"I told you the real story, Miguel."

"Maybe, but not all of it."

"OK. His name is Nick Gallagher. I met him when I worked in Michigan. He was a temporary faculty member in the Psych Department at

Grand Valley State University. We got married. He didn't get the 'forsaking all others' part. We got divorced. It wasn't fun for either of us. We both had some growing up to do. He stopped by to ask me to forgive him. I did. End of story."

His dark eyes were dancing with excitement. "No, no, *chica*. That sounds like the beginning of the story." I knew that his imagination was concocting a Lifetime movie scenario.

"No. Stop right there. We are not star-crossed lovers. He did not ask me to take him back. I did not say 'I've always loved you.' He said he was sorry. I said it's OK. And that's that. Now, I met my part of the deal. Tell me what you found out."

He wanted to talk more about Nick, I knew, but I set my face in an expression that said *no way*. He put his curiosity aside for another day.

"It wasn't very busy at the salon today. I listened to lots of bad husband stories. But no Garrett Whiting."

"That's all right. I—"

"No, wait. You are so *impaciente*. It was quiet, until I did the shampoo and conditioner for Mrs. Caldwell."

"Traitor. You gave a Miguel special to that nasty woman who tried to get me fired?" Georgia Caldwell is the ex-wife of Miller Caldwell, the lawyer Isabel had identified as one of Garrett's oldest friends. He's nice. She isn't.

"Commerce, *chica*. Got to keep the customer satisfied. I had to massage her head. But it didn't mean anything. I thought about you the whole time. Don't you want to hear what she said?"

"Yes, you know I do."

"I just did a little chatting about Garrett Whiting, how sad the suicide was, and she took over from there." He nodded, pleased with himself, as he put a handful of popcorn into his mouth.

"C'mon, c'mon, tell me already."

He finished chewing and said, "She didn't like Dr. Whiting."

"So she didn't like him. So what? She doesn't like anybody."

"She likes me," he said with a slightly smug smile.

"Don't make me question her judgment. What did she tell you about Garrett?"

"He was handsome, and he chased women."

"Anyone in particular?"

"She said, and this was not so nice, 'garden variety sluts.' And the worst one was Francesca Saxon."

"Frankie Saxon? I know her. She's a counselor at the high school. I like her," my mother said.

"I know the name, too," I said. "Isabel told me she helped get her brother Jamie into rehab. She didn't say her dad dated her."

"Maybe she didn't know," my mother said. "In my experience, children often find it hard to believe their parents aren't past all passion."

"Oh, that's your experience, is it? Miguel, was this a recent relationship?"

"I didn't get a chance to ask. She just said that Frankie was an Italian witch who got what she deserved."

I was pretty sure that Georgia Caldwell had not said "witch." But Miguel is very circumspect with his language, which I admire but find hard to emulate.

"What did she mean by that?"

"*No sé.* An old scandal, maybe? Georgia's stylist came and got her, so I didn't get any more."

"I don't remember the details. There was some kind of drama there years ago, but I didn't pay much attention. You don't have to dredge up some malicious old scandal, do you?"

"Mom. I work for the *Himmel Times,* not *The Daily Mail.* There will be no scandal writing. But it's interesting. Well done, Miguel. Thanks."

"*De nada.* Anytime. I'm happy when you are, *chica.*" He grinned, getting up to leave. Then he turned back, "You're coming to my Christmas party, aren't you? Both of you?"

"After your *Cinco de Mayo* soiree, I'm not sure I should."

"*Chica,* you have to. Anything can happen."

"That's what I'm afraid of."

"You and Paul are coming aren't you, Carol? It's gonna be *fabuloso!*"

"No doubt, Miguel. But that's the night Paul and I are going to *La Folie* in Madison. He's been planning it for weeks."

"*Muy elegante.* Very fancy! Come by after."

"We'll try."

"Now you, *chica*. Promise. Two weeks from tomorrow. You can bring a friend. Maybe an old boyfriend? An old husband? Whatever you like. The theme is holiday sparkle."

"You're not selling me on it." His face fell and I felt bad. Don't rain on Miguel's party parade.

"Just kidding, Miguel. I'll be there. I'm just not sure what I'll wear. Sparkle isn't a big part of my wardrobe."

"It's not what you wear, it's who you're with. I can hardly wait. Now, I have to go. The *Caliente* Club waits for no man."

———

"So, I didn't know you and Paul were going to *La Folie*. That's pretty swank. What's the occasion?"

"Nothing special. Paul's been wanting to go ever since it opened. It's really hard to get reservations, and he's really looking forward to it, so I can't say no. I'd rather go to Miguel's, actually."

"Soft music, candlelight—sounds pretty romantic. Maybe I better ask him what his intentions are. He might be planning a marriage proposal."

"Don't even say that. That's not what's happening."

I looked up from rearranging my blanket and putting my popcorn within easy reach, surprised at the vehemence in her voice.

"OK, OK. Just kidding."

"Well, don't. Now, are we going to watch this movie or not?"

"Yeah, sure." And we did, but I kept stealing glances at my mother, trying to figure out why a little light teasing had irritated her so much.

12

I RARELY SLEEP IN, even on a day off, unless I'm sick. So, I was already show-ered, dressed, and eating Honey Nut Cheerios when my phone rang at 8:30 Saturday morning. Given the way I'd left things with her, I was surprised to see Isabel's name pop up.

"This is Leah."

"Hi. Don't hang up, please. Let me say this first. I am really sorry I didn't tell you everything. I know I can't expect you to help me when you can't even trust me. It's just that you were the only person who would even listen to me. I didn't want you to brush me off, too. I'm not making excuses; I'm just saying, that's why. But it was wrong, and I totally understand why you're so angry at me."

She sounded resigned and really, really sad. And I wasn't angry anymore. That's one benefit of a quick temper—it doesn't last long.

"Isabel, I can see why you did it. I'm sorry I blew up at you. But you've gotta know that your father's illness adds a whole lot of credibility to the suicide verdict—and it was already on pretty solid ground."

"I know that's how it seems, but you didn't hear my dad that night. He wasn't a man about to commit suicide. He wasn't, and I don't care what you or anybody else believes. He wasn't!"

"Take it easy. Actually, I did come across something after I left that's making me rethink things."

"You did? What?" I winced at the hope in her voice, because I was pretty sure the thing that made me change my mind wasn't going to go down very well with her.

"Isabel, how sure are you that Jamie's story for that night is solid?"

"Jamie's story? He didn't have much of one. You don't when you're as messed up as he was. He just came home, passed out, and woke up to find dad was dead."

No point in dancing around. I came straight to it.

"Someone saw Jamie driving toward town around 3:15 a.m."

"That can't be right."

"Maybe it isn't, but your neighbor, Mrs. Wright, believes she saw Jamie's car, when Jamie says he was passed out at home."

"She's wrong, that's all. She's very scattered. If she saw a car, it wasn't Jamie's."

"You do understand that I'm going to have to talk to Jamie."

She rallied. "Yes, sure. Of course. You'll see, when you meet him. Jamie isn't the violent type. He and my father didn't always see eye to eye, but he would never, ever hurt him."

"There's another thing. You mentioned Francesca Saxon. You didn't say she and your father were lovers."

"That old gossip? My father was a single, good-looking doctor. A lot of women threw themselves at him. Maybe he and Frankie were involved once, but if so, it was a long time ago. If it's true, I don't think it was any big romance. He was pretty old for that." I remembered my mother's comment about children and their parents' love lives.

"Doesn't matter. But I'll be checking it out. Maybe she knows more about your father than you thought."

"I don't care who you talk to, as long as you keep asking questions. I know Jamie had nothing to do with it, and I doubt Frankie did either. But the more you ask, the more you'll see I'm right. I know we can prove my father didn't kill himself."

"OK. But you need to understand something."

"What?"

"This isn't about you and me against the world. This is about a reporter chasing down leads and following them wherever they go. It might end up that the police were right, or it could be that your father was murdered—but this investigation has a life of its own now. I won't be checking with you to see if you're cool with it. And I'm going to follow it through until there's no more for me to find out."

Big words that I'd have a tough time following up on if Rebecca decided to block my way. I could do it without her support, even with her opposition, but it can get pretty tiring running against the wind all the time. I had to bring her in on it, now that I'd committed the full force of her paper's senior reporter to the story.

"I get it. I'm not worried. Find out the truth. I trust you."

"OK then. I'll talk to you soon."

"So you want to pursue a theory you have that Garrett Whiting was murdered, based on what again? Your instincts?" Rebecca's eyes still focused on the spreadsheets she had continued to study while I updated her on Isabel. She often spends Saturday morning at the paper doing important Rebecca things in her office.

"That's right." I struggled to keep my voice level. What I wanted to say was, *"Yeah, instincts. Reporter's instincts. Something a paper pusher like you wouldn't know anything about."*

"But my instincts are based on the facts I just gave you."

"Are they really facts, Leah?" She finally looked up and pulled off her glasses, the better to impale me with her icicle stare. "You've outlined an alternative theory of how Garrett was killed, and you've pointed out holes in the son's story, but you also discovered a major motive for suicide and a reason for the children to push a murder agenda. They do not pass GO, do not collect $1 million, if daddy killed himself."

"I know, you're right. But sometimes it isn't one or two major reveals, it's a whole bunch of little inconsistencies that tip you to the real story. I know you're worried about upsetting advertisers and getting the sheriff's undies in a bunch—" Oops. Wrong tack to take.

"You really do enjoy your self-righteous role as the last real reporter in captivity, don't you? Yes, I have to think about advertisers and subscribers and budgets. That doesn't mean I don't care about journalistic integrity and the truth. So, don't patronize me talking about your 'instinct' and your ability to go where no journalist has gone before. Bottom line, you do your job and I'll do mine. You turn up something more substantial than 'inconsistencies' and gut feelings. If you don't, the story is dead. Understood?"

"Yeah, OK. Understood."

"Anything else?" She had put her glasses back on and her eyes were once more cast down, looking at the lines of numbers.

"No. No, that's it." I left without saying goodbye, and Rebecca didn't seem to notice. I had gotten what I wanted, the go-ahead to pursue the story without active obstruction from Rebecca. But somehow it felt like I had lost.

"Won't you come in?"

It was nearly five o'clock that afternoon when I followed Francesca Saxon into the living room of her house on Pine Street. It was the room of a reader, with stacks of books and several magazines on end tables. In front of me on the coffee table, a book was turned face-down with a pair of glasses and a half-full wine glass beside it.

"Thanks for seeing me on such short notice, Mrs. Saxon."

"Just Frankie. Please, sit down." She pointed to one end of a green sofa.

The name was tomboyish, conjuring up freckles, skinny legs, and short, ginger-colored hair. This Frankie had dark brown tresses caught up with a clip, a few tendrils escaping and curling softly at her neck and in front of her ears. A light fringe of bangs drifted across her forehead, and she had the beginnings of fine laugh lines fanning from the corners of her brown eyes. She wore leggings with flats and a tunic-length ivory sweater. So, this was the woman Garrett had dumped. She couldn't be much older than me. She was beautiful.

"Would you like a glass of wine?"

I almost said no, but caught myself. Sharing a glass is a way to get the conversation, and sometimes the truth, flowing.

"Yes, thank you. Pinot Grigio if you have it, but any white is fine with me."

She left the room and returned in a minute carrying a nearly full bottle and a glass into which she poured a generous amount. She went to the sideboard and topped her own glass off from a bottle of red wine. Then she sat down next to me, one leg tucked under her. She leaned back a little against the throw pillows in the corner of the couch.

"So, you're writing a story about Garrett Whiting's life?"

"Actually, I'm looking into his death."

"His death? I don't understand."

"The family isn't completely satisfied with the suicide verdict. Some of the questions they have made me curious enough to see if there was more to the story."

"The family? Isabel and Jamie?" She seemed taken aback.

"Yes. That surprises you?"

"Not that they don't want to believe their father killed himself. But surely you don't—Jamie and Isabel—don't think their father's death was an accident? I don't understand how you could accidentally shoot yourself in the head."

"No, not an accident. Murder." I said the last word with a little dramatic spin, like a television attorney trying to jolt an incriminating statement from a complacent witness. It didn't work.

"Murder?"

"It's possible."

"No, I don't believe that," she said, shaking her head so vehemently she spilled a few drops of red wine on her pale sweater.

"According to Isabel, Garrett wasn't the kind of person to commit suicide."

"What 'kind of person' is that? Suicide isn't restricted to a type." Her voice was sharp.

"You're right. I didn't phrase that very well." I backed off a little. "I'm just trying to get a handle on what motivated Dr. Whiting, what pressures he may have been dealing with, what his relationships were like. That's all."

"I really wouldn't know anything about that," she said, taking a sip from her glass—because she was thirsty, or to buy some time?

"I know you helped him get his son into a drug rehabilitation program a couple of years ago."

"Yes, I did. But that was in a professional capacity. I'm a counselor at the high school, and Jamie was a troubled student. I helped his father like I would have helped any parent."

"I see. But you knew Dr. Whiting before that, didn't you?"

Another drink before she answered. "I've known him for a long time, yes."

A flush crept up her flawless olive skin, though that could have been the wine. I went in another direction to keep her off-kilter.

"I guess it must have been pretty upsetting when Jamie relapsed, after all the work you and Dr. Whiting put in helping him."

"Relapsed?"

"Yes. Didn't you know? Isabel said he started using again a month or so before Dr. Whiting died."

I couldn't read the look on her face—surprise, disbelief?

"I didn't hear anything about that."

"Dr. Whiting didn't ask for your advice? That's odd. So you hadn't talked to him in quite awhile?"

"We weren't social friends. We weren't in regular contact."

I nodded. "So, you wouldn't have any way of knowing if Dr. Whiting was suffering from depression. You probably didn't know that he was seriously ill?"

"Ill?" Either she was very good, or this really was news to her.

"Yeah. Parkinson's. He was diagnosed not long before he died."

"I had no idea."

"It must feel weird not knowing what was going on with someone you used to be so close to. I mean years ago, way before Jamie's problems."

A cornered look came into her eyes. It's what I'd been looking for. But I didn't feel very good about it.

"I already said I knew Garrett for years." She fussed with her wine glass, setting it on the table, then picking it back up.

I put my own glass down and half-turned on the sofa so that I was facing her directly. In a quiet voice, I said, "You more than 'knew' him, didn't you, Frankie? You and Dr. Whiting were lovers once. What happened?"

She downed the rest of her wine. Got up, went to the sideboard again, and poured another. Came back, sat down, and stared into it, as though looking for the answer there. I waited. Then she blew out a long sigh before looking up.

"It's not exactly a secret. More of a forgotten scandal. At least I hoped it was forgotten. What happened is that 10 years ago we fell in love. Or rather, I did."

"Were you still married?"

She nodded. "He wasn't. But I was. Jerry and I were high school sweethearts. He was the only boy I'd ever dated. Marissa was born seven months after we were married. She was a beautiful baby. We did all right at first. Jerry had a good job at a factory, he had his bowling, his buddies, his beer. But I didn't want to let go of my dreams. I was only 19. I thought I'd be the first person in my family to earn a college degree. I wanted my parents to be proud of me, not disappointed in me."

The words were tumbling out now, as though she couldn't stop them.

"When I started college, Jerry hated it. I agreed to have another baby, my son Caleb, because I thought it would make Jerry feel more secure, less resentful. But then I graduated and got a teaching job, and he hated it even more. He didn't like my new friends, he didn't like my new interests, he didn't like that he and the kids weren't 'enough.' His words, not mine. We fought all the time. It was exhausting. Then I met Garrett."

"Was it serious, your relationship with Garrett?"

"I thought it was. He said he loved me. He was intelligent, witty, charming. He was much older. I couldn't believe a man so sophisticated could fall in love with me. He made me feel like we were soul mates. It turned out he specialized in making women feel that way." She gave a humorless laugh.

"What happened?"

"He'd already broken it off with me when my husband found out. Jerry went crazy. Went to the country club one night, when Garrett was receiving a civic award. He made a huge scene, threw a punch, had to be escorted out.

Half the town saw it, and the other half heard about it." She closed her eyes as through reliving the humiliation.

"Then he filed divorce papers on me at work. Right in my classroom. Tried to keep me from sharing joint custody because of my relationship with Garrett. Told everyone I abandoned him, neglected the children, flaunted my lover. I nearly lost my job when one of the school board members wanted to invoke the 'moral turpitude' clause in our contract. If it weren't for Father Lindstrom, I would have. He intervened with a couple of the board members, and they changed their minds. It was the worst time in my life. And my kids. My poor, sweet kids. They were too young to really understand, but they knew something was very wrong."

"I'm sorry. I'm sure it was hard on everyone."

"Yes. It was. You make your choices, and you have to accept the consequences. But not your kids. Your kids shouldn't suffer for something you did. You're not going to write about this, are you?"

"I'm not planning to write about an affair that happened a decade ago, no. I'm sorry if I upset you." And I was. But it didn't stop me from pressing on.

"Were you surprised when you heard that Garrett had committed suicide? Did that jibe with the man that you knew?"

"I was stunned. Garrett was exciting, brilliant, self-centered, egotistical. When I knew him, I never once saw self-doubt, or depression, or anything but absolute self-satisfaction."

"How did you find out about it?"

She paused before answering. "I think I got a text from a friend that Monday, the day after. Yes, I'm sure that's how I heard about it. I ran in a 10K in Lake Neshaunoc on Saturday. I try to do that one every year."

I nodded, and her voice picked up speed as she went into greater detail, twisting a strand of hair as she spoke. "It's a pretty trail, really spectacular when the colors are changing. I decided to make a long weekend of it. I took a personal day on the following Monday so I could stay up there, relax, visit some antique shops. I really enjoy antiquing, but I didn't find anything this time. But the weather was beautiful. And I did some shopping. My mother's birthday is coming up, and I drove out to look at some quilts at a really nice little place outside of Lake Neshaunoc. She's looking for a wedding ring pattern in a particular shade of green. So, that's why I wasn't here when I got the news. It was such a shock."

My antennae had gone up slightly. People not used to lying often offer up too much information. They get nervous and start rambling, as though piling on details will make their story sound more credible. All it does is give them more ways to trip themselves up. But before I could follow-up, she stood and set her wine glass on the edge of the table, where it teetered precariously for a second.

"You'll have to excuse me. I just remembered I have to pick up my daughter. I'm sorry I wasn't able to help you. I really do have to go."

With that she lifted my half-full glass out of my hand, plunked it down on the table, reached for my jacket, which she had laid across a chair earlier, and hustled me to the foyer. I was at the front door, still wriggling my arm in my sleeve, as I said, "Of course, all right. Thank you for—"

"You're very welcome. But I've really told you everything I know, and it's all too upsetting to talk about again. And I would appreciate your discretion about my relationship with Garrett." And the door was closed.

13

As I started to pull my car out of the driveway, a tall, dark-haired girl came down the sidewalk. I waited for her to pass before backing up. Instead, she turned and walked up the path to Frankie's house. On impulse, I turned off the car and got out.

"Hi. I'm Leah Nash. I'm a reporter with the *Himmel Times*. I was just talking to your mother for a story I'm doing."

"I'm Marissa. Marissa Saxon. You're a reporter? That's cool. Are you doing a story on my mother?" She was puzzled, but interested.

"No, about Garrett Whiting. You probably know his kids, Jamie and Isabel?"

"I know who Isabel is, but we never hung out or anything. I know Jamie though. He's a pretty cool guy."

"He had some problems though, right?"

"Yeah, that's true. He was into drugs for awhile, but my mom helped him get into a program. He seems fine now. I mean, as far as the drug stuff, of course, not about his dad." The wind blew a strand of long dark hair across her eyes, and she pushed it out of the way.

"So, you knowing Jamie, his dad's death, that must have been pretty upsetting to you, too."

"Totally. I came home early that Monday to check on Mom. She was just sitting in bed crying. It really freaked me out. She told me Dr. Whiting was dead. That he shot himself. It was surreal."

"You had to check on your mother? Why was that?"

"She got really sick at this big race she runs in. She came home Sunday night; we were already in bed. But when I got up in the morning, she told me she thought she had food poisoning or the flu. She looked so bad that I wanted to stay home with her. But she said the worst was over; she just wanted to sleep. I came home at lunch to see how she was doing. I'm glad I did because she just got the text about Dr. Whiting, and she was really upset."

Before I could ask anything else, the front door opened. Busted.

Marissa looked up. "Hi Mom, I—"

"Honey, come on in, I need you to help me with something." She spoke to her daughter, but she was looking at me.

"Right. Well, good to meet you, Marissa."

"Yeah, you, too." She was a nice kid.

"Thanks again, Frankie," I called. She didn't answer, just stood there waiting for her daughter. As soon as Marissa crossed the threshold, the door closed.

So, Frankie was home Sunday night, the night Garrett died. And she lied about it. And she hadn't needed to pick up her daughter today, and she definitely didn't want me talking to Marissa. Too late.

On Monday, I had a couple of interviews in the morning and then a lunch meeting of the Himmel Holidays Committee to cover. Feeling pretty virtuous about my productivity, I decided to use part of the afternoon to make a visit to the Whitings, in hopes of catching Jamie at home. But first I stopped by the paper to pick up a camera. I try not to go anywhere without one. A wild art shot of a cute squirrel or a kid walking his dog has rescued more than one *Himmel Times* front page when a planned-for story fell through.

When I walked in, Miguel was leaning over the front counter chatting and laughing with Courtnee. Both of them sprang apart and stared at me.

"What? What are you guys looking at?"

"*Chica*, it's what *you'll* be looking at."

"It's on your desk. Go look on your desk!" I hadn't seen Courtnee this animated since Taylor Swift's last album came out.

"Why?" Suspicion was heavy in my voice. A few months ago, after I wrote a story someone didn't like, I'd received a box of still-steaming dog poop. I was not up for such high jinks today.

"Come on, *andalé*, just go!" Miguel grabbed my hand and pulled me into the newsroom, Courtnee hard on our heels. There, in the middle of my desk, sat a big bouquet of red roses.

Oblivious to the look on my face, Courtnee was bouncing up and down with the wonder and amazement of it all. "Leah! You got flowers! Roses! Who would ever, ever, ever think someone would send you flowers?"

"All right, Courtnee, that's one too many 'evers' there. I've gotten flowers a time or two."

She gave me the kind of look the prom queen might bestow on the head of the clean-up committee.

"What? I have."

"I know you have, *chica*, but who are these from? And so many!"

I had an inkling, and I surreptitiously slipped the card tucked into the flowers into my jacket pocket. But not stealthily enough.

"Read it, Leah, read the card!" Courtnee commanded.

I opened it and read aloud, "'Super story on Grandma's shot glass collection. Thanks, the Chumley Family.'"

"That's not what it says."

"Yes, it is, and very nice of the Chumleys it was," I said, as I collected the camera for a quick getaway.

"No." She put a hand on my arm to stop me. Closing her eyes halfway to aid her powers of recall, she said, "The card says, 'Leah, your forgiveness means everything, Nick.'" Her voice went up in a little squeal.

"Courtnee, you read my card? You opened my personal mail?"

"I had to. I mean, like, the delivery guy said they were for you, but I was pretty sure that couldn't be right. So, I had to look at the card. I was being proactive. Isn't that what you're always telling me to do?" Her tone was self-righteous and long-suffering at the same time. "Besides, it wasn't the mail. I mean, it didn't come from the Post Office. It was more like a note. Like a Post-it note, really."

"A Post-it note inside an envelope marked 'Leah.' "

She pouted. "You're always yelling at me. 'Think, Courtnee, think!' Like I'm stupid or something. Then, I try to, like, do what you want, and you're still all up in my grill."

"You violated my privacy."

Miguel could contain himself no longer. "Yes, yes, you're right, *chica*. Courtnee, you shouldn't have done that. But Nick. Your ex-husband sent you flowers!"

"Ex-husband? Leah was married?" Apparently, Miguel had saved that tidbit for the big reveal.

"Yes!" He leaned in to give her the lowdown, and as she cross-examined him excitedly, I managed to slide out from under their gaze and dash to my car.

Flowers from Nick. He was always a fan of the over-the-top gesture, and roses are his favorite. Tulips are mine.

It was after 1 p.m. when I reached the Whiting house a few miles outside of Himmel. Jamie's Mini Cooper was in the driveway. I rang the doorbell, but instead of Isabel or her brother, a middle-aged woman wearing jeans and a long-sleeved T-shirt, her hands encased in thin plastic gloves, opened it.

"Yeah?"

"Hi. I'm Leah Nash. I was hoping to see Jamie or Isabel?"

"Which one do you want?" Her voice was nasal and slightly twangy.

"Uh, well, Jamie, I guess. Is he here?"

"Sleeping. Most days he's not up before 2."

"Is Isabel up and around?"

"Her? She was gone when I got here." Her hand shifted slightly on the door as she got ready to close it.

"Oh. Well, it's almost 1:15. Would you mind just checking to see if Jamie's awake and could talk to me?"

She sighed in annoyance, then motioned me in. "I guess. Follow me."

She led me past the living room where I had talked with Isabel. I saw that the furniture was moved, cushions were piled high, and the air was redolent with the smell of furniture polish. A large vacuum sat in the middle of the floor.

"I'm cleanin' in there," she said unnecessarily.

She led me down a hallway to a room that I immediately recognized as Garrett's study. Not exactly the receiving room I would've chosen for guests, but then the housekeeper bore a closer resemblance to Mrs. Danvers than to Mrs. Potts. The room showed no evidence of its grim recent past. Various sized boxes sat on the floor, partially filled with books. One armchair was gone. The other had a box on it. The wall had obviously been repainted.

She rolled the padded leather executive chair out from behind the desk and put it in the middle of the floor. "You can sit there."

"Thanks, Mrs. ...?" I knew who she was from reading the police report, but I was trying to get a little conversation going.

"Godfrey. Evelyn Godfrey. I'm the Whiting's housekeeper."

"Looks like you've got your hands full today."

"Isabel, she finished goin' through her dad's stuff and it set there for weeks. Then all of a sudden she decides stuff has to get moved today. She left me a note this morning."

"You've got to move all these boxes? Today?"

"Well, no," she admitted grudgingly. "She's not done yet. But she wants me to take this one here." She pointed to a large box on the edge of the desk. "She wants it dropped off to Dr. Whiting's office manager. Way across town. It's my regular day to clean the living room and the kitchen, plus I gotta make something for supper. I don't know how I'm going to get that to that office today. And I'm not supposed to lift anything real heavy." Her voice was aggrieved, and the lines that bracketed her mouth deepened as she pressed thin lips together.

"I'm going to town after I talk to Jamie. If it's just the one, I can drop it off. Would that help?" It wasn't just the latent Girl Scout in me that prompted my offer. The office manager, Elaine Quellman, was one of the people Isabel had suggested I talk to.

"I guess maybe it would," she said, unwilling to give up a grievance so easily.

"No problem then. Where's the office?"

"It goes to Elaine Quellman." She gave me the address and then reached into another box and brought out a roll of packing tape. "Here, you can seal it up with this."

"OK. Will do." She stood, waiting for me to apply the tape. For someone who had such a tight schedule she didn't have time to drop off a box, Mrs. Godfrey seemed reluctant to leave. I wanted to get a look inside before sealing it shut.

"OK then, Mrs. Godfrey. You know what, I wouldn't mind a cup of coffee if you've got it." I began pulling off a length of tape as though ready to seal the box and laid it across the top.

"I'd have to make it." She spoke in the same overwhelmed tone I might use if asked to produce Thanksgiving dinner.

"That's fine," I said, my voice as chipper and cheery as I could make it. "I don't mind the wait. And that will give you time to let Jamie know I'm here."

Any goodwill my volunteer delivery service had engendered vanished.

"It's gonna be awhile."

"No problem."

As soon as she left the room, I lifted the tape up and pawed through the box. It was wide but not very deep. I pulled out a bubble-wrapped pen and holder—the Montblanc I'd seen in the crime scene photos. Then the silver-framed photo that had sat on the desk, also swaddled in bubble-wrap. What kind of a narcissist kept a photo of himself on his desk? At the bottom of the box was a leather portfolio that I opened without much hope. Another bust. Just a pad of pristine paper. And that was the sum total of the box. No patient files, no secret diary, no second set of books.

I was putting everything back in place to seal the box when a voice behind me made me jump.

14

"FINDING EVERYTHING ALL RIGHT?"

As I finished rewrapping the photo and putting it back in the box, I tried to assume a casual tone. "Jamie. Hi. Leah Nash, we haven't met officially." I held out my hand. "Mrs. Godfrey asked if I'd drop this box off at your dad's office. I was just admiring his Montblanc pen. Really beautiful."

"Yeah. I know who you are." He took my hand with a firm grip, but let it go quickly. He ran his fingers through thick, slightly curly blondish-brown hair, ruffling it up a little. He and Isabel had the same slim build, and they were about the same height. He was good-looking in an ethereal, hot vampire kind of way–slender, with long-lashed blue eyes under straight brown eyebrows, and a thin, sensitive mouth. "So. You wanted to see me. Here I am."

"Would it be easier to talk in a different room?"

"You mean because my old man died here? I don't believe in ghosts."

OK, then.

"Isabel has some concerns about your father's death." I sat down on the chair Mrs. Godfrey had dragged out for me, while he moved a box off the armchair and took a seat.

"Yeah, I know." He slouched down in the chair, stretching out his legs and sticking his hands into the pockets of his jeans. He wore a tan v-neck sweater over a white T-shirt. His long feet were bare. He definitely looked like he'd just woken up, but his eyes were steady and clear.

"I realize this is hard, Jamie. I—"

"It's not hard. It's just bullshit. My father was an asshole. He wasn't Izzy's favorite when he was alive, either. The truth is, he didn't care about either of us. Especially not me. That wasn't a picture of us on his desk, was it? Just him, the way he liked it. He would've been happier if we were never born. Talking about him isn't hard. It's just pointless."

"You don't care that he's dead?"

He shrugged and sat up a little, taking his hands out of his pockets and rubbing one thumb over the other. "I learned to stop caring after he never went to a parent-teacher conference, never showed up for a school play, never watched me run cross country. Was never there, period. Except to criticize everything I did and tell me what a disappointment I was. I've been clean and sober for over two years. But he never once said he was proud of me. What can I tell you? We weren't close. He didn't even bother to tell me he had Parkinson's. I found out from Isabel after he died. What does that say about our 'relationship'?"

"That he wanted to protect you?"

I've never actually seen a sneer, but the look he gave me seemed to fit the bill. "Right. Because he was such a great father. He wasn't trying to protect me; it just never occurred to him to include me in anything in his life. Most of the time he didn't even remember I existed."

"Is that why you got into drugs? To get your father's attention?"

"You've been watching too much Dr. Phil. Thanks, but I don't need pseudo-analyzing. I did drugs because I liked how they made me feel." His tone was belligerent, but I tried again.

"OK. Can we talk about how your father died? Your sister—"

"Yeah, I know. Isabel's convinced herself it wasn't suicide. That Garrett wouldn't do that to us. She's delusional."

"That's pretty harsh."

"Look at the way he died. A nice blurry mix of rum and Coke with some Kpin to take the edge off, then a single bullet to the head. Clean, calculated, in control. Just like he was."

"He hurt you a lot, didn't he?"

"I got over it." His words were dismissive, but anger and pain were evident in his eyes. He must have realized that, because he lowered them as he shifted position, crossing an ankle over his knee. He began picking at a loose thread on the hem of his jeans.

"You say your dad didn't care about you. But he had a life insurance policy that would pay you and Isabel $1 million when he died. That seems to say 'I care' in a big way."

"Yeah, well, excuse me if I don't get all teary eyed about his generosity. Especially since he'd already stolen $100,000 from me. And he made sure neither Isabel nor I would ever collect on his insurance."

"What do you mean your father stole $100,000 from you?"

"My mother left me the money when she died, and my father was trustee until I turned 21. Which I will next month. Then a few weeks before he kills himself, he tells me that he made some 'unfortunate' investments, trying to 'strengthen' my portfolio, and it's all gone. It wasn't enough for him to lose his own money; he had to take mine too."

"What about Isabel, did he lose her inheritance too?"

He looked confused for a minute, then embarrassed. "She didn't have one. Not from our mother."

"It wasn't my idea," he added defensively. "She was always—distant to Isabel. She got heavy into prescription drugs when we were young—runs in the family," he said, with a self-mocking aside. "When she left, she never looked back. I was shocked that she left me anything. Doesn't really matter now though, does it? Garrett evened things out. Right down to zero. Killed himself just six months short of us collecting. Typical dick move of his."

"You seriously think your father timed his death so you couldn't collect the insurance? Wouldn't it have been a lot easier to cancel the policy?"

"Do you think you're funny? Because you aren't. You don't know the first thing about my father. But this time the joke's on him. I don't care about the money, and I'm happy he's gone."

"I talked to Frankie Saxon today. She made it sound like your dad came through for you when it really counted, when you had your drug problem a couple of years ago."

For the first time, he gave a genuine smile. "Frankie's a good person. A really good person."

"She and your dad were pretty close at one time."

He stopped picking at the hem of his jeans and looked up. "Are you talking about the 'affair' they had?" He shook his head. "That's old news."

"You don't think it might have started up again?"

"No way. She'd never be with my dad again. Frankie's way too smart for that."

"It's not about how smart you are. You can't always choose who you love." A little voice in the back of my mind snorted—I have a very obnoxious inner voice—*Who are you trying to convince, yourself or Jamie?* I squelched it by veering in a new direction.

"You told the police you got wasted the night your father died. Why did you? After all that time sober, I mean?"

"No reason. I have to choose to be sober every morning. And every night, and every time someone offers me something to get high. I made a bad choice that night, that's all."

"Was there anything that happened that day? A fight with a girlfriend, an argument with your dad, something that triggered your fall off the wagon?"

"I told you no. Just stupid, just testing the limit. I just felt like it. Why is this any of your business?"

"Why does my asking make you so mad?"

"I'm not mad. I just don't see the point."

"I want to make sure that I've got things straight, that's all. The police report says you went to a party, got pretty messed up, and left with a friend after a neighbor threatened to call the cops. You got home around 4 a.m. Is that right?"

"Yeah, I guess. Like I told the cops, my memory of the night isn't very clear."

"You must've really been out of it. You didn't notice a light on in here?"

"I came in the back and went up to my room. I thought you said you read the report." His irritation was growing. I pretended not to notice.

"I'm just trying to figure out what your father's frame of mind was. If you take yourself back in your mind, you might remember something now that didn't seem important at the time."

"I didn't see anything. I didn't notice anything. I hadn't even been home for three days before he killed himself."

"So, you were at the family cabin in Eau Claire for the weekend. By yourself? Wasn't that kind of lonely?"

"I like to be alone up there. It's peaceful. I do some writing, some hiking in the woods. I wasn't coming home until Monday, but I forgot my charger and my phone went dead. So, I came home Sunday instead. I was almost here, but I needed gas. When I stopped to fill up, I ran into Keegan. He asked if I wanted to party, and I said yes."

"So, you have this Thoreau weekend and get all one with nature and all, then you come home and party your brains out?" My voice was heavy with skepticism. I switched to a more understanding tone, trying to play both bad cop and good cop myself. "You know, Jamie, even if you had a fight with your dad before you left, you don't need to feel guilty. Your fight didn't make him die."

"Nothing happened. I don't feel guilty," his voice had risen to an angry shout as he jumped to his feet. "Stop pretending you care about me, or Isabel, or my father's suicide. You're just after a story. And the bigger, the messier, the dirtier it is, the better!" He towered over me, clenching his fists so hard I knew he wanted to take a swing at me. I stood up and moved in close, into his space. Time for bad cop to return in a big way.

"What is it you don't want me to find out? You might as well tell me, Jamie, because one way or another, I will find out." The problem with that approach was that I wasn't a cop, and he wasn't scared of me. But he sure was mad.

He grabbed me by the shoulders and shoved me aside as he left the room. I lost my footing and slipped, hitting the edge of a small table as I fell. He didn't even look back. By the time I got to my feet, Mrs. Godfrey was standing in the doorway. She held out a cup to me.

"You want that coffee now?"

15

OUT IN THE DRIVEWAY, I loaded the box into my car and cast a quick glance up at the windows. No sign of curtains twitching or Jamie glowering down from the third floor.

I walked over to his yellow Mini Cooper, found a hand sanitizer in my purse, and squirted some on the grime-encrusted passenger's door, then wiped it off with a wad of Kleenex. Squatting down, I looked it over carefully for signs of a run-in with Mrs. Wright's mailbox. I rubbed my fingertips lightly over the midsection of the door. There it was. A slight indentation, a small concave spot that should have been smooth. I peered closer. Just to the left was a long, light surface scratch and what could be a speck of red paint. The decapitated mailbox had been red.

Conclusive? No. It could have been the aftermath of a close encounter with a car door in a parking lot. But it was suggestive. As was Jamie's out of control behavior at the end of our interview.

I got into my car and drove toward town. Why had Jamie gotten so angry at me? What had happened the night Garrett died? Had he seen something—or done something?

He hadn't looked like he was in the throes of a relapse—though a person can fake sobriety. Then again, he can fake being drunk or high, too. What if Jamie wasn't out of it at all that night? If Garrett was the sadistic son-of-a-bitch that Jamie described, if he'd been undermining his son's confidence his whole life, and then actually stole $100,000 from him, maybe Jamie decided he'd had enough.

Maybe he spent the weekend thinking about his dad and how he'd never been good enough. And what he could have done with the money his mother left him. Maybe he got angrier and angrier. I was a witness to his temper. There was a lot of fury inside that kid. Maybe he came home earlier—and far less drunk—from the party than he said and decided to do something about it. I let the scene form in my mind's eye.

He gets home from his party well before 4 a.m., and he's not near as wasted as he pretends later. And he's got a plan. He sees the light on in his father's study as he drives up. He comes in through the kitchen like always, only this time he slips a pair of the housekeeper's plastic gloves into his pocket. He takes out some of the Klonipin he's bought or stolen and grinds it up, then stirs it into a rum and Coke. He grabs a bottle of water for himself. Then he heads for the study. He apologizes to his father for disappointing him. He offers his dad the drink and says he's sticking to water, proving what a clean and sober son he is. Maybe Garrett responds the way Jamie feels he always has, with criticism and sarcasm, removing any doubt from Jamie's mind about what he's going to do.

When Garrett starts to nod off, Jamie puts on the gloves, takes the gun out of the drawer, wraps dear old dad's hand around it, and pulls the trigger. Then off to bed it is, maybe after a fortifying beer or two for verisimilitude to bolster his alibi. And he's finally free. And, he thinks, he'll be half a million richer when the insurance money comes through—that can make up for a lot of adolescent angst. What a crushing blow when he finds out about the suicide exclusion. No wonder he's so pissed off at the world.

But wait a minute—what about the Mini Cooper that Mrs. Wright had seen that night? What did that have to do with anything?

I didn't realize the light had turned green until a horn honked behind me. I took my foot off the brake. Instead of going straight to the office, I turned and headed toward the Himmel Police Department. I needed Coop to help me think this through. But when I stopped by the front desk, Melanie said he had the afternoon off.

"Is he at home, do you know?"

"Couldn't tell you," she said, patting the odd poof of curls that was apparently now a part of her standard hairdo. The phone rang and she turned away to answer it.

I tried his cell as I stood there, but it went straight to voicemail. I didn't bother to leave a message. When I got to the parking lot, an involuntary groan escaped me. Dale Darmody was warming his backside against my car, chowing down on a burger in the sunlight of an unseasonably warm day.

"Hey, Leah. Long time, no see." As he spoke, a bit of burger tumbled out of his mouth, bounced off his jacket and hit the pavement.

"Hi, Darmody."

"Old Charlie Ross hit you with a sucker punch on that Whiting file, didn't he?" Darmody started laughing, and then he started choking. It's no testament to my character that I hesitated for a second before I slammed him on the back, and he dislodged the piece of bun that was impeding his airway.

"Yeah. It was hilarious. Thanks for rubbing it in."

"Aww now, hey, don't be like that. I'm not the one that did it. Fact of the matter is, I told the lieutenant as soon as Charlie told me what he was up to." He coughed a little, and his blue eyes watered from the effort. He had taken his hat off and set it on the roof of my car, as he used the hood for a picnic table. A light breeze ruffled the rapidly-diminishing strands of gray on his head. The sun in his face highlighted fine hairs sprouting randomly from his ears and nose. Somehow, that was a little endearing. Darmody is like a beat cop in a 1940s movie. Jovial, friendly, just not all that smart. Still, he loves his job, and he loves his town, and I've known him since I was 10 years old.

"Never mind, it's all right, Darmody."

He smiled then, and I did, too. "Haven't seen you around much lately."

"I've been around. It's Coop who's MIA. What's up? Is he working on some big undercover operation or what?"

He laughed, a little nervously, I thought.

"What? Is he? Come on, you can trust me."

"Well, I prob'ly shouldn't say anything. I mean the lieutenant—"

"Dale!" From across the parking lot came a voice that could peel paint.

Darmody snapped to attention in a way I was sure he never did for a senior officer.

"Hi, hon. I was just keepin' Leah company while she ate her lunch." He quickly shoved the bag he was holding into my hand and shot me a pleading look.

"Dale, the doctor said you are not supposed to eat red meat. Your cholesterol is sky high." By this time Angela Darmody had reached us. She stretched her tiny five-foot frame to the max and pulled Darmody's head down to her level, sniffed, pushed him back, and said, "Hamburger!" She turned a fierce gaze on me that I tried to avoid.

"Don't look away, Leah Nash. You are aiding and abetting Dale right into a heart attack."

"Sorry, Angela. Won't happen again. I asked Dar—Dale to share lunch with me. He just did it to be polite."

"Hmph!" She wasn't buying it, and I wasn't about to stand around waiting for my turn while Darmody got reamed out.

"Good to see you, but I've got to go." With that I handed Darmody his hat from the roof of my car, tossed the burger bag into the nearest bin, opened my door and scooted onto the seat, all before Angela finished reading him out. I'd have to wait another day to find out what Coop was up to—or ask him myself. Though if I were the sensitive type, I might think he was avoiding me.

I was heading toward the paper when I remembered the box in the back seat of my car and my promise to Mrs. Godfrey. I made a U-turn and drove toward Hickam Avenue. A sort of mini-medical row had built up in the last 10 years in the blocks surrounding Caldwell Memorial Hospital. Several medical practices had offices there, a few dentists, an optometrist. A couple of buildings housed specialists like dermatologists, oncologists, nephrologists, and others who practiced at larger hospitals in Madison or Milwaukee, but kept office hours once every week or two in Himmel. The surgical practice of Garrett Whiting, M.D. was located there.

The waiting room had that smell peculiar to a doctor's office, a combination of antiseptic and anxiety. I approached the sliding glass window, lugging the box with me. I set it down and tapped gently on the glass to get the attention of the receptionist. She was frowning as she stared at her computer screen. She opened the window without looking up and said, "Sign in please, include the time. Fill out this form, and we'll call you in a few minutes." She slid a clipboard and a pen toward me and closed the window. I tapped again. This time she looked up with the pained expression of someone who has heard one too many stupid questions that day.

"Yes? Do you need help with the form?"

I used the clipboard to block the window so she couldn't shut me out again if she were displeased with my answer.

"I'm not a patient. I'm delivering a box for Dr. Whiting's family. His daughter Isabel asked me to drop it off for his office manager, Elaine Quellman."

"She's not here. But you can take it through that door." She pointed to her right. "Janelle is working in her office, and she can help you." She moved the clipboard and shut the window before I could bother her again.

Hefting the box, I used it to push the door open and walked through. As she had indicated, there was an office immediately to the left. I tapped on the half-open door and walked in.

"Hi, I'm delivering a box from Dr. Whiting's daughter, for Elaine Quellman. Where should I put it?"

The woman sitting on the floor surrounded by file folders and banker boxes was young, maybe early 20s. She had gone a little heavy on the liner and eye shadow, but she was very pretty with long red hair tucked behind her ears and a dusting of freckles on her short, straight nose.

"Miss Quellman isn't here. I guess you can put it over there in the corner." She pointed to one of the few empty spaces on the carpet. I dumped the box unceremoniously, then dropped down beside her and held out my hand. "I'm Leah Nash. I'm a reporter with the *Himmel Times*."

"Janelle Bigelow." She gave my hand a limp squeeze.

"Will Miss Quellman be back tomorrow?"

"I doubt it. She's all emotional, because of Dr. Whiting and all."

"She's still not coping?"

"I know, right? It was like a hundred years ago."

"Actually, more like six weeks ago."

"Well, still. Get over it. So, she came back to the office and everything, but then when we had to start transferring patients and closing out Dr. Whiting's files, she flipped out. She's been off forever, and I'm the one stuck doing everything."

"So. She and Dr. Whiting were close? Were they..." I let my voice trail off, waiting to see if Janelle would fill in with details of a long-standing office romance. To my surprise, she burst out laughing.

"Doctor and Miss Quellman? Not hardly. She's got to be like 100. She was like his hover mother. Always all over us about his special coffee, and his special pen, and his special paper, and his special self. My grandma is kinda like that with my dad. Drives my mom crazy. So, what's in the box? More junk for me to take care of, I suppose."

"No, just some things from Dr. Whiting's desk at home. I think his daughter wanted Miss Quellman to have them as keepsakes."

"Someone will have to take them to her house. Probably me. No one else ever does anything around here. She only lives over on Newton Street, but it's totally the opposite direction from my place. The newspaper office is over by there, isn't it?" She looked hopefully at me.

I ignored her subtle suggestion that I be the one to deliver the box.

"Is his associate Dr. Bergman going to keep the office open?"

"I hope so. He's seeing patients and stuff, but we've been transferring a lot of Dr. Whiting's patient records, so I don't know. And there was, well, that thing."

She stopped, but her eyes begged me to ask more. I recognized the look, having received it from Courtnee many times before. There was gossip to be had.

I leaned in and lowered my voice to show her I knew how this was done. "What aren't you saying, Janelle?"

She met my lean with an incline of her own, so that our heads were nearly touching and she spoke in a lowered voice, as though we were in a crowd of people, instead of the only occupants of a small room. "I heard Dr. Whiting yelling at Dr. Bergman. 'You have f'd up for the last time. But I'm damned if my reputation is going to be f'd up with you!' Only he didn't say 'f'd,' he just dropped the whole f-bomb."

"What did he mean?"

"I don't know. I only overheard them because I ran back in to get my coat. The office was just closed. But that old bag-head Miss Quellman was standing at the back door like, 'Hurry up, Janelle. You don't have business in there after hours.' Like she's the big sheriff of the office. Well, she is kind of, I guess. They were still going at it, but I had to leave," she said, her regret evident.

"When was this?"

"I'm not sure exactly. But not very long before Dr. Whiting killed himself."

"Did you tell anybody else?"

"Just a couple of the girls, but then Miss Quellman heard me, and said she'd fire me if I didn't stop gossiping. It wasn't gossip. It was true," she said virtuously. I was beginning to think that I had found Courtnee's spiritual doppelganger in Janelle.

"What did you think of Dr. Whiting?"

She didn't hesitate. "Bossy old bastard. Not like Dr. B."

"And what's Dr. Bergman like?"

"Hot. I mean the car, the clothes, he flies his own plane. He's super sexy."

"But you don't know if he's planning on buying the practice for himself?"

She shook her head. "I'd be the last one to know. Nobody tells me anything."

"OK, then. Well, I'd better let you get back to work. Sorry I interrupted you," I said, standing up.

"It's OK. I needed the break."

Judging from the half-hearted way she'd been moving files around, I doubted it.

"Yeah, I'll bet. You know what? Let me take that box over to Miss Quellman for you. That's one less thing you have to take care of."

"Her house is right next to the Presbyterian Church on Newton. It's gray with white shutters," she said as I lifted the box again. "Here, let me get the door for you."

16

As I reached my car, a shiny black Mercedes pulled into the parking lot. I watched a man who defined the term "metrosexual" get out. He had a bronzed face, despite Himmel's seasonal lack of sunshine, and subtle highlights in his layered dark brown hair. A luxurious camel hair coat covered his tall, lean frame. As he pressed the lock button on his key fob, I tossed the box into my car and called out, "Dr. Bergman!"

He paused, and I hurried up to him. He seemed vaguely familiar. As I got closer, I realized he looked a lot like the movie star Johnny Depp—without the facial hair and glasses.

"Dr. Bergman, hi, I'm Leah Nash, a reporter with the *Himmel Times*. I'm working on a story about Dr. Whiting's death—" His expression, which had been merely curious, now looked wary.

"Garrett's suicide? Why would you be doing a story on that now? It happened weeks ago."

"I know, yes, but his family is concerned the death was investigated too quickly. They—"

"I don't understand why that would be."

"There are some unanswered questions."

"Not that I'm aware of. If you'll excuse me please, Liz, is it?"

"Leah. Leah Nash."

"Right. Sorry. But I do have to go." He turned toward the building. As he did, I put my hand on his arm. He gave me a withering look. If we were in elementary school, he would have accused me of having cooties at that point.

"I'm sorry. I'm sure it's hard to talk about losing a friend."

"We weren't friends. Dr. Whiting owned the practice. He was a mentor and a very good surgeon. I'm sorry he's dead, but it wasn't a personal loss. Again, please excuse me." He was getting away. Time to bring out the big guns. I spoke to his retreating back, and what I said made him stop and turn around.

"I heard he could be pretty rough on you. Someone said you guys had some harsh words not long before he died. Must be tough, one of your last memories of him being a shout down."

"I don't know what you're talking about." His voice was as cold as the winter wind off the Himmel River, but I had his attention now.

"He didn't say, 'You have f'd up for the last time. But I'm damned if my reputation is going to be f'd up with you!'?"

"Who told you that?"

"Is it true?"

Now it was his turn to grab my arm. "If I ever hear that you've repeated that lie I will sue you and your paper for everything you have. If you ever come on this property again, I will have you arrested for harassment, trespassing, and slander." For emphasis, he gave my arm a hard twist, then he flung it away and walked quickly into the building.

Well, well, well, now we were getting somewhere. Dr. Hal Bergman just joined Jamie Whiting and Frankie Saxon on the persons of interest list. And, mostly just because I didn't like the smug bastard, I put him right at the top.

―――――――――

"Elaine Quellman?"

"Yes, that's right. You are?" The woman who opened the door wore a white turtleneck and navy trousers. Her salt and pepper hair was cut in a bob with straight bangs that grazed her eyebrows and focused attention on her amazing aquamarine eyes. Though clearly well into middle age, she was far from the "old bag head" Janelle had described.

"I'm Leah Nash, a friend of Isabel Whiting's. I have a package for you from her," I said, shifting the box slightly. It wasn't that heavy, but it was a little unwieldy to hold.

"Oh! Really? She didn't mention it. Well, please come in." She waved me into her living room. "You can put the package on the coffee table, if you would."

As I did, she went to a desk in the corner and retrieved a letter opener. I watched as she used it to slice open the box. She hadn't asked me to sit, but then again she hadn't asked me to leave. So I waited, noting the room's cool gray walls hung with modern art reprints, the light oak floors, and the uncomfortable-looking low sofa and chairs. She pulled out and unwrapped the pen and the photograph. When she came to the portfolio, she gave a little cry and looked up at me.

"What a lovely, thoughtful thing for Isabel to do. I gave this to Garrett years ago." She ran her fingers lightly over the embossed initials on the cover, like a blind person reading a message in braille.

"It's beautiful."

"He always carried it with him. He refused to use the computer for notes and correspondence. Always a Montblanc pen and a sheet of lined paper. That's why I bought this portfolio for him. To hold his pads of paper."

"He didn't use email?" That hardly seemed possible.

"It's not as though he didn't know how to use email. He preferred not to. He had beautiful handwriting, very precise." Her voice had taken on a distinct chill at the perceived criticism of her boss.

I tried to warm her up a little.

"You and he worked together really well, I guess."

"We did. For over 20 years. We were often at the office together on Sunday mornings. We both enjoyed the quiet time to catch up. The last time I saw him was at the office, the day he died." Her voice had softened.

"What was he doing? What kind of mood was he in?"

"Well, he wasn't suicidal, if that's what you're asking. I certainly would have done something if he were," she said, her voice tinged with annoyance again.

"No, of course. I'm sure you would have. I've been talking with Isabel, his daughter, and she's been trying to piece together his last day. I just thought maybe I could tell her how he spent that morning."

"It was just the same as always. He made calls, did some correspondence. We had coffee together. I noticed he'd used the last page of his pad of paper on a letter he'd written, so I brought him a new one. He thanked me. I picked up the mail to take to the Post Office, and we walked out together. He told me to have a good day. Just ordinary, just like a hundred times before. I had no idea it was the last time I'd ever see him." Her eyes glistened.

"I'm sorry," I said.

"Yes. Well." She flicked a tear away, assumed a brisk tone, and said, "Thank you for bringing these to me. I was about to have coffee. Can I offer you some? Leah Nash, you said your name was?"

"Yes, that's right. Thanks, that would be nice."

"Of course." As she turned to get it, I followed. If she were disconcerted to have me at her heels like an imprinted duckling, she had the good manners not to show it. I hoped that if we were seated together at the kitchen table, the intimacy of the setting would help her open up a little.

She pulled cups from the cupboard, then poured coffee from an already brewed pot.

"Don't I know your name? Aren't you the reporter who exposed the chicanery at DeMoss Academy?" She sat down across from me as she asked.

"Yes. I'm a friend of Isabel's, but I also work for the *Himmel Times*. I'm actually investigating the death of her father. Isabel doesn't believe he killed himself."

"I don't either."

I hadn't expected flat-out agreement.

"You don't? Why?"

"He wouldn't have left without saying anything." She gave a small, sad smile.

"You mean, you don't think he killed himself, because he didn't leave a note?"

She didn't answer my question directly. "I loved him. Oh, not like some of those nitwits at the office think. I'm aware they called me his office wife, laughed behind my back, thought I was a deluded old maid. It wasn't like that."

"What was it like?"

"I didn't harbor any romantic dreams about him. I wasn't 'in love' with him. I loved his skill, his confidence. He was arrogant, and he could be cold and even cruel sometimes, but he was brilliant. People like Garrett are rare. They demand the best of themselves and of others. They deserve special care and attention. It was my pleasure to give it to him."

"So you think he couldn't have suffered the self-doubt or depression that could lead ordinary people to suicide?"

"That's not what I said. I realize he was subject to human frailties. But I don't believe he would end his life without making a statement. It wasn't in his nature. He would have written a suicide note."

"You knew about his financial losses?"

"Of course. He trusted me with everything."

"Then you knew he had Parkinson's, too?"

"What? No. He didn't."

"Yes, he did."

"That can't be right. Garrett would have told me. He wouldn't keep that from me. From everyone else, perhaps, but not from me." Her voice faltered as she processed the information and its implications. The man she idolized and trusted had not trusted her with his secret.

"I was his right hand. He always said, 'Elaine, you're the glue that holds this place together.' I know he trusted me. He did!" She said it with defiance.

"I'm sure he did, but the diagnosis must have been devastating to him. He probably didn't want to tell you until he'd come to terms with it. He wouldn't want you to suffer along with him." I highly doubted that, from what I'd been learning about Garrett Whiting, but I wanted to offer her a little comfort.

"Yes. Yes, you're right." She rallied, taking a breath and composing herself. "I know he would have told me. I wasn't just his office manager. I was his trusted confidant." She said it with pride, but it struck me as sad that she had settled for what seemed to me so little.

"Is it possible that his financial losses, combined with his illness, might have driven Dr. Whiting to take his own life?"

"Not the money. No. It was never about the money. It was always the work. And I don't believe the Parkinson's would have either. Garrett was a strong man, a brave man. He wouldn't give up, not without a fight." Her voice had risen and I wondered if she were trying to convince me or herself.

"Did the sheriff's department talk to you?" I didn't recall seeing a statement from her.

"They didn't come to me after he died. But I finally called them. I felt I had to tell them about Dr. Bergman, but they weren't interested."

"What about Dr. Bergman?"

"He was stealing prescription pads and sample drugs. Quite possibly he still is. Either for himself or to sell. Perhaps both."

"Did Dr. Whiting tell you that?"

"I told him. Drugs were missing from our sample closet. And our prescription pad counts and order numbers didn't match."

"Why did you suspect Dr. Bergman? Did you confront him?"

"Only three people had unrestricted access to the locked cabinet where they were kept and the authority to order them. It wasn't Garrett. It wasn't me. That left Dr. Bergman. I didn't approach him about it. Garrett told me to let him handle it. He didn't want me involved."

"So, Dr. Whiting confronted Dr. Bergman. That's why he said Dr. Bergman was f'd, and he wasn't going down with him, or words to that effect."

"I see you've spoken with Janelle. Garrett didn't want the practice dragged into Dr. Bergman's mess. And Dr. Bergman begged Garrett to give him an opportunity to put his affairs in some kind of order, perhaps a chance to make some kind of deal with the authorities."

"And Dr. Whiting agreed?"

She nodded. "I didn't think it was wise. But Garrett wanted to handle it as quietly as possible, without tainting the practice. That Sunday before he died, he told me not to worry, that everything was taken care of as far as Dr.

Bergman was concerned. I took that to mean that Dr. Bergman was going to the police. Or that Garrett was."

"But Dr. Bergman didn't confess and go the authorities, did he? And Dr. Whiting didn't either. He died. Do you think Dr. Bergman had something to do with his death?"

She stopped short of that. "I don't know. But after Garrett died, I called the sheriff's department. I talked to the detective on the case and told him what I knew about the prescription drugs."

"And?"

"He wasn't much interested in what I had to say. He told me that Garrett's death was a suicide, period. He thanked me for the information on Dr. Bergman and said they would follow up. He also advised me not to discuss it with anyone. He said if I did, it could impede their investigation into Dr. Bergman. I could see the wisdom of that, so I haven't. But that was weeks ago and nothing's been done."

My mind was teeming with possible directions to go here. OK, even that moron Ross would've had to check out the prescription drug story, or he would've turned the lead over to the Himmel Police Department. Unless he didn't need to, because they already knew. Maybe that's what Coop was up to. He was part of a multi-agency task force cracking down on prescription drug rings. Ross was sure Whiting's death was a suicide. He was in no hurry to act on Miss Quellman's tip because he knew the task force already had Bergman in their sights. I pulled my thoughts back to the present.

"So, why are you talking to me now?"

"Because Dr. Bergman is still in practice and that isn't right. A brilliant man is dead. Dr. Bergman can't be allowed to continue as though nothing happened. He can't be allowed to get away with no punishment. I respect what you did for your sister. I believe you'll make something happen here, too."

Oh, I was going to make things happen. I just wasn't sure what things and to whom.

"I'm certainly going to try. If you think of anything else, please call me, any hour. Trust me, I will be following up on this." I handed her my card, and as she took it, her hand shook a little.

She hadn't told me to call her Elaine, so I didn't, but I said, "I'm very sorry for your loss, Miss Quellman."

"Thank you," she said, accepting the condolence as her due. And after 20 years of faithful service to a man few seemed to miss, maybe it was.

"Those are beautiful flowers."

I had hoped my mother would be in her room, or doing laundry or something, so I could slip them into my bedroom without being noticed. No such luck.

"Yeah."

"Where did you get them? From your guilty expression, it looks like you stole someone's funeral arrangement."

"Funny. They're from Nick. I only brought them home to stem the tide of Miguel and Courtnee's endless speculation."

"Nick? Why?"

"I don't know. A gesture of thanks, I guess, for not taking his head off. Let it go. It's been a really long day." To distract her I launched into a recap of my adventures.

"Rebecca's not very impressed, but at least she didn't tell me to stop. I wanted to talk to Coop about things, but he was out again. I saw Darmody and he started to tell me that Coop's doing something secret. I think it might be something with the Drug Enforcement Agency. There's a rumor that there's a task force operating in the area. I could've gotten it out of Darmody, but Angela came by and started in on him before he could finish. I guess he's got high cholesterol. No surprise really. Though he's so scared of Angela, I can't believe he won't toe the line." My rambling did not distract her.

When on the scent, my mother has the tenacity of a bloodhound. "Those are very expensive flowers. Are you sure Nick is thanking you, not courting you?"

" 'Courting' me? Yes, he is Ma. And I hope you and Pa will let us sit in the front parlor and spoon when he comes to call. No. He's not 'courting' me."

"You know, sarcasm is not attractive. Is he trying to get back together with you?"

"I don't think so. Remember, Nick always favors the excessive gesture. And apparently he's forgotten that I hate getting things like that at the office. Miguel and Courtnee haven't given me a minute's peace. That's why I brought them home. Out of sight, out of mind. Except no, now you've got to start in."

She didn't say anything for a minute, but I could see the wheels turning behind her dark blue eyes, calculating just how far she could take this. When she spoke, it surprised me.

"I'm sorry. Whatever is going on —" She held up her hand to stop me as I started to interrupt, "No, let me finish. Whatever Nick's intentions are, they're none of my business. You're right. I just don't want to see you hurt again, but that's all I'm going to say about it." I doubted it, but decided not to say so. She was the one who changed the subject.

"Thanksgiving is Thursday, you know. Paul and Miguel and Father Lindstrom are coming. Is Coop?"

"No, I thought I told you. He's going to his sister's, but he said he might stop by later to watch the game."

"OK. There's some leftover roast beef in the fridge if you want to make a sandwich for dinner. We're running low on just about everything. I'm going to the store and then stopping at Paul's for a minute. Do you want anything?"

"We're out of Honey Nut Cheerios. Otherwise, no, I'm good. I'll probably be in bed when you get back. I'm beat."

———

And so it was. At 9 p.m. on Monday night, I was tucked in my bed and in my jammies when I got a text from Isabel.

Jamie is really mad. What happened?

I'm not sure. He just went off. Saw Dr. Bergman today. Interesting.

Meaning?

Bad blood between him and your dad. Could be something there.

What?

I'll talk to you later this week.

She sent another text, but I was done. I understood why she wanted to know all the details, but I couldn't do my job if I had to report back to her every step of the way. I'd have to remind her of that. My glance fell on the giant bouquet sitting on my chest of drawers. I really should thank Nick, but I wasn't up for another conversation with him. I texted instead.

Thanks for the flowers. Very pretty.

Glad you like them. I should have done more of that when we were married.

No, just less of a few other things.

Ouch. Moving on. Getting anywhere with Dr. Whiting story?

Maybe. Talked to someone today. Definitely had the means. Whiting's partner. Maybe the motive too.

Want to meet for drinks Thursday or for dinner?

It's Thanksgiving.

I forgot. No plans.

This I knew was my cue to say *"Why don't you come to dinner?"* But for several reasons I didn't. First, my mother would kill me. Second, the new Nick was an improvement over the old, but I was leery of his let's-be-friends schtick. Third, my mother would kill me.

OK. Got to go. Later.

Maybe dinner Saturday?

I didn't answer. But since I was in the texting mood, I shot one off to Coop.

WTF? Why are you never around?

Can't talk. In the middle of something.

Later this week?

I'll see you Thursday, when I get back from Tracy's.

That definitely felt like a brush off, and very not like Coop. It made me think that I was probably right. He was working on a DEA task force. Rural areas are prime locations for under-the-radar drug rings, because of the isolation and the limited law enforcement budgets and manpower to combat them. So, the DEA sometimes sets up a task force that uses their personnel with local cops to pool resources and expertise. If Coop was assigned to work on one, that would explain why he'd hardly been around lately. And why he wasn't giving me any answers.

17

FATHER LINDSTROM looked a bit nonplussed when he pressed the buzzer on our front door and *All About That Bass* boomed out, but he took it in stride.

"Sorry, Father, Mom changed up her doorbell tunes, but she left the volume a little high. Happy Thanksgiving. At least she didn't start dancing it out with you."

"Very catchy song, Leah," he said with a distinct twinkle in his eyes.

My mother gave him a quick hug and led him into the living room where Paul and Miguel were already sitting. She handed him a glass of the wine Miguel had brought, and they all sat back to watch the endless pre-football programming, while I helped Mom finish up in the kitchen.

Thanksgiving dinner was predictably epic. My mother is a great cook, and Paul knows his way around a green bean casserole.

"Wonderful meal, Carol," Father Lindstrom said. "I'm afraid I may have flirted with the second deadly sin today. Gluttony," he added, for those of us not well-versed in the Baltimore Catechism.

"I'm sure God will forgive you," I said. "Jesus himself would have a hard time resisting Mom's turkey stuffing."

"Great job, sweetheart." Paul leaned over and kissed my mother on the cheek.

"*Tan bueno*. Thank you, Carol."

My mother stood and took a small bow. "Thank you. I'm just glad so many of my favorite people could be here. Who's ready for pie?"

A collective groan went up.

"How about later, when we're watching the game? We need some time for this to digest," I suggested.

As everyone was nodding in agreement, Paul, Miguel, and Father Lindstrom started clearing the table. My phone rang. Isabel. I'd forgotten to get back to her like I had texted I would on Monday. I just had so much work to cram in at the paper because of our early holiday deadline.

"Hey, Isabel."

"Hi, Leah. I'm sorry, I know it's Thanksgiving, but this will just take a minute. When we texted earlier this week, you were going to call and talk to me about Jamie. He's been in a terrible mood ever since you questioned him, and he's barely talking to me about anything. And then today he just took off. I'm worried about him. I just thought if there was any more you could tell me, maybe I'd know what to say to him. And—you know what? This is stupid. You're with your family, it's a holiday. Forget it. We can talk tomorrow."

Her voice was both wistful and apologetic. I felt a stab of guilt that I hadn't called her, or even spared a thought for what this first family holiday without her father might be like.

"No, no, that's okay. I'm sorry I didn't get back to you. It was crazy busy at work, but how about if I run out to see you now?"

"Oh, no. You don't have to do that. Not on Thanksgiving. It was stupid to call."

"No. It wasn't. I'm practically on my way. See you shortly." I hung up and realized that my mother had been listening.

"You're leaving?"

"Just for a little while. I feel like a jerk. Isabel is all alone in that house. I never even thought about her. I'll be back before Coop gets here to watch the game."

"Why don't you take her a plate of food and some pie?"

"Yeah, I guess I could. She might like that."

"Good. I'll make enough for both her and her brother. And I'll make one for Vesta too. You can drop it off on the way."

"Whoa. Wait a minute. I told you I was out of the delivery game as far as Vesta is concerned, after last time."

Vesta Brenneman is an elderly eccentric who lives in a tumbledown house on the outskirts of town. She spends her days riding her bicycle all over the county with her little dog Barnacle in the front basket. Even winter doesn't deter her, as long as the roads are plowed. She hardly ever speaks, and when she does, it's mostly to quote Bible verses. She should probably be in an assisted living home, but she'd fight for her independence tooth and nail. And she'd never, ever give up her dog. My mom and some of the other women from St. Stephen's look out for her with gifts of food and clothing, and someone makes sure she always has her heat on.

"She chased me right out the door last time. And she's way on the other side of town from the Whitings."

"Oh, stop it. It will take an extra 15 minutes, just run it in. Think what a nice treat it will be for her."

"*Chica*, I'll go with you. I'm parked behind you anyway. It'll be fun. I'd like to meet Vesta."

Ten minutes later I was in the car with Miguel. Mom's Thanksgiving boxes of goodies for Vesta, Jamie and Isabel sat in the backseat. Rain had fallen off and on during the morning and early afternoon, but the temperature had dropped, and now it was turning into a light, silvery sleet.

As we came to a stop sign, Miguel's car fishtailed a little, and the Thanksgiving bounty slid and shifted on the backseat.

"Hey, take it easy, unless you want to accessorize your outfit with a slice of pumpkin pie on your shoulder."

"Sorry, *chica*. Black ice. Which way to the famous Vesta's house?"

"She lives on Birch Street, the last block, the only house left standing." We were both too full of turkey and trimmings to talk much as we neared the southern edge of town. As we turned onto Vesta's street, out of the corner of my eye, I saw her pedaling toward us on her bike. I started to unroll the window to hail her down, just as her bike wobbled and leaned precariously over. She managed to keep it upright, but her dog, Barnacle, bounced out of the basket, staggered, then ran yipping across the road right in front of us.

"Miguel!"

He slammed on the brakes. The wheels locked and the car spun out on the slippery street as he lost control of the steering wheel. A blue pickup, coming in from a side street, blared its horn and tried to swerve out of our path, but too late. As Miguel's Toyota caromed off the side, the airbags deployed, hitting us both in the face. Then we were bouncing across a vacant lot strewn with broken concrete, old tires, and potholes, each more jarring than the last. Finally, blessedly, the car came to a stop. We both took a second to get our bearings, coughing and choking on the chemical dust that shot into the air along with the airbags.

"Are you OK?" I managed to croak, undoing my seatbelt and turning to look at Miguel.

He nodded.

"Let's get out of here. Can you move?"

"Yes, yes, *chica*, I'm fine." He smiled, but his grin looked as shaky as I felt. When Miguel tried to open his door, it was jammed shut. By now the truck driver had run over to us, and he yanked my door open so fast I almost fell out.

"You guys all right?"

"Yeah, yeah. Fine. The driver's door is jammed shut though. Miguel, can you slide over, get out on my side?"

It wasn't easy with his long frame, but he managed to wrestle with the deflated airbag, scoot across the console, and squeeze out the passenger door.

"I already called 911," the truck driver said. He was a big man in a Carhart coat that hung open over his well-stuffed flannel shirt. "I'm Gus Lundquist. You're sure you're all right now, the both of you?"

"Leah Nash, Gus. This is my friend Miguel Santos." We extended our hands and Gus shook each of them in his bear-size paw. It was then I noticed Vesta hovering behind him, Barnacle shivering in her arms.

"Are you all right, Vesta?"

" '*O thou afflicted, tossed with tempests*,' " she said. Then surprisingly, she scurried forward and took my hand, pulling me in the direction of her house.

"Now hold on there, ma'am." Gus turned to her. "We got the police and the ambulance comin.' These folks need to be checked out."

" 'Out of the South cometh the whirlwind, and cold out of the North.' " She continued to tug on my arm.

"Let's all go with her," Miguel said. "It's freezing out here." His teeth chattered in testament to the fact.

"Vesta's house is right across the street," I said.

"You go ahead then. I'll wait in my truck for the cops; it's plenty warm for me. I'm gonna call back and say that's a negative on the ambulance, though, unless you two feel worse than you look."

"I'm fine," I said.

"Me, too."

"All right then. You go with the lady there."

So there we were, Vesta in the lead, holding Barnacle in one arm, tugging me with the other, while I grabbed onto Miguel's hand to reassure myself that he really was all right.

Once inside the oddly furnished little house, Vesta flipped a switch. Two bare lightbulbs hanging overhead came to life and threw faint light into the gloomy space. She gestured for me to sit on her iron-framed bed, made up with a faded and frayed pink chenille bedspread. She gently set Barnacle down in a basket on the floor, near an ancient wall-mounted gas furnace that sent welcome hot air into the room. She moved to the small stove and turned the burner on under the teakettle, then set out two cups and retrieved a withered teabag from a saucer on her small counter.

Next, she turned her attention to Miguel. She pulled him to the sink and turned on the porcelain handle of the hot water faucet. She reached for a slightly grimy washcloth that she lathered with a yellowed and cracked bar of soap. She moved it gently over his forehead.

"Ouch!" He jerked back a little, and I saw that Vesta's ministrations had uncovered a quarter-sized abrasion on his forehead. She stopped, a stricken look in her eyes. Miguel saw he had alarmed her.

"No, it's fine, Vesta. Thank you. *Gracias*. It feels much better, thank you," he said in a soothing voice and smiled. She smiled back.

"You saved Barnacle," she said, in the most coherent sentence I'd ever heard her utter. At the sound of his name, the little dog leaped from his basket and ran to her feet. She picked him up and cradled him in her arms. As she stood there in her baggy, raggedy pants at least a size too big, her grubby fisherman's knit sweater hanging down on her skinny thighs, still wearing her hooded yellow slicker, a tear ran down her weathered cheek. She nuzzled her face in Barnacle's fur and looked very small and very vulnerable. I reached out to touch her arm in a gesture of reassurance and kindness. It was not reciprocated.

" *'You are strangely troublesome,'* " she said, turning an accusatory glare on me. The quote came from *Henry VIII*. I know my Shakespeare better than I do my Bible. Apparently, she couldn't find a verse there to sufficiently express her irritation with me. She may have made room in her heart for Miguel, but clearly there was no vacancy where I was concerned.

"We almost got killed because of you and your dog, and I'm the troublesome one?"

Her only response was to hug Barnacle closer and edge a little nearer to Miguel, who appeared oblivious to the combined odor of sweat and menthol Vesta was exuding as she warmed up. As she smiled at him again, the teakettle whistled. She put Barnacle down, turned it off, and poured hot water into each of the cups she'd set out. I watched as she dipped the used teabag back and forth into the water in the two cups. Miguel and I exchanged a glance, but knew there was nothing to do but accept Vesta's version of a tea party. Satisfied that the brew had reached maximum potential, she squeezed the bag with her fingers over each cup, then put it back on its saucer and handed us each a mug.

"*Salud!*" Miguel said, as he clinked his cup with mine. I closed my eyes and swallowed, trying to focus on the warmth not the flavor, which was reminiscent of dirty dishwater and essence of Vesta.

"What is all this, Vesta?" Miguel asked. He gestured toward the feather and stone-filled plastic bags on the windowsill; the naked, bald plastic baby dolls piled in a jumble on the top of a tall dresser; and a woven basket on the floor that held tightly crunched shiny balls of aluminum foil in varying sizes.

"My collections." She preened a little as he complimented her on her specimens. "She doesn't have collections," she said with a disdainful nod in my direction. "Do you, boy?"

I saved Miguel from disillusioning his new friend by announcing that the police had arrived, and we should go outside.

He nodded agreement, then turned to Vesta. "*Gracias* so much for taking care of us."

But before she let him leave, Vesta carefully applied a Cookie Monster Band-Aid to Miguel's forehead. Me, she ignored. Which actually was an improvement over chasing me out the door.

18

WHEN WE GOT TO THE CAR, our truck driver friend Gus was already talking to the cops.

"You go ahead, Miguel. You and Gus need to exchange insurance information. I'm going to call Isabel and tell her what happened. I'll be over in a minute."

Isabel picked up on the first ring, and I explained the situation.

"Yeah, we're OK, but Miguel's car is in pretty bad shape. He's definitely not going to be driving away from this one. Hold on just a second." I gestured to the cop, who was looking my way, to indicate that I was wrapping things up.

"OK, sorry. I better go."

"I'll come get you and take you home."

"Hey, no, you don't need to do that. I'll just call my mother; we only live a few miles away."

"Too late, I'm pulling out of my driveway. This wouldn't have happened if I hadn't called you. The least I can do is give you a ride. What's the address?"

It was still sleeting, my hair was getting wet, my hands were freezing, and I didn't feel like arguing. I gave her Vesta's address.

"Be there in a few minutes."

I walked over to talk to the officer and added what I could to Miguel's account. He was pretty nice and let him off without a ticket. It may have been because it was Thanksgiving, or maybe because of the extremely sad expression on Miguel's face as he watched the wrecker come and load up his car. Gus, our pickup-driving friend, had stayed around to the end.

He clapped Miguel on the shoulder as the tow truck pulled away. "Looks totaled to me, *amigo*," he said. "Still, you walked away; that's gotta be a good feeling."

"*Sí*. That's true," Miguel said, as he tried to rally from his loss. "Thanks, Gus, for being so cool. I'm so sorry I hit your truck."

The big man shook his head. "Couldn't be helped. Glad you didn't hit the old lady's dog. You take 'er easy now, buddy." He climbed back into his pickup and gave a beep on his horn as he pulled away. Just then a green Escalade came driving up the street.

"Who's that?" Miguel asked as he watched the car pull up and park in Vesta's driveway.

"Isabel is giving us a ride back to mom's."

She parked and stepped out of the SUV. Vesta came barreling out of her house as we walked toward Isabel and planted herself in front of her.

" '*When the enemy shall come in like a flood, the Spirit of the Lord shall lift up a standard against him.*' "

Isabel took a half-step back.

Miguel went for Vesta as I came up behind Isabel.

"Thanks for coming. Don't be alarmed, Vesta doesn't like strangers."

"I can see that," she said, her nose wrinkling slightly as *eau de Vesta* wafted her way.

"Vesta, *cálmate*. It's fine. This is Isabel. She's not here for you. She's taking us home. But first let me take you inside. It's too cold out here for you." He whisked her back into the house before she could protest.

"Now, there's an odd couple. What is Miguel doing with her?"

"We were just dropping off some Thanksgiving dinner my mother sent her. It went the same way yours did, all over the car. Sorry."

When Miguel came back out, Isabel gave him a hug.

"Miguel! It's been a long time. Since high school, I think. It's nice to see you."

"Hi, Isabel." His greeting was more subdued than usual. "I'm sorry about your *papá*," he added.

"Thank you. Well. Why don't you both get in the car? The heater's on high, and you look like you need it."

As we approached my house, I saw Coop's car parked out front.

"You can park in the driveway, Isabel. Where Miguel's car would have been. He won't be needing the space anymore."

He emitted a sound between a whimper and groan. "*Chica,* you have no heart."

"Too soon?"

"No, I shouldn't come in," Isabel said. "You've got company, you've just been in a car wreck—"

"Please, come in. I know my mom would like to meet you."

The predictable pandemonium broke out as we entered and my mother got a good look at us. Somehow, between introducing herself to Isabel, demanding to know what had happened, plying Miguel with a big fluffy towel to dry his hair, and handing us both a shot of Bailey's in a cup of coffee, she managed to put together a plate of food for Isabel and sit her down at the kitchen table. I slipped off at the height of the activity to stand in a hot shower for five minutes. When I emerged, Coop was talking to Isabel at the table, and Father Lindstrom was offering Miguel a ride home.

"*Gracias, padre.* But I don't want you to miss the game."

He waved off Miguel's polite resistance. "I'm taping it, and I should be getting home anyway. Early day tomorrow. You might find an early night and a hot shower of benefit as well."

"He's right, Miguel. If not for yourself, do it for your hair." His usually perfectly styled hair was hanging down in his eyes, and he looked fried.

"What are you going to do about your car?" Coop asked.

"I don't know. My Aunt Lydia and Uncle Craig only have the one car. I can't borrow theirs, because what if my uncle got the call for a kidney? *Ándale*, they'd have to go. I can't be 30 miles away with their car. I have to check with my insurance. I don't know." He sounded uncharacteristically down as the full implications of being without a car hit him.

"Don't stress, Miguel, we'll figure it out. Get your hair back to normal and everything will look better in the morning."

He gave me a half-hearted grin, and then he and Father Lindstrom took off.

"I should go, too," Isabel said.

"Oh, have a piece of pie, won't you? It came out pretty well if I do say so myself."

"Well... "

"I'm going to take-off, too," Coop said, pushing back from the table. "Good meeting you, Isabel."

"Hey, don't go, Coop. I've hardly seen you in weeks. I want to tell you—" I stopped because part of what I wanted to tell him and ask him and debate with him were the various leads in the Whiting story. And I wasn't ready to share all those with Isabel yet.

"I know. I want to talk to you, too. It just didn't work out today. How about Saturday? We could grab some lunch?"

"Saturday? OK, yeah, that would be good. Meet you at the Elite at noon?"

"Yep, that works."

I walked him out.

"I know that you're involved with some big secret investigation. How about some details?"

"Not going to work, Leah. I told you, we'll talk Saturday. Sounds like we both have information to share. Until then, you'll just have to wait."

"Then, you are working on something big, aren't you? Something with the DEA? Just tell me. I bet you have a cool windbreaker with DEA stenciled on the back. Are you wearing a DEA super agent T-shirt under that sweater?" I made as if to lift it up, and he laughed and pushed my hand away.

"Saturday. OK?"

"Got it. OK. But there better be a big reveal to make all this waiting worthwhile."

He gave me look I couldn't quite read and said, "There will be."

Bemused, I wandered back into the kitchen where Isabel was telling my mother and Paul about meeting Vesta.

"Those crazy eyes and that hair and that outfit. She looked like something from a horror movie." Her graceful hands fluttered as she talked, and her voice ascended into a passable impression of Vesta squawking out a Bible quote. She was a good mimic, but after witnessing Vesta's vulnerability this afternoon, I didn't feel like laughing. I could see my mother didn't think it was so funny, either.

"Vesta was a college professor years ago. When her sister was diagnosed with Huntington's, she took care of her. It's a terrible, terrible illness. After Dora died, Vesta had a complete breakdown. She never really recovered. Just became more and more eccentric and alone. It's a sad story."

Isabel looked abashed. "That's awful. I'm sorry. I didn't mean anything by what I said. I didn't know."

"Well, how would you?" my mother relented. "Can I get you another piece of pie?"

"No, it was delicious. Everything was. But I should get going. I just wanted to talk to Leah for a minute."

"Sure. Paul, let's see how the game is coming." The two of them returned to the living room, and I sat down next to Isabel.

"Jamie's pretty mad at me for getting you involved in this."

"I got that impression when we talked. He and your dad—Jamie seems to hate him."

"He doesn't mean it, not really. My father wasn't the warm, fuzzy type. But he loved us. I know he did." She said the last part emphatically, though whether to convince me or herself, I wasn't sure.

"Isabel, you didn't mention that your mother left money to Jamie, but none to you. Why didn't she leave you anything?"

"She never thought of me as her 'real' daughter, even though she adopted me. I was used to it. And it's not like I ever expected anything from her."

"And your father lost Jamie's inheritance?"

"Not all of it. He used part of it for Jamie's rehab. Private boarding schools are very expensive."

"You should have told me that."

"I didn't think it mattered."

"Isabel, everything matters. You can't be the one who decides what counts and what doesn't, not if you want me to find out the truth. It seems to me Jamie has some pretty good reasons to be angry with your father."

She waved it off as though it weren't worth talking about and changed topics.

"Mrs. Godfrey told me you took the box of my father's things over for Miss Quellman. Thank you for that. Did you find out anything from her? Or when you talked to Frankie?"

She seemed desperate for anything that would take the spotlight off Jamie.

"The more I dig, the more odd things I'm turning up. Let's just say I'm very curious about Dr. Bergman. And I caught Frankie in a lie, but I don't know what that means yet."

"What? What did you find?"

"I'm not getting into specifics right now. And I'd appreciate it if you don't share with anyone—especially Frankie and Dr. Bergman—what I've said." I was regretting my information share, scant though it was, already.

"I wouldn't say anything! But you really think Frankie is lying about something?"

"I know she is. But the question is why. She struck me as one of those women who just can't get it right when it comes to men." *Unlike you who has such a stellar track record,* said that snide, inconvenient internal voice. I hate that voice.

"But does that mean you don't think Jamie had anything to do with it? Because he didn't, I'm sure."

"Isabel," I said with a touch of exasperation, "that's why it's probably best if I don't give you any details. You're too close to things, and you're going to worry and imagine and try to second-guess, when I don't even know where things are going yet."

"I'm not pushing you. Even though it probably sounds like it. I do appreciate that you're helping me. I really do."

She stood. "I should go." She raised her voice so my mother could hear her. "Thanks so much for the dinner, Mrs. Nash."

"You're very welcome, Isabel." I noticed she didn't tell Isabel to call her Carol. She must still be a little miffed about Isabel's Vesta mimicry. My mother doesn't forgive and forget as easily as I do.

19

NEXT MORNING, I went to the office early to do some checking on Frankie's story about her weekend race. The weather was weird. Yesterday's freezing drizzle had turned into dense fog and a light rain, but the temperature was a balmy (for winter Wisconsin) 45. I left without even a jacket, despite my mother's protests. The *Times* wasn't officially open. We always take a long holiday weekend at Thanksgiving, but I half-expected Rebecca to be there. She wasn't. I parked out front and went through the big double doors. The reception desk, as expected, was Courtnee-free. I had the blissful silence of an empty office to myself.

Of course, if anything came in on the scanner, given Miguel's car situation, I'd have to roll. But if it didn't, I could really get some work done on the Garrett Whiting story, which I hadn't touched since earlier in the week.

The first thing I did was bring up the *Lake Neshaunoc News* online. It's a weekly with an even smaller circulation than the *Himmel Times* and an even smaller staff. Which was good for my purposes, because it meant that the paper printed just about everything handed to them by the community. That should include a very thorough description of the Fall Fun 10K Run. If Frankie Saxon had been there, I should be able to find her name in a story.

I dug into the online archives. The results included the names of all the entrants, listed in order by their times for finishing the race. I checked it forward and backward. Twice. No Frankie Saxon, no Francesca Saxon, no F. Saxon. No Saxon at all.

The write-up also included the name of the race organizer and a phone number. He answered on the first ring.

"This is Gil Teed."

"Gil, hi, this is Leah Nash at the *Himmel Times*. I was wondering if you could give me some information about the 10K run you organized a couple of months ago."

"What kind of information?"

"Do the runners all have to enter beforehand?"

"We try to enforce that. We have prizes and gift bags donated by local merchants, so we need a good count. Once in awhile someone just shows up though, and we usually let them run."

"Do you have a lot of no-shows?"

"Hardly any. They pay the fee in advance, so they lose it if they don't come."

"You know, I know someone who was telling me she really enjoys your event. Tries to run every year."

"Really? Who's that?"

"Frankie Saxon."

"Oh, sure. I know Frankie. Real nice gal. I was sorry she didn't make it this year. She signed up, but she was one of the no-shows."

"Yeah, she was ill, I think. Well, thanks, Gil, this has been really helpful."

Frankie didn't come home that Sunday night because she was ill. She never even went to the race. She could have been in town the whole weekend. Which meant she had no alibi for Garret's death. And her elaborate lie about what she had done that weekend was an indicator that she might have needed one.

I was just getting ready to put in a call to Garrett's friend Miller Caldwell when I heard someone tapping on the glass doors of the front entrance. I went out, hoping it wasn't Betty Meier, lost again. Instead, Isabel stood there holding two steaming paper cups in her hands. She smiled when I opened the door and waved her in.

"I stopped by your house. Your mother said you were here. I thought you might like a coffee break. Chai latte is your favorite, isn't it?"

"Yeah, sure. C'mon back." I noticed then that in addition to holding the refreshments, she was clutching a hoodie under her arm. She saw my glance and said, "Your mom asked me to bring you this. She said you left without a jacket."

"She's cold, so *I* need a hoodie." I took it from her.

"Well, it's getting colder out there; you might be glad to have it. But, oh, it's sure warm in here."

"Yeah, the furnace has two settings: Arctic Circle and Hell." She handed me my chai, then shrugged out of her hoodie, which was identical to mine. I took it and laid both of ours on Miguel's clean desktop.

"It's not what I thought a newspaper office would be like," she said, looking at the sparsely furnished, slightly dingy newsroom, with its two beat-up desks, plastic visitor chairs, and dinged-up beige filing cabinets.

"Not exactly the *New York Times*, right? But you did catch us on an off day. We're actually closed. I'm just here taking advantage of the peace and quiet."

She pulled up a plastic chair and sat beside my desk. She took a sip of her coffee, then said, "I'm sorry to bother you again, but I didn't want to say anything with everyone around last night. I have to tell someone. I'm pretty sure Jamie's using again."

"Why do you think so?"

"Well, that would explain why he got so mad at you. That's not like him. Not like the real Jamie anyway. He's quiet and kind of shy. Really sweet. And he's been taking off, won't tell me where he's going. He's dropped all his classes at UW."

"Could be that's just how he's coping with his loss. He seemed pretty clear-eyed to me. Pretty mad, but he definitely wasn't high."

"Maybe. I hope so. You already know he didn't feel the same way about Dad that I did. Dad was always tough on Jamie. I think to make up for the way our mother treated me—like I didn't exist. But Dad loved Jamie. I don't think Jamie ever believed that. Anyway, I don't want you to get the wrong idea about him."

"What idea is that?"

"Well, you know. You said Mrs. Wright saw Jamie's car driving away from the house the night Dad died. And he got so mad at you, and he told me he sort of shoved you and everything. I don't want you to think that he was mad because he had something to hide."

She was obviously used to being the protective older sister. A role with which I was very familiar.

"I'm not coming after Jamie, Isabel. True, I'd like to know why his car—or what looked like his car," I amended as she started to protest, "was seen driving away from the direction of the house that night at the time that he says he was at a party in town. But there are lots of other things I want to know too, involving other people."

"You mean like Frankie and Dr. Bergman?"

I put my hands up in the time-out sign. "Isabel, I've already told you all I'm going to say about my research for right now. Please stop trying to wheedle it out of me."

"Sorry."

I lightened up a little.

"It's all right. Let's not talk about it anymore. This chai is really good, thanks."

We made small talk for a few minutes, and when we had finished our drinks, she said, "I'll let you get back to work. No, don't bother." She waved her hand as I started to get up. "I can find the way out." She grabbed her hoodie and then turned back as she reached the door. "I won't call you. You call me, OK?"

"Deal," I said. "As soon as I have something to tell you."

I had no luck reaching Miller Caldwell, but left messages at his office and on his home phone. I didn't have a cell number for him, and his secretary wasn't inclined to give it to me. I wasn't quite ready to call Frankie yet and confront her with what I'd found out. Besides, that would be better done in person. Instead, I stepped away from the Garrett Whiting story for awhile and tackled something that might actually earn me a brownie point or two with Rebecca: filling out my mileage and expense reports before the end of the month.

As I emailed the forms to Courtnee, I felt extremely pleased with myself. In celebration of my mastery over paperwork, I decided to call it a day and check in on Miguel. I stood and started to pull my hoodie on, then realized something wasn't quite right. Besides smelling faintly of Isabel's perfume, the zippered sweatshirt was extremely soft inside, with the fluffy quality of a new, never-washed hoodie. And it was at least a size too big. I like mine roomy, but the sleeves on this one came well past my wrists.

Isabel must have taken mine by mistake when she left. I'd have to call and arrange for an exchange later. I walked down the hall and pushed open the door. As it slammed behind me, a chilly gust made me thrust my hands in my pockets and admit that my mother might have been right. I jogged to my car, head down against the wind.

When I pulled out my hand to open the door, I also pulled out a piece of paper that fluttered to the ground. I picked it up and smoothed it out. An ATM receipt for a $500 withdrawal. I looked closer at it. The time stamp was Oct. 13, 3:30 a.m. The day Garrett died. And the ATM location was JT's Party store, a straight shot down the road from the Whiting house. What was it doing in Isabel's jacket, when she told me she didn't arrive home until 8:30 a.m.?

20

My phone rang before I had time to process the thought.

"Leah, hi, this is Isabel. I just realized I must have grabbed your hoodie when I left. Can I come down and switch it with you? The thing is, it's really Jamie's. He isn't even awake yet, so I'll get it back before he gets up. He hates it when I borrow his things without asking."

Jamie's hoodie. Not Isabel's.

"Leah? Hello? Is it all right if I come down now?"

"Uh, yeah, sure. I'll see you in a few."

Back at my desk, I laid the ATM slip out and stared at it. Jamie's jacket. Jamie's ATM slip. Jamie, who told police he was at a party until 4 a.m., so wasted he didn't remember anything. Had he instead used the party and the drunken, hazy memory of a friend as his alibi? Had he gone home much earlier and killed his father, set up the suicide, and then taken a quick and cold-blooded trip to the nearest ATM?

"Isabel, can you explain why this was in Jamie's pocket?" I shoved the ATM withdrawal slip over to her. "Look at it. It's date-stamped just 15 minutes after Mrs. Wright saw Jamie's car driving away from your house. When Jamie said he was at a party in town."

"I don't understand. He *was* at a party. Keegan was with him. Ask him. He'll tell you. They didn't leave until 4 a.m. He couldn't have been at an ATM at 3:30. Besides, this says it was a $500 withdrawal. Jamie doesn't have $50 in his account, let alone $500."

"But I'm sure your father did. I bet if you look at his account, you just might find a $500 withdrawal from it. Made when he was already dead. That's quite a trick."

"What are you saying? That Jamie killed our father for $500? That's crazy. Anyway, how would he even know Dad's pin number?"

"Your father kept a list of his passwords and pin numbers taped to the bottom of his keyboard. I'll bet you and Jamie both knew that." She didn't deny it.

"But Jamie was with Keegan. They left the party at the same time. He couldn't have been at the ATM at 3:30."

"If your best witness is a guy who was drunk off his ass, that's not very reliable."

"But the police believed him."

"And the police believe your dad committed suicide. So they're totally wrong about that, but infallible when it comes to assessing a witness? And there's the Mini Cooper driving away from your house."

"Mrs. Wright is an old lady who can't hear and probably can't see either. It was dark, it was late, who knows what kind of car she saw. If she even saw a car."

"Jamie pretty much told me he hated your father. He described him as manipulative, verbally abusive, neglectful, incapable of loving his own son. And Jamie was very angry that your father took the one thing that he got from his mother, his inheritance, and pissed it away on bad investments. Your brother might have felt he had some pretty good reasons to kill his father that had nothing to do with $500. That may just have been a bonus."

"No. My father loved Jamie. It wasn't his fault he got taken in by an investment scam. A lot of people did. And besides, I told you, Jamie's rehab was really expensive, and Dad was having cash flow problems then. He had to use the money. But he took out the insurance so we'd have something to fall back on." She was twisting her hands in her lap, her voice tight with anxiety.

"Maybe so, but Jamie didn't know that, did he?"

"Jamie didn't hate our father. He didn't kill him. I want you to stop saying that. I want you to stop it right now." She reached out and grabbed me by the shoulders, thrusting her face close to mine. "Do you hear me? Stop saying that. Stop, stop, stop. And stop investigating."

She released me and began to sob. After a minute, I handed her a Kleenex, and she blew her nose noisily. When she looked up, the only evidence of her crying jag was a little dampness around her large brown eyes and a slight hiccup to her breathing. In similar circumstances, I would have presented with an ugly red nose, swollen eyelids, and a thread of snot running down my chin.

"Leah, please. Promise me you won't go to the sheriff. It's already done, right? They said it was suicide. I was just crazy to think it wasn't. This other stuff, you're just guessing. You don't know anything. It doesn't matter."

"Yeah, it does. I can't just stop cold because you don't like where it's going."

"Well, at least will you talk to Keegan before you go to the sheriff? He was with Jamie. He'll prove Jamie couldn't have done it. And maybe the ATM slip wasn't even for my father's account. We don't know that for sure. I bet when I check his bank statements there won't be any withdrawal. Like I said, maybe Jamie found that slip and picked it up, you know, just stuck it in his pocket. Couldn't that have happened? Don't go to the sheriff. Please, talk to Keegan at least."

I hesitated for a minute, but in the end, it wasn't that hard to agree. Not so much because of my tender heart, but because I was walking a fine line here. I thought about the information I had dug up: Jamie's car on the road, his attitude about his father, his probable lie about where he was and what mental or physical state he was in. It all added up to something I knew I should take to the sheriff's department. But if I did, would it just get tossed aside, especially after the funny "joke" Ross had pulled on me? I didn't have a lot of credibility there.

If I took a little more time, I might be able to get the real story from

Jamie's friend Keegan, or even better, I might be able to get security video of Jamie using the ATM.

"All right. I'll talk to Keegan. But you do something for me. Check your father's bank statement, see if there was a withdrawal of $500 the night he died. And don't talk to Jamie. Not yet. Agreed?"

"Agreed."

"I'm serious."

She gave a solemn nod. And then we both went on our way.

I called Coop at his office.

"Sorry, Leah, Coop has the day off today. Do ya want to leave a message?"

"No, that's OK, Melanie. I'll try his cell."

I had no luck. It went straight to voicemail. I didn't bother to leave a message. Instead I texted him.

Hey, any chance we can connect today? Things are getting interesting on the Whiting story.

I tried Miguel next.

Hey, I need you to help me think. I'm at the paper.

No luck there, either. I considered my next move. I didn't want to text or talk to Rebecca, but I probably should. I was leaning toward not contacting her when, in a surprise takeover, the keep-your-job part of my brain won. I texted Rebecca. I hoped Coop would respond first, because I'd like to get his take on things before I took on Rebecca.

I was three for three with no answers. I focused again on the ATM slip. Time for a trip to JT's Party Store.

JT's rundown building near the railroad tracks still has the same dented yellow aluminum siding it had when I was a kid. The faded red awning over the door is still positioned so that rain, snow, or sleet slide merrily off it and right onto the heads—or down the necks—of entering customers.

When I was a kid, JT himself, a big bald man with a belly that rested comfortably on the low counter, kept a watchful eye on the grubby-handed kids who lusted after his stock of sugar-laden treats. The store had since changed hands, but the new owner kept the name.

The emphasis now was on more adult-friendly treats—lottery tickets, liquor, cigarettes, and, I heard, fairly decent coffee. I hadn't been there in years. When I pushed through the heavy glass door, the scent of over-cooked hot dogs rotating slowly on a glass-encased rotisserie hit me. But it was the sight of the person behind the counter that stopped me in my tracks. Cole Granger. Part-time drug dealer, part-time conman, full-time asshat.

21

HE LOOKED UP as the bell over the door rang, then gave an insolent grin.

"Well now, if it ain't Miss Hot Shit reporter. I hear you got you a big book deal. Gonna be real famous, ain't you? Did you come here to get some quotes from me? Gonna tell everybody how grateful you are for me helpin' you get the real story on that little sis of yours?" He looked pretty much the same as the last time I'd seen him a year ago—slicked-back, mud-brown hair, yellow-flecked green eyes, thin-lipped mouth always on the verge of a cocky grin. His dragon tattoo, which I knew stretched up one arm, was covered by the long-sleeved T-shirt he wore. It stretched tautly across his thick-muscled chest and over the beginnings of a belly that would rival the original JT's one day.

"I thought you left town."

"I'm real touched at you keepin' tabs on me, but you're a little behind the times. I did leave town for a while. Had me some business opportunities. Unfortunately, they didn't work out. So, here I am. Just another cog in the wheel of commerce." Cole and his then-girlfriend Delite had given me vital information about the death of my sister Lacey, in exchange for every dollar I had and a few Miguel contributed, too.

"Cole, just knock it off. I'm working on a story. I'd like to talk to the owner about his ATM machine."

He ran his thumb and forefinger down either side of his chin before he answered.

"That would be my Uncle Chaz. He ain't here right now. Fact is, he won't be back 'til spring. He and Aunt Florinda, they got a nice little condo in Alabama for the winter. You could say I'm in charge." Cole didn't speak with the typical middle Wisconsin accent—a combination of brusque Germanic tones oddly laced with a light Scandinavian lilt. Instead, he retained the drawling cadence of the Kentucky hills his family came from and used a vocabulary that showed he wasn't as dumb as he looked.

"You're in charge? Why do I find that hard to believe?" He had a history of petty theft, small time drug dealing, and general bad behavior. I doubted even an uncle blinded by family feeling would leave him in charge of a business where money changed hands regularly.

"I'd just have to say that's because of your judgmental nature, Leah. Now why, I wonder, do you want to know about our time machine?"

Anyone not from Wisconsin might be taken aback with Cole's reference to something that seemed to belong in *Dr. Who* or an episode from a *Rocky & Bullwinkle* cartoon. But here in the land of milk and cheese, when ATMs were first introduced they were promoted as Take Your Money Everywhere (TYME) machines. The name stuck with some people, even as the acronym faded. So, it's not unheard of for someone to refer you to the "time machine" in the lobby. Though it might be a letdown to discover that you're only making a cash transaction, not booking a trip to another dimension.

"I told you, it's for a story. What kind of security camera do you have on it? How long do you keep the recordings?"

"It's a fine piece of equipment. Real safe and secure for our customers. 'Course it don't exactly have a security camera on it. This is what you call a gently used older model. Doesn't have all the bells and whistles. Little cheaper that way, and Uncle Chaz is very economy-minded. But like he says, we keep a real sharp eye on it, so our customers got no problems with it."

"You don't have any video?" My heart sank. I'd been sure that if I could get security footage from the ATM, it would show Jamie there in the early morning hours after his father died.

"Hold on there. I didn't say we got no video. Just we don't have video on the ATM. Happens we got a real deluxe video surveillance system right here in the store. Look up there, see? That camera right behind me? And that one over there by the machine?"

"So, you do have video? Would you have it from October 13th, early morning? How long do you keep it?"

"I'm not sure I should be tellin' you all our security measures. Might give the wrong element an idea about how to take advantage of things. I don't think Uncle Chaz would like that."

"I really need to see that video."

He assumed a baffled expression, tilting his head to one side and raising an eyebrow. "Now, what's that got to do with a story about ATMs?"

"The video. Please." It took all I had to plead, but he had the advantage. And I'm willing to grovel, if it gets me the information I need.

"Sorry. Don't have anything to show you."

"But you said you have store surveillance video."

"Now, see, that's why you ain't in the big time anymore, Leah. You just don't listen. I said, we got a video surveillance camera, but I never said we had the video. This here system records on SD cards. Like I told you, Uncle Chaz, he's real economy-minded. We only keep 'em awhile, maybe a few weeks, and then I reformat and we reuse 'em. That video from, what did you say, six weeks ago? I'm pretty sure that one's long gone."

"Pretty sure? But maybe it isn't? Could you look?"

"Well, I'm awful busy right now, as you can see."

He stopped, and I stepped aside as a woman came up carrying a six-pack. I waited with mounting impatience while he checked her ID and rang her out.

When she left, he leaned forward, his hands on the counter.

"Now, what were you sayin'?"

"Couldn't you check, see if you might still have the SD card for the early morning of Oct. 13th?"

"October 13th, huh? My mama's birthday was October 12th. Had a real nice party for her. But I had to leave early. Had to work at 11 that night."

"Come on, Cole, give me a break. Just look and see if you still have the card."

"Well now, I don't see as how it's worth my while. I'd have to go into the office, get down the box we file 'em in. Look all through it. Put it in the computer. I mean, you're askin' a lot, Leah, on such a busy day, too. I just can't see how there's any percentage in that for me."

I knew what he was getting at, but even if I had the cash, I couldn't use it for this story. I'd wiped out my bank account to find what he knew about Lacey, but that was personal. It wasn't for a story. I couldn't pay a source for information. Not and have it be worth anything.

"I don't have any money, and if I did, I wouldn't pay you for it."

He gave a fake wince. "Now you're hurtin' my feelin's, sweetheart. I don't believe I said anything about money. I just said I'm awful busy, and I don't think I have what you need. Leastwise, not in the technology department. I'm sure I could meet your needs in other ways." I glared at him and he laughed.

The door opened again, and two college-age boys came in, followed by a group of teenagers laughing and shoving each other.

"Now, as you can see, I got some customers need my attention. Can I help you find anything, or are you all set?"

"Thanks. For nothing." Defeated, I turned to go. He gave a nod and a smirk.

He was messing with me. I'd tipped my hand and let him know how much I wanted it, so he took pleasure in toying with me. I had to find some leverage, something that would make him let me see the footage for that night. What, I didn't know at the moment.

Back in the car, I pulled out my phone. 2:45. I was bursting to talk to Coop or Miguel about what had turned up, but neither had answered my text. Not even Rebecca, who I really didn't want to talk to but probably should, had responded. I drummed my fingers on the steering wheel while I thought, then went back to the paper to track down an address for Jamie's friend Keegan.

22

THE COLLEGE-AGE KID WHO OPENED the door was big. I mean line backer big, with a thick neck, heavily muscled arms, and a really large head. His belly was big, too, pushing out between the bottom of his Milwaukee Brewers T-shirt and the top of the drawstring sweatpants he wore. His blue eyes had suspiciously large pupils. As he struggled to focus, he blinked and gave a shake of his head, like a befuddled buffalo.

"Yeah?"

"Keegan Monroe? Hi. I'm Leah Nash. I'm a reporter with the *Times*. Can I come in for a minute?" I spoke briskly and already had a foot in the door before he had time to say no. He stepped back a little, and I squeezed through the opening and into a studio apartment that looked even smaller because of his massive size.

The single room with a tiny kitchen in one corner was littered with pizza boxes and empty beer cans. A tangle of sheets and blankets lay on the open hide-a-bed sofa in the middle of the floor. A trail of tiny styrofoam pellets leaked from a vinyl beanbag chair. The only other seat, which he gestured for me to take, was a wooden chair with two spindles missing from the back.

He dropped down on the edge of his unmade bed, making it jump up from the floor on the other side. A faint sweet odor lingered in the apartment, and I noticed an ashtray holding the stubs of several joints. Keegan rubbed his fingers lightly over the stubble on his jaw and nodded slowly at me, as though he didn't dare execute a rapid head movement.

"I'm hoping you can help me, Keegan. I'm doing a story on Garrett Whiting, and I'm trying to put together his last day."

His expression remained befuddled. He got up and lumbered to the refrigerator for a Coke, then grabbed a bag of chips off the counter. He chugged down the drink, followed it with a loud burp, reached into the bag of chips, and tried talking around the mouthful he had shoved in.

"Sorry. I didn't really know Dr. Whiting."

"But his son, Jamie, is a friend of yours, right? I talked to him the other day, and I know you were with him the night his father died." I compressed several bits of information together and hoped that he would assume Jamie had given me that information, not the police report.

"Yeah. Yeah. We were at a party." He spoke slowly, as though measuring each word. I couldn't tell if that was his natural speech pattern or the result of the weed he'd just smoked.

"It's almost unreal, isn't it? I mean you and Jamie, out having a good time at a party, and right across town, there was his dad so depressed he took his own life. Makes you think, doesn't it?"

Clearly, not very much could make Keegan think right at the moment, but he gave it a try, drawing his thick eyebrows down and tilting his head slightly. "Yeah. Absolutely. Want some chips?" He extended the bag toward me, his latent sense of hospitality apparently having awakened.

I shook my head. "No, but thanks. You go ahead. You and Jamie have been friends for a long time?"

He knew this answer without any thinking at all. "Yeah. Since kindergarten."

"It must have been rough, watching him go through all that happened these last few years. His mom dying, I mean, then the drug issues, and now his dad commits suicide. Unbelievable."

"Yeah. Heavy stuff." He frowned at the Coke can he was holding in his thick, meaty fingers. I'd been worried that he'd be wary of talking to me, intent on protecting Jamie's alibi, but whether it was the relaxing embrace of a marijuana high, or a naturally non-inquisitive nature, he didn't seem to have any problem with my questions.

"Jamie doesn't really remember much about that night. Maybe it's a good thing. If he weren't so out of it, he might have been the one to find his dad's body. What time was it that you guys left the party?"

"The party?" He looked around as though a group of fellow stoners previously unnoticed might be found lounging in the corners.

"The party you and Jamie went to that night? Remember, he ran into you at the gas station, you invited him to go with you to somebody's place. Got kind of loud and everybody was pretty wasted?"

"Ohhh. Yeah, the gas station. Jamie always takes it to the max. Wait a minute, I mean the min, right? His gas tank, I mean. He was runnin' on empty or I wouldna seen him that night. 'Cause he was getting gas."

"Right. Yes. But about the party you went to?"

"Yeah. The party. Wow. That was a party." He paused and grew silent, perhaps reliving the happy event. I prodded again.

"So, you were there with your friends, having a good time. Now, what time was that?"

"Jamie was really out of it." He laughed. "Me, too. I had such a good time, I don't even remember most of it. If Isabel didn't remind me about it, I probably wouldn't remember anything."

"Isabel?"

"Yeah, she called to tell me about Dr. Whiting. Said Jamie was really messed up. She was kind of mad at me. But, hey, I didn't make him come. I mean, I just asked, but it was like, his choice. Do you think it's, like, my fault Jamie got wasted?"

"No, I don't. Keegan, are you saying you didn't actually remember when you and Jamie left the party until you talked to Isabel?"

He shifted a little and looked slightly abashed. "No. Yeah, kinda, I guess. I was kinda hazy, but it came back. Isabel, she like, refreshed my memory."

"How could she 'refresh' your memory if she wasn't there? She wasn't, was she?"

He laughed. "Not her thing. But she said we musta got back really late, because Jamie was still pretty out of it when she got home. She said the cops were gonna make a hassle for him if he couldn't remember when. So, like we talked about the party for awhile, and that kinda helped bring it back. Besides, 2 in the morning, 4 in the morning? What's the difference anyway?"

"So, you told the police you left at 4, but you didn't really remember it?"

"Yeah. Sure. I mean, I didn't tell them I didn't remember. Like, I did remember, after Isabel reminded me, just not at first. What's it matter? Jamie's my bro. I got his back. Who cares what time we left? Jamie and me, we were both pretty turnt up. He couldna stopped his dad anyway, no matter what time he got home."

It was clear Keegan wasn't the brightest star in the Monroe family firmament. And that it hadn't occurred to him he had been pushed by Isabel to give Jamie an alibi for murder, regardless of the fact that he had no real memory of how the evening played out. Why she did it was obvious.

Isabel arrived home, found her father dead and her brother in bed. She didn't believe her dad had committed suicide, but if it were murder, she wanted to be sure Jamie wasn't a suspect. When she woke him up, and he said he couldn't remember anything, she believed him. But she knew the police might want more than his word. Enter Keegan, a willing stooge, ready to stand by Jamie. She got the two of them on the same page, and it worked. She pushed me to Keegan because she thought it would work again. Maybe it would have, if he hadn't been high, and I didn't already have serious suspicions about Jamie.

The silence between us had stretched on for some seconds as I processed this, but Keegan was unperturbed by the quiet. He dug lustily in his bag of chips, then polished it off by tipping the open bag over his mouth and shaking the last crumbs down his gullet. He got up and came back with a bag of M&Ms, and attacked them with the gusto of someone in the grip of major munchies. He did politely hold the bag out to me. This time I accepted a few.

"I don't suppose you remember who was at the party?"

"Dude, I don't even remember where the party was. Some guy's house, somewhere around here. Had to be kinda close, 'cause I walked home. It was just, you know, organic. Some guys are hangin' out, and then somebody texts somebody else, and then somebody else, and before you know it, you got a whole lotta people, and a whole lotta party. It's not like we had sign-in sheets." And then he started laughing at his own joke, probably picturing a party of drunk kids smoking weed, wearing nametags, and exchanging business cards.

One last question came to mind. "So, do you and Jamie still get your stuff from Cole Granger?"

He gave me a knowing smile, like we were all stoners together. "Might be worth checkin' out. He's got like, what you call it? A small client base. Works out of a party store in town. JT's. But you gotta have an in, or he won't deal. Tell him Keegan sent you."

I may just have gotten that leverage I was looking for.

"Thanks, Keegan, you've been great!" I said with such enthusiasm that he blinked.

"No problem, man." The smile on his good-natured face made me smile in spite of the situation.

It was almost four o'clock, and I started for home, then decided to swing by the paper on the off chance that Rebecca or Miguel had stopped in. I was anxious to talk to somebody, and I really did think I'd gathered enough to get even Rebecca a little excited about the story.

As I drove into the parking lot, I didn't see either of their cars. I did see one that brought me up short. Jamie Whiting's Mini Cooper. His door opened even before I pulled into a spot. By the time I got out, he was standing in front of me, so close I could feel his breath on my cheek. He had me backed up against the car, and I didn't like the feeling. I put my hands up and pushed, not hard, but the surprise move threw him off balance and gave me time to move away from the car and reestablish my personal space.

"What can I do for you, Jamie?"

"You can quit telling my sister that I killed our father." His voice shook and his fists were clenched at his side.

So, Isabel had told him. It was probably too much to expect that she wouldn't. I doubted I would keep something like that to myself either. Not if my brother were at risk.

"I didn't say you killed your father. I'll ask you what I asked her. Why did you have an ATM receipt in the pocket of your hoodie? Date and time stamped when you and your friend Keegan told police you were at a party?"

"I don't know what you're talking about. And I don't owe you an explanation." His eyebrows were drawn down in a ferocious frown. "You're taking advantage of Isabel. She's all messed up about Garrett. You need to stop."

We were out in the open on a reasonably busy street, so although I wasn't very comfortable facing down an angry Jamie, I was pretty sure he wasn't going to do me bodily harm.

"Isabel came to me; I didn't approach her. But now that I've started, I'm going to finish. You don't have to answer my questions, that's true. But there are too many of them for me not to go to the police. And they'll ask more questions, not just to you, but your friends, your sister, your school, your neighbors. The truth will come out. All of it."

"I'm telling you the truth. I didn't kill my father. I don't know why you think I did. But if you don't leave this alone, people are going to get hurt." With that he turned on his heel and walked toward his car.

"Wait, Jamie. What people? Who's going to get hurt? Why?" My questions were drowned out in the roar of his engine as he peeled out of the parking lot and down the street.

23

My phone had pinged a couple of times with text messages as I drove home, and I checked them as I walked into the kitchen.

Sorry. Can't get away. See you at Elite tomorrow.

Well, Coop was unavailable. The next text didn't have any better news.

Chica, out with friends tonight. Details tomorrow.

Miguel was out of reach as well. I started to give a shout to my mother, who I assumed was in her room, when I noticed the note on the bar.

Leah, Paul and I went to Omico shopping, and then we're going to see a movie. Plenty of leftovers in fridge.

Great. My entire support system was AWOL. Even Rebecca had ignored me. I briefly thought about buzzing over to Father Lindstrom's, but decided to wallow in aggrieved self-pity instead. I piled a plate high with yesterday's bounty and sat down at the table to enjoy it. When I finished, I cut myself a piece of pumpkin pie, buried it in whipped cream, and slowly savored it.

My mother makes a pumpkin pie that is as close to a religious experience as I am ever likely to come. The cool sweetness of the whipped cream contrasted with the spiciness of the pie filling and the crisp crunch of flaky pie crust—pure bliss. By the time I finished, I felt somewhat less alone in the world. I was also so full that it was time for either yoga pants or pajamas. I chose pajamas, even though it wasn't even five o'clock yet. Then, I sat down with my laptop to review what I knew.

Things that say suicide

- Garrett's fingerprints on gun
- Absence of struggle
- Absence of other fingerprints
- Health problems
- Financial problems
- Klonipin and alcohol in his blood, easy for doctor to get the drug

Things that could say murder

- Isabel's phone call with her father the night he died
- Garrett's book order, why would a suicide order a book the night he plans to die?
- No history of depression
- No note

Knowledge that if he killed himself, Isabel & Jamie would be SOL for the insurance

- Possible for someone else to administer Klonipin/alcohol mix, then pull the trigger

People who had reason to kill him

- Frankie—past affair, woman scorned?
- Dr. Bergman—drug use/fraud/sales—fear of exposure
- Jamie—suppressed rage over years of emotional abuse; anger over loss of inheritance
- Other??

Case against Frankie

- She lied about where she was that weekend. Why?
- Weak—she could be lying because she's having an affair, she's hiding a secret for someone else?

Case against Bergman

- He denied fight with Garrett, but was furious when I pressed, threatened lawsuit/arrest
- Miss Quellman's belief he was abusing/selling drugs
- So-so—need more information on drug situation

Case against Jamie

- His car or its twin seen driving away from house at 3:15 a.m.
- ATM slip stamped 3:30 a.m., crumpled up in Jamie's hoodie
- Keegan's inability to corroborate Jamie's story
- Jamie's violent reaction to my first interview with him
- His $100,000 inheritance, lost by his father
- An insurance policy that would give him financial freedom
- Question: did Jamie know about suicide clause?

I got up and grabbed my notebook. Riffled through the pages and found the notes I'd taken when I'd called Charlie Ross to eat crow. I always take notes when I'm talking to a source, even on background, unless it spooks them too badly. Sometimes, I even take notes when I'm talking to a friend or to my dentist's office. I feel more comfortable communicating with a pen in my hand.

While Ross was gloating and rubbing it in about the insurance policy, he'd given me the name: Security Mutual Life. I knew Marty Angstrom was the agent; he was our insurance guy as well. I looked at my watch—4:55 on a Friday. What were the chances? Still, I made the call.

"Marty, hi! It's Leah Nash. I'm surprised I caught you."

"What can I do you for real quick, Leah?" I always like talking to Marty, because he's got that "up north" Wisconsin accent, which is stubbornly resistant to the homogenizing influence of television and a wired world.

"I'm hearing that Garrett Whiting had a life insurance policy with you that won't pay out for his kids, because it had a suicide clause. Is that true?"

"That's pretty confidential stuff there, ya know?"

"But your client is dead, Marty, and I got the information from Charlie Ross. Are you saying he got it wrong?"

He mulled that over for a second. "No, no. Charlie's right. But it's a standard clause, ya know? I don't want you puttin' anything in the paper, makin' the company look bad."

"This isn't for print, Marty." I moved on quickly before he thought to ask exactly what it was for. "Did Jamie and Isabel know about the suicide clause?"

My phone flashed a text message coming in. I ignored it.

"That was bad. Real bad. Real tough visit to make."

"So you had to tell Isabel and Jamie? They didn't already know about the clause?"

"Yah. Yah, I did. They said no. Jamie, he just kinda laughed. He's a strange sort of young fella. That suicide clause, when it kicks in, that's a tough one. Ya gotta think a guy was real far gone in his thinkin' to do that. Real hard on the families when they think they got some financial security, then find out they don't. Only had to break the news a coupla other times."

"But Garrett, he definitely understood about the clause?"

"He sure shoulda. I explained it all real clear when I wrote it up. If he had any questions, he coulda called me anytime. I had a long talk with him a few months ago about changin' up his house insurance. He had some real good questions, but he never mentioned the life insurance. And I never talked to him again. Is that it, Leah, or no? Only I got to stop by the store real quick, pick up some brats for dinner, is all."

"Yeah. That's it, Marty, thanks."

Things weren't looking any better for Jamie. If he'd known about the insurance, but not the suicide clause, and set up his father's "suicide," no wonder he was freaking out over Isabel pushing for a murder investigation. OK, so he didn't get the money he expected, but at least he was going to get away with murder, unless Isabel didn't give up.

I clicked on the text that had come in. Not from Coop with a change of plans, as I'd hoped. From Clinton, my agent, with a pointed question about whether or not I would have the page proofs of my book done by Sunday, as I'd promised. And a reminder that I was a new author who couldn't afford to clog up the production schedule.

He was right. And I pride myself on meeting deadlines. I sighed, then put everything else away and grabbed the page proofs sitting on top of the bookshelf. I worked steadily until I finished, sometime after midnight.

My mother was still sleeping when I left the house Saturday morning around 10. Coop and I weren't supposed to meet until noon, but I couldn't wait any longer. I drove over to his house, prepared to roust him out of bed. Enough of this elusive act. I needed some face time with him.

I pulled in the driveway behind his car, which struck me as odd, because he always parks it in the garage. Unless he's building a new piece of furniture. His detached double garage serves as housing for both his car and workshop. He's really pretty good, and sometimes his projects get pretty ambitious.

I went through the breezeway to the side door, gave a quick knock, and walked on in like I usually do. But what I saw inside the kitchen as I stepped in wasn't usual at all.

Rebecca was standing at the counter, wearing one of Coop's blue work shirts and, it appeared, nothing else. Coop was sitting at the table in a white T-shirt and jeans. All three of us stared at each other for a minute, frozen in position like action figures abandoned in the middle of play.

Rebecca was the first to reanimate.

"Good morning, Leah. Care to join us?" She held out the coffee pot she was about to pour from.

"Uh, no. No, that's all right. Actually, I should go, I just—"

I glanced at Coop, who seemed to think that was a fine idea.

"Don't be ridiculous. Have a seat while I go get my day clothes on." She set the pot down on the counter and left the room.

Coop still hadn't said anything, and I burst out with the first thought that came to mind. Not a good idea.

"Rebecca?" I hissed. "Are you freaking kidding me? Is that the big secret stuff that's been going on? You've been seeing Rebecca?" My words ended on something between a squawk and an outraged yelp that seemed to jolt Coop into a response.

"Settle down, Leah. Yeah, Rebecca and I have been seeing each other for a while."

"So listening to me tell you how impossible she is, how controlling, how micromanaging, how she's always on my back—that makes you think, 'Wow, that sounds hot. I'd really like to date the woman who's making Leah miserable?' "

He stood up and walked over to where I was rooted to the floor.

"I know you and Rebecca don't see eye to eye at the paper. And I respect your feelings. That's why I didn't tell you before. I really like Rebecca. I wanted to tell you, but I wanted to do it the right way. I've been having a hard time trying to figure out what that was. You and I just see her differently."

"I'll say."

Rebecca returned then, wearing a sweater that clung to her lean frame tightly enough to make clear it was hers, and not Coop's, over a pair of skinny jeans. Her blonde hair was pulled back and she'd slipped on her glasses.

"I'm sorry you found out like this. David and I talked about how to tell you, and we really didn't want it to be awkward, but, well, here it is. Awkward."

"Don't worry about it."

"David and I?" Nobody but his mother had called Coop "David" since we were in seventh grade. *"David and I talked?"* I hated that she and Coop had talked about me and had jointly decided what to tell, or not tell, me. I hated that they discussed me like I was some kind of external problem. I was his best friend, not some awkward situation.

"It's probably a good thing you're both here. I wanted to talk to you both about Garrett Whiting." True enough, though my choice was Coop first, to help me filter and reframe the facts for Rebecca's consumption. That wasn't going to happen. I plunged in and went over what I'd found out, wrapping up with the lists I'd put together last night.

"I have to give you credit. You've made a reasonable case for murder instead of suicide. I take it your money is on the son, Jamie?" Rebecca asked.

"At this point, yes."

"What are your chances of getting cooperation from this Cole Granger? The one you think might have access to video of Jamie using the ATM?" Before I could answer, Coop interrupted.

"Don't count on anything there. Cole's a conman from way back. He's just stringing Leah along, trying to see what he can get from her. Or even just to jerk her chain."

"I know the type," Rebecca said. And suddenly my story was the focus of a conversation that excluded me.

Stung, I interjected, "Excuse me. I think I know when a source is stringing me along. Cole knows something. I just may have an incentive that will make him talk."

"Now, what does that mean? Don't do something stupid. He's a garden-variety lowlife, but he can still be trouble." Coop was frowning at me, and his gray eyes held a warning.

"I don't need you to tell me how to do my job."

"No, that's my job," Rebecca said. "I agree with David. You need be careful with this Cole character."

"You're planning on sharing all this with Charlie Ross, aren't you?" Coop interfered in the conversation again.

"Yes, Coop, of course I am. Though that isn't exactly your call," I said testily. Before I could get any further unnecessary input from either of them, I made my exit.

"Well, I think we can skip the lunch date. It looks like we've both shared our news already, so I'll get going. See you guys later." I was moving toward the door as I talked and was already through it as I heard Coop say, "Leah, wait—"

I was in my car when he came barefooted onto the driveway. He looked so forlorn there, his naked feet on the freezing concrete, his arms waving to stop me, that I had to smile at the sight in my rearview mirror. It wasn't until I was several blocks away that I realized my eyes were watering. Damn allergies.

24

"WHY DID IT HAVE TO BE such a big deal secret? That's what I don't get."

"Don't you, Leah?" Father Lindstrom sat across from me at the Elite, which was empty except for us in the late morning lull before lunch. I'd called him after my meet-up with Coop went bust, because I wanted to talk my feelings through but couldn't deal at the moment with Miguel's exuberant curiosity or my mother's probing questions.

"No. I don't. You don't lie to people you care about. He said he wanted to tell me 'the right way.' That was just an excuse to not tell the truth."

"Oh?" He gave me a quizzical look. "People keep things hidden for many reasons, not all of them bad. And not sharing private information isn't the same as lying."

I understood what he was saying. I just wasn't having any of it.

"This is different," I said stubbornly.

"All right." He took a sip of his tea, then set the cup down and finished off the apple strudel he'd ordered.

"So, we're done talking about it? You don't think Coop was wrong?"

"I think that it's not my place to judge Coop."

"Or mine either?"

He didn't answer. This was not going the way I'd planned.

"You're a priest. It's kind of your job to make moral judgments, isn't it?"

"No wonder you left the Church, Leah, if that's what you think the role of a priest is. I'm sorry if I disappointed you. I believe you'll figure this out on your own, in time. I would only urge you to remember there are things you can change and things you cannot. And now, I must go. I've got a wedding this afternoon." With that, he pushed his chair away and reached for his wallet.

"No, no way. I invited you. My treat. Sorry if I was a little snippy. Whoa, and I'm sorry I just used 'snippy' in a sentence. When did I become my Aunt Nancy?"

He touched my hand as he left and said, "Thank you, Leah. You weren't snippy, maybe just a little frustrated." His smile held so much warmth that I felt better than I had since I'd opened Coop's kitchen door.

———

Dinner offer is still open, any takers?

Yes. What time?

Really? I'll pick you up at 6.

Not at the house. I'll be at the paper.

Some people might say I'd changed my mind about dinner with Nick because I was pissed at Coop. Which, of course, would be an absolutely stupid reason to go out with my ex. And which, of course, was absolutely true. But despite being born of petty anger and self-pity, it turned into a pretty good evening. I had Nick pick me up at the *Times* to avoid the gimlet-eyed stare of my mother, and he took me to McClain's. Sherry sashayed over to check out the new talent and impart what she thought was a bombshell of information.

"Hi, I'm Sherry. I'll be serving you tonight. What's your pleasure?" she said, batting her admittedly long and lustrous lashes at Nick, while ignoring me.

"I think I'll have a Sam Adams and the lady—well, what will the lady have, Leah?"

"Jameson on the rocks."

"Coming right up." She smiled at Nick and then leaned in toward me for the kill.

"So, guess who came in for lunch today, and they were very cozy."

"Kim and Kanye."

"Coop and your boss Rebecca! What does he see in that blonde bitchsicle?"

Nick was watching our exchange, and I took care to keep my expression neutral. "To each his own."

"Well, I just thought you should know."

"I already knew, Sherry. I had coffee with them this morning." Not strictly true, but close enough. And it pleased me to see the deflated look on her face. She recovered quickly though, flashed a smile at Nick, and said, "Be right back with your drinks."

"What was that about?"

"Sherry's had a crush on Coop since high school. She's upset because he's dating the ice queen. My boss, Rebecca Hartfield."

"She seemed to think it would bother you."

"It doesn't."

"Hmm."

"Hmm, what?"

"Nothing. Just the way you always talked about him. Why didn't you get together with him when you came back?"

"We're together. As friends. You know, men and women can be friends, Nick. I realize that's a foreign concept to you, but trust me it can be done."

"Ow! I think you drew blood with that one." We were both quiet then, until he said, "I've got an idea. Let's have a moratorium on the verbal jabs. We'll pretend we just met." He held out his hand. "Hi, I'm Nick Gallagher."

I hesitated for a second, then shook it. "Nice to meet you. I'm Leah Nash."

It was silly and kind of stupid, but kind of fun too. We proceeded to ask each other about our jobs and our lives and listened with the care and curiosity you accord interesting new acquaintances. Nick was witty and charming and on his absolute best behavior. No matter how flirty Sherry was whenever she came to our table—and she came way more often than she needed to—he treated her with absolute politeness and nothing more. I refrained from making any snarky comments.

He told me stories about work and his colleagues and the research he was doing. I brought him up-to-date with my own career trials and tribulations. He asked me about the book that was coming out soon, and if he could read it before publication. We stayed very carefully away from recounting memories of our past life together, good or bad. And some were really very good. We sat talking long after we'd finished eating, and when I looked at my watch, I saw that it was after nine.

"I probably should get going."

"Oh, not yet. Let's go over to that little park you took me to once. I'll push you on the swings."

"Riverview Park?"

"Yeah, that's the one."

Dinner had been fun, and it felt like I hadn't had a relaxing evening in a long time. I wasn't anxious for it to end.

"All right, let's do it."

The park was deserted under a clear night sky with a few stars beginning to appear. We followed the sidewalk that ran through the park, walking into pools of light cast by the old-fashioned lampposts, then out again into the shadows, all the way to the swings. Only to discover they weren't there, apparently unhung and stored for the winter.

"Too bad. I guess we'll have to go down the slide instead." He pointed to a tall stand-alone slide with metal steps and handrails all the way up and a small platform at the top from which to launch yourself. It was the one relic of a less safety-conscious era that hadn't been replaced since I was a child.

"You're kidding."

"Why not? We're both dressed for it." He was wearing jeans, like me, and we both had on winter jackets.

"All right, let's do it. I'll race you there." I got there first, probably because I'd taken off before he realized we were in competition, and clambered up the ladder. The sharp cold of the metal bit into my gloveless hands. I sped up and reached the top, then swung myself onto the steel slide, its smooth and slippery surface hurtling me down until I shot off the end into the soft wood chips at the base. Nick was right behind me. Before I could get up from the half-crouch I'd landed in, he careened into me and we both wound up on the ground entangled and laughing. His face was so close to mine I could feel his breath on my cheek, and suddenly we both stopped laughing. He bent toward me and kissed me softly on the lips. I kissed him back for a second.

Then I pulled back quickly and jumped up, brushing bits of damp wood chips from my clothes and chattering nervously.

"Well, that was quite a ride. Not quite as high as I remembered it from the last time I went down the slide, but still high enough. That metal was really cold, wasn't it? I wonder if you can get frostbite in under 30 seconds? You know, we used to take pieces of waxed paper and rub down the slide to make it more slippery, so we could go faster. Sometimes we'd sit on a square of it, too. We'd really fly off the ends then! My fingers are freezing. How about you? Are your hands cold?"

He had stood up too and was silent until I finally wound down.

"I'm not going to apologize, because I'm not sorry. But I won't do it again. You'll have to make the next move, Leah, if you want to."

"Nick. It's been a really nice night, but I—"

"But you don't trust me. I understand. I can wait."

I didn't want to let him think there was even a slight chance I'd reopen that door.

"Nick, it's not going to happen. I really had fun tonight. And I can see that you're trying hard, and maybe you've changed. But so have I. I'm not willing to be that vulnerable to anyone, ever again. But, we can be friends. Real friends. After all, we already know the worst about each other, right?"

I put my hand on his and looked up, hoping the doubt and confusion I felt didn't show in my eyes. I knew that getting back with Nick would be a very bad idea. But right at the moment, I was having trouble remembering why.

I was a little disappointed when he didn't protest. Instead, he turned his hand over so it clasped mine and gave a firm shake. "OK. Friends it is. Hey! Your hands are like ice!"

"Yours aren't much better."

"Let's stop at the party store across the way. It might feel good to wrap our hands around a warm cup of coffee. Then, I'll take you back to your car."

"That, my friend, is a great idea."

25

INSIDE JT'S there was a bit of a rush. Several teenagers were attempting to convince the clerk that they had forgotten the IDs required to purchase the case of beer they'd hauled up to the counter. A whiskery-faced old man wearing a battered John Deere hat waited for his turn at the register, holding a pint of Jim Beam and a bag of peanuts. At the coffee station, we stood behind two women in scrubs who were pouring coffee into large containers, doubtless fortifying themselves for a long shift ahead at the hospital. Out of the corner of my eye, I saw a familiar figure at the back door give a quick glance right and left before stepping out. That was odd. Why would Cole take a break in the middle of a rush, and why was he so furtive about it?

"Oh, Nick, I left my phone in the car. I'll just run out and get it. Can't be a reporter without being in constant contact, right?"

Before he could answer, I was out the front door. With luck, I would catch Cole doing something illegal, like selling a bag of weed or something worse to one of the "special" clients Keegan had mentioned. Maybe I could even get video of it. Anything that would give me leverage enough to get him to give up the video of the night Garrett died. I circled around to the back, coming up behind a dense thicket of evergreen bushes that gave me some cover. I crept up as close as I dared, stooping down low in the poky shrubbery to stay unseen. About 20 yards away were two men. One of them was Cole Granger. The other was Dr. Hal Bergman.

They kept their voices low, so I could only make out a word here and there, but their posture and gestures made it clear they were arguing. I waited a couple of minutes, holding very still to avoid their attention. Then, I tried to move just a little farther forward to catch at least some of their conversation. A vicious branch nearly poked my eye out. I pushed it away. The branches and dried leaves around me crackled and rustled.

Both men turned in my direction. I flattened myself down as low as I could go. I lay absolutely still, unless you counted the way my heart was jumping around in my chest. My eyes were at ground level, so I could only see a pair of feet coming my way. I calculated how quickly I could escape the tangle of shrubbery and run toward the light and safety of the parking lot out front. He was only steps away. I'd never make it. I steeled myself to stand up and avoid the indignity of being hauled from the bushes. And I prepared to yell really loud. Just then the blaring of a car alarm rent the air with repeated whoops of ear-shattering sound.

The feet stopped. Cole muttered something. I heard the thud of a car door and the smooth start-up of a luxury engine. The alarm continued. Cole's footsteps retreated. I waited a second, then backed my way out like a crawling baby in reverse. I hightailed it to the bright lights of the front parking area.

Nick was standing beside his car, fumbling with a key fob, as several people shouted advice on how to shut down the alarm. He saw me coming, and suddenly the horn stopped.

"There, got it. Sorry for the nuisance, everyone."

I hopped into the SUV and he did the same. As we pulled out, I said, "Nicky, you just saved my butt. Thank God you hit the panic button by accident." The nickname I had used in happier days slipped out of its own volition. I hoped he wouldn't notice.

"Freud says there are no accidents."

I stared at him. "Are you saying you did that on purpose?"

"I do know you, Leah. I saw you watching the clerk who left out the side door. And then all of the sudden you needed your phone? When you didn't come back by the time I paid for the coffee, and neither did he, I put the cups in the car. Then I walked to the back edge of the building and looked around the corner. I saw him and another man arguing, but no you. I heard a noise and saw the bushes shaking. One of the men started walking toward the thicket, and I thought a diversion might be in order. So, I hit the panic button."

I was speechless. For a second or two. "Were you this smart when we were married?"

He smiled. "And I brought you coffee then, too. Now, can you tell me why that butt of yours needed saving?"

As we drove to my car, I filled him in. When I finished, Nick let out a low whistle.

"So, you think the son Jamie killed his father?"

"I did. I'm not sure now. I never expected to see Bergman there. Now, I'm wondering if Cole and Bergman are partnered up. Bergman could be part of a much bigger drug distribution operation. That would explain his connection to Cole. But Jamie's kind of a wild card. He was probably one of Cole's customers in the past—and maybe still is. If Cole and Bergman are connected, then there's a link to Jamie, too."

"You think both Jamie and this Bergman are linked to Garrett Whiting's death?" He sounded doubtful. That was OK, I was pretty unsure myself.

"I don't know. All of the leads were pointing in one direction: Jamie. But Bergman had a strong motive to want Garrett dead, and Jamie did too. Maybe they worked out something together."

"Leah, if I were you, I'd just hand it over to the police."

"That's because you don't know Ross. This will go nowhere if I don't give it to him tied up with a big bow. And I owe it to Isabel to get it right."

"That's what it's really about, isn't it? You know you're a fraud, don't you? Underneath that tough reporter act, you're a softie, an easy mark for anyone in distress."

"I'm not. I just want to do the job right. And yeah, OK, I'd like things to work out for Isabel. I want to help her. Is that such a bad thing?"

"Helping is different from rescuing. You're putting yourself at risk when you get so emotionally involved. You did what you told Isabel you'd do. Now, you can let it go to the police."

"But that's just it. I didn't do what I promised. I said I'd follow it through to the end. It's not the end yet."

He sighed. "I can see there's no point in arguing with you. But at least be careful. I might not be there to save you next time."

And because I owed him, I let it pass.

But I didn't make any promises, either.

"OK then. Thanks, Nick. For everything. You were great."

True to his word, he made no move to swoop in for a goodnight kiss, for which I was very glad. Or so I told myself.

"Leah? Is that you?" My mother's sleepy voice called down the hallway. No matter how quiet I was, she could always hear me coming in.

"No, Mom. It's a psychotic killer."

"Don't be such a smartass. Good night," she said sleepily.

I went straight to bed and fell immediately asleep. Until, that is, I sat up with a start at 2 a.m., fully awake, with the knowledge that I had dropped my phone in the bushes behind JT's. Clearly, at some level, my mind had registered that when I scrambled out of the thicket, my phone wasn't in my jacket pocket, bumping against my hip as I walked. But my subconscious has always preferred to wake me up out of a sound sleep, rather than alert me at the time the crisis happens. I couldn't leave it lying in the bushes. I groaned, got up, put on my clothes, and crept silently out of the house. I didn't worry about waking my mother when I started the car, because once she believes I'm safely moored at home, she sinks into a sleep that a hibernating bear would envy.

I didn't pull into the lot at JT's. Instead, I drove a little way down the street to avoid attention, parked, and got my flashlight out of the glove compartment. Then, I jogged up the sidewalk until I got to the outer edge of the party store's property. The lone light in the back cast a glow that faded long before it reached the shrubbery. I walked quickly over, then crouched down and turned on the flashlight as I entered the bushes.

I soon realized I'd have to do this search on my hands and knees. I didn't relish rooting around in the dead vegetation and debris, but I wouldn't find my phone otherwise. I held the flashlight in my mouth and crept forward, my hands stretched out in front of me feeling the ground. I made one forward pass with no luck, then stood up and moved over a little to try another crawl heading from front to back. My hands were cold and wet and encountered old beer cans, candy wrappers, discarded cups and straws and a couple of slimy things I didn't want to think about. The earth smelled dank and loamy, and the wet ground was penetrating the knees of my jeans.

I couldn't give up. It had to be here. My light grew dimmer as the batteries in the flashlight weakened. I shook it impatiently as though that would re-energize them. It must have worked, because all at once I could see better. Then a voice I knew well spoke, and I realized the light source wasn't from the flashlight I was holding.

"Whyn't you come on out of there, Leah?"

There was nothing to do but back ungracefully out of the bushes. I turned and faced Cole, who was holding a Maglite flash in one hand. In the other he jiggled my iPhone on his palm.

I reached out to grab it, but he snatched it away.

"Not so fast. Ain't there some kind of a reward? This is a valuable piece of equipment. And how do I know it's yours?"

"Yes, how do you know it's mine?"

"Well, outside of you crawlin' around in the bushes lookin' for it like a pig rootin' out grubs, there's the fact that I saw you lurkin' in this very thicket earlier tonight. And when I come back out after you left, there it was."

"Give me that!" I said, grabbing for it again. But his grip was tight and I wasn't about to engage in hand-to-hand combat with him. I took a breath. "All right, Cole, what is it you want?"

"I want to know what you heard when you were sneakin' around eaves-droppin' on private conversations tonight."

"I didn't hear anything. You were talking too low."

"And what did you see?"

"Just you talking to some guy. I couldn't tell who it was."

"Hmm. Now, I wonder why I don't think you're tellin' me the truth?"

"Because you have a suspicious nature."

"You are right. I surely do. It comes from a sad life of hard livin.' But that isn't why I'm doubt'n' you, Leah. I think you don't have confidence in my goodwill and changed ways. I think you don't trust me enough to tell the truth, and that makes me feel real bad."

"Right. Look, it's 2:30 in the morning. You have my phone. Either give it to me, or don't, but I'm not standing here arguing with you anymore."

"Oh, I'm gonna give it to you, Leah. And I'm gonna throw in a free piece of advice, too. You best forget you saw anything at all tonight."

"Is that a threat?"

"It pains me to hear you say that. I am not threatnin' you. I am suggestin' that there are things that are none of your business. There are forces at work you know nothin' about. Sometimes it's a good thing when the right hand don't know what the left hand is doin.' And sometimes we think we know, and we don't. There are people in this world not as committed to nonviolence as I am. And they will not take kindly to your interference."

He flipped the phone to me then, and I caught it with both hands. Before he left I played my only card, the only thing I could think of that might make him give me the SD card.

"What do you suppose Coop will say when I tell him you're still dealing?"

"Now, why would you go sayin' somethin' like that?"

"Well, I just hear things, you know."

"Yeah?"

"I understand you're the man to see for weed, pills, a full range of high quality products. Is that really wise? It would be a shame if you got arrested again. That new circuit judge is really tough, especially on repeat offenders."

"What's this about, Leah? Are you still tryin' to get hold of that SD card? I wonder what's on it that could make you want it so bad you're tryin' to extort an old friend like me?" He shook his head. "That makes me right sad. 'Specially when you think about how I saved your ass not three hours ago. That nameless gentleman is not someone you want to cross."

It almost sounded like he really *was* trying to warn me.

"Cole, I think there's something on that SD card that ties Jamie Whiting to his father's death."

"You think Jamie killed his old man?"

"I'm not saying that. I'm not saying anything except quit playing with me. This isn't a game. I really need to see that video."

"Now, I told you—"

"You told me you didn't have it, but I don't believe you. And now I have something to make it worth your while to find it."

"You got nothin'. So what if you tell the cops you heard I was dealin'? Hearin' don't make it so."

"With your record, I suspect the cops will definitely take some extra interest in you. Stop by unexpectedly and frequently. Coffee's good here. Maybe JT's is about to become Cop Central, the place to be for a late night cup of joe and a chat with the friendly staff."

He squinted, and I could tell he was running the odds in his mind. What did I really know? How much trouble could I cause him? What would Bergman do to him if JT's really did become Cop Central? After a few seconds, he said, "Like I said, I don't believe we still have that particular SD card you want, but I'll go take a look."

"That's really nice of you," I said, following him in and to the office in the rear of the store. He didn't ask, but I took a seat behind the desk on which sat a laptop computer. I waited while he got a step stool, reached to the top shelf of a wall cupboard, and pulled out several small plastic storage cases. He set them down on the desk and opened the first one. I saw it contained multiple SD cards.

"I thought you didn't keep the cards longer than a couple of weeks."

He didn't answer, just flipped through the box, closed it and reached for another, searching until he found the card he was looking for. He slipped it into the computer and said "There. Anythin' else I can get you?"

"Some popcorn would be nice."

The bell on the door rang as he shook his head and went to the front of the store. I turned my attention to the video. I fast forwarded, stopping whenever anyone approached the ATM. In the early part of the evening, there was a mother with tired eyes who held a toddler on her hip; an older man who weaved back and forth and took multiple tries to steady his hand enough to put in his card; then later a shift worker in a hurry, holding a cup of coffee in one hand and punching in her numbers with the other.

And then nothing, nothing, nothing, nothing. Until a figure in a hoodie suddenly appeared on camera, head lowered and hood pulled forward so his features weren't visible. He walked quickly to the machine, slid in a card and hesitated a second (trying to remember his father's code?) before punching in the numbers. Even though his face was hidden, I was sure I was looking at footage of Jamie Whiting. The hoodie, identical to my own, the height, the build, the furtive air to avoid being recognized. It was him. And here was the link to the ATM slip.

I stopped the video and ejected the SD card. As Cole came in, I was putting it into my purse.

"I take it you found what you were looking for."

"Yes, I did. I'll make a copy and get it back to you."

"That there belongs to my Uncle Chaz. You can't just take it."

"I'll get it back to you. Look, I really need this."

"Sometimes we don't know what we need—or what we got. It's a real complex world we live in. Full of surprises, 'specially if we don't keep our eyes open. You think on that."

"Whatever. I'll make a copy and get this back to you," I repeated. I was in motion the whole time I was talking, closing my purse, standing up, turning from the desk, and before he could stop me, I was out of the office and at the front of the store.

I pushed out the door and held it for a cop who was coming in.

"Hey, Officer Kline," I said to the young cop who'd given me a speeding ticket the month before. Cole looked at me as though I had assumed magical powers and conjured up a friendly policeman just when I needed him.

If my happy greeting surprised the patrolman, I didn't stick around to find out. I ran to my car, my brain going faster than my feet. Jamie had the ATM slip in his pocket, and I had the video to put him at JT's at 3:30 a.m. He had lied to Isabel, to the cops, to me. I couldn't think of a single plausible explanation for the fact, other than that he killed his father and cared so little that he stole the man's ATM card and slipped out to get some quick cash. But was there anything to a Bergman-Cole-Jamie connection? Was that what Cole meant about the right hand not knowing what the left was doing? Was I missing something?

The first thing I did when I got home was go straight to my room and make a copy of the SD card on my computer. Then I took the card, put it in a plastic baggie, and put it in my purse along with the ATM slip. In the morning, I'd take them to the sheriff's department. I pulled on my pajamas, brushed my teeth, and was just pulling back the covers when my phone chimed. Who would be texting me at 4 in the morning? I grabbed the phone off my nightstand. I had to read the text twice to take it in. And even then, it didn't make sense.

Jamie is dead.

26

WHEN I DROVE UP, Ross was coming out the Whiting's front door, his head down and his phone to his ear. I noticed Jamie's car in the driveway. Had Isabel found him here? But if that were true, the area would be full of police and crime scene technicians. There was only Ross's car next to Jamie's. I parked my Focus off to one side of the wide driveway and scrambled out as he ended his call.

"I heard Jamie's dead. Is he inside? What happened?"

He looked up in surprise. I realized he hadn't even noticed me until I spoke. When he answered, he sounded more tired than hostile, and he gave me the information straight, no gratuitous insult thrown in.

"Nah. His car's outta gas. He took the dad's SUV to the county park. Two 12-year-old kids found his body around midnight. Sneaked into the park on some damn dare after the gates closed for the night. Ridin' their trail bikes. Stupid, dangerous. Those trails got tree roots, rocks; they coulda broke their necks."

"Is that what happened to Jamie? Did he fall on one of the trails?"

"His head was pretty well stove in on the right side. We found a rock tossed off the trail. Could be the weapon. M.E. won't commit 'til after the autopsy, but it looks like somebody whacked him a good one."

"Did the medical examiner give you a time?"

"Won't go closer than late afternoon to 10 p.m. Rigor's set in, but bein' cold like it is, doesn't mean much."

"Ross, who would want to kill Jamie?"

"I thought you might have something to say about that, Nash."

I didn't trust him; I didn't believe that he was capable of untangling this case. He was even less capable of admitting that he'd screwed it up in the first place. I didn't want to give him anything. But I knew I should. After all, he was the investigating officer, he had more resources than I did, and it was his job. Still, I hesitated. Then I looked into his eyes. Yes, they were piggy with a trace of truculence, but despite their appearance and rude manners, pigs do have a reputation as intelligent animals.

"Yeah. Yeah, I do."

He motioned toward his car.

"All right, then. Get in there. I want to hear everything you've been doing, everyone you've been talkin' to, everything you think you know."

He turned the car on, and the heater enveloped us in a rush of warm air and an odd sense of intimacy. He pushed his seat all the way back to accommodate his size and half-turned, so he could look at me while I spoke. I went over the facts that led me to believe Garrett didn't kill himself and why I had suspected Jamie. I didn't mention that I'd seen Cole and Bergman together earlier in the evening. I didn't say anything about Frankie, either. Although this was as close as Ross and I would probably ever come to a kumbaya moment, I wanted to see how he responded to what I'd said before I gave him everything.

He sat very still as I spoke. Not surprising, maybe. After all, the facts I'd laid out were a litany of his incompetence. He must be beating himself up over the way he'd mishandled things. Even after all the history between us, I felt a little sorry for him.

"Goddammit, Nash. You went around double-checkin' everything we did? You just gotta be the smartest person in the room, don't ya?"

OK. Detente officially over.

"Not hard when the only other person there is you. Look, I'm not saying I had everything right. I really thought Jamie had killed his father. But maybe he's dead because he knew something that made him a danger to someone."

"You ever consider that kid is dead because you had to be the big detective, the superstar reporter? You should've come to me with this information a long time ago. When are you gonna get you got no business mixing in an official investigation and withholding evidence?"

That was so grossly unfair it took my breath away. Though I still managed to eke out a few words. "Oh, no. No. Don't even try to go there. There was no 'official investigation.' You had already written Garrett Whiting off as a suicide. You didn't believe me about Garrett; you sure as hell weren't going to listen to me about Jamie. Don't you try to put this on me. You missed one murder completely. Then when I started investigating, started doing the job you couldn't be bothered to do right, all you did was make me the butt of your stupid joke.

"Your ego is so big you couldn't admit that you might have been wrong. Again." I was shaking and it wasn't from the cold. Why hadn't I followed my instincts? There was no way Ross was going to take any theory I had seriously. Not unless I could provide very specific, very solid, very irrefutable proof. Ross was so committed to believing I was out to get him that he wouldn't accept a winning lottery ticket from me, let alone a crime theory that ran counter to his.

"You're holding possible evidence. You get me that ATM slip and that video, and you better be ready to make a signed statement at the department first thing in the morning. And you stay the hell away from this investigation, or—"

"Or what? Here's the ATM slip." I unzipped a pocket in my purse and pulled out the clear plastic bag I'd slipped it into. "And here's the SD card." I handed it to him before he could demand it. "I'll be there to make a statement tomorrow. Right now, I'm going to see Isabel. Her brother just died. Remember?"

He was still talking as I stepped out of the car. He leaned over to the passenger side and looked up at me before I could slam the door shut. "You do anything to mess up this investigation and you're gonna regret it."

"The only thing I regret is having to read you in."

Isabel opened the door and all but collapsed in my arms. She seemed to have all the weight of a dry leaf, and I had the odd sensation as I walked her to the kitchen that if I didn't hold tight, she'd blow away. Once there, I sat her at the table, rummaged in the cupboards for cups and tea, then put the kettle on.

All the while she sat without moving, staring into space, not crying exactly, but with tears streaming down her cheeks from a seemingly endless well of grief. The expression in her eyes was something I'd seen in the mirror once, a long, long time ago. When the water boiled, I poured it over the teabags and set the cups on the table, taking the seat across from her. She looked at me then and for the first time she spoke.

"Leah, why is this happening?"

I covered her hand with mine. "I am so sorry, Isabel."

"It's my fault. If I had never called you, this wouldn't have happened. If I had just let things go. Now, Jamie's dead, and my father's dead, and I'm all alone. Jamie and I had a fight Friday and then a really bad one yesterday. The last time I ever saw him, and I ended up screaming at him."

"What were you fighting about?"

"On Friday I did what you said. I looked at dad's bank statement. There was a withdrawal. I confronted Jamie. I told him what you said. I'm sorry, but I had to ask him. I had to hear what he said. I knew he had to have an explanation for it."

"Did he?"

"He said he didn't know what I was talking about. He said you'd say or do anything, hurt anybody just because you wanted a big story. I begged him to tell me how the slip got there, but he just left. He didn't come home until really late. When I went to bed at 1:30, he still wasn't here. But on Saturday, yesterday, morning he was in the kitchen when I came down around 11. He'd made coffee for us both, and he asked me to sit down with him and talk. I was so happy. He said he was sorry we'd been fighting so much. He said. He said. He said." She kept repeating the words, her voice stuttering, unable to go on. She stopped herself and took a deep breath, then tried again.

"He said we only had each other. We shouldn't be arguing. He said again that he didn't know where the ATM slip came from. He begged me to believe him. He said that you were driving a wedge between us. I told him no, that we had to know what really happened to Dad. He got mad again then, got right in my face and started yelling.

"And I got mad right back. I said some terrible things. I told him he never cared about anything or anyone except himself, that he messed up his own life with drugs, and that he was probably using again. I said, 'Why do you want Leah to stop so bad? Maybe she's right. Maybe you did have something to do with it.' He didn't say a word. He just turned and walked out. That's the last time I saw him. That's the last thing he ever heard me say. And I didn't even mean it."

"When was this?"

"Around noon or so. After he left I couldn't stop pacing, couldn't calm down. I couldn't believe I'd said such awful things to him. He was right, there was only us left. And I was driving him away. I had to get out of the house, had to calm down, had to think. I decided to go for a hike on Patmore's Ridge and then try to talk to him when he came back. I left a note for him. I told him nothing was worth losing him. I told him I was done trying to find out what really happened with Dad. I said I would get you to stop. I said I was sorry."

"Do you have any idea what Jamie was doing at the county park?"

She nodded miserably.

"It was me. He came to find me. My note—I just said, 'going for a hike.' I didn't say where. I do usually hike at the county park, but yesterday I felt like climbing. And it was beautiful, the air was cold, but so clear. You know you can see for miles from the top of the ridge. Everything seems so much less important up there, you know? I just felt like we'd be able to get through this. I thought maybe we would just sell the house and get away. Maybe go somewhere together, for a while anyway, just to start living again." She stumbled over the last words and started crying. I handed her a tissue and waited.

"I just feel like, if I hadn't left that note, he wouldn't have come after me. He wouldn't have been in the park. He wouldn't be dead."

"Isabel, stop. Don't do that. You don't even know for sure that Jamie came back home and saw your note. Listen to me, please, this is not your fault."

Ignoring my reassurances, she asked, "What's going to happen now?"

"Well, the sheriff's department will investigate, there'll be an autopsy to determine official cause of death. And they'll look for potential witnesses, talk to you, to his friends, try to figure out who had a motive for killing Jamie."

She gave a bitter laugh. "So, now I've got what I wanted. A full-fledged police investigation. But I never thought it would be into Jamie's death. And you. You thought Jamie killed our father. Are you happy now that he's dead?" Her voice had risen and had a slightly hysterical edge.

"No, of course, I'm not. I want to find out what happened and why as much as you do. Jamie's death could be connected to your father's. Or maybe to his drug use. And the investigation could lead them to reinvestigate your dad's death. That's what you wanted, isn't it?"

"But not this way. What does it matter now?"

"Look, why don't you come home with me for the rest of the night? In fact, you could stay with us for a few days, even. As long as you like. You shouldn't be here alone."

She shook her head. "I'm sorry, but I just don't want to be around a happy family right now. It would be harder for me at your house. You go on. Get some sleep. I'll be fine." She stood up and I could see she wanted me to go.

"All right. But call me if you need anything. I mean it. Any time."

27

I DIDN'T SLEEP MUCH after I got home. Around 6 I got up and showered and dressed. My mother came into the kitchen as I was finishing coffee.

"You're up early for a Sunday. Planning to go to Mass with me?"

"Hardly. But it wouldn't hurt to say a prayer for Isabel Whiting."

"What happened?" She stopped in mid-pour of her own cup of coffee.

"Her brother was killed yesterday. Now she's got no one." I filled her in on some, though not all, of the details. "I tried to get her to come home with me, but she said it would be too hard."

She nodded. "I understand that. You know, after Annie died and your father—well, when it was just the three of us, you and me and Lacey, it seemed like everywhere I looked there were happy families living the life that I was supposed to have. Everyone was kind, but I felt so isolated and angry. And, I'm not proud to say, jealous. I couldn't stand to be around people who got to be happy and carefree when my life was shattered. It took a long time before I could let go of the self-pity and resentment and accept that it was just my turn. And someday it would be someone else's, while I carried on with my own happy life."

"I didn't know you felt like that."

She sat down across from me and smiled. "Thank you, hon, that's the best thing you could have said to me. I didn't want you to know. Lacey was so young; she didn't realize what we'd lost. But you did. I didn't want you to see me struggling, too. Luckily, you had Coop to keep you out of trouble—more or less. He was such a good kid. He was a good influence on you." She said the last part in a teasing tone to lighten the conversation and get a rise out of me. She did, but it wasn't what she expected.

"Too bad I don't have more influence on him. He's making a big mistake."

"Really, what?"

"Not what, *who*. Rebecca." It pained me to say it, but I'd better get used to it. "They're in love or in lust or whatever. I wouldn't know, because Coop didn't even tell me until I stumbled on them myself. Apparently, it had to be some big secret until Coop could tell me 'the right way.' Seriously, what's the right way to tell your best friend you're dating the person who's making her life miserable?"

A visitor might have been surprised when my mother burst into song at that point, but I took it in stride. She has a great voice and a vast catalog of song lyrics that she's prone to belting out as musical examples of her point. This time it was "When a Man Loves a Woman." I waited 'til she got past the part about the guy being willing to turn on his best friend if he disses his woman.

"OK, OK, I get it. I know. It's not my call, and I have to accept Coop's choice."

"Exactly. Besides, maybe you're wrong about her." She held up her hand as I started to object. "I know she's hard to work for, but frankly, honey, she doesn't seem that bad to me. She must have something good about her if Coop is attracted to her, right?"

"Well, yeah, sure. She's attractive if Elsa is your fantasy girl." My mother gave me an exasperated look, and I grudgingly admitted that Miguel liked her, too. "Apparently, she told him some sad story about her miserable childhood—her mother committed suicide when she was a kid, she lived in foster homes, physical abuse, no family—she's a regular Dickens poster child. Miguel is convinced there's marshmallow creme under her tough cookie coating. Father Lindstrom said kind of the same thing. But then, he likes everybody."

"They may be right. And maybe you two don't get along because you're too much alike." I was too shocked at the comparison to retort before she went on. "You'll just have to wait and see what happens. If she's not what he thinks she is, Coop will come to his senses. Just like you did with Nick."

An uncomfortable silence followed.

"Yeah. About that." It seemed as good a time as any to own up to my dinner with Nick, which seemed way longer ago than the night before.

It did not shock me that her sage 'live and let live' advice went right out the window when it came to telling me what to do.

"Leah Marie, why would you do that? What possible good can come from it? You know how hard it was for you to recover when he cheated on you. You were a basket case."

I squirmed uncomfortably. I don't enjoy reminders that I'm not as emotionally invulnerable as I like people to believe. And my mother knows exactly where the chinks in my armor are. Fortunately, I had enough presence of mind not to fall into her trap and offer any defense. I really wasn't up to being on the witness stand in Carol's Court, at which she sustains all her own objections and overrules mine.

"Thanks, Mom. I appreciate your concern, but I've got this," I said, as I put my cup in the dishwasher and grabbed my coat off the hook. "I'm going to the paper. I have to call Rebecca and update her, get in touch with Miguel, check on Isabel, and I have to stop by the sheriff's department and make a statement. I'll catch you later."

And I left her in a position that my mother truly hates: having a whole lot to say and no one to say it to. I suspected a call to Paul was in the offing.

I stopped at the sheriff's department. Ross wasn't in, so another detective took my statement. I still didn't mention the meeting I'd witnessed between Cole and Bergman. I didn't feel like giving any more leads away—or like being ridiculed for thinking it was a lead. When I was finished, he told me that Sheriff Dillingham wanted to see me. The door to his office was half-shut, but when I tapped lightly, he called for me to come in.

I pushed the door all the way open and saw that he was on the phone, though it appeared he was just wrapping up his conversation.

"Yeah, that's right. I'll see what I can do on this end, but I just thought you should know. You might be better equipped to handle the situation. Real good, then. Bye." He hung up the phone and turned his attention to me.

"What situation needs handling, Sheriff?"

He ignored my question. "Appreciate you coming in to make your statement so prompt, Leah. Sorry Charlie wasn't here to take it."

"That makes one of us. What can I do for you?"

He nodded his head a couple of times and then gave me a smile that looked more like a grimace of pain. I smiled back and waited. He shifted his weight, bringing his chair upright so he could lean forward, his arms resting on the desk in front of him.

"Leah, you know I like you. I don't hold it at all against you, what you did on your sister's case. Though I'll be the first to say you are a royal pain in my backside sometimes. If you'da come to us, we maybe coulda moved things along a little faster and less dangerous for you." He paused and smiled again, to show there were no hard feelings. As my contribution to our friendly chat, I refrained from pointing out that his department had, far from helping me, tried to arrest me. And that we'd had a very similar conversation just a few weeks ago when I'd picked up the Whiting file.

"I feel the same way about Charlie Ross. Really like the guy, but I'll be the first to admit, he can be a pain. But what I don't understand is why the two of you are always crossways with each other." He shook his head slowly, to emphasize his bewilderment over the fact that Ross and I weren't best friends. "But I'm tellin' you for your own good, you need to stop it. You got to trust him. I understand you did some follow-up on your own with that ATM slip you found." I started to interrupt, but he made a tamping down gesture with his hands and continued.

"No, now let me finish. You know Cole Granger is a pretty lowlife character. You don't want to have dealings with him. You let us take care of things. If you don't, you just might get hold of the wrong end of the stick here. Could be there's more to this case than you think. And it's got nothing to do with us makin' a mistake on Garrett Whiting's death, because we didn't."

"Well, tell me what's going on, then."

"It's need to know, and right now, you aren't one of the people who need to know. There's things going on, and I don't want you getting in the way." The pseudo-affability was gone now, and his irritation with me was clear.

"Sheriff, I'm not trying to make Ross look bad, or make your job harder, but two people in one family are dead now, and I think there's a connection. If you're honest, I think you'll admit that, too."

He shook his head in frustration. "You are one stubborn girl. Don't make me call your boss. I told you, when there's something to know, I'll tell you. Is that so hard?"

"Sorry, Sheriff. It doesn't work like that."

Back at the office I did a little copy editing while I waited for it to be late enough on a Sunday to call Rebecca or text Miguel. And I did a lot of thinking about who had picked up a rock and bashed Jamie Whiting in the head. And why.

How would Jamie's killer know he was going to the park? He wouldn't. Unless either he or Jamie had set up the meeting. The more I thought, the less I believed Jamie going to the county park had anything to do with misunderstanding Isabel's note. No. Jamie was there to meet someone. I could think of three possibilities. One, Jamie did kill his father and the person he met was blackmailing him, and something had gone wrong at the meet up. Two, Jamie didn't kill his father, but he knew who had, and he was trying some blackmail of his own that worked out badly. Three, Jamie's death had nothing to do with Garrett's. He had a history of drug abuse; he could've been involved somehow with Bergman and his prescription drug theft. Maybe Cole was involved too.

Which brought me back to my suspicion that Coop was involved in a rural DEA task force. Bergman and Cole could be part of something larger than a small-time local drug operation. And Coop, as well as someone from the sheriff's department, could be part of a DEA task force trying to bring down a much bigger network. That could be why Sheriff Dillingham warned me away, and why Coop was so insistent on me steering clear of Cole Granger.

Jamie's history with drugs could have brought him into contact with Cole and possibly Bergman. If Garrett found out there was a link between Bergman and Jamie, then all bets were off. Wouldn't he go straight to the cops, regardless of his concerns about the reputation of his practice? And if Bergman was connected to a bigger drug operation, he had more to worry about from Garrett than career loss and jail time. Bergman's drug bosses would kill him to prevent exposure of their operation. Bergman couldn't let them know that was a risk. So, he could've killed Garrett for the most elemental of motives—to save his own skin. Or, he might have played on Jamie's anger toward his father and manipulated him into doing it. Then Jamie got cold feet, and Bergman had to take him out, too. I didn't have that many suspects, but there were a hell of a lot of motives.

"Gaarrgghhh! Why can't I figure this out?!" I shouted out loud and hit the top of my desk with the palm of my hand, sending my phone clattering to the floor just as it started ringing. I grabbed it and said a slightly breathless hello.

"Leah? Miller Caldwell. I have a note here from my secretary, Patty. She said that you've been trying to reach me. How can I help you?"

"Hey, Miller. Thanks for calling back. I really need to talk to you, but I'd rather do it in person. Could I stop by your house later today?"

"You can come by my office right now if you want. I'm going through a stack of things Patty left me. I just got back last night."

"That'd be great."

"The front door is unlocked, just come straight through to my office."

Miller Caldwell is a big, handsome man who resembles Robert Redford in his prime. His brown hair has grown a lot grayer in the past year, and there's a look of wariness in his blue eyes that wasn't there before, but he still has the easy manner of a natural politician. Which he almost was a year or so ago. That's when he upended his run for state senate by announcing that in addition to being a Catholic, married father of two teenagers, and president of the Bank of Himmel, he was also gay.

Confession may be good for the soul, but it had taken a toll on his professional and personal life. He was forced to step down from the bank, and he withdrew from his political activities. His wife divorced him and his children were just coming to terms with the new reality of their father's life.

About six months ago he reopened his law practice, and I knew he did consulting on business deals for a small group of clients. He wasn't hurting financially—his family had major money—but losing your professional identity, your political ambitions, and your family life in one fell swoop had to be pretty hard to take.

He stood as I came into the office carrying two cups of coffee and two rugelachs from the Elite.

He smiled as he took them from me and cleared a space on his paper-strewn desk.

"You're a lifesaver. Jet lag just sneaked up on me about 10 minutes ago, and I've got a lot of paperwork to go through before I call it a day. Mrs. Schimelman's coffee will get me through."

"So, you were what? In China? Every time I called, your secretary said you were unreachable. She made it sound like the President personally sent you on a trade mission and that me asking to talk to you was both untoward and impossible."

"Patty tends to overstate my importance. I think it's to convince herself that I'm worthy of her. Which I absolutely am not. Best secretary ever. Anyway, my contact with the State Department was very routine, had to do with a Wisconsin company that an old friend of mine owns. He's going to expand its operation to several sites in China, and he asked me to consult in a few areas. I jumped at the chance, and it was the trip of a lifetime."

"When did you leave?"

"About six weeks ago. We took advantage of some time to travel in the rural areas of the country before we had to settle down to business."

"So, you were gone when Garrett Whiting died?"

"Yes. Actually, I left the night he died. I didn't know that then, of course. Why are you asking about Garrett?"

"I'm sure you know his death was ruled suicide, but it's looking like that might not be true. Especially in light of what happened yesterday. Jamie Whiting's body was found in the county park."

"Jamie! He's just a boy. What happened?"

"It's not official yet, but I got it from the investigating officer. Jamie was killed. It looks like murder."

"Murdered? But why? By whom?"

"I don't know, but I was hoping you could help me figure part of it out. You and Garrett were friends, right? You were his lawyer?"

"We've known—we knew—each other for a long time. Georgia and I and Garrett and his wife Joan used to socialize years ago. My daughter Charlotte and his daughter Isabel played on the tennis team together in high school. But I haven't been his lawyer for years, not since I took over at the bank. And I can't say we were close friends. I don't know that he had any, really. He was good company, witty and amusing, though his humor could be a bit cutting. I saw him now and then, and we had the odd drink together over the years. That's about it."

"So, you didn't know he had Parkinson's?"

"No, I had no idea. When I heard he committed suicide, it surprised me, but if he had Parkinson's... His work meant everything to him. I can see why he might take his own life. But you don't think he did?"

I explained in general terms about the things that didn't fit. "I thought Jamie might have something to do with his father's death. He was evasive and angry when I talked to him, and when I checked it out, his story about where he was the night Garrett died didn't hold up. But now that he's been killed, I don't know if it was because he was somehow involved in his father's death, or if there's another reason."

Miller didn't respond, and he had a somewhat dazed look on his face.

"I'm sorry, I know this is a lot to take in. I just really want to get some answers for Isabel as soon as I can, and I don't have much faith in Detective Ross's ability to do it."

"No, no, I understand. It's just—" He shook his head the way you do when you're trying to clear out the cobwebs. "If I'd had any idea there was any question—I thought I was just respecting their privacy." His last few words trailed off into a half-whisper.

"Miller, what is it? Whose privacy?"

He sat up straight and put his coffee cup down on his desk. He leaned forward as he spoke.

"The night Garrett died, I drove by his house on my way to Chicago. I had an early morning international flight to catch. I meant to get away sooner, but I got caught up in some things here and didn't leave home until after 11. Garrett had offered me his noise canceling headset for the flight. I decided if there was a light on at his house, I'd stop, even though it was late. When I was almost to his driveway, I saw a car parked there, and the inside light came on as the door opened. I recognized the person who got out." He stopped. If it were me talking, the pause might have been for dramatic effect. In Miller's case, I was pretty sure he was still debating whether or not to tell me who he'd seen.

"Who? Who was in the car?"

"It was Frankie. Francesca Saxon."

28

"FRANKIE WAS AT GARRETT'S HOUSE? Why didn't you tell anyone that you saw her there?"

"I was on my way to China, remember?" He said it in a much calmer tone than I'd used. "I didn't hear Garrett had died until a week or so later, and I was told it was suicide. It didn't occur to me that it might be important."

"Oh, it's important, all right. It means Frankie was at the scene that night. She could be the killer. I know she wasn't where she said she was, and I can't think of too many reasons she'd be at Garrett's the night he died."

"Maybe for the reason I assumed. That she and Garrett were in a relationship again. Why would she kill him?"

"Jealousy, revenge, I don't know. But the thing is, she lied to me. She told me she was out of town when Garrett died. And now I know exactly where she really was. You need to talk to Ross. No, wait, make it the sheriff. He won't be happy, but I don't think he'd try to cover anything up. I think they've got the wrong angle on this, and you could help set them right."

Miller was quiet as I rattled through the list of instructions I had for him. He was so quiet that I eventually wound down. Belatedly, it occurred to me that I actually had no authority to tell him to do anything, that he was used to being the "bosser," not the "bossee," and that he might not like me switching it up.

But when he spoke, it was without any sign of irritation.

"I can't believe Frankie had anything to do with Garrett's death. She's a very warm person, and she was extremely kind to our son Sebastian when Georgia and I divorced. Charlotte was away at school, so she was out of the fray, but Sebastian really struggled. It was Frankie who helped us get our relationship back on track."

"Hey, I think she's a nice person, too. I'm not saying she killed Garrett." Although his lifted eyebrow reminded me that I had, in fact, pretty much said that a few minutes ago. "I know, but I was just thinking out loud. It's a possibility. I'm not saying she did it. The thing is, she was there that night. And she lied. At the very least, she's hiding something that might help solve two murders."

"It could be as simple as the fact that Frankie didn't want anyone to know she was involved with Garrett. Maybe she was just there for a few minutes, and he killed himself hours after she left."

"It's possible. 11 p.m. to 3 a.m. is the time of death window. But Frankie still might have seen something or heard something that should be brought out. Protecting her secrets doesn't trump finding out what really happened to Garrett. And Jamie."

"I agree, and I'll call the sheriff. I just hate to see all that old gossip revive. Small towns can be vicious." He spoke from firsthand knowledge, I knew.

"I understand that, but I think it's too late for Frankie to preserve her privacy. She might have some important answers. I know there are some questions I'm going to be asking her."

"Shouldn't you leave that to the sheriff's investigators?"

"Let's just say I'm performing a fail-safe function. Because if they don't find out what Frankie knows, I will."

"*Híjole, chica!* I can't believe it!" I'd finally connected with Miguel. We were in the newsroom eating a fast food lunch following my conversation with Miller.

"Which part? Coop and Rebecca? Me and Nick? Jamie's death? Frankie at Garrett's the night he died?"

"All of the above. Coop and Rebecca. So, that's why she started taking those long lunches, yes? A little afternoon delight."

I shuddered. "Don't go there."

"Why not? I think it's nice."

"Nice? You think it's nice that Coop is hooking up with the ice queen?"

"*Sí.* I do. Rebecca is OK. She just doesn't warm up to people very fast. But Coop, he must know how to get her temperature rising." He said it with a lift of his eyebrows that was more Groucho Marx than Latin lover. I couldn't help laughing.

"Shut up. It wouldn't have been so bad if Coop had told me. I felt so stupid running right into their big fat secret. And Rebecca was so condescending. 'David and I,' and 'We didn't want this to be awkward.' My ass."

"Hey, if he's happy and she's happy, then you better get happy. Don't make Coop choose."

"You sound like my mother. I wanted him to find someone better for him. He deserves it."

"*Qué será será.*"

"Thank you, Doris Day."

"Don't be so *enojona, chica*. Being salty gives you wrinkles. Now, what about you? Nothing like a night chasing bad guys to bring a *chico* and *chica* together."

"Nick and I weren't 'chasing' bad guys. He just helped me out of a tight spot with Cole and Bergman. We're just, I don't know. Friends, I guess."

He nodded in a knowing way that I found more than a little annoying. I made an abrupt return to the real news.

"So, anyway, I left a voicemail for Frankie. If she doesn't call me back, I'm just going to drop in on her. I'd like to talk to her before Ross does."

"What do you need me to do?"

"Well, you could stop by and see Isabel. She may not be very receptive, but I think she needs the company. I texted her awhile ago, but she didn't answer."

"Sure, I can do that, but I mean reporting, investigating, that's what we do, right?"

"I don't suppose you want to meet with Rebecca instead of me? She'll be here in an hour or so."

"No thanks, *chica*. That one's for you."

"Kidding. Sort of. You know, you could check out Miller's story for me. See when his flight was, chat up his secretary Patty, see if you can corroborate the timeline he gave."

"You don't believe Miller?"

"Yeah, I do. I just don't want to get sandbagged by something unexpected. Just in case Ross decides to do some actual detecting. I want to be sure I'm moving ahead on solid ground. You know the reporter's code, Miguel. 'If your mother says she loves you—' "

"Check it out," he finished for me.

"Also, see if you can find out anything about Cole Granger selling prescription drugs, maybe hooked up with a local doctor. Bergman is who I'm thinking."

People sometimes dismiss Miguel as a lightweight because he's so upbeat and funny. That's their mistake. You don't grow up in a neighborhood full of gangs in Milwaukee and not learn a lot about the darker side of life.

"OK. *Lo tengo*. I've got it. I'm gonna bounce before Rebecca gets here. Good luck!"

"I'm not sure you understand the editor/reporter dynamic, Leah. You don't make decisions about what and how we cover things, I do."

The light glinted off her lenses, so I couldn't read the expression in her eyes. I didn't need to. Rebecca's frosty voice conveyed her displeasure pretty clearly.

"I know that. That's why I just brought you up to speed, that's why I gave you an update yesterday morning, remember?"

"But it wasn't a very complete update yesterday morning, was it? You said you believed Jamie Whiting had killed his father. You didn't say you were following up on a lead with Miller Caldwell, you didn't even tell me that you suspected a connection between Dr. Bergman and Cole Granger. And now Jamie is dead, and you've got more theories than a conspiracy website. Maybe it's Bergman, maybe Bergman and Cole are working together, maybe Jamie's death was about drugs and had nothing to do with his father, maybe Jamie knew something about his father's death and that's why he was killed. Maybe Francesca Saxon is involved."

She took off her glasses and stared at me. Looking in her eyes was like looking into a glacier crevasse, just as cold, blue, and forbidding.

"Maybe, Leah, it's time for you to step back and report on what the police find, not try to prove you're smarter than they are. You're too emotionally involved in this."

"Come on, Rebecca, that's not fair. I told you what I knew for sure yesterday. A lot happened between the time we talked and this morning. Sure, I'm fired up about the story, but I'm not attached to how it comes out. I can be objective. Things pointed to Jamie Whiting, but there were always other possibilities. I've got no stake in which one pans out."

"Can you honestly say you're not hoping to make Detective Ross look like an idiot? And let's not forget you've got a book coming out in a couple of months. Maybe you're a little too distracted for your news judgment to be reliable. Can you admit that's possible?"

"Seriously? I've barely thought about my book the last few weeks. Just ask my agent. As for having it in for Ross, the answer is no. I can't help it if I keep stumbling over his incompetence. I'm not out to get him. But I'm not going to watch from the sidelines while he screws things up."

"And I'm not paying you to conduct a personal vendetta on the paper's dime. No. The *Times* is going to pull back from this story. We'll wait and see what the investigation into Jamie's death turns up, but there are plenty of other things to work on. We're a community paper, not a supermarket tabloid. Miguel can handle it from here."

I was stunned. I tried to salvage things.

"Wait a second. You don't have to do that. Ross may be a little pissy with me, but I can still get the story. Don't take me off this, please."

"Leah, I've had a call from the sheriff. He's unhappy with the way you've been interfering with his investigative team, and he can make it hard for us to get the basic information on the things our readers want to see every week. The B&Es, the accident reports, the drunk driving arrests. When the sheriff's ready, he'll give us the results of their investigation. I have to ask, are you fighting me so hard on this because you feel like I've already taken something important away from you?"

I didn't like where this was heading.

"I know you're not happy that David and I are in a relationship. You have to learn to separate the personal from the professional. I've made up my mind. I'm pulling you off this story. Any future developments, Miguel will cover."

"I can't separate the personal and the professional? Why are you even bringing Coop up? Your relationship with him is your business and his. And what kind of an editor waits to be handed information? We're supposed to be watch dogs, not lap dogs."

"I understand you're upset, but you're dangerously close to the line. One more word and you'll be over it."

"Then you'd better get out of the way, because I'm about to take a running leap. You're terrible at your job, and I shouldn't have stayed here this long. No need to fire me. I quit."

29

"So, you really quit your job."

"Yes, Mom. I quit my job. Why do you keep repeating that?" She was sitting in the living room when I came storming in from the office, and had listened to my story while I got out glasses, ice, and poured each of us a generous measure of Jameson. Now, we sat across from each other in the living room, she on the couch, me on the wingback chair. I took a large sip from my glass, closed my eyes and sighed as the icy burn went down my throat.

"I'm just trying to get used to the idea. What are you going to do?"

"I don't know."

"That sounds like a good plan."

"How about a little support? Something like 'I can't believe you lasted so long with that incompetent woman. You're twice the reporter she could ever think of being.' That would be nice." I took another sip, smaller this time.

"Sorry. How about 'I'm sure when your book comes out in a few months, you'll be rolling in money and fame, and Rebecca will be holding a sign on a street corner, begging for food.' Is that supportive enough?"

"Look, I had to quit or kill myself. I've been sweating blood over this story, and because it developed faster than I expected and she didn't have minute-by-minute bulletins from me, she decides to pull me off it and give it to Miguel."

"You're sure she wasn't on to something when she said you were bent out of shape over her relationship with Coop?"

"With 'David,' you mean? No. Absolutely not. Yeah, I wish he were with someone else, but whatever, it's his life. I can deal with it. Taking me off the story doesn't make any kind of sense. I know it inside out. So, she doesn't like me, so what? I don't like her either, but she's not stupid. She has to see that I'm on to something. And she knows Miguel is good, but he doesn't have the experience."

"Maybe it just doesn't matter that much to her. Why does it to you?"

I stared at her, the answer so self-evident I couldn't believe she was asking. "Because, Mom, I'm a reporter. There's a story. I need to find out what's going on."

She retreated a little in the face of my intensity. "Fine, Nellie Bly. So, what are you going to do now?"

"I'm going to get the story. I already talked to my friend Lisa at the *Milwaukee Journal*. You remember her, don't you? She was at the *Green Bay Press* the same time I was."

"You're working for the *Milwaukee Journal*? That was a quick job hunt."

"Not working. Lisa said she'd look at it on spec."

"Oh. On spec." She paused and took a sip from her own glass. "So, that means you're going to investigate it and write it, but you don't have any real commitment that they'll print it or pay for it, right? You might wind up writing it and get nothing for it, right?"

"Well, yeah, basically. What else can I do?"

"Let it go? Call your agent, tell him you're ready to roll on whatever promotion things he thinks you should be doing. Start thinking about another book?"

"Maybe this story will be the second book in my new life as Leah Nash, true crime writer. Have a little faith. I'm on to something, and I'm going to run it down."

The phone rang and I looked at it, prepared to send it to voicemail. I'd already ignored multiple texts from Miguel and a call from Coop. But when I saw the caller ID, I picked up.

"Leah, this is Frankie Saxon. Is it true? Is Jamie Whiting dead?"

"Yeah, it is. His body was found in the county park last night."

She gasped and then started breathing rapidly.

"Frankie? Are you all right?"

She took in a big breath and held it before she answered. "Yes. I'm all right. But I need to talk to you. Can you meet me at the EAT tonight?"

"Yes, sure. When?"

"I'll be there at 9."

The EAT HEARTY restaurant, known locally as the EAT, is a Himmel institution that's been on the decline since it opened 30 years ago. The only explanation for it still hanging on is that, though the food is terrible, it's cheap. And a certain number of Himmel residents will tolerate a hot mess of beige on a plate if the price is right. It's a good place to meet if you don't want to be seen, because there never seems to be anybody there. The coffee isn't bad though, and I had already downed a cup when Frankie pushed open the heavy glass door. The collar of her trench coat was pulled up like a spy's in a bad movie, and her dark eyes behind tortoise shell glasses darted back and forth looking for me. I lifted my hand and she nodded, then hurried toward me and slid gracefully into the booth.

"What happened to Jamie? People are saying he was murdered." Her knuckles were white as she gripped the tabletop.

"People are right. Someone hit him in the head with a rock. Or that's how it looks right now."

"But why?"

"I thought maybe you could tell me, Frankie."

The surprise in her eyes seemed real. "Me? How would I know?"

"Come on. We both know you've been hiding things. You didn't run at Lake Neshaunoc the weekend Garrett was killed. In fact, you were in Himmel, at his house, the night he died. If I can find that out, so will the police. You lied to me about being involved with Garrett again. Oh, I get it. You didn't want to start all the gossip again, maybe you didn't want your ex-husband to know, so you decided to keep it on the down low. What happened?

"Was Garrett true to form? Did he have someone else on the side? Did he make a lot of promises and break them again? I can see why you'd be angry. Jealous, even. From what I've gathered, Garrett wasn't a very nice man. He pushed you too far this time, right?

"You felt like a fool falling for him again. You'd had enough. You went to his house that night, but you didn't confront him. Instead, you said you wanted to talk, and you offered to make him a drink. You slipped in a little Klonopin that you confiscated from one of your students. Garrett got really woozy and out of it. It wasn't hard after that, was it? Just slip on the gloves, pull out the gun, and one quick shot, you're good to go."

She was staring at me, not as I'd hoped, dumbstruck by my awesome reconstruction of the crime, but as though I had lost my mind.

"I wasn't having an affair with Garrett."

"Come on. Miller Caldwell saw you at his house at 11 p.m. the night Garrett died."

She shook her head. "No. Not Garrett. It was Jamie. I was in love with Jamie."

If she'd said she was having an affair with Father Lindstrom, I couldn't have been more surprised.

"Jamie? But—"

"But he was 17 years younger than me? But I'd had an affair with his father years ago? Yes, I know, it sounds like a bad plot from a romance novel. But it wasn't like you think."

"Oh? What is it that I think?" The disapproval was plain in my voice and probably my expression. But come on, she was the kid's teacher. His counselor, really, which made it even worse.

"That it was tawdry and exploitative and maybe even illegal. It wasn't any of those things."

"OK. Tell me how it was."

"Ohhh," she expelled a long sigh. She pulled off her glasses and set them on top of her head, then rubbed the bridge of her nose with long, graceful fingers. She fidgeted, started to speak, then stopped herself. Finally, she began rubbing the fingers of one hand across the palm of the other, and that seemed to soothe her enough to talk. She started off slowly, with information I already had.

"When Jamie got into trouble with drugs, I helped Garrett find a program for him. It was strictly professional—as though Garrett and I had never been intimate. That was fine with me. He listened to my advice. Jamie did his senior year at a residential school for kids with drug issues. And he did really well. I sent him a card when he graduated to congratulate him and tell him I was proud of what he'd accomplished, and that was that."

"Well, obviously not."

"No, but I didn't see him again until this past summer. He stopped by one day when he saw me working in the yard, just to say hello. He told me he'd finished at Himmel Tech, and he was transferring to UW in the fall. It was really nice to know he'd kept himself straight. While we talked, he just started bagging up the grass I'd raked, and then he kept working alongside me. I invited him in for an iced tea. After that he started dropping by a few times a week. He was funny and smart, and I enjoyed his company. And I needed the help. The kids were at their dad's for the summer, and there was a lot to do in the yard."

"He wasn't bad looking either, was he? Now let me think, how old was Jamie, 20?" I shook my head. "And what about his relapse? It didn't bother you that he was using again?"

She flushed, and I felt a little bad for shaming her.

"He wasn't using drugs. I don't know why Garrett would say that. And don't make our relationship sound like something it wasn't. Jamie wasn't my student, and he wasn't a child. He was a young man. We worked together, and we had fun together. We laughed and we talked about books and music and movies. And we fell in love. Maybe it was clichéd, and maybe it wasn't realistic. But it wasn't tawdry. It was real. For both of us."

I saw the pain in her eyes. Maybe she really had loved him.

"OK. What happened?"

"Garrett found out."

"How?"

"I don't know. But he called me about a week before he died. He was furious. He said I was taking advantage of Jamie, that I would ruin his life, that I was ridiculous. But I really think he was angry that Jamie was happy. I can understand a little now, since you told me he had Parkinson's. His life, as he wanted to live it, was over. And Garrett was never what you'd call an unselfish man. I think he was jealous that Jamie had his whole life in front of him."

"Nice dad."

"But surely you've learned that's how he was. He said if I didn't break it off with Jamie that he'd ruin me. Everyone in town would be talking about the cougar teacher who took her student as a lover. My kids would find out. The school board would find out. My ex-husband might take my son, Caleb. I couldn't go through that again. And I knew that he was probably right. Deep down, I knew all along it couldn't last."

"So, you broke it off?"

She nodded. "The weekend I told you I was at the fun run, Jamie and I had gone to his family's cabin. I didn't tell Garrett I was taking that last two days with Jamie. It was the only time that we actually spent time away together. I waited until Sunday evening to tell him. It was so hard."

"Did you tell him why?"

"No. It was part of the deal with Garrett. Besides, I didn't want to damage his relationship with his father any further. I told him that he was too young, and we didn't have enough in common. I told him I was bored with him. That was the worst lie I ever told in my life. He just, he just stared at me in such utter bewilderment it broke my heart." Tears had welled up in her eyes and were spilling down her cheeks, but she didn't move to wipe them away.

"He got angry then, asked me if any of it was true, if I'd ever cared about him. I said yes, of course, but that it was time to move on. I needed someone older, more mature. He called me terrible names, and I let him, because I deserved it. I loved him, but I knew it could never work in the real world. I indulged myself, and I hurt him so much." She started actually crying then with quiet sobs. I reached for the napkin dispenser and pulled out a handful to hand to her.

"Frankie, what were you doing at Garrett's that night?"

"I had to tell him I'd done it. That I'd broken things off with Jamie. I had to be sure he knew, had to be sure he wouldn't tell my ex-husband or my kids."

"And what did he say?"

"He didn't answer when I rang the bell, but the light was on in his study. The front door wasn't locked, so I went in and called out to him. I went to his study. He was at his desk writing something. He actually jumped when I spoke. He put down his pen, and he said, 'Did you do it?' I told him I had and begged him to keep his word.

"He said, 'Don't worry, no one will hear about it from me. Goodbye, Frankie.' I stood there for a minute. I'd expected more anger, or more recriminations, more warnings to stay away from Jamie. But he was so calm and so distant. I just said, 'OK,' and I left."

I wanted to believe her, but she had a big fat motive to kill him. He could destroy her life. And Garrett wasn't exactly a trustworthy man. He'd set her up for a fall before, and she had to wonder if he'd do it again, despite what he'd said.

"You said he was writing. What? A letter, a list, a report?"

"I don't know. I couldn't really see. Later, I assumed it was his suicide note. Then, I started worrying that maybe he'd written about me and Jamie as a cruel last trick. But when nothing came out, I knew he hadn't."

"Nothing came out, Frankie, because there wasn't any note. Are you absolutely sure you saw him writing something?"

"I—well, I—," she faltered. "I think so. Yes, I'm sure." But her voice was tentative.

"You know you need to go to the police."

A panic-stricken look came into her eyes. "I can't. I can't have all this come out. What good would that do now?"

"Miller Caldwell saw you. He's probably already talked to them. And they're going to come to you."

"But I didn't do anything! I don't know anything! Please, you have to believe me."

"It's the police who have to believe you." It was a little cold, but I was irritated by her weakness, her poor judgment, her failure to see the conse-quences of her actions. She was too soft. And she kept making the same mistake. Choosing the wrong man, over and over. And maybe I was more than a little irritated that if Garrett really had been writing something, I might be the one who had been making a big mistake.

"I'm sorry, Frankie, but you'd better get ready to answer some pretty tough questions."

30

As I DROVE THROUGH TOWN, my thoughts careened off each other like bumper cars.

What if Isabel and I were wrong all along? Garrett is determined to take control of his illness before it takes control of him. He decides to kill himself, and he's so angry about Jamie and Frankie that he doesn't care if suicide means both Jamie and Isabel will lose the insurance money. Not very fair to Isabel, but nothing new in that family. Only Garrett can't let go completely. He uses his suicide note for one last attempt at control by destroying Frankie's life, by further tormenting Jamie, by ensuring that Bergman is caught at whatever he's doing? Maybe all three. If Jamie found it, taking it away would protect Frankie. It could also give him information to blackmail Bergman.

But Frankie could be mistaken about a note. She had an emotional personality and that night her feelings would have been at fever pitch—fear, resentment, guilt, and grief. Was she really seeing and remembering things accurately? Even if she were, maybe Garrett was writing up case notes or a reminder to himself about a meeting or something he had to do, and then filed the note away. Or was he writing something incriminating that his murderer took with him?

Then again, was Frankie flat out lying? There never was a note. She made the whole thing up to make it seem as though Garrett killed himself, once she knew that someone saw her and she needed to explain away her presence at the Whiting house. But if that were true, that would mean Frankie wasn't the vulnerable, emotion-wracked woman she seemed, but a much stronger, more calculating thinker.

When I pulled in the driveway, I reached for my phone to call Coop. As soon as my fingers wrapped around it, I dropped it back in my purse. Not a good idea. We'd been on the outs before; in a 20-year friendship it happens. But this time it was a complete break in understanding. He had lied to me. The firm ground of our relationship had shifted. And there was no doubt about it. Reasonable or not, it hurt.

I turned my thoughts back to the problem at hand. Was there a note, or wasn't there? How could I find out?

My phone rang, and I was actually glad when the caller ID said Nick.

"Hey."

"Hi. Just thought I'd check in and see how you're doing."

"Well, you missed a big day in the little town of Himmel. Jamie Whiting was murdered; I joined the ranks of the unemployed, and my Garrett Whiting murder theory is on life support." I spilled out to him what I would normally have told Coop.

"I can understand why you quit. Rebecca sounds pretty vicious."

"Thanks for the solidarity. She's probably not as bad as I'm making her sound. But pretty close."

"I don't doubt it. A colleague and I did a study in a corporate setting last year. We were looking at saboteurs in the workplace. Psychopaths really. They're not always violent, you know. Sometimes they get their thrills destroying other people's lives—and careers. We're presenting our findings at a conference next March."

He said the last with a clear note of pride in his voice.

"That's great," I said, and it was, but at the moment my interest was forced. I really wanted to pick Nick's brain about Frankie.

"What are the odds that Frankie is remembering what she saw that night accurately?"

He switched gears with me, and I made a mental note to ask him all about his conference as soon as things settled down. He really was being very nice.

"Well, memory isn't a digital recorder. It doesn't take in unfiltered data and play it back when you press the right button. Eyewitness accounts are notoriously unreliable, because our minds fill in the gaps between what we actually see and what we think we should be seeing."

"Say again?"

"Frankie sees Garrett that night. She's in a highly stressed state. Later, she's told he committed suicide. Her mind reconstructs the memory, but it's based not only on what she saw, but on her expectations. She expects that the arrogant, controlling Garrett she knows wouldn't commit suicide without leaving a note. So she 'remembers' he was writing something at his desk."

"Then she's making it up."

"Not what I said. Our minds interpret what we see and hear. Sometimes the interpretation and the actual event matches, but sometimes it doesn't. That's why a victim can swear that she recognizes her rapist and believes it, but years later DNA evidence proves it couldn't be him."

"You're not helping me."

"Sorry. I live to serve, but there isn't a black and white answer. Is it better if Frankie's right or if she's wrong?"

"Could be better for her if she's right. But it could be good for me, too. If Garrett was writing a suicide note, then Frankie would be off the hook. On the other hand, if he was writing a note that incriminates his killer, that would sure make things easy for me. My problem now is there's no way to know if a note existed, let alone what it might have said... " My voice trailed off and I fell silent.

I was thinking about Elaine Quellman, Garrett's office manager, running her hand over his leather portfolio like a blind person reading braille. Only not braille. Indented writing. I wasn't aware I'd said the words out loud until Nick repeated them.

"Indented writing?"

"Garrett used a lined pad of paper in a leather portfolio to write down lists, notes on patients, personal correspondence."

"And so?"

"So, she—Elaine Quellman—the office manager has the portfolio. Isabel gave it to her as a keepsake. And she said she'd put a new pad of paper in it for him at the office. The morning he died."

"OK. I'm still not following this."

"Indented writing! Remember Jane Barstow? She was a forensic document examiner for the Michigan State Police Crime Lab? She opened her own practice in Grand Rapids, and I did a feature story on her?"

"Vaguely."

"She told me that it's possible to get handwriting from the impressions made in the paper below the one you're actually writing on. In fact, you can get impressions off as far down as four pages, maybe even more. She uses an ESDA machine—an Electrostatic Detection Apparatus. She demo'ed it for me. It was pretty amazing."

I explained how Jane had taken a piece of paper that looked totally blank to me. I couldn't see dents from heavy pressure of a pen, nothing like that. She put the paper on the platen of her machine and covered it with a clear film, sort of like plastic wrap. Then she turned on a vacuum in the machine, and it basically sucked the film onto the paper so the two were melded together.

"Then, abracadabra, she waved an electrified wand over it. I'm not sure, but I think she chanted a spell, too. The wand leaves a heavy static charge in the indented areas of the document. When she sprinkled a little pixie dust over the whole thing—actually, she said it was more like toner—it settled into the impressions in the paper. The 'invisible' writing on the paper showed up, and I could read what I couldn't even see before."

"You mean like on TV, when someone rubs a pencil over a blank piece of paper and brings up the killer's address."

"That doesn't work in the real world, or all forensic document examiners would need is a supply of number two pencils. It just ruins the paper so the tests that do work can't be used. Jane's ESDA is magical."

"So, you're saying—"

"Yes! If Garrett wrote the suicide note Frankie says she saw, he would have written it on his portfolio pad. Elaine Quellman has the portfolio. I can get the pad from her and ask Jane to do her forensic magic. Then I can read whatever Garrett wrote."

"Including something that might tell you who the killer is, or at least point you in the right direction."

"Exactly."

"It sounds like a Hail Mary play, but I hope it works for you. How about meeting me for coffee after I teach on Thursday night? You can tell me how it comes out."

I was already scrolling through my phone, focused on finding Jane Barstow's number.

"Maybe. Text me later."

The only number I had for Jane was her business phone, so I left a voicemail and asked her to call me back in the morning. I wanted to head over to Elaine Quellman's house to borrow the portfolio, but when I looked at my watch I saw it was 11 p.m. I might have a better chance of persuading her if I didn't roust her out in her pajamas. It could wait until morning.

At home, my mother was already in bed. My phone had been chiming with text messages from Miguel with increasing frequency, so I finally sat down and called him. I had to hold the phone away from my ear when he answered.

"*Díos Mío*! You quit? Why? What's wrong?"

"What did Rebecca say?"

"She said I should ask you."

"Typical. I quit because she accused me of being unprofessional, because she killed the Whiting story, and because she's terrible at her job."

"But, Leah, I don't want to work there without you." He almost never called me Leah, always *chica*. He sounded so sad.

"I'm sorry, Miguel. I planned to leave anyway, just not this soon. You'll be fine. Rebecca will find someone to take my place and then you can be the bossy senior reporter. And I'm not gone out of your life, just out of your newsroom. Maybe she'll promote Courtnee." Fortunately, his naturally sunny temperament responded to my feeble attempt at humor, and he gave a small laugh.

"I know. But it won't be the same."

"Nothing ever is."

"What are you going to do?"

"I'm still working on the Whiting story. I'm going to do it on spec for a friend at the *Milwaukee Journal.*"

"Oh, I almost forgot. Word is your *amigo* Cole Granger has been selling prescription drugs out of JT's. Not a lot, just as a favor to some old customers. I don't know who he's getting them from."

"It's got to be Bergman. Why else would he and Bergman even be talking to each other?" I filled him in on Miller and Frankie and what she'd told me about Jamie. And about Frankie seeing Garrett writing something before he died, and my plans for the portfolio.

"You know, I'm starting to rethink Frankie Saxon as a suspect."

"Remember, you only know what she told you. What if Dr. Whiting forced Jamie to break up with her, not the other way around? She killed the *papá* for revenge, and Jamie found out. He was gonna tell, so she had to kill him. Or, what if she did tell Jamie that his *papá* wanted them to split up? Maybe she pushed him to get rid of his father. But then he got scared, and she was afraid he'd confess, and they'd both be arrested, so she has to kill him, too."

"Listen to you, being all grown up with your theories. It could have happened. What you're saying could be true, but the more I think about Frankie, the less I think so. Nothing in her life says she's capable of master-minding that kind of crime. She's too impulsive, I think, and she doesn't have the killer instinct. When her husband verbally abused her, she tried to appease him by having another baby. When Garrett dropped her, she slunk quietly away until her husband kicked up a public ruckus. When Garrett ordered her to drop Jamie, she did it without any pushback. I think even if it were reversed, and Jamie dumped her, she'd go into hiding to lick her wounds, not plot a revenge killing. No, Miguel, there's something I'm not seeing, something that ties this whole thing together, but I can't get hold of it. Yet."

31

I woke to the sound of voices in the kitchen and jumped up with a start. My clock said 8 a.m. I was going to be late for work. Wait a minute. I didn't have "work" anymore. I wasn't late for anything. But I was curious about who my mother was talking to, so I brushed my teeth, pulled my hair up into a clip and walked to the kitchen. When I saw Coop sitting at the table, I almost walked back out.

"Coop said he's had trouble getting hold of you. I told him you'd be up in a few minutes and here you are. You want some eggs and toast?" She sounded a little nervous, as well she should after setting up an ambush for me.

"No, thanks, that's OK." I turned to Coop. "I did get your calls and your texts. And I wanted to call you back, but now why didn't I? Oh, yeah. I was waiting to call you back the right way, seeing how I know you're very particular about doing things 'the right way.' "

"I think I'll go put in a load of laundry. Good seeing you, Coop. Don't be such a stranger." My mother scurried off, her part in the set-up over.

"Leah, sit down. Please."

I dropped into the chair across from him, folded my arms across my chest, and said, "Well?"

"Look, I'm sorry for the way it came out about me and Rebecca."

"You lied to me. By omission if not outright. You told Darmody? But you didn't tell me? How do you think that makes me feel?"

"I didn't say anything to Darmody. Why would I tell him?"

"Well, he knew. The real question is, why wouldn't you tell me? Don't give me that 'I thought you'd be upset' excuse either."

"But you are upset. Rebecca and I thought it would be better if we waited to see if our relationship was going anywhere. She knows you don't like her, and she knows how important you are to me. She didn't want you upset for nothing, if things between us didn't work out. And I wanted to tell you the right way, at the right time."

"Yeah, you said that already. So, I take it that things are 'working out' then?"

He nodded with a stupid grin on his face.

"I'm glad you're so happy. But things aren't going so well for me. Your girlfriend fired me yesterday."

"That's not exactly how I heard it. She said you quit."

"I had to. She may slay you, but she was killing me. She's a piss poor editor, who wouldn't admit I had a great story if the Pulitzer Committee handed me the prize."

He ignored the trash talk about his girlfriend and tried to lighten the mood with a little teasing. "Oh, think this Whiting story is going to be a Pulitzer, do you?"

"Maybe. I'm still going to write it, you know. Only I'm going to sell it to the *Milwaukee Journal*. Probably be top of the fold." I cringed inwardly at the desperate-sounding bluster of my words.

"Hey, that'd be great." His voice held the same condescending note of pity that my teacher's had, when I told her my dad was on a secret mission for the CIA and that's why he couldn't come to Dads and Daughters Day at school. I hated it coming from Mrs. Bole then. I hated it especially coming from Coop now.

"Yeah, I've got a line on a tie-in with a prescription drug ring in the area. I think I know who two of the players are. And one of them is linked to Garrett Whiting. But you probably know something about that already?" I was baiting him, trying to get a reaction other than complacent patience. Because that's the kind of immature asshat I am.

"What do you know about the investigation?" He wasn't complacent anymore, and though I was going in blind, I was pretty sure I'd hit the mark.

"You mean the DEA Task Force you've been working on?"

"Darmody told you," he said in disgust.

"No. I asked, but he didn't give you up. He just stammered and stopped talking. No wonder. You were a busy boy, hooking up with Rebecca and working a major drug case. Poor Darmody wasn't sure which secret life I was asking about. You and Rebecca or you and the DEA. No worries, I'm an investigative reporter, right? I found out both."

"Darmody didn't know about Rebecca. I didn't tell anyone and neither did she." I felt a tiny bit of forgiveness slip into my soul. At least he hadn't confided in Darmody.

"But what about the DEA? He knew about that, didn't he? But you didn't even give me a hint. You know I can protect a source."

"Not my call. I can't be your source on this. I'm just one guy on the task force, and we're all under strict orders to keep the lid on tight. We're closing in on a big one. Any leak could ruin months of work."

"So, who local is involved in the task force? You and a couple of guys from HPD? Someone from the sheriff's department? How close are you to cracking it?"

He didn't answer.

"Coop, come on, I'm just asking for a general heads up. How about this, I'll give you a name and you blink your eyes if I'm right. Is Dr. Hal Bergman involved?"

"Leah, when there's something to tell, you'll be the first reporter I call. That's all I can give you."

The first reporter. But not the first person. That would be Rebecca. This was it, the moment when our friendship was redefined. I remembered something Father Lindstrom had said a few days ago. There are things you can change and things you can't. This looked like one of things I couldn't change. And if I didn't stop trying, I might lose what I wanted most, Coop's friendship.

"All right. I understand."

"Do you?"

OK, now that was uncalled for. There I was prepared to take the high road and there he was pushing me right back on the low road.

"Yes. I understand that you aren't going to help me on this. I understand that you want me to back off. Now, you better understand, I'm going to do whatever I have to do to get the story. Thanks for stopping by. I've really enjoyed the update on your personal and professional life. I've got to get a shower now. You can let yourself out."

When I got out of the shower, my mother was gone. Coward. I checked my phone and saw a voicemail had come in from Jane Barstow.

"Leah, just listened to my office messages. I'm in the airport, on my way to a family reunion cruise. Won't be in the office until Dec. 11th. But I'd be glad to take a look at the pad you mentioned when I get back to Michigan. Just package it carefully and send it registered mail. Oh, and if you have samples of the victim's handwriting—business or personal letters would be good—include them. If I'm able to bring up anything on the portfolio pad, then I can compare the writing and authenticate it as being written by him. Got to go. Bye."

Well, good news and bad. Good Jane would look at it, bad I'd have to wait 10 days or so. I called Elaine Quellman and explained what I needed. She wasn't happy to give up custody of the portfolio, but I assured her it would be returned in perfect condition. By the end of the conversation she had volunteered several letters she had from Garrett, handwritten as per his eccentric preference, too. While I was talking to her, a text came in from Rebecca, instructing me to turn in my keys and pick up my things, which I had neglected to do while making my grand exit.

Courtnee was munching on Junior Mints when I walked through the front door.

"I was looking for the Donniker anniversary photo in your desk. I found these." She held the box out to me, and I shook my head. "You shouldn't leave them in the drawer. The mint part gets all hard instead of creamy if you leave them too long," she said, displaying no guilt about searching my drawers or being caught with contraband candy.

"Mrs. Donniker was all, like, up in my business, but I told her you probably lost it. But she just kept, like, talking about how she needed it back."

"I put the Donniker picture in your in basket three weeks ago, after I scanned it. It's your job to mail photos back, not mine."

"Well, I have a lot of jobs around here, especially now that you got fired." She tilted her head and cast her slightly protuberant blue eyes upward, a signal that she was thinking, or at least as close as she ever came to it. "Maybe it got filed in the Missing drawer." I briefly considered asking why she kept a drawer labeled "Missing," but decided that way madness lay.

"I think it was really mean of Rebecca to fire you. Especially after she stole your boyfriend."

"She didn't fire me. I quit. And Coop wasn't my boyfriend."

"Ohhh. I get it." She nodded. "That's what my Aunt Darlene said after her boss let her go for stalking her ex-fiancé from her work computer. We're not supposed to talk about it. It's still in court."

"Courtnee, Coop wasn't—never mind. I'm just going back to pick up my stuff. Is Rebecca in?"

"No. She went to an early 'lunch' with Coop." She made air quotes with her fingers, which I ignored. I went into the newsroom to pack up my things, but Courtnee followed me.

"Are you still going to Miguel's Christmas party? I am. My outfit is super cute. I've got a picture on my phone, do you want to see it?"

"No." I found a box and started taking things off my desk, my back to her, but she was undeterred.

"You should go to Miguel's with Nick. I mean, since Coop is Rebecca's bae, you should have somebody. But don't get all thirsty with him, Leah. Guys don't like girls who are desperate."

"I'll keep that in mind."

"Guess what?" She didn't wait for my response. "I saw Jimmy Fallon going into the Sunny Side Market yesterday."

"No, you didn't."

"Yes, I did." Ever since Courtnee and her father had spotted Brett Favre on a trip to Himmel to visit his cousin, she's been convinced that a continuous stream of celebrities is making incognito visits to town.

"Did anyone else see him?" I didn't know why I was even having the conversation, but Courtnee has a way of luring me in.

"Well, no. He was, like, in disguise."

"OK." Sometimes you just have to know when to walk away. "Well, that's it, I guess." I turned as I hoisted my box and held my keys out to her with one hand. "I'll see you around."

To my surprise she leapt toward me, knocking my small carton of personal items to the floor as she gave me a hug. I was taken aback, but I returned it gingerly.

"I'm sorry you screwed up and got fired. I'll try to find the picture you lost. And I'll tell Mrs. Donniker you got fired, too, so that'll make her feel better. On account of you had consequences for losing her anniversary photo."

"Thanks, Courtnee. I guess." As she turned to leave, I could have sworn her eyes were damp. I actually felt a little verklempt myself.

Without the structure of a daily job with deadlines, I felt a little lost. I picked up the portfolio from Elaine Quellman, packaged it, and sent it from the Post Office. I stopped by St. Stephen's where my mother worked several days a week in the parish office and had an unsatisfying discussion of her role in ambushing me that morning. She didn't argue with me, just shook her head and said, "Oh, Leah. I'm sorry you're hurting." Which made me feel bad for yelling at her and worse that she didn't understand this wasn't about hurt feelings, it was about honesty and loyalty.

I called Isabel to see how she was, but she didn't answer, so I just texted that I was thinking about her. I ran into the Elite and bought five rugelachs and a coffee, then drove to Riverview Park and ate them all while I thought about the time Coop saved me from an oncoming train, and what an ass he was now. At last, when my stomach was so full I could hardly breathe, I went back home. I collapsed on the couch, exhausted as though I'd actually done something that day. Self-pity takes a lot out of you.

Finally, I got up and made dinner as a peace offering to my mother. Then, while it was in the oven, I started pacing up and down the hallway, talking out loud to myself. Which I do when I've alienated everyone else and I need to get my thinking in order.

"All right. Coop's in the Rebecca zone now, so get over it. He'll see what she's like, or he won't, but I can't do anything about it. I can, however, move forward on this story. I need to review my notes, make a plan, and get going." Sufficiently buoyed by my self-generated pep talk, I went to my room and pulled out my notebooks, but within minutes my mother got home, the timer dinged, and I got caught up in serving large helpings of twice-baked potatoes, green beans, meatloaf, and apologies.

"I'm sorry I got so mad at you. It's not your fault Coop is being so stupid, and you're right."

"Wait a second, could you say that again? I'm not sure I heard you."

I made a face, but I was way happier to be talking to her normally than to be angry at her. "You heard me. You're right. Coop's girlfriend is Coop's business, and it will only make things worse if I keep criticizing her. I'm done. Pretty much."

"I think that's wise. You've got enough on your plate with your book and this story on spec you're trying to do. How's that coming?"

"I feel like all the threads running through this thing—Garrett's death, Jamie's murder, the sheriff warning me off, Dr. Bergman and his connection to Cole Granger, Jamie's visit to the ATM at JT's—are somehow connected, but I can't quite knit them all together."

"Interesting metaphor, given your aversion to the homemaking arts, but I get your drift. So, you don't think Frankie Saxon is involved?"

"Not really. I hate to say it again in such a short span of time, but I think you were right. I don't think she has it in her, at least not to kill Garrett so dispassionately. And I believe she really loved Jamie."

There was a knock at the kitchen door and Miguel came in, stamping his feet from the cold.

"Mmmm, it smells good in here."

"Leah made dinner; pull up a chair."

"Really, *chica*? I didn't know you could cook."

"There are lots of things you don't know about me." I stood up and got him a plate of food and handed it and silverware to him.

"*Qué tal*? Are you doing OK?"

"Not that great."

"Me either. Ohhh, this is so good! I might ask you to marry me."

"I might say yes. Why is your day not so good?"

"We are *muy ocupado* at the paper. We miss you, *chica*. Rebecca had Courtnee shoot pictures at the Middle School today so I could run cops. She took video instead of photos. I can put a clip on the website, but I have to go in and grab a still for the paper. And I so don't have time. And my insurance called. My car—a moment of *silencio*, please—is totaled."

"Oh, no. I'm sorry, Miguel. I feel responsible. If I hadn't asked you to take dinner to Vesta, it might not have happened."

"That's true, Mom. It is kind of your fault."

"No, no, no, Carol. Don't let her tease you. It just happened. No one's fault, but I don't know what I'm going to do. I still owe on my car, and now I have to get a new one."

"You can borrow Mom's car for awhile, since it's really her fault. She and I can make do with mine. Now that we're both not working."

"Yes, Miguel, please."

"No, no, don't worry. *Está bien.* I can manage. I have the rental car for another week. I'll figure something out. So, *chica*, your turn. Why is your day so bad?"

"It really isn't, I guess. I'm just having trouble figuring out what to do next. I was going to take a look at the security video from Cole again, want to see it?"

"You two go ahead, I'll clean up here."

"*Sí*, sure."

I took him to my room, where my laptop was set up with the SD card already inserted. I skipped ahead to the part where Jamie approached the machine.

"See, it's him. He's wearing the hoodie." We watched as he entered the pin number. The lighting was terrible, the angle was bad, and the video quality was poor. But it was Jamie. It was proof he was there, but what good did that do now?

"I don't know, *chica*, you can't really see his face. Lots of people wear Badger hoodies." As someone who would never make a hoodie a staple of his wardrobe, he shuddered slightly. "Couldn't someone else have taken

Garrett's ATM card before he was killed? You know, maybe he lost it, or left it in a machine and somebody picked it up, then tried to use it?"

"But I found the ATM slip in Jamie's pocket. The time stamp matches the time here on the video."

"But why would he go to the ATM in the middle of the night?"

"Add that to the pile of things I don't know."

"Oh, I have something for you. Jennifer at the sheriff's department told me they brought Frankie Saxon in for questioning today, but they let her go."

"They brought her in, or Frankie came in on her own?"

He paused and looked abashed. "I'm not sure. When Jennifer told me they were questioning Frankie, I didn't ask. Not very good reporting."

"It doesn't really matter, I was just hoping Frankie would go in herself. It might help a little if she took the initiative. But maybe not. Her affair with Jamie is going to look like a big fat motive to Ross. I hope she had a lawyer with her."

He sighed and changed the subject. "Are you still coming to my party?"

"I don't know, I—"

"*Chica*, you have to! My car is ruined. My finances are ruined. Don't ruin my party. Here, let me look in your closet and find you something fabulous to wear." He pulled open the door, flipped through the clothes hanging there, then said, "Never mind. We'll go shopping tomorrow. You can't hide from Rebecca like a scared little bunny."

"I'm not hiding."

"Then prove it. Promise you'll be there."

"Fine. I'll be there. But—" Miguel's phone rang and I waited while he took the call. I couldn't get much from his side of the conversation, but from the way his face lit up, I knew it was good news. He hung up and turned to me with a wide smile.

"That was my Aunt Lydia! There's a kidney for Uncle Craig. We have to go now!"

"Go, go on, get out. Good luck. Keep in touch!" He was gone before I finished. And I smiled because he was so happy, and because now Rebecca had no one but Courtnee to help her get the paper out, and deadline was only two days away. Oh, that was too bad.

32

I TRIED ISABEL AGAIN on Tuesday morning and this time she picked up.

"I just wondered how you're doing, if there's anything you need?"

"I'm all right. But, Leah, something really strange happened yesterday. Detective Ross came to see me. He asked me about Frankie Saxon and Dad. I told him I was just a kid then. I knew there was kind of a scandal because Frankie was married, but it didn't really have any impact on us. But then he started talking about Jamie and Frankie and if I thought they were close. And I told him Jamie really liked her, and I did, too, because she's the one who really made Dad get involved and help Jamie get straight. But he made it seem like he thought they were having an affair! Why would he ask me that?"

"Because they were, I guess. At least according to Frankie. I wasn't going to tell you yet; I thought you had enough to deal with just now."

There was silence for a few seconds.

"But does that mean they think Frankie had something to do with Jamie's death?"

"I'm not exactly in the loop, but I imagine so."

"She was his teacher, his counselor! She slept with our father and then she slept with Jamie? That's sick! Did she kill Jamie? And my father, too?"

"Hold it, hold it, hold it. We don't know anything yet. Ross is just asking questions. That's his job."

"But he must suspect something. Why would he even be asking if he didn't have some evidence? You know, don't you? Please, tell me what's going on."

"All right, but this may not mean anything. Miller Caldwell saw Frankie in the driveway of your house the night your father died."

"Frankie? Frankie killed him?"

"No, Isabel, not necessarily. Frankie admitted she was there, but she said your father was alive when she left. And I think I believe her."

"Why? You could believe that Jamie killed his own father, but you can't believe that Frankie killed someone?"

"She could have, but it just doesn't fit with her temperament. Anyway, I'm still checking some things out."

"What?"

"I'll tell you if they work out. In the meantime, try not to think about this too much." I realized how ridiculous that sounded as soon as I said it. How could she not think about it?

What she said next, and the way she said it, almost broke my heart.

"Detective Ross told me something else. He said." She stopped and tried again. "He said they're going to release Jamie's body today."

"Oh, Isabel. I know how hard that's going to be. I could go with you to make arrangements. You shouldn't do that alone."

"No, it's all right. I've already talked to Mrs. Delaney at the funeral home. There won't be any service. Jamie wasn't religious and neither am I. We don't have any extended family to speak of. No, I'm having him cremated. And then, I don't know, maybe later I'll scatter his ashes at our cabin. He was really happy there."

"Are you really sure? You've had a tremendous loss. A service might help you—"

"Help me what? Get 'closure'? Nothing is going to help me get past this, nothing will bring me closure. I just—oh, never mind. I know you're trying to help. But there isn't any help."

"No, you're right. I'm sorry. That was stupid. But will you call me, please? I'd like to do something, anything."

"Yes. I will."

But I knew she wouldn't. There are some things so terrible, some grief so searing that no one can help.

It's how I felt when Annie died, and when my father left. It's how Isabel must feel now.

I was just starting to highlight and organize some of my notes, in search of that elusive connecting thread, when my phone rang. It was my agent, Clinton Barnes. I'd almost forgotten I was writing a book.

"Leah, the final pages look great. Wonderful job. The story is really compelling. We're all set for launch: interviews, book signings, podcasts. You'll be a busy girl for awhile. Do you have a stylist?"

"A stylist?"

"You know, a person to help you get your look right. Clothes, accessories. You want to project a certain image."

"Um, sort of," I said, thinking of Miguel, but not at all liking the thought of my "image" and how I needed to look. I hadn't considered the promotion part of book publishing much.

"You need to get working on that. I have someone if you don't. Let me know. And we need to talk about your author photo for the back cover."

"I sent you the photos two weeks ago. Didn't you get them? You can choose either one you want. I trust you."

"The thing is, I think we want to go a little more awesome with them. Maybe you standing on the cliff where Sister Mattea went over. I see you maybe staring out at the horizon, looking kind of pensive but determined. You know, a Katniss Everdeen vibe going."

"You're kidding."

"I'm not. It goes with the narrative. You know, sister protecting sister, strong, confident."

"I am not posing like the heroine of a young adult novel."

"It's very in now. Very on fleek."

"'On fleek?' Clinton, I hate it when you talk millennial to me. English, please."

"Well, don't worry about it. We have time. We'll talk again. We want everything to be right. *True Crime: Unholy Alliances* could be a blockbuster."

"Really?" Clinton's words made my current unemployed state a little easier to take.

"Absolutely. I know you were a little disappointed with the advance, but we got you a great contract. This could be a very good deal for all of us, Endres Press, you, me. In fact, we need to talk about your next book. We want to capitalize on the momentum. Any ideas?"

"Well, what about the Mandy Cleveland murder?" That was the original story I'd queried Clinton—and a thousand other agents—about a few years ago. He'd taken me on but hadn't been able to sell it. "I thought you said that we could try that again."

"We will, we will. Not yet. It's a good story, but maybe a little too complex, a little too nuanced at this stage of your career. We want to follow *Unholy Alliances* with another fast mover. It's what your readers will be looking for."

"I don't have any readers."

"You will. What about this murder you're working on now? Could that be your next book?"

"I guess, maybe. Depends how it plays out. I don't have any idea how this ends, yet."

"Get me an outline as soon as you can, and I'll start pitching it. Well, got a meeting, got to go. Let me know about reshooting the author photo."

"I already let you know, I said—" But I realized I was speaking to dead air; he'd already hung up. I'd only met Clinton face-to-face once; everything else was text, phone, or Skype, and it was always twice as fast as any normal human being communicated. He was in constant motion. But I really liked him, and I appreciated his faith in me. There would be no posing on a cliff, but I might give some thought to the Garrett Whiting story as a book. If I could ever figure out the ending.

I went back to my notebooks again, and when nothing struck me, I pulled out the case file I'd gotten from the sheriff's department. This time I read the phone records more carefully than I had the first time. I looked at all of the calls for the preceding week, thinking maybe I'd see Frankie's number, or one that could be Bergman's. But aside from a few 800-number market-ing-type calls, there was only one other local number listed. It looked vaguely familiar, but as I started to punch in the numbers to see who answered, a text came in from my friend Jennifer at the sheriff's department.

Frankie Saxon was arrested.

I knew I wouldn't get anything walking into the sheriff's department. In addition to being *persona non grata* to both Sheriff Dillingham and Ross, I didn't even have the quasi-official status of a newspaper affiliation. I texted Jennifer back.

Can you take a break and meet me in the Court House parking lot? 10 minutes?

Yes

I had just pulled into an out-of-the-way spot next to the trash dumpster when Jennifer opened the passenger door and slid in.

"I can't stay. I'll be in big trouble if the sheriff or Ross know I'm talking to you."

"What's going on?"

"They arrested Frankie this afternoon."

"You already texted me that. What's the evidence?"

"Frankie didn't have a lawyer yesterday when they interviewed her. She talked too much. She said she was there at the Whiting house that night. She admitted Garrett had found out about her and Jamie and that he told her to break it off."

"But they let her go yesterday."

"That was part of the plan. Get her shook up, then let her go home and think she's off the hook, then reel her in again. She's got a lawyer now, but it's Jim 'let's-make-a-deal' Gilroy." She rolled her eyes, and I knew why. Jim Gilroy is a not-very-ambitious lawyer who never met a client he didn't want to plead out.

"So, what happened today? Why'd they arrest her?"

"They've got phone records that show a call from Jamie's cell to

Frankie's home phone on Saturday. They think either Jamie actually helped her kill his dad, or he knew that she had. Either way, he got a bad case of nerves, and he told her he was going to the police. She set up a meeting in the park, told him they'd talk about it, maybe even go in together. Instead, she killed him."

"That's not good."

"No kidding."

"Jen, I don't think she did it."

"Well, good luck with that. They're all doing a victory lap around the office right now. They wrapped up a murder case in three days. The only thing keeping Ross from kissing himself all over is he has to admit Garrett Whiting didn't commit suicide. But he's so fired up over catching a double murderer, I think he's gonna be okay with that."

"This is moving too fast. They're totally ignoring any other suspects."

"You got someone in mind?"

"As a matter of fact, yes I do. What do you know about the DEA Task Force?"

"And that's my cue to leave," she said, reaching for the door handle and sliding out.

"Wait a second."

"Nope. Sorry." Jennifer didn't mind giving me the inside track on Frankie; she knew most of it would be released in a back-patting press conference soon, or I'd get it from Frankie herself. But she'd never give up details on something as hush-hush as a drug operation, regardless of how much time we spent together in the kindergarten time-out corner. Nevertheless I tried, giving her my most compelling stare, one eyebrow raised.

"Quit trying to pressure me with 'the look.' I'm not telling you. Why don't you ask Coop?"

"Not gonna happen. We'll do lunch, I'll tell you all about it. C'mon. Just give me a crumb."

"Well, there is one way you might get some information."

"Yeah?" I leaned in toward her a little closer.

"The sheriff's still looking for a date for the Elks Club Christmas dance. If your mom's not busy?"

"Goodbye, Jennifer."

"You should run it by her at least. Lester's been trying out a new after-shave. It's pretty intense. Could be sparks would fly. Maybe some intel, too. Who knows, you could get the information and a new stepfather, too." She was still laughing as she shut the door. Not funny. Well, OK, a little funny, but I wasn't in a laughing mood.

33

On impulse, I drove out to the Whiting house. If Isabel didn't know already, she'd soon hear the news. I didn't think she should be alone.

"Leah, it's over. The police arrested Frankie. Detective Ross just called me." She sounded different. Jubilant, almost. Looked different, too. Her eyes had lost their dullness and were a clear, warm brown again. I followed her into the living room. As we sat down, she said, "Thank you, for all you did, and for sticking by me. I know I didn't make it easy."

"You seem a lot better."

"I didn't think anything would make a difference. But it does. Knowing who killed Jamie and my father, well, it's as though something shifted inside me. I don't know how to explain it. It's like, there's an ending. It won't go on and on and on, with me never knowing why. And I know now that Jamie wasn't at the park because of my note. It wasn't my fault. He went there to meet Frankie."

"Isabel—" I started to tell her maybe it wasn't over. That Bergman had a strong motive and was much more likely than Frankie to commit a calculated crime like Garrett's murder. I stopped myself, because I didn't want to take away whatever comfort she was finding at the moment.

"What?"

"Nothing. I, uh, I'm just. I'm glad you feel better about things." But she was too perceptive not to hear the hesitation in my voice.

"You don't think Frankie did it, do you? You still think Dr. Bergman had something to do with it? Isn't that what you said the other day?"

"I just don't see Frankie having the temperament for a cold-blooded killing like your father's."

She didn't answer right away, and I thought she might be angry at me.

"Leah, you've done so much for me. Not just investigating when no one else would, but you really cared. I'll never forget that. But maybe you cared too much. Maybe it's just hard for you to realize it's over. Frankie killed them both, I know she did." She reached out and touched me on the arm. "But I don't want to argue with you. Can we just not talk about this for awhile?"

"All right, sure." I nodded agreement. What was the point of trying to convince her? She felt a little better and I didn't have any hard evidence, so couldn't I just back off for once? Yes, I could. Coop would be proud of me. As if that mattered.

"Good. I want to ask you about something else," Isabel said.

"What's that?"

"Do you think Miguel would want Jamie's car? I know his was pretty wrecked the night you guys were coming to my house."

"The Mini Cooper? He'd love it, but he couldn't afford it."

"I wasn't planning on asking much. I have three cars now. Mine, my dad's, and Jamie's. I need to get rid of two of them. And I don't like seeing the Mini in the driveway. It just reminds me of Jamie. Do you think he could afford $500?"

"I think so, yeah, but that's a ridiculously low price."

"It isn't really. It has a lot of miles on it—it was mine before it was Jamie's. Actually, it still is mine; we never transferred the title. The other thing is, it's pretty bad inside. Jamie wasn't exactly a neat freak. And the police went through it too. It's beyond messy. But I can't make myself clean it out. So, Miguel would have to take the car as-is."

"Isabel, if you're sure you want to do this, that wouldn't be a problem." In my mind, I saw Miguel sitting in the yellow convertible. He'd be ecstatic. "If you're serious, text him and see what he says."

"I will. Thanks."

I stuck around for awhile longer, hating to leave her in that big house alone, but she insisted she was fine. On the way home, I got a call from Marissa Saxon, Frankie's daughter.

"Leah, they arrested my mother!"

"I know, I heard. I'm sorry."

"But she didn't do it!"

"Marissa, I can't imagine what you're feeling."

"No, that's right. You can't. It's your fault."

"My fault?"

"You tricked me into telling you she was home the night Dr. Whiting died. You made me break her alibi."

"No, Marissa. That's not why she was arrested. Someone saw her at Dr. Whiting's the night he died."

"I know all about that," she interrupted. "And I know about Mom and Jamie. She told me after you talked to her that day I met you. She got scared I'd find out. She wanted me to hear it from her. We had a huge fight. It was so totally gross. She and Jamie. But it was Jamie's fault, too. It's not like she came on to him."

I was touched that she was defending her mother for something that must seem to her pretty indefensible. It's hard for a kid to admit her mother has a sex life. Finding out that she's been having it with someone a lot closer to your age than hers would be even worse.

"And she didn't kill him, either. She wasn't even in Himmel on Saturday. She was at the mall in Madison all afternoon. She didn't get home until dinner, and we were together all evening. Someone must be trying to set her up."

"Marissa, there's a record of a phone call between her and Jamie on Saturday."

"I know, but it wasn't her. I'm the one who took the call."

"What?"

"Mom was gone. The phone rang, and I saw it was Jamie. He needed to leave her alone. I picked up the phone, but he didn't wait past hello. He started saying 'Frankie, I have to talk to you. You're not picking up your cell. I need you—.' I didn't let him finish. I told him to leave her alone, and not to call her ever again. And I hung up. But I never told Mom he called. Don't you get it? I didn't tell her. She didn't make any plan to go meet him at the park, because she couldn't have known he was there."

"Did you tell that to Detective Ross?"

"I tried to. He didn't believe me. He thinks I'm lying to help my mother."

"What about her cell phone? If tracking was on, it would show where she was."

"She's got this new app that really drains the battery, and she didn't realize her phone was dead until she got home. Jamie said she wasn't picking up her cell. That's because it wasn't ringing! Don't you get it? She never talked to him, didn't even know he was trying to call. And because the battery was dead, the GPS tracking doesn't work. She can't prove where she was."

"Marissa, your mother was at the Whiting house the night Garrett died," I repeated.

"I know that." Her voice was hard, angry. And scared. "But that doesn't mean anything. He was alive when she left. She told me! She didn't kill him, and she didn't kill Jamie! What's going to happen to her? Mom can't be in jail all alone. They won't even let me see her." Her anger crumbled and she started to cry.

"Listen, she hasn't been arraigned yet. That will probably happen tomorrow or Thursday. She may get bail, and then she'll be able to come home while she waits for trial. You're not alone, are you?"

"No. But grandma's just saying the rosary and crying her head off. I'd rather be here alone. It's because of you. If you left it alone, my mother wouldn't be in jail for something she didn't do. And we won't be able to afford bail. They're not going to just let her go. This is your fault, and I hate you for it!" She hung up before I could say anything. And really, what would I say?

It was 4:30 when I got home. My mother was sitting in the living room, a glass of wine beside her and a pensive expression on her face. There was no sign of anything happening meal-wise in the kitchen.

"Hey. Want to order a pizza for dinner?"

She didn't answer. "Earth to Mom, earth to Mom. Hey, are you hungry? Because I'm starving. I haven't eaten since breakfast."

"What? Oh, no, not really." Her tone was distracted, and it was most unusual for her not to ask for details of my day. I tried a small test.

"I thought I might call Nick and see if he wants to come over tonight to watch a movie." When she didn't immediately start telling me why that was a bad idea, I knew something was up.

"OK, what's going on? Why are you acting so weird?"

"I'm not. What did you say about pizza?"

"I said let's order one. But I'm gonna need something first. Like I said I'm starving. And this has been a terrible, horrible, no good, very bad day." I put together a plate of cheese and crackers as I spoke. I poured myself a healthy shot of Jameson and carried both into the living room. I needed something to blur the edges.

Her cell phone was sitting on the end table next to her chair, and it pinged with a text message just as I passed it. I reached to hand it to her, but she leaped up and snatched it out of my grasp.

She walked into the kitchen to read it, and I could hear her furiously tapping something in response as I gave myself over to contemplating the delicious smoked Gouda on my cracker. Say what you will about Wisconsin, but we've got some mighty fine cheese.

I vaguely heard some additional frenzied typing and then she walked back into the living room.

"What was all that mad texting about? Updating your *Plenty of Fish* dating profile again?" She didn't even smile at the small joke.

"I was just texting with Louise. She asked me again at the last minute to make a sheet cake for a funeral dinner. I told her no. I'm tired of it, that's all." Her voice had risen slightly, and she looked way more tense than the situation seemed to warrant.

"Mom, I have to tell you, you seem a little over the edge. It was just a cake, right?"

"Do I? Well, I'm sorry if I'm not reacting the way you think I should. It's nothing you need to worry about. I have to go check my email." She turned and went to her room.

OK, this was seriously strange. I wondered if she'd had a fight with Paul. Maybe the text was from him? I took a long sip of my drink and felt it send its warmth through my entire body. At least some things were reliable. Then, because the cheese and crackers had barely penetrated my hunger wall, I phoned in my pizza order. While I waited for delivery, I got a call from Miguel.

"Uncle Craig is doing great!"

"Oh, Miguel, that's so good. I'm so happy for you guys."

"And also, Isabel texted me. She wants me to buy Jamie's car. For $500!"

"Yeah, I know, she told me. That would be perfect for you. I can just see you buzzing around town with the top down on your little Mini Cooper."

"Yaaasss! But..." Hesitation had crept into his voice. "I don't think it's totally fair. The car is worth way more *dinero* than that."

"Hey, you're not cheating her. The car has a lot of miles on it, and she wants to get rid of it. She told you it reminds her of Jamie, right? And that's hard for her."

"*Sí*, she did."

"So, take it already!"

"I will!"

"When are you coming back?"

"My grandma is here and my *mamá* and some of my cousins. Aunt Lydia needs us. So, I told Rebecca I couldn't come back until Friday. She wasn't so happy."

"Don't worry about it. You're the only reporter she's got right now, so she's not going to fire you." She was, however, going to have a few more tough days without him. So sad.

"How are you doing?"

I told him about Frankie's arrest and Marissa's phone call.

"*Chica*, you can't fix everything. Frankie, it's not your fault."

"I know, but I feel for the kid. And I believe her, about Jamie's phone call."

"What are you going to do?"

"Look into where Bergman was the night Garrett died. Find out what he was doing on Saturday when Jamie was killed."

"I don't know, *chica*. Coop said—"

"Coop told me to stay away from his task force. I will. I'm just trying to see how Bergman fits into the Whiting murders. If he even does. C'mon, Miguel, I can't let Frankie go on trial for something she didn't do."

"*Comprendo*, but still. Just wait until I get back, let me help."

"No, you don't need to get tangled up in this."

"*Chica*, why don't you let me help more? I'm your *amigo*. I told you before, there's no Thelma without Louise, no Butch without Sundance, no Ben without Jerry, no—"

"Hey, did you just call me butch? No, I know, I get it. Let's see where I am when you get here Friday. For now you need to focus on your aunt and your uncle and your grandma and your mom and your million cousins. I'll see you soon. Bye." I hung up before he could extract any promises of nonaction from me.

34

I KNOCKED ON MY MOTHER'S DOOR after the pizza arrived, but she said she had a headache and wasn't hungry. She clearly wasn't in the mood to talk, either, so I left her alone.

As I ate my pizza, I thought about Marissa's description of Jamie's phone call to Frankie. It didn't sound to me like Jamie was accusing Frankie or threatening her. It sounded more like he was asking for her advice or her help. Had Jamie made arrangements to meet Bergman at the park to accuse or blackmail him even, but he got scared? Had he wanted Frankie to know where he was, so he could tell Bergman that someone knew who he was meeting and would know who to blame if anything happened to him?

This was getting me nowhere. And meanwhile, Frankie was sitting in jail and her daughter was enduring probably the worst night of her young life. I sighed. And maybe it was the extra-large Jameson affecting my judgment, but I decided to call Coop.

"I'm surprised to hear from you." His tone was cool.

I felt for the first time that the fissure in our friendship could grow into an unbridgeable chasm. And it scared me. I gritted my teeth and said words I didn't really believe, but I knew I had to speak.

"I wanted to apologize for the way I reacted to you and Rebecca. And how I was this morning. And I'm sorry I was so mad at you about the task force. We don't see things the same way, but that doesn't make you wrong or me right. It just means we have different perspectives." God, it was painful to say that. Because, of course, he was wrong, but he sure wasn't ready to hear it yet.

"It's all right. I'm sorry, too, that things came out the way they did."

"I suppose you know Frankie Saxon was arrested."

"I heard."

"Coop, I don't want us to fight again, and before you say it, I don't want to do anything to hurt your investigation, but could we just talk for a minute about Frankie?"

Silence.

"I just want to run something by you."

"Leah, c'mon. I'm not involved in that."

"I understand. But just listen, just for a minute. Let's say that Frankie didn't kill Jamie. Or Garrett either. Her daughter Marissa says *she* took the phone call from Jamie, on Saturday, not Frankie. That Frankie was shopping in Madison all afternoon and into the evening. If that's true, then how would she know where Jamie was?"

"That's 'if,' Leah. Marissa wouldn't be the first person to lie to protect someone she loves." An impatient note had crept into his voice, a note I wasn't familiar with. He got frustrated with me sometimes, and angry sometimes, but he'd never before sounded like he was tired of talking to me.

"Yes, I know. But Frankie's history, her pattern of dealing with issues, isn't confrontation, it's running away or caving in. She's emotional; she's high-strung. She doesn't have the kind of cool thinking it would take to kill Garrett, or the cold-blooded self-preservation she'd need to kill someone she really loved like Jamie."

"Frankie had a strong motive for both murders. She killed Garrett because he was splitting her and Jamie up. Then Jamie found out what she'd done, and he turned against her. She had to kill him. Self-preservation is a pretty strong instinct."

"But listen, Coop, Bergman was stealing drugs and prescription pads, and Garrett gave him an ultimatum. I think the threat of jail, financial ruin, and the end of his professional life are pretty strong motives to kill the person threatening you. That's definitely self-preservation. I know you won't say, but I'm pretty sure Bergman is connected to the drug ring you're looking at."

"No, stop there. I'll tell you this much. Bergman's on our radar. But he didn't kill Garrett Whiting. We know he was out of town at a medical conference the weekend Garrett died."

"Well, but he could've left the conference, driven back here, killed Garrett and driven back."

"No, he couldn't. It was in Sioux Falls, South Dakota. That's six hours away, maybe even a little more. He was an after-dinner speaker at the closing banquet Saturday night. He didn't leave the dais until 9:30. If he drove like hell, he might've made it to the Whiting house by 3:30 a.m. but that's outside the window the ME gave. Besides, he was in Sioux Falls Monday morning at 8 a.m. for a consultation with another surgeon. The timing just doesn't work."

I'm not so good with the story problem timetables, so I dropped that for the moment.

"What about Jamie then? Where was Bergman this past Saturday?"

"Leah, I don't owe you any more information. I'm just telling you, it wasn't Bergman. You need to trust the sheriff's department got it right. Frankie's the logical killer."

"I disagree," I said, careful to keep the anger and frustration I was feeling out of my voice.

"Understood. But that doesn't change things. I've told you more than I should. Now, stay away from Bergman. I don't want him to catch wind of the fact that we're looking at him because you're poking around. I want to get him for the crimes he's actually committed, not lose him because you're chasing him for ones he didn't." I heard someone in the background talking to him, but I didn't catch what was said. Probably Rebecca.

"I have to go. I'll talk to you later."

"Yeah. Sure. Bye."

The perfect ending to a perfect day.

In the morning, my mother announced she was going to visit my Aunt Nancy in Michigan for a few days.

"That's a little sudden, isn't it? Is Aunt Nancy all right?" My Aunt Nancy likes to have everything planned out at least 10 years in advance. A spontaneous visit wouldn't normally be on her list of happy surprises. In fact to her, surprise and happy are two words that don't go together.

"She's fine. I've just been thinking about her, and I haven't seen her in a while. So I thought I'd just get in the car and go."

"OK, well, when are you leaving?"

"This morning. I'm already packed; I was just waiting for you to get up to say goodbye. It's one of the benefits of being unemployed. I can go where I want, when I want." I was surprised when she didn't burst into the Mama's and the Papa's "Go Where You Wanna Go." One of her favorites.

"Well, have fun, I guess. Tell Aunt Nancy hi. And make sure she knows this wasn't my idea." I gave her a hug, and there was something in the way she held on just a second longer than usual that made me pull back and ask, "Mom, are you OK? Not still upset about the sheet cake wars, are you?"

"What? No, of course not. I just feel like seeing Nancy, that's all. I'll be back probably late next week. I'll call you when I get there."

I walked to the door with her and stood waving goodbye until her car turned the corner and disappeared.

I couldn't stop thinking about Frankie. Or Marissa. Isabel was at peace now, but Marissa was in her own special hell and so was Frankie. But I couldn't figure out a way around Coop's confident assertion that Bergman was in the clear for Garrett's death. When I couldn't stand going in circles anymore, I put on my coat and went for a walk.

The air was cold and a brisk wind made it even colder. I turned up my collar, curled my fingers up inside my mittens, and half-trotted down the street. The faster I moved, the warmer I got, and after a few blocks, I began to enjoy the clear sky and the bright sunshine. In a half hour or so, I felt better and turned homeward.

As I reached the front door, the roar of a low-flying single engine plane was so loud, I looked up to see if it was about to land on the street. It wasn't. But when I looked away, I had an idea. Inside the house I got the box of things I'd taken home when I cleaned out my desk. I flipped through the pages in one of the notebooks and reread the notes I'd taken at the Board of Supervisors meeting weeks ago—the one Grady O'Donnell had appeared at to defend his private airfield against noise complaints from his neighbors. Then, I looked at the notes I'd written up after talking to Janelle at Bergman's office.

When I got to Grady's house, his wife told me I'd find him in the hangar working on a plane. She pointed me down a private dirt road that ran from the back of Grady's barn for about a quarter of a mile before jogging to the east for another quarter mile. It ended at an airfield with two large hangars. I could hear banging and other mechanical sounds coming from the nearest building as I got out of my car.

The door was open and I called out.

"Hey, Grady, how you doing?"

He was standing on a short ladder, bent over the open engine compartment of a plane. He straightened and looked up at the sound of my voice.

"Real good, Leah," he said, pulling his cap off his head, revealing a bald head damp with sweat. He rubbed his forehead with the sleeve of his blue work shirt before replacing his hat. "What can I do for you?"

"Well, I was just going over my notes from that Board of Supervisors meeting last month. I thought maybe I'd do a follow-up on your operation here." Mostly true.

"I gotta tell you, I'm not real anxious for more publicity. The board just kinda talked around things, and I'm hopin' to keep a low profile and see if things don't just fade away. Vi and Harvey Schmidt, that's the ones who complained, they got some new four-wheelers that make a lot of racket. I'm thinkin' we might be able to strike a deal between us—we don't bellyache about their machines runnin' all through the countryside, and they don't fuss about a few planes takin' off and landing. Besides, one of my renters who flies the most, he's takin' himself a long vacation, so things should be pretty quiet the next few months."

"Oh? Who's that?"

"Doc Bergman. This here's his Beechcraft. Real sweet plane. Me and Doc took it out for a spin one day, got up to 200 mph. Don't tell Beverly that. I still can't get her reconciled with me flyin,' and it's been near 30 years."

"I know Dr. Bergman. He flies a lot, does he?"

"Oh yeah, most every weekend."

"Just up and around local, or does he like to fly long distances?"

"You wouldn't have a plane like this if you weren't doin' some serious flying. Couldn't tell you where all he goes. The pilots keep their own logs and all. I just furnish the airfield and the hangars."

"So, you don't have to, I don't know, sign them in and out, or run a radio tower or whatever for air traffic control?"

He laughed. "This isn't exactly O'Hare, Leah. Basically, alls I do is keep the landing strip in good shape, plow it in the winter, make sure the runway lights are good, and keep the hangar clean and secure."

"And you don't necessarily know when they're using their planes and when they're not?"

"That's right."

"And you said you have lights on the runway, so that means they fly in at night, too, right?"

"Oh sure, yeah. That's what got old Harvey all shook up. Sometimes they come in kinda late at night. Bev and I both sleep like the dead, so we didn't notice. But Harvey said the missus sleeps real light, so the planes wake her up. Hard work and a clear conscience, that's how you get a good night's sleep. I sleep good every night," he said with a grin.

"I'll bet you do."

So Bergman's plane could fly 200 mph. He could come and go from Grady's airfield without any attention being paid. He could make a 500-mile trip in three hours easy. Coop was wrong. Bergman would have had plenty of time to fly back to Himmel, kill Garrett, and fly back to Sioux Falls.

"So, anyway like I said, I'd appreciate if we could just kind of let sleeping dogs lie. Not do that follow-up piece."

"Sure, I understand, Grady. No problem."

The sound of a well-tuned car engine caught my ear, and both of us looked out to see a black Mercedes coming down the road. When it parked, Hal Bergman got out and walked toward the hangar.

"Hey, Doc, we were just talkin' about you." Grady seemed not to notice the scowl on Bergman's face when he saw me.

"I can't imagine why."

"Not really about you, Dr. Bergman. More about your plane. Grady was telling me it can travel 200 mph. Amazing. You know, I really hate long car rides. A plane like this would be great. I mean, instead of driving five or six hours from Himmel to Sioux Falls, I could be there in three hours, right? Heck, I could go there and back in less time than it takes to drive one way."

Something flickered behind his eyes. I wasn't sure if it was fear or anger or just distaste. He turned from me without commenting and addressed Grady.

"Were you able to get that part?"

"No problem, Doc, it's all set. Everything else checked and she's good to go any time. When you takin' off?"

"Not quite sure, Grady. So, I'd like to settle my account today."

"I'm not worried about that, Doc. I know you're good for it."

"You know, I might have to look into a plane one of these days. It sure makes coming and going easy, doesn't it, Dr. Bergman? Yep, I'm definitely gonna do that. Get a plane when my ship comes in."

Bergman stared at me but didn't say anything.

Grady finally picked up on the tension between us and laughed uneasily. "That's a good one, Leah. Get a plane when your ship comes in."

"I assume you're here bothering Grady and harassing me because you don't have anything else to do. I understand you were fired from your job, and I can see why."

Grady's face showed surprise and a little confusion, but he stayed out of it.

"I'm still working, Dr. Bergman. Just not at the *Himmel Times*. I'm on a big story right now. You remember, I'm sure. Garrett Whiting's death."

"I know that the high school teacher was arrested for his murder. I would assume the story is over."

"Oh, twists and turns, Doctor, twists and turns. You never know how things will come out in the end. Stay tuned. You might find it interesting."

I turned then and left before I edged any closer to the boundaries Coop had laid down about Bergman.

35

ALL RIGHT. Now I knew Bergman could have made it back to kill Garrett. But what about Jamie? Had Bergman killed him because of something to do with his drug activities, or because Jamie knew Bergman had murdered Garrett? How could I get more on Bergman without screwing up the DEA investigation? There was no way I could talk to Coop about it. Or anything else. I needed to do something different for a while and let my subconscious turn things over, because my conscious brain was drawing a blank. And I knew just what would take my mind off it. I called Isabel.

"Hey, I talked to Miguel yesterday. Did he get back with you?"

"He did. He's going to buy the car for $500."

"Well, I've got a thought, if it's all right with you." I explained that I'd like to surprise Miguel by cleaning the car, so it was all ready for him when he got back on Friday. That way he could just take possession, get his insurance, and drive his happy little self around town.

"Would that be OK?"

"Yes, sure, that's a great idea. Is tomorrow soon enough? It's an easy switch. He already electronically deposited the money with me. I'll sign the registration and bring it to you with the car."

"So, you doing all right?"

"Yeah, I'm OK. I'm just more sure every day that I need to get things straightened out here, and then I need to get away. I'm thinking about graduate school out east maybe."

"Yeah? That could be really good for you." I wondered if she ever thought about connecting with her birth family. Maybe her biological mother would welcome contact with her. Then again, what if her birth family didn't want to hear from her? What if they were worse than her adopted family? Though that hardly seemed possible. But it definitely wasn't the time to even mention it. But maybe something else would help.

"Isabel, my mother's out of town, and you're on your own—how about getting some dinner tonight?"

She hesitated.

"Come on. It'll be good for both of us."

And it was. We didn't talk about anything that mattered. She teared up a few times, but that was all right. You just have to let each wave of grief wash over you. It recedes and you have a little space where it doesn't hurt so much. If you're lucky, over time, the spaces between get bigger. At the end of the night, I think she felt a little better. At least she seemed to.

Isabel and her housekeeper dropped Jamie's car off in the morning. As I started working on the clean up, I thought again how much fun Miguel was going to have with this car. If ever a boy was made for a bright yellow convertible, it was him.

The inside was as bad as Isabel had said. Fast food wrappers and bags were crumpled and tossed in the back, empty soda cans, a stack of books, a magazine, flashlight, jumper cables, unopened mail. I tossed everything in a sack to go through later and determine what should go back to Isabel. Then I got seriously busy dusting, wiping down, cleaning the chrome and leather. I was major head sweating by the time I got to the vacuuming.

I pushed the driver's seat all the way back to give me full access to the floor and found an envelope wedged underneath. Had that kid ever cleaned this car? I tossed it into the bag as my cell phone rang. I pulled it out and saw the call was from Paul, my mother's boyfriend.

"Leah, can I talk to you?"

"Sure. Aren't we doing that right now?"

"No, I'd like to see you in person. It's important." That alarmed me a little.

"Paul, what's it about? Have you heard from Mom?" I'd spoken to my mother the day before when she arrived at Aunt Nancy's and she'd sounded fine.

"No, that's not it. Well, that is it, but not exactly." Curiouser and curiouser. Paul was not the stammering, stuttering type, but he was having a hard time getting his words out.

"OK, sure. When?"

"I had a cancellation. A root canal, so I've got an hour to spare right now. Can you meet me at the Elite in 10 minutes?"

"All right." I put the vacuum away, shoved the bag in the corner of the garage and went inside to do something with my hair. My head sweating had caused it to hang limply, and pieces of it were plastered to my skull. Not a great look. A hair clip was the only remedy in the time allotted, so I changed my shirt, slammed in the clip, and ran out the door.

Paul was already sitting at a table when I got there, his normally cheerful face fixed in a worried frown. He pushed a chai latte over to me as I pulled up a chair. He already had coffee, but it didn't look as though he'd drunk any.

"What's up?"

He ran his hand through his curly brown hair before he answered.

"I think your mother is having an affair."

Now, of all the things that had run through my mind since he called, that was definitely not one of them.

"You're kidding, right?"

"Do I look like I'm kidding?" And no, he did not. His brown eyes, which were usually alight with laughter, were serious and there were dark circles under them.

"Why would you say that? Mom thinks the world of you. And even if she didn't, she'd never do anything like that. She wouldn't hurt you that way."

"I'm crazy about her, Leah. You must know that. Heck, everybody must know that. I thought she felt the same way. But these last few weeks, she's been, I don't know, different. Sort of distant, and when I bring it up, she says I'm imagining things. And she always seems to be busy when I suggest we do something, like she's avoiding me."

"Even if that's so, it's a big leap to an affair, Paul. How would she hide something like that, not just from you, but from me, too? I haven't noticed any hang-up phone calls or late night rendezvous." Though I, too, had noticed my mother behaving a little oddly, like the night we were watching a movie and she practically snapped my head off when I teased her about Paul's "intentions." Then there was the text that upset her so much a few nights ago. The one she said was from Louise about a funeral cake.

"She called me this morning from Michigan. She didn't even tell me she was going. Said she was sorry, but she wouldn't be able to go to La Folie on Saturday. Leah, I made reservations weeks ago. I was going to ask her to marry me. Now, I can't even get her to tell me why she doesn't want to see me."

"She didn't say that, did she?"

"No," he admitted. "But I asked her when she was coming back. She said she wasn't sure, maybe a week or so. I asked her why she went, and she was vague and said something about just feeling like a getaway. That's not like Carol. I got a little angry at her, and I asked her what was going on. She said nothing. I told her I didn't like where we were in our relationship. And she said she was sorry, but maybe we should take a break. I said yeah, maybe we should. But I don't want to, Leah. I just want Carol to tell me straight out. If she doesn't love me, if she has someone else, I just need her to tell me."

"Paul, Mom doesn't have anyone else. I'm sure of that. She is not having an affair. But as for the rest of it, I don't know. That's something you two are going to have to figure out."

"But couldn't you talk to her, maybe find out—"

"No," I said without hesitation. "I can't get in the middle of this." He looked so dejected I put my hand over his and said more gently, "I want this to work for you both, I do. But you have to figure it out for yourselves. I don't know what else to tell you."

I almost called my mother after I left, despite what I'd said to Paul about being Switzerland and staying out of it. But I didn't, because I knew that my mother, despite her predilection for diving feet first into my life, was very feisty about keeping her own private. Still, it worried me. I knew she wasn't having an affair, but what on earth was going on? A chill went through me. What if she was ill? What if something was seriously wrong, and she was pulling away from Paul because she didn't want to burden him? Maybe she went to see Aunt Nancy to tell her and get advice? I pushed the thought away. I refused to believe that whatever guiding force there is in the universe could take away the last part of my family that I had left. No. That wasn't it. But what was it?

I spent most of the afternoon putting the finishing touches on Miguel's new car. While I worked, I pushed thoughts of my mother and Paul out of my mind and focused instead on how I could find out where Hal Bergman was the day Jamie was killed. If Coop's super-duper DEA team could miss the fact that he had a private plane that could have allowed him to get to Himmel, kill Garrett, and get back to his conference, then who knows what they'd missed or assumed about his movements on Saturday. I didn't have to prove Bergman committed either crime, but if I could kick up enough reasonable doubt for Frankie's attorney to work with, maybe she wouldn't spend the rest of her life in jail.

By late afternoon the Mini Cooper was pristine inside and out, and I'd even found a cleaning product that left the interior smelling like a new car. He was going to be so happy. And that made me happy. And I had generated so much good karma with my cleaning frenzy on Miguel's behalf that I actually came up with a way to find out more about Bergman.

I'd go to Cole. If things were starting to heat up for Bergman, Cole might be ready to cut his ties and bail. On his way out, he just might toss me a bone and give me something I could use against Bergman. Of course, that would put me in his debt; not a great place to be, but I was willing if I could get something useful from him.

I was tired and sore and dirty, and I decided that what I needed even more than answers was a hot shower, a bowl of Honey Nut Cheerios, and a night spent listening to '80s power ballads.

36

FRIDAY MORNING I texted Miguel and asked him to stop by my house before he went home, once he got back into town. He answered right away to say he was already on the road and he'd be here by 10. "*Mucho* to do for the party tomorrow. And I have a surprise for you!"

That could mean anything from a match he'd found for me on craigslist personals, to a gift certificate for a makeover at Making Waves. Or anything in between.

I buzzed over to JT's party store on the off-chance that Cole was working the day shift. He was not. I had no idea where he was living, probably with one of the many women he seemed to be able to charm into supporting him. Though charm wasn't exactly the right word. Maybe mesmerize, the way a cobra hypnotizes his prey.

Nadine, or so her name tag read, was running the register. She was young but had a hard edge. Her eyes were heavy with liner and her lashes spiky with mascara; her blonde hair showed dark at the roots. She tapped aqua-tinted fingernails on the counter to signal her impatience with me.

"Do you know when Cole will be in again?"

"I don't make the schedule."

"Do you have his phone number?"

"What do you want it for?"

"I just need to talk to him."

She looked at me suspiciously, perhaps gauging whether I was a rival for Cole's affection, or maybe one of his "special" customers.

"Can't give out his number. It's against store policy." I highly doubted that JT's had anything close to a "policy," but I could see I wasn't going to get anywhere with Nadine.

"All right. But could you get in touch with him for me? Just ask him to call Leah? Please, it's important." I handed her my card, which she took reluctantly.

"Just get it to him, please. Tell him I've got something he needs." It was really the other way around, but I hoped he'd be curious enough to call.

"Yeah?" She looked me up and down. "I doubt it."

I got home in time to check over the car and rub out any stray smears. Just as I finished, I heard Miguel's rental car in the driveway. I ran out to meet him, and as he got out, I commanded, "Close your eyes until I tell you to open them." I led him through the side door of the garage. The Mini Cooper sat in the center of the floor, directly under the overhead light.

"OK, open them!"

There was a sharp intake of breath as he took in the shiny yellow car, and he promptly burst into tears.

"Oh! She's so beautiful! I can't believe it."

"Get in, get in, let me take a picture."

I took several shots with his phone, so he could text them to his mother and grandmother, and then he wanted to drive around town. With the top down, of course.

"Miguel, it's 25 degrees out!"

"C'mon, *chica*. Just ride with me to get the plates and insurance. Then, I'll put the top up until spring. I just have to do this one time. Quick, before Rebecca knows I'm back in town," he added with a grin.

"All right, all right. Let me get my jacket. And hat. And scarf. And mittens. And blanket."

After a very cold, but very fun drive through town to the DMV to register the car in Miguel's name, we clambered back in and drove to the A+ Independent Insurance Agency. As we walked up, I noticed the lettering on the glass door had been redone in a modern font. The extra-large phone number caught my eye and reminded me that I'd forgotten all about tracking down the local number I'd seen on Garrett's phone record. I didn't need to now, because it was right in my face.

Marty Angstrom's office number was the local phone number I'd seen in Garrett's phone records. But when I'd called him about Garrett's life insurance, Marty said he hadn't talked to Garrett for months before he died. In fact, he made a point of telling me that. Marty was holding something back. What? I felt a little thrill of excitement run through me. Sometimes breaks in an investigation come from the most unexpected places. Maybe I was going to get one. Finally.

"So, you got a fancy new car. Hope you take better care of it than you did your Toyota." Ivah Rollins, Marty's secretary, waggled her head in disapproval at Miguel as we walked through the door. Her large bun of steel gray hair didn't budge. She'd anchored it with a pair of chopsticks, from which dangled a fishing lure. At least that's what it looked like. Ivah has her own sense of style.

"I couldn't help it. But the Mini Cooper, she's not just a fancy car. She's my passion. I will let nothing bad happen to her, ever!" Miguel said, with a dramatic sweep of his hand to his heart.

Ivah raised her eyebrows and looked stern, but I saw a grin tugging at the corners of her mouth.

"C'mon, Ivah, don't scold Miguel. The accident wasn't his fault; he was trying to save a little dog. And he didn't get a ticket, remember. Hey, is Marty in? I need to ask him something." Maybe face-to-face he'd be more forthcoming—or truthful—than he had been on the phone with me.

"No, he's over to his in-laws in Oshkosh. He won't be back until Monday." My disappointment must have shown on my face, because she continued. "Don't worry, I can take care of anything you need."

"Thanks, Ivah, but I don't think so. I really need to see Marty."

Her tone shifted from helpful to slightly affronted. "I know everything that goes on here. Marty might be the agent of record, but I know everything he does about insurance."

"Oh, I know you do. But it's not about insurance. I just wanted to ask him about a phone call he made to Garrett Whiting the week before he died. Afraid you can't help me."

"Well, you're wrong there. Marty's the one can't help you. I called the doc. Marty wasn't even in the office. He was out with the shingles for better than two weeks."

The little thrill of excitement I'd felt a few minutes before disappeared. Still, I didn't give up completely. Marty couldn't tell me anything more about Garrett, but maybe Ivah could.

"Did you call about his life insurance policy? Did Garrett want to change it? Did he ask about the suicide clause or anything?"

"No, nothin' like that. That little girl of his got herself in a pickle with a fender bender she had up to Eau Claire last 4th of July. She tried to take care of it under the table, because she already had one claim from a deer accident over to Michigan last winter. Then Mr. Shyster that she hit changes his mind, starts talkin' whiplash and disability, and I got nothin' on the accident. I must've called her five times. Never returned a message. Finally, I calls the doc. He was pretty unhappy, I can tell you that. And Lady Isabel, she wasn't too pleased either that I called her dad. Came in not long after her dad died, cancelled her insurance, took her business elsewhere. Suit yourself, I told her."

So, that's all it was. A stupid parking lot accident and a guy who tried to take advantage of Isabel's fear of rising insurance rates. Sometimes a cigar is just a cigar, and a phone call is just a phone call. One of the hard lessons of investigative journalism.

At least Ivah had been working all the time she was talking, and now she pushed some papers over to Miguel to sign. "Well, there you go Mr. Mini Cooper. Here's your proof of insurance. Put that in your fancy car. And you drive safe this time, or I'll have to get in there and give you a lesson one day."

"*Gracias*, Ivah. You can teach me any time. You'll look *muy bonita* riding in my convertible with a yellow scarf to match my yellow car."

"Cheeky!" Ivah said, but she flushed with pleasure. "I could teach you a thing or two, I can tell you that."

———

"Do you like it, *chica*?"

I held a very sparkly, and what I suspected would be rather clingy, gold top in my hands, which I'd lifted from the beribboned box Miguel handed me as we sat on the couch at my house.

"Um. Wow. It's really, really shiny. And pretty. Yes. So pretty." I felt now exactly as my mother must have felt when I presented her with a birthday gift of the world's biggest, shiniest fake diamond earrings and matching necklace. Torn between horror at the gaudiness of the gift and a rush of intense affection for the giver who was so excited to present it.

"It's for my party tomorrow night. Remember, it's all about the sparkle. When I looked in your closet, *chica*, no, not happening. So, I bought you this. You can wear your Amish black pants with it, so you won't feel so nervous. But you will look so hot! You love it, yes?"

"I love you for giving it to me, Miguel. It's amazing. I don't have words."

"You don't have to be nice. I know it's outside your 'comfort zone.' But you're way too comfortable there. You got to break free. You got to move, move, move. You got to groove, groove, groove." He grabbed my hand, pulled me off the couch, and started doing exaggerated dance moves with me around the room. Until finally we were out of breath from dancing— and laughing.

"Oh, *chico*, you got the wrong Nash here!" I said, as we flopped down on the couch.

"No, you just have to learn to let it go."

"No, don't even—" But it was too late. He had already launched into a spirited rendition of Elsa's theme song.

Which I have to admit I joined in. Despite my voice deficiencies, I got the music in me—and my mother's propensity for bursting into song at a moment's notice.

"All right, all right. I'm going to your party. I'm wearing this very outside-the-box sparkly top. Are you happy now?"

"Well, if you promise to find a nice pair of gold high-heeled sandals, put a little makeup on those fantastic hazel *ojos*, don't pull your hair back in the clip like that, and come to my party happy, I will be *exstático*."

"I give up. All right. I'll dress up like your life-size Barbie doll, but only because I'm so happy everything went so well for your uncle and aunt, and because I'm really glad you're back," I said, giving him a hug. And it was true. I felt more light-hearted than I had in weeks. Miguel has that effect on me.

"Me too, *chica*. But I better bounce. Need to check in at the office, and then I've got lots of things to do for my party tomorrow. Now, *recúerdate*! Remember what you promised."

37

I RANG THE DOORBELL, shivering slightly in my skimpy gold top, black pants, and gold high-heeled sandals, purloined from my mother's closet. My hair had been cut and styled at Making Waves. It hung in a silky, shiny, coppery-brown curtain that swung out like a shampoo commercial when I tossed my head. Too bad there wouldn't be many reasons to whip my head from side to side at the party. I'd taken extra pains that night to do Miguel's faith in me justice, and I was pretty happy with the results. I'd never be a cute little curvy thing like Sherry, or a willowy, icy blonde like Rebecca, but for a sturdy upper Midwestern chick, I looked pretty good.

"*Chica!*" Miguel threw open the door and pulled me inside, taking my coat from me and hanging it in the closet with one fluid motion. He wore black trousers and a black and white striped shirt with silver cufflinks that had a glittery stone in the center. His dark hair was artfully messy, and his eyes shone with the excitement of one of his favorite things—hosting a party for a million people.

"You look amazing. But you're a touch subtle on the sparkle," I said.

"You know me, *chica*, I'm all about the subtle. *Además*, it's not good manners to outshine my guests." He gave me a smile with plenty of dazzle. "But you have just the right amount of shiny. You are on fleek! *Perfecto*." The doorbell rang again, and he touched me lightly on the arm as I drifted into the house.

A Christmas tree twinkling with white lights stood in Miguel's living room. Candles in glittery glass holders flickered on tables and window ledges, and the fireplace mantle was festooned with gold and silver garlands that shone and winked in the light. A long table laden with food held wine bottles that had been liberally rolled in glitter. The house shimmered with light and hummed with laughter and conversation. As always at a Miguel soiree there was an eclectic mix of young and old from all strata of Himmel society. Miller Caldwell stood in a corner holding a glass of punch and talking to Courtnee—with an understandably bemused expression on his face. Miguel's current boyfriend, Adam, was sitting at the piano next to Mary Beth Delaney, who with her husband Roger owned the funeral home.

Sherry had broken completely with her McClain's waitress uniform of tight white shirt and black pants and had draped herself on the arm of a chair to show off her charms in a tight red-sequined dress. Insurance agent Marty Angstrom appeared delighted with the effect, but from the way his wife Noreen was bearing down on them, it looked like Marty's enchanted evening would be short-lived. There were lots of other people I recognized, and some I knew by sight only, and many whom I had no idea who they were. Miguel has never met a man, woman, or child he didn't want to get to know better, and it appeared he'd invited all of them within a 50-mile radius tonight.

I said hello to various friends and acquaintances as I made my way to the kitchen in search of the Jameson that Miguel keeps in his cupboard for me. I felt I needed to be fortified with something stronger than punch before I ran into the two people I dreaded seeing, but who were sure to be there. Fortunately, I had a drink in my hand when I felt the presence of someone tall looming over my shoulder.

I turned with a forced smile to say a civil hello to Coop and Rebecca. Instead, I felt a genuine grin spread across my face. "Nick! I didn't know you were coming!" I'd never been happier to see him, and if he was taken aback by the quick hug I gave him, he didn't hesitate to return it.

"I almost didn't. Miguel invited me a couple of weeks ago, but I've got an exam to finish writing for the class I'm doing at Himmel Tech and final papers to grade for my regular classes at Robley. But there are only so many freshman term papers you can read before your red pen starts to drip blood."

"Grab a drink and a plate of something. I'll find someplace for us to sit. Looks like there's a vacancy coming up on the corner of the couch and the chair next to it." Suddenly the night looked a little more fun, and I was actually enjoying the jazzy version of "Walkin' In A Winter Wonderland" Adam was playing on the piano. And, really, who knew Mary Beth had such a strong alto?

But my happy Christmas glow was short-lived. The smell of Chanel Allure wafted toward me, and my worst fears were realized. Rebecca was just steps away. I looked a little wildly for Nick, but he was at the buffet loading up plates.

"Leah. How are you?" Rebecca was wearing a short ice blue dress with a shimmery shawl covering her bare shoulders. I stood up quickly, taking a slight lurch in my unaccustomed strappy sandals.

"Fine. You?"

"Busy. We're a little short-handed at the *Times*."

I looked for, but didn't detect, any sarcasm in her voice.

"I understand you're writing a piece on spec for the *Milwaukee Journal.*"

"Yes."

We stared at each other for a few seconds, neither having anything to say, and neither willing to cede any ground. Then Coop walked up behind Rebecca and put an arm around her shoulder. She looked up at him, but not without smiling the victor's smile at me first.

"Leah, hi. You look nice."

"Thanks. New do. You look pretty good yourself." Coop had made no concessions to 'the sparkle.' He wore a dark gray herringbone blazer that had Rebecca's fashion advice all over it, but his tie was one I gave him for Christmas a few years ago, so score one for me. Though I wasn't sure exactly what game she and I were playing.

I smiled with relief as Miguel came up and said "Rebecca! C'mon, you have to meet Chloe. She's the new marketing director at the hospital. You look *fabuloso!*" He hustled her away before she, or Coop, could say anything. But not before he winked in my direction.

"So, you here alone?"

"Nick is here. Somewhere." Of course, I hadn't come with Nick; I was just noting that he was there. Coop could infer whatever he liked. I looked around then, realizing Nick was taking an awfully long time to get a plate of food, then spotted him trapped in a doorway by Courtnee. From the confused look on his face as she rattled on, I assumed she was detailing her latest incognito celebrity sighting.

"Oh. Nice." He nodded and I smiled. I took a drink of my Jameson and wished it were a little stronger. This was agony. I wanted to talk normally to him, tell him what I'd found out about Bergman's plane from Grady, how I'd had to drive around town with Miguel in the freezing cold so he could show off his new convertible, discuss my mother's odd mood, and Paul's bizarre suspicion about why. All the regular things I'd say if things were like they had been. But they weren't. So, I didn't. Out of the corner of my eye I saw Nick break away from Courtnee and make his way over. Thank God.

"Nick, you remember Coop, don't you?"

"Absolutely. How are you?" he said, handing me the high-piled plate of food he'd carried over, then shaking Coop's hand.

"Good. I hear you're teaching at Himmel Tech this term."

"Almost done. Filling in for a friend. My day job is teaching psychology at Robley College."

"Good school." Coop nodded.

"Yes, I'm really enjoying it. Not as exciting as your job, but it has its moments."

"Well, you know. What's the saying? Police work is hours of boredom interrupted by moments of sheer terror."

"That sounds like academia, if you substitute complete despair for sheer terror." He smiled to show he was joking, and Coop chuckled to show he was polite.

Rebecca reappeared at that moment, and I introduced her to Nick. The four of us chatted in a stilted way for a few minutes. Then Nick and Rebecca discovered they had mutual friends at Grand Valley University, where Nick had taught before moving to Wisconsin.

"Yes, Ingrid and Erik Solberg are old friends. Ingrid and I met years ago in a fitness boxing class." *Of course they did*, I thought. Rebecca likes fitness training almost as much as she likes destroying newspapers, and I had to admit that her long, lean, strong body showed it. How could such a physically perfect human being have such a corroded soul? Somewhere there had to be a Dorian Gray-style portrait of her shriveling its way to monstrous deformity.

She was droning on about visiting her friends in Michigan every year and yada yada, and I tried to catch Coop's eye for a subtle raised eyebrow, then caught myself and remembered that he saw her very differently than I did. In fact, he seemed to find her inane conversation fascinating. I did not. I was getting ready to break free with a trip to the secret Jameson cupboard for a refill when she touched Coop's arm and said, "I really hate to do this, but I'm getting a massive headache. I need to get home and get my medication before it turns into a full-blown migraine."

He jumped up, and they were on their way with a quick goodbye.

"Nick, what's your professional opinion? Is Rebecca a narcissistic sociopath?"

He laughed. "It's a little hard to make a diagnosis after five minutes of party conversation. Although after 30 seconds with Courtnee, my professional opinion is that she's deranged. She was telling me some story about seeing Johnny Depp at the county park."

I shrugged. "Courtnee's hobby is seeing celebrities who aren't there. I'm pretty sure she's certifiable, but mostly we just ignore it. So, Rebecca was on her best behavior tonight, very charming to you, very civil to me. You fell under her spell, right?"

"How about we stop trying to analyze your former boss, and let's go over to the piano and see if Adam knows 'Last Christmas.' "

"Hey, you remembered. My favorite holiday guilty listening pleasure." We circulated for the next couple of hours. Nick met a lot of the people I knew, and sat in Miguel's new car, and took over the piano from Adam, and was very engaging and a lot of fun.

"*Chica,* he's pretty good for second prize," Miguel whispered in my ear, as Nick played "All I Want for Christmas is You."

"Who's first?"

"You know. But Coop, he's got it bad for Rebecca."

"For the millionth time, I don't want Coop for my boyfriend. I just want him back for my friend."

"Then go after Nick. Make him your own. Again."

"It's complicated."

"No. It's easy. You're complicated."

Around midnight people started leaving. I asked Nick if he'd like to come to the house for a cup of coffee.

"I'm not sure I'm up for Carol's disapproving glare."

"She won't be there. She's in Michigan visiting Aunt Nancy."

I could tell by his expression he was trying to determine if this was just a friendly invitation to coffee talk, or something more. I wasn't sure enough myself to help him with the answer.

Just as he started to say yes, I heard the familiar chirp of a text.

Got some information for you. Meet me at ice rink warming house. 12:30.

A phone number I didn't recognize. But the message I was waiting for. Cole. It had to be. Nadine must have come through after all.

"I'm sorry. That was Isabel. She really needs to talk. I have to go see her."

"So late?"

"She's in a really bad place right now. Rain check?"

He looked disappointed but said, "Sure, no problem. Hey, there's a faculty end-of-term party next Friday night. Want to go?"

"Yeah, maybe. Look, I better get going; I'll text you later."

38

I FELT A LITTLE BAD about lying to Nick, but he might have wanted to come, which just wouldn't fly with Cole, I knew. I didn't have time to go home and change, so I headed straight to the park.

The ice rink in Founders Park hadn't opened for the season yet. But I knew the warming house was good to go. A few weeks earlier I shot pictures of the city crew moving park benches inside to serve as winter seating and stacking up the firewood for the large open fireplace.

Once we had multiple consecutive days below freezing, the rink would be ready for future figure skaters and hockey stars who would be on the ice every weekend. When their toes were frozen and their fingers numb, they'd head for a break inside the old wooden building, jostling for a place nearest the warmth of the fireplace. The concrete floor would ring with the sound of ice skate blades, and the big room would smell of wet mittens, sweat, hot chocolate, and coffee—the sound and smell of many a childhood weekend for me.

Tonight, however, the park was deserted and the warming house, contrary to its name, was freezing and dark. I checked my watch and saw I had another 10 minutes to wait. I paced around in front of the building, but the icy gusts of wind penetrated even my heavy wool coat, and I was losing feeling in my feet. I cursed Miguel for talking me into the flimsy, fanciful gold party shoes. I tried the heavy wooden door of the building, expecting it to be locked, but it swung inward noiselessly.

I lit the way to a bench near the fireplace with the flashlight on my phone. I turned off the light to avoid draining the battery. Then I sat down, brought my legs up on the bench and pulled my coat down over them. I wrapped my arms around my knees, then rested my chin on them in a futile attempt to encase the little body heat I had left.

I hoped what Cole had to share would be worth it. Had he decided Bergman and his "associates" were too dangerous to deal with? Was he getting out? Did he know something about Garrett's murder—or Jamie's? Could he place Bergman at the scene for either one? What would he want in exchange for telling me? There always had to be something in it for Cole. Unless there was an altruistic side to his nature that had never surfaced before. Then again, he hadn't outed me to Bergman in the parking lot, and he'd warned me about him. Sort of.

The wind had picked up speed outside, and overhead the bare branches of trees scraped the metal roof of the building. I thought I heard a car door slam. I got up and opened the door, peering into the darkness, ready to call to him that I was inside. There was only blackness and the wail of the wind.

I walked back to my bench and huddled up again. I looked at my watch. 12:35. I hoped Cole wasn't going to stand me up. I leaned against the wooden slats of the bench and closed my eyes. It was so cold. My eyelids fluttered. I tried to keep them open, but it was as if a gentle hand was pressing them shut. I nodded off, until my chin dropped and I woke with a start. I shook myself, changed position, and looked at my watch. 12:45. Five more minutes and I was out of there. I yawned. My eyelids drooped.

Pain from a sharp blow on my upper arm jolted me awake. My head jerked up and my eyes flew open.

"Mind your own business, bitch!" The raspy whisper from behind a ski mask was hard to understand, but the bat the dark figure held aloft made the message perfectly clear.

I rolled to the right and scrambled under the bench. The bat hit the wooden slats with a cracking sound. I curled into a fetal position under the bench. The bat came down again and slammed in frustration the wooden seat I'd just vacated.

Before he could turn the bench over, I kicked out as hard as I could with my left leg, the sharp spike of my heel making contact with bone and flesh. I felt the heel of my shoe give way. The bat dropped to the floor as my assailant groaned and stumbled back. Still under the bench, I rolled onto my back, pressed both hands palm side up on the slats and pushed as hard as I could. The bench tipped on its side and I scooted out from underneath. I kicked off both shoes and ran to the door without looking behind me, focused on getting through the door and away. I pounded down the concrete sidewalk in my bare feet, my coat swinging out behind me.

I ran flat out, and I could hear footsteps close behind me. I did then what Satchel Paige counseled so wisely against. I looked back and saw the dark figure right at my heels. I tripped over my own terror as much as over the uneven sidewalk beneath me. I desperately tried to stay upright, but I'd lost my equilibrium. I felt a thump on my mid back as the tip of the bat made contact. It wasn't a hard blow, but enough to throw me completely off-balance. I hit the ground and curled into a ball, covered my head with my hands, and yelled as loud as I could. I braced for the next blow. Instead I heard a voice.

"Hey! What's goin' on there? You! Stop right there!"

The bat clattered to the ground and landed several yards from me as my attacker sprinted away, shin injury notwithstanding.

"Stop, police!"

Sweeter words were never shouted. I tried to sit up, but the pain in my left arm was so intense I settled for rolling onto my back to get my bearings.

"Stop! Oh, shoot."

Wait a minute. Shouldn't that be "Stop, or I'll shoot"? Not "Stop, oh shoot"?

I gritted my teeth as I struggled to a sitting position. My rescuer rushed to my side and slipped an arm around my waist to help me stand. I leaned for support into his very round, but surprisingly firm, belly. When I was fully upright, I looked into the eyes of my guardian angel. Dale Darmody.

"Holy smokes, Leah. Who was that?"

I managed to persuade him not to call my mother, but he insisted on taking me to the hospital despite my protests that I would be fine. There I was subjected to poking, prodding, and a few admiring whistles—not at me, but at the size, swelling, and deep red hue of the bruise that was engulfing my left bicep. After my doctor, a sharp-featured man with bright black eyes, looked at my x-rays, he pronounced me free of broken bones.

"You've got a severe contusion of the bicep. A pretty impressive one, but that's all. Your thick wool coat probably saved you from worse. You're a very lucky woman. Ice your arm and rest it at least 48 hours. Expect it to be pretty sore. You can take some ibuprofen for the pain. See your family doctor if it doesn't start to feel better in a few days."

Darmody was in the waiting area when I came padding out in a pair of thick hospital socks with rubber grippers on the bottom. My shoes—my mother's shoes, that is—were back at the park.

"What are you still doing here? I thought we finished my statement?"

"Well, ya can't go home alone. I called the Father and I'm just waitin' 'til he gets here."

"What? You woke him up in the middle of the night? Darmody, come on. I told you I was fine."

"You told me not to call your mother, and I didn't, but you shouldn't go home alone tonight. I know half the town was at Miguel's party and are probably three sheets to the wind. So, I called the *padre*. He'll be here in five minutes."

I pulled my "sparkle" top as high up as the low neckline would go.

"It's too late to argue then, I guess. Maybe he'll run me to the park to get my car."

"Nope. The doc said you're supposed to rest. We'll get it back to you tomorrow."

"Just because you're my hero doesn't mean you can boss me around," I said. "You know, you really did save me tonight. Now, tell me how you happened to be there just when I needed you."

"It's my prostrate. I tried that pill that's supposed to make you not have to pee all the time, but it's not workin' for me. I was patrolling the road around the park. It was quiet tonight and I was just heading out, when bang. I hadda go. You know, it just hits a man and you can't wait. It's a terrible feelin,' I'm tellin' you, Leah—"

"No, that's OK. You don't have to tell me that part. Just what happened after."

"Well, I parked the car and I found a place to pee, an' I was just zippin' when I heard you—well, I didn't know it was you—but I heard hollering over by the warming house. I takes off and I see this guy standin' over somebody on the ground, gettin' ready to swing a bat or a pipe or somethin'. I shouted, and he dropped it and took off. I knew I wouldn't catch him, and I hadda see how you were. I shoulda got him, though."

"Darmody, you did great." Words I never expected to hear myself utter. But there'd been a lot of unexpected things happening lately.

"I wish I woulda at least seen his face, but it was dark and he was all in black, and he never turned around. Just ran. I'm gonna hear from the lieutenant about this. Maybe I should sign up for that fitness class Angela wants us to take."

"I can't describe him either, and I was a lot closer than you were. He had a ski mask covering his face, just eyeholes and a mouth. And his hoodie pulled down over his head. I told you, I'm pretty sure it was someone Bergman sent. I went because I thought it was Cole, but this kind of thing, that's not him. Lying, stealing, scamming, conning, yes. Violence, no. Besides, Cole's got a thicker, squattier body. This person was lean, trim. With a really good swing."

Out of the corner of my eye, I caught sight of Father Lindstrom, his fluff of white hair more tousled than usual, hurrying toward us.

"Leah! Are you all right?"

"Yes, Father. I'm so sorry you got called out in the middle of the night. I'm fine."

"Nonsense." He turned to Darmody. "Dale, thank you for calling me. What a fine, brave thing you did tonight. Leah is blessed that you were there."

Darmody's grin was priceless.

"Awww, Father. Just doin' my job. Protect and serve. It was a pretty dangerous situation there though. I had to use all of my trainin' and—" He launched into a retelling of the night's events, this time with a few more flourishes. I sensed that a legend was being born. Darmody would repeat the story many times, but however he might exaggerate and embellish, there was a core truth I wouldn't forget. Darmody had been there when I needed him.

Father Lindstrom listened, nodding, and expressing appropriate levels of admiration, all the while skillfully helping me maneuver into my coat and gently moving Darmody toward the door. When we reached the parking lot, I thanked him again and gratefully got into Father Lindstrom's car.

39

"LEAH, THIS IS VERY DISTURBING. Who would do this to you?" Once inside the house, I shuffled off to my room to put on my pajamas, robe, and a pair of fuzzy slippers to warm up my freezing feet. I stopped in the bathroom to wipe the remains of my party self off my face. When I got to the living room, Father Lindstrom had made me a cup of tea and one for himself. As I took a sip, I realized he'd laced it with whiskey and honey. I love him.

"I think it was someone Hal Bergman sicced onto me, because he's afraid I'm going to prove he had something to do with Jamie Whiting's death. And Garrett's, too."

"Dr. Bergman?"

I liked so much how he asked me with normal surprise, instead of with the kind of patronizing disbelief I'd been getting from everyone else. I gave him a brief summary of why I suspected Bergman. I didn't say anything about Coop and his DEA task force.

"Despite what Miller saw, I don't think Frankie Saxon killed Garrett or Jamie. I think both deaths are connected to Bergman, and both probably have to do with his drug activities. And I kind of let him know that when I saw him the other day. And he wasn't very happy. By the way, you know I'm not working at the paper any more, right?"

"Yes, I heard that from your mother. But Leah, I'm very concerned. If you're correct, you've crossed a very dangerous man. And even if your theory about Dr. Bergman is wrong, you've alarmed someone who is intent on inflicting serious harm on you. Or worse."

"No, see, Father, that goon who came after me tonight wasn't supposed to kill me. He was supposed to scare me. Mission accomplished, by the way. But if he'd really wanted to do me in, he could have. He had a bat, I had nothing. But I got away with a sore—really sore—arm. Bergman wants me to back off. Which proves I'm on to something."

He was shaking his head. "Leah, I understand and applaud your desire to help Frankie. I believe in her innocence, too. But she wouldn't want you to sacrifice yourself to clear her name."

"No, that's just it. I don't have to. Bergman isn't as smart as he thinks he is. By trying to scare me off, he just brought the kind of attention he doesn't want from the Himmel Police Department. They're going to investigate, and they're going to find a connection to him. And then they're going to ask why he wanted to hurt me."

He still looked worried.

"I'm fine. And I'm sure Darmody will drive by here a few times before his shift ends. Nothing more is going to happen. Definitely not tonight. Now, please, promise that you won't call Mom. She'll just freak out and come home, and frankly, I'm not sure I'm ready to deal with that drama right now. Something's going on with her and Paul and I think she could use the breather—without worrying about me. She'll be home next week, and I'll tell all then. Right now, I could use about 10 hours of sleep. And you've got early Mass in just a few hours."

For added leverage, I made a quick sign of the cross and said, "Bless me, Father, for I have sinned. You just heard my confession, so you can't say anything."

"That isn't exactly how it works, Leah, as I know you're aware. But all right. I'll leave you to get to bed. And I'll promise not to call your mother, if you promise to call Coop and get his advice on this."

"Yeah, OK, I'll call him. Tomorrow."

I crawled into bed, pulled up the comforter, and didn't move until almost noon. When I did, my arm was seriously hurting, so I took some ibuprofen, took a shower, left my hair to dry on its own, and sat down with coffee and toast.

I put off calling Coop despite my promise, because I was sure he'd have heard by now and would be calling or stopping by to check up on me. But the day stretched on, and there was no call or text.

My arm hurt. Bad. Coop must know what happened. He'd have seen the reports, and Darmody definitely would have told him. Apparently, he didn't care if my arm had to be amputated, which at the moment, that's what it felt like it was telling me. *"Leah, arm speaking here. I'm too far gone. Can't make it. Cut your losses. Goodbye."*

I got up and put some ice in a baggie and dutifully applied it to my bruise, which by the size and color really did deserve the name "contusion," instead of plain old bruise.

I got my phone and called JT's on the off-chance Cole might be there. He wasn't. I got Nadine instead. "I told you, I don't know when he's comin' back to work. I put your message on the desk. If he wants to call ya, he will."

I texted Miguel, and he didn't answer. I texted Nick.

Want to come over?

Sorry, papers to grade. Tomorrow?

Sure.

I'll bring pizza.

I didn't relish telling Nick that I'd lied to him about the text I'd received at the party, but it seemed that would be better coming in person. I did the ice thing again. At least when my arm was frozen, it wasn't throbbing. The color had changed from angry red to a rather pretty deep indigo shade. I flexed it experimentally, then stopped. Too soon.

Why didn't Coop call? Or come over? Or text me? Or why didn't Miguel? Maybe he was still cleaning up from the party. Maybe Coop and Rebecca and Miguel were off having brunch together, while I was alone and crippled with pain, a possible target of a drug lord. I texted Miguel. No answer.

I turned on the television and landed in the middle of a rerun of *Pirates of the Caribbean*, watched 'til there was a run of commercials, then turned it off. Finally, I went to my room and pulled out my notebook and worked on my Bergman theory.

Garrett's murder

- Motive—selling drugs, exposure, bosses higher up want Garrett shut up
- Means—easy for him to get Klonopin, easy to arrange meeting with Garrett
- Opportunity—he could use his plane to get back and forth to Himmel in plenty of time

Jamie's murder

- Motive—Jamie knew about his prescription business and was trying to blackmail him, or
- Jamie had discovered that Bergman killed his father and wanted to blackmail him, or
- Jamie killed his father in partnership w/Bergman, then got cold feet
- Means—crude but effective, a rock to the head. No weapon to dispose of, nothing special required
- Opportunity—that was still a question

I knew he was in town; I saw him at JT's that night. But Jamie was dead by then. Where had Bergman been in the afternoon? Was that what Cole and Bergman were arguing about? Had Bergman told Cole he'd had to get rid of Jamie? Was that why Cole warned me off?

I had to find Cole. He knew what Bergman had been up to. Maybe that's why he was making himself scarce. He was hiding out. Or something had happened to him. I texted Coop again. No response. I almost called Rebecca, but I couldn't quite bring myself to do that.

I wished Nick had been able to come. Maybe I should have told him about my close encounter with a baseball bat last night. Then, the doorbell rang. "Who Are You?" was the current tune my mother had set up. I opened it and Isabel immediately stepped inside and wrapped me in a hug that left me howling with pain. She was a deceptively strong girl.

"Owww!"

"Oh, I'm so sorry. How stupid of me. I just heard about what happened."

The jungle drums were beating then. "From whom?"

"I stopped for coffee at JT's, and a couple of people were talking about you."

"Who?"

"I don't know, I just overhead 'Leah Nash' and 'beating.' What happened?"

"Bergman happened. Come on, we don't have to stand in the doorway. Would you like tea or coffee?"

"Let me make it. You sit down and tell me everything."

When I finished, she was sitting across from me, her eyes wide and troubled, her own coffee untouched.

"You think Dr. Bergman beat you up with a baseball bat?"

"Not Bergman himself. The person wasn't tall enough, and besides, he wouldn't run the risk himself. He's warning me to back off. Nothing else makes sense."

"I don't know, Leah. The police have evidence against Frankie. No one even brought Dr. Bergman's name up, except you."

"All right, then listen to my evidence." I outlined how and why Bergman could have killed her father.

"I guess it's maybe possible. And if he was in town like you said, I suppose he *could* have killed Jamie as well. But Miller Caldwell actually saw Frankie at the house the night my father died. And Detective Ross said that Jamie called Frankie from the park the afternoon he was killed. There isn't any witness to what you say Dr. Bergman did, nothing that really links him."

"Then why did he have me attacked last night? No, Isabel, I know I'm right. I—wait a minute." I grabbed my phone and punched in Courtnee's number.

"Leah! I heard you were in a coma. Everybody's saying you got airlifted to the hospital in Milwaukee. My mom said Marge Leary saw you at the E.R., and you were barely conscious. Are you calling from Milwaukee?"

"Yes, Courtnee. I was in a coma, and the first person I wanted to talk to when I woke up was you."

"Really?"

"No, Courtnee. I wasn't in a coma; I got hit on the arm by some thug with a baseball bat, but I'm all right. I'm at home. Courtnee, Nick said he talked to you at the party last night—"

"He's pretty hot, Leah. I think you should try to get him back. I told him how Ben dumped you, and then Rebecca stole Coop, and really, you'd probably be a lot nicer if you had a boyfriend. My mom says—"

"Courtnee, did you tell Nick you saw Johnny Depp at the county park last Saturday?"

"Why are you asking? So you can tell me how I didn't? He was driving a black Mercedes. Isn't that the kind of car a movie star drives? Yes, it is."

"Did you see him actually in the park?"

"Almost."

God help me, please.

"What do you mean almost?"

"Well, I was driving by on my way to my friend Shawna's. She lives out on River Road. And anyway, I looked over and I saw Johnny Depp, just sitting in his Mercedes on the side of the road, talking on his phone! If I didn't have to get to Shawna's with her emergency hair color kit—she always wants to be blonde like me, but I tell her 'Shawna, mine is natural. You have to pay big money to get this; you can't just do it yourself.' But no, she never listens and this time, her hair turned kind of green. I mean not cute-on-purpose green, I mean hair-falling-out-pea-green. So obvs, I had to get there to help. She's just kind of basic, but she is my bestie, so you know—"

I had tried to interrupt the flow several times to no avail. Finally, I shouted, "What time was this?"

"I don't know. Like, 3:30, maybe. Or maybe earlier. Or later."

"OK. Bye, Courtnee."

"But—" Whatever she wanted to say was lost in the ether.

Isabel was looking very confused, as well she might. "Johnny Depp?"

"Courtnee is the Haley Joel Osment of celebrity sightings. She sees famous people, all the time. Only they're always just regular people, who may or may not bear a resemblance to the actor or singer or TV star she's sure they are."

"And so?"

"So, who does Bergman look like? Johnny Depp. I noticed it the first time I met him. Courtnee didn't see Johnny Depp by the side of the road; she saw Dr. Bergman. And that puts him at the park at the same time Jamie was."

She put her hands up on either side of her face and held her head with her eyes closed for a second. "Leah, I don't know. I just can't handle this. I want it to be over. And that's not much to go on. I don't think that will convince anyone."

I was about to say that maybe the DEA task force had Bergman under surveillance because of the drug operation. If so, that might put him at the park. I stopped myself in time.

"I know Courtnee's not a good witness, but it's a start. Maybe I can dig up someone else, or probe into that scary brain of hers and get something more. I could start looking for people who saw shiny black cars at the county park. I'm not sure what I'm going to do. I have to think some more."

After Isabel left, I did sit down for some serious brain exercise.

Realistically, unless our relationship took an upturn, Coop probably wouldn't be sharing anything about Bergman's whereabouts with me. If he even could. Maybe I could go to Frankie's lawyer, Jim Gilroy. He didn't have to prove she wasn't guilty; he just had to prove there was reasonable doubt. And putting Bergman in the mix could give him something to go on. Though, he'd still probably advise Frankie to plead out instead of go to trial. Maybe I could convince Frankie to get a different lawyer.

I started feeling tired, even though I'd done basically nothing all day. I lay down on the couch and promptly fell asleep. When I woke up, the house was in darkness. I was disoriented, unsure if it was night or day, uncertain even where I was. As I rolled over on my left side to get up, the sharp pang in my arm brought it all back to me. What time was it? I stumbled over to the lamp and turned it on, then looked at my watch. 7:30 p.m. Now that was an epic nap. I downed two ibuprofen, then my phone rang. I was tempted to let it go to voicemail, but knew I'd have to deal with it sooner or later.

"Hi, Mom."

"Leah, are you OK? I just heard—"

"Yes, I'm fine. No serious damage."

"No damage? You're beaten up in an alley by a gang of thugs, and you expect me to believe there's no damage?"

"That's not what happened, Mom."

"Well, I wouldn't know that, would I? Because I had to hear about it from Courtnee's mother. What is going on?"

"It's fine. Just listen." I ran through an abbreviated version of what had happened, and why I didn't think anything else would be forthcoming from Bergman. She wasn't totally convinced, but I sensed she was wavering.

"What does Coop say?"

"I haven't actually had a chance to talk to him about it yet."

"He hasn't been over to see how you're doing?"

"He's all wrapped up in something at work. I'm sure Darmody filled him in and he knows I'm fine." I hoped that was true, but it bothered me a lot that he hadn't answered my texts. But I didn't want to hear my mother tell me I brought it on myself by not falling all over his new girlfriend, so I changed the subject.

"So, I talked to Paul a couple of days ago. Mom, he thinks you're having an affair."

"What?" She sounded completely mystified.

"Yeah. He's worried. Says you've been avoiding him, making up reasons to not go out with him, and then when you took off this week, he was really upset."

"I don't want to talk about this right now, and Paul shouldn't have involved you."

"Mom, you're not sick or something, are you?"

"Leah, why are you asking me that?"

"Well, I know you'd never have an affair. But I know something's been on your mind, and I—"

"And so you thought I had some deadly illness and was trying to spare you? No. I'm perfectly healthy. Don't worry about it. I'll talk to Paul when I get back. But, please, don't get involved."

"I'm not planning to."

We chatted a little about Aunt Nancy and some of the cousins, and I reassured her a few more times, and then I wound things down. "OK, Mom, see you soon. Have fun. I love you."

"I love you, too."

It's a good thing, I thought sourly. Because apparently no one else did. No word from Miguel, nothing from Coop. Nick was too busy. Fine. I was perfectly capable of taking care of myself. I cued up the "sad bastard" playlist on my iPod, so-named by Miguel because it's a set of mostly melancholy tunes. Then, I sat back with a bag of potato chips. After an hour or so, and multiple checks to make sure I hadn't somehow not heard the phone ring or a text come in, I tottered off to bed with an icepack to soothe my throbbing arm and an aggrieved sense of self-pity.

40

In my dream, someone was leaning in very close to me. All I could see was a mouth that kept saying "Who? Who? Who?" in a sharp staccato demand. It was a minute before I realized that the front doorbell was being hit repeatedly, resulting in an extremely jerky rendition of the ringtone of the week, "Who Are You?," which had invaded my sleep.

As soon as I opened the door, Miguel burst in.

"What time is it?"

"*Chica*! You'll never guess! *Qué emocionante*! Amazing! Everything, all over. The big papers, the television news, radio, everything! A big drug bust!"

Belatedly, he took in my bedraggled appearance, the soggy icepack that in my stupor I'd clutched in my hand, and the incomprehension on my sleep-drugged face.

"Oh, your arm! Come on, come on, let's go sit down." He gently steered me to the kitchen where he put on coffee and put the loaf of bread he'd been carrying on the counter.

"*Chica*, oh, *lo siento*. I didn't forget you, but Rebecca, she was on fire yesterday. We were running like crazy all day. And Darmody, he told me you were OK, just had to rest. Oh, *perdóname*. I brought you ciabatta bread from Argento's. Your favorite. I'll slice some and make you toast. Forgive me?" The stricken look on his face as he handed me coffee was comic.

"Hey, I'm all right. I'm not so needy I can't go without daily contact. I figured you must be busy. I just didn't know on what. Sounds like a killer day. Put the knife down; don't bother with the toast. I'm not awake enough to be hungry yet." I smiled, even as I felt guilty for my doubts about Coop and Miguel. No wonder I hadn't heard from either one of them.

He still looked unsure.

"It's OK. Really. I'm fine. But could you tell me at less than warp speed exactly what's been going on?"

Reassured, he immediately jumped back up from the table—apparently to ensure he had sufficient scope to wave his arms and bounce around the room as he told his story. His expressive eyes shone with excitement.

"Imagine, *chica*. A DEA Task Force, with Coop, sheriff deputies, *policía* from other counties, federal agents! They took down a big prescription drug ring. Huge. *Enorme!*" He spread his arms to indicate the humongous size of the operation.

"It started early yesterday. Raids on houses, pharmacies, even people in church. At the same time, bam, bam, bam, people getting scooped up in Milwaukee, too."

"So, is that where the drug ring was headquartered?"

"*Sí.* The big drug *jefe* was there. He had all these *chicos malos*, really bad guys, selling all over in the rural counties. They can make, like, $50,000 on one prescription pad, a DEA agent told me."

"So, were they selling the drugs or just the prescriptions?"

"Both. Some recruit people to fill the fake prescriptions so they can get the product to sell. Some sell the prescription sheets or the pads. It was a big enterprise, *chica*, lots of layers and lots of players. All over south central Wisconsin and east to Milwaukee."

"Wow, that's a big story for the *Times* to get a piece of."

"I know! Everybody rolling out, bringing in suspects, booking, interviewing. So exciting. I was running around trying to get the pictures, the interviews, send tweets for the paper, it was intense." I could see that he'd loved it. Any reporter would.

"Was there was a lot of press there?"

"Yes! It was so big. But I was the *primero*. The first! But there was the TV and online and the radio, and a reporter from Omico and Hailwell. Oh, also, Dr. Bergman, he was arrested!"

"Maybe now that he's in custody, and I've had the crap beaten out of me, Coop will take what I've found seriously."

"*Chica*, you said you were fine. Did you get more hurt than your arm?" He looked at me with such concern, I felt bad.

"OK, well, not exactly the crap beat out of me. But look—" I pushed up the sleeve of my shirt and showed him the quite spectacular blue and green bruise covering my bicep.

"*Ay mierde!*"

"Yes. But it's getting better." Which, I realized, was true. "Hey, what about Cole Granger, did he get rounded up, too?"

"No, he didn't."

"He must've skipped town before everything went down, then."

"*Chica*, I'm sorry. I have to get in to work. I already posted some video on the web, but Rebecca, she—"

"I know. Go. Go! I'll see you tomorrow."

"You're sure you're fine? When is Carol coming home?"

"Not until later this week. Honestly, I'm fine. Coop will probably stop by later, and Nick's bringing pizza for dinner."

Only Coop didn't come over later. Father Lindstrom did, and brought me a chai latte, and told me Frankie Saxon hadn't been able to make bail. It was set really high because of the charges. My mother called while he was there, and I put him on the phone to reassure her, which worked, and so that was one good thing. But then he left, and Coop still hadn't called or come over. I tried his cell, and he didn't answer. I called HPD and Melanie said he was in his office, but he couldn't be disturbed. I understood, sort of. A bust that big brings paperwork even bigger. But I really, really wanted to talk to him about Bergman.

Around 5 the doorbell rang. Nick with the pizza. I was so ready. I was in the laundry room doing a one-armed wrestle with the washing machine, so I stuck my head out and yelled, "Come on in, door's open. Get that pizza in here, please. I'm starving."

But when I walked down the hall to the kitchen, it was Coop I saw, not Nick.

"Hey! Congratulations on the drug bust. That's really great. I called a couple of times, but I guess you were pretty hung up with..." My voice gradually wound down as I finally registered the look on his face. It did not read *"So glad you're OK, sorry I wasn't here sooner."*

"What's the matter? Come on, let's sit in the living room."

He shook his head. "No, thanks. I won't be here long. Leah, why did you tell Darmody you thought Bergman was behind whoever took a swing at you in the park?"

"Because he was. Because he had to be. He knew I was on to him, that I knew he was a murderer."

"And how would he know that?" He didn't give me a chance to answer. "He'd only know that's what you thought if you disregarded everything I asked you not to do."

"Coop, I didn't try to talk to Bergman after you told me not to. I can't help it if I ran into him at Grady's. I went there to talk to Grady, to find out about planes. And, Coop, that's the thing. Bergman could have gotten back and forth from his convention in plenty of time to kill Garrett, because of his plane. I know the drug ring is a big deal. I know it's important. But Bergman killed two people, and Frankie Saxon is under arrest for crimes she didn't commit. Isn't that important too?"

He ignored what I'd said.

"I didn't come or call until now, because I was so angry I knew I couldn't be in the same room with you. Do you realize we had to pull the trigger before we were ready, because of you and your fixation on Bergman? You jeopardized an investigation that took us months to put together. Do you have any idea of the man hours, the expense, the danger that involved? For our team? For our CI's? Do you care how many kids have gotten hooked because of this drug ring? How many lives ruined? How many families shattered? You're damn lucky we were so close to shutting it down. Once I heard from Darmody, I knew we had to move or we'd lose Bergman, and maybe a lot more."

"Yes, of course I care! I told you, I didn't go after Bergman, he just showed up where I was. And you're not listening to me. He used his plane to get back and forth from the medical conference. His alibi is no good."

"Listen to me carefully." He spoke slowly, enunciating each syllable. "Bergman did not kill Garrett Whiting. Yes, he could have flown back and forth in his plane. But we know he didn't."

For the first time my confidence in Bergman's guilt wavered. "But Coop, Grady said pilots come and go day and night out there. Bergman's plane goes 200 mph. He could easily have flown to a private airport near Sioux Falls and flown back again the night he killed Garrett. I haven't checked it all out yet, I'll probably have to drive to Sioux Falls myself to talk to somebody—"

"Don't bother. Bergman didn't fly his plane anywhere. He was with a woman that night. Another doctor at the conference. Her husband was having her followed by a private investigator. Suspected she was cheating on him. She was. With Bergman. We've got time and date-stamped pictures of the two of them together. Plus the PI's testimony. There's no way Bergman killed Garrett."

My throat had gone dry, and I was finding it a little hard to breathe. "Then, maybe he got Jamie to do it. Bergman needed Garrett to be quiet about the prescription drugs. Jamie hated his father, and he could've been connected to Bergman through the drug ring. Then, the guilt got too much, he wanted to confess, and Bergman killed him. It's possible. I think Cole Granger knows something. You need to find him—"

"Cole is one of our confidential informants. He's been feeding us information on Bergman for months. That video you thought was so important, the one you kept badgering him about? I told him to give it to you. I hoped that would keep you busy and away from Bergman. But then Jamie died, and you were right back tramping all over our operation."

"Cole was your CI? But you said he was a conman, a liar, a—"

"What do you think a confidential informant is? Cole's ex-girlfriend worked in Bergman's office. Stole a pad. Bergman caught her. Instead of firing her, he wanted in. He and Cole were small timing it at first, just the two of them with Cole recruiting people to get the scrips filled and selling the product. Then, Bergman wanted more. Cole hooked him up with a big operation out of Milwaukee. Then, things got a little too big, a little too physical for Cole. He wanted out, but knew they wouldn't let him just walk away. He came to us. He gave us Bergman and a lot more.

"But because you always know everything, you're always right, you had to push ahead. He probably *was* behind your beat-down at the warming house. Maybe because he wanted to scare you into backing off, but more likely because you pissed him off. He's a bad guy, and he's a mean guy. He knew any poking around that you did could be trouble for him, especially if his bosses got wind of it. So, he decided to cut his losses and run. We picked him up at Grady's airfield yesterday morning. He almost got away."

"But that doesn't mean he didn't kill Jamie, or use Jamie to get to Garrett."

"Look, we got Bergman, we got his boss, we got dozens of his associates. The bad guys are in jail, and now it's up to Ross, and the sheriff, and Cliff Timmins to decide what happens to Frankie Saxon and their investigation. It's not my business, and it sure isn't yours."

"And you're OK with Frankie being charged with a crime I know she didn't commit."

"Oh, how do you 'know?' That famous 'reporter's instinct?' That sixth sense that makes you so infallible? Funny, it looks to me like you've chalked up a lot of mistakes on this investigation." His voice was scathing, and it evoked an equal measure of anger in me.

"Don't you dare talk to me like that. You've been so wrapped up in this DEA thing, you couldn't see anything else. And to prove you're so smart, and I'm so stupid, you're not going to lift a finger to help Frankie." He started to say something, but I rolled right over him.

"No, you listen to me for a minute. Maybe I did get some things wrong about Bergman, but I know that Frankie had nothing to do with Garrett's or Jamie's death. If it wasn't Bergman, I'm going to find out who it was. Don't be surprised if it turns out that he's in the mix somehow."

"You've always been bull-headed, but you are way beyond that now. Darmody said you got hit in the arm, not the head. I have to wonder. I'm sorry that you got hurt by one of Bergman's guys. And we'll do our best to get him for that. But Rebecca's right, you put your own damn self in his sights. You're all in for Frankie like you've been all in for Isabel all along. Why? Because you ran some Leah litmus test and decided she's telling the truth?"

"Rebecca's right?" I choked out the words.

"No, my turn."

I was so incensed I could hardly speak anyway, so I waited for him to finish.

"You won't admit that Isabel is using you to get what she wants, which is a murder verdict on her father, so she can collect the insurance. Rebecca saw it before I did. Isabel is always lying to you. She lied to you about her dad's illness, the insurance, Jamie's alibi, and who knows what else. She's a user, and you can't see it. OK, fine. That's your business. But you can't give me the same respect I'm giving you. I'm involved with someone you don't like, and it's always your way or no way. Not this time. Rebecca matters to me. If you can't accept that..."

"*Isabel's* a liar? At least she was trying to get justice for her father. What's your excuse for lying to me? Because Rebecca told you it wasn't time for me to know about your relationship? You wouldn't tell me jack about the DEA investigation. If you'd been honest, told me what you really had on Bergman instead of 'mansplaining' to me how stupid I was, and how I needed to just trust your superior judgment, maybe the takedown would have unfolded the way you planned. And if you would give half the credence to what I say that you give to your precious Rebecca, maybe an innocent woman wouldn't be charged with murder. You're willing to toss me into the trash can because Rebecca tells you to."

"Rebecca has never once told me what to do, or how to do it, or said anything mean or undermining about you. Unlike the way you talk about her. She's gone out of her way to take your feelings into consideration, she—"

"Please, you're making me physically ill. You are so besotted, you can't see that she's vicious, ruthless, self-centered, and manipulative. She's manipulating you right out of our friendship. No, wait, I'm giving her too much credit. She couldn't make you do that if you weren't willing." I finished, almost out of breath with the rush of angry words.

Coop stared at me for a minute. Then, in a voice that was so soft it was almost a whisper, he said, "Goodbye, Leah."

He turned and left. I just watched him walk out the door.

41

NICK ARRIVED about 15 minutes later. As soon as I opened the door, he said, "What's wrong?"

"Nothing's wrong. Why would anything be wrong?" Apparently my answer was not as bright and breezy as I'd tried to make it, because he set the pizza box down, put his hands on my shoulders, and leaned down a little so he could peer directly into my face. His touch was light, but my arm was sore and I gave an involuntary wince. He let go immediately.

"Leah? What's going on? What's the matter?"

"Oh, my arm's kinda sore. I got a little beat up the other day."

"What do you mean you 'got a little beat up'?" He was frowning, and I knew there was no way this explanation was going to go well. Might as well get it over with.

"You know that text I got at the party? The one from Isabel? Well, it wasn't from her. I lied, because I thought it was from Cole Granger to give me some information I need. And I thought you'd want to go with me or try to talk me out of it. So I, well, I just lied. I'm sorry."

I braced myself for my second verbal battering of the day. Oddly, it didn't come.

"My God, Leah, are you all right?"

"Mostly." I pulled up my sleeve and showed him. He gave a low whistle.

"It looks worse than it feels. Well, no, that's not true. It feels pretty bad, but it's getting better. They told me just to ice it and rest for a couple of days, so that's what I've been doing."

"How about this? I won't lay into you for lying to me, in exchange for you telling me everything you've been up to."

"Deal."

He took the pizza into the living room while I grabbed a couple of sodas from the fridge. Nick sat on the wingback chair, and I sat on the couch across from him. When we were settled, I launched into my story. I told him everything right up to and through the reaming out I'd just taken from Coop.

"So, now Coop has washed his hands of me. And he's never going to help me help Frankie. And I won't be able to get within a million miles of Bergman. And Ross is not about to listen to me, and the most I can do is talk to Frankie's lawyer, who is not what you'd call a strong advocate. And so, everything is worse than before I started. If I'd left it alone, everyone would have thought Garrett killed himself, Jamie might still be alive, and Frankie Saxon's life wouldn't be in ruins. So, that happened." I finished with what I'd intended as a bitter laugh, but it caught it my throat and sounded more like a sob.

"I'm sorry, Leah." Nick put his pizza down and came over and sat next to me on my good arm side. I didn't answer, because I was too busy blinking and sniffling, trying to keep from crying.

"Hey." He put a finger under my chin and lifted my face up. "You made some mistakes because you put yourself out there, you always do. That's not a bad thing. It's not always a good thing either, but it's who you are. You don't have to feel guilty about it."

I didn't say anything, just swallowed hard.

"You are so fearless. You just jump right in if you think it's the right thing to do. You fight for what you believe in, for yourself, and for other people as well."

"Don't stop. I'm liking this."

He shook his head. "I'm not joking. You're a good person, Leah. And you're smart and you're funny and—"

"Makes you wonder why you found Cherubim so attractive, doesn't it?"

But instead of responding in kind to my teasing, he said, "Yes. It does."

I quickly moved us back to the subject at hand. "Well, I'm not sure what I'm going to do to clean up the mess I made. If I could get to Cole Granger, I think he might be able to help. If he would. And I'll have to talk to Frankie and let her know maybe there's a little hope. I just don't trust her lawyer to do much with what I can give him."

"That's one of your problems, Leah. You don't trust anyone, not really. I understand why—you had a childhood trauma that still affects the way you see the world. I—"

"You know, I liked that other part of the conversation. You know, where I'm a good, smart person? I'm not up for a stroll through the darker recesses of my psyche. Why don't we talk about you? Tell me more about that paper you're presenting next spring. What's it called? 'Psychopaths Walk Among Us: The Rebecca Hartfield Story?' "

"Something like that. But you know, let's not. Let's watch a movie instead."

"OK. Here, you have the power. And that's not something I give up lightly," I said, handing him the TV remote. "Find something good on Netflix while I take care of our pizza leavings."

When I returned from the kitchen, we engaged in a short debate over what constituted "something good" on Netflix, but finally settled on *Love Actually*, a romantic comedy. I wondered if he remembered that we'd watched it on our first date. We'd walked out of a really awful movie and decided to go to his place to watch a DVD instead. I had been secretly impressed that he showed no embarrassment about owning what most people would call a "chick flick." It was a good night.

And, despite the terrible fight with Coop that had preceded it, so was this night. When the movie was over, I said, "Thanks, Nick. I feel much better than I did when you got here."

"Well, you know, Nick Gallagher's my name, mental health's my game."

"Nice. I'll get you a T-shirt with that on it."

"Please don't."

And then, because I didn't want to be alone, or I didn't want the evening to end, or maybe just because I remembered what it felt like to be crazy in love with him, I reached up and pulled his head down and kissed him.

I woke in the morning and took a cautious but satisfying stretch before opening my eyes. My sore arm still ached, but not nearly so bad. Extending my body from tip to toe felt good. I lay there in a pleasant stupor, gradually returning to full consciousness, eyes still closed. It was the sound of voices in the kitchen that made my eyelids pop open and caused me to leap out of bed. Memory came flooding back, helped along by the unfamiliar pair of shoes I tripped over as I scrambled into my robe and stumbled to the kitchen. But it was just as I feared and already too late.

Miguel and Nick sat at the kitchen table, laughing and eating scrambled eggs.

"*Chica! Buenos días.* I stopped to check on you on my way to work, but I can see everything is fine." His wide smile was innocent, but his eyes were alight with suppressed laughter.

Nick rose from the table and came to me, bending to plant a kiss on my cheek that I turned my head to avoid. He stepped back with a hurt look. I tried to cover the uncomfortable moment by making a major production out of pouring myself coffee and putting bread in the toaster, talking all the while.

"So, are you getting things under control at the paper? Rebecca settle down any? I saw Coop yesterday afternoon. Have you heard anything more about Frankie Saxon?"

Miguel's grin had faded, and he looked back and forth between Nick and me. Nick didn't say anything. Miguel stood, saying, "Oh, I forgot! I have to shoot a photo at the hospital this morning. Gotta go. Looking good, *chica*. *Gracias* for the coffee and eggs, Nick. See you later."

As the door closed behind him, I buttered my toast and took it and my coffee to the table, frantically trying to think of what to say to Nick, who deserved some kind of explanation for my ridiculous behavior.

"Nick." He was still standing in the middle of the kitchen, watching me.

"Nick," I tried again, "about last night. It was nice." The feel of his gentle hands on my back, the tenderness as he carefully—and athletically—avoided pressure on my sore arm flashed in my mind and mocked the inadequacy of the word "nice." I steeled myself and continued. "But it didn't mean anything."

Still, he said nothing. And the less he said, the wordier and stupider I got.

"I mean, of course it meant something. It's not like I go falling into bed with every good-looking psychologist I meet. And, well, I didn't 'meet' you. We were married, right? You're a different person now. Nick 2.0. The same great operating system, but with upgrades like sensitivity and honesty. And, seriously, where did you learn to do that thing with your tongue? No, never mind, what am I saying? I don't want to know that. But, uh, you see, yesterday I was just. You were so. And everyone else was—" I foundered on my own inarticulateness and petered to a halt, staring at my coffee to avoid looking at him.

"Leah, it's OK." He pulled up a chair next to me and tucked a lock of hair behind my ear. I turned to face him, my cheeks flushed with embarrassment, my whole self full of confusion and regret.

"Last night was great. But I know what you're trying to say. You were lonely, upset, your support system wasn't there—your mother's away, Coop is angry, Miguel was busy, even Father Lindstrom was otherwise engaged. I wanted to be there for you, to help you any way you wanted." He smiled. "And I have to say, given choices like make tea, bring pizza, just listen—I liked the option you chose."

"You're making me feel worse. Like I used you."

"Well, maybe you did, but I was a willing participant. I knew what you were doing, and why. And I know why you're feeling strange now."

"Oh? Why's that?" I was slightly irritated at his presumption that he knew what was going on in my head. When I wasn't entirely sure myself.

"You're in a vulnerable place right now. You've lost your job; you're blaming yourself for Frankie Saxon's problems; you don't see a clear way to fix it. And the best friend who's always been there for you, isn't. And you're still not sure you can trust me, and you don't want us to fall back into old patterns—great sex, terrible relationship. How am I doing?"

"Pretty good. You should look into this for a career."

"You're going to have to come to terms with all that yourself. But you don't need to add feeling guilty about last night onto your list. I wanted to be with you, and last night you wanted to be with me. We're adults, neither of us is in a relationship, and we didn't do anything last night we haven't done hundreds of times before."

"Well, there were a few new things," I said, and finally looked up at him with a small smile. "Why are you making this so easy for me? I feel like I'm playing the jerky guy part of the morning after a hook-up."

He shrugged. "Maybe I'm just paying something on my karmic debt. Nothing has to come of this. No strings. Are we OK?"

"Yeah," I nodded. "Yeah, we're OK."

"All right then. I'll get out of your way now. Still have papers to grade, faculty meeting to attend. Are we on for the faculty Christmas party Friday night?"

I looked at him blankly.

"At Miguel's, I asked if you'd like to go, you said you'd text me later? I'm here now so—"

"Yes, sure, I remember. Yeah, OK, let's do it. What time?"

"I'll pick you up around 7. It's casual."

For a second I thought he was reiterating the state of our relationship, then realized he meant the party attire.

"Got it."

As he went back to my room to get his shoes and socks, I cleaned up the kitchen. In the old days, Nick would have pouted because I'd been so focused on a story that I'd forgotten to answer his invitation. I would've had to apologize a hundred times, and even then, he might still feel aggrieved. Old Nick would have loved the no-strings relationship, except he would want to be the one deciding that, not me. Maybe people really can change. I had to hope so, because there were definitely a few tweaks that needed to be made to my character. He came back into the kitchen.

"All right then, I'll see you Friday. I'll be pretty much buried in finals and grades until then, but text me if you need anything."

Then he took my hand and turned it palm-side up, and placed two shoe strings in it. I looked at him, uncertainly. He pointed to his feet, wearing brown leather shoes without laces.

"See? No strings."

"Leah, I was just going to your house to call on you. Are you sure you should be out and about?"

"Yes, Father. I feel much better. I just wanted to bring you a little thank you gift for taking care of me Saturday night."

"Nonsense. I was happy to do it. After all, it's my job to take care of my flock."

"Well, I wandered away from the herd quite awhile ago. I think you're excused from shepherding duties where I'm concerned."

"You know the story of the lost lamb, Leah. I'll always go searching for you."

When I looked in his eyes, I felt my own welling with tears. What was wrong with me? This weepy side of my personality was something new. I didn't like it. I pushed the bag into his hand, and as he opened it, he gave a delighted chuckle.

"Benedictine B&B!"

"I don't understand how you can like that herby brandy stuff, but I know you do. So, enjoy."

"Oh, I will, thank you, Leah. Someday I'll make a convert of you. Now, sit down for a minute, won't you?"

"Just for about that long. I've got some stuff to get done today. So, did you hear about the drug bust?"

"Indeed. It's the talk of the town. Someone said that Dr. Bergman had been arrested. So, your suspicions about his drug activities were correct. Do you think that will help Frankie Saxon?"

"Maybe, but I've got to find out more."

"Isn't that a job for the police?"

"It would be, if they were interested in finding out who really killed Garrett and Jamie. But Frankie fits the bill as far as they're concerned. And you know my history with Detective Ross."

"Perhaps Coop could serve as a liaison?"

"Don't think that's going to happen. Coop is not exactly in my corner. He and my ex-boss have decided that I'm a vengeful screw up, and I'm probably lucky if they don't put out a restraining order on me."

"I see," he said, though he clearly didn't.

"Believe it, Father. But I don't really want to talk about it today. Like I said, I just wanted to tell you thanks." His phone rang then, and he excused himself to answer it. I stood and put my coat on, then popped my head in his office just to wave goodbye. He held up his hand and motioned for me to stay. I waited as he wrapped up his conversation.

"Yes. Yes, I see. Of course. All right. I'll see you later then."

"Betty Meier passed away. That was her daughter, Deborah. Seems she wandered away from the nursing home yesterday. She died of hypothermia."

I flashed on Betty Meier, sitting at my desk in the newsroom, confused and a little frightened.

"Poor Betty. How could she just wander away?"

"I don't know exactly what happened. Deborah was quite distraught. I'm going to meet with her now to plan the service."

"Sure, yes. I'll see you later, Father."

42

I WAS BACK HOME icing my arm, which had started throbbing after I left Father Lindstrom's, when the phone rang. The caller ID showed the *Himmel Times*, so I picked it up, thinking it was Miguel.

"Leah, did you know your crazy old lady friend, Betty Meier, died?"

"Yes, Courtnee, I heard Betty died. She wasn't crazy; she had Alzheimer's."

"Same thing, right? Anyway, her obit came in from Delaney's Funeral Home today, so I thought you'd want to know about the visitation." That was oddly thoughtful of Courtnee. "The funeral is Thursday at 11, but visitation is tomorrow from 2 to 4 and from 6 to 8 at the funeral home."

"Courtnee, how did Betty get lost?"

"My cousin Jasmine is a CNA at Valley Manor. She said there was, like, a fire and smoke, and the sprinklers went off and the alarm, and they had to get everybody out. All these old people with walkers and wheelchairs, and kinda crazy, I mean Alzheimery. I guess your friend, Betty, she just kinda walked away when nobody was looking. She was a wanderer, Jasmine says."

"How bad was the fire? Did people get displaced?"

"Well, there wasn't one, was there? I said there was *like* a fire. Don't you ever listen, Leah? Just the alarm went off."

"But you said there was smoke—"

"It was just in a wastebasket. They think one of the old people got a cigarette and dropped it in the basket to hide it or something. They're not allowed to smoke. But Jasmine said you'd be surprised what goes on. She said that she walked into a room once and there was this grandpa guy and this old lady in bed, and they were—"

I tuned her out as I thought about Deborah, and how she must be feeling. After the fire at Betty's house, she'd had her mother admitted to Valley Manor to keep her safe. And it turned out she was less safe there than she'd been at home.

"And so she says to the grandpa guy, 'Get your pants back on, Mr. Harris, and—' "

"Thanks for calling, Courtnee. I have to go. Bye."

"Deborah, I'm so sorry. I know you're going to miss your mom so much." I gave her a hug. I had arrived early on Wednesday afternoon so I could talk to Deborah a little before the visitation got too crowded.

"Thank you. Everyone keeps saying she's not suffering anymore, and she had a good life, and I know they're right. These last two years have been so hard. I thought it wouldn't hurt so much when she died, but it does." Her eyes were red-rimmed, and her voice shook a little.

I nodded, because I didn't have anything wise or helpful to say.

"Did you know she wandered away? It isn't just that she died. It's the way she died—alone, confused, frightened. They found her in the storage shed at her old house. We had the house torn down after the fire, but we left the shed. And that's where she was. She just wanted to go home." Her voice broke on the last words, and as she started to cry, I put my arms around her again. After a minute, she pulled away and swiped at her eyes and nose, and when she spoke, it was in a firmer tone.

"I don't blame the nursing home, not really. She sometimes slipped out when we were with her ourselves. Well, you know that, right? My brother Keith called her the Houdini of Halston Street." She gave a watery smile. "But I don't understand how she could get so far. That's miles away."

"Alzheimer's is funny. Mostly people are in a fog, but sometimes they have startling moments of clarity. Your mother wanted to go home. And she did." I thought of the day Betty had gripped my arm so fiercely, and the bright light that had burned in her eyes for a minute. What had she said? *"We're all dying."* Well, she was right about that.

Just then an elderly man in a shiny brown suit walked up to talk to Deborah. I excused myself and went to look at the picture boards set up to highlight Betty's life. There she was, a little girl, leaning back on a swing, blonde curls flying, laughing over her shoulder at a tall man in suspenders pushing her. Her father probably. A hundred pictures of a happy life—First Communion, birthday parties, high school graduation, a wedding photo, pictures with her husband and children in the yard, on vacation, gathered around a Christmas tree.

The second board was smaller and clearly dedicated to her professional life. There was a picture of her graduation from college, and another of her resplendent in an old-school nursing uniform—white dress, white shoes, white stockings, white cap with a black stripe. One photo appeared to be Betty instructing a Lamaze class, another of her getting an award. In one picture that looked like it had been clipped from a newsletter, Betty stood in front of a large "Happy Retirement" banner as a distinguished looking man handed her a gaily wrapped package. I bent in to read the cutline. "Retiring nurse Betty Meier receives congratulations and a surprise gift from Dr. Martin Rosen on behalf of the St. Cyprian's Transplant Center."

A voice at my elbow made me jump. "She was a real nice gal."

"Yes, she was." I turned and saw that I was speaking to a solidly built man, probably in his 60s, with light blue eyes under thick, bushy eyebrows. "I'm Ed Slade. Betty was a friend of my wife's." He held out his hand and I shook it.

"Leah Nash. I've known Betty for years." I started to withdraw my hand, but Ed held firm. I noticed his eyes were bloodshot and the large nose over his gray mustache was red-tipped and blotchy, as though he had a cold.

"I'm from Chicago. My wife Gail worked at St. Cyprian's with Betty. Alzheimer's. A terrible thing."

"It is. Is your wife here today?" I had managed to extricate my hand, but Ed gave every sign of being a long talker. If I could steer us in the direction of his wife, I might be able to make a polite exit.

He hesitated a second, then said, "No. No. Gail passed away six months ago." He cleared his throat and said, "It's why I came. Gail would've wanted me to." His voice broke, and he reached in his pocket for a handkerchief to mop his eyes.

"Oh, I'm so sorry." I felt like a jerk for trying to ditch him, and I touched his sleeve. It seemed to be the signal for him to unleash the sadness he was trying to contain.

"She was only 56. We were going to Hawaii for our anniversary. She went shopping for vacation clothes, and she, she—" I expected him to say she was in a car crash, or had a heart attack or a stroke. Instead he said, "She fell from a subway platform. You know, someone just goes out shopping, you don't worry, you don't say 'be careful,' like they were going on a long trip. You expect them to come back, they should come back. But the platform, it was just so crowded and everyone was pushing forward and..."

"Oh, my God. That's so unbelievably awful."

He nodded miserably, tears streaming down his plump cheeks. He dabbed at them again.

"I'm sorry. I shouldn't have blurted it out like that. I think I've got it under control and then... well, and then I don't."

"Don't worry about it." I touched his arm as he took several deep breaths and pulled himself together. Just then, Deborah walked up to us and said, "Ed, I thought that was you! I'm so glad you came. I'm sorry we didn't get there for Gail. When we heard about it, Mom wasn't doing so well. I just wasn't sure she could manage. I don't—didn't—ever really know how much she was taking in. Especially the last year, so—"

"That's fine, that's fine." He patted her on the back, and they both teared up. Now seemed like a good time to leave. "It was nice to meet you, Ed. Deborah, again, I'm so sorry." I gave her hand a quick squeeze and left.

───────

At the moment, I didn't have much to do. I had called Frankie's lawyer, but he was out of the office until Friday. I didn't want to bug Miguel again; I'd already asked him to find out anything he could about where Cole Granger might be, and I knew he was really busy as deadline day approached. Cole and Frankie's lawyer were the two major items on my agenda.

When I pulled in the garage, I noticed the bag from my clean out of Miguel's Mini Cooper. I hadn't finished sorting stuff that day because Paul had called me to talk about my mother. I should get it done and return what seemed meaningful to Isabel.

I dragged the bag in and sat at the kitchen table, separating things into "keep" and "trash." I tossed out the old food wrappers, dried out pens, and other detritus. A couple of CDs, a book of poetry, and a copy of *On The Road* I put in the keep pile.

When I was done, I picked up the garbage bag I'd been pulling things from and turned it upside down to shake it out and make sure I hadn't missed anything. A jaggedly torn envelope came floating out. It was the one I'd found under the seat and tossed in the bag when Paul called. I picked it up and read the writing on the front. The return address was preprinted. *Garrett Whiting, MD, PC* with his office location. A yellow return-to-sender-not-deliverable sticker was just below the mailing address, which read:

Dr. Martin Rosen
4914 Howard Street
Willow, Wisconsin

I felt a start of recognition. That was the name of the guy in the newsletter photo with Betty.

When I looked at the postmark, a little shiver ran through me. October 13. This must be part of the mail that Elaine Quellman had taken to the post office for Garrett that Sunday when she left the office.

I Googled the name and the town and found a Dr. Martin Rosen at 4194 Howard Street, not 4914 as Garrett had written. Where was the letter? Why did Jamie have the envelope? What had Garrett written to Dr. Rosen the day he died?

It was only 3:30. Willow was about three hours away. I felt the sudden urge for a road trip.

43

I PULLED INTO THE DRIVEWAY of a two-story brick house flanked by tall fir trees. Light shone through gaps in the curtained windows on the first floor. The night air was damp with the promise of snow to come. I rang the bell. No response. I was about to press it again when I heard the slow thump and measured pace of someone using a cane or crutches. A man leaning slightly on a cane in his right hand opened the door. Despite the device, his posture was erect. He looked at me directly with beautiful cornflower blue eyes behind silver, wire-rimmed glasses. He had a full head of thick white hair.

"Yes?"

"Dr. Rosen, I'm Leah Nash. I'm a friend of Garrett Whiting's daughter, Isabel. I wonder if I could speak to you for a moment?"

"You're Garrett's daughter?"

"No, I'm a friend of his daughter's. My name is Leah Nash. I wanted to talk to you about Dr. Whiting."

"I'm sorry. It's a cold night to keep you on the doorstep. Come in, please. Can't get used to this damn hearing aid." He lifted a hand to his ear and fiddled with it, trying to adjust it. "Come in, come in."

He moved aside and then led me to a cozy study with a crackling fire burning in the brick fireplace. He gestured for me to take a seat on one of two upholstered chairs while he took the other, turning it slightly so he could face me directly. "You want to talk to me about Garrett?"

"I don't want to take up too much of your time. Garrett's daughter, Isabel, asked me to look into her father's death—I'm a reporter. She doesn't believe it was suicide."

"Garrett's dead?" He looked surprised.

"I'm sorry. I didn't realize you hadn't heard. Yes, he died in October."

"I had a stroke in September. I've been staying with my niece in Chicago for the past two months. I just returned home a few days ago. You said suicide? No, you said it wasn't. I'm sorry, my thought processes are a little slower these days. It was an accident then?"

"No. Dr. Whiting was murdered."

"Murdered? Who would want to murder Garrett?"

For the moment, I ignored the question. "He sent you a letter the day he died, but it was never delivered, because he addressed it incorrectly. Do you have any idea why he wrote to you?"

"No. I haven't heard from Garrett in years. But you have the letter. What does it say?"

"That's just it. I don't have the letter, only the envelope. It was empty when I found it, in the car that belonged to Dr. Whiting's son, Jamie. And I can't ask him about it, because he's dead, too."

He was looking slightly alarmed, and I realized that I sounded more than slightly strange. I took a step back and started again, giving him a brief explanation of Garrett's death and what I'd turned up.

"But today, I was at the visitation for Betty Meier, and I saw a picture of you and her when she retired from St. Cyprian's. Then I saw your name on an envelope I found in Jamie's car, with Garrett's return address. It got sent back because he got the house numbers wrong. It was mailed the day he died. It just seemed, that is, I thought, if you had any idea what he wrote to you about, I felt I should talk to you," I finished a little lamely.

But Dr. Rosen, though he hadn't asked any questions, had been paying close attention. His eyes were bright and alert. "I don't know why he wrote to me, but I can tell you why he wrote to me."

OK, so maybe those bright eyes were deceptive. Maybe the stroke had affected his speech? He saw my confusion.

"I'm sorry. That was very unclear. What I meant was, I know why he communicated with me by letter. Quite possibly he called, but I don't have an answering machine. I hate the damned things. And, of course, I was away. So, he could have tried several times and never reached me. If he really wanted to contact me, a letter might have seemed his only option."

I was thinking hard. "You don't have an answering machine, but does your phone track missed calls?"

"Yes, it does, but I don't pay much attention to the feature. My friends all know they'll have to call back if I'm not here."

"Could I take a look at it?"

"Certainly. It's on the desk over there."

When I scrolled through the call list, I found a number with a Himmel area code and prefix listed several times. It wasn't the Whiting's home phone. I pulled out my phone and googled Garrett's office number. It was a match.

"Garrett did try to call you, more than once. But you said you weren't in regular contact with him?"

"No. The only member of the team who stayed in touch with me was Neal Dawson, one of the nurses."

"Team?"

"Yes, the Kidney Transplant Team at St. Cyprian's. We—the first members—got things off the ground there. It was an exciting time." As he spoke, he leaned over and pulled out a drawer on the end table and sorted through some things in it. When he sat back up, he held a photograph out toward me. As I crossed the room and took it, he said, "That's our transplant team, as it was originally composed."

Seven people stood in a row in front of a sign that said "St. Cyprian Kidney Transplant Center." From the clothes and hair, it looked like a late 80s or early 90s photo.

"I know Betty Meier, and I recognize Garrett Whiting, but is this you?" I pointed to a man with thick gray hair and dark-framed glasses.

"Yes. Next to me is Gail Slade, our social worker. That fellow with the cocky grin is Neal Dawson, another transplant nurse, like Betty. Next to him is Bill Lessing, the nephrologist. The one on the end is Greg Lindstrom. He was chaplain at the hospital then. Not technically part of the team, but he worked with the families and the team quite often. Some decisions we had to make were extremely troubling."

I pulled the photo closer. I hadn't realized Father Lindstrom had once been a ginger. But beneath a copper-colored head of wispy hair, I identified his sweet smile. "Yes, I know him. He's a priest in Himmel. And I remember now, he did mention he'd worked with Garrett a long time ago."

"Nice fellow. All of the team were good people. But you said you were at a visitation for Betty?"

"She passed away just a couple of days ago. She had Alzheimer's." I felt like the angel of death's recording secretary, but figured I might as well tell him about Gail Slade as well.

"Gail Slade died, too. I met her husband at Betty's visitation this afternoon. About six months ago. An accident. She fell from a subway platform."

His eyebrows drew together in a frown of concentration. "But that would mean...that would be...I don't understand." His face had lost some color, and the fingers he put to his temple shook a little.

"Dr. Rosen?" I half-rose from my chair.

"No, no," he waved me back. "I'm all right. I'm just having trouble taking this all in."

"Of course, I understand."

"No, I don't think you do." He looked at me with an odd expression on his face.

"Neal Dawson died of an allergic reaction last Fourth of July. I went to his funeral in Eau Claire. We used to go trout fishing in April every year. He's the only team member I stayed in touch with. Last March, I received a solicitation for a scholarship in Bill Lessing's memory. It said he'd died in a hit and run accident in January. Do you see what I'm saying? There are only two of us left."

My brain was racing. "*We're all dying.*" That's what Betty had said to me weeks ago in the newspaper office. That day there was a fire at her house. Five people in a group of seven, all dead in less than a year? Five people who had made "troubling" decisions. Life and death decisions.

"Dr. Rosen, you said some of the decisions the transplant team had to make were troubling. What did you mean?"

My abrupt change of subject didn't fluster him. "Organs are in such scarce supply that we had to make sure that a transplant would be a long-term success. We had to weigh not just physical matches, but also consider the financial and psychological state of the patient."

"Financial?"

"There is Medicare coverage available, but it only covers 80 percent of the cost for anti-rejection drugs, and then only for three years. The drugs are necessary for the lifetime of the patient."

"So, you would turn people down because they were too poor?"

"With such a shortage of organs, we had to consider not only how sick patients were, but whether they could afford the anti-rejection drugs on a long-term basis. Or the kidney would essentially be wasted."

"You said psychological, too. Did you turn down people with mental illnesses?"

"It wasn't cut and dried. If a mentally ill patient was stable and compliant with his medication, that wouldn't be a reason to turn him down. But if he were noncompliant, again we had to consider the likelihood of long-term success. A patient who didn't conform to the strict drug regimen would endanger the ultimate success of the kidney transplant."

"I imagine it's very hard to give a dying patient the news that he's not eligible for a transplant."

"Yes. The entire team makes the decision. It's a very heavy burden. I'm convinced one of the decisions we made broke our team apart."

"Really? What was it?"

"A single mother. Amber Pelly. Very beautiful young woman. Her kidneys were irreparably damaged by a suicide attempt with a large dose of acetaminophen. She had a pattern of going on and off her mood stabilizer drugs. She was in financial distress as well. We turned her down. The repercussions of that decision took a toll on all of us."

"What repercussions?"

"She killed herself. She jumped from a bridge in her hometown. Sandersville, in the western part of the state. I remember because that's where I spent summers as a child. Amber's mother blamed us, the team, for her daughter's suicide."

"That must have been pretty terrible. For everyone."

"Yes. Despite the process we followed, we all felt some measure of guilt and regret. It was a very hard time. There was some adverse publicity, some accusations from Amber's mother that we had only rejected her because she was poor. That wasn't true, but as I said, it's a factor in every transplant decision." He sighed heavily, and I noticed his hands were still shaking slightly. I pointed to the crystal decanter and glasses sitting on a nearby table.

"Are you allowed to have alcohol? You look like you could use a drink."

"A small glass of brandy would be very good medicine for me right now, I think, my dear."

"Let me get it for you."

"Please, pour one for yourself. If you're not a brandy drinker, there's an excellent scotch there as well."

"Thanks, but I've got a long drive back tonight." I handed him a small glass of "medicine." I waited as he took a sip and some color returned to his cheeks.

"It's so gratifying to match a patient with a donor organ. But it's devastating, every time, to tell a patient there is no kidney for them, for whatever reason. Garrett seemed to take it particularly hard. He was almost physically ill with the stress of Amber's death. He actually met personally with her mother, though our attorney advised against it. I always thought it was his deep sorrow that persuaded her to drop the legal action she threatened. He left the team not long after. Eventually, everyone moved on." He took another sip and settled back a little in his chair.

"What about Amber's child?" An idea, fragmentary and bizarre, was forming in my mind.

He thought for a moment, then said, embarrassed, "It was a daughter, I'm sure of that, but I, I just can't recall anything else. It seems as though she was school age, certainly. But, perhaps younger? Is it important? I just can't retrieve information as readily as I once did, I'm afraid."

"That's all right," I said, although his memory lapse frustrated me. I knew that I was upsetting, even badgering, him, but I had to find out. "Do you remember, did she go to live with Amber's mother, her grandmother?"

"No. Amber's mother accused us not only of killing her daughter, but also of ruining her granddaughter's life. I believe the grandmother suffered from ill health and couldn't care for the child. My recollection is she was placed in foster care. Or perhaps adopted?"

"Do you remember her mother's name?"

"Yes, it was Wilson. Goldie Wilson."

"I just have one last question. What year did Amber die?"

"1994."

"All right. Thank you, that helps a lot. But there is something." I hesitated, not wanting to upset him any more than I already had. But I had no choice.

"I don't want to alarm you, but I think you need to take some precautions. You mentioned a niece in Chicago. Maybe you should go to her for awhile."

"What? Why would I do that? I just got back in my own home."

"I understand, but realize what we've been talking about. Five of seven people on your transplant team are dead. Someone is after you. All of you."

44

IT TOOK SOME CONVINCING, but by the time I left, Dr. Rosen had been on the phone with his niece and told her he felt he wasn't quite ready to be on his own. She arranged to pick him up the next morning. I could tell from his side of the conversation that she had been requesting him to stay with her longer anyway.

"I have to talk to some people, but I'll get back to you as soon as I know something for sure. I may be wrong, this may be crazy, but I don't want to take a chance, and you should be fine with your niece."

I wished I felt as confident as I sounded, but in my car on the way home I knew this was a big fat mess. And a dangerous one, too. I reached for my phone and automatically started to call Coop, then stopped.

He wasn't going to believe me. I hardly believed me. But I knew I finally had it. Nothing else brought everything together. I'd made a huge mistake. I'd been looking at Garrett's death all wrong. He wasn't killed because of who he was as an individual or what he knew. He was killed because he was part of the transplant team that had killed Amber Pelly. Or so her daughter believed.

Betty had told me that in my office. *"We're all dying."* The funeral that Deborah had taken her to, not long before she showed up at my desk—it must have been Garrett's. In some elusively lucid part of her brain, Betty made a connection. Garrett was the fourth member of the team to die. Amber's mother had blamed the team, and Amber's daughter had absorbed that anger. It didn't matter that the team made an ethical decision. The end result was that Amber Pelly had died. Her young daughter hated the people she believed responsible.

I called Nick.

I told him about Amber and the daughter she left behind.

"Listen. This is what I think happened to Garrett and Betty and three other members of the original St. Cyprian Kidney Transplant Team. I think Amber Pelly's daughter killed them."

"I'm stunned."

"But you don't think it's impossible?"

"No. It's definitely not impossible. But if you're right, you're talking about a psychopathic personality. Someone with a strong sense of entitlement and an enormous capacity for narcissistic rage. She'd have to be high-functioning to have escaped detection, which means she's very, very dangerous."

"So, she's smart. Angry, but not crazy, right? She wants to get away with these murders."

"Not only that. She positively thrives on the knowledge that she's more clever than anyone else. And, to give her due justice, she's pretty damn smart. A series of accidents in widely different locations, victims not easily linked—that's a good way to go. The only death that breaks the pattern is Garrett Whiting."

"I've been thinking about that. What if Garrett somehow stumbled onto the connection? Dr. Rosen said the team had split up and not stayed in touch, but he got a letter for a scholarship fund after Dr. Lessing died in a hit and run accident. Maybe Garrett did too. And in his case, maybe he had some other information that made him suspicious. He wanted to talk to Dr. Rosen but couldn't reach him, so he sent him that letter."

"Possible, but it still doesn't explain why and how Amber's daughter killed Garrett and faked a suicide."

"But she wouldn't want it to look like murder—it would ruin her clever planning. None of the other deaths were investigated as suspicious, because they looked like accidents. If Garrett discovered her identity and thought he was smarter than she was—which, of course, he would, because he thought he was smarter than anybody—he might have invited her to meet him. Maybe she even liked the challenge. She turned the tables on him, but she had to make it look like suicide. A murder investigation might have turned up something that could lead to her."

"And Jamie? Do you think she killed him, too?"

"I don't know. But the empty envelope was found in his car. If he read the letter from his father, he may have decided to take matters into his own hands. He didn't have much faith in the police, or in me. She agrees to meet with him, and when she realizes what he knows, he's got to go. That's a big risk. But then psychopaths are risk takers, right?"

"Yes. Now, your next call is going to be to the police, right?"

"Soon. Very, very soon."

"Leah—"

"Come on, Nick. You're only half on board, and you like me. Ross is going nowhere near this. I can just imagine what he'd say if I told him a mystery woman killed Garrett, and she's killed five people altogether. And I can't blame him, really. It's not like I have a great track record on this one."

"Hey, I'm fully on board. I just think you should expand your crew. What about Coop?"

"No."

"What are you going to do then?"

"I'm going to find Amber's daughter."

"OK, wait a minute. What about 'she's killed five people' makes you think it's a good idea to confront her?"

"I didn't say I was going to confront her. But I have to find out who she is, where she lives, what she does. Besides killing people."

"And then what?"

"Then I give the police something solid to go on."

"How will you do that?"

"Well, I know that her mother was from Sandersville. Her grandmother might still be alive. She might even be in touch with Amber's daughter. So, I guess I'm going to find grandma."

"Leah—"

"Thanks for everything, Nick. I'll talk to you soon. Bye."

I ignored the incoming call from Nick as I waited for Miguel to pick up.

"*Chica!* Where are you? I stopped by your house, but nobody was there. And you didn't answer my text."

"I'm on my way back from Willow. And I need your help, bad."

I explained what I'd figured out.

"I have to find Amber's daughter, fast. First thing is to find out her name. Can you check online, the Sandersville paper, maybe the local library? Try to get the story that ran when Amber killed herself; the daughter's name might be in that. Also, see if you can find Goldie Wilson. I don't even know if she's still alive, but if she is, she could have some answers."

"Maybe the *abuela* knows where her granddaughter is?"

"That would make things easier. But, Miguel—"

"I know. Don't let Grandma Goldie know I'm trying to find her granddaughter. *No problema.* If she knows, she'll tell me, and she won't even realize she did."

"I'm counting on you. There are only two people left on the team. I think I have Dr. Rosen squared away. But I'm worried about Father Lindstrom. I'm going to call him now, but I can't explain everything on the phone. Can you meet me at his house when I get back? If we tag team him, maybe he'll take it seriously. I should be there by 11 or so."

"For sure, I'll be there."

Father Lindstrom didn't answer his home phone, and I didn't bother to leave a message, because it was way too much to explain. I tried his cell without much hope. He does carry one, but he's not a big fan, and he's always forgetting to turn the ringer back on after he turns it off. I'd have to try later.

I drove as fast as I dared on the two-lane highway, but the snow that had threatened earlier had started to fall in big, wet flakes that gave my wipers a workout trying to keep the windshield clear. Then, I got behind a car going 30 miles an hour on a long, curvy no-passing stretch of road. I had my phone GPS reroute me, but instead of saving time, it took me onto a series of dirt roads that finally dead-ended at a lake. By the time I backtracked and got back on the main road to Himmel, I'd lost over an hour. At least the snow had stopped. But there was no way I'd get back to town by 11 p.m. I texted Miguel, told him we should skip tonight and meet at Father's at 8 a.m.

When I pulled into town, I was about three adjectives past very tired. I really wanted to go home and go to bed, but I couldn't yet. I knew he was probably fine, and he might as well have one more night of untroubled sleep before I told him he was the target of a psychopath. But I had to go by Father Lindstrom's house, just to check and make sure that all was well.

45

HIMMEL AFTER MIDNIGHT is pretty quiet. Most of the houses are dark; a couple of party stores and the bars are still open, but almost everything else is shut down tight. I like driving down the deserted streets, seeing the occasional light in a window, wondering if someone is up with a new baby, or a sick child, a new boyfriend, or a broken heart. The silence, interrupted only by the occasional bark of a dog or the wail of a passing train, was so peaceful, all the stress of the day temporarily stilled. It was so calm, in fact, that I felt a little silly as I drove toward Father Lindstrom's, but I couldn't not check on him.

The stoplights had already switched to flashing red and yellow, an acknowledgement of how the traffic slows at night. But as I turned onto Father Lindstrom's street, a car blew past me. A silver Miata. Rebecca. I couldn't see her face, but with that car and that entitled attitude, it had to be her. Probably going home from Coop's.

Father's house is a small brown bungalow on a corner. It's a nice location, because he's got an empty lot on one side, St. Stephen's on the other, and a parking lot that takes up a big chunk of the block. It's quiet and private, and he has plenty of yard for all the bird feeders he likes to set up. It's a buffet of sorts—for the neighborhood cats. As I approached the house, I saw smoke coming out of his chimney. Maybe he was up after all. But still, I thought I'd go home without stopping. I was so tired.

But when I pulled in the driveway to turn around, I noticed the windows were all dark. Why would he have a fire in the fireplace and then go to bed? Then, I saw it. A red-tipped flame showing through a basement window. It was coming from the back of the house. Then a bright yellow flicker visible in the living room. My fingers shook as I called 911.

"A fire. A fire at 529 Church Street. There's a man. Father Lindstrom. I think he's inside." The phone slipped from my sweaty hand. I could hear the dispatcher talking, but I couldn't answer. I couldn't move, my breath was coming in short gasps, my heart was thumping so loudly I couldn't think. I stared in horror, but I wasn't seeing Father Lindstrom's house. It was our house, my mom and dad's house. And the fire roaring through it had ignited more than 20 years ago.

It started while we slept. I shared a room with my little sister, Annie. She was 8 years old, just two years younger than me. Mom was holding the baby, Lacey, when she came to wake us up. Dad wasn't home.

Confused and stumbling with sleep, we held hands and followed her. She carried Lacey and shepherded us across the street to a house kitty-corner from ours. Mom pounded on the door, and Mrs. Nussbaum answered, wearing curlers and a purple velour bathrobe. Her hand went to her mouth as Mom told her our house was on fire. She held Lacey while Mom ran in to call the fire department. Soon other lights went on in the neighborhood, and a crowd began to gather on the Nussbaum's lawn.

We weren't scared anymore. We were excited to be up so late, to be so brave—that's what Mrs. Nussbaum said as she handed us each a cookie—we were such brave, good girls. Lacey started crying. Mom told us to stay put while she went in to change the baby's diaper. We could hear fire trucks and police sirens in the distance. Our eyes opened wide as we watched flames shoot out of the roof of our house. Annie tugged at my sleeve. She was worried about her cat, Mr. Peoples. I told her it was all right. He always went out for the night through the cat door in the basement. He wasn't even home.

David Cooper, a boy from my school, came up and asked me what happened. Breathlessly, I told him how we had escaped, dodging flames with fire chasing after us. That wasn't true, but I wanted my story to match the keyed-up atmosphere on the lawn. Then I heard my mother call. I reached to grab Annie's hand. But she wasn't there. My eyes quickly scanned the crowd in the yard. Mostly grown-ups standing in twos and threes, a few kids, but not Annie. I turned and saw my mother waiting on the doorstep. I looked across and down the street. The fire trucks had pulled up and in their bright headlights I saw a flash of pink squeezing through the tiny opening in the hedge that surrounded our yard. Annie!

I took off at a run, dashing between the chattering adults, dodging past Mr. Nussbaum who had reached out to stop me. I heard my mother calling me, but I ran faster than I ever had. I slipped through the narrow gap in the hedge. I started screaming Annie's name. Window glass had shattered and flames pushed out through the open spaces. Loud crackling pops rent the night air. I could feel the heat on my face. Annieeeee! Annieeeee! Annieeeee! I ran toward the back of the house. I heard the yowl of a cat and saw Mr. Peoples in the far corner. I looked wildly around the yard. Annie? Annie? I ran toward the back door, but someone scooped me up from behind. A firefighter carried me away from the fire as I struggled and screamed for Annie. Out in the street, Al Porter, the fire chief, was holding my mother and she was sobbing. When she saw me, he let her go. She swept me up in her arms, gasping and laughing with joy.

Suddenly, her laughter stopped as she asked, "Where's Annie?" I stared at her. I couldn't speak. After what seemed like a long, long time, a fireman came out with a small pink bundle in his arms. My mother jumped up. Then she saw the limp limbs, the lolling head, the tears streaking the smoke-stained face of the fireman. And she began to wail.

All of that flashed through my mind in seconds as I sat there, sweating, panting for air, watching the flames move toward the front of the house, hearing the first shatter of glass from the basement windows, knowing Father Lindstrom was inside. I was crying now, sobs that came from deep within and rattled through my body, expelled in jagged barks of fear and frustration.

I have to do this. I have to go in there. I can't do this. I have to do this. I forced my hand to open the car door. I didn't let myself think. I ran to the front steps and up to the landing. I touched the door. It wasn't hot. That was good. I fumbled with the knob. Not locked, but the door stuck.

I twisted to heave my good arm and shoulder into it. As the door swung inward, a billow of smoke came out. There were no flames, but the hallway was filling with smoke. I dropped to my hands and knees, my eyes burning. I pulled my sweater up over my nose as a filter.

"Father! Father!" The thick yarn muffled my voice. I called again. No answer. The smoke was so heavy it was hard to see. I crawled down the hallway, my eyes glued to the baseboard to guide me. I turned the corner toward his room and saw him. Lying face down, one arm stretched out in front of him. *Please, God. Please, God. Please, God. Please, please, please. Not this time.*

I reached out and grabbed his wrist. I shook his arm. "Father, Father."

He coughed and turned his head slightly. He was still alive.

"OK. You're OK. It's OK. Come on now." I moved beside him. I put my arm across his back and tried to get him into a crawling position.

"Come on now, stay down low." I spoke quickly, in short bursts to save my breath. He struggled into position. I tugged to help him. My head jerked up. I felt the heat buildup above us. I knew what that meant. There's not much heat in a smoke-filled room. If you feel it increase, that's a bad, bad thing. When it gets hot enough, all the combustible fuel—wood, insulation, furniture, carpeting, everything—goes up in a flash. Including anyone who's in the room.

"Come on." This time I yanked on him as hard as I could. He was up on all fours and I said, "All right. We're moving now. You can do it."

He was coughing, weak and obviously confused. But he followed my simple commands. One arm, one leg, other arm, other leg. We were only inches from the door. I could see the smoke-free air outside. Then his arm collapsed. He sank down. "Can't. Can't."

"The hell you can't."

I moved behind him. He was still on his knees, though the front of his body had collapsed to the floor. I tucked my head down into my chest. I leaned back on my legs. Then I sprang forward, keeping my head low. I plowed into Father Lindstrom's backside. The force propelled him forward, but I'd knocked him off-balance. He lay crosswise at the threshold, his head and shoulders partially out of the opening. He was so still. I knew he wasn't conscious any longer.

I took a quick look up, then gasped. Above the thick gray shroud of smoke that surrounded us, black smoke was rolling back into the hall at ceiling height. Fire darted snake-like out of the blackness. I heard the scream of sirens coming nearer. It wouldn't be soon enough for us. We had about 10 seconds before the hallway flashed over and burst into flames.

I scrambled over him onto the outside landing. Still kneeling, I reached under his chest. I grabbed up the folds of his pajamas, his robe, and his belt. Then, I held tight as I launched into an off-kilter sideways somersault that sent us tumbling down three steps. We landed in a heap at the foot of the stairs. The fire flashed over inside the house, shooting out a wall of flame. Father Lindstrom wasn't moving. I didn't know if I'd saved him or killed him. I reached for his wrist. His pulse was thready, but it was there. I stood up and started tugging him away from the house. I was coughing and wheezing as firefighters and two paramedics came running up.

"I'm OK," I managed to cough out as I pointed in Father Lindstrom's direction. "He's not doing so well."

The little priest was lying on his back, breathing shallowly, his shock of silvery-white hair coated in soot and ashes.

"Is he going to be all right?"

Neither answered. They got him on a gurney, covered his face with an oxygen mask, and quickly wheeled him away.

"He's going to be OK, right?" I called after them.

"Don't worry. They know what they're doing." Al Porter, the fire chief, was standing next to me. I didn't even see him walk up. "Come on, Leah, you need to move back, let the guys get in here. That house is fully engulfed." I looked back then and shuddered as I saw orange flames shooting out of every window.

Al half pushed, half pulled me away. I stumbled, and he put an arm around me. I leaned against him gratefully.

"You OK, Leah? You know you did a really brave, really stupid thing going into that building. A few more seconds and ..."

"I had to. I had to make a different ending. I couldn't just watch, not again."

He shook his head. "Leah, your sister. That wasn't your fault. You were a little girl. There was nothing you could do."

"But I'm not a little girl anymore. And there was something I could do. This time I got it right."

We had reached the street where the scene was controlled chaos as fire-fighters in turnout gear, helmets, and masks grabbed equipment and set up hoses. More trucks continued to arrive.

I saw an ambulance pulling away. "Al, my car, I have to get to the hospital."

He shook his head and pointed toward the garage and driveway. His crew was already shooting hundreds of gallons of water at the house and garage out of huge high pressure hoses. "You're not gonna get anywhere near that little car of yours. Tell you what, I'm gonna give you to Janice over there; she's gonna check you out."

"But I don't need—" He was gone before I finished. Janice, a paramedic with a no-nonsense haircut and the sturdy appearance of a beef-fed woman, appeared at my side.

"Hi there, I'm Janice. Understand you had a close call with a fire tonight. Let's just get you checked out here. What's your name?"

"Leah Nash. I'm OK, if I could just have a little water?" My throat felt so dry and tight it hurt to swallow.

"We'll get you some real quick there, Leah. Just let me look over a few things. Why don't you hop up here." She had produced a gurney as if by magic, and I scooted myself up onto it. Her voice was calm and slow, but her hands were quick and efficient as she checked my pulse, my blood pressure, my breathing, looked in my nose and down my throat. Finally, she handed me a bottle of water. "Take it easy."

I took a long, slow drink. It was the coolest, sweetest tasting liquid I'd ever had. I might not ever drink anything but water again. "I love you, Janice."

"I get that a lot. Now, how long were you in the house?"

"I don't know, maybe four or five minutes. Felt like four or five hours. I'm not sure. But I'm OK. And I really have to get to the hospital."

"Now, that's a real funny thing. That's just what I'm thinking. I'm just gonna have you lie back here, get this oxygen mask on you. That'll get some real good fresh air right into your lungs. You're a pretty tough little cookie, but we want to get your CO and CN toxicity checked, just make sure there's nothing going on."

She deftly slipped the mask over my face and gently pushed me into a prone position. I gave up protesting. It was one way to get to the hospital fast.

"Leah! Leah!" A shock of happiness zipped through me as I turned my head and saw Coop running toward me. As he reached the gurney, I sat up and pulled off the mask.

"We have to quit meeting like this," I croaked.

He stopped in front of me and grabbed me by the shoulders, bending down to look into my face. "I heard it on the scanner. The fire. You were in the house. Are you all right? What were you thinking? Jesus, Leah!"

"Don't be mad at me again. I had to do it. I couldn't let another goddamn fire swallow up someone I love. And I didn't. I was so scared, but I did it, Coop. And I'll never let myself be that scared of anything again."

He hugged me then, bending down and smooshing my face into his chest. When I pulled back, I saw that I'd left a wide smudge of dirt and ashes on the front of his jacket.

"I'm sorry. Looks like I ruined your coat."

"You're quite a hero, Leah. I admire your courage. That was an amazingly brave thing to do." I hadn't even noticed Rebecca, but at the sound of her voice Coop dropped his arms and stepped back.

Before I could say anything I'd regret, not that I had many regrets when it came to insulting Rebecca, Janice reasserted herself.

"Sorry, folks. I need to get this gal to the hospital."

"Leah, we'll meet you there."

"No, Coop. No need. I'm good. I just want to check on Father Lindstrom. I'll talk to you later."

"She's right, David. We'd only be in the way. And I have to get some photos and talk to the fire chief. Miguel chose a bad time to be out of town."

I laid back down with a secret smile on my face. Miguel, I knew, was busy working for me.

46

WITHIN MINUTES OF ARRIVING at the hospital, I was in an examining room. No waiting time, I guess, when you arrive by ambulance. But none of the people who came in and out would admit they knew anything when I asked about Father Lindstrom. That worried me.

Then the doctor, the same guy who'd treated my arm the week before, came in with the lab results. "You're a lucky girl. Your blood work is fine. I think we can let you go. I have to say, I had no idea writing was such a dangerous profession," he said in a deadpan voice.

"What about Father Lindstrom? Is he going to be all right?"

"He's in intensive care."

"Will he be all right?"

"He has significant carbon monoxide saturation in his blood—the result of prolonged smoke inhalation. There's some airway injury and respiratory compromise. He's receiving high flow oxygen and an IV. He's been intubated as a precaution. Airway obstruction is a possibility over the next 24-48 hours. He'll have a series of chest radiographs because of his exposure to the toxins in the smoke. He has a second degree burn on his left forearm."

Each piece of the information I had been so hungry for hit me with the force of a blow. A heavy weight had settled in the middle of my chest. My eyes must have shown the bleak fear I felt, because the doctor patted my hand.

"For a man his age, Father Lindstrom is in very good health. He is conscious and responsive—though he's not able to speak just yet. He's not out of the woods by any means, but he's holding his own."

"Can I see him?"

"He's not allowed visitors—"

"I—"

"But," he continued smoothly, "I think we might make an exception. Very briefly. For the person who saved his life."

The intensive care unit was dimly lit and eerily quiet, except for the whoosh and soft beeps of various medical equipment. Two people were working at the nurse's desk, which provided a clear line of sight to a series of small glass-walled patient rooms that encircled the area. One of them looked up as I approached.

"You must be Miss Nash. The doctor said you can see Father Lindstrom, but you can only stay a few minutes. He's sleeping right now, so please don't wake him."

"No, I won't. I just need to see him."

He was lying in a hospital bed with tubes coming out of his nose, his mouth, and his arm. A blood pressure cuff attached to one arm periodically inflated and deflated. A machine beeped off each beat of his heart, its screen tracing the electrical pattern. The only light came from a small fixture over his bed.

"Oh!" I gave an involuntary gasp at the sight of his pale face. His beautiful silvery-white hair, usually fluffing out in multiple directions, was matted and dull. Without the sparkle of his light blue eyes, his face looked old and worn.

"He's doing better than when he came in." I had forgotten the nurse at my side.

"Can I stand by the bed? I won't disturb him, I promise. Just for a minute."

She nodded and left me alone with him.

I stood and stared down at him through tear-filled eyes.

"I'm so sorry, Father. I should have left a message. I should have tried harder to reach you. I know why this happened. And I'm closing in fast. You rest, and you'll be better before you know it." I paused to give my voice a chance to steady. Hard to impart confident optimism when you're choking up.

"And guess what? I'm signing both of us up for the St. Stephen's talent show. I think we've got a real chance of winning with our new stunts and tumbling routine. But next time we'll use dry ice for the smoke and no flames."

I might have imagined it, but I thought his eyelids fluttered.

"It's time to go," said the nurse who had again appeared at my elbow.

"Yes, OK."

I turned back to the bed. "I'll see you tomorrow, Father."

On the way out, I asked, "So, do I need special permission to get in tomorrow?"

"No, you're on the visitor list now, and unless there's a no-visitors order, you can come by. But visits are restricted to 10 minutes."

"How many nurses are taking care of him?"

"We have a 1:1 staffing ratio here, so each patient is assigned a nurse. We're monitoring all the time. If he shifts position, we know it. If his blood pressure drops a millimeter, we know it. If his stomach starts to growl, we know it. We'll take the best care of him. He's pretty special to you, isn't he?"

I swallowed hard and just managed a husky, "Yeah, he is."

"Well, don't worry. Nothing is going to get past us. We'll take very good care of him."

"You have no idea how comforting that is."

Father Lindstrom was about as safe as he was going to get, short of having a personal bodyguard. Which, if he got out of here and I still didn't have Amber's daughter, I was perfectly willing to get for him. No one was going to get in who wasn't on the list. And I really didn't see the killer trying again tonight. It would be impossible to go unnoticed in the ICU. So, while I wanted him out of there as fast as possible, at the same time, it wasn't a bad place for him to be.

I had to get in touch with Miguel, but I'd dropped my phone in my panic attack in the car. There was a visitor's phone in the hospital waiting room, and I used that, but his cell went straight to voicemail.

"Don't have my phone. Come to the house. Go on in, the door's not locked." OK, now I had to find a ride home. There is no taxi service in Himmel, and the city-run Dial-A-Ride shuts down at 8 p.m. My usual go to people—my mother, Coop, Miguel, Father Lindstrom—were unavailable for various reasons. My second-string favor granters, Jennifer Pilarski—she had little kids, there was no way I'd roust her at 2 a.m.; Miller Caldwell? No, a non-emergency middle-of-the-night phone call was pushing it too far. I needed to work on my friend-making skills.

Isabel. I hated to wake her, but I knew she'd be glad to do it. And, actually, given everything that had happened in her life lately, she probably wasn't sleeping too deeply anyway.

"I feel bad getting you up in the middle of the night," I said, sliding into the passenger seat of her car.

She took in my bedraggled appearance, my stained and smelly clothes. "What happened? You sounded terrible when you called, and you look even worse. No offense," she added.

"None taken."

"Are you all right? What's going on?"

"Listen, Isabel, I found out something today that changes everything. Frankie didn't kill your dad; Bergman didn't kill your dad; Jamie didn't either. It wasn't anyone from his present. He was killed by someone from his past."

"I don't understand."

"You will." As she drove toward my house, I tried to lay it out coherently, but between my exhaustion and the urgency I felt, it came tumbling out in a way that I feared made no sense. The pictures at Betty's visitation, the empty envelope I found in Jamie's car, Dr. Rosen, the transplant team deaths, the suicide of Amber Pelly, the fire at Father Lindstrom's. By the time I finished, I was almost breathless, my mouth was unbelievably dry, and we were standing in the kitchen of my house. Isabel looked shell-shocked.

"I don't know what to think. Some stranger killed my father and all those people? But why, what would she gain?"

"Revenge. Satisfaction. A warped justice for what she thinks the members of the transplant team took away from her. She's had a lifetime to hate everyone she blames for her mother's suicide. Why should they have happy lives? Why should they have wives, children, husbands, love, a good life? They took the possibility of all that away from her mother and from her. They went on with their nice little lives, and she was left with nothing."

She was shaking her head. "I don't know, Leah. What do the police think?"

"I haven't told them. And judging by the way you're looking at me, that's probably just as well. I know I'm not helping you take me seriously, standing here ranting and waving my arms. But you have to, Isabel. You could be in danger, too. Who knows how warped this chick is? Look, can you stay a little while? I just want to hop in the shower, get into some clean clothes, and I'll try it again. With a touch less crazy, OK?"

"Sure, I can stay. Go on. I'll make some toast and eggs for you. And some tea."

Suddenly food sounded like a great idea. I couldn't remember the last time I'd eaten. "Thanks," I said, as she found a knife in the drawer and started slicing bread for toast from the loaf Miguel had brought on Monday.

47

I STOOD UNDER THE HOT WATER, scrubbing the ash and grime off my body and out of my hair. The water ran black for a few minutes. When it was clear, I raised the temperature and turned the nozzle on the shower head so that a hard stream of hot water hit my shoulders. The steam rose around me, and the only sound was the beat of the water. It wasn't hard to let my mind float. For 10 minutes. But then the hot water started to run out; the air was chilly outside the shower, and my "moment of Zen" began to dissipate. I toweled myself off quickly, ran a comb through my hair, and went into my room to pull on jeans and a sweater. The light on the cordless phone was flashing. Miguel.

I pressed the voicemail button—my mother's antique cassette tape answering machine had finally died, and we now had the latest technology. From 15 years ago. Voicemail accessible from all the extensions.

I played the message twice, unable to take in what he said the first time. It wasn't any easier the second. I called him back and it went to his voicemail.

"I'm here with Isabel. Come as soon as you get this."

I walked slowly back to the kitchen. Isabel was just closing the kitchen door.

"I just ran out to roll up my window. I left it down to get rid of the smoky smell, but now it's starting to sleet." A plate of eggs and toast sat at my place. "Let me get that tea, you look like you need it."

I sat and didn't say anything. Her back was to me as she put a tea cup in the microwave. I noticed then that she was wearing a hoodie. She half-turned and saw me looking at her.

"Hope you don't mind. This was hanging on the hook, so I just grabbed it to keep the rain off. How many minutes for the tea?"

"Two."

She turned back and began punching in the digits on the microwave keypad with her left hand. As I watched her entering the numbers, wearing my hoodie, identical to Jamie's, a montage of half-registered memories surfaced and fast-tracked through my mind.

The crime scene photo showing Garrett's computer mouse on the left side of his PC, though he was right-handed, like Jamie. The ATM slip in the pocket of the hoodie Isabel had "accidentally" switched for mine. Jamie's friend Keegan, telling me Isabel "helped" him remember when Jamie left the party. Her repeated referrals to Jamie's past drug use and relapse, though I'd seen no signs, nor had Frankie. How she goaded Jamie into confronting me by telling him I found the ATM receipt.

Her story that Jamie had misread her note and gone to the wrong park to find her the day he was killed. Ivah at the insurance office telling me Isabel's car was hit by a deer in Michigan last January. And that she was in Eau Claire July 4th, the day Neal Dawson died. Cole's cryptic remark about the left hand not knowing what the right hand was doing. All those clues, half-noticed or ignored, because I was sure Isabel needed a champion. The angry words Coop had hurled at me, that Isabel was manipulating me, that she was always lying to me. Lies that I excused, because I was giving Isabel what she really needed. Not a champion. A chump. Me.

I was so lost in my thoughts that I jumped when she set the tea down for me. She waved her hand in front of my face.

"Hey, anybody in there?" She smiled.

"The day's catching up with me, I guess. I'm a little slow on the uptake. Thanks." I pulled the tea closer, knocking over a vase filled with chrysanthemums. I grabbed it before all the water ran onto the floor. Isabel jumped up and got a dish towel as I righted it.

"Hey, you're kind of wobbly, aren't you? Do you want to call it a night? We can always talk tomorrow," she said, mopping up the spill.

"No, I'd like to talk awhile." How long would it be before Miguel got my message?

"All right. Just take it slow then. Eat something, why don't you?" I hadn't touched anything on my plate.

"I'm not as hungry as I thought I was."

"It's probably the smoke. Drink some tea. I put some honey in it. I like it that way. It'll be good for your throat." She took a sip of her own.

I nodded and lifted the cup to my mouth and swallowed.

"Leah, I've been thinking about what you said. I guess if this daughter really believes the transplant team killed her mother, I can understand her anger. But the idea that she could get away with killing five times, and no one caught on? Could she really be that smart?"

"It wouldn't take a mastermind."

"You're kidding. Someone kills five people and doesn't get caught, and you don't think she's super smart?" She laughed, shaking her head, but I could tell she was irritated.

"It's just a riff on the plot of *Strangers On A Train*. How do you get away with murder? Kill people you have no obvious connection to. No one on the team knew Amber's daughter. The members themselves went their separate ways 20 years ago. So, when the individual team members began dying "accidentally" one by one, with no common cause of death, no red flags went up."

"If you're right, I think what Amber's daughter did took an amazing amount of intelligence. She'd have to be really clever."

"Look, if she has the IQ of a potato and an internet connection, it wouldn't be hard for her to find the team. And just google 'accidental deaths,' and you've got a hundred different ways to go. I'm not saying she doesn't have nerve, but smarts? Not buying it."

"But she got away with it."

"Almost, but not quite. And that's thanks to you."

"Me?"

"Sure." This was starting to be fun, playing cat and mouse with her as she tried to figure out if I was the cat or the mouse. I wanted to goad her narcissistic self into such a fury that she'd blurt out the truth. And she had no idea Miguel and Coop were on their way. *At least you hope they are.*

She took several long drinks of her tea before setting it down. Her brown eyes fixed on me, but they were now the hard, shiny color of a cockroach's shell.

"If you hadn't wanted justice for your dad, to prove that he didn't commit suicide, nothing would have come out. Amber's daughter had already killed three people. But she made a mistake with your father. Instead of an accident, she tried to make it look like suicide. But you saw through it."

"But that doesn't mean she's the killer. Don't killers stick with a pattern? Why would she switch from accident to fake suicide?"

"Maybe she had to. Maybe somehow Garrett found out what was going on, and she had to improvise. And that might have worked. It was very well done, I admit. But she didn't count on you. You knew your father, and you knew he wouldn't kill himself. And I finally got lucky, finding that envelope in Jamie's car. Otherwise, I wouldn't have connected Betty and Dr. Rosen and the rest of the team to Garrett's death."

"The envelope was empty though. The letter could have been about anything. I don't see how that matters." She got up with her empty cup and my untouched plate of food. She tossed the eggs and toast into the trash can, then turned to the sink, her back toward me as she started rinsing the dishes.

"If it didn't matter, why wasn't the letter in Jamie's car? If it wasn't anything important, why didn't he just crumple it up and toss it in the backseat with the Burger King wrappers? No. I'm sure Garrett was trying to tell Dr. Rosen what he suspected. That he was warning him. And when Jamie read it, he realized what your father knew. That's why he went to the park, to meet Amber's daughter. That's why he called Frankie, so she'd know where he was and what he was doing, in case anything happened."

"You haven't told anyone else your theory yet?" She raised her voice slightly over the running water.

"No. Not yet. I just figured it out, and I've put so many wrong theories out there, I want to at least find out who Amber's daughter is and prove the connection. I don't think it will take long, now that I know who I'm looking for. Then, I'll give up everything I know."

When she turned around, the bread knife was in her hand. And she was pointing it at me.

"Oh, I think you know who Amber's daughter is, Leah."

"It took me long enough, didn't it? What are you planning to do? Go full Manson on me in my own house? How do you think you'll get away with that?" *Where the hell was Miguel with my reinforcements?*

"I'm sure I'll figure out something. I always do." She took a step toward me. "You know, I always liked you, Leah. This isn't personal. You just know too much, and you never stop. You just can't help yourself, can you?"

"I don't know as much as you think I do. Why don't you tell me more? How did you find out Garrett was your father?" I was stalling, hoping she couldn't resist the chance to demonstrate her brilliance.

"Last Thanksgiving a water pipe burst in the basement. I went through the boxes that were water damaged. I found a picture in one of them. A woman, who looked a little like me, holding a toddler, who looked a lot like me. On the back it said, *Amber and Lynette, Sandersville Centennial, 1991.* I already knew I was adopted. It wasn't that hard to figure out who was in the picture. I went to the Sandersville library, looked through the high school yearbooks. There in the Sandersville 1988 *Tiger Tales* was a picture of Amber Pelly, Homecoming Queen, with her mother Goldie Wilson.

"It's a small town. I didn't have any trouble finding my sweet Grandma Goldie. She was finishing a fifth vodka when I got there. She could hardly stand. But she could talk. I told her my name, and she said she'd been waiting all these years for me to find her. Right. She told me all about my mother, and that bastard doctor who got her pregnant, and the transplant team he was on that killed her. Then she had a crying jag, then she passed out.

"I looked through the house. Found bank statements with regular deposits from my father's bank. It was all pretty clear then. I wasn't sure what I was going to do then, but I warned Goldie to keep quiet about my visit, or the money would dry up. I think it's time for me to visit her again."

She blinked rapidly, then squeezed her eyes tight for a moment. She gave her head a shake, as though trying to bring something in focus. Then, she took two quick steps toward me and stuck the point of the knife in the space between my ribs.

"Get up. Get up!" If I made a sudden move, she could slice right through me.

"OK, OK, I'm getting up. You have to move back. I don't have room to move my chair out."

She inched back a little, but the knife tip still poked at my side.

"So, how do you think you're going to get rid of me?" I asked, as I slowly rose and pushed the chair back with my knees.

"Shut up." Only she slurred her words, so that what came out was "Shub ut." I felt her wobble. I turned abruptly. She stumbled. The knife skittered across the floor. We both lunged for it. I grabbed it first. I pointed it at her, suffused with primal rage and the urge to hurt her as she'd hurt someone I loved.

"You tried to kill Father Lindstrom." Anger coursed through me, and my hand clenching the knife shook.

"Wha. Wha gonna do? Gonna do abou, about it?" She swayed. I sprang forward. Then, her eyelids fluttered and she gave a soft sigh, like air leaking out of a tire. She slumped, and as she hit the kitchen floor, the door flew open. I turned, the knife still in my hand.

"*Díos mío, chica*! You killed her!"

48

"*Híjole, chica, you scared me.* I saw that knife in your hand and Isabel lying on the floor—" Miguel shuddered. It was two hours later, and Isabel was in the hospital sleeping off the Klonopin dose she'd intended for me. We were in the conference room at the Himmel Police Department, waiting to sign the statements we'd just given.

"I can't believe you'd think I'd kill her in my own kitchen. I'd at least do it somewhere I could hide the body." I was giddy with relief that Isabel was at least temporarily out of the picture, and when I had checked, the hospital said Father Lindstrom was showing signs of improvement.

"You did so good tonight, Miguel. You found Amber's mother, and you got her to talk. I can't believe she told you so much."

"*Chica,* you know the ladies, they love me." He grinned. Then, he got serious. "I found the story online about Amber's suicide, then I got an address for the grandma, but no phone number. I used a reverse directory and found one for a neighbor. I called her, and she told me Goldie goes to the Comet Tavern every night. So, I drove to Sandersville."

"Now, that's good reporting, my friend. Most people wouldn't drive two hours at eight o'clock at night on the off chance of finding someone."

"You would," he said. "And that's my mantra, WWLD—What Would

Leah Do? I knew I'd be late, but then I got your text, so I knew it didn't matter. And the *abuela*, she had a lot to say."

Despite the extremely late—or was it early?—hour, he was energized. Chasing down a lead can make you feel that way. I could tell he wanted to relive his reporting prowess for me, and he deserved to.

"Tell me again what happened."

"OK. You know, the grandma was at the *taverna*. And she was pretty *borracha*. Pretty drunk. She was crying, crying. The bartender told me 'Goldie is either cryin' or cussin', no in between.' I bought her a drink and asked her about Garrett Whiting. She said he was a *bastardo* who took her granddaughter. '*Dígame*, tell me why did he do that?' And she said—" Here he paused to add some dramatic tension to his tale. He resumed with a deep frown, a sweep of his hand, and the solemn intonations of Darth Vader, "Because, he is her father!"

I doubted Goldie had delivered it with such flourish, but Miguel does tell a good story.

"I didn't know everything, *chica*, but I knew you needed to know. So, I called your cell and no answer. And texted and no answer. And I called your house and no answer, but I left a message. Then, when I came into town, I saw the fire, so I had to drive by."

I nodded. It's in the blood. You have to check out a fire.

"I saw your car. Chief Porter told me you were at the hospital with Father Lindstrom. But when I got there, you were gone. I was getting worried. Your call came in when I was checking with Coop, but it went to voicemail before I caught it. After I listened, we came right over. And saw you trying to stab Isabel."

"I could have. I thought the Klonopin she tried to give me would never kick in. I switched the cups when I knocked over the flowers, and she drank the whole thing, but she didn't go down easy."

The door opened and Coop came in, followed by Detective Ross and Sheriff Dillingham. I had to go over everything again for them.

"Once I put it all together, I knew Amber's daughter had done it. And I thought Father Lindstrom might be next. And I was sure none of you would believe me without more evidence. I had Miguel check out Amber and her mother. I drove straight to Father Lindstrom's. When I got there, his house was already on fire. It wasn't until I got home and heard Miguel's message that everything fell into place."

"So, you're sayin' that you've been withholding information that would've helped me find a serial killer?" Ross leaned menacingly across the table. He had held in his anger and resentment for as long as he could. But then, so had I.

"No. I'm saying that Christopher Columbus with a GPS couldn't help you find your own ass. I knew there wasn't a chance in hell you'd listen to me, unless I could give you Amber's daughter on a silver platter. So, that's what I did."

Ross slammed his hand down on the desk so hard that Miguel jumped. The sheriff intervened.

"That's enough, Charlie. Nobody's covered in glory here. In fact, it looks like we got a world class FUBAR to try and figure out. Let's calm down. I'd like to have something in my back pocket when the prosecutor gives it to me in the neck this morning. Miguel, you want to tell me what you did tonight?"

After Miguel finished, Ross didn't say anything, and the sheriff just nodded and sighed. Then he said, "OK, Leah, now did Isabel Whiting confess to you tonight? Seeing as you had her at knifepoint as I understand?" For just a second I thought I saw a flash of laughter in his weary blue eyes, but that was probably just a trick of the light.

"How we gonna prove any of this stuff?" Ross's tone was belligerent and his cheeks were bright red from the effort of holding in his hostility. I felt no such constraint.

"Geez, Ross, isn't there any part of your job I don't have to do?"

His beefy face reddened even more. Coop stepped in.

"I think everybody's pretty tired. Leah, why don't you and Miguel go home, get some rest. The sheriff and I need to get ahead of this thing as much as we can, and we've got a lot of catch up to do."

49

WHEN ISABEL WOKE UP later that morning, the first thing she did was ask for a lawyer. When I woke up that afternoon, the first thing I asked was, "How's Father Lindstrom?"

"Much better. They moved him to a regular room a little while ago." My mother was sitting on my bed, having just woken me up by asking me if I was still sleeping.

"Leah, I don't know whether to kiss you or smack you." She settled the question by doing a little of both, planting a kiss on my cheek, enfolding me in her arms as I sat up, and then hitting me lightly on my arm.

"Hey! That's my sore bicep."

"You don't want to go there. Why didn't you tell me you'd been beaten within an inch of your life?"

"Because I wasn't, there wasn't anything you could have done, and you'd only worry."

"With good reason."

I had groggily promised when she had arrived home at 10 a.m. to tell her everything, if she'd just let me sleep. But I dreaded the thought of going through the whole complicated story again. She read the look on my face.

"Don't worry. I've got the gist of it. I talked to Coop and Miguel, and I went to see Father Lindstrom early this afternoon—though he doesn't remember much." Abruptly, she turned serious. Her dark blue eyes searched my face. "Honey, how did you manage to go into that burning house?"

"I don't know, Mom. I just kept thinking about Annie, and, and, and—" I took a breath to stop my voice from quavering and tried again. "I felt like I was right back at our house. The night of the fire. I couldn't fail again. This time I had to do it."

"Oh, Leah." She took hold of my hand. "Honey, you did everything you could. Just like you did last night. But you were a little girl then. And now you're a grown, amazing, brave woman, and you saved Father Lindstrom's life. I am so proud of you."

"He wouldn't have needed saving, if I hadn't been so stupid."

"All right, now. That's enough of that. I can tell you need some four-cheese macaroni, a nice green salad, and apple crisp for dessert. Fortunately, I've got all three going in the kitchen. You get up, get showered, get dressed, and there will be no more talk of what you could have or should have done. You did wonderfully well." She hugged me again, and I did as I was told.

A lot happened over the next week; unfortunately, none of it involved Isabel confessing to multiple murders. Father Lindstrom got steadily better. The *Himmel Times* ran a huge story on the drug bust and Dr. Bergman's involvement, and a small story about the fire at Father Lindstrom's. The sidebar on my "heroism" in rescuing him was a little embarrassing. I'm sure that was Miguel's idea, not Rebecca's. I spent some time that week helping my mother and some of the other St. Stephen's parishioners fix up a little house for Father Lindstrom, so he'd have a place to go when he got out of the hospital.

On the night before his release, she and I went grocery shopping to stock his refrigerator and cupboards for his return home on Friday. As we worked together putting things away, I tried once again to get her to talk about how things were going with Paul. I'd made several attempts since she got home, but she had adroitly avoided my questions by parrying with questions of her own, about what I wanted for Christmas, or whether I was going ahead with my freelance story for the *Milwaukee Journal*, or if everything was set for my book release in February. If she were really desperate to get me off the topic of her and Paul, she'd ask me how Nick was doing and what our long-term plans were. A sure way, she knew, to get me to leave the room.

But she hadn't seemed any less tense or stressed than she'd been before she went to Michigan. She was still preoccupied, a little short tempered, and sometimes I caught her staring into space with a worried look on her face that she always briskly denied when I pointed it out. But we were alone at Father Lindstrom's new place and there was nowhere for her to run.

"OK, what's going on with you and Paul?"

"Nothing. Everything's fine."

"Then why haven't I seen him all week? Why hasn't he called?"

She busied herself putting cans of soup in the cupboard before she answered. When she did, it was in a forced, breezy voice. "Nothing's wrong. We've both just been busy."

"Mom."

She sighed but still didn't say anything.

"I'm not going to stop asking, and you're not leaving this room until I know."

"All right. Fine. Paul asked me to marry him. And I said no."

"What? Why? Why would you do that? You're perfect for each other."

"No, we're not."

"Mom."

"Leah, I don't want to talk about it."

"Paul is wild about you. You guys love spending time together. It may not look like it, but seriously, I can take care of myself. It's about time I got a place of my own anyway. And—"

"Stop it."

"But you're just being—"

"I can't marry him, that's all." Her eyes were bright, and I realized she was trying hard not to cry.

"Yes, you can, Mom. Paul must be crushed. You have to tell him you changed your mind. Well, at least you told him there wasn't another man, right?"

She looked like a deer caught in the headlights.

"Mom? There's not another man, right? That's not why you can't marry him?"

"Enough. I'm not talking about this with you anymore. I don't want you asking me, and I don't want you talking about this to anyone else. Do you understand? Do you promise?"

"All right! OK, I promise. I promise." I let it go, because she was as upset as I've ever seen her. Later that night, she was in the shower for a long time. And mixed in with the noise of water beating down on the fiberglass tub surround was the unmistakable sound of heart-wrenching sobs. And worse than hearing them, was knowing that she wouldn't tell me why.

50

On Saturday morning Coop called and asked me to meet him at the Elite. That I was surprised and that he didn't just drop by the house to talk to me were both indicators of how far apart we'd grown.

He didn't notice me as I came through the door, and I had a chance to look at him unobserved. He wasn't wearing his usual HPD cap, and I could see that he'd grown his hair out so that it was a little longer on the front and shorter on the sides. It looked good. Rebecca's influence, no doubt. He was staring into his coffee cup, and he looked tired. He glanced up then and smiled, and for a minute it was like the last few weeks had never happened.

"Hey. I got you a chai," he said, pointing to the cup in front of me as I sat down at the table.

"Thanks." We sat in silence for a minute, then both started talking at once.

"Coop—"

"Leah—"

"No, me first."

"All right."

"OK. I want us to be friends. I'm sorry I made such a mess of everything —Garrett's murder, Isabel, the DEA investigation, you and Rebecca. Sometimes I get so focused on the way I see things, I forget everyone else doesn't share my vision."

"Oh, really? I hadn't noticed."

"Yes, really. So, anyway, I've made a lot of mistakes. Bad ones. I'm sorry. I'll try to do better. No, I will do better. I've missed you."

"Same here."

"Wait a minute. I had to do a whole mea culpa, and you get away with ditto?"

"You wanted to go first. Then, you said it all. Like usual."

"Shut up."

And we were back. Maybe not the same way. There was Rebecca now, but that was something I just had to accept. I would do better. I would.

"So, what's going on with Isabel?"

"That's the second reason I wanted to talk. Charlie Ross arrested her for Garrett's murder about an hour ago."

"Just Garrett's? What about Jamie?"

He shook his head. "The prosecutor didn't think there was enough evidence."

"Cliff Timmins is a politician, not a prosecutor. He doesn't want any case that doesn't come with a signed confession."

"He's got a decent chance of winning on Garrett's case. There's just not enough on Jamie. Yet, anyway."

"What about the rest of them?"

"Come on, you know jurisdiction is in three different places. There's not much Cliff can do about that. We're sharing information with the other departments, but so far they're not overwhelmed by the evidence. There isn't anything solid linking her to those other deaths."

I slumped down in my seat. "So, she'll get away with all those?"

"Maybe. She did cross state lines though."

"Yeah, so?" And then I got what he was driving at. "That means she could be prosecuted in federal court. The FBI could assume jurisdiction and link all the murders together." My voice rose with excitement.

"Take it easy. The operative word is 'could.' Doesn't mean they will, but it's possible. Right now, be happy she's going on trial for killing her father."

"Who's her attorney?"

He grimaced. "It's Aiden Kennedy."

"That's bad. He's good. Probably the best criminal defense attorney in the state."

"No doubt. But Isabel had two of the top five motives for murder: money and revenge. Ross dug up cell phone tower records that put her within three hours of Himmel when she talked to her father. And there's a security camera at a toll booth near Hammond, Indiana, with a nice picture of Isabel's car to corroborate that she was actually in that area. She had enough time to get home and kill him within the window the ME gave."

"That's good news," I said, my spirits lifting. "And there's the video from JT's and the ATM slip."

"Yeah. There's a lot a jury's gonna like. And if Cliff can get in that Isabel tried to frame her own brother, that's going to have an impact. Though there is one tricky part to this case."

"What's that?"

"Convincing a jury that Isabel set up a fake suicide for Garrett, then tried to make it look like murder. The defense may argue that if she'd killed her father and got away with a suicide verdict, there's no way she'd focus attention back on the crime. After all, she's the one who pushed to have the investigation reopened. Kennedy could argue that it doesn't make sense. Why didn't she leave it alone? That's the question Cliff will have to answer."

"But that's easy. She thought suicide would be the cleanest way, but she slipped up. She either forgot, or didn't know there was a suicide clause. Or she didn't realize the two years hadn't run out on it yet. She went through Garrett's papers after she killed him, and oh-oh, she's not going to get the money she thought she was. And Isabel is a greedy girl. So she created a murder scenario on the fly. She worked backwards to re-stage things, and as an added bonus, to implicate Jamie, so he'd get the blame."

"Good argument. I like it."

"Thank you."

"But Ross didn't follow her plan. It looked like a straight up suicide. He made a classic error, and he didn't investigate it the same way he would a homicide. I'm not sure I would have either."

"Yes, you would, Coop."

"Well, it's easy to second guess. Anyway, he didn't, and nothing Isabel set up panned out. He didn't find the clues. She was too clever for her own good."

"So, then she calls me, because I'm like one of Pavlov's dogs, salivating at the sound of injustice. I jump in with both feet and do exactly what she wants me to do."

"Not exactly, because she definitely didn't want you to go beyond suspecting Jamie. But she didn't realize that Leah Nash never does what anyone wants her to do. She's pushy, know-it-all, stubborn, and she won't be bossed. And she's maybe the best reporter I've ever seen."

"OK. Now I want to thank you and to punch you in the arm. Why do you have to tangle up a compliment with a list of my flaws?"

"Take 'em where you can get 'em. You did a good job, Leah, you really did. You made some mistakes. So did the rest of us. But you got there in the end."

"Thanks. Hey, Frankie's out, right?"

"Yep. This morning."

When I checked my phone after leaving, I saw an email from Jane Barstow, the forensic document examiner. I stared at it blankly for a second. With everything that had happened the last few days, I'd forgotten all about the portfolio.

I finished the indented writing tests. I'm FedExing the original materials back to you, as well as my formal report. Attached is the text I was able to recover. Interesting. Best, Jane.

I clicked the attachment open.

To the investigators of my death—

I have taken my own life. I apologize for the unfinished business I'm leaving.

My daughter Isabel Whiting, born Lynette Pelly, is a multiple murderer. Isabel is my natural daughter, the result of a brief sexual liaison with a woman named Amber Pelly. I didn't want the child; Amber didn't want anything but the child. We parted. She never contacted me. However, in 1994 while I served on the St. Cyprian Kidney Transplant Team, Amber was a candidate for transplant. I was ethically obligated to recuse myself from the decision process. I didn't. No one on the team knew of my connection to Amber. She was turned down because of mental instability and financial problems. She killed herself shortly after.

Her mother, Goldie Wilson, threatened legal action against the team and the hospital. Then, she met with me personally to say that she would report me to the medical board unless I agreed to her conditions. Exposure would have ruined my life. I did as she wanted, paid her, and took the child she didn't want to raise. I had no further contact with Goldie Wilson other than recurring quarterly payments until recently. She phoned to tell me Isabel had learned her real identity and my role in her mother's death. In her drunken state, Goldie had concluded I would pay her for that information. I allowed her to think that. I had already determined I was going to end my life. But what she said disturbed me. An unsettling suspicion began to take hold. After some research, it became a conviction.

Isabel discovered the truth of her parentage, and the fate of her mother, last January. Last spring, I learned a colleague on the transplant team, William Lessing, was killed in a hit and run accident jogging near Grand Rapids, Michigan. A few months later, another colleague, Gail Slade, was killed in an accidental fall from a crowded subway platform in Chicago. Last month I heard that Neal Dawson, yet another team member, had died in Eau Claire on the 4th of July, the result of an allergic reaction. Isabel was in each place at the time the incidents occurred, and she had lied to me each time about where she was.

Lest you think my conclusion is histrionic, please know that Isabel was an accomplished liar and manipulator from an early age. Her beauty and intelligence hid a ruthless nature. People who thwarted her suffered—accidents, damage to reputations, loss of treasured possessions. I suspected, and I sometimes knew, she was the cause, but I did little. Parenting was never an interest of mine. However, I never imagined she was capable of what I am convinced she has done.

Still, I didn't want my brief time left taken up with investigations and infamy. You have the information now to do with it what you will. In any case, I've ensured that Isabel will suffer some punishment. By committing suicide, I void my life insurance. Isabel will get nothing from that source. Neither will my son, Jamie, but it will do him good to stand on his own.

There is one other matter. Dr. Hal Bergman, my associate, is involved in prescription drug fraud; how deeply I'm not sure. Elaine Quellman can provide the information we have. I leave on my own terms, without regret.

Garrett Whiting

Holy shit. Holy shit. Holy shit.

Isabel hadn't committed the only crime she was arrested for. She really didn't kill Garrett. He killed himself.

Charlie Ross had been right all along.

51

On Monday, I received the FedEx package with the originals and the document Jane had recovered from the indented writing on the portfolio pad. I still hadn't told anyone about the report. If I gave the material to the prosecutor, it would mean Isabel would go free. If I didn't, she could be convicted for the one crime she didn't commit.

When my phone rang at 11, it was Miguel telling me Isabel had been arraigned, but she was still in jail. She couldn't make the $500,000 bond the judge set. Then, I made a phone call of my own.

"Hello, Leah." Isabel said it as though she were receiving me in her living room, not sitting at a beat-up table wearing handcuffs. Even in the standard jail uniform, without make-up, she was stunning. Her big brown eyes were warm and guileless, her dark blonde hair framed her face. She looked like the angel on top of a Christmas tree.

"I'm surprised you agreed to see me."

"I was curious. What do you want?"

"I'd like some answers."

"I didn't kill my father. That's the only answer I'm prepared to give."

"Yes. I know."

"So, now you believe me? What changed your mind?"

"I have your father's suicide note."

"You can't have it! I de—" She stopped abruptly.

"You what? Destroyed it? Yeah, I'm sure you did. Have you ever heard of indented writing, Isabel?"

Her expression was wary, her eyes narrowed and calculating. "No. What's that got to do with anything?"

"I have your father's portfolio. The one you gave to Elaine Quellman. There was a pad of paper in it. Miss Quellman put it there herself the Sunday Garrett died."

"And so?"

"So it's the one he wrote his suicide note on."

"There's nothing there. I—"

Again I interrupted. "You checked, right? Yeah, I didn't see anything either. But that's the thing. Indented writing isn't always visible. I sent it to a forensic document examiner. She was able to bring up the impressions his pen made on the pages beneath the one he wrote on. That means I have a copy of your father's suicide note. It's pretty clear you didn't kill him."

She made a sudden move to grab my wrists and was brought back to reality by her shackled hands. She settled back in her chair, but her voice was sharp and commanding when she spoke.

"You have to give it to my lawyer, now!"

"Actually, no, I don't. See, I'm the only one who knows it exists. Well, the expert who examined the portfolio does, but I have the original materials. Maybe she could testify on your behalf, but it would be pretty hard with the originals gone." I paused for effect. Her knuckles were white from the effort of controlling herself, but she didn't say anything.

"I have to tell you, I'm not the most careful person in the world. Anything could happen. Maybe I'd set the documents on the roof of my car. And then I could forget and drive away. They'd fly right off, maybe into the river if I was crossing a bridge, and never be found again. Then again, I'm a little clumsy, too. I might be looking at them while I was drinking a cup of tea and then, oops, I spill it all over them. The paper would be ruined. Nothing could be recovered from that."

"You can't do that. I'll tell the prosecutor and my lawyer what you just said."

"Oh, I wouldn't do it on purpose. But like I said, I'm very careless. But even if nothing happened to the documents, and I turned them in, you might not be home free. Remember the note? Your father says that you killed all those people on the transplant team."

"That doesn't matter. I can't be prosecuted for a crime that never happened. He wasn't murdered. He committed suicide. Anything else he wrote is just a product of his damaged mind. The Parkinson's, the Klonopin he took, the stress he was under, it all affected his thinking."

I knew that's what her lawyer would argue. And she'd make a very attractive defendant—young, beautiful, bereft. Hell, Lizzie Borden got away with it, and she wasn't half as appealing as Isabel.

"Could be. But without Garrett's note, Cliff Timmins has a pretty good case against you for murder, you have to admit. And juries don't like kids who kill their parents."

"What do you want?"

"I want you to tell me what you did. And I want you to promise that if the murder charge is dropped, and you manage to escape the consequences for the other murders you committed, you will never, never come within a hundred miles of Father Lindstrom again. Or Dr. Rosen, either."

"No matter what I say here you won't be able to use it, even if you could prove it. You're extorting a confession from me. You're making me admit things I didn't do, in exchange for evidence that will prove I didn't kill my father."

"That may be true. But no one is going to see the documents if you don't tell me what you did. And if no one sees them, you might just go away for first degree murder. I think I can live with that. Do you want to risk it?"

"Give me the documents first."

"No. You tell me what you did. And you promise me that you will not hurt Father Lindstrom or Dr. Rosen. Then, I'll turn them over to Cliff Timmins and to your lawyer."

"How do I know I can trust you?"

"I guess you'll have to take a chance. Just like me."

Surprisingly, she laughed.

"I do like smart women, Leah, and you're almost as smart as I am. I think I can agree to your terms. Father Lindstrom and Dr. Rosen are both old men. I can let nature take its course. But I have a condition, too. You agree that your next book will not be the story of my father's death, and you will not write anything that tries to link him, or me, to the transplant team deaths. I'd like to put this chapter of my life behind me. A book by you would make it hard to do that, even though I'd sue you for libel and win."

So, she was a little rattled, despite her cool demeanor. That was a good thing. In truth, I had no plans to make the Whiting case the subject of my next book. She'd been too smart—though I would never tell her that—and too lucky. There was almost zero chance of finding evidence that would hold up in court linking her to the transplant deaths. But if she was just a little worried that I might keep trying, it might be enough to keep her away from Father Lindstrom.

"All right. Agreed. Now, let's hear it."

"First of all, I want to say that you don't have any idea what my life has been like. It was no fairy tale, growing up in the Whiting house. Once my father agreed to my sweet grandma's blackmail terms, he deposited me with Joan and never gave me another thought. He was too busy with his women and his practice. Joan hated me, and she treated me like dirt. Plus, she was strung out on prescription drugs most of the time. They were quite a pair of parents. I had to fight for the right to exist. And Jamie, that whiny little brat. The only fun I ever had in that 'family' was setting him up for things I'd done. He was so trusting and stupid, he fell for it every time."

"That's a really sad story, Lynette. I can see why you had to kill six people. Let's get back on track with what happened. Start with the night your father died."

I saw the flash of anger in her eyes at my use of her "real" name, but she controlled it quickly.

"All right. This is all hypothetical, and I'm not admitting anything. I'm just going to tell you how things might have happened. Hypothetically."

"OK, fine. Just get to it."

"I told you that I was driving home from the Adirondacks that Sunday, that part was true. But I said that I stopped outside of Cleveland for the night. I didn't. I drove as far as Hammond, Indiana, and stopped there. I was less than three hours away when Garrett called me. He didn't even know I'd started for home. He thought I was still in New York. I didn't tell him any different. He told me he'd been diagnosed with Parkinson's, and he didn't see any point in living if he couldn't be a surgeon. I was surprised he was confiding in me, because we didn't really have that kind of daddy-daughter relationship.

"But then he also told me that he knew what I'd done. He was so proud of himself for working things out, and even prouder that he'd figured out a way to destroy me. He told me he was leaving a note for the police telling them everything. And then he laughed. Because he knew I wouldn't be able to get home from Blue Mountain Lake before the housekeeper found his body in the morning and the police were called—not even if I drove all night. Then he hung up, leaving me helpless to save myself—he thought. But the joke was on him. I had plenty of time to get home and destroy his suicide note, because I was three, not 14 hours away.

"When I arrived around 2:30 a.m., Jamie's car was there. I went right to my father's study. The light was on. He was dead. I read his suicide note and realized Garrett had tried to outmaneuver me to the very end. By killing himself, he voided his insurance policy. I wouldn't get any insurance money, and he owed me that. He died thinking he'd checkmated me, but that was never going to happen. I destroyed the note, and I decided to make his suicide look like murder. And to let Jamie take the blame. I'd get all the money, and Jamie would get payback for being Joan's precious favorite. $100,000 to him and nothing to me? He deserved to suffer. I went to Jamie's room, found him passed out, and I knew he wouldn't be a problem.

"I set up the Hook's cheese, ordered the book, flushed an old Klonopin prescription I had down the toilet, and put the bottle in Jamie's room. Then, I drove Jamie's car, sideswiped that nosy old bat's mailbox, and went to the ATM wearing Jamie's hoodie. When I got back home, I hid the ATM slip in Jamie's desk, and waited. Everything pointed to Jamie. At 8:30 I woke him up. I told him I just got home and found Garrett dead in his study.

"He couldn't take it in. He was confused, couldn't remember anything except he went to a party with Keegan. He didn't know when he got home."

She paused for a second, and looked at me expectantly. When I didn't say anything, she gave an impatient sigh.

"Don't you see? This part was pure genius. He didn't remember, so I knew if I worked it right, I could make him think he didn't get back until much later than he did. And he'd tell the police that and use that moron Keegan as his alibi. All I had to do was convince Keegan that it was 4 a.m., not 2 a.m. when they left the party, and tell him it was important for Jamie that the police knew it was 4 a.m. I knew Keegan wouldn't be able to keep the story together if the police questioned him. Then, I had another piece of 'evidence' that Jamie was guilty. His alibi wouldn't hold up. He could easily have left the party much earlier than he said, killed Garrett, and made a run to the ATM.

"Then the police came, and everything fell apart. That detective, Ross, he was sure it was suicide as soon as he saw the body. He believed Jamie's story, he barely questioned Keegan, they didn't search Jamie's room, so they didn't find the ATM slip, so it didn't lead them to JT's, or the security camera footage, or Mrs. Wright's stupid mailbox. And when I tried to convince them it was murder, Ross just dismissed me. I didn't have any choice. I had to call you.

"And that worked out perfectly, at first. You followed the clues beautifully. I wanted to get that ATM slip to you, but I had a hard time figuring out how. Then your mother dropped it into my lap by asking me to bring you your hoodie. I zipped back home, put on Jamie's hoodie, stuffed the ATM slip into the pocket, and then I pulled the switch at the paper. It was so fun to watch you try to convince me that my brother was a murderer, when I was trying to convince you of that very thing. It was all coming together.

"Until Jamie picked up the mail that Saturday. He opened the letter I didn't even know my father had sent to Dr. Rosen. He went to the county park—I really did leave a note, but I said I'd gone for a hike at the county park, not at Patmore's Ridge like I told you. I rode my bike out, and he saw it parked at the start of one of the trails. He found me, and he confronted me. He really didn't leave me a choice. But even that turned out all right, because he'd made that call to Frankie. And you found out about their affair, which I didn't even know about. When Detective Ross arrested her for both deaths, I thought I was home free.

"But I admit, I made a mistake. I should have stopped then. If I hadn't gone ahead with Betty, you never would have put things together. But I thought she would be so easy, and she was. I just put on some scrubs, set a small fire in a wastebasket at the nursing home, and pulled the alarm. In all the confusion, I took Betty to my car and I drove her home. That's where she kept telling me she wanted to go. I had to come back in the morning and unlock the shed she was in, to make sure she was dead, but that was no problem."

"You're a monster."

"And the people who killed my mother weren't? They took away something that belonged to me. They had to pay, that's all."

"Why did you go after Father Lindstrom? He just advised the team. He wasn't part of the medical decision making."

"He let them kill my mother. Probably told them it was all right, they were doing their duty, making the hard choices. But it wasn't all right. And it wasn't fair. They had happy lives. They had families. They had what I deserved. They took it away from me, so I took it away from them. It was justice."

"What about the others? How did you get rid of Dr. Lessing?"

"It wasn't hard to find out he was a jogger. Hit and run accidents, they happen all the time."

"Gail Slade?"

"She was on Facebook. Not good with privacy settings. Said she was going shopping at Neiman Marcus. I knew where she lived, and I knew the subway line she'd take."

"Neal Dawson?"

"That was tougher. But his daughter is on Tumblr, and she tells the world everything. It took a little effort, but I managed to switch his coffee for one laced with peanut oil. It only takes a tiny amount. It was so crowded no one even saw me. But then that insurance bitch had to call my father. Every step of the way my planning was perfect, but my luck didn't hold up, that's all."

Her narcissism was boundless.

"But now my luck's changed. You found the note that's going to set me free."

"We're all through here," I said as I got up and knocked on the door. The guard opened it immediately and walked over to Isabel.

"You're going to do what you promised, aren't you?" I enjoyed the fearful suspicion in her voice.

I shrugged.

She twisted away from the guard, but he grabbed her quickly and shoved her roughly forward. "What are you going to do, Leah? You'd better keep your promise." She hissed out the words.

Now, it was my turn to lie.

"I don't know, Lynette."

52

BUT I DID KNOW. I turned everything over to the prosecutor. I had played God once before, and I still wasn't easy with what I'd done. This time, I couldn't do it.

I did, however, have an ace up my sleeve. An old friend of mine, Jess Patterson. I'm pretty good at finding people, but Jess is the best PI and skip tracer I've ever met. And Jess owed me. Big. It was time to collect. Through Jess, I would always know where Isabel was, and what she was doing, no matter how far away she went or what she called herself. I'd be able to keep my eye on her for years. And she'd never know.

I pretty much avoided people for the rest of the day, not wanting to explain myself, or listen to Miguel's upbeat chatter, or even to Coop's commiseration or Nick's comforting words. I went to McClain's for a burger by myself before the evening rush started.

I was enjoying the solitude in my dark corner booth. Then Ross walked through the door. I tried donning my cloak of invisibility. It didn't work. He spotted me and came over.

"Mind if I sit down?" That was a switch–a polite inquiry instead of an aggressive demand.

"Suit yourself."

"Isabel Whiting got out this afternoon. Prosecutor dropped the charges.

I heard you turned over the suicide note." I waited for him to tell me what a dumbass I was, how I let a killer go free.

"Yep."

"There was nothin' you could do. You had to turn it in, but it hurts like hell, doesn't it?"

"Yeah, it does," I said cautiously. I wondered what the catch was. Surely such empathy didn't come for free?

"We're still investigating Jamie's death. Doesn't look good though. No witnesses, nothin' at the scene. Well, the DEA surveillance guys did put Bergman near the park, like your goofy friend said, but not at the right time and he never even got out of his car. That empty envelope you found in Jamie's Mini Cooper? Timmins says it's 'suggestive,' but we can't prove anything."

"And the other deaths?"

"Betty Meier belongs to HPD. Coop musta told you; they can't find anything but some crazy old guy at the nursing home who saw her walkin' away with a nurse. The other three deaths belong to three different departments, and nobody's very interested in trying to dig up new evidence on cases they already ruled accidental. Maybe if we had a serial killer slittin' throats, we might be able to get the FBI to take an interest, but we don't." His shoulders sagged, and I knew he was as frustrated as I was.

"I talked to the fire marshal. He said the fire at Father Lindstrom's house started in the basement. It could've been set, but it could've been that the stacks of old newspapers down there were too close to a gas water heater. They can't tell for sure."

He shook his head. "We can't make anything stick to her. It's like she's made outta Teflon."

I didn't say anything, just took a bite of my burger and chewed it slowly. Though as I tried to accept the reality of Isabel walking away, I had a hard time swallowing. I took a sip of my soda.

"Look, Nash. I think we both got some things wrong here. But, uh, in the big picture, you know, you were more right than I was. You didn't totally screw up." His face was sweating, no doubt with the effort of giving me a semi-compliment.

"Well, you didn't either, Ross. In fact, you saw Garrett Whiting's death for what it was from the beginning. I got distracted and taken in by all the fake clues Isabel was strewing all over the place. Your instincts were right."

"Yeah well, like I told you, if it walks like a duck and quacks like a duck, it's a duck. And that duck—"

"Yeah, I know, was 'quackin' suicide'."

"Still, I missed that portfolio. I mean, we looked at it, but there wasn't anything there. I made a mistake. I should've had it tested. But it looked like suicide—"

I interrupted. "Because it was suicide. Everybody makes mistakes. Don't beat yourself up."

"You, either." He sat there for a few seconds, then put his hands on the table and used it to support his slide out of the tight confines of the booth. As he stood he said, "Yeah. OK, then. I just wanted to say that you, uh, weren't all wrong. And you did good with the Father."

I looked at him, a stocky middle-aged man with little squinty eyes and a too-tight collar pinching the fat rolls on his neck. And for some reason, another one of Father Lindstrom's favorite quotes popped into my head. "*Everything that irritates us about others can lead us to an understanding of ourselves.*" Ross was stubborn, and didn't let people in, and held fast to his own point of view, and he made a lot of mistakes—just like me. Maybe there was something to that. Maybe.

"Thanks, Ross. See you."

"Yeah, see you."

"Hey, Father. You would've been proud of me last night."

It was Tuesday evening, and like any wild and crazy woman in her early 30s, I was having a drink with an elderly priest. Various people in town had donated items to furnish his new living room, and the result was definitely eclectic. I sat on a posh leather sofa provided by Miller Caldwell.

Father Lindstrom was enthroned on a plaid recliner that was a gift from the high school football coach, whose wife had declared there was no room for a king size chair in her new family room. Someone else had donated a glass-topped coffee table and a Tiffany style floor lamp.

The little priest's color was good, and his light blue eyes had regained their sparkle. But sitting in the big chair that threatened to swallow him up, he looked very small, all of his 70+ years and then some.

"Leah, you saved my life. I'm more than proud of you. I'm indebted and grateful for your bravery."

"Yeah, well, OK." I reddened slightly and continued my initial thought. "No, seriously. It's like I was channeling you." I told him about my conversation with Ross at McClain's.

"I'm very glad. But you weren't channeling me, you know. You have a very deep vein of loving kindness inside you."

"OK, no. I think you see people the way you want to see them, not how they really are."

"You're quite wrong. I have exceptionally clear vision where human nature is concerned." He wasn't in a reclining position, but his short legs barely touched the floor. He took a drink.

I did the same from the glass in my hand. And made a face. "You know that conversion thing? To Benedictine B&B? It's not happening."

He smiled but didn't answer, and I took another sip of the nasty stuff to please him.

"Do you think you could turn your 'exceptionally clear vision' on my mother?"

"What do you mean?"

"Something's wrong. I promised her I wouldn't talk about it to anyone, so I can't say specifically. But it's really upsetting her. I heard her crying the other night. I don't know what to do."

"Sometimes there's nothing you can do. I know that's hard for you to hear, but you can't solve everyone's problems, no matter how much you want to."

"Do you know anything about it? Has she talked to you?"

The look he gave me was kind and full of concern. So full, that I was sure he knew the truth. My mother had told him, and he couldn't tell me.

"You know, don't you?"

He took a sip of his drink and didn't answer.

"Father, please. Give me something to go on, something I can use to help her. Please."

"The only way you can help her is to respect her wishes. Your mother is in good health. She is not in trouble, nor is she in danger. Beyond that, there's nothing I can tell you. I'm sorry. You must be patient. When she's ready, she'll tell you herself."

There was no point in badgering him. He's small, but he's mighty when it comes to protecting confidences, in the confessional or otherwise. I had to let it go. So, we talked quietly and laughed some. In the soft glow of the lamplight, I began to feel that things were finally righting themselves in my world.

Coop and I were friends again. Rebecca and I were civil to each other. My first book was coming out. Nick and I were doing surprisingly well. My mother was troubled, but she was healthy and she was safe, and she would tell me, eventually, and I would help her. And everything would be all right.

I had no premonition then that in the months ahead, everything I thought I knew about myself, my family, my life, was going to change forever.

DANGEROUS PLACES: Leah Nash #3

Vanished Without A Trace

Teenager Heather Young disappears from the small town of Himmel, Wisconsin. Everyone believes her boyfriend killed her, but no one can prove it. Twenty years later, Leah Nash is pulled into the cold case by an old friend. She finds the answer—and the shocking truth shatters her world.

Dangerous Places is the third standalone book in the Leah Nash series of complex, fast-paced murder mysteries featuring quick-witted dialogue, daring female characters, and plots with lots of twists and turns.

Get your copy today at SusanHunterAuthor.com

LOVE READING MYSTERIES & THRILLERS?

Never miss a new release! Sign up to receive exclusive updates from author Susan Hunter.

Join today at SusanHunterAuthor.com

As a thank you for signing up, you'll receive a free copy of *Dangerous Dreams: A Leah Nash Novella*.

YOU MIGHT ALSO ENJOY…

Leah Nash Mysteries

Dangerous Habits

Dangerous Mistakes

Dangerous Places

Dangerous Secrets

Dangerous Flaws

Dangerous Ground

Never miss a new release! Sign up to receive exclusive updates from author Susan Hunter.

SusanHunterAuthor.com/Newsletter

As a thank you for signing up, you'll receive a free copy of

Dangerous Dreams: A Leah Nash Novella.

ACKNOWLEDGMENTS

IT TAKES A VILLAGE to edit a book. I'd like to thank all of my beta readers and proofers who gave their time, attention, and insights willingly and cheerfully.

Also, thanks to Jane Lewis, MFS, D-ABFDE, forensic document examiner nonpareil, who generously shared her expertise about indented writing and also allowed me to appropriate her first name for my fictional forensic document examiner. Any mistakes with reference to forensic document examination are entirely my own.

And it goes without saying, but never should, thanks to my husband Gary Rayburn for his unflagging encouragement, patience, and love.

ABOUT THE AUTHOR

Susan Hunter is a charter member of Introverts International (which meets the 12th of Never at an undisclosed location). She has worked as a reporter and managing editor, during which time she received a first place UPI award for investigative reporting and a Michigan Press Association first place award for enterprise/feature reporting.

Susan has also taught composition at the college level, written advertising copy, newsletters, press releases, speeches, web copy, academic papers and memos. Lots and lots of memos. She lives in rural Michigan with her husband Gary, who is a man of action, not words.

During certain times of the day, she can also be found wandering the mean streets of small-town Himmel, Wisconsin, looking for clues, stopping for a meal at the Elite Cafe, dropping off a story lead at the *Himmel Times Weekly*, or meeting friends for a drink at McClain's Bar and Grill.

For more information
www.SusanHunterAuthor.com
Susan@SusanHunterAuthor.com

DISCUSSION QUESTIONS

1. What's the most important part of a mystery/thriller to you—characters, action, plot, dialogue? Which aspects does the author focus on in *Dangerous Mistakes*?
2. How important is setting to *Dangerous Mistakes*? Is Himmel a place you feel like you've been—or would like to go? Why?
3. Besides the main character, Leah Nash, which other characters in the book stood out? Who was your favorite? Why?
4. Part of the fun of a mystery is guessing "whodunit." Who was your prime suspect early in the book? Did your guess change as you read further?
5. What red herrings threw you off the track of "whodunit?"
6. Leah experienced loss and abandonment at a young age. How does that affect her relationships with others and her approach to life?
7. Do the characters in *Dangerous Mistakes* act consistently with what you learn about their personalities? Were their motivations believable?
8. Is Leah any different at the end of the book than at the beginning? If yes, how?

9. Leah has to make a choice at the end of the book. How did you feel about the choice she made? In her place, what would you have done?